PB

ROSIE THOMAS

All My Sins Remembered

Bantam Books
NEW YORK · TORONTO · LONDON · SYDNEY · AUCKLAND

ALL MY SINS REMEMBERED
A Bantam Book / October 1992
Bantam paperback edition / January 1994

PUBLISHING HISTORY
First published in the United Kingdom in 1991
by the Penguin Group

ISBN-0-553-56368-8
Published simultaneously in the United States and Canada

Bantam Books are published by Bantam Books, a division of Bantam Doubleday
Dell Publishing Group, Inc. Its trademark, consisting of the words "Bantam
Books" and the portrayal of a rooster, is Registered in U.S. Patent and Trademark
Office and in other countries. Marca Registrada. Bantam Books, 1540 Broadway,
New York, New York 10036.

PRINTED IN THE UNITED STATES OF AMERICA

RAD   0 9 8 7 6 5 4 3 2 1

For John,
who was there when it counted

THE FAMILIES

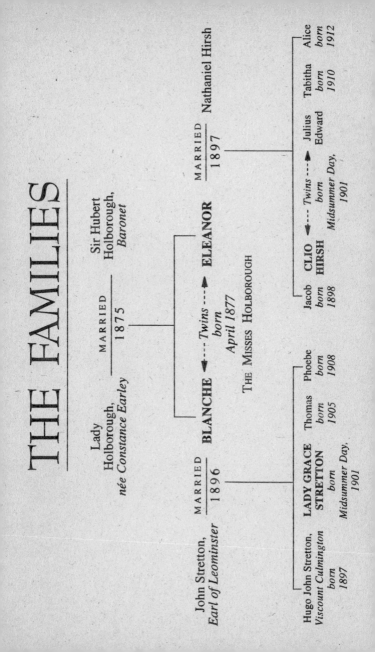

John Stretton, *Earl of Leominster*
    MARRIED 1896
Lady Holborough, *née Constance Earley*
    MARRIED 1875
Sir Hubert Holborough, *Baronet*

BLANCHE ◀---- *Twins* ----▶ **ELEANOR**
born April 1877

THE MISSES HOLBOROUGH

Nathaniel Hirsh
    MARRIED 1897

Hugo John Stretton, *Viscount Culmington born 1897*

LADY GRACE STRETTON *born Midsummer Day, 1901*

Thomas *born 1905*

Phoebe *born 1908*

Jacob *born 1898*

CLIO HIRSH ◀--- *Twins* ---▶ Julius Edward
born Midsummer Day, 1901

Tabitha *born 1910*

Alice *born 1912*

London, 1990

IT WAS A LIE, BUT it was not a lie that could do any damage.

The writer reflected on the relative harmlessness of what she was doing as she waited on the step for the doorbell to be answered. It was a cold and windy autumn afternoon, and the trees that bordered the canal in Little Venice were shedding their leaves into the water. She had turned away to look at the play of light in the ripples drawn behind a barge when the door opened at last behind her.

There was a smiling nurse in a blue dress. "Mrs. Ainger, hello there. Come in, now."

"How is she today?" Elizabeth Ainger asked.

"Not so bad at all. Quite clear in the head, as a matter of fact. She even asked when you were coming."

"She's getting used to me," Elizabeth said. "I'm glad it's one of her good days."

The nurse showed her into a drawing room at the rear of the house with a view of a small garden through double doors. There were porcelain ornaments arranged on the marble mantelpiece, a little blue painting of an interior hanging above them, embroidered cushions and faded rose-patterned loose covers. These neat, traditional furnishings were faintly at odds with the picture that hung on the wall behind the old lady's chair. It was a double portrait, in oils, of two young women. They were looking away from each other, out of the frame of the picture, and there was tension in every line of their bodies. The painter's peculiarly hectic style owed something to Picasso, and something to Stanley Spencer.

It was so quiet in the room, away from the noise of the traffic, that the occupant might have been sitting in some cottage in the country instead of in the middle of London.

"Hello, Aunt Clio," Elizabeth said. The nurse withdrew and closed the door behind her.

The tiny old woman in the velvet-upholstered chair was not really Elizabeth's aunt, but her grandmother's first cousin. But it was to "Aunt Clio's" house in Oxford that Elizabeth had been taken on visits with her mother when she was a little girl. She could just remember the rooms, with their forbidding shelves of dark books, and her childish impression that Aunt Clio was important but in some way not easy.

When Elizabeth was seven, her American father had taken his wife and daughter back to live in Oregon, and there had only been birthday cards and Christmas presents from Oxford after that. By the time Elizabeth was grown up herself and had come back to live in the country of her birth, the links had been all but broken. Until this series of visits had begun, the two women had not met for thirty years.

Clio turned her head a fraction to look at her visitor. "It's you, is it?"

Elizabeth smiled and shrugged, deprecatingly held out her tape recorder.

"I'm afraid so. Do you feel too tired to talk today?"

"I am not in the least tired."

She did not look it, either. Her body was tiny and frail, but her eyes were bright and sharp like fish caught in their nets of wrinkles. She watched Elizabeth Ainger sitting down, adopting a familiar position in the chair opposite her own and fiddling with her little tape recorder.

"I just wonder why you are not bored to death with all these old tales?"

With a show of cheerful patience the younger woman answered, "You can't tell me anything that will bore me. I am your biographer, remember?"

That was the lie, but it came out fluently enough.

The biography was not of her relative, Clio Hirsh, although she would not have been an inappropriate subject, but of Clio's first cousin.

Lady Grace Brock, née Stretton, was Elizabeth's maternal grandmother. She was the daughter of an Earl, a famous socialite in her day and then one of the first women Members of Parliament.

Elizabeth had never met her, but she was fascinated by her. Elizabeth's mother and the rest of the family had warned her at the outset that Clio was famously reluctant to talk about her cousin and friend. The defenses that the old lady duly put up against Elizabeth's first casual inquiries were infuriating and impregnable, but she needed her cooperation, and so Elizabeth had pretended that it was a family biography that she was researching, with particular emphasis on Clio's own life.

Elizabeth was invited to call at the house in Little Venice. The first visit had led to a series of interviews, and Elizabeth had patiently waited and listened.

It would not matter if the finished book were not what had been promised. Books took a long time to write, and Clio was very old and no longer reliably clear in her own mind.

Clio said irritably, "I bore myself. Who could possibly want to read anything about me? I wish I hadn't agreed to this rigmarole."

"But you did agree."

"I know that. And having agreed to it, I am doing it." She was tart, as she often was on her lucid days.

"We were talking about Blanche and Eleanor, last time I was here," Elizabeth prompted.

"You know it all. You've seen all their letters, the papers. What more do you want to hear?"

"Just what you remember. Only that."

The old woman sighed. She was almost ninety. She remembered so many things, but she had forgotten more. The firm connective tissue of memory that once held the flesh of her life together had all but dissolved. There were only incidents to recall now, isolated like the tips of submerged rocks rearing out of a wide sea.

Then, in a stronger voice, Clio suddenly said, "I remember my Aunt Blanche's scent. White lilac, and burnt hair. They frizzed their hair, you know, in those days, with curling tongs that the maid heated red-hot in the fire. I remember the smell of burning hair."

Elizabeth pressed the record button, and then sat quietly, listening as Clio talked. This was the pattern of her visits.

One

THE OLD WOMAN SAT PROPPED in her nest of cushions and rugs. Her hands rested like small ivory carvings on the rubbed velvet arms of the chair. The visitor waited, watching her to see if she would doze, or sit in silence, or if today would be a talking day.

Clio said to Elizabeth, not looking at her but away somewhere else, a long way off, "I remember the holidays. There were always wonderful holidays." She tilted her head, listening to something that reminded her.

When she thought about it, she supposed that had been Nathaniel's doing. Nathaniel applied the same principles to holidays as to his work. He could turn the radiance of his enthusiasm equally on the business of enjoyment or the pleasures of academic discipline. And Nathaniel's enthusiasm infected them all, all of his children. When the time came for the family migrations, excitement would fill the red-brick house with high-pitched twittering, like real birds. Clio could hear the starlings out in the garden now. It must be their chorus that had taken her back. The nurse would have tipped the crusts of the breakfast toast on the bird-table.

"Where did you go?" Cressida's daughter Elizabeth asked.

"Different places." Clio glanced at her, suddenly sly. "Grace and the others used to come with us, too." It amused her to see how the mention of Grace sharpened the other's attention. It always did.

There had been different holidays, but almost always beside the sea. They would take a house, or two houses if one was not big enough for Hirshes and Strettons together, with their retinue of nursemaids and attendants. The children and their mothers would stay there all the long summer, and the two fathers would visit when they could.

Only they almost never came at the same time. Nathaniel would go away for some of those summer vacations on reading parties with his undergraduates, or on visits to Paris and Berlin. And John Leominster had the estate at Stretton to attend to, and business in London, and the affairs of his club.

It was Blanche and Eleanor who were always there.

Clio and Grace and the boys ran over the expanses of rawly glittering sand, or hung over the rock pools, or dragged their shrimping nets through fringes of seaweed before lifting them in arcs of diamond spray to examine the catch. It was the mothers they always ran back to, to show off the mollusc or sidling crab, Jake pounding ahead with Julius at his heels, and shoulder to shoulder, the two girls, with their skirts gathered up in one hand and their sharp elbows sticking out. If one of them could manage a dig at the other, to make her swerve or miss her footing, then so much the better. It would mean reaching the boys first, having the chance to blurt out with them the news of the tiny discovery, while the loser came sulkily behind, forced to pretend that nothing mattered less.

The two nannies sat with the nursemaid in a sheltered corner at the top of the beach. The little brothers and sisters, Hirshes and Strettons, played at their feet or slept in their perambulators. These babies were beneath the attention of the bigger children. The flying feet swept past, sending up small plumes of silvery sand, heading for the mothers.

Blanche and Eleanor sat a little distance apart, beneath a complicated canvas awning. They were protected from the sun and the sea breeze by panels of canvas that unrolled from the roof-edge. The little pavilion was carried down to the beach every morning and erected by Blanche's chauffeur, who also brought down their canvas chairs and spread out the rugs on which they rested their feet. One year Hugo Stretton had made a red knight's pennant to fly from the top of the supporting pole. This spot of scarlet was the focus of the beach, however far the children wandered. The twin sisters sat beneath it in the canvas shade, watching their families and mildly gossiping. Sometimes there was a husband nearby, either Nathaniel Hirsh, with his black beard bristling over a book, or John Leominster, bowling at Hugo who stood in front of a makeshift wicket and squinted fiercely at the spinning ball. But if neither husband was there, Blanche and Eleanor were equally content. They found each other's company perfectly satisfactory, as they had always done.

It was always Jake who reached them first.

"Look at this, Mama, Aunt Blanche. Look what we found."

Then Julius would plunge down into the sand beside him. "*I* found it. It came up in my net."

And one of the girls would drop between the two of them, panting for breath and grinning in her triumph. "Isn't it beautiful? Can we keep it for a pet? I'll look after it, I promise I will."

The second girl would stumble up, red-faced and pouting. "Don't be silly, you can't keep things like that for pets. They aren't domestic," Clio would say scornfully, because it was the only option left open to her. It was usually Clio. Grace was quicker and more determined in getting what she wanted. She usually won the races. *It isn't fair,* Clio had thought, almost from the time she had been able to think. *Jake is my brother and Julius is my* twin. *They're both mine, Grace is only an outsider.*

But Grace never behaved like an outsider, and never behaved as if she owed her Hirsh cousins any thanks for her inclusion in their magic circle. She took it loftily, as her right.

The children knelt in a ring at their mothers' feet. Jake put his hand into the net and lifted out their catch to show it off. Blanche and Eleanor bent their identical calm faces and padded coiffures over him, ready to admire.

One of them gave a faint cry. "It is quite a big one. Don't let it nip you, Jacob, will you?"

Hugo was digging in the sand nearby. His curiosity at last overcame him, and he left his complicated layout of moats and battlements and strolled over to them, his hands in the pockets of his knickerbockers.

"It's only a stupid crab," he observed.

"Stupid yourself," Clio and Grace rounded on him, united in defense. "Just because you didn't catch it."

"I wouldn't have bothered. It'll die in five minutes in this sun."

Hugo turned his back on them, returning to his solitary game. Hugo was Grace's elder brother. He was good as an extra player in field games, or for Racing Demon, or to perform the less coveted roles in the rambling plays that Clio and Julius wrote, but he never belonged to the circle. There was room for only the four of them within it.

Hugo would have said, "I'm not interested in stupid clubs. They're for little girls."

Knowing better, none of them would have bothered to contradict him.

Eleanor or Blanche would say, soothingly, "It *is* very handsome. Look at those claws. But I think Hugo may be right, you know. It will be happier under a rock, somewhere near the water. Shall I walk over there with you, so we can make sure it finds a safe home?"

Then, whichever mother it happened to be would stand up, smoothing the folds of her narrow bell skirt and the tucked and pearl-buttoned front of her white blouse. If it was a hot day, she would shake out the folds of her little parasol and tilt it over her dark head before following them across the shimmering sand. The hem of her skirt trailed on it, giving a rhythmic, languid whisper. The mothers' feet were always invisible, even beside the sea. Even though she knew Blanche really wore elegant narrow shoes in suede or glacé kid, Grace used to imagine that her mother's gliding step was the result of wheels smoothly revolving beneath her rustling gowns.

When they came to the rocks, the children hunched together, watching as Jake slowly opened his hands and laid the crab in the narrow slice of shade. The creature seemed to rise on its toes, like a ballerina on points, before it darted sideways. They watched until the crimped edge of the green and black shell disappeared under the ledge. Julius flattened himself on his stomach and peered after it, but he couldn't see the stalky eyes looking out at him.

"It's gone," they said sadly.

The mother or aunt reassured them. "It will be happier, you know. A crab isn't like the dogs, or Grace's rabbits." And seeing their miserable faces, she would laugh her pretty silvery laugh and tell them to run over to Nanny and ask if they might walk to the wooden kiosk at the end of the beach road for lemonade.

When was that? Clio asked herself. *Which summer, of all those summers? Grace and Julius and I must have been nine, and Jake eleven.*

Nineteen ten.

And where?

It might have been Cromer, or Hunstanton. Not France, that was certain, although there had been two summers on the wide beaches of the Normandy coast. That had been Nathaniel's doing, too. He had made the plans and chosen the solid hotels with faded sun awnings and ancient, slow-footed waiters. He had supervised the exodus of the families, marshaling porters to convey brass-bound trunks, seemingly dozens of them, and booming instructions in rapid French to *douaniers* and drivers. It had all seemed very exotic. Clio was proud of her big, red-mouthed, polyglot father. Uncle John Leominster seemed a dry stick beside him, and Clio glanced sidelong at Grace to make sure that she too was registering the contrast.

But if Grace noticed anything, she gave no sign of it. She would look airily around her, interested but not impressed. Her own father was the Earl of Leominster, *milord anglais,* and she herself was Lady Grace Stretton. That was superiority enough. Clio writhed under the injustice of it, her pride in Nathaniel momentarily forgotten. That was how it was.

Eleanor and Blanche enjoyed Tròuville. They liked the early evening promenade when French families walked out in chattering groups, airing their fashionable clothes. The Hirshes and Strettons joined the pageant, the sisters shrewdly appraising the latest styles. The Countess of Leominster might buy her gowns in Paris, but Eleanor, a don's wife, couldn't hope to. She would take the news back to her dressmaker in Oxford.

The two of them drew glances wherever they went. They were an arresting sight, gliding together in their pongee or tussore silks, their identical faces framed by huge hats festooned with drooping masses of flowers or feathers. Their children walked more stiffly, constrained by their holiday best, under the benign eye of whichever husband happened to be present. Grace liked to walk with Jake, which left Julius and Clio together. Clio was happy enough with that, but she would have preferred it if Jake could have been at her other side.

They were all happy, except for Uncle John, who did not care for Abroad. Blanche never wanted to oppose him, and so the experiment was only repeated once. After that, they returned to Norfolk.

Nineteen eleven was the year of the boat.

The summer holiday began the same way as all the others. The Hirshes and their nanny and two maids traveled from Oxford to London by train and stayed the night in the Strettons' town house in Belgrave Square. It was an exciting reunion for the cousins, who had not seen each other since the Easter holiday at Stretton. Clio and Grace hugged each other, and then Grace kissed Jake and Julius in turn, shy kisses with her eyes hidden by her eyelashes, making the boys blush a little. Hugo watched from a safe distance. He was already at Eton and considered himself grown up. The other four sat on the beds in the night-nursery, locking their circle tight again after the long separation.

The next day, the two families set off by train from Liverpool Street station. There were three reserved compartments. The parents traveled in one, the children and nannies in another, and the maids in the third. The nannies pinned big white sheets over the seats, so the children's hair and clothes didn't touch them.

"You never know who else has been sitting there before you, Miss Clio," Nanny Cooper said, compressing her lips. They ate their lunch out of a big wicker picnic basket, and afterward the smaller children fell asleep. Tabitha Hirsh, the youngest, was still a tiny baby.

At the station at the other end, the Leominster chauffeur was waiting to meet them. He had driven up from London with part of the luggage.

That year, there was one big house overlooking the sea. It was a maze of rooms opening out of each other, with a glassed-in sun room to one side that smelled of dried seaweed and rubber over-shoes. The children ran through the rooms, shouting their discoveries to one another while the maids and nannies unpacked.

Later, in the early evening, there was the first scramble down onto the beach. The clean air was full of salt and the cries of gulls. Nathaniel put on his panama hat and went with the children, letting them run ahead to the water's edge and not calling them back to walk properly as the nannies would have done. From the high-water mark, where the girls hesitated in fear of wetting their white shoes, they looked back and saw Nathaniel talking to a fisherman.

"What's he doing?" Julius called. "Can we go fishing?"

When he rejoined them, Nathaniel was beaming. "Surprise," he announced, waving his big hands. The children surged around him.

"What is it? What?"

"Look and see."

They followed him across the sand. There was an outcrop of rock draped with pungent bladder wrack, and an iron ring was let into the rock. A rusty stain bled beneath it. A length of rope was hitched through the ring, and the other end of it was secured to a small blue dinghy beached on the sand. A herring gull perched briefly on the boat's prow, then lifted away again.

Grace stooped to read the faded lettering. "It's called the *Mabel.*"

"Your *Mabel,* for the summer," Nathaniel told her.

"Ours? Our own?"

"I'll teach you to row."

Hugo was already fumbling with the rope. "I can row."

Nathaniel and the fisherman eased the dinghy down to the water's edge, steadying it when the keel lifted free and bobbed on the ripples.

"Six of us. You'll have to sit still. Hugo in the front there, Jake and Julius in the middle. Leave room for the oarsman. The girls at the stern." He ordered them fluently, and they scrambled to his directions, even Hugo. The fisherman in his tall rubber waders lifted Clio and swung her over the little gulf of water.

"There, miss. Now your sister's turn." He went back for Grace and hoisted her too.

"She's my cousin, not my sister," Clio told him quickly.

"Is that so? She's like enough to be your twin."

"He's my real twin." Clio pointed at Julius.

"But he's nothing like so pretty." The man twinkled at her. Clio was sufficiently disarmed by the compliment to forget the mistake. Nathaniel dipped the oars, and the *Mabel* slid forward over the lazy swell.

There had been boat rides before, but none had seemed as magical as the first trip in their own *Mabel.* They bobbed out over the green water into the realm of the gulls. Only a few yards separated them from the prosaic shore, but they felt part of another world. They could look back at the old one, at the holiday house diminished by blue distance and at the white speck of a nanny's apron passing in front of it. Out here there were the cork markers of lobster pots, a painted buoy with another gull perching on it, and the depths of the mysterious water.

Grace leaned to one side so that her fingers dipped into the waves. She sighed with pleasure. It was the first day of the holidays. There were six whole weeks to enjoy before she would be returned to Miss Alcott and the tedium of the schoolroom at Stretton. Jake and Julius were here. She was happy.

Nathaniel bent over the oars. The dinghy skimmed along, and the sea breeze blew the railway fumes out of their heads.

Jake said, "I can see Aunt Blanche. I think she's waving."

Nathaniel laughed. He had a big, noisy laugh. "I'm sure she's waving. It's our signal to make for dry land."

He paddled vigorously with one oar and the boat swung in a circle. When it was broadside to the sea, a wave larger than the others slapped against the side and sprayed over them. The girls shrieked with delight and shook out the skirts of their white dresses.

"Rules of the sea," Nathaniel boomed, as the *Mabel* rose on the crest of the next wave and swept toward the beach.

The rules were that no child was allowed to take out the dinghy without an adult watching. The girls were not allowed to row unless one of the fathers came in the boat. The boys would be permitted to row themselves, once they had passed a swimming test that would be set by Nathaniel.

The boys often bathed in the summer holidays, wearing long navy-blue woollen bathing suits that buttoned on the shoulders. To their disappointment, the girls were not allowed to do the same, because Blanche and Eleanor had never done so and didn't consider it desirable for their daughters. They had to content themselves with removing their shoes and long stockings and paddling in the shallows.

"Are the rules understood?" Nathaniel demanded ferociously.

"We understand," they answered in unison.

The keel of the dinghy ran into the sand like a spoon digging into sugar. The fisherman had gone home. The boys jumped ashore, Nathaniel lifted Clio, and Grace launched herself into Jake's arms. He staggered a little with the weight of her, and a wave ran up and licked over his shoes.

They all laughed, even Clio.

As they trudged back up to the house Grace said to Clio, "I must say, I think your father can be splendid sometimes."

"So do I," Clio answered with pride.

The days of the holiday slipped by, as they always did.

John Leominster was in Scotland for the shooting. Nathaniel went away to London, then came back again. Blanche and Eleanor stayed put, happy to be together, as they had been since babyhood. They wrote their letters side by side in the morning room, walked together in the afternoons, took tea with their children when they came in from the beach and listened to the news of the day, and after they had changed in the evenings, they ate dinner alone together in the candlelit dining room, the food served to them by the manservant who came from Stretton for the holiday.

The children, from elsewhere in the house, could often hear the sound of their laughter. Clio and Grace listened, their admiration touched with resentment at their own exclusion. They knew that the two of them could never be so tranquil alone together, without Jake, without Julius.

For the children there were races on the beach, picnics and drives and hunts for cowrie shells, and, that year, rowing in the *Mabel*. The boys passed their swimming tests and became confident oarsmen. They learned to dive from the dinghy, shouting to each other as they balanced precariously and then launched themselves, setting the little boat wildly rocking. The girls could only watch enviously from the waterline, listening to the splashes and spluttering.

"I could swim if they would just let me try," Grace muttered.

"And so could I, easily," Clio affirmed. "Why isn't Pappy here, so that we could at least go in the boat with them?"

They weren't looking at each other when Grace said, "We should go anyway. Prove we can, and then they'll have no reason to stop us anymore, will they?"

"I don't think we should. Not without asking."

Grace laughed scornfully. "If we ask, we'll be told no. Don't you know anything about older people? Anyway, Jake won't let anything happen."

It was always Jake they looked to. Not Hugo, even though Hugo was the eldest.

"I'm going to go," Grace announced. "You needn't, if you're scared."

"I never said I was scared."

They did look at each other then. The fisherman had been right, they were alike as sisters. Not identical like their mothers—the resemblance was not as close as that—but they had the same straight noses and blue-gray eyes, and the same thick, dark hair springing back from high foreheads. When they looked, they seemed to see themselves in mirror fashion, and neither of them had ever quite trusted the reflection.

Grace turned away first. She lifted her arm and waved it in a wide arc over her head. The white sleeve of her middy-blouse fluttered like a truce signal.

"Jake," she called. "Ja-ake, Julius, come here, won't you?"

Jake's black head, glistening wet like a seal's, appeared alongside the dinghy. He rested his arms on the stern, hoisting the upper half of his body out of the water. He was almost thirteen. His shoulders were beginning to broaden noticeably under the blue woollen bathing suit.

"What?"

Hugo and Julius bobbed up alongside him. Hugo's head looked very blond and square alongside his cousins'.

Grace's arm signal changed to a beckoning curl. "Come in to shore for a minute."

Jake began lazily kicking. Julius and then Hugo dived and swam. Under Jake's propulsion the *Mabel* drifted toward the beach. Clio thought, *They always do what she wants.* She turned to look up the sand. The two nannies were sitting as usual on a blanket on the lee of the sea wall. Tabitha's perambulator stood close by. The two younger Strettons, Thomas and Phoebe, were playing in the sand. They were turning sand castles out of seawater-rusted tin buckets. Hills the chauffeur had put up the canvas awning ready for the mothers, but they had not come down yet. They would still be attending to their volumes of correspondence. Their empty steamer chairs sat side by side, and Hugo's red pennant flew bravely above them in the stiffening breeze.

Clio saw the fisherman a little farther up the beach. He was busy with his coils of nets.

When she looked behind her again, it was to see the boys plunging through the shallows in sparkling jets of spray. *Mabel* rocked enticingly at the end of her painter.

"It isn't fair," she heard Grace saying. "You have all the fun in the boat. I think you should take me out now."

"Us," Clio insisted, and Grace looked at her but said nothing. She stood characteristically with her hands on her hips, her chin pushed out. Hugo laughed and Julius began to recite Nathaniel's rules of the sea. Jake stood and looked at Grace, smiling a little.

Grace fixed on him. "There are grown-up people on the beach, the nannies and the fisherman. You three have been rowing and swimming all week. What difference will there be just in having us in the boat? And once we've been, they won't be able to stop us going again, will they? The rules are petty and unfair."

"That's true, at least." Support came from Hugo, who was never anxious to accept Nathaniel's jurisdiction.

"But we were told," Julius began.

"Stay here with Clio, then."

The twins shook their heads, and Grace smiled once more at Jake. "Wouldn't it be fun for all of us to go out together, on our own?"

He put out his hand and took hers, making a little bow. "Will you step this way, my lady?"

Grace bobbed a curtsey and hopped into the dinghy as Hugo held it. Her white cotton stockings twinkled under her skirts. Clio followed her, as quickly as she could. Julius sat in the prow, and Hugo and Jake took an oar each. The rowlocks creaked, and the *Mabel* turned out to sea. The nannies were still watching the babies.

It was exhilarating out beyond the breakers. The swell ran under the ribs of the dinghy, seeming to Clio like the undulations of breath in the flank of some vast animal. The waves looked bigger out here than they had done from the shore, but Hugo and Jake pulled confidently together and the boat rode over the wave-breaths like a cork. On the beach Nanny Brodribb suddenly stood up and ran forward, with her white apron molded against her by the wind. She was calling, but none of the children heard her or looked around.

Grace let her head fall back. Her even teeth showed in a smile of elation. The satisfaction of getting her own way together with the sharp pleasure of the boat ride and Jake bending in front of her made her eyes bright and her cheeks rosy.

"You see?" she murmured. The question was for Clio, wedged beside her in the stern. "I was right, wasn't I?"

They rowed on, turning in an arc away from the horizon, and once again a wave caught them broadside and washed in over them. This time, instead of laughing, Clio gave a small yelp of alarm. The water seeped in her lap, wetting her legs and thighs. It was surprisingly cold.

"Don't worry," Jake told her.

"Don't worry," Grace sang. She was filled with happiness, the sense of her own strength, after being confined on the beach with the women and the babies. She saw the blue sky riffled with thin clouds and wanted to reach it. It was joy and not bravado that made her scramble up to stand on the seat with her arms spread out.

Look at me.

They did look, all of them, turning their faces up slowly, as if frozen. All except for Clio, whose eyes were fixed on Grace's feet planted on the rocking seat beside her wet skirts. She saw the button fastenings, and the rim of wet sand clinging to the leather. A second later the dinghy pitched violently. There was a wordless cry, and the shoes flew upward.

Jake shouted hoarsely, *"Grace."*

Clio looked then. She heard the cry cut off and the terrible splash. She wrenched her head and saw the eruption of bubbles at the stern of the *Mabel.* Grace was gone, swallowed up by the sea. The boat was already drifting away from the swirling bubbles. It pitched again, almost capsizing as Jake and then Hugo launched themselves into the water. The boat began to spin helplessly. The sun seemed to have gone in, the brilliant morning to have turned dark.

"Take an oar. Steady her," Julius screamed.

Clio was still staring into the water. In that instant she saw Grace, rising through it. Her face under the greenish skin of the sea was a pale oval, her eyes and mouth black holes of utter terror.

"Row," Julius was shouting at her.

"I don't know how to." Clio was sobbing. She stumbled forward, took up the wooden oar, warm from Jake's hands, and pulled on it.

Grace's head had broken the surface. She was thrashing with her arms, but no sound came out of her mouth. Then she was sinking again, and Hugo and Jake plowed on through the swell to try to reach her.

"Pull with me," Julius instructed. Clio tried to harness her gasping fear into obeying him. She stared at his white knuckles on the other oar, dipped her own, and drew it into her chest. Out, then in again.

When she looked once more, Jake and Hugo had Grace's body between them. She was lashing out at them with the last of her strength, her staring eyes sightless, and for a long moment it seemed that all three of them would be submerged. A wave poured over them, filling Grace's open mouth. Jake flung back his head, kicking toward the *Mabel* and trying to haul her dead weight with him. She hung motionless now with her head under the water.

Julius rowed, and Clio battled to keep time with him. Her teeth chattered with cold and terror and she repeated over and over in her head, *Help us, God. Help us, God.*

The gap narrowed between the boat and the heavy mass in the water. Hugo had his arm under Grace's shoulders. *"Come on,"* Julius muttered. On the beach the two nannies had run to the water's edge. Their thin cries sounded like the sea gulls. Julius saw too that the fisherman had shoved out in his much bigger boat, the one he used to row around the lobster pots. The high red-painted prow surged through the breakers.

Hugo and Julius were closer. Grace was between them, a tangled mass of hair and clothes and blanched skin.

"Ship your oar," Julius ordered Clio. He leaned over the side, tilting the boat dangerously again, stretching out his arms. His hand closed in Grace's hair. He hauled at her, feeling the terrible weight, and another wave flung the dinghy upward so that his oar rammed up into his armpit. Hugo was choking and flailing now, and Jake's lips were drawn back from his teeth as he gasped for breath.

"Hold her," he begged Julius. In spite of the pain Julius knotted his fingers in the sodden hair and felt the body rise as Jake put his last effort into propelling Grace toward him. Between them, they forced one dripping arm and then the other over the dinghy's side.

Julius took another handful of the back of her dress, and her head rolled, pressing her streaming cheek against the blue ribs of the *Mabel*. Jake and Hugo could do no more than cling onto the same side. Clio leaned out the other way as far as she dared.

She was dazed to realize how far out to sea they had been carried. The beach and the headland and the houses seemed to belong to another world, a safe and warm and infinitely inviting place that she had never taken notice of until now, when it had gone beyond her reach. The words started up in her head again, *Please God, help us*.

The red prow of the fisherman's boat reared over Jake and Hugo and Grace. The man lifted one oar and paddled with the other, maneuvering the heavy craft as if it were an eggshell. He leaned over the side, and Clio saw his dirty hands and his thick brown forearms. He seized Grace and with one movement lifted her up and over the side of his boat, her legs twisting and bumping. The fisherman laid her gently in the bottom of his boat. The sight of the inanimate body was shocking and pitiful. Clio knew that Grace was dead. She forced her hand against her mouth, suppressing a cry.

With the same ease, the fisherman hauled Hugo and Jake in after Grace. They sank down, staring, huddled together and trembling. Their hair was plastered over their faces, fair and dark, and seawater and spittle trailed out of their blue mouths.

The man leaned across and lifted the trailing bow-rope of the *Mabel*. He made it fast to the stern of his own boat and then lifted his oars again. The two boats rose on the crest of a wave and plunged toward the beach.

A little knot of people had gathered, watching and waiting. As soon as the red boat came within wading distance, two men splashed out and hoisted the bundle of Grace between them. They ran back and grimly spread her on the sand, rolling her onto her belly, lifting her arms above her head.

Clio let herself be lifted in her turn, and then she was set gently on her feet. She wanted to run away up the beach, away from the sea that gnawed at her heels, but there was no power in her legs. She almost fell, but someone's hands caught at her. Part of the murmuring crowd closed around her, and then she heard the very sound of the warm world, the lovely safe world. It was the faint crackle of starch. She lifted her head and saw Nanny's apron, and half fell against it. The scent of laundry rooms and flatirons and safety overwhelmed her, and she looked up and saw Nanny Cooper's face. Her cheeks were wet, and her eyes were bulging with fear.

The boys had been hurried ashore. Jake and Hugo were shrouded in rugs, and all of them became part of a circle that had Grace at its center. The desperate business of the men with their huge hands, who bent over her and pounded at her narrow chest, seemed in futile contrast with her stillness.

Nanny Brodribb stood beyond them, her hands pressed against her face, her mouth moving soundlessly.

They waited a long time, only a few seconds.

Then Grace's mouth opened. A flood of watery vomit gushed out of her. She choked, and drew in a sip of air. They saw her ribs shudder under the soaked dress.

The crowd gave a collective sigh, like a blessing. They closed in on what had become Grace again, living and breathing. Julius stumbled forward and tried to kneel beside her.

"Give her room, can't you?" one of the men said roughly.

They turned Grace so that she lay on her back, and her eyes opened to stare at the sky.

Clio became aware of more movement beyond the intent circle. Blanche was coming, with Eleanor and Hills the chauffeur just behind her. The strangeness of it made her lift her eyes from Grace's heaving ribs. There was no elegant glide now. Blanche's head was jerking, she was hatless and her ribbons and laces flew around her. Clio had never seen her mother and her aunt running. It made them seem different people, strangers.

The two women reached the edge of the crowd, and it opened to admit them to where Grace lay. Blanche dropped on her knees, giving a low moan, but no one spoke. They were listening to the faint gasps of Grace's breathing, all of them, willing the next to follow the last. Jake and Hugo stood shivering under their wrappings of blankets. Nanny Cooper moved to try to warm them, with Clio still clinging to her apron. The other nanny began to trudge up the slope of the beach to where the small children had been left under the nursemaid's eye. Clio took her eyes off Grace once more, to watch her bowed back receding.

They were all helpless, most noticeably the mothers themselves, kneeling with the wet sand and salt water soiling their morning dresses. They looked to the fishermen for what had to be done.

Grace's stare became less fixed. Her eyes slowly moved, to her mother's face. She was breathing steadily now, with no throat-clenching pauses between the draughts of air. The fisherman lifted her shoulders off the sand, supporting her in his arms. Another of the men came forward with a pewter flask. He put it to her mouth and tilted a dribble of brandy between her teeth. Grace shuddered and coughed as the spirit went down.

"She'll do," one of the men said.

Another blanket materialized. Grace was lifted and wrapped in the folds of it. Blanche came out of her frozen shock. She began to cry loudly, trying to pull Grace up and into her own arms, with Eleanor holding her back.

"All right, my lady," another fisherman reassured her. "I've seen enough drownings. This isn't one, I can promise you. Your boys got to her quick enough. Not that they should have took her out there in the beginning."

In her cocoon of blanket, Grace shook her head. Her face was as waxen as if she had really died, but she opened her mouth and spoke clearly. "It was my fault, you know. Not anyone else's."

The fisherman laughed. "You're a proper little bull-beef, aren't you? Here. Let's get you inside in the warm. Your ma'll want to get the doctor in to look at you, although I'd say you don't need him any more'n I do."

He lifted Grace up in his arms and carried her. Blanche followed, supported by Eleanor and Hills on either side, and the children trailed after them, back to the big house overlooking the sea.

As soon as she was installed in her bed, propped up on pillows after the doctor's visit, Grace seemed too strong ever to have brushed up against her own death. For a little while afterward the boys even nicknamed her Bull-beef.

Clio remembered it all her life not as the day Grace nearly drowned, but as the day when she became aware herself that all their lives were fragile, and temporary, and precious, rather than eternal and immutable as she had always assumed them to be. She recalled how the land had looked when they were drifting away from it in the *Mabel,* and now that inviting warmth seemed to touch everything she looked at. The most mundane nursery routines seemed sweet and valuable, as if they might stop tomorrow, forever.

There must have been some maternal edict issued that morning for everything to continue as normal, more normally than normal, to lessen the shock for all of them. So the nannies whisked the older boys into dry jerseys and knickerbockers and made Clio change her damp and sandy clothes, and by the time they had been brushed and tidied and inspected and had drunk hot milk in the kitchen, the doctor had been and gone without any of them seeing him, and it was time for the children's lunch. There was fish and jam roly-poly, like any ordinary day. No one ate very much, except for Hugo, who chewed stolidly. Clio wanted to cry out, *Stay like this. Don't let anything change.* She wanted to put her arms around them all and hold them. But she kept silent and pushed the heaps of roly-poly into the pools of custard on her plate.

Later in the afternoon, Clio found the two nannies together in the cubbyhole where the linen was folded. There was the same scent of starch and cleanliness that had drawn her back on the beach into the safe hold of childhood, but now she saw that both of the women had been crying. She knew they were afraid they would be dismissed for letting Grace go out in the boat.

"It isn't fair," Clio said hotly. "You couldn't have stopped her. I couldn't, nobody could. Grace always does what she wants." Anger bubbled up in her. Nanny Cooper had been with the Hirshes since Jake was born. She came from a house in one of the little brick terraces of west Oxford. The children had often been taken to visit her ancient parents. It was unthinkable that Grace should be responsible for her being sent away.

"Don't you worry," Nanny tried to console her. But it was one of the signs of the new day that Clio didn't believe what she said.

In the evening Nathaniel arrived off the London train, summoned back early by Eleanor.

He called the three boys singly into a stuffy little room off the hallway that nobody had yet found a use for. They came out one by one, with stiff faces, and went up to their beds. When it came to Clio's turn to be summoned, she slipped into the room and found her father sitting in an armchair with his head resting on one hand. His expression and posture were so familiar from bedtimes at home in Oxford that her awareness of the small world's benevolent order and fears for its loss swept over her again.

Nathaniel saw her face. "What is it, Clio?"

She had not meant to cry, but she couldn't help herself. "I don't want to grow up," she said stupidly.

He held out his hand and made her settle on his lap as she had done when she was very small. "You have to," he told her. "Today was the beginning of it, wasn't it?"

"I suppose it was," Clio said at length.

But she found that her father could still reassure her, as he always had. He told her that there was no question of any blame being placed on Nanny Cooper for what Grace had done. And he told her that the changes, whatever they were, would only come by slow degrees. It was just that from today she would be ready for them.

"What about Grace?" Clio asked. "Is today the first day for her, as well?"

"I don't know so much about Grace," Nathaniel said gently. "I hope it is."

Clio wanted to say some more, to make sure that Nathaniel knew Grace had insisted on going out in the *Mabel,* and that she had just been showing off when she leaped onto the seat. She supposed it was the same beginning to grow up that made her decide it would be better to keep quiet. She kissed her father instead, rubbing her cheek against the springy black mass of his beard.

"Goodnight," she said quietly. As she went upstairs to the bedroom she shared with Grace, she heard Nathaniel cross the hallway to the drawing room where the sisters were sitting together, and then the door closing on the low murmur of adult conversation.

Grace was still lying propped up on her pillows. Her dark hair had been brushed, and it spread out in waves around her small face. A fire had been lit in the little iron grate, and the flickering light on the ceiling brought back memories of the night-nursery and baby illnesses. Clio found herself instinctively sniffing for the scent of camphorated oil.

"What's happening down there?" Grace asked cheerfully.

Clio didn't return her smile. "Jake and Julius and Hugo have been put on the carpet for letting you out in the boat."

"It can't have been *too* serious," Grace answered. "Jake and Julius have just been in to say goodnight. I thanked them very prettily for saving my life. They seemed quite happy."

"Aren't you at all sorry for all the trouble you caused?"

Grace regarded her. "There isn't anything to be gained from sorrow. It was an accident. I'm glad I'm not dead, that's all." She stretched her arms lazily in her white nightgown. "I'm not ready to die. Nothing's even begun yet."

Clio didn't try to say any more. She undressed in silence, and when she lay down, she turned away from Grace and folded the sheet over her own head.

In the night, Grace dreamed that she was in the water again. The black weight of it poured over her, filling her lungs and choking the life out of her. When she opened her eyes, she could see tiny faces hanging in the light, a long way over her head, and she knew that she was already dead and lying in the ground. She woke up, soaked in her own sweat and with a scream of terror rising in her throat. But she didn't give voice to the scream. She wouldn't wake Clio or Nanny, who was asleep in the room next door. Instead she held her pillow in her arms and bit down into it to maintain her silence. She kicked off the covers that constricted her, too much like the horrible weight of water, and lay until she shivered with the cold air drying the sweat on her skin.

At last, with her jaw aching from being clenched so tight, she knew that the nightmare had receded and she could trust herself not to cry out. Stiffly she drew the blankets over her shoulders and settled herself for sleep once again.

Downstairs, after Clio and the boys had gone up to bed, Nathaniel went into the drawing room where his wife and sister-in-law were sitting together. They had changed for dinner, and in their gowns with lace fichus and jewels and elaborate coiffures, there was no outward sign of the day's disturbances. He had not expected that there would be. Blanche and Eleanor were alike in their belief that civilized behavior was the first essential of life. Nathaniel had been fascinated from the first meeting with her to discover how unconventional Eleanor could be, and yet still obey the rigid rules of her class. She had married him, after all, a Jew and a foreigner, and still remained as impeccably of the English upper classes as her sister the Countess. He smiled at the sight of the two of them.

Nathaniel kissed his wife fondly and murmured to Blanche that she looked as beautiful as he had ever seen her, a credit to her own remarkable powers of composure after such a severe shock. Then he strolled away to the mahogany chiffonier and poured himself a large whiskey and soda from the tray.

"I still think we should try to reach John," Blanche announced.

Nathaniel sighed. They had already agreed that John would have been out with the guns all day, and that now he would have returned, there was no real necessity to disturb him. "What could he do?" he repeated, reasonably. "Leave the man to his pheasants and cards. Grace is all right. I have dealt with the boys."

Blanche closed her eyes for a moment, shuddered a little. "It was all so very frightening." Her sister rested a hand on her arm in sympathy, looking appealingly up at her husband. Nathaniel took a stiff pull at his drink. He didn't like having to act the disciplinarian, as he had done this evening to the three boys, particularly when he saw clearly enough that it was Grace who had been at fault. The business had made him hungry, and he was looking forward to his dinner. He was congratulating himself on not having to sit down to it with fussy, whiskery, humorless John Leominster for company. He did not want him summoned now, or at any time before he had conveyed himself back to Town or to Oxford.

"It's all over now," he soothed her. "Try to see it as a useful experience for them. Learning that rules are not made just to curb their pleasure."

And I sound just as pompous about it as Leominster himself, Nathaniel thought. He laughed his deep, pleasing, bass laugh and drank the rest of his whiskey at a gulp.

"I'm sure you're right," Eleanor supported him, and at last Blanche inclined her elegant head. The little parlormaid who performed the butler's duties in the holiday house came in to announce to her ladyship that dinner was served. Nathaniel cheerfully extended an arm to each sister and they swept across the sand-scented hallway to the dining room.

Nathaniel orchestrated the conversation ably, assisted by Eleanor, and they negotiated the entire meal without a single mention of death by drowning. At the end of it, when the ladies withdrew, Blanche was visibly happy again. There was no further mention of calling John back from his sport.

Nathaniel sat over his wine for a little longer. He was thinking about the children, mostly about Grace. He had not tried to lecture her, as he had done the boys. He had sat on the edge of her bed instead. Grace had faced him with the expression that was such a subtle mingling of Blanche and Eleanor and his own dreamy, clever, ambiguous Clio, and yet made a sum total that was quite different from all of them. He thought he read, behind her defiant eyes, that Grace had already been frightened enough and needed no further punishment.

They had talked instead about the girls learning to swim. He had made her laugh with imitations of the mothers' reaction to the idea.

Now that he was alone Nathaniel let himself imagine the threat of Grace's death, the possibility that he had denied to the women. His fist clenched around the stem of his glass as the unwelcome images presented themselves. It came to him then that he loved his niece. There was determination in her, and there was something else, too. It was an awareness of her own female power and a readiness to use it. She was magnetic. It was no wonder that his own boys were enslaved by her, Nathaniel thought. And then he put down his glass and laughed at himself.

Grace was ten years old. There would come a time to worry about Grace and Jake, but it was not yet.

Nathaniel strolled outside to listen to the sea. He sat and smoked a cigar, watching the glimmering whitish line of the breakers in the dark. Then he threw the stub aside and went up to his wife's bedroom.

Eleanor was sitting at her dressing table in her nightdress. Her long hair hung down, and she was twisting it into a rope ready for bed. Nathaniel went to her and put his hands on her shoulders. He loved the straight line of her back, and the set of her head on her long neck.

Very slowly he bent his head and put his mouth against the warm, scented skin beneath her earlobe. Watching their reflections in the glass he thought of Beauty and the Beast. His coarse black beard moved against her white skin and shining hair as he lifted his hands around her throat and began to undo the pearly buttons.

"Nathaniel," Eleanor murmured. "Tonight, of all nights, after what has happened?"

"And what has happened? A childish escapade, with fortunately no damage done. All's well, my love." He reassured her, as he had reassured Clio.

All's well.

His hands moved inside her gown, spreading to lift the heavy weight of her breasts. He loved the amplitude of her, released from the day's armor of whalebone and starch. She had a round, smooth belly, folds of dissolving flesh, fold on intricate fold. Eleanor gave a long sigh. She lifted her arms to place them around her husband's neck. Her eyes had already gone hazy.

Eleanor had had four children. Even from the beginning, when she was a girl of twenty who barely knew what men were supposed to do, she had enjoyed her husband's love-making. But it had never been so good as it was now, now when they were nearly middle-aged. Sometimes, in the daytime, when she looked up from her letters or lowered her parasol, he could meet her eye and make her blush.

He lifted her to her feet now so that she stood facing him. Nathaniel knelt down and took off her feathered satin slippers. Then he lifted up the hem of her nightgown to expose her blue-white legs. His beard tickled her skin as he laid his face against her thigh.

An hour later, Eleanor and Nathaniel fell asleep in each other's arms. In all the dark house, Grace was the only one who lay awake. She held on to her pillow and waited for the water and her fears to recede.

Two

"MY MOTHER WAS A HOLBOROUGH, you know," Clio said.

Elizabeth did know. She also knew that Clio's grandmother had been Miss Constance Earley, who had married Sir Hubert Holborough, Baronet, of Holborough Hall, Leicestershire, in 1875. Her daughters had been born in April 1877.

Lady Holborough never fully recovered from the stress of the twin pregnancy and birth, and she lived the rest of her life as a semi-invalid. There were no more children. Blanche and Eleanor Holborough spent their childhood in rural isolation in Leicestershire, best friends as well as sisters.

Elizabeth knew all this, and more. She had the family diaries, letters, Bibles, copies of birth and death certificates, the biographer's weight of bare facts and forgotten feelings from which to flesh out her people. She thought she knew more about the history of their antecedents than Clio had ever done, and Clio had forgotten so much. Clio could not even remember what they had talked about last time they met.

And yet Clio possessed rare pools of memory in which the water was so clear that she could stare down and see every detail of a single day, a day that had been submerged long ago by the flood of successive days pouring down upon it. Elizabeth wanted to lean over her shoulder and look into those pools too. That was why she came to sit in this room, with her miniature tape recorder and her notebook, to look at reflections in still water.

"A Holborough. Yes," Elizabeth said.

"Mother used to tell me stories about when she was a little girl."

When Blanche and Eleanor were girls, a hundred years ago.

"What sort of stories?"

Clio gave her a cunning look, to show that she was aware of the eagerness behind the question. "Stories . . ." she said softly, on an expiring breath.

There was a silence, and then she began.

"Holborough was a fine house. Not on the scale of Stretton, of course, but it was the first house in the neighborhood. There was a maze in the gardens. Mother and Aunt Blanche used to lead new governesses into it and lose them. They knew every leaf and twig themselves. They would slip away and leave the poor creatures to wander all the afternoon. Then the gardeners would hear the pitiful cries and come to the rescue."

Elizabeth had visited Holborough Hall. After it had been sold in the Twenties, it had been a preparatory school and then in wartime a training camp for Army Intelligence officers. After the war it had stood empty, then seen service as a school again. Lately it had become a conference center. The famous maze had survived, just. It looked very small and dusty, marooned in a wide sea of tarmac on which delegates parked their cars.

"Can't you imagine them?" Clio was saying. "Identical little girls in pinafores, whisking gleefully and silently down the green alleys?"

Elizabeth smiled. "Yes, I can imagine."

"They had to make their own amusements. There were no other children. It wasn't like it was for me, living in the middle of Oxford, with brothers and cousins always there."

But it had been a happy childhood, Clio knew that, because Eleanor and Blanche often spoke of it. There had been carriage drives and calls with their mother, when she was well enough. There had been outings in winter to follow the hunt, with their father's groom. Sir Hubert was an expert horseman. There had even been visits to London, to shop and to visit Earley relatives. There had been nannies and governesses and the affairs of the estate and the village. But most important of all, there had been the private world that they had created between them.

It was a world governed only by their imaginations, a mutual creation that released them from the carpet-bedded gardens and the crowded mid-Victorian interiors of Holborough, and set them free. They made their own voyages, their own discoveries, even spoke their own language. The intimacy of it lasted them all their lives, even when the intricate games were long forgotten.

Their imaginary world of play was put aside, reluctantly, when the real world judged that it was time for them to be grown up.

Blanche and Eleanor accepted the judgment obediently, because they had been brought up to do as they were told, but they kept within themselves a component that remained childlike, together.

Eleanor's husband Nathaniel thought it was this buried streak of childishness that gave them their air of unconventionality buttoned within perfect propriety. He found it very alluring.

When the twins reached the age of seventeen, Sir Hubert and Lady Holborough decided that their daughters must do the Season. Constance had been presented at Court as a debutante, and in the same year she had been introduced to and then become engaged to Hubert. There had been little Society or London life for her in the years afterward, because of her own ill-health and her husband's addiction to field sports, but they were both agreed that there was no reason to deny their daughters their chances of a good marriage.

Constance was apprehensive, and her nervousness took the form of vague illness. But still, a house was taken in Town, and more robust and cosmopolitan Earley aunts were enlisted to launch their nieces into Society.

The twins brought few material or social advantages with them to London in 1895. Their father was a baronet of no particular distinction, except on the hunting field. Their mother came from an old family and had been a beauty in her day, but she had not been much seen for more than fifteen years. There was no great fortune on either side.

But still, against the odds, perhaps because they didn't care whether they were or not, the Misses Holborough were a Success.

They were not beautiful. They had tall foreheads and narrow, too-long noses, but they had handsome figures and large dark eyes and expressive mouths that often seemed to register private amusement. Nathaniel Hirsh was not the first man to be attracted by their obviously enjoyable unity in an exclusive company of two. They began to be invited, and then to be courted. Young men joked about declaring their love to a Miss Holborough on one evening, and then discovering on the next that they had fervently reiterated it to the wrong one.

The joke was more often Blanche and Eleanor's own. It amused them to tease. From infancy they had used their likeness to play tricks on nannies and governesses, and it seemed natural to extend the game to their dancing partners. They wore each other's gowns and exchanged their feathered headdresses, became the other for a night, and then switched back again. They acquired a reputation for liveliness that added to their appeal.

One evening toward the end of the Season there was a ball at
Norfolk House. Blanche and Eleanor had received their cards, and
because Lady Holborough was unwell, they were chaperoned by
Aunt Frederica Earley. Sir Hubert escorted them, although he had
no patience with either dancing or polite conversation. He was
anxious for the tedium of parading his daughters through the
marriage market to be over and done with, so he could return home
to Leicestershire and his horses. He had already announced to his
wife that he considered the whole affair to be a waste of his time
and his money, since neither girl showed any inclination to choose
a husband, or to do anything except whisper and giggle with her
sister.

The Duchess's ballroom was crowded, and the twins were soon
swept into the dancing. Their aunt, having married her own daughters, was free to watch them with proprietary approval. Blanche
was in rose pink and Eleanor in silver. They looked elegant and
they moved gracefully. They had no particular advantages, the
poor lambs, but they would do. Mrs. Earley was not worried about
them.

She was not the only onlooker who followed the swirls of rose
pink and silver through the dance.

There was an urbane-looking gentleman at the end of the room
who watched the mirror faces as they swung, and smiled, and
swung again. The room was full of reflections but these were
brighter; their images doubled each other until the ballroom
seemed full of dark hair and assertive noses and cool, interrogative
glances.

The gentleman inclined his head to one of the ladies who sat
beside him. "Who are they?" he asked.

The woman fastened a button at the wrist of her long white
glove.

"They are the Misses Holborough," she answered. "Twins,"
she added unnecessarily, and with a touch of disapproval in her
voice that made it sound as if it were careless of them.

"They are interesting," the man said. "Do you know their
family?"

"The lady in blue, over there, is their aunt. Mrs. Earley. I am
acquainted with her. Their mother is an invalid, I believe, and their
father is a bore. I would be happy to give you any more information, if I possessed it."

The man laughed. His companion had daughters in the room
who were not yet married and who were much less intriguing than

the Misses Holborough. He asked, "And may I be presented to Mrs. Earley?"

A moment later, he was bowing over another gloved hand.

"Mr. John Singer Sargent," Mrs. Earley's acquaintance announced.

"I should very much like to paint your nieces, Mrs. Earley," the artist said.

Mrs. Earley was flattered and agreed that it was a charming idea, but regretted that the suggestion would have to be put to Sir Hubert, her brother-in-law. When Sir Hubert reappeared in the ballroom, he was still smarting from the loss of fifty-six guineas at a friendly game of cards, and he was not in a good humor. Fortunately, Mr. Sargent had moved away and was not in the vicinity to hear the response to his proposal.

Sir Hubert said that he couldn't imagine what the fellow was thinking of, wanting him to pay some no doubt colossal sum for a pretty portrait of two silly girls who had never had a sensible thought in their lives. The answer was certainly not. It was a piece of vanity, and he wanted to hear no more about it.

"You make yourself quite clear, Hubert," Mrs. Earley said, pressing her lips together. No wonder Constance was always indisposed, she thought.

The ball was over. Blanche and Eleanor presented themselves with flushed cheeks and bright eyes and the pleasure of the latest tease reverberating between them. The Holboroughs' carriage was called and the party made its way home, to Sir Hubert's obvious satisfaction.

The end of the Season came. The lease on the town house ran out, and the family went back to Holborough Hall. Blanche and Eleanor were the only ones who were not disappointed by the fact that there was no news of an engagement for either of them. They had had a wonderful time, and they were ready to repeat the experience next year. They had no doubt that they could choose a husband apiece when they were quite ready.

The autumn brought the start of the hunting season. For Sir Hubert it was the moment when the year was reborn. From the end of October to the beginning of March, from his estate outside the hunting town of Melton Mowbray, Sir Hubert could ride to hounds if he wished on six days of every week. There were five days with the Melton packs, the Quorn, the Cottesmore, and the Belvoir, and a sixth to be had with the Fernie in South Leicestershire. There were ten hunters in the boxes in the yard at Holborough for Sir

Hubert and his friends, and a bevy of grooms to tend them and to ride the second horses out to meet the hunt at the beginning of the afternoon's sport.

The hall filled up with red-faced gentlemen whose conversation did not extend beyond horses and hunting. They rode out during the day, and in the evenings they ate and drank, played billiards, and gambled heavily.

Now that they were out, Blanche and Eleanor were expected to join the parties for dinner. They listened dutifully to the hunting talk, and kept their mother company after dinner in the drawing room, while the men sat over their port or adjourned to the card tables in the smoking room.

"Is this what it will be like when we are married?" Blanche whispered, trying to press a yawn back between her lips.

"It depends upon whom we marry, doesn't it?" Eleanor said, with a touch of grimness that was new to her.

Then one night there was a new guest at dinner, a little younger and less red-faced than Sir Hubert's usual companions. He was introduced to the Holborough ladies as the Earl of Leominster.

They learned that Lord Leominster lived at Stretton, in Shropshire, and that he also owned a small hunting box near Melton. The house was usually let for the season, but this year the owner was occupying it himself with a small party of friends. Sir Hubert and his lordship had met when they enjoyed a particularly good day out with the Quorn, and both of them having failed to meet their grooms at dusk, they had hacked part of the way home together.

Lord Leominster had accepted his new friend's invitation to dine.

On the first evening, Eleanor and Blanche regarded him without much favor. John Leominster was a thin, fair-skinned man in his early thirties. He had a dry, careful manner that made an odd contrast with the rest of Sir Hubert's vociferous friends.

"Quiet sort of fellow," Sir Hubert judged. "Can't tell what he's thinking. But he goes well. Keen as mustard over the fences, you should see him."

Lady Holborough quickly established that his lordship was un-married.

"Just think, girls," she whispered. "What a chance for one of you. Stop smirking, Eleanor, do. It isn't funny at all."

The girls rolled their eyes at each other. Lord Leominster seemed very old and hopelessly shriveled from their eighteen-year-old standpoint. They were much more interested in the cavalry officers from the army remount depot in Melton.

But it soon became clear that the twins had attracted his attention, as they drew everyone else's that winter. Against the brown setting of Holborough they were as exotic and surprising as a pair of pink camellias on a February morning. After the first dinner he called again, and then became a regular visitor.

It was also evident, from the very beginning, that he could tell the two of them apart as easily as their mother could. There were no mischievous games of substitution. Eleanor was Eleanor, and Blanche was the favored one.

John Leominster became the first event in their lives that they did not share, did not dissect between them.

Eleanor was startled and hurt, and she took refuge in mockery. She called him Sticks for his thin legs, and before she spoke she cleared her throat affectedly in the way that Leominster did before making one of his considered pronouncements. She made sure that Blanche saw his finicky ways with gloves and handkerchiefs, and waited for her sister to join her in the mild ridicule. But Blanche did not, and they became aware that a tiny distance was opening between them.

Blanche was torn. After the first evening she felt guilty in not responding to Eleanor's overtures, but she began to feel flattered by the Earl of Leominster's attention. She was also surprised to discover how pleasant it was to be singled out for herself alone, instead of always as one half of another whole. As the days and then the weeks passed, she was aware of everyone in the household watching and waiting to see what would happen, and of Constance almost holding her breath. She saw her suitor's thin legs and fussy manners as clearly as her sister did, but then she thought, *The Countess of Leominster* . . .

One night Eleanor asked impulsively, "What are you going to do, Blanche? About Sticks, I mean?"

"Don't call him that. I can't do anything. I have to wait for him to offer, don't I?"

Eleanor stared at her. Until that moment she had not fully understood that her sister meant to accept him if he did propose marriage.

"Oh, Blanchie. You can't marry him. You don't love him, do you?"

Blanche pulled out a long ringlet of hair and wound it around her forefinger. It was a characteristic mannerism, familiar to Eleanor from their earliest years. "*I* love you," Eleanor shouted. "I won't let him take you away."

"Shh, Ellie." Blanche was deeply troubled. "We both have to marry somebody, someday, don't we? If I don't love him now, I can learn to. He's a kind man. And there's the title, and Stretton, and everything else. I can't turn him down, can I?"

Eleanor shouted again. "Yes, you can. Neither of us will marry anyone. We'll live together. Who needs a husband?"

Slowly, Blanche shook her head. "We do. Women do," she whispered.

Eleanor saw that her sister was crying. There were tears in her own eyes, and she stood up and put her arms around Blanche. "Go on, go on then. Make yourself a Countess. Just have me to stay in your house. Let me be aunt to all the little Strettons. Just try to *stop* me being there."

Blanche answered, "I won't. I never would."

They cried a little, shedding tears for the end of their childhood. And then, with a not completely disagreeable sense of melancholy, they agreed that they had better sleep or else look like witches in the morning.

There came the evening of an informal dance held in the wooden hall of the village next to Holborough. The twins dressed in their rose pink and silver and sighed that Beecham village hall was a long way from Norfolk House. But there was a large contingent of whooping army officers at Beecham, and there was also John Leominster. While Eleanor was passed from arm to arm in the energetic dancing, Blanche agreed that she would take a respite from the heat and noise and stroll outside the hall with her partner.

Lady Holborough inclined her head to give permission as they passed the row of chaperones, and Blanche knew that all their eyes were on them as they passed out into the night. It was a mild evening, but she drew her fur wrap tightly around her shoulders like a protective skin. She was ready, but she was also afraid. They walked, treading carefully over the rough ground.

"Blanche, you know that I would very much like you to see Stretton, and to introduce you to my mother."

Blanche inclined her head, but she said nothing.

John cleared his throat. She was irresistibly reminded of Eleanor's mimicry, but she made herself put Eleanor out of her mind and concentrate on what was coming. It was, she knew, the most important moment of her life. If it seemed disappointing that it should have come now, outside the barnlike hall at the end of a rutted country lane, then she put her disappointment aside and waited.

"I think you know what I want to say to you. Blanche, my dear, will you marry me?"

There was nothing more to wait for. There it was, spoken.

"Yes, John. I will," Blanche said. Her voice sounded very small.

He stopped walking and took her in his arms. His lips, when they touched hers, were soft and dry, and they did not move. That seemed to be all there was.

"I shall speak to your father in the morning," John said. He took her hand and they turned to walk back toward the hall. "You make me very happy," he said.

"I'm glad," Blanche answered.

After the engagement was announced, his lordship seemed to become aware of the bond between his fiancée and her twin sister. It was as if he could safely acknowledge its existence, now that he had made sure of Blanche for himself. He reminisced about how he had first seen them, coming arm in arm into the drawing room at Holborough.

"As lovely as a pair of swans on a lake," he said, surprising them with a rare verbal flourish. Blanche smiled at him, and he put his hand on her arm. He took the opportunity to tell the sisters he wished to have their portrait painted. The double portrait would mark his engagement to Blanche, but it would also celebrate the Misses Holborough. He had already chosen the artist. It was to be Sargent.

When the spring came, Lady Holborough and her daughters removed to London. Blanche's wedding clothes and trousseau needed to be bought, and there were preparations to be made for Eleanor's second Season. They settled at Aunt Frederica Earley's house, and in the intervals between shopping and dressmakers' appointments the twins presented themselves for sittings at Mr. Sargent's studio.

They enjoyed their afternoons with the painter. He had droll American manners, he made them laugh, and he listened with amusement to their talk.

The portrait, as it emerged, reflected their rapport.

The girls were posed on a green velvet-padded love seat. Blanche faced forward, dressed in creamy silk with ruffles of lace at her throat and elbows. Her head was tilted to one side, as if she were listening to her sister's talk, although her dark eyes looked straight out of the canvas. Her forefinger marked her place in the book on her lap. Eleanor faced in the opposite direction, but the painter had turned her so that she looked back over her own shoulder, her eyes following the same direction as her sister's. Their mouths were painted as if they were on the point of curving into smiles, the eyes were bright with laughter and the dark eyebrows arched questioningly over them. Eleanor wore sky-blue satin, with a navy-blue velvet ribbon around her throat.

Their white, rounded forearms rested side by side on the serpentine back of the love seat. It was a pretty pose.

The girls looked what they were, identically young and innocent and good-humored. There was no need for Mr. Sargent to soften any of the sharpness of his vision with superficial flattery. He painted what had first attracted him in the ballroom at Norfolk House, twin images of lively inexperience.

"You have made us look too pretty," Eleanor told him.

"I have painted you as I see you," he answered. "I can do no more, and I would not wish to do less."

"We look happy," Blanche observed.

"And so you should," John Sargent told her, with the advantage of more than twenty years' longer experience of the world. "You should be happy."

Even then, the girls understood that he had captured their girlhood for them on canvas, just at the point when it was ending.

The Misses Holborough was judged a success. John Leominster paid for the double portrait, and after the wedding it was transported to Stretton where it was hung in the saloon. Blanche sometimes hesitated in front of it, sighing as she passed by.

Eleanor was often at Stretton with her, but she could not always be there. Blanche missed her, but she was also occupied with trying to please her husband, and with the peculiar responsibilities of taking over from her mother-in-law as the mistress of the old house. The separation was much harder for Eleanor.

The dances and dinners of the second Season were no longer a novelty. They were also much less amusing without Blanche, who was away in Italy on her wedding journey all through the height of it. A small compensation for Eleanor was a new friendship with her cousin Mary, the younger daughter of Aunt Frederica Earley. Mary had married a languid and very handsome man called Norton Ferrier, and the Ferriers were part of a group of smart, young, well-connected couples who prided themselves on their powers of intellectual and aesthetic discrimination. They called their circle the

Souls, and they spent weekends in one another's comfortable houses in the country, reading modern poetry and writing letters and diaries and discussing art.

Mary was kind-hearted and generous, and she began to invite her young cousin to accompany Norton and herself on their weekend visits. Constance was glad to let her go, and there could be no objection to Eleanor making excursions in the company of her older married cousin.

The Souls were sophisticated and underoccupied. Once their conventional marriages had set them free, they were at liberty to wander within the limits of their miniature world and amuse themselves by falling in and out of love with one another. Most of them had one or two young children. They had done their family duty, and they left their heirs at home in their nurseries while they traveled to one another's houses to play, and to talk, and to pursue their romantic interests. At night the corridors of the old houses whispered with footsteps. The mute family portraits looked down on the secret transpositions.

There was one house in a village near Oxford that Eleanor liked particularly. It was an ancient gray stone house, set in a beautiful walled garden. Eleanor liked to wander on her own along the stone paths, breathing in the scents and bending down to examine a leaf or a tiny flower beside her shoe. At Fernhaugh she was perfectly happy to leave the Souls to their books and their mysterious murmurings, and to enjoy herself amongst the plants.

She was, she told herself with a touch of mournful pride, learning to be by herself. And at the same time she wondered if she could persuade Blanche to begin the creation of a garden like this somewhere in the Capability Brown park at Stretton.

One Sunday morning at Fernhaugh, Eleanor was walking in the garden. There had been rain overnight and the perfume was intensified by the damp air. She knew that some of the house party had dutifully gone to church to hear their host reading the lesson, but that most of the Souls were not yet downstairs. There were guests expected for luncheon, but the drawing room with the French windows looking out on the terrace was still empty. Even the gardeners would not appear today. The green enclosure in all its glory was hers alone.

Eleanor wandered, breathing in the richness, letting her fingers trail over dewy leaves and fat, fleshy petals. She felt for a moment as if she might at last aspire to the sensuous abandon of the real

Souls. She let her eyes close, feeling the garden absorb her into its green heart.

From close at hand, too close, an unfamiliar voice asked, "Are you all right?"

Eleanor's eyes snapped open.

She saw a man she had never met, a big man in odd black clothes made even odder-looking by his big, thick black beard. He must have come silently over the grass, although his feet looked big enough to make a clatter on any surface.

"I am perfectly all right. Why should you think I am not?"

"I wondered if you were going to faint. Or worse, perhaps."

It came to her how she must have looked, drooping with closed eyes between the soaking leaves, and her face turned red.

"Thank you, but there's no danger of anything like that. Unless as the result of shock. From being pounced on in an unguarded moment by a perfect stranger."

"By a peculiar-looking person far from perfect, don't you mean?"

The man was smiling. His beard seemed to spread around his jawline. The smile revealed his shiny mouth and healthy white teeth.

"I don't mean anything," Eleanor said, retreating from this newcomer. "Will you excuse me? I should go and make myself ready for luncheon."

To her surprise, the man turned and began to walk with her across the grass toward the house. He strolled companionably with his hands behind his back, looking from side to side.

"This garden is very beautiful," he said. And then, peering sideways at Eleanor with unmistakable mischief, he recited, *"Sed vos hortorum per opaca silentia longe Celerant plantae virides, et concolor umbra. Do you know the lines?"*

Blanche and Eleanor's governesses had had to negotiate too many other obstacles at Holborough. There had been little time to spare for Latin verse.

"No," Eleanor said. She was thinking that the man was not such a misfit at Fernhaugh as his appearance suggested. No doubt the Souls would all be familiar with the verse, whatever it was. Or would at least claim to be.

"No? It's Marvell, of course. He is addressing Innocence. He finds her in the shaded silences of gardens, far off, hiding among the green plants and like-colored shadow."

"Thank you so much for the translation." Eleanor took refuge in briskness. They had reached the terrace, and the open doors of the drawing room were only a few steps away. "Don't let me detain you any further in your search for Innocence amongst the rose bushes."

The man was smiling again, looking full into her face. He seemed very large and dark and exotic in the English summer garden. He wouldn't let her go so easily. "In the absence of our hostess, may I introduce myself? I am Nathaniel Hirsh."

"Eleanor Holborough."

The man's hand enveloped hers. The grip was like a bear's.

"And now you must excuse me."

Eleanor mounted the two steps to the terrace level and passed out of the sunshine into the dimness of the drawing room. Nathaniel watched her go. He was thinking with irritation that although he had been born in England and had lived in England for most of his twenty-six years, he would never make an Englishman. He could never get the subtle nuances of behavior quite right. He could never even get the broad principles. Today he had arrived for luncheon at least an hour too early. Then he had seen a striking girl daydreaming in the wonderful garden. An Englishman would have approached her with some stiff-necked platitude, and she would have known exactly how to respond. But instead he had pounced on her with some clumsy joke. And then he had begun declaiming in Latin. Innocence amongst the green plants and like-colored shadow, indeed.

Yet that was how she had looked.

"You will never learn, Nathaniel," he said aloud. But he was humming as he leaned over and picked a yellow rose from the branch trailing over the terrace wall. He slid the stem into his buttonhole. He had liked the look of Eleanor Holborough. He had liked even better her cool admission of ignorance of Marvell's *Hortus*. Nathaniel did not think many of the other guests at Fernhaugh would have acknowledged as much. He liked Philip Haugh well enough, but he did not have much patience with the rest of the crew.

He reminded himself now that he had accepted Philip's luncheon invitation in order to come and observe the idle wealthy at play, and to be amused by them. He could see Lady Haugh beyond the drawing-room doors, so he judged that it was at last the acceptable time to arrive. Nathaniel felt familiar exasperation. How could he have known that the fashionable hour was so much later than stated?

But now that he was here, he would go in and be amused, as he had intended, and at the same time he would take the opportunity of seeing where Eleanor Holborough fitted into this languid coterie.

When Eleanor came into the drawing room again, the rest of the guests were assembled. She looked around quickly and saw Nathaniel Hirsh. He was talking to Philip Haugh and Norton Ferrier. Beside Philip's well-bred colorlessness and Norton's perfectly sculpted feminine beauty, it surprised her to see how very large and disheveled and red-blooded he looked. From time to time his huge, booming bass laugh filled the murmuring room. Eleanor sensed that the other guests had to restrain themselves from turning around to stare. And to her surprise she felt her sympathy was with Nathaniel, rather than with Mary and Norton and their friends. What had he said or done to make her feel that they were a special minority of two?

Nathaniel had seen her, but he made no effort to navigate his way through the party to her side. Eleanor concentrated very hard on the conversation immediately around her, and wondered why not.

She need not have worried. Nathaniel had already discovered from Lady Haugh that they were to be seated together at the luncheon table. He was waiting for his chance.

There was no formal taking-in at Fernhaugh, but when Lady Haugh leaned elegantly on Norton Ferrier's arm and drifted toward the dining room, Nathaniel materialized at Eleanor's side. Philip Haugh murmured the briefest introduction. Nathaniel took her hand and bowed over it, as though they had never seen each other before. On his arm Eleanor felt small and light, as if the toes of her shoes barely touched the floor.

"Now then," he said as they sat down, "we can talk. Tell me exactly who you are, and what you are doing here."

Eleanor told him, and he listened intently. For the first time, she talked about herself without referring to Blanche. She laid out the bare facts of her life as if it had been hers alone, and just as Blanche had done, she discovered that it was agreeable to be reckoned with for herself, instead of as one half of a whole. It was more agreeable still just to sit with this unusual, suddenly solemn man looking into her eyes. The food came and went. The partners on their opposite sides were brutally neglected. Mary Ferrier caught Lady Haugh's eye, and they exchanged a small, surprised *moue*.

"I have a twin sister," Eleanor said at length, touched by a finger of guilt. "She was married earlier this year."

"You miss her," Nathaniel remarked, as if stating what was obvious.

"Yes, I do."

"Are you very alike?"

"We are identical."

Nathaniel's thick eyebrows drew together. When he opened his mouth, Eleanor saw the movement of his tongue and the elastic contraction of his lips. She had never been so sharply aware of anyone's physical nearness, of the few inches of air and layers of cloth between them. She should have glanced away, but she let his eyes hold hers.

"I don't think so," Nathaniel said softly. "I believe you are unique."

Eleanor did look away, then. She turned deliberately to her neighbor on the other side and began a conversation about architecture. She did not turn back until she was sure of herself, and when she did speak to Nathaniel again, it was in an attempt to take control.

"You haven't told me who or what you are. It's your turn to confess now." To her disgust Eleanor knew that she sounded arch rather than commanding. Nathaniel's mouth twitched in the depths of his beard.

"I am a teacher. I live in Oxford."

That was all. Lady Haugh was standing up. Eleanor rose and followed her. When they sat down in the drawing room with their coffee cups, Eleanor found herself on a sofa between Mary and her hostess.

"What did you think of our friend Mr. Hirsh?" Frances Haugh asked her, ready to be amused.

"I liked him," Eleanor said. She hadn't learned the Souls' way of pretending to feel less, or more, or something different. "Who is he?"

"He's a friend of Philip's. He is very clever; last year he was elected a Fellow of All Souls. He is a don, a linguist, I believe. Eccentric in the way that people of that sort often are. And he is Jewish, of course."

Eleanor had met plenty of Jews during her two Seasons. There were dozens of them in the new aristocracy. Many of them were rich, and most of them were good company. They were invited everywhere, and hostesses were pleased to welcome them while congratulating themselves at the same time on their own enlightened attitudes. Now that she thought about it, Eleanor realized that

of course Nathaniel Hirsh was a Jew. And at the same time she
knew that he was different from the bankers and financiers and
manufacturers she had met in the London ballrooms. They were
indistinguishable except by name from the old families.

Nathaniel was distinguishable. Nathaniel was distinguishable
from everyone else she had met in her life. She didn't want to label
him, Jewish or not, suitable or otherwise. He was, she understood,
above that.

When he came to claim her from between Mary and Frances,
Eleanor went with him. Mary watched them go out into the garden,
then shrugged her pretty shoulders.

"Whatever will Aunt Constance think?" she wondered, and
laughed faintly.

Eleanor and Nathaniel walked the shady paths together. They
could never remember afterward what they talked about, only that
there was a great deal to say. The sun moved and dipped behind the
garden's fringe of elms.

When it was time for Nathaniel to leave, he took her hand. He
lifted it to his mouth and held it there. The beard was soft on her
skin, black against the whiteness.

"May I call again tomorrow?"

"I go back to Town tomorrow afternoon, with my cousin."

"I will call in the morning," Nathaniel said.

Eleanor smiled at him, and he saw all the light of the day in her
face.

That evening, Eleanor sat down at the writing table in her
bedroom and began a letter to Blanche. She had been intending to
tell her sister everything; about how Nathaniel Hirsh had appeared
in the garden at Fernhaugh and had immediately occupied the
middle of her private landscape. He had made her see how bland
the scenery was before he came. But then she thought of Blanche
and John Leominster together, and of the tentative, sometimes
puzzled way they seemed to defer to each other. She had never seen
John Leominster look the way Nathaniel had looked at her today,
and she didn't believe Blanche had ever known the mixture of
happy anticipation and certainty and dazzlement that she felt tonight.

Eleanor sighed, resting her chin in her hand and thinking of the
miraculous day that had produced Nathaniel. Then she put down
her pen. She never completed the letter.

Nathaniel went slowly back to Oxford. He was considering the
other women he knew, the dark, exuberant daughters of his

mother's friends and the few University ladies and the wives of his colleagues. None of them had Eleanor Holborough's air of opposites combined, of originality within the conventional, of passion contained by propriety. None of them even seemed to Nathaniel to be as perfectly beautiful as Eleanor.

He had accepted the invitation to Fernhaugh intending to listen and watch, and he came back having fallen in love.

The next morning, when he was leaving her again, Nathaniel kissed Eleanor on the mouth. She turned her face up to his, and kissed him back. There was no reason not to. They were honest with each other. Afterward, when he had gone, Mary and Frances looked speculatively at her. They were too discreet to ask direct questions, and Eleanor had enough self-possession to give nothing away. But her senses were sharpened by the feelings Nathaniel had stirred in her. She looked around Fernhaugh and suddenly understood what she saw.

As they were leaving the old house and Norton Ferrier bent his sleek head to kiss Frances Haugh good-bye, Eleanor felt as if her eyes had been opened. There was plenty for her to think about on the journey back to London.

"What will you tell my mother and Aunt Constance about Mr. Hirsh?" Mary asked slyly.

"The truth." Eleanor was composed. "When the right time comes."

They wrote to each other every day of the next week, letters of deepening affection. Eleanor discovered that Nathaniel was steeped in Goethe and Dante as well as Andrew Marvell, and her own responses seemed stilted and childish in answer to the fluently romantic pages he poured out to her. But Nathaniel answered that he loved her letters and would keep them forever. He also warned her, as gently as he could, that there might never come a right time to announce to their families that they intended to marry.

Nathaniel was right to be apprehensive. The news was greeted with even stronger opposition from Levi and Dora Hirsh than from the Holboroughs. The Hirshes wanted a Jewish daughter-in-law and Jewish grandchildren even more than Lady Holborough wanted another Countess in the family.

There were months of separations, and tearful reunions, and bitter family arguments.

In the end, Eleanor's conviction that all would finally be well was justified. The Holboroughs capitulated first and agreed that their daughter could throw herself away on a teacher, a foreigner, and a Jew, if that was what she really wished for. The Hirshes took a little longer to give way, but at last they consented to welcome Eleanor into their family. And then, once the decision had been made, she was received with much more warmth than Nathaniel was ever to know from the Holboroughs.

Miss Eleanor Holborough was married quietly in London to Mr. Nathaniel Hirsh, of New College, Oxford, on June 28, 1897. It was almost exactly a year since they had met in the garden at Fernhaugh.

The Countess of Leominster was in an interesting condition.

Blanche was at Stretton, preparing for the birth of her first child. When the time came, Eleanor traveled north to be with her sister. She had only been married for three months, and it was hard to leave Nathaniel. But Blanche was begging her to go, and Eleanor couldn't think of refusing.

Nathaniel consoled her, when he took her to the station for the Shrewsbury train, with a promise that while she was away he would find a house for them to buy. Nathaniel had given up his bachelor rooms in college, of course, and they had spent the first weeks of their marriage living in a little rented house at Iffley. Homemaking in it had reminded Eleanor of dolls' house games with Blanche. She protested that she was quite happy where they were, but Nathaniel had other ideas.

"We need a big house," he told her. "A proper house, for a family. A real home. I'll find it, and when you come back you can tell me if you approve. Then all we will need is children to fill it up."

"Nathaniel," whispered Eleanor, looking around to see if anyone might overhear. But she was only pretending to reprove him. Nathaniel wanted a big family, and she knew quite well that they were doing everything possible to achieve the beginning of one. They did it in the mornings, and in the quiet afternoons when Nathaniel came back from his tutorials, as well as in the proper shelter of the night. They regularly created their own world of feather pillows and tangled black hair and white skin, and Eleanor was surprised by how natural and how good it felt.

On her wedding night she had known next to nothing, and Nathaniel had no more practical experience than she did. But he knew what to do, as he seemed to know everything else, and he guided her confidently.

They learned quickly, together.

Eleanor had been ashamed, at first, of the way her body led her. She had believed that she should be passive and reticent, and meekly let Nathaniel do whatever it was he needed to do to her. But then she had discovered another Eleanor within herself, this Eleanor who would not be subdued except by what her husband did. It was not a matter of allowing him, as she had imagined, but of meeting him halfway. Sometimes, to Nathaniel's delight, it was more than halfway. Then she heard the other Eleanor scream out in the intensity of her response.

She had been ashamed until Nathaniel told her that there was nothing they could do together, in the seclusion of her bed, that was either wrong or unnatural. She believed him, as she believed everything he said.

"Come back soon," Nathaniel whispered, when he had installed her trunk and boxes in the train with their little Iffley housemaid who would be her lady's maid at Stretton. "I wish I was coming with you."

He did wish it. He liked to see his wife and her twin sister together. The double vision intensified his pleasure in the secret Eleanor known only to him, as well as tantalizing him with a sense of the other secrets the sisters shared only with each other. He thought, sometimes, of what it would be like to have the two of them together. . . .

"That would be quite unsuitable," Eleanor rebuked him. "This is a time for women."

"Not when my children are born. You won't banish me then."

"You will have to wait and see what happens when the time comes, Nathaniel."

The train was on the point of departure. Eleanor smiled up at him from under the brim of her feathered hat. She suspected that they would not have so very long to wait.

"Come back *soon*," he ordered her. "I didn't marry you to have to spend more than a day without you."

"I will," she promised him. "As soon as I'm sure Blanche doesn't need me any longer."

Nathaniel stood on the platform waving until the train was out of sight. At Shrewsbury, Lord Leominster's groom was waiting with the carriage to drive Eleanor to Stretton.

The approach to the house was by a winding carriage drive through the trees of the park. By this time, Eleanor was familiar enough with the view to be ready for the sight of Stretton itself, but the size of it still made her catch her breath at the first glimpse. The trees suddenly gave way to reveal a lake and a bridge and the house standing on a vast slope of grass beyond the water.

The original house was very old, but in the eighteenth century an ambitious Earl had commissioned Robert Adam to extend it and impose the appropriate grandeur on the south front. Now two short wings curved outward from the main body, and a dome had been added to crown the new composition. The centerpiece of this symmetrical arrangement was a porch raised on eight stone pillars, reached by a pair of stone staircases that rose from the graveled drive. The effect was magnificent, but the Leominster fortunes had never properly recovered from the expense.

The comparison of Stretton's creamy stone bulk with her cottage at Iffley made Eleanor smile a little as she was handed down at the porch steps.

The butler who swept down to meet her assured her that her ladyship was waiting anxiously upstairs. Eleanor almost ran in his stately wake. She found Blanche in the doorway of her own small drawing room on the first floor, and the sisters fell into each other's arms.

"You look so well, and pretty," Eleanor exclaimed when they were alone. Blanche did look well, dressed in a loose blue robe that almost hid her bulk. She rested one hand proudly on the summit of it.

"Sir John says that it will be any day." Sir John Williams was her obstetrician. "I wish it would come."

"And this is so cozy." Eleanor walked admiringly around the room. It was decorated in pale blue and eau-de-nil, with watercolor landscapes on the paneled walls. It was new since her last visit, and she thought how well it suited Blanche. The Adam interiors of the rest of the house were very fine, but they had been left untouched for a hundred years. The fabrics were beginning to decay, and there was an air of chilly gloom.

"John ordered it for me. It is so comfortable to have somewhere pretty and warm to sit. I spend all my days in here. Oh, *Eleanor*, how glad I am that you are here." Blanche sat down on her blue sofa and patted the place beside her. "Let me look properly at you." With her head on one side, she examined her sister's face. She saw contentment in every line of it, and something else too. There was a richness, a new luster that she had not seen before.

"And I can see that you are well."

Eleanor smiled. "I don't feel so very magnificent. I suffer from sickness. I believe—Blanchie, I haven't even told Nathaniel yet, but I think I may be in the same condition as you are."

After hugging and exclaiming, the sisters sat back to look at one another again. They felt that as married women, both carrying children, there were matters to be discussed that they could not have touched on before, for all their closeness.

Blanche said delicately, "Tell me, Eleanor, how do you find the *married* part of marriage?" She saw that her sister's mouth looked fuller than it had been, and her eyes were soft. There was color warming her neck and cheeks.

"Surprising, at first," Eleanor said. And then, laughing, "But afterward, like . . . finding out the answer to a riddle. A rather good riddle, with a particularly satisfying solution."

"A riddle?" Blanche was staring at her, uncomprehending.

"Yes, just that. One that you have half overheard, and never understood before. And you?"

"John is very good," Blanche answered, aware that it was no answer, any more than Eleanor's had seemed. But John *was* good, she told herself. He did not trouble her so very often, and when he did materialize in her bedroom, sliding in in the darkness to lie briefly on top of her, he seemed so insubstantial, so thin and light that she wondered if he was completely there. Afterward he would whisper to her, "I'm sorry, my dear. Will you forgive me?"

Blanche had no idea why her forgiveness should be necessary, because she had not felt particularly violated, but she gave it readily. She was fond of her husband, and recognized his kindness.

After waiting a moment, Eleanor realized that Blanche would say no more. She murmured, "Yes. I'm sure he is." She was remembering the letter she had started to write to Blanche on the night of meeting Nathaniel. She had known then that it was not the right thing to finish and post it.

Eleanor stood up and went to Blanche. She kissed the top of her head, in the middle where the dark hair parted to reveal the white skin beneath. Then she wandered to the window and looked down at the wide park.

"Will the baby be an heir for John and all this?"

"I am quite sure it is a boy, and so is John," Blanche said composedly.

Blanche's son was born a week later, and named Hugo John. By family tradition he took his father's second title, Viscount Culmington.

It was an easy, uncomplicated birth. Eleanor stayed with her sister until she was well enough to leave her rooms, and then she traveled back to Nathaniel with her own news.

Seven months later, in April 1898, Jacob Nathaniel Hirsh was born in Oxford, arriving as quickly and easily as his cousin Hugo had done.

Before his son's birth Nathaniel had found the family house he had always intended to own. It was to the north of the city, in the Woodstock Road, in the heart of an area of solid new houses colonized by the first generation of University dons who were allowed to marry and live outside their colleges. It was a tall red-brick building that reared up from its newly planted garden and loomed over the quiet road like a Gothic castle in miniature. There were arched windows at a dozen different levels, doors in unexpected recesses, and a round turret topped off with its own pinnacle of purplish slate. Inside there was a good deal of stained glass and polished mahogany, and short flights of shallow stairs leading from one mystifying level to the next. It had ten inconveniently sited bedrooms and only one bathroom; it cost much more money than they could afford; and Eleanor and Nathaniel both loved it.

The new house stood on an oddly shaped three-quarters-of-an-acre plot, which Eleanor claimed at once as her own, with the garden at Fernhaugh as her model. By the time Jacob was born, she felt her house and her garden fitting around her as comfortably as a shell enclosing an oyster. She told Nathaniel that he had better find that it suited him too, because she had no intention of ever living anywhere else.

"It is too big," Nathaniel protested. "All these rooms, just for us and Jakie and his nurse and a couple of maids. We need more children, Eleanor. We need to fill up the house. I want a dozen children, a whole team, a chamber orchestra."

Eleanor laughed at him. "A dozen? How will we feed them all?" The Hirshes had very little money.

"Leave that to me. I shall be Professor Hirsh before you know it." Eleanor didn't doubt it. She was proud of her husband's growing academic reputation, and she was glad to see the students who began to flock to their house to hear him talk.

"A chamber orchestra it shall be then," she agreed with mock obedience. Nathaniel loved music almost as much as he loved books.

In the next year Eleanor made a long summer visit to Stretton, taking Jake with her, and the sisters sat tranquilly in the shade of Capability Brown's trees with their babies beside them. Blanche

came to Oxford in her turn and discovered how much she enjoyed
the Hirshes' unconventional domestic life after the formalities of
Stretton. Eleanor often forgot to order food; the Irish cook was no
more reliable; Nathaniel could turn up with two or twenty hungry
undergraduates at any hour of the day; but the odd corners of the
red-brick miniature castle were full of the twins' laughter all
through Blanche's visit.

Their only regret was that their husbands would never be
friends. John Leominster was courteous, but he clearly regarded
Nathaniel as a dangerous barbarian. And where Eleanor had made
gentle fun of her brother-in-law, Nathaniel's jokes were sharper,
rooted in his mistrust of the English aristocracy itself. But both
men liked to see their sisters-in-law, and Eleanor and Blanche
contented themselves with that much.

Toward the end of 1900, when Jake was well out of babyhood
and Nathaniel was beginning to be anxious and impatient, Eleanor discovered that she was expecting another child. Her husband's delight at the news touched her deeply, and she
remembered his wish to be the father of an entire orchestra. She
could only be pleased for Nathaniel's sake when her doctor told
her a little later that she should prepare for twins. The news was
no great surprise. There were generations of twins in the Earley
family.

"Twins!" Nathaniel exclaimed. "A pair of violinists for the
Bach Double Concerto." Eleanor had never seen him look so
happy.

"And two more children to read their way through some of these
books. Jake will never manage it alone," she told him.

An added satisfaction was that Blanche was pregnant again too.

The weeks of the second pregnancy passed slowly. Eleanor grew
so large that she could hardly move. She sat in her garden through
the spring and into the early summer, watching Jake play and
waiting for news from Blanche, whose confinement was expected
before her own.

Then, early in the morning of Midsummer's Day 1901, almost a
month before she had expected it, Eleanor went into labor. The
twins, a black-haired boy and girl, were born that afternoon within
fifteen minutes of each other. They were small babies, but perfectly
healthy. Nathaniel knelt by his wife's bedside, crying tears of
gratitude.

That evening, the news reached the Woodstock Road that
Blanche had given birth to a daughter. She had been born at

midday, two hours before the Hirsh twins, at the Leominsters' town house in Belgrave Square.

All three deliveries had been quick and uncomplicated once again. Unlike poor Constance, the Holborough girls with their stately, ample figures were excellent breeders.

Eleanor lay weakly back against her pillows, half dazed with exhaustion and relief and happiness. "I can't believe it," she said, over and over again. "My daughter, and Blanche's, born on the very same day."

"You don't have to believe anything," Nathaniel said sternly. "Rest is all you have to do."

The three babies were christened together at the house in Belgrave Square. The girls were given each other's names, as well as their aunts' and the new Queen's. Their mothers had no doubt that their old communion would be passed on to the new generation. Lady Grace Eleanor Alexandra Clio Stretton and Miss Clio Blanche Alexandra Grace Hirsh would share everything that their mothers had shared. Julius Edward, the real twin, was after all a boy, and boys were different.

"They will be more than friends and more than sisters," Blanche said, leaning over the cradles to look at the tiny faces.

"Twins," Eleanor answered, her voice full of affection. "Like us."

Three

CLIO LAY ON HER BACK on her bed, her knees drawn up, following with her eyes the pattern of cracks in the ceiling. She was listening to the familiar sounds of the house, disentangling the various layers as they drifted up to her attic bedroom.

Closest to hand was the sound of Julius practicing. He ran up a scale and down again, up and down, the chains of notes left hanging in the air to be overtaken by their successors. Clio knew that he would be standing with his eyes shut, his face closed with concentration and his black hair falling over his forehead as the bow dipped and rose. As she listened the scale stopped and Julius launched into a piece of Bach. Clio nodded and folded her hands behind her head.

From below her, in the nursery, she could hear Alice begin to cry, and then the creaking footsteps of Nanny Cooper crossing the room to pick her up, or retrieve her ball, or whatever it was that she needed.

The baby Alice was only two years old, the last-born of the Hirsh children. The next-youngest, Tabitha, had been born in 1910, when the twins were already nine and Nathaniel had long given up hope of his chamber orchestra. After the twins, Eleanor had suffered two miscarriages and had been sure that there was no hope of another child. But then Tabitha had come, a big, contented baby who lay in her crib and smiled at the world, and two years later Alice arrived. Alice never seemed to sleep or to rest and she had a shrill, frequent cry, but she was also endlessly inquisitive and resourceful in comparison with her placid sister. Nathaniel loved all his children, but he knew that Alice was almost certainly the last baby and she was his adored favorite. It was Alice he looked for first, after Eleanor, when he came into the house, and he had infinite patience with her.

In return, Alice would do anything Nathaniel wanted her to, even go to sleep, while refusing the overtures of everyone else in the family.

There were two younger children in the Stretton family too, Thomas and Phoebe, born four and seven years after the arrival of Grace. But all the younger children, cousins and siblings from Thomas right down to Alice, were always impatiently dismissed by the older ones as the Babies. For Jake and Julius and Clio and Grace only reckoned with themselves, or with Hugo as an occasional extra.

Downstairs, Alice's screaming stopped abruptly. Nanny must have done something to pacify her. Clio strained to discern the other more distant noises. A door opened somewhere, and Clio thought she could just catch the *click click* of her mother's heels across the colored tiles of the hall. She would be walking quickly from her drawing room to Nathaniel's study, perhaps with an armful of flowers from the garden, or the post to put on the corner of her husband's desk. Clio smiled. At the heart of the house there was an absence of noise, the silence of Nathaniel working. He would be sitting at his desk or in the decaying armchair beside it, his beard sunk on his chest and his reading spectacles pinching the bridge of his nose. When he took the spectacles off, he would massage the reddened place where they had rested.

The other noises were the ordinary sounds of the house in the Woodstock Road. The wood paneling and the floorboards creaked and protested under so many feet. The metallic rattle might be one of the two housemaids carrying an enamel jug of hot water to the nursery. The muffled thumping could be Jake descending the stairs, or Tabby banging her wooden blocks, or Mr. Curler the handyman performing some repair job in the back scullery. And all these domestic sounds were wrapped in the outside whisper of the breeze in the garden trees. They made Clio feel comfortable; she had been hearing them all her life.

Now she turned her head, trying to distinguish the other sound that she was waiting for. The rattle of a car drawing up in the Woodstock Road would be an intrusion, the beginning of much more serious intrusions. Everyone else in the house was waiting for the car too, but the difference was that everyone else was looking forward to its arrival. Clio sighed. The car would bring Aunt Blanche for two days, and Hugo and Grace for much longer: their summer visit to Oxford.

Julius must have been listening too. He stopped playing in the middle of a bar, and it was two beats longer before Clio heard the throaty mumble of the idling engine at the curbside.

A door opened inside the house, and Jake's voice rose up the stairwell. "They're here!"

Clio swung her legs over the side of her bed and stood up, smoothing the layers of her skirts. She looked at herself in the small mirror hung over her plain wooden dressing table; a long look, without a smile.

Grace stood on the tiled path that led up to the front porch. She tilted her head back to gaze upward at the Gothic windows and the pointed eaves and the absurd round turret under its witch's hat of purple slate. Grace was smiling. She was glad to be here, she was always glad to be with her cousins. Jake ran down the steps from the front door, and she held out her hands to him. He took them in his and leaned closer, to kiss her cheek, as he always did. Grace slid away from him, leaving his lips pursed against the air, and she looked at him with amusement from under her eyelashes.

"Hello, Jake," she said, acknowledging him and demanding his acknowledgment too that she was older, prettier, more adult than she had been the last time they met, at Christmas. She had been silently practicing the exact note all the way in the car. She was pleased to see that he did look again at her, with a different expression, still holding her hands.

Julius came out, with Eleanor and Nathaniel behind him. Julius was as tall as Jake but thinner, and he moved more tentatively, without his brother's good-humored confidence. Julius kissed Grace as he had always done. Grace did not try to demonstrate any changes to Julius, nor did she know that there was no need to because he saw them at once. Julius saw everything about Grace and remembered, storing up the precious hoard of memories.

Hugo had held back to help his mother down from the car. Hugo was nearly seventeen, almost grown up. He was fair like his father, even his coloring setting him apart from the others. Hugo shook hands heartily and automatically; Julius had once said that it made him feel like one of the Stretton tenants.

The sisters had kissed and Nathaniel had embraced Blanche before Clio appeared in the doorway. She came slowly down the stairs, listening to the confusion of greetings, and stood at the top of the front steps looking down. She saw that Grace's navy-blue tucked linen dress was crisp, and that her own was creased from rolling on the bed. She also saw that Grace had done her hair differently, drawing it back over her ears to show more of her face.

"Clio, oh *Clio,* I'm so happy to see you."

Grace ran up the stone steps and flung her arms around her cousin. She hugged her, almost swinging her off her feet in her exuberance. At once Clio felt pleased and flattered and ashamed of her own reluctance. It was impossible not to love Grace for her warmth and enthusiasm and all the life in her. Clio hugged her back, murmuring that she was happy too. She was only thinking that Jake and Julius loved Grace, of course they would do, but that in return she behaved as if they were hers, by some seigneurial right.

They are not hers, Clio reiterated. She was fiercely proud of her brothers, and the pride was coupled with possessiveness.

"You can have no idea how boring it has been at Stretton all these months," Grace was saying. "How much I have longed for company, died to be with you all. I would look out of the windows at the trees and grass and emptiness and *moan* with misery."

"What nonsense you talk, Grace," Hugo said briskly.

"How would you know about misery, or ecstasy, Hugo, for that matter? When you are only concerned with cricket?"

Grace linked her arms through Jake's and Julius's and drew them up into the house with her. Clio followed thoughtfully behind, leaving Hugo to accompany the parents into the drawing room.

The four of them climbed to the playroom, their old headquarters near the top of the house. Over the years they had played and plotted across the worn carpets and horsehair sofas, and the scuffed tables and bulging cupboards showed the scars of imaginary battles and voyages. The room was so familiar to them all that none of them even glanced around. Jake dropped at full length onto one of the sofas, letting one long leg swing over the arm. Clio and Julius sat on the club fender, one on either side of the empty grate. They were alike, with the same narrow faces and the same peak of hair springing from their foreheads, but the family resemblance was just as strong between Clio and Grace.

Grace stood in the middle of the room, with their eyes on her. "Now, tell me the news," she insisted. "All the news."

"Jake is going to be house captain next term," Clio said proudly.

Jake and Julius were boarders at a school near Reading. Clio attended a girls' day school in Oxford. Only Grace was being educated at home, by a governess, just as her mother and aunt had been at Holborough. She was quick-witted and had an excellent memory, but she guessed that she was not academically clever like her Hirsh cousins. She also knew that by comparison with them she was undereducated; Nathaniel was a great believer in the power of learning, whereas John Leominster considered it quite good enough just to be born a Stretton, especially for a mere girl.

The Woodstock Road house had always been full of books and atlases and globes of the night sky, taken for granted by the Hirsh children. Grace had concealed her ignorance by always trying to take the lead, directing the talk or the game onto ground that was safe for her. She preferred Kim's Game to quizzes, fantasy to fact. She looked down at Jake now.

"Isn't that rather Culmington?" she demanded.

Grace had coined the term from Hugo's title. In the beginning they had used it to describe the qualities stoutly advocated by Hugo himself: decency and fairness and a willingness to play the game by the rules. There was no malice against Hugo in it, it was simply that the circle considered themselves more imaginative and less conventional than the Viscount. By extension, the term had come to refer to doing the right thing, public spirit, duty and virtue. To dullness.

Jake waved languidly. "One has to accept these tasks." He said to Clio, "Grace didn't mean that kind of news." He knew that Grace was asking him to offer his equivalent of what now seemed so obvious and intriguing about her, evidence that he had grown up.

"What kind, then?" Clio demanded.

Grace began to walk to the window, measuring her steps. "News of life. Love."

"Love?" Julius sniggered; reached across the gap of the fender to nudge Clio. Julius was still a boy, only thirteen.

Grace's eyes met Jake's, and they smiled. Watching, Clio knew that her cousin had created a pair with Jake, and that she and Julius were excluded.

At the window Grace spread her hands on the sill and looked down into the road. There was a grocer's delivery cart clopping by, her mother's car with the chauffeur polishing its gleaming nose, almost no one else to be seen. Oxford was asleep in the depths of the Long Vacation. But after Stretton, the Woodstock Road looked as busy as Piccadilly.

"What shall we do?" she asked.

"You choose. It's your first afternoon," Julius said politely, wanting to cover up his lapse.

"Pitt-Rivers, then," Grace answered.

They left the playroom and chased down the stairs, as if they were children after all.

Blanche and Eleanor were drinking tea together. Hugo had gone out, announcing that he wanted to look around the place. The next year at Eton would be his last, and he planned to go up to Christ Church. His attitude to Oxford was already calmly proprietary. The other children laughed at this embodiment of Culmington.

They met Nathaniel at the bottom of the stairs. He had shrugged himself into his light summer coat, and carried his panama hat in one hand and a leather bag full of papers in the other.

"We're going to Pitt-Rivers, Grace has chosen. Where are you going, Pappy?"

"Into College, just for an hour. If you would like, I will meet you at Pitt-Rivers, and we can walk in the Parks."

"Yes, yes, we can do that. Only don't forget about us as soon as you get to College and sit there for hours and hours, will you?"

"I'll try not to," Nathaniel said, not denying the possibility.

They left the house and walked toward the city, through the patches of shade cast by the big trees lining the road and out into the sunshine again. Nathaniel walked quickly, taking long strides, but the children easily kept pace with him. When they came to the red-and-yellow bulk of Keble, with its chapel looking—as Clio always said—like some animal on its back with its legs in the air, they turned into Parks Road and Nathaniel left them.

The Pitt-Rivers loomed across the road. They hurried over to the arched entrance, and the yawning attendant in his booth nodded them in. They passed through the door and into the museum.

The smell descended around them. It was compounded of dust, formaldehyde, and the exudations of rumbling hot-water pipes, animal skins and bones, and mice. The air was thick from being long enclosed, and the dim light hardly illuminated the exhibits in their glass cases. The silence was sepulchral.

The cousins breathed in; looked up into the wooden galleries rising above their heads where the occasional shuffling don might be glimpsed, and fanned out ready to make their tour of inspection.

They had been visiting the museum ever since they were old enough for Nathaniel to bring them, on wet winter afternoons when their woollen hats and mufflers steamed gently and added to the miasma. It had been an outing, a place where Nathaniel told stories sparked off by the sight of a gruesome shrunken head or a decorated shield, a mysterious treasure cave remote from the humdrum Oxford, and for Grace a source of information that she secretly gathered to herself. Grace knew about the earth's mineral deposits because she had learned the display labels beside the glittering chunks of quartz and mica and hematite.

Later, when they were a little older, the Pitt-Rivers had become a place of refuge away from the house. No one ever objected to their making the short walk to the museum. They had drifted between the tall cabinets, peering in at the jumble of trophies within and then at their own reflections in the murky glass, waiting for something to happen.

Each of them had their favorite exhibits and they visited them in ritual order, jealously checking to make sure that each item of the display was intact. Jake liked the Mammals, a small collection of stuffed arctic foxes and ermines and skunks with mothy hides and bright glass eyes, their stiff legs and yellow claws resting on wooden plaques garnished with little fragments of tundra. Julius preferred the Story of Man, a Darwinian series of tableaux culminating in Modern Man, a wax dummy complete with bowler hat and starched collar. Clio headed for the Dinosaurs, peering upward through the ark of a rebuilt ribcage and sighing over the great empty skulls.

Grace's favorite was Geology, considered very dry by the others. She could stand for hours looking at the black slabs stained with ochre iron, at polished golden whorls and salty crystals, and at an egg of gray rock split to reveal the lavender sparkle of raw amethyst.

She found that her rocks were all in their places, the labels beside them only a little yellower and the spidery handwriting fading into paler sepia. She rested her forehead against the glass, transfixed by the mathematical purity of hexagonal prisms of quartz. She was thinking that her mother's diamonds came from the same source, from rocks like these chipped out of the deep ground somewhere. Grace liked the diamonds although they would be worn by Hugo's wife, not her, but she preferred these other crystals still half embedded in their native rock. They gave her a vertiginous sense of the earth's prodigality, her own smallness in comparison.

She was still leaning her head against the case when Jake came up behind her. He stood at her shoulder, looking down at the eternal display of stones. Then he shifted his gaze to Grace's hair, a thick ringlet of it lying over her shoulder, and the lines of her cheek and jaw. He saw that her breath made a faint mist on the glass. He reached up with his finger and touched the haze, and it seemed such an intimate part of Grace herself that the blood suddenly hammered in his ears and he opened his mouth to suck in the thinned air.

With the tip of his finger in the mist Jake traced the letter *G*.

Grace turned to look at him then with color in her face that he had never seen before. Jake felt as if a fist had struck him in the chest, but he looked steadily back at her. He saw the faint bronze flecks in the brown of her eyes.

Something had happened, at last.

Then they heard Clio calling them in the sibilant whisper that stood for a proper shout in the vaults of the Pitt-Rivers. "Grace, Jake? Where are you? We've been here for an hour. Pappy will be waiting."

"We had better go," Grace said.

Jake stumbled after her, blinking, out into the July sunshine.

Nathaniel was sitting on a low wall reading a newspaper. His panama hat was tipped forward to shield his eyes from the sun and his leather bag stood unregarded at his feet.

They called to him, "Pappy, Uncle Nathaniel, we're sorry to keep you waiting, don't be vexed. . . ."

Nathaniel did not look up. He was reading intently, his thick eyebrows drawn together and the corners of his mouth turned down in the springy mass of his beard.

"Pappy—"

He did look up then. He was still frowning, but he folded the newspaper carefully into its creases, smaller and smaller still, and poked it away out of sight between the books and papers in his bag.

"Here you all are," he said, tipping his hat back as if he were glad of the distraction they provided. His frown disappeared a moment later, and he stood up, swinging the bag over his shoulder by its leather strap and holding out his other arm to Grace. "Is everyone ready? Then off we go."

They turned through the big iron gates into the University Parks. There was a vista of heavy-headed trees and smooth grass, and flowerbeds subsiding into high-summer exhaustion. The scent of mown lawns was welcome after the thick atmosphere of the museum.

"We should have called in for Tabby and Alice," Nathaniel said. He enjoyed having all his children around him. "They love the Parks."

"No, *not* the Babies," the older ones groaned.

Grace walked with her arm in Nathaniel's, chattering to him. Clio and Julius and Jake walked close behind, following their shadows over the grass. Jake felt as if his eyes and ears had been suddenly opened. The colors were almost painfully vivid, and he could hear bees humming, even the splash of the river over the rollers beyond Parsons' Pleasure. He struggled to listen to what the twins were saying, and to frame ordinary responses.

They came to the river rippling under a high arched footbridge. Clio and Julius ran up the steep slope of the bridge and hung over the metal railing to peer into the depths. When they were small, they had dropped stones and twigs to race in the winter currents. Today the river was sluggish, deep green in the shade of the willows. Jake caught the whiff of mud and weed.

Nathaniel said, "If you would like to walk up to the boathouse, we could take out a punt."

Clio and Jake were enthusiastic. Punting was always popular with the Hirshes, and on a hot afternoon it was pleasant to lie back on cushions and glide over the water. Only Grace said nothing, and Julius was quiet too, observing her. Nathaniel led the way along the river path under the branches of the willows, to the point where the punts were tied up. The boatman scrambled across the raft of them, setting the boats rocking and the water slapping against the flat bottoms. Feather pillows were handed into one of the boats, and Nathaniel selected a hooked pole, weighing it critically in one hand.

Grace stood on the sloping jetty, watching Clio sit down and spread her skirts. She wanted to step in too, but she couldn't move. The sight of the rocking boat and the sound of slapping water froze her, as they had done ever since the *Mabel*. Grace hated to be afraid, but she couldn't conquer this fear. She recoiled from the innocent river as if it might flow up the jetty and engulf her.

Julius and Jake hesitated beside her. Julius knew what held her back, because his senses were highly developed where Grace was concerned. Jake was looking at her curiously.

"I think, Uncle Nathaniel, I would rather walk on the bank today. If you don't mind, of course?" Grace's voice was clear and steady.

Nathaniel saw what was the matter and blamed himself for his insensitivity. "Walk by all means, Grace. We will keep pace with you."

"Don't hold back on purpose. Perhaps Jake will walk too, to keep me company?"

"Good idea. Thank you, Jake," Nathaniel said. Julius scrambled into the punt after Clio, without looking around. The twins sat facing each other amongst the piled cushions, and Nathaniel stationed himself at the back. He dropped the pole into the water, pushed, and twisted it to lift it free. The punt shot forward, and drops of spray scattered concentric circles in its wake.

Grace and Jake began to walk, side by side.

Jake could think of nothing to say, now he had the unthinkable chance of being alone with her, out of earshot of noisy siblings and all the busy demands of the Woodstock Road. He wanted to say everything, to pour out his astonishment that Grace, who was only his cousin and ally, had suddenly turned into an intriguing mystery. He wanted to ask her if she felt the same, to compare and confide, to draw her closer, this unknown Grace. The clumsy words jammed in his head. He could only manage, thickly, "It's all different, all of a sudden. It is, isn't it?"

Grace seemed calm, as if she understood everything. She nodded her head once, very slowly. "Yes. Everything is different."

"You're not just Grace any longer."

"Nor are you *just Jake*." Her voice was very low, almost inaudible.

Jake could hardly breathe. So Grace felt it too, then, this naked and painful awareness? The intimacy of it was terrifying, and intoxicating. They were walking very close together. Their arms almost brushed, and then Jake's fingers hanging loosely at his side touched the tips of Grace's. A current shot up his arm. Their hands groped, in the folds of Grace's blue skirt, then clasped together. They walked on, linked together, staring straight ahead of them at Nathaniel's back as he bent and straightened to the pole.

Clio sat facing them, her expression unreadable at this distance. It was like holding Clio's hand, Jake thought. This hand was the same shape as Clio's, there was the same warmth in the palm of it. But there was the sudden, startling difference. Bewildered, Jake tried to work out what he did feel.

He wanted to take Grace and hold her against the ribbed trunk of one of the trees; he wanted to rub his face against her and push his hands into the blue dress. He felt like an animal, like one of the museum's Mammals in rut, in the grip of terrible instincts. He was disgusted, and ashamed, and confused by what had been set off within him.

He believed that what he was thinking about Grace was almost as bad as thinking it about Clio.

Jake's skin burned and his vision blurred, but he went on walking stiffly, staring ahead of him, all the heat of him concentrated in the palm of his hand.

Grace was silent too. She was thinking, *If he tries to kiss me, what will I do?* She wanted him to kiss her, she wanted him to *admit,* although she couldn't even have defined what the admission would be. She knew that she had suddenly acquired some power, but now she had sensed it, she was afraid of using it.

She thought, *I'll let him, and then I'll break away from him and run. I'll know he loves me, he'll be* mine *then....*

Jake didn't try to kiss her. He walked on, miserably, his eyes fixed on Clio and Nathaniel and Julius on the river, but he held on to Grace's hand as if he would never let go.

At last they saw Nathaniel draw the pole in a wide arc from the stern of the punt. The long nose swung across the river until it pointed back toward them. It was time to head home again. Jake and Grace jumped guiltily apart. They stood awkwardly until the punt drew level and Clio's accusing eyes settled on them.

"Are you enjoying the walk?" Nathaniel boomed.

"Yes, thank you," Grace said.

They turned together and began to follow the punt once more. Instead of all the things he wanted to say and couldn't, and all the banalities he might have settled for instead, Jake blurted out, "Are you afraid of boats?"

It was the first time since the *Mabel* summer that Grace had been obliged directly to refuse to go out on to the water. Usually, with some ingenuity, she was able to evade the possibility well in advance. Now she thought how inadequate Jake's words were. "Afraid of boats" took no account of the nights when she bit the insides of her mouth to stop herself falling asleep, so the dreams couldn't come, nor of the waking cold terror of the sound of the waves, of the simple smell of salt water.

She said, "I think you might be too, if you had almost drowned."

"Why didn't any of us know? Haven't you told anyone?"

Grace considered. "I think Julius guessed."

Jake didn't want to hear about Julius now. Grace went on, "I haven't told anyone. Only you."

Jake gave her such a look of happiness and gratitude for singling him out that Grace forgot her humiliation over the punt.

"You mustn't worry about it, Grace, I'll look after you, there's no need to be afraid of anything."

She smiled, looking up at him, tasting some of the satisfaction of power. "Thank you, Jake," she whispered. He was her admired cousin, their longtime ringleader, and she wanted his allegiance to her alone, that was the admission. And it came to her that although

Jake was sixteen and clever and she was three whole years younger and had been taught nothing, she still knew more than he did.

Behind the folds of her skirt she reached her hand to touch his again, and he took hold of it as though it were the Grail itself.

The twins and Nathaniel were waiting at the jetty. Julius looked from one of them to the other, with resignation. Clio stared straight ahead, and even in his confusion, Jake saw that she was jealous. He took care to walk beside her on the way home. Only Nathaniel seemed oblivious to what had been happening. He had taken the newspaper out of his bag again, and he beat the rolled-up tube of it against his leg as he strode along.

When they came home, Eleanor was waiting for Nathaniel. "Oswald Harris is here," she said. "In your study."

Dr. Harris was one of Nathaniel's colleagues, a specialist in Romance languages and an old family friend. He was a particular favorite of the Hirsh children, and Clio's face brightened at the mention of his name.

"Oh, *good*. Will he play something with us?"

"Not now, Clio," Nathaniel said abruptly. "Off you go, all of you." He went into the study, and they saw Dr. Harris jump up to greet him without his usual smile. Eleanor and Blanche were left in the hallway, their clothes dappled with colored light from the stained-glass panels in the front door.

Afterward the cousins recalled that evening at the end of July as the first time they heard adult talk of Serbia and Austria, and the first time they overheard the murmured word *Crisis*.

They paid little attention to it, then.

That year Hugo and Jake were considered old enough to join their parents for dinner, but the twins and Grace still had to sit down with the Babies for nursery supper. Jake was hanging up his jacket in the boot room and Nanny Cooper was already calling the rest of the children to the table when Grace appeared in the doorway. The boot room was a place of discarded galoshes and fraying straw hats and croquet mallets, and she looked around it with a brilliant smile.

"You're *here*," she whispered. Her eyes were shining. She closed the door silently, and came straight to him. She put her hands on his forearms, and then she reached up and kissed him on the mouth.

It was a long kiss, soft-lipped and tasting of strawberries.

Jake almost fainted. When she drew back he croaked, "Grace,

come here again, *please* . . ." but she was already at the doorway, easing open the door and checking the corridor beyond.

Her lips looked very red, and her smile dazzled him. "If I don't go, Nanny will be down here to find me. But this is a good place, isn't it? We can meet here again. There's all the summer, Jake."

Then she disappeared.

Dinner was interminable. All Jake wanted was to escape to his bed, to think in privacy and silence, but the adults and Hugo seemed disposed to sit with grave faces and talk all night.

"It must come," Dr. Harris judged. "I cannot see how it can be avoided now that Germany and France have mobilized."

"There must not be a war. Think of our poor boys," Blanche whispered.

"If it does come, and I agree with Dr. Harris that it must," Hugo intoned, "then I shall enlist at once. It will be over by Christmas, and I don't want to miss it."

"Hugo, you can't possibly. You are only sixteen years old."

"Almost seventeen, Mama, quite old enough. What do you say, Jake?"

Jake was startled out of his own thoughts, and unreasonably irritated that international events should disturb him now, when there were other things to consider. When there was Grace, with her strawberry mouth . . .

"Jake, are you all right?" Nathaniel asked.

He said stiffly, "Perfectly. I don't believe there should be a war. I don't believe that men should go out and kill each other over an Archduke or Serbian sovereignty or anything else. There should be some other way, some civilized way. Men should be able to demonstrate that they have higher instincts than animals fighting over their territory." He was reminded of the Mammals, and the Pitt-Rivers, and Grace's breath clouding the glass of the display case. He was made even angrier by the realization that his face and neck were crimson, and that Hugo was eyeing him with superior amusement.

Nathaniel said gently, "I think you are right, Jake. But I do not believe that very many people share our views."

At last the evening was over. Jake escaped to his bed, but there was no refuge in sleep. He lay in the darkness, rigid and sweating, envying Julius's oblivious, even breaths from the opposite bed. He could only think of Grace lying in her own bed, in her white nightgown with her hair streaming out over the pillow, just a few yards away.

She is your cousin, he told himself hopelessly. *Almost your sister.* But she had come to seek him out in the boot room, and there had been that precious, inflammatory kiss. . . .

Jake groaned in his misery and rolled over onto his stomach. He did not touch himself, although he knew that there were men who did, plenty of them at school. But they had been issued with severe warnings, some more explicit than others, and Jake had been disposed to believe them.

The pressure of the mattress made it worse. He rolled over again and pushed off the blankets so that he only felt the touch of the night air. It was already light when Jake finally fell asleep.

On August 1, 1914, Germany declared war on Russia, and the first shots of the European conflict were fired.

John Leominster came from London to fetch Blanche. As always when his brother-in-law was at hand, Nathaniel became noticeably more beetle-browed and clever and Germanic. After so many years of marriage, the sisters had become adept at defusing the tension between their husbands with inconsequential talk, but on this somber evening the only real topic was the likelihood of Britain entering the war. After the long-drawn-out family dinner Jake wandered away, but Hugo and John retired with Nathaniel to his study. Nathaniel poured whiskey and soda, diluting Hugo's until it was almost colorless and Hugo blinked in protest.

"This can't be easy for you, Hirsh," John said.

"It isn't easy for any of us. War does not have the reputation of ease."

"I meant for you in particular, with your, ah, antecedents."

John Leominster knew quite well that Levi and Dora Hirsh had settled in Manchester from Bremen in the mid-1860s. Levi was a scientist, an industrial chemist, and he had prospered with England's manufacturing prosperity. Levi and Dora had family spread across most of Europe, but after fifty years they would not have considered themselves anything but English.

"My antecedents? I was born here, Leominster. I am as British as you are, my dear fellow."

It was a favorite tease of Nathaniel's. Leominster could trace his descent from Henry VII, and his pale face darkened with annoyance now. "Not quite, but let us not argue about it."

"By all means not. More whiskey, old chap?"

Hugo held up his glass too. "What do you think will happen, uncle?"

Nathaniel sighed, relinquishing the pleasure of baiting Leominster. "I think Britain will be at war with Germany in a matter of days. I feel great sadness for Germany and the German people, and for all of Europe. I feel the most sorrow for Jake, and you, even Julius. It will not be a short war, Hugo. You need not be afraid that you will miss it."

"Don't feel sorry for me. I shall join just as soon as I can, in any case."

John put down his glass. "You may enlist when you are eighteen, Hugo, not before. I shall be proud to send you off then."

Hugo asked eagerly, "And Jake? Jake is only seven months younger than I am."

"Jake must speak for himself, Hugo. But I understand that he feels as I do, that it should not be necessary for civilized peoples to kill and maim one another's young men, and to leave a whole generation lying bleeding on some battlefield. I do not believe that Jake will want to go and slaughter his German cousins, and I am ashamed of the politicians and the leaders who will oblige him to make such a decision. I pray that he will have the courage to do what he believes is right, and I am sure he will find a way to be of service to our country."

Nathaniel stood up, slowly, as if he were tired, and replaced the whiskey decanter on the tray on his desk. The top of the desk was a drift of papers covered with his tiny handwriting, and he seemed to gaze longingly at it.

The Lords Leominster and Culmington exchanged glances. "And to show the damned Kaiser that Britain means business," Leominster muttered.

Nathaniel was still looking at his papers. There was the ordered world of scholarship, beckoning him. He put his hand up to rub his beard around his mouth where gray fronds were beginning to show amongst the wiry black. "If you wish," Nathaniel said absently.

"Where is Jake?" Hugo demanded.

"I don't know. I think Jake has problems of his own, just at present."

Jake was standing at the upstairs landing window, looking down from one of the unpredictable angles of the house to the Woodstock Road below. A gas lamp on top of a tall iron post beyond the gate threw light on the evergreen shrubs beside the gate and tipped the points of the iron railings that bounded the front garden. A cyclist swooped silently past, and for an instant the street lamp laid a monster's wavering shadow on the road before him.

Jake was not thinking about the war, or reflecting on duty and service to his country. He was wondering what his cousin Hugo did in circumstances like his own. Hugo was fond of hinting that he was a man of the world, but Jake couldn't work out what that meant. He didn't know either whether it was more Culmington nobly to resist temptation and think pure thoughts, or not to think at all and so avoid anxiety, as well as shame and guilt. Jake was not sure that there was any way of asking Hugo.

It was soothing to be alone in the dark, at least. He had been with Grace for most of the day, but he had never been alone with her for a second. Clio was always there, however mutely Jake willed her to take herself off. And Julius too; Julius had stayed close to them, seeing everything and saying nothing. For the first time, there was a break in the magic circle.

Jake sighed. There had been no chance to exchange a private word with Grace, let alone another kiss, a caress. They had contented themselves with looks. And he had seen that Grace looked happy, with rosier cheeks and brighter eyes than when she had arrived.

Perhaps that was enough, Jake thought. With the tender new concern he felt for her, he wanted Grace to be happy as much as he wanted his own happiness. But his own happiness, or satisfaction at least, seemed to depend on the unthinkable. He remembered the boot room again, and the smell of galoshes and waterproofs and the taste of Grace. It was better that she should be happy, he told himself, and that he should suffer. It was the only solution, Culmington or otherwise.

Eleanor came up the stairs on her way to bed and saw Jake silhouetted at the window. He did not hear her approach, and he jumped violently when she spoke.

"Jakie, what is it? Is it the war?"

"Yes," Jake lied. "The war." Even in his mother's face he saw the shape of Grace's features. Eleanor and Blanche and Clio. Sisters, family. And yet.

"I was proud of what you said," Eleanor told him.

Jake found that he could barely remember what it was he had said. Some pompous diatribe about man's higher instincts. Upon which, he thought, he was hardly in a position to pronounce.

"But you are only sixteen. You are only a boy, Jake. Going to fight is for men, and so is taking the decision not to fight."

Jake mumbled, "I know. I'm quite all right. I'm not worried about it."

Eleanor put her hand up to his face. Jake stood a head taller than she; she wondered exactly when it was that this unfathomable man had emerged from the soft pupa of her child. He suffered her caress stiffly.

"Go to bed now." Eleanor sighed.

Jake went obediently, and lay thinking about Grace.

By August 4, Britain was at war with Germany.

News came of crowds gathered outside Buckingham Palace and Downing Street, cheering and singing the national anthem. Hugo pored over the newspapers that carried pictures of young men flocking to recruiting offices. He ached with impatience to join them, and sighed over his misfortune in being just too young. The prospect of having to return to school for the next half while other men marched to glory filled him with despair.

It was odd to find that outwardly, visibly, nothing changed. The cousins discovered that Oxford looked exactly as it always did in the middle of the Long Vacation. The High was deserted except for plodding dons and dons' wives shopping, and only the windows of the men's outfitters replaced their displays of academic robes and College ties with military tunics and officers' caps. North Oxford drowsed beneath its canopies of trees, and there was the summer round of tennis parties and picnics and croquet games, no different from any other year.

Jake bore the sociable routine half impatiently and half gladly because it occupied the four of them and allowed him to be harmlessly near Grace. Grace was very lively. Her vivacity made Clio look like her smaller shadow.

There were no more meetings in the boot room, because Grace did not look for the opportunities. Jake realized that he was shadowing her like a patient dog, hoping for a scrap of intimacy. She rewarded him with private smiles and with the touch of her hand sometimes, when no one else was looking. He was tormented by the inadequacy of their contacts, and at the same time relieved that he did not have to control himself as he would if they were to find themselves alone.

The long days of August passed quickly, even for Hugo in the agony of his inactivity.

At the end of the month there was a picnic beside the river at Iffley, when the Hirshes and their cousins were joined by Dr. Harris and his wife and small children. Nathaniel and Oswald Harris spread rugs and a white linen cloth in the shade of the trees, and

Eleanor and Mary Harris unpacked wicker baskets and spooned raspberries into glass dishes. The small children ran and fell over in the grass, and Hugo and Jake and Julius swam in the river. Their shouts and splashings were swallowed prematurely by the still, heavy air. Nathaniel predicted that the day would end with a thunderstorm.

Clio and Grace, in white dresses and straw sunhats, walked arm in arm along the footpath. Grace unraveled coarse strands of goose-grass from the hedge and twisted them into sticky garlands for their straw hats.

"You look like a girl in a painting," she told Clio. "Raspberry juice on your chin and leaves in your hair. It ought to be red wine, and vine leaves, and you could pose for Bacchus. He is the god of wine, isn't he?"

"Revelry, as well. He's Dionysius in Greek. Painters give him crowns of grapes and vine leaves, yes." When she had delivered her speech Clio regretted her pedantry, but Grace seemed as always to be glad of the information.

"Mmm, you'll do for him, then. What shall I be?"

"Helen of Troy," Clio said. She would have gone on to make some wry observation on the distinction between her brother and Paris, but Grace good-humoredly interrupted her. Grace didn't seem to know anything about Helen of Troy.

"Listen, Dr. Harris is calling. They must want us for something." She held out her arm again and Clio took it. There was no sense in being resentful of Grace. Grace herself did not harbor resentment. But then, Clio reflected, she had no reason to.

Oswald Harris was directing preparations for a wide game. He waved his arms in excitable sweeps, ordering children in different directions. Hugo forgot his dignity and ran with Julius and Clio and the Harris children.

"You are the quarry," Dr. Harris called after them. "Run, now."

He turned back to the depleted circle gathered around the remains of the picnic. "Jake and Grace, you are the hunters. Give them five minutes exactly."

They waited, not looking at each other, paying exaggerated attention to counting the seconds.

Eleanor and Mary Harris leaned against the trunk of an elm tree, talking in low voices. A little distance away Nathaniel lay on the rug, propped on one elbow. Tabby had fallen asleep beside him, and he had placed his old panama hat to shade her head. He was watching Alice, who made little lunging rushes to and fro through the tufts of tall grass. He saw her tilt her head backward to follow the flight of a white butterfly, and as it rose she leaned too far backward and overbalanced. She lay on her back, staring at the sky from under the brim of her cotton sunbonnet. The butterfly still hovered above her, and in her fascination she forgot to cry.

Nathaniel saw the wide meadow dotted with sheaves of corn, and the willows on the opposite bank of the river, and Jake vaulting the gate into the next field before opening it to let Grace through. He heard the women murmuring, and the creak and splash of a skiff on the river, and one of the Harris children, a long way off, calling a taunt to the hunters.

Along the borders of Eastern Prussia, the Russian soldiers of General Samsonov's Second Army were being cut down by German shellfire. With the sun hot on his bare head and the afternoon's warmth beginning to build into oppressive stillness, Nathaniel imagined the thunder of the guns, and the stench of burning, and sudden death.

The same world contained these two realities: the picnic and the battlefield, and Nathaniel knew that the threads that bound them together were tightening, drawing them closer every day.

At home in London the exhibition hall at Olympia had been converted into a camp for aliens. Hundreds of Germans living in England had been rounded up and imprisoned there, and many more had suffered the ransacking of their homes on suspicion of being enemy spies. Only two days earlier, a policeman had come to visit Nathaniel. He had left his bicycle leaning against the stone steps leading up to the front door in the Woodstock Road, and when the outraged housemaid had shown him into Nathaniel's study he had stood awkwardly on the threshold, turning his helmet over and over in his hands.

"I'm sorry, Professor Hirsh," he kept saying.

"What do you want to do?" Nathaniel asked him. "Search this room for coded messages to General von Hindenburg? Arrest me for treason?" The conversations he had had with John Leominster seemed prophetic now, not comical at all.

"Of course not, sir," the man said miserably. "It's a matter of formality. It's this DORA, isn't it?"

Nathaniel wondered what else the powers of the Defense of the Realm Act might bring, and what his children would have to suffer for bearing a name that he was proud of.

In the sunny meadow he scrambled to his feet and ran to where

Alice lay on the grass. He scooped her up and touched his lips to the warm baby flesh at the back of her neck.

"I love you," he murmured to her. *"Ich liebe dich."*

Jake and Grace stood face to face in an angle of the hedge, hidden from the world by a green buttress of hawthorn branches.

"I love you," Jake said hotly. The taunting calls of their hidden quarry filled the heavy air like the cries of birds. Jake didn't care about anything except Grace, and the dampness of her skin under the weight of her hair, and the pulse of her throat just above the white collar of her dress. He fixed his eyes on the fluttering beat of it.

"Jake . . ."

She touched his face, and then his black hair, still slick and wet with river water. The gesture reminded him of his mother's and he snatched her wrist and held it.

"Don't say anything," he begged her. "Just be here. Just like this. . . ."

He put his hands around her waist. It was narrow, the fragility of her body surprised and stirred him. He could feel the curve of her ribs, and the soft small swellings above. His hands rested there, he didn't dare to move them, and he was afraid that his knees would give way beneath him.

Jake bent his head, darkening her face with his own shadow. He touched her mouth with his own and his tongue found her teeth like a barrier, and then she opened her mouth and it was hotter and wetter than his own. He kissed her, drinking her in as if he had been dying of thirst.

Her head fell back, baring her throat, and her straw hat with its wilting Dionysian garland dropped off and lay at their feet.

Grace almost toppled under his leaning weight, but he caught her, and they half fell and half lay down in the grass under their hawthorn hedge. Jake pressed himself on top of her, and his hands found the hem of her white dress and the folds of her petticoat, all the mysterious layers of feminine apparel, and then the little mound between her legs, tight and innocent like the smooth rump of a small animal.

"Jake, *Jake,*" Grace was almost screaming. For an instant she was stronger than he was. She pushed him aside and scrambled up, snatching her crushed hat from beneath him. There was grass caught in her hair and in the tucks of her dress. She crammed her hat on her tumbled hair and ran away, toward the voices, her own cry rising to theirs, "Coming to find you. Coming to *find* you."

Jake rolled onto his side and lay staring through the stalks of grass, reduced to the same level as the insects that crossed his limited field of vision. The grass was damp against his cheek, but he was sticky with heat and he found that he was panting for breath. He lay still until his breathing steadied again, watching the miniature world inches from his face.

The voices were a long way off now; he knew that he was alone. Grace had run away from him, and a kind of carelessness replaced his anxiety. He found that he didn't mind that she was gone, that he was even relieved. Dreamily, still watching the waving blades of grass, Jake undid his clothes. It felt indecent to be exposed in the open air, in daylight, but the air was deliciously cool. He stretched out, flattening himself against the earth, his thoughts stilled.

He closed his fingers around himself, tentatively at first, and then with a firmer grasp.

After a month, a long month of suppressing himself, it did not take much. He was not thinking of Grace, or of anything at all except obeying his instincts. The pleasure of the orgasm raced all through his body, wave after wave, but the satisfaction and relief that followed it was better. It was like a blessing. His limbs felt heavy and soft, like a baby's, and he curled on his side listening to the empty air.

Jake opened his eyes again on the grass world, and then on the sky over his head. Heavy, piled clouds had rolled over the sun, but the margins of them were still rimmed with gold. He smiled, and raised himself on one elbow, then sat up and spread his arms until the joints cracked. He saw that there were pearly drops on the grass where he had been lying, bending the blades of grass. They didn't look ugly, or unnatural, or in any way unclean. They seemed shiny and quite innocent. Jake waited for the waves of guilt to come, echoing the pleasure, but nothing did. He only felt calm, and comfortable.

He stood up then, buttoning his trousers up. Then he bent down and tore some handfuls of the long grass, and dropped them over the evidence of himself in the sheltered angle of the hawthorn hedge. He felt light and springy, full of energy. He had done nothing wrong, it occurred to him. He was right, and all the murky advice and warnings he had been given were wrong.

He lifted his head and called loudly, "Coming to find you."

Nathaniel had been right about the thunderstorm. It broke in the early evening, sending Tabby and the housemaids scuttling to

Nanny in the nursery and making Alice break out in wails of uncomprehending protest.

Clio and Grace sat in their bedroom while the rain drummed on the roof and bounced in fat drops off the streaming Woodstock Road. Grace was humming and brushing Clio's hair, long rhythmic strokes that made it spark and crackle. In his room, Julius was practicing the Mendelssohn violin concerto. Clio loved the music but Julius kept breaking off in the same bar, repeating a handful of phrases with his perfectionist's concentration.

"Your hair is prettier than mine," Grace said, breaking off from her humming. "It's silkier. I'll give it one hundred more brushes, and it will *shine*."

Clio sighed languorously. She felt happier this evening than she had done since the beginning of the holiday. Jake and Grace had appeared separately during the game; they could have been together, but she was sure they had not. Jake had looked ordinary, too, instead of always covertly peering at Grace and then glancing hastily away in case anyone noticed him doing it.

Grace herself had been friendly, perhaps a little quieter than usual. Clio thought that the atmosphere between them all was as it used to be, except that Julius watched what went on and said nothing.

The intimacy created by the storm and the hairbrushing and Grace's humming made Clio feel bold, and she said, "I think it's stupid, all the boy and girl business. Like you and Jake sighing and staring at each other. It spoils everything."

There were two or three more brush strokes, and silence, while Grace seemed to consider. Then she laughed, putting the hairbrush down and leaning over Clio's shoulder so that she could see their twin reflections in the mirror. "Do you know what? I think you're right. It does spoil everything."

In a month, since the Pitt-Rivers day, she had seen Jake change from the admirable leader and innovator she had hero-worshipped almost from babyhood into a duller, slower twin of himself. Jake blushed now, and hovered awkwardly, and tried to catch her in corners. She wanted to be admired and singled out and even kissed, but by the old glamorous Jake, not the new hesitant one. And then today, when he did catch her, he hadn't acted as he was supposed to act. Grace wasn't exactly sure how that was, except to do homage to her in some way, perhaps kneeling down, perhaps eloquently declaring that he would love her forever, would go to the war and fight and die for her sake.

Instead he had frightened her, and she had frightened herself. She wasn't supposed to feel like that, when he touched her *there*, was she? She had run away, run in real terror, back to the other children and the rules of the game.

It was cozy in Clio's bedroom with the two white beds turned down and the night-light burning on the table between them. Clio would turn it out when they went to sleep, but for now it gave the room the look of the old night-nursery at Stretton.

Grace picked up the hairbrush again and began the long smooth strokes through her cousin's hair. Clio looked pleased and Grace smiled over her shoulder at her reflection. "Look at us. We are alike, aren't we?"

Clio did look, at Grace's face behind her own, a pale moon in the dim room. The rain was still hammering down outside.

She said, "I don't know. I suppose we are, a little."

The same night, in bed listening to the rain, Jake repeated what he had done under the hawthorn hedge. The sensation was less surprising and so even more pleasurable, but it was the sense of calm and relief afterward that affected him most strongly. He knew that he would sleep, and that images of Grace and Clio and even Blanche and Eleanor would not rise up to torment and reproach him. His bed felt soft and safe, like arms wrapped around him. He began to speculate drowsily about his own unpredictable body, quiescent at last, however temporarily. He realized that he knew almost nothing about what made it work, or why he had been obliged to suffer for a month, or why it was considered wrong or dangerous or wicked to do what he had just done, so simply and satisfyingly. He knew even less about Grace's body, even though he had speculated furtively about it for so many leaden days. What did Grace feel, what did Grace know? He did feel ashamed that he had frightened her.

And yet, Jake thought, he knew Latin and classical Greek, and the planets of the solar system, and algebra and trigonometry, and the countries of the world and their rivers and mountains and principal exports. Why such ignorance about himself, his own insistent flesh and blood?

Just before he fell asleep, an idea came to him.

In the morning he found Nathaniel in the breakfast room, *The Times* folded beside his plate. They were the first members of the household to come down. Jake helped himself to ham and eggs from the silver dish on the sideboard and sat down beside his father. He ate hungrily, watching Nathaniel frowning over the news from Europe. Then he said, "May we discuss something, Pappy?"

Nathaniel put his newspaper aside. "Of course."

"I have been thinking about what I should do. It's time I had an idea. Even Hugo knows that he wants to be a soldier."

"Even Hugo," Nathaniel agreed seriously.

"I would like to study medicine. I should like to be a doctor."

"You have never talked about this before."

"I have been thinking. I know something about so many things, and nothing about myself. Anatomy, physiology, chemistry. It came to me that nothing would interest me more than to learn, and then to apply that knowledge. The world will need doctors. I could be a doctor, not a soldier."

Nathaniel looked hard at him. He had been thinking that Jake had shaken off his preoccupation of the last weeks, regained his old animation. Whatever his problem had been with Grace, he must have found the answer to it. Nathaniel trusted his son enough to be certain that it was the right answer.

He said, "If you are serious, I think it is a fine idea. I will talk to the medical man at College."

Jake beamed at him, as pleased as a small boy. "Thank you," he said simply. He went back to the sideboard and mounded his plate with a second helping of ham and eggs.

Nathaniel turned back to his newspaper, but the gray print blurred. He was thinking about Julius and hoping that when his turn came for Grace's attention, if it did come, he would deal with it as sensibly as Jake had done.

Four

BLANCHE FOLLOWED HER HOUSEKEEPER THROUGH the *enfilade* of rooms that ran along the south front of Stretton. The long vista was dim because the shutters were closed. The few bright beams of sunshine that pierced the cracks and fell across their path seemed solid enough to trip her, much more solid than the furniture invisible and shapeless under its dust covers. She stepped through one of the golden rods, and the finger of it ran over her face and then fell back over the floor behind her.

Blanche had flinched when the beam of sunlight touched her. She was thinking of Hugo, who had gone at last to join his regiment in France.

She knew that he would be killed, she knew it with unshakable certainty, and when she thought of him, as now, the air itself seemed to bruise her with its weight of terror.

Blanche had to force herself to concentrate on Mrs. Dixey's broad back marching in front of her, to harness her thoughts to Stretton and these dim shuttered rooms. They were closing them up until the end of the war.

If the day ever comes, Blanche thought. *And if I could close up the fear, as if it were the saloon or the yellow drawing room. . . .*

"The china from these rooms is all packed in the chests now, my lady," the housekeeper said. "And stored in the billiard room, like you ordered."

"Very good," Blanche said automatically. The silver had been taken away to the security vaults, and the better pictures had been lifted down from the walls. There were darker rectangles on the faded silks and damasks, showing the places where generations of Strettons had stared down on their successors.

But in the saloon, the Sargent portrait still hung in its accustomed place. John Leominster himself had given the order for it to be left. "I like to know it's there," he had said gruffly. "In the place where it belongs, even if nothing else is."

Blanche had not asked him why, because to ask or answer such a question would not be part of their expectations of each other, but she guessed that he thought of it as a kind of talisman. Perhaps he attached some superstitious importance to it, imagining that the old, prewar order it seemed to stand for would somehow exert its benign influence over Hugo's fate.

She paused beneath the picture now, looking up into the innocent faces. *As if it could*, she thought bitterly. As if a society portrait of two silly girls could have any effect on Hugo in the trenches.

But even as she dismissed the picture, she felt a wave of longing for the days it recalled, for the measured, orderly prewar times that she was afraid were gone forever. Her own bright painted face, and Eleanor's mirror of it, seemed to belong to a different generation.

"Not *this* portrait, you know," Clio had said once to Elizabeth Ainger, during one of her rambling monologues.

Elizabeth had barely glanced up at the picture that hung behind the old lady's velvet chair. It was the work of a painter no longer very much admired, and she did not herself care for the violent expressionistic style. She knew the history of it, from family stories, and its title, *The Janus Face*. That was all.

"I'm talking about the Sargent," Clio went on. "His portrait of Eleanor and Blanche. *The Misses Holborough.*"

"I know," Elizabeth said. The Stretton family had sold the picture in the Fifties, and it was now housed in a private collection in Baltimore. She had never seen the famous Sargent itself, only reproductions of it. She had suggested to her publishers that they might try to obtain permission to use the double portrait as a frontispiece for the book.

It was a pity, she thought, that the later picture, the one of Grace and Clio, was not more attractive or at least more celebrated.

"This picture, the one of me and—and your grandmother, was intended to hang at Stretton alongside the other. But old John Leominster never liked it, and your . . ."

Clio paused and squinted sideways at Elizabeth, smiling a little. Elizabeth thought that she looked very old, and rather mad.

". . . the painter refused to sell it to him. He loaned it to my father, and there it stayed, in the Woodstock Road, for years and years."

Clio's head fell forward then, so that her chin seemed to touch her chest, and Elizabeth thought she might have fallen into one of her sudden sleeps. She could see the shape of her skull under the thin hair and paper skin, and she was touched with pity for her.

But then the skull-head jerked up again, and the surprisingly bright eyes flicked to her. "Such a lot of years, eh? Why are you interested in so much long-ago, forgotten nonsense?"

"It's my trade," Elizabeth answered. "I'm a biographer."

The pity was still with her and she could not make herself say, "Your biographer."

Blanche turned her back on the mocking optimistic faces. She looked around the shadowy saloon again, up at the great glass chandelier that had been swathed in burlap, and at the ghostly shapes of gilt chairs and console tables under their dust sheets.

The huge house seemed already dead. The clocks had been allowed to run down, and not even their ticking disturbed the silence. Blanche imagined that she could hear the dust settling.

In September 1916, John Leominster had decided that it was his patriotic duty to free as many men as possible from his house and estate to help with the war effort. From the outbreak of the war the house had been run by a minimum of staff, but now Stretton was being entirely closed up. The land and the farms would be left in the care of a manager who would oversee the growth of food crops, and the family was migrating to London, to the Belgrave Square house.

"You have done a very good job, Mrs. Dixey, you and the men."

The butler and two of the footmen, all too old for active service, were accompanying the family to Belgrave Square. Mrs. Dixey and her husband, in their quarters at the far end of one wing, would be left as the sole guardians of a hundred lifeless rooms.

"Thank you, my lady," Mrs. Dixey said.

They hesitated, unbalanced for an instant in their familiar relation to each other by this dislocation of the house. The housekeeper saw the expression in Blanche's eyes and understood it, because two of her own boys were in France. She wanted to put out her hand to touch her employer's arm and say, "God will watch them for us." But she knew her place too well and stood silently instead, waiting to see if there would be any more instructions.

Blanche sighed. John was waiting for her in his office. "I think that will be all," she said. She crossed beneath the portrait without looking at it and walked slowly back over the thin bars of light.

John was sitting at his desk, staring into the pigeonholes with their neat sheaves of paper, but when Blanche came in, his face lightened. He stood up and put out his hands to rest on her shoulders, then drew her closer to him. Blanche let her head droop until it rested against him. They stood still, finding comfort in one another.

Blanche and John had not founded their marriage on words, because John had never been able to express his thoughts or feelings. Instead, Blanche had learned to interpret the different languages of their silence. She knew that he heard her fear, and shared it with her. She began to cry helplessly, her face pressed against the rough tweed of his coat.

Upstairs in the schoolroom, Grace was sitting alone on the floor. Nanny had taken eight-year-old Phoebe away to the nursery, to select whatever books and toys must be packed up and sent by the carrier to the London house. She had given Grace instructions to prepare her own belongings, as well as Thomas's, who had returned to his prep school.

But Grace had not even opened the doors of any of the tall, brown-varnished cupboards that lined the room. She sat in a patch of sunlight with her legs stretched out in front of her, scanning the familiar surroundings.

At the old desk she had sat to listen to Miss Alcott, or one of her predecessors, stifling her yawns over the atlas or the French grammar. She wondered, if all the minutes were added together, how many hours of her life she must have spent staring out of the window, over the trees of the park toward the brown hills.

When they were both very small, she had had Hugo for company. But then Hugo had gone away to school, and all through the long termtimes she had suffered the governess alone. She had always hated her isolation and the unfairness of what she considered to be her imprisonment. The Babies had been no consolation. Even now, at eleven, Thomas was no more than an infuriating little boy.

Grace smiled suddenly. The holidays had been different. The holidays had always meant the Hirsh cousins, and when they were all at Stretton, this room had been their headquarters.

She scrambled to her feet now, and went over to the desk. It had a sloping wooden seat, worn shiny, connected to the desk part by braces of cast iron. The metal had been rubbed shiny too, by her own restless feet. Grace lifted the white china inkwell out of its round hole and turned it upside down. The ink had dried out, and

Miss Alcott was gone. Grace was fifteen, and she was finished with the schoolroom.

She lifted the lid of the desk. One wet afternoon Jake had carved his initials with a penknife. She could see his face now, his tongue protruding slightly as he worked and a thick lock of black hair falling into his eyes. Grace ran her fingertips over the JNH. The letters were deep, and even. Julius had taken the knife from him after that. JEH was fainter, scratched rather than carved, but with curlicues extending from the arms of the H. Grace followed the flourishes of them with her fingernail, her eyes half closing.

After that it had been the girls' turn. They had bickered about who was to go first, and then they had carved their semi-alphabets with laborious care. GEACS and CBAGH. Clio's carving was better than her own, Grace saw now.

When the initials were all complete Jake had taken a pair of dividers and scratched a circle to enclose them all, the magic circle.

"Grace? What are you doing?"

It was Nanny, calling from the nursery. Very gently, Grace traced the circle and then she lowered the desk lid, hiding the carvings once more.

"Packing," she answered.

Grace didn't want to move to London. The London house was gloomy, and the rush of the city outside seemed only to emphasize her isolation within it. Grace understood her own position perfectly well. She was too old for the schoolroom and too young to go out in Society, even the restricted version of Society that was all the war allowed. She knew that she was facing a prospect of suitable war-work under Blanche's supervision; days of packing dressings for the Red Cross, or knitting socks, with walks in Hyde Park and tea with the daughters of Blanche's friends regarded as adequate diversions.

Grace wished she had been born a boy. Then she could go to the front, like Hugo. She was quite sure that Hugo would come home again, so certain of it that she did not even bother to try to define why. He would come home, probably with a medal, and all the glory would be heaped on him.

There was no glory in rolling bandages. There was no glory, Grace thought, in any of the things she might do.

She wandered to the window and looked down. The trees showed the first yellow and ochre of autumn. Soon the frosts would come and there would be the scent of woodsmoke and apples, but she would be in London looking out into Belgrave Square.

It isn't fair. I wish I were someone else.

It was a new sensation, for Grace, to be dissatisfied with her position in life. Until now she had always felt able to direct matters to suit herself, to arrange the world according to her own requirements. But she understood suddenly how small the world of her childhood had been, and realized that she was about to exchange that world for an adult one, no bigger and circumscribed by propriety and convention.

Grace lifted one fist and banged it against the glass of the schoolroom window. Then, out loud, she said the worst word she knew. The pointless syllable fell away into silence.

"When will this war be over?" she demanded of the empty room. She meant, When will everything else begin? Impatience budded inside her like an ulcer.

"Grace, you haven't done one single thing."

In the doorway, Phoebe appeared and Nanny Brodribb behind her, standing with her hands on her hips. Grace knew that meant she was angry. She also knew that she could easily wheedle her back into a good humor.

"Please, Broddy, will you start on it for me? I don't know where to begin. I just want to go downstairs for five minutes and then I'll be back, I truly promise."

"Will you, now?"

Grace went, leaving Phoebe clicking her tongue in imitation of Nanny. "Grace is very lazy," she heard her say.

The marble stairway that circled under the central dome was littered with woodshavings, curled like severed pigtails, and the wide marble expanse of the floor below was cluttered with boxes. An old man in a green baize apron was labeling each crate. Grace loved Stretton and had never considered that it would not stay the same forever. She hated to see it dismantled like this, being packed away like a Whit Monday fairground.

She found her parents in her father's study. As she hesitated at the door and saw them turn away from each other, it occurred to her that they might have been embracing. The notion was embarrassing, and she forgot it as quickly as she could. She also saw that Blanche had been crying. The tears were for Hugo, of course. Grace shrugged, awkwardly, wanting to reassure her out of her own fund of certainty that Hugo would not be killed, but there was something in her mother's defeatism that irritated her and diffused her sympathy.

"Yes, Grace, what is it?" John said. He had never been easy with his daughters.

As meekly as she could, Grace asked, "I wondered if I might go to Oxford, to be with Clio. Instead of staying by myself in London?"

John was never in favor of other people's suggestions, particularly his children's, and he stared at her now as if she had suggested removing to Australia. "What can you mean? You will not be by yourself. Your mother and I will be there, and your sister, and Thomas in the school holidays. As well as the rest of the household."

Blanche looked at her daughter. She had expected that Grace would grow up to be calm and controlled, and pliant where necessary, but Grace was none of those things. She was eager and strong-willed, and so full of impatience and the taste of her own needs that Blanche was sometimes afraid she might split her own skin, showing the soft pulp beneath like a ripe fruit.

"I think Aunt Eleanor has enough to worry about."

Except that her sons were safe. Jacob had kept to his declaration of pacifism. He had deferred his entry into medical school and was serving in France as an orderly in a field hospital. Julius was on the point of entering the Royal College of Music.

"She wouldn't need to worry about me. Perhaps I could help her. Perhaps I could even go to Clio's school for a few months. Until the war is over."

"I don't know," Blanche said.

Grace did. She also knew when to save her ammunition. She smiled acquiescently now. "Well, perhaps," she said. She went back upstairs to the big brown cupboards and began laying out her own possessions and Thomas's ready for transporting to London and Oxford.

Julius and Clio sat on a bench underneath the walnut tree in the garden at Woodstock Road. They were reading, and they sat turned inward toward each other, their profiles identically inclined over their books. Grace had no book, and she had already walked the flagged paths between Eleanor's flowerbeds.

"You are very lucky," Grace said to Clio. "Do you know how lucky you are?"

The twins looked up at her, and it seemed to Grace that they smiled the same patient smile.

Grace had never felt jealous of Clio before. She had envied her the relative freedom of life in the Oxford house, and the constant company of her brothers, and her easy confident store of knowledge, but she had never before thought that it would be preferable to be Clio Hirsh than to be Lady Grace Stretton.

But now, it seemed, Clio had everything that she did not.

Jake was no longer at home, of course, but Clio still had Julius, and the bond between the twins had strengthened since Jake had gone away. When Blanche set her free at last, on a long visit to the Oxford family, Grace had plenty of time to observe her cousins. Watching them, seeing how comfortable they were together and how they seemed to know without speaking what the other was thinking, Grace felt her own solitude like an affliction. She wished that she could share the same intimacy with someone.

She found herself reaching out to Clio, on this visit, as she had never done before.

Without even admitting it to herself, Grace had begun to dismantle the old barriers. She stopped trying to be better, or quicker, or louder, and she started to follow Clio's lead. She wanted to be like a sister, like a third twin to Clio and Julius, instead of merely sharing the accident of a birthday.

Since the beginning of the war Clio had grown up and away from Grace, who knew she had done no more than mark time in the schoolroom at Stretton. Unlike Grace, with her undirected impatience and energy, Clio had acquired a sense of purpose. Encouraged by Nathaniel, she had decided that she wanted to study for an Oxford degree in modern languages and was planning to enter one of the women's halls. She worked hard at her books, making Grace feel stupid and aimless in comparison.

Clio also had useful practical work to do. The house in the Woodstock Road was no longer filled with a stream of undergraduates coming to visit Nathaniel and to sit talking and arguing until Eleanor fed them. Most of the students had been swallowed up by the war, and those few who remained were quieter and more jealous of their time. The house had seemed unnaturally empty and quiet until Eleanor had offered it as a convalescent home for wounded officers.

The men came in twos and threes, physically more or less repaired but in need of rest, and comfort, and security. Eleanor and Clio nursed them, but they also talked and read to them, and Julius played chess, and Tabby and Alice ran in and out of their rooms, and so the men were drawn into the family. They seemed to thrive in the warmth of it. Each time one of them became well enough to leave, the Hirshes said good-bye with as much affection as if he were a son or a brother.

Grace saw all this, and she admired it. She was always clear-sighted enough to know what was worthy of approval. She was generous in her open admiration of Clio, and Clio responded to her generosity.

For the first time, Clio became the leader and arbiter, and in a matter of days she lost the layers of her own resentment and jealousy of Grace that had built up over all their years together. They became friends, knowing that they had never truly been friends before.

"Why am I so lucky?" Clio asked, still smiling. "I've got three pages of French translation to do, and an essay on Robespierre, and there's an ink stain in the front of the skirt of my good dress."

"You're a Hirsh, and a twin," Grace answered seriously.

They both knew how impossible such an acknowledgment would have been only a few months ago.

Clio slid sideways on the garden bench, drawing up her serge skirt to make room, and held out her hand to Grace.

"You're a Stretton. *Sursum corda,*" she said. "Lift up your hearts" was the Stretton family motto, and the cousins considered it appropriately Culmington. "And you *are* a twin."

Julius had put his book down, and he moved to one side too as Grace sat between them. He put his arm across her shoulder and Grace leaned back, resting her head against the sleeve of his coat. She sighed, then turned her face so that she could look up at him.

"Am I, Julius?"

Julius contemplated the sheen of her pale skin, and the fine hairs at the tail end of her eyebrow, and the small vertical cleft beneath her lower lip that she had inherited from her father, and he knew that he loved her as much as he loved Clio, and that she filled a space in his life that was not sisterly at all, but much more intriguing and enchanting. He could not remember even how long he had loved her, but he knew the roots of it went a long way back, and deep within him, and that the love was very important to him, but it carried no sense of threat because he knew it was immutable.

"Is that really what you want to be?" he asked her, teasingly, because that was the language they used with one another.

Grace said, "Yes."

"Then consider it a fact," Julius told her.

"Thank you." She lifted her head and kissed him on the

cheek. Being physically close to Julius always made Grace feel happy. There was a wholesomeness about him that she liked very much. His olive-colored skin smelled good, and he gave and received kisses and hugs quite naturally, as if they were a matter of course.

Jake did not, she remembered. Jake jumped and started as if something hurt him, and then he clutched with overheated hands and frightened her. When she was not frightened, she recognized an avid, beseeching kind of eagerness in him. It embarrassed her and made her want to laugh, and that was not what he wanted from her at all.

Jake and Grace had not seen very much of one another since the summer at the beginning of the war, and when they had met, they had ignored the few opportunities of being alone together, as if by mutual agreement.

And yet, since he had been at the hospital in France, Jake had written to her three or four times. They were extraordinary letters that didn't seem to speak with Jake's familiar voice. Grace kept them tied with a piece of braid in a pocket of her writing case. She did not take them out to reread when a new letter came, but quickly undid the braid and then fastened it up again.

Grace kissed Clio too, then sat back with satisfaction between the two of them. It was comfortable with Julius's arm around her, and with Clio on the other side, companionable instead of challenging.

I was lonely, Grace thought, *and now I'm not lonely.* She felt sleepily grateful to Clio and Julius.

Clio picked up her book again. "May I finish my French, please?"

It was the middle of October, and the lawns and flowerbeds were overlaid with a brown mosaic of fallen leaves, but the bench was sheltered by a high wall of red brick and the afternoon sun was warm. For once, Grace felt glad that there was nothing else to do but sit here, resting her head against Julius's shoulder.

At the beginning of her visit, wanting to prove her good intentions, Grace had repeated her suggestion that she might perhaps accompany Clio to her day school in Oxford. But most of the girls were the studious daughters of dons, and Grace had seen at once from the reactions of Nathaniel and Clio herself that she would be hopelessly out of her depth in a class with her own age group. She had no desire to be relegated to studying with the twelve-year-olds, and so she added quickly, "But my father might not want that, and perhaps I could do something here for Aunt Eleanor that would be more useful than mathematics?"

"Nothing is more useful than mathematics, except possibly Latin," Nathaniel had said severely. But the Hirshes had agreed that Grace would be a valuable assistant for Eleanor in looking after the convalescents. Lately it had become her job to lay trays and to hurry upstairs with them, to cut up food and to carry hot water in jugs, and to do whatever she could to save her aunt's legs and the energies of the overworked housemaids.

The men liked Grace, although she did not find it easy to be relaxed and happy with them and to forget what they had suffered, as Clio seemed able to do.

The middle of the afternoon, once the luncheon trays had been cleared away, was the quiet part of the day. The convalescents were sleeping, or reading, and even Tabby and Alice were resting.

It was good, Grace reflected, to be busy enough to find a break in the afternoon sunshine so welcome.

Julius stirred beside her. "Are you asleep?" he whispered.

"No. Just thinking."

Of all Grace's moods and humors, and he could have listed a score without any effort, Julius liked her contemplative manner best. He felt closest to her then, as if they could exchange ideas without words, across some invisible membrane. "Serious thoughts?"

She smiled at once, skimming away from him. "Not very. Not at all."

Clio jammed her fingers into her ears and hunched closer over her textbook. "I'm trying to work. *Please.*"

Julius lifted his arm from Grace's shoulders, yawned, and stretched his long legs. "And I have to go and practice."

Grace said, "May I come and listen?" She liked to be the audience, sitting silently through the music and applauding when he reached the end of a piece. Sometimes Julius played to his audience of one, tucking his violin under his arm and making a deep bow, and sometimes he lost himself in the music and forgot her altogether.

"You certainly may," Clio answered for him, and Julius and Grace laughed and walked back through the garden to the house.

Julius's room was bare, like a monk's cell. The papers and sheets of music on his table were laid in neat piles and squared off at right angles to each other. The covers on the iron-framed bed were drawn up with the same geometric precision. The only ornament was an engraving of the head of Mozart hanging on the wall next to the window.

Grace hesitated between the smooth bed and the upright chair in a corner, and opted for the chair. She sat down, straight-backed, and folded her hands in her lap.

Julius lifted his violin and tucked it beneath his chin. Grace saw how it became part of him. With the tip of his bow he indicated the sheet music on the music stand. "The *Rondo Capriccioso,* Camille Saint-Saëns," he announced formally. And then he added, "It's rather difficult, in parts."

It was one of the pieces his teacher had recommended he work up for his Royal College audition. The flying staccato run in E major still made him feel sweaty when he thought of it. "It calls for practice, Julius," his teacher had advised him. He took a breath now and lifted his bow.

Grace listened, intently at first, but then her attention began to wander. There was a fast section, where the notes seemed to climb and tumble over each other, and each time he played it, Grace was sure that this time Julius would be satisfied with it and move on. But each time he broke off and jerked his bow away from the strings, closed his eyes to refocus his attention, and then began again, over and over.

Grace could not even hear what it was that displeased him.

She would have been incapable of such perfectionism herself. All her own instincts would have led her to scramble through the awkward passage somehow, anyhow, and then to hurry on, aiming for the end in one triumphant rush.

Julius stopped yet again, and patiently began one more time. He had forgotten she was there. She watched his face with its shuttered look of intense concentration.

She knew that Clio's school friends considered Julius to be handsome, and she had agreed with their judgment without giving it very much thought. Now, as she studied him with detachment through the skein of music, she noticed that he had heavy rounded eyelids that looked as if they might have been sculpted and a deep upper lip with a strongly defined margin, and that his perfectly harmonious features were more feminine than conventionally handsome. He looked like Clio, of course. And so there was much more than an echo of her own face in Julius's. She had known it, but now she catalogued the similarities as if she had never been aware of them before, the color of eyes and skin, the shape of mouth and ears and the height of cheekbones. Grace smiled faintly.

The music flowed on. This time, she realized, there was no stopping. The logjam of tumbling notes broke up and was carried away in the stream of the melody. Grace found herself leaning forward on her hard chair and willing him on, holding her breath for him as if it would help him to reach the release at the end of the piece.

The music swelled, filling her head and the bare room until she sat on the edge of her seat, her lips apart and her eyes fixed on Julius's blind absorbed face. The echo of the last chord vibrated in the stillness before she realized it was finished, and then Julius raised his head and she saw his shining eyes. He was panting for breath.

"Bravo," Grace shouted. She jumped off the chair and clapped her hands until the bones jarred. "Julius, bravo. That was wonderful."

He nested his violin carefully in its case, then straightened up again. "It was better, anyway," he gasped.

"No," Grace said seriously. "It was wonderful." She meant it, and he heard it in her voice, and he crooked his arm around her shoulders again.

"Thank you," he said.

Empty of the music, the room seemed very silent. They stood side by side, next to the window, looking down into the garden. Clio's bent head was visible beneath the walnut tree at the far end, and beyond her were the trees of other gardens with bare branches beginning to poke through their faded summer covering, and the gables and slate roofs and brick chimneys of North Oxford. Grace liked the domesticity of this view, after the emptiness of Stretton Park and the grimy, pompous expanse of Belgrave Square. It amused her to imagine the blameless academic lives that were lived behind all the blandly shining windows.

Julius had no attention to spare for the view. He was too conscious of Grace's warm shoulder and arm beneath his own. He had grown rapidly in the last year—he was taller even than Jake now—and he stood a head higher than Clio and Grace. Grace seemed very slight and fragile next to his own lumbering bulk. He turned his head very slightly, breathlessly, so that he could look down on the top of her dark head. Clio still wore her hair in a long plait that hung down her back, but Grace had put her hair up in a shiny, smooth roll that showed her ears. He could see the pink rim of her ear now, and the whiteness of her neck in the shadow of her blouse collar.

He felt a spasm of tenderness for her, and at the same time a startling, fierce determination that he would never allow anything to hurt her.

He moved around so that he stood in front of her, blocking out the vista of trees and rooftops. Grace looked up at him, her mouth opening a little, surprised but unafraid.

Julius wanted to take her face between his hands and hold it, so that he could study all the contours of it, but he felt too clumsy to trust himself. Instead he bent forward, slowly and stiffly, and kissed the corner of her mouth.

"It's all right," he said, afterward.

"I know it is," Grace answered. She was at ease with Julius. She didn't feel any of the fear or fascination that Jake had set off inside her two summers ago. Julius was safe. His smooth skin smelled faintly of honey, she identified it now. He carried an aura of cleanliness with him. She knew that he loved her, and she loved him back, a love with clearly defined parameters.

Julius blushed. He was suffused with happiness that made him feel weak and light-headed, but he also felt quite calm and secure. There was no rush, no cause for anxiety. Grace was here, and there was plenty of time. If he had made himself analyze it he would not have been able to define what exactly there was time for, now or in the mysterious future, but the rush of happiness defeated logic. He wanted to lift Grace up in his arms and swing her around, laughing and shouting, but the knowledge of his own clumsiness restrained him again. Instead he reached out and touched her shoulder, near where the collar of her blouse folded against her throat. Immediately all the sensation in his body concentrated itself in his fingertips. The fabric seemed ethereally soft, as if it might melt under his touch. He shook his head, slowly, in amazement.

Grace reached up and took his hand. She turned him gently so that they faced the window again, and then settled herself against him, in the crook of his arm. To Julius, the gesture seemed wonderfully natural and confiding. He held her, and they went on looking out at the view together.

He didn't know how long it was they stood there, but it seemed a long time.

At last, they heard Tabby running down the linoleum corridor outside the door. She was calling for Eleanor, and there was a clatter as she jumped three steps in the angle of the passage and skidded along the slippery stretch to the nursery. Another door slammed somewhere else in the house, and Grace and Julius remembered that they were not the only people in the world.

Grace stepped to one side and put her hands up to her hair, smoothing it where it was already smooth. Julius loved the womanly economy of the gesture. He was thinking, *I will remember this, the look of her, the way she is outlined in the light against the window.*

"I must go and help Aunt Eleanor," she said.

Julius watched her go, and watched the door for a long moment after it had closed behind her. Then he picked up his violin again. He could play the Rondo now, he wasn't afraid of it any longer.

Nathaniel came home, bringing the evening papers with him. Eleanor hurried to meet him as she always did, as soon as she heard his key in the lock. Their eyes met, telling one another, *No bad news. Not yet.* Only then did Nathaniel kiss her. Tabby and Alice came running, and he lifted them up in turn and swung them in the air, growling like a bear to make them laugh and then scream to be put down again. Julius came more slowly down the stairs and Nathaniel clasped him briefly. They were the same height, now.

Evenings in the Woodstock Road belonged to the family. It was one of the things Grace particularly liked about staying with the Hirshes, that there had never been the starching and combing before the stiff half-hour visit to the drawing room that was always the routine at home.

Before dinner Eleanor and Nathaniel always sat in the big, comfortable room at the back of the house that looked down over a narrow wrought-iron balcony into the garden. Nathaniel sometimes played Pelmanism with the children, all of them ranged in a circle around the mahogany table. A lamp with a shade of multicolored glass threw flecks of different-colored light on the ring of faces. On other evenings Eleanor played the piano or Julius his violin, and the children took it in turns to sing. Nathaniel particularly enjoyed the singing, and would join in in his resonant bass. His voice was so unsuited to the sentimental Victorian ballads that Eleanor favored that the children would have to struggle to avoid collapsing into furtive giggles.

At other times there were the general knowledge games that Grace dreaded because she seemed to know even less than Tabby, and she would hurriedly suggest charades or recitations as a diversion. Jake's special piece had always been a theatrical rendering of "How They Brought the Good News from Ghent to Aix"; when she closed her eyes on this evening's tableau of Eleanor sewing and Julius and Nathaniel playing cards with the little girls, Grace could hear him intoning "I sprang to the stirrups." He always snatched up the invisible bridle and bared his teeth like a brigand.

There was no Jake tonight, of course. They felt his absence. With her new empathy Grace knew that Clio, hunched over a book in the corner of the room, was not reading but thinking about him.

Jake's place was taken by two of Eleanor's convalescents. They sat near to her, talking quietly. But for this difference the well-worn room looked just as it always did, with its sagging seats and piles of books and newspapers, and the murky picture of steamers on the Rhine that always hung on the wall facing the French windows.

But Grace was possessed by the realization that everything was changing. The war had crept in here, into the Woodstock Road as well as Stretton; she had not even understood how significantly. She tasted a mixture of resentment and apprehension, dry in her mouth.

When Clio's eyes wandered yet again from her book, they met Grace's. Even the old ground between them was changing its contours, but they were both glad of that. They needed their new friendship now.

Before dinner, Nanny came to take Alice and Tabby back up to the nursery. Nathaniel poured sherry into little cut-glass thimbles for the men, and there was general talk until it was time to go in to dinner.

Tonight, one of the housemaids had placed the evening post on a silver tray that stood on the hall table. When the family crossed the hall on the way to the dining room they saw that there were two thin blue foreign envelopes lying side by side.

Eleanor moved with surprising speed. She scooped up the two letters from Jake and then, seeing the inscriptions, she held one of them out with a little involuntary sigh of disappointment.

"One is for you, Grace."

It was the first letter she had received in the Woodstock Road. The others had been addressed to Stretton, or Belgrave Square. She took it, feeling the harsh crackle of the envelope between her fingers. She put it straight into the pocket of her skirt, without looking at it. She felt that the Hirshes were watching her, as if she had taken something that was rightfully theirs.

"Shall we go in?" Nathaniel murmured at last.

Eleanor opened her letter and had read it before the maid placed the soup tureen on the table in front of her. She looked up from the single flimsy sheet of paper.

"He's well," she said. "There is—there was when he was

writing, rather—a kind of lull. He calls it the calm before the next storm."

There were tears plainly visible in Eleanor's eyes, but no one was careless enough to see them. She refolded the letter and handed it down the table to Nathaniel, and then began briskly ladling soup.

Captain Smith, one of the convalescents, said, "I admire what your son is doing, Professor. I was in one of those hospitals before they sent me back home. They do a fine job."

He wanted them to know he understood Jake's beliefs, wanted them to be aware that he didn't consider him a shirker. It was not the Captain's fault that he sounded like Hugo. Grace's eyes met Clio's again.

Nathaniel lifted his head. "Of course," he said.

The letter passed to Julius, then to Clio. They were greedy for the news, there was no question of politely waiting until dinner was over.

Grace felt the generosity of it when Clio passed the blue paper to her in her turn. She was aware of the second letter burning in her pocket.

Jake wrote of the work he was doing, but only as numbers, how many casualties arriving, how many hours on duty, how few hours' sleep. The rest of the letter was taken up with his thoughts on John Donne, whose poems he had been reading, and with reminiscences of home. He recalled the day of the picnic beside the river.

Grace gave the letter back to Eleanor. "Jake will be a good doctor," she said to fill the silence, but the random remark struck a chord of optimism. It looked ahead to a better time, beyond the necessity of survival. Eleanor's face softened.

"I believe so," she said.

The maid came to clear away their soup plates.

After dinner, it was usual for Grace to sit with Clio and Julius while they read or worked, but tonight she left the table and went quickly up through the odd layers of the house to the room she shared with Clio. She half sat and half leaned against her high bed, and opened the envelope.

The letter was longer. There were three sheets of the flimsy paper, each one closely covered with Jake's black handwriting. Grace bent her head and began to read.

The words burned off the page. There were no careful sentences here, nothing like the letter he had addressed to Nathaniel and Eleanor. Jake had simply written what he felt, disjointed snatches of it, letting the raw suffering lie where it spilled. It was these images that had informed his earlier letters, the awkward and troubling missives that she had not wanted to look at again, but Jake had kept them veiled, somehow, saving her eyes. Now he had passed some last point of endurance, and Grace saw clearly what Jake was seeing.

Oh, Grace, the horror of it. Grace, do you hear me? I hold on to your name, like a clean white river pebble in my fingers.

They come in all day and all night, stretchers, cargoes of what were once men, pulp and jelly of flesh, turned black, bones like splinters.

Crying and screaming and praying, or lying mute like children.

I am afraid of each day, each death.

We are close to the lines here, I can hear the guns.

We run like ants, doctors and orderlies and bearers, like ants over the blood heaps, but we can do so little. Death keeps coming, the tide of it. Some of the men I work with indemnify themselves with a kind of terrible laughter, but I can't laugh, Grace. All I can see and hear and smell is the suffering. Each separate pain, loss, life gone or broken.

The deaths are all different. We have to leave them, most of them, to the chaplains or themselves. There was a boy like Hugo, younger, who screamed and cursed. His anger poured out of him as fast as blood. As hot. And another man, an old Cockney, wept for his mother. Like a baby cries, like Alice.

I have tried to read. I know there is beauty and order somewhere, but I can't recall it. I look at the words on the page, and I see death. I try to see your face, Clio's face, my mother's.

I am afraid of death, I am afraid of life like this, I am afraid for us all. I think of Hugo, under the guns. I think of all our deaths, yours and mine and the others; the same deaths, over and over, each of them different.

I have tried to assemble the disciplines of logic, and marshal the proofs of what human suffering has won for humanity, but I can find no logic here. There is only madness. I am afraid that I am mad.

Grace, you should not have to hear this. Forgive me.

I think of you, and of home. Julius and Clio. Of you, especially.

All this will end, it must end. But when it is done, whatever the outcome, nothing can be the same as it once was. I am sad for what we have lost, for what we are losing every day.

Grace lifted her head, but she didn't see the room with its two white beds and her own gilt-backed hairbrushes laid out beside Clio's on the dressing table. She could only see Jake, and after a moment she looked down again at the last page.

The black handwriting had deteriorated so much that she could only just decipher the words. Jake was writing about Donne again, but not in the detached, analytical way he had done in Eleanor's letter. As far as Grace could understand, he had taken some of the poems as speaking directly to him. They had taken on a significance for him that she could only guess at.

There is one, "A Nocturnal upon St. Lucy's Day," do you know it? It is about loss and grief. There is one couplet: "He ruined me, and I am re-begot Of absence, darkness, death; things which are not."

It runs in my head, all the time, while I am doing my antlike scurrying. We are all re-begot as nothingness by this war. The evil of it, the waste.

I have to go now. We live in a canvas shelter, and I sit on my camp bed to write this on my lap by candlelight. Perhaps you can't even read the words. Perhaps I should not send them to you, but I need to reach out. It is another weakness. I am afraid of my own cowardice, too.

You are so clean and white, Grace, like nothing here.

When will it all end?

For some reason Jake had signed not his name but his initials. It made Grace think again of the schoolroom at Stretton, of their old secure and undervalued world.

She said aloud, "You are not a coward."

The window opposite her had been left wide open after the warmth of the day, but the night air was icy now. It rolled in like a hill mist, and Grace shivered as it touched her bare shoulders.

She did not move, or fold the letter into its creases again. She knew that she would never forget the way Jake spoke to her out of it.

It was the letter's fusion of two voices that touched her most profoundly. There was the old Jake, who had whispered their secrets to her in the hot summer before the war began, and from whom she had in the end retreated. Out of fear of the unknown, out of childish impatience. And there was the Jake she did not know, who had witnessed the field hospital. The images of it came to her now, in Jake's disconnected words, *pulp and jelly of flesh, bones like splinters* . . .

And just as Jake had become two Jakes, boy and man, so the world had split into two worlds, old and new. Not only for herself, Grace understood that, but for all of them.

Images of the old world were all around her. There was this room with its mundane evidences of their girlhood, and in the framed snapshots on Clio's tallboy there were memories of Christmases, holiday games at Stretton, beach cricket in Norfolk or Normandy.

The new world was obliterating everything that had once been familiar. Jake and Hugo in France were part of the fearsome new world, and the officers who came to mend themselves in this house, and so were the newspapers with their black headlines and their casualty lists, and even the women who served behind shop counters where there had once been men were part of it too.

For a long time, for almost two years Grace realized, she had thought of the war as a momentous event that touched them all, but as an episode that would eventually be over, leaving the world to continue as before.

It was on that day in October 1916, the day of Jake's letter, that she understood there could be no going on as before.

If Hugo came home again, he would not be the same boy who had marched off in his fresh uniform. Jake would not be the boy who had kissed her in the angle of the hawthorn hedge. For all of them, whatever they had done, there would always be the speculation: If there had been no war. If part of a generation had not been lost.

Grace read the last, scrawled page of the letter once more.

> *I am re-begot*
> *Of absence, darkness, death; things which are not.*

But then she put the pages aside. The blackness of the lines stirred an opposing determination in her. Grace found herself making a bargain with a Providence she had never troubled to address before.

Let them come home, she bartered, and we will make something new out of "things which are not." We don't cease to exist, those of us who are left. We'll make another world.

She could not have said what world, or how, but she felt the power of her own determination as a partial salve.

Behind her, the bedroom door creaked open and Clio slipped into the room.

"Grace? It's so cold in here." She went to the window, closed it, and drew the curtains over the square of darkness. She did not ask, but Grace picked up the pages of the letter and gave them to her.

"Read it," she said in a low voice.

Afterward, Clio sat down beside Grace on the edge of the high bed. She was ashamed that amidst all her love for Jake, and fear for him, there was a shiver of jealousy that he should have written in such a way to Grace, not to herself, or Julius. And yet she understood that in the terrible hospital Jake needed to reach out to his ideal of whiteness and cleanliness, his smooth river pebble. That was not a family entity, and so Jake turned to what was closest to home, to Grace. So she told herself.

The two girls let their heads rest together, the smooth roll of hair and the thick plait the same color and texture, side by side. They were still sitting in the same position when Julius found them. He took his place next to Grace, making the same arrangement as on the garden bench.

He still felt happy, remembering that he had kissed her.

The letter did not surprise Julius, neither the horror of it nor Jake's image of Grace. His vivid imagination had led him closer to the reality of what Jake was suffering, and he loved Grace to the point where he would have been more surprised to find that his brother did not.

It did not occur to Julius to feel jealous.

"I wish he would come home," Clio said savagely.

"He will, and Hugo," Grace promised. "Everything will start again. We'll make it."

When Eleanor came up, the letter was hidden in the folds of Clio's dress. All three of them knew that it was for the magic circle alone. They felt that for even Eleanor to see it would be a betrayal.

That night, although she had not had the nightmare for years, Grace dreamed of her own death by drowning.

Five

THE TURRET ROOM WAS GROWING familiar. As he lay in bed the soldier had learned the contour of it, the regular square of one side and then the hemispherical opposite bulge where the tower was grafted onto the red brick absurdity of the house.

He had looked up at the turret, blinking his sore eyes at the white winter sky, when they wheeled him into the house from the ambulance. Since he had been brought home from Cambrai, he had seen nothing but the rigid lines of the hospital ward, and this apparition of a house with its crenellations and gables had made him momentarily afraid of hallucinations again. He had gripped the wooden arms of the wheelchair and found them solid, and had looked again to see that the house was solid too, an architect's fantasy castle planted in the North Oxford Street. There were bare-branched cherry trees in the front garden, and a child's discarded wooden engine beside the path.

As they lifted him up the steps, a woman had come out to greet him. She was statuesque, dressed in a plain gray afternoon dress, with her coils of dark hair put up in the prewar fashion.

"I am Eleanor Hirsh," she said, smiling at him. When she held out her hand, it was as if they were being introduced in a London drawing room. After the months in the trenches and the indignities of hospital, the simple gesture was like a benediction. When he took her hand, he saw that there were no rings except for a thin wedding band and a small diamond, and that the fingers looked as if they were accustomed to harder work than writing invitation cards.

"And you are Captain Dennis."

Peter Dennis forgot, momentarily, that he was in a wheelchair with his head bandaged and all his senses dislocated. He made a little bow from the waist that was almost courtly.

"Welcome to my house," Eleanor said.

The nurses and the driver who had come with him from the hospital half pushed and half carried his chair up into the house. There was another nurse here, and Peter Dennis had a confused impression of a dark-brown hallway, many more stairs and passages, children's faces solemnly watching him, all blurred by renewed pain as he was lifted out of the wheelchair and carried up to the turret room.

He heard that his attendants called the dark-haired woman Madam or Mrs. Hirsh, but that the children's voices rising up through the house cried "Mama . . ."

The room they put him into was blessedly quiet and filled with the reflections of light from the pointed windows in the turret. The new nurse helped him into the high iron-framed bed, and he lay back against the down pillows and closed his eyes.

Eleanor took Tabby and Alice down to the kitchen with her. "You mustn't make too much noise," she told them. "Captain Dennis has been very ill, and now he will need to rest quietly."

"May we go and see him?" Tabby asked. "I could show him my sewing."

"Perhaps, in a day or so."

"Did a German shoot him, as well?" Alice demanded. It was her standard question.

"Captain Dennis was very brave. He was fighting to defend what he believes in, and he was wounded. But the German soldier who fired at him was probably just as brave, and defending his own in the same way."

It was a variation on Eleanor's standard reply. With her own pacifist sons, her husband's German blood, and the male Strettons' fierce jingoism to reconcile, she felt it was the best she could do.

"Like Hugo?"

"Yes, of course, like Hugo," Eleanor answered. That was safer ground. She did not object, for once, to Cook handing out iced biscuits to the little girls. They took their prizes and ran out into the garden before Eleanor could change her mind.

Eleanor instructed Cook that the driver and the nurses who had accompanied the ambulance would probably require tea before returning to the hospital. Then she saw that Mrs. Doyle had already put the kettle on the hot plate of the big black range. The kettle sighed, and a wisp of steam issued from the curved spout. Eleanor nodded her satisfaction, and the two women smiled at each other. Their relationship was unconventional, but Eleanor did not run a conventional household.

Mrs. Doyle had been widowed in the first year of the war and had left her husband's Oxfordshire village shortly afterward to return to service. Before her marriage she had been employed as a parlormaid in a great house, and had no experience in the kitchen. But Eleanor had lost a series of cooks who could not adapt to Madam's haphazard housekeeping, and she was glad to offer the post to the capable-looking Mrs. Doyle. Her instincts were correct. Mrs. Doyle proved herself to be a naturally talented cook, producing the sweet cakes and pastries that Nathaniel loved as well as economical ragouts and vegetable pies, and managing to direct the shopping and weekly menus for the family while giving the impression that Eleanor was really in charge. Everyone ate much better food, and a new state of calm overtook the household.

The secret of their relationship was not a secret between the two women. They felt a comfortable and open respect for each other, and as the war continued they also became friends. Mrs. Doyle's dependability freed Eleanor to concentrate on her convalescent nursing work, and as the time passed the Woodstock Road house became less a rest home than a hospital extension.

By the beginning of 1918, the flow of casualties was so relentless that there were never enough hospital beds available. Eleanor and Nathaniel had begun to accept into the house men who were still seriously ill, simply because their taking a man who could be nursed at home meant that a bed was freed for another who could not.

One trained and one volunteer nurse now came to the Woodstock Road every eight hours, in shifts around the clock, but it was still Eleanor who took responsibility for the recovery of her patients. They did recover, almost all of them had done, some with a rapidity that surprised the doctors.

"You should have been a professional nurse," Nathaniel proudly told his wife. "You have a great gift for it."

"Can you imagine my dear mama countenancing anything so dreary and dangerous? Permitting her daughters to do any work at all, however genteel?" Eleanor sounded cheerful, but she was touched by a wistful sense of opportunity missed, of an unexperienced life running parallel to her own that she could only imagine, never know for sure. She consoled herself with the fact that she was doing what she could, now that it was needed, although it seemed so little.

Nathaniel had laughed and refolded his newspaper. "I can *not* imagine," he had said.

Eleanor and Mrs. Doyle now had enough experience of both nurses and ambulance drivers to know that they needed tea, and slabs of cake as well. Mrs. Doyle set out the plain white kitchen cups and cut a cherry cake into symmetrical pieces, and Eleanor welcomed Captain Dennis's escorts into the kitchen.

"Is he comfortably settled?"

"The journey's taken it out of him, all right," one of the nurses said. "But I reckon he'll do well enough when he's rested himself." There was no "Madam." She spoke with a brusquely businesslike air, one professional to another. Eleanor noticed it and felt a mild satisfaction. Only Mrs. Doyle frowned and held up the big brown teapot as if to threaten the woman with it.

"Won't you sit down, if you have time?" Eleanor invited.

They settled themselves around the scrubbed table, and Eleanor sat down with them. She took a cup of tea from Mrs. Doyle and paid her a joking compliment about the even distribution of the cherries in the sponge. Only the driver stared and looked uncomfortable, but he was the only one who had never been to the Woodstock Road before.

The nurses talked about patients and their prospects. Eleanor stayed just long enough to drink her tea, and then she said a smiling good-bye and went off upstairs to see if her newest patient was comfortable.

"She's the lady of the house, is she?" the driver sniffed. "Funny sort of a set-up you've got here, the mistress sitting drinking tea with our sort, isn't it?"

"More of a lady than you're ever likely to encounter," the cook snapped. "And a finer household, too."

The man appeared not to have heard her. He rubbed his whiskers with the palm of his hand. "It's the war, isn't it? Changing everything, all the old ways." He shook his head lugubriously, ready to insist that no change he had ever experienced had ever been for the better.

Nathaniel came out of the Examination Schools and began to walk up the honey-walled curve of the High. He had been lecturing on Old French vowel shifts, and his mind was still busy with the fascinating labyrinths of word formations and Germanic borrowings. It was the middle of the afternoon and Oxford was at its busiest, but Nathaniel was oblivious to the cyclists who swept past with their gowns fluttering, the tradesmen's vans and carts and omnibuses and private cars that clogged the road, and even the fellow dons who passed in the opposite direction and glanced at him in the expectation of a greeting. He had forgotten to button up his overcoat and it flapped around his legs as he walked, but Nathaniel didn't notice the cold wind either.

If he had stopped to look around him, it would have been to notice, with the same sadness even though it was for the thousandth time, that the faces of the undergraduates who swept by him were either too young, no more than boys, or else they were much older, and shadowed with experience. There were only one or two young men of the right age, and they were in khaki uniforms.

Still preoccupied with his own thoughts, Nathaniel passed the golden front of Queen's and hurried on, intending to cross Radcliffe Square in the direction of the Bodleian. But when he reached the corner of Catte Street, he had to wait to allow a brewer's dray to pass ahead of him, and while he stood hesitating, something made him look sideways, across the High.

Through the traffic he saw two young women. They were balanced on the edge of the curb, one of them leaning on a bicycle, the other carrying a shopping basket. They were laughing, their heads held close together, and their rosy faces were bright with happiness. They looked very alike.

His first response was abstract admiration. An instant later he thought of Eleanor and Blanche, with their lifelong conspiracy of friendship. These two reminded him of the older twins. And only then, emerging from his preoccupation, did he see that the two were not strangers at all, but Clio and Grace.

He realized with a little shock that they were grown up, not children any longer. And as soon as the pair of faces dissolved into familiarity he lost the sense of how similar they were.

Clio was wearing her school coat and a dark felt hat with a colored ribbon, and her schoolbag was fastened to the front of her bicycle handlebars. Eleanor allowed her to cycle to school now, because Clio insisted that all the other girls did. By contrast, Grace wore one of the well-tailored suits that Blanche's dressmaker made for her. From somewhere, probably her mother's wardrobe, she had purloined a fur tippet and cut it up to make a turban. The fur made a dark cloud around her face. The shopping basket was an incongruous accessory. It looked very heavy.

Nathaniel changed course and ducked through the passing traffic to greet them. They swung around at once with pleased cries of "Pappy!" and "Uncle Nathaniel!"

"What's the joke about?" he asked, wanting instinctively to be a part of it. The girls looked blankly at him.

"I don't think there was a joke, really," Grace answered. "We were just laughing. I've been to the Lending Library. Look." The basket was full of books. It was one of Grace's responsibilities to select novels for the patients. She chose out of the depths of her ignorance, with results that varied from inspired to comical.

Nathaniel tilted his head to one side to read the titles on the spines. "*Martin Chuzzlewit*, mmm, mmm, *Zuleika Dobson*. That's interesting. All very suitable. And where are the two of you going now?"

"Home. Unless we can come with you? Out to tea?"

Nathaniel had been planning to do some work in his rooms, but the idea of tea was tempting.

Clio begged, "Please, Pappy? Tea at Tripps'? You know it's meatless day today. That means vegetable sausage for dinner, doesn't it?"

The Hirsh household always obeyed the government's edict for helping with food shortages by doing without meat on at least two days a week. But even Mrs. Doyle's version of the invariable vegetable sausage was no great favorite.

"Tripps' it is," Nathaniel said briskly.

The tea shop on the corner of the Broad was an old favorite. Nathaniel had first taken Eleanor there long ago, before Jake was born. The crooked floors of the little rooms and the dark oak furniture and faded yellowish walls seemed exactly as they had always been; the difference was that the cakes were brought by waitresses in caps and aprons, whereas there had once been waiters like family retainers in dark jackets with white napkins folded over their arms.

Tripps' appeared to be unaffected by food shortages. There were still tiny sandwiches cut into triangles and circlets, and chocolate roulade and ginger sponge and almond slices. Ceylon or China tea came in big silver-plated pots.

"Heaven," Clio said greedily.

Nathaniel had been eating and looking around the room. The tables were occupied by groups of pink-faced boys, by mature men, usually alone and absorbed in a book, and by young ladies from the women's halls, always in pairs.

Clio and Grace looked quite old enough to be one of those pairs, he thought, and then remembered that it was only another year or so before Clio would embark on her degree course. He was proud of her. When he finished his inspection of the room and looked back at their two faces, he felt proud of both of them, the way they reflected each other, like two bright coins. He felt the same pleasure in their company as he had always done with Eleanor and Blanche. He was glad that the two of them seemed to have become such good friends. He would not have cared to place a bet on it when they were younger.

"Penny for your thoughts?" Grace invited.

"I was thinking," Nathaniel teased, "that the two of you are almost as beautiful as your mothers."

He was amused to see that they were both still young enough to look disbelieving, and then to blush fetchingly. Grace put her hands up to her hat, adjusting the fur cloud around her face. There was no echoing gesture from Clio in her old school felt.

"Only *almost*?"

Grace had recovered herself. There was something so provocative in the curve of her mouth that Nathaniel was confused now by the dissimilarity between the two of them. Clio was still a little girl, Grace was not.

He was pleased that Jake and Julius had gone on, out of the family circle. And Julius had survived his period of Grace-enchantment admirably well, Nathaniel thought. His music studies would give him enough to think about from now on. "As yet," Nathaniel answered.

They had finished their tea. Nathaniel began to look forward to reaching home. He wanted to see Eleanor and to play for an hour with Alice. He loved his work, but the center of his life was his wife and children. "Time to go," he announced.

Grace and Clio might have hoped for more cake, but they knew Nathaniel better than to argue. When they stood up to leave, Nathaniel noticed how the men's eyes followed Grace. Clio must have some proper clothes, he decided. He would talk to Eleanor about it.

The three of them came out of the tea shop into the greenish, fading afternoon light. Clio's bicycle was propped against the wall nearby.

"I'll be home first," she called. "Lovely tea, Pappy." She swung away from them toward Cornmarket. Nathaniel took Grace's arm, and they began to walk.

It was a long way along St. Giles and up the Woodstock Road. So it happened that Clio was the first to meet Captain Dennis.

She almost collided with Eleanor negotiating the stairs from the kitchen with a tea tray. Clio took the tray from her mother automatically, and Eleanor leaned to kiss her cheek.

"Hello, my darling. Will you take it up to the turret for me? Nelly and Ida are both so busy, and Grace is at the circulating library. Then come down and have some tea yourself."

"We met Pappy. He took Grace and me to Tripps'."

"Oh, how lucky." Eleanor was truly envious. She would have loved to sit in the tea shop and gossip with her husband. Clio smiled at her, understanding as much.

"Tell him to take you. Has someone new arrived?" She nodded down at the tray.

"The ambulance brought him this afternoon. His name is Captain Dennis. He was shot in the head, poor boy, but they say now that he will recover completely. Isn't that marvelous?" Eleanor was completely happy again, contemplating the good news.

Peter had watched the light fading in the corners of the room, letting himself grow familiar with the opposite contours of square and semicircle, and then he had drifted into sleep. The soft knocking at the door woke him into momentary disorientation.

"What is it?" he called.

"Clio Hirsh. I've brought your tea."

"Come in," he said, not much the wiser.

The door opened, and he saw a dark-haired girl with wide eyes and pink cheeks. She came into the room sideways, carrying a tray of tea things. She was not a nurse, or an orderly, although she was wearing some kind of uniform. Peter blinked, feeling the mists of confusion threatening him. A kind of convalescent home, they had told him before he left the hospital. He longed suddenly for his real home, and the sight of his mother, but they had also told him that Inverness-shire was too far for him to travel yet.

The girl set the tray down and then turned shyly to look at him. Peter saw that she was perhaps three years younger than himself.

"I expect you wish you really could go home," she said. It was not a particularly profound insight, but in his weakness Peter was amazed and grateful. He had an uncomfortable moment when he was afraid that he might cry. He made himself smile instead. "It's a very long way."

Clio was gazing at him. One side of his head had been shaved, and where it was not hidden by the white lint dressing, she could see the new growth of hair. It was a kind of fuzz, darker than the old hair.

Apart from the red pucker of a healing scar that ran upward from his cheekbone and under the pad of bandages, his face seemed undamaged. She wanted to look at his face, but she felt constrained by her shyness. She turned to the tea tray instead and found that her hands were shaking.

"I'm sorry," he said. "It isn't a very pretty sight."

"I didn't mean . . . It isn't that." She couldn't say that it was nothing, because he had suffered it, but it wasn't his wound that she had been thinking about at all. "What happened to you?"

"I stuck my head above a parapet. A sniper got me. The bullet sliced a furrow through the bone. Missed my brain, more or less." Economical words, that was all. He wouldn't tell her about the mud and the noise and the specter of death, any more than he had told his father and mother when they came to see him in the Oxford hospital. That was past now, and he was alive. "What did you say your name was?"

"Clio Hirsh."

She had a wonderful smile, and skin like ivory satin. Her throat was very white where it was swallowed by the collar of her severe blouse. He knew that he wanted to touch it. The strength of his inclination startled him.

Clio felt his eyes on her, and put her hand up. "It's my school uniform. I have to wear it. This, and the tunic."

She was a schoolgirl. Peter Dennis's schooldays, only two years behind him, seemed to belong to another lifetime. "You look very pretty in it." It was an unimaginative compliment, he thought, and Clio's smile was more of a reward than it deserved.

"Do you know, that is the second time today I have been told I look pretty?"

Peter tried to sit upright. "And who is the other man?"

"My father."

It made her happy to see him laughing, and she laughed too.

"Let me give you some tea," she said when they had finished.

She was going to hand him the cup when she saw that he had slipped down against the pillows. She leaned over instead and rearranged them for him. Then she put her arm behind his shoulders.

"Can you sit up some more?"

She lifted the weight of him, and his head rested against her for an instant. Looking down, she saw the line where his natural hair met the fuzzy new growth. She was suddenly aware of the eggshell vulnerability of the naked skull. It was terrible to think of the bullet smashing into it, the hairsbreadth distance from the soft brain. She felt a shiver of horror traveling through her limbs. Her awareness of her own body was immediately heightened. The business of muscles and tendons and blood vessels instantly struck her as precious and miraculous, all the more so for never having been considered before.

She withdrew her arm, very carefully, aware of the infinitesimal warmth of their contact.

Peter's head flopped back against the plump pillows. "I'm so damned weak."

"You will get strong again," she made herself say, with composure. She handed him the white and gold teacup. The mundane gesture was invested with importance.

There was another knock at the door, and the day nurse came in. She was a square-jawed, middle-aged woman who wore a long starched apron and a cap of starched and folded linen. She was carrying the dressings box, and a tin jug of hot water.

"Good afternoon, Miss Hirsh. How are you, Captain Dennis? It's time for your dressing."

Clio knew that she was dismissed. She was disappointed, but she nodded meekly. "Good-bye, Captain."

He ignored the nurse. "Peter," he said. "Will you come back tomorrow?"

Clio gave him her smile once more. "Of course I will."

Only when the door had closed behind her did he lean back, ready to submit. The nurse bent over him, crackling, and began to peel the old dressing away from the weeping furrow in the side of his skull.

Nathaniel and Grace were home. Clio could hear Tabby and Alice clamoring for their father's attention. Grace was coming swiftly up the stairs. She glanced up and saw Clio hovering at the top, as if she had a secret. "What is it?" Grace called.

Clio had been thinking dazedly that here was a man, a man who was neither a brother nor a cousin. She had met hardly any men except the other patients, and she knew with certainty that Peter Dennis was absolutely unlike any of those.

"Nothing," Clio answered innocently.

Grace came up the stairs, and stopped on the stair level with her. "What's the new patient like?"

"Quite nice, I think." She went on down, with every appearance of calm, and left Grace on the landing.

It was the next afternoon, when Clio was at school, before Grace met Peter Dennis. She was making a visit to each of the patients, distributing the new books she had brought home in her basket. The turret room was the highest in the house and the last one she came to.

When she came in, Peter saw her dark hair and eyes, and remembered the color of her skin. There was a faint blur of light around her silhouette, but he knew that was a trick played by his own damaged eyesight. He smiled at her. "Clio? I hoped you'd come today."

Grace saw that he moved his legs a little to one side under the white covers, in the expectation that she would sit down beside him. The intimacy of the small gesture struck her first, and then came a tide of other impressions. She saw that he was good-looking, even though his head was bandaged and partly shaven, and she felt disappointed that Clio had claimed his friendship first. She understood at once that he had eagerly mistaken her for Clio, and it was a ferment of mischief and pique and residual boredom that made her smile back and answer, "Of course I have come."

As she said it, she sat down on the bed, in the space his long legs had made for her. She was remembering the stories that Blanche and Eleanor used to tell of confusions at evening parties when they were girls. Her smile widened, and grew brilliant.

Peter Dennis was dazzled by it.

"It's my job to go to the library and bring back books. You must tell me what you like to read. I'm afraid there's only one left today."

"What is it?" He had been unable to read for a long time. The print blurred and ran down the page like tears and made pain slice through his head. But now he felt that he wanted to read again. He would have liked the volume of Tennyson that had been in his tunic pocket.

Grace held out the book. "It's *Zuleika Dobson*."

"I've read it," Peter said. And then he added, "But I would love to read it again." *This* was Zuleika, he thought lightheadedly, sitting on his bed with a rainbow around her hair. He knew that he would happily throw himself into the river for her sake.

"Do you know the story?"

Grace hesitated. She did not, but she had no doubt that Clio did. It would not be easy, passing herself off as her cousin. The challenge enticed her. "Not very well," she hedged.

"Zuleika is the most beautiful girl in the world. All the young men in Oxford drown themselves in the river for love of her."

Their eyes met.

"How stupid of them," Grace said softly. "What a waste."

In the moment's silence that followed there was nothing for Peter to do but lift her hand from where it lay on the bedcover. He turned it in his own, examining the fingers, the dimples over the knuckles and the knob of bone at the wrist. It seemed extraordinary that this girl should be here, with her clean apple-scented skin and shiny hair, extraordinary that he should be here himself, in this room that smelled of lavender and fresh linen and polished oak boards. He wondered if he would wake up and find himself lying in a shell hole, the sky over his head blackened with smoke.

He closed his eyes, then opened them again.

Grace was looking steadily at him. "Are you tired? Does your head hurt?" Her voice had turned gentle.

"No. I'm not tired."

He lifted her hand and held the palm of it against his lips.

As if drawn by an invisible thread, Grace leaned toward him. She leaned closer, until her cheek rested against his head. She could feel the silky texture of his natural hair and the rougher prickle of the new growth. She rubbed her cheek, turning her head so that her mouth was against his skull, and her chest seemed to tighten and expel the breath out of her lungs in a ragged sigh.

He said, "Clio," and she was startled because she had forgotten the deception.

To exclude it once more she drew her hand back, away from his mouth, and put her own lips in its place. Peter breathed in sharply, but then when her mouth opened a little, he tasted the slippery heat of her tongue. He put his arm around her shoulders, pulling her so close to him that he could feel her small breasts against his chest. He pushed his tongue between her teeth, his own mouth widening. He was thirsty, and ravenously hungry.

Grace thought, *What did Clio do yesterday?*

It came to her that she didn't know her cousin nearly as well as she had thought, and then that for now she was Clio, looking out from inside her. Or controlling her from above, like a puppet. The notion was intriguing, and oddly exciting. It was more exciting than what was actually happening to her.

Grace didn't feel frightened by Captain Dennis, not in the way that Jake had frightened her with his furtive desperation. She felt pleasantly alive, and stimulated by his kisses, without being afraid that she might not be able to control him, or understand her own response.

She knew what she felt about this. She enjoyed being kissed by the damaged hero, she liked the way that he seemed to give himself up to her, with blind concentration. She was relieved to find now the first surprise was over that she felt cool, almost detached. She reached up and stroked back his hair, away from the stark white dressing.

Had Clio done the same thing yesterday?

When Peter opened his eyes, her face was momentarily shot into bright and dark fragments, prism-edged, like broken mirror shards. He waited for the visual disturbance to subside, and her features reassembled themselves. For another instant there was a complete image but it was a double one, so that he saw two of her. Then the dark heads slid together and coalesced, and she was smiling at him, soft-lipped. They were both panting a little.

"You are really here, aren't you?" he asked.

For answer she held out her two hands for him to take. They were warm and quite solid. He kissed the knuckles of each one in turn.

"I can't believe you," he said delightedly. "You are a miracle."

"If I were a miracle, I wouldn't have to go now and do the tea trays." Clio would be home soon.

He was anxious immediately. "Will you come back again?"

"Of course I will. When I can."

After she had gone, Peter Dennis lay back against his pillows and slipped into an erotic reverie of the kind he had not had for two years. Love and sex had been a part of the old world, the one he had exchanged for the trenches. He was astonished to find that he could reenter the old kingdom so easily.

And in her turn Grace might have been amused to know that Peter's imaginings were set in an idyllic water-meadow backed by a hawthorn hedge.

When the starched nurse came in, she looked sharply at her patient and then pronounced, "You are looking very much better, Captain Dennis."

"I am feeling very much better, Nurse, thank you," Peter agreed with her.

Clio came home from school, bumping her bookbag down on the console table in the hall and sending the cards and papers piled on it whirling to the floor. "I've so much work to do. Miss Muldoon is a tyrant, a vile tyrant. I wanted to be free on Saturday, and now I shall have to plow through a thousand pages of Racine. You're so lucky, Grace, you just don't know."

"I'll do your chores for you, if you like," Grace offered.

Saturday was important. It was Alice's sixth birthday, and there would be a family party. Jake and Julius were coming home for it.

Clio's face lightened. "Will you, really? If I go straight up and start on it now, I might just finish it by Friday. You are a true friend, Gracie. I'll remember you in my will."

Grace had been intending to confide in her. She had imagined that they would enjoy the mischief of the confusion together, playing at being each other as Eleanor and Blanche had done in the ballrooms twenty years before.

But she watched Clio unpacking her books, and said nothing. Clio could play at being Grace, of course, as easily as she could play at being Clio. There was a different, darker satisfaction in keeping the secret just for herself. Clio was preoccupied with her languages, busy and productive, while Grace had no such focus. The image of the puppeteer manipulating the strings came back to her.

There was a moment when she could have said, Something quite funny happened when I took a book in to Captain Dennis. Then the moment was gone.

"Here I go," Clio sighed.

"I'll bring you up something to eat when I've done the trays."

Clio blew her a kiss from the foot of the stairs. Grace did the extra work with an assiduity that made Nelly and Ida exchange surprised glances behind her back.

Later, when the girls were preparing for bed, Clio asked, "Have you met the new patient yet? Captain Dennis?"

Grace concentrated on her own reflection in the looking glass as she brushed her hair. She shook her head.

Clio was smiling, wanting to offer something, a confidence, in exchange for Grace's earlier generosity. "He's—interesting. Rather beautiful, in a way."

"The damaged hero, you mean? Another one."

"Oh, no. Not another, not at all. He is quite different."

In the glass Grace saw that there was warm color over Clio's throat and cheeks, and her eyes were shining. Clio was ready to fall in love, and Grace felt the allure of responsive strings in her fingers. The temptation was too strong to resist. The chance to influence Clio's love affair more than compensated for not having a love of her own. Grace didn't think beyond that. For two or three days, until Alice's birthday, she enjoyed the challenges of her complicated game.

Clio's attention was torn between the books waiting on her desk and the turret room. For the first time in her life she experienced the thrill of neglecting what she was supposed to do and indulging in what she was not. She would wait in agony for what she judged to be the safest moment, then quietly close up her grammar and slip through the shadowy house to Peter's door. He would look up when she came in, with a mixture of anticipation and uncertainty, and when she sat on the edge of the bed he would put his arms up around her neck and draw her down beside him.

Sometimes they would kiss; more often they would lie quite still, their mouths just touching, talking in whispers. Clio told him everything, about Jake and Julius and their childhoods, about Blanche and Eleanor and their different marriages, and Stretton and what had happened to Hugo, and about Grace.

"Why haven't I seen Grace yet?" Peter asked once.

"I think she's piqued because I've claimed you for my own," Clio said, not pursuing the topic. She was quite happy for Grace to keep her distance.

At other times, Peter would begin to talk about the war. From the way his words came, reluctantly but inevitably, Clio understood that he could never close his mind to what he had seen and done. He tried to obliterate it, but he could not. She felt it always there, a long shadow between them.

Sometimes he would remember the men in his company, recalling their jokes and their idiosyncrasies and smiling at the memory so that he looked much younger, the boy that he must have been. Almost always, it seemed, these reminiscences ended with Peter saying, "He was killed, not long after that."

"What was it really like?" Clio asked once, her whisper almost inaudible.

There was a silence before he answered her.

Then he said, "Like nothing you should ever know about."

He turned her face between his hands, so that he could look into her eyes. It was difficult for him to focus on her face, so close to his. He could see the dark fringe of her eyelashes, the glint of reflected light in her pupils. Her breath was warm and sweet. He felt in this safe place that he was bathed in happiness, like sunshine.

"I love you," he told her.

"I love you too," Clio breathed.

Grace had to plan her own visits with even more care. She watched and waited, and then flitted like a shadow up the stairs and passageways that led to the turret: she had to avoid the nurses, and Eleanor on her rounds, and Nelly and Ida with their clanking hot-water jugs, and Clio herself.

The best time was the quiet middle of the afternoon, when Eleanor was resting in her bedroom and the maids had retired to sit with Cook in the kitchen. The nurses withdrew too, to what had once been the housekeeper's parlor at the back of the house, where they could be summoned by an ancient system of brass bells if any of the patients needed them.

On the first afternoon Grace had thought of putting on one of Clio's school tunics, but she dismissed the idea as too difficult to explain away if anyone else in the household should catch sight of her. She made do with a plain linen blouse and flannel skirt, and she plaited her hair in a long braid, like Clio's.

"Don't you have to go to school? It is a weekday, isn't it? Or have I lost count?" Peter asked in puzzlement.

"It's Wednesday, all day." Grace laughed. "I'm supposed to be working at home. Preparing for examinations." She changed the subject quickly, not eager to be questioned too closely about which examinations.

She quickly discovered that it was easier not to talk very much at all. There were too many potential pitfalls in conversation. She stretched out beside him instead, measuring her supple length against him. And at the beginning, he was a willing participant. He was even the leader in their explorations of each other.

Peter was a virgin, technically. But there had been a girl at home, the daughter of one of the tenant farmers on his father's estate. In the summer after he had left school, before he joined his new regiment, the girl had taken a fancy to him. He could still remember the smell of dust and saddle soap and horse sweat exuded by the blanket that they spread on the floor of the barn loft, and see the dreamy, intent expression on the girl's face as she unbuttoned his clothes and took hold of him with her cool hand.

"Please," he had begged her. "Please, let me."

"No-o," she whispered. "I darena'. What would I do wi' a babby?"

"I'll be careful," he said in his innocence. The girl only giggled.

"For sure you will. But I'll not let you, whatever. Look, this is what you do. It feels just as good, I tell you."

She had guided his hand until his fingers slipped in the silky wetness and rubbed against a hard nub of flesh. She had stretched out on the blanket then, with her skirts up around her waist, exposing her thin white legs and a patch of dark red hair. She had closed her eyes, sighing and lifting her narrow hips under his hand. It seemed to Peter that she took her pleasure and achieved satisfaction with the same uncomplicated innocence as the cats in the farmyard.

"That's right," she said afterward. "Now I do it for you, see?"

She did, with quick, businesslike strokes, and he groaned when the milky jet spurted over the blanket to lie in glistening clots between their bodies.

Peter knew that it was not as good as burying himself inside her, but it was good enough. There were variations, too, they discovered together before it was time for him to leave for France.

Part of him longed to rediscover all those variations with this miraculous Clio. When she wasn't with him he thought of it constantly. But when she did come to his room, he was immediately and painfully conscious of every creak and whisper in the old house, imagining a footstep outside the door, voices intruding on them, staring eyes and shocked exclamations.

"What's the matter?" Grace whispered. "Don't you like it when I do this?"

"I like it too much," he answered, half-ashamed.

She was much braver than he was, much more reckless. She seemed to have no fears of discovery. Her hand brushed against him, and he felt that it was hot through the thin sheet.

Peter had begun to be puzzled. He admired her, he was captivated by her in all her moods, but he was confused by her capriciousness. Sometimes when she came she was demure, even shy, seemingly happier to lie in his arms and whisper disarming confidences than to touch and tease. She said, I love you, and he believed her. And then at other times she was evasive, except in the matter of her thin, smooth body. The heat in her seemed almost febrile. He would follow her lead, and then he would shiver with the fear that someone would come in and discover them.

If he told her he loved her then, she would only smile and look at him from beneath her dark eyelashes.

He felt more comfortable with her innocent, confiding manner, but it was the other one he dreamed of when he was alone.

He lay in his room, and for all his satisfaction otherwise his thoughts circled around the mystery of it, as if he could not keep his tongue away from an aching tooth.

At last he said to her, when she slipped into the turret room on Friday evening, "Wicked Clio, today, is it?"

Clio was in her bedroom finishing her translation. Alice was being put to bed in a state of furious overexcitement, and the rest of the household was preparing for the birthday party and the arrival of Jake and Julius. Grace had stretched out full-length on the bed beside Peter, her head propped on one hand. Unusually, her hair was loose and a strand of it lay across Peter's shoulder.

She hesitated only for an instant. Then she looked full at him. "What can you mean by that?" she asked, in her teasing voice. "I am never wicked."

His eyes met hers. She saw that he was serious.

"You know what I mean."

Grace had sensed his confusion, almost from the moment he had become aware of it himself. She had understood that whatever it was that Clio and Peter did or talked about together, it was different from what she did. She was not finding out what it was like to be Clio, only setting herself further apart from her. She was not directing anything, and she had no power at all. She was simply involved in a mean and sordid piece of trickery.

The realization had made her feel miserable and defiant. It was worse because she had grown to like Peter Dennis and to wish that he might like her for herself, rather than for her inept version of Clio.

She wondered now if she had said or done something obviously wrong, or omitted to do something else, and so given away her wretched secret. She had already decided that it was time to stop her visits. She would change her clothes and give herself an elaborate coiffure, and reintroduce herself as Grace. If it was not already too late.

She answered warily, "I don't think I do know."

She saw that he hadn't guessed, but that he must do soon.

Peter sighed. "It doesn't matter, then."

Grace sat up. "I'd better go. Mama needs help downstairs."

He held her wrists then, unwilling to let her go in either of her incarnations. "Stay." He wanted to force her back against the white pillows, shutting out her life that he didn't know beyond the door of the turret room. He wanted her to belong to him, with all her inconsistencies.

A little of Grace's confidence flooded back. She did have her own power that was nothing to do with Clio. She had learned that from Jake and Julius.

"I'll come tomorrow," she promised. One last time, she told herself. She leaned over and kissed him, and for a moment the dark veil of her hair obscured the light.

In the morning Clio said happily, "I'm so looking forward to you meeting my brothers."

She had brought his breakfast tray. Instead of her school uniform she was wearing her best dress, hyacinth-blue crêpe de Chine with the faint traces of an ink stain in the front panel of the skirt. The bodice had slightly too many fussy ruches and pleats, but Peter thought she looked beautiful. He wanted to reach out for her, but the morning nurse was bustling in and out with her thermometer and hot water. They contented themselves with touching hands when her back was turned.

"I'm looking forward to it too," he said.

Clio had talked a lot about her brothers. He knew that Jake had finally been invalided home from a hospital in France, suffering from pneumonia and exhaustion. He was a medical student now, at University College in London.

He knew about Julius the violinist, too. Clio talked less about her twin, but he guessed that it was because there was a closeness between the two of them that went deeper than words. He was particularly curious to meet Julius Hirsh.

While they were talking, they could hear Alice's high-pitched voice rising excitedly through the house. Now she materialized in the open doorway and blinked at Peter. Her springy black curls had been pulled back into a tight braid, and her round face suddenly looked older.

"I'm six," she said importantly. "My cousin Grace did my hair grown-up for me. It's my birthday."

"I know it is. May I wish you many happy returns of the day?"

Alice had firm likes and dislikes, not always logically based. She included Peter amongst her likes. "Thank you. Did you buy me a present?"

Clio remonstrated, "Alice!" but Peter held up his hand.

"I am afraid I didn't. It isn't very easy for me to buy presents, lying here like this."

"Pappy and Mama gave me a doll's house. *With* furniture."

"I see. Is there a dog kennel?"

"Of course not."

"All doll's houses need a dog to guard them, and a kennel for him to live in. I will carve you one. I happen to be a very fine woodcarver."

Alice beamed. "That would be very kind of you."

A moment later she was gone.

It delighted Clio that her love was generous to her little sister. He had told her that he had two younger sisters of his own, at home in Scotland. She liked to think of him as part of a family, belonging to a warm nexus like her own. She looked at him now, with the nurse bending over him and the asymmetrical crest of his hair spread out on the pillow, and thought that she had never felt happier in her life than she had done since Peter Dennis had come.

"What time will your brothers be here?"

"On the eleven o'clock train from Town. Pappy will go to the station to meet them."

Peter heard the excitement of the arrival.

He was alone, watching the progress of the squares of sunlight across the polished floor. Then he heard the chugging of a taxicab, and running feet and excited voices. Alice's shrill cries were the most clearly audible, but it sounded as if the entire household had spilled out of the front door and down the steps to greet the returning sons.

After the hubbub was over and the house had swallowed the voices up once more, it was a long, slow hour and more before Peter heard them coming along the passage to his room. He sat up against his pillows, watching the door.

Clio was the first to appear, with pink cheeks and bright eyes, as he had first seen her. She was followed by two tall young men who had to stoop to pass under the door lintel.

Peter's first impression, born out of his upper-class Anglo-Scots prejudice, was that they looked large and strange and exotic, unmistakably Jewish. He had noticed none of this strangeness in Clio. The two young men were like their huge, black-bearded father, and Clio took after her aristocratic mother. But then, when they came closer to shake his hand, he saw the strength of the family likeness. It was especially marked between Clio and

Julius. It was as if the addition of her brothers made him see Clio afresh, in a different context. Her duality seemed less puzzling, then.

Jake was friendly and direct. He sat on the end of the bed and talked to Peter about where he had been fighting, and about his injuries and recovery. Julius was quieter. Peter noticed that his wrists protruded from the sleeves of his coat, and that his hands were long and pale with broad, spatulate tips to the fingers. He asked if Peter played chess and diffidently offered to give him a game, later, after the birthday party.

Clio looked from one to the other of the three faces, with a mixture of pride and anxiety. It seemed very important that they should all like one another.

Eleanor called them. "Jacob! I need you to help to move this table. Why is poor Grace left to do all the work?"

They stood up obediently. "Can't you come down and join the party?" Julius asked.

"Peter's eyesight is affected, he has to keep still, the doctors won't let—" Clio broke off, blushing, knowing that she had betrayed her loving concern. Her brothers grinned.

"Next time," Peter said, smiling at her. "But I would like to meet Grace. To complete the set." He saw, in the three faces, three different reactions to her name. Julius's was the least ambivalent.

"You will," Clio promised. "I'll make her come up."

Alice sat at the head of the long table. She was wearing her best white muslin dress and a crown that Tabby had made for her out of gold paper. Tabby was always happier to celebrate other people's birthdays than to be the focus of attention on her own. Nathaniel and Eleanor sat on her right and left hands, and down the length of the table were the Hirsh children, Julius and Jake vying with each other to make Alice laugh and encouraging her to an even higher pitch of excitement, three or four little girls who were Alice's friends and who stared at her brothers with big, round eyes, and Oswald Harris and his wife and children. Grace sat at the far end, facing Alice.

On the white linen cloth there were the remains of jewel-colored jellies and iced cakes, with ribbons and favors and fondant sweets. Grace watched Mrs. Doyle come in with the birthday cake. It was chocolate and cream, with a ruff of the same gold paper as Alice's crown.

Nathaniel beamed with paternal pleasure as Alice seized the bone-handled knife from Mrs. Doyle. He looked across the table at his wife, celebrating in the exchanged glance another year of family life, Jake's safe return and recovery, the quiet continuation of the domestic happiness.

"My cake! I cut it," Alice shouted.

Grace thought that she could not stomach much more of this joyful family harmony. In a little while there would be singing, and then noisy party games. Just for the moment, she had had enough of Hirsh good humor and wholesome merrymaking. Birthdays and family occasions at Stretton and Belgrave Square were more somber, restrained events. This party, today, made her feel rebellious and contrary.

She pushed her chair back and slipped away from the table, murmuring an inaudible excuse. Only Julius saw her go.

It was pleasant to be out of the overheated room. She wandered slowly up the stairs. The upper part of the house was cool and silent. She came to the door of the turret room, and gently pushed it open.

Peter was asleep. Grace stood beside the bed, looking down at him. He was rather beautiful, she thought. He looked like a marble knight on a tomb. She had to lean down, until her face almost touched his, before she could hear the faint sigh of his breathing.

Grace smiled suddenly. She wanted to warm the cold marble and bring the effigy to life.

It was her last visit. She had no idea, still, what it was like to be Clio, and she understood that the notion was ridiculous. After this she would be Grace entirely. But for now, in this hour while Alice's party went on downstairs, she felt that she was anonymous.

She reached up to the buttons that fastened the neck of her dress. It was her best afternoon dress, silk in tiny stripes of lavender and cream. She undid the pearl buttons, and the dress rustled down around her ankles. Grace stepped away from it, feeling the cool air on her bare arms and shoulders. She lifted the bedcovers and Peter stirred in his sleep. Grace lay down beside him, and drew the covers over them both.

Then she turned to him and put her arm around his neck. She felt that her own body was a matter of soft curves and recesses, whereas Peter's was all bone and sharp angles. She let her breath warm his cheek, and then she reached with the tip of her tongue to the corner of his mouth.

Peter opened his eyes and looked directly into hers. She was afraid that he could see straight through into her head.

As soon as he woke up, Peter knew that it was not Clio in his bed. This girl did not look like Jake and Julius. She was rounder, fuller-lipped, more English. There was a dress lying on the floor, in shadow now but where he had watched the square of light move that morning, and it was not Clio's hyacinth blue.

Peter was used to dreams, to apparitions that were more vivid than dreams. This one was as welcome as the others were unwelcome. He didn't try to talk, or to define the mysterious boundary between sleeping and waking. He put his arm around her waist, and his mouth against her bare shoulder.

"Zuleika," he whispered.

Outside in the Woodstock Road a car drew up. It was a dark green Bullnose Morris, driven by a young man in flying goggles and leather gauntlets. He jumped from the driver's seat and strolled around to open the door for his passenger, another young man. The passenger put one hand on the driver's shoulder and carefully negotiated the high step to the ground. Then he held on to the polished chrome door handle while his friend took a pair of wooden crutches from behind the seats and fitted them under his armpits.

"Very good of you, Farmy," Hugo said. "Won't you come in and have a drink? My aunt and uncle will be glad to see you."

"No, thanks all the same, Culmington. Little girls' birthday parties are not quite my métier. Big girls quite different, of course. Let me just see you to the door, won't you?"

Hugo moved quickly on his crutches. One leg of his flannel trousers, empty, was rolled up and pinned neatly just below the knee. He was already ringing the bell when Farmiloe held up a parcel.

"Don't forget the present. Enjoy yourself."

Nelly opened the front door. Through the open drawing-room door beyond Hugo could see a line of cushions, and a dozen pairs of flying feet. Someone was thumping out a Strauss waltz on the piano. The games were in progress.

"Hugo, *Hugo*."

Alice saw him first. Musical bumps were abandoned as the Hirshes came flooding out into the hall.

"Happy birthday, miss." Alice was a favorite of Hugo's. He held the present above her head, so she had to jump for it.

"Be careful, Alice," Eleanor scolded. "Hugo, this is wonder-fully good of you."

"I'm not an invalid, Aunt Eleanor, I don't know about good. College tea is a poor show on Saturdays. Is there anything left?"

Grace and Peter did not hear the new arrival. They only heard the rasp of each other's breathing, and the rustle of clothes, and the small squeak of the iron bedstead.

They could not have heard Hugo asking, "Where's Grace? Not in a sulk, somewhere, is she?"

But if they had been listening they would have heard the quick clicking of Eleanor's heels as she came along the linoleum corridor. She had not been able to find Grace in the garden, nor in her bedroom, so she could not have retired with a headache. The only possibility was that she had looked in to see if any of the patients needed anything. Eleanor was thinking that it was considerate of her, with the rest of the household so busy elsewhere.

When it opened, the door seemed to admit a wedge of cold blue light into the room. Peter felt it touch him, and freeze him. Eleanor stood in the coldness of it, staring at them in silence, for what seemed an eternity.

"Grace."

He understood then, but only then.

"Nemesis was swift and awful," Jake said afterward. He was the only one of them who could joke about it; even much later. For Julius, it was the time when he began to understand that he was a spectator in Grace's concerns, not a participant.

Grace was sent back to London, to Blanche, in the deepest disgrace. She spent the remainder of the year, until the war ended, yoked to a series of chaperones and fulfilling a round of charity work and visits with her mother.

She always claimed thereafter that those months were the most miserable of her life.

Peter Dennis returned to the hospital, and Nathaniel wrote a stiffly worded letter to his commanding officer. Before the ambulance came to take him away, defiant and dry-eyed Grace managed to insinuate herself into his room for the last time. She was supposed to be folding linen in a cubbyhole downstairs, but she had walked through the house with her head held up and no one had come out to intercept her.

"I wanted to say good-bye," she told him. "Even though we haven't been properly introduced."

Peter stared at her in incomprehension. He could not imagine what it was that drove Grace to pretend carelessness, even comedy, when he could see that she was miserable. He was wondering how what had seemed with Clio to be innocent and natural should have become a matter for shame and public humiliation, because of Grace. He felt ashamed when he remembered what he had done with this mutinous girl, letting himself believe that she was Clio.

"I suppose the gentlemanly course would be to ask you to marry me." He thought sentimentally of marrying Clio, the impossible outcome.

Grace gave a harsh spurt of laughter. "I'm not ready to marry anyone yet. I'm sorry."

"Don't feel that you should apologize."

Grace didn't seem to flinch. She held out her hand. "Won't you say good-bye?"

There was something determined about her, a toughness that he disliked but could not deny. At last he held out his hand in return. Grace shook it, and then turned without another word and went back to folding the linen, waiting for her father's chauffeur to come and take her away.

In the hours before the ambulance arrived Peter waited and wished, but Clio didn't come.

It was Clio who suffered most. She could not bring herself to go up to the turret room again, imagining Grace there. She didn't want to see her brothers' sympathetic, speculative expressions, or her mother's anxiety, or Nathaniel's disappointment. She wanted to be with Peter as they had been before Alice's birthday party, and that possibility was gone forever. She sat in her bedroom, listening to the timid sounds of the shocked household, until Grace came.

No one overheard what passed between Clio and Grace before the chauffeur came, and neither of them ever talked of it afterward.

It was Clio's anger that made Grace realize the final absurdity of having tried to imitate her. She had expected tears or temper, but nothing like the bitter fury that Clio turned on her. For all their seventeen years together, she had never properly known her cousin.

"You have to have everything, don't you?" Clio had whispered.

Her eyes were like black holes in her white face. "You have to take everything for yourself. You don't really want it, because you don't know what you want, but you can't bear anything to belong to someone else.

"That was how it was with Jake and Julius, wasn't it? Not loving them for themselves, but just demonstrating that you could have them, mesmerize them."

Grace tried to laugh. "I'm not a hypnotist." But Clio's cold face froze her.

"No. You're a liar, a deceiver. And you saw what I felt about Peter, so you had to wreck it, didn't you?"

"Clio, that's not true. He mistook me for you. I thought it would be like Blanche and Eleanor, when they were girls. It was a way of being closer to you. . . ."

There was too little time, and Grace knew at once that the hasty elision of what she had really felt was the wrong explanation.

Clio spat at her. "You are not close to me. I hate you, Grace. I want to kill you."

Grace faltered. "No, you don't. I did something stupid and thoughtless, and I regret it. I'm sorry. I'm sorry."

Clio shook her head. The anger inside her seemed to expand, stretching taut the skin of her face, tightening her scalp over her skull. The blood throbbed behind her eyes, and she wanted to reach out her fingers to Grace's throat, to squeeze the soft, startled smile off her face.

In a small smothered voice she said, "After all this time. After living here, with us. I hate you. I could easily kill you."

Grace's own anger rose up in response. "Living here? With you complacent, condescending Hirshes? Who are you, after all? What do you know?"

"Go away, Grace. Go away now, before I hit you." Clio ran across the room, and flung the door open. Ida the housemaid's frightened face was revealed on the other side, her hand raised to knock.

"The car is here, Lady Grace," Ida mumbled.

From her window, Clio watched Grace's boxes being stowed in the dicky. She didn't move until Grace had taken her seat, stiff-backed, until the chauffeur had closed the door on her and swung his starting handle, until the car had rolled away and out of sight down the length of the Woodstock Road.

Two hours later, from the same place, she saw Peter's wheelchair rolled up the ramp into the high-sided ambulance. She didn't know where they were taking him.

Six weeks later, a small parcel came addressed to Alice. Inside it was a tiny carved dog kennel, and a miniature china cocker spaniel. A single line on an otherwise blank sheet of paper wished Alice a belated happy birthday. There was no address.

After some thought, Eleanor and Nathaniel allowed Alice to keep her present.

No letter came for Clio. She would have written to him if she could, she wrote a thousand letters in her head, but she never put one down on paper. She knew that Captain Dennis would rather forget what had happened in the turret room.

Six

JULIUS FASTENED THE BOW OF his white tie and spread the butterfly ends between the points of his starched collar. He pulled down his white waistcoat and then shrugged himself into his tailcoat. The coat had once belonged to Nathaniel, who had distinctly broader shoulders, but the length of it at least was approximately right.

Eleanor had told him to take the coat to a tailor, but Julius had answered that he was perfectly happy with it as it was, and he didn't want to spend time waiting in a fitting room like some debutante.

"When I make my concert debut," he told her, "*then* you can kit me out with new evening clothes."

He inspected himself briefly in the wardrobe mirror, noting the unfamiliarly brilliantined hair and patent leather slippers, and turned away without interest. His violin was lying in its open case on the table, and he took it up and ran his finger across the strings. Julius sighed. The prospect ahead of him was less inviting than a concert. He was on his way to Clio's and Grace's coming-out dance at Belgrave Square.

Downstairs, at the end of the narrow brown-linoleum hallway, the doorbell rang. Julius laid his violin in its plush nest once more, draped a white silk scarf around his neck, and went out, locking the door of his rented rooms behind him. On the landing he met the woman who lived opposite, a thirtyish redhead who worked at some job with very irregular hours. She raised her eyebrows when she saw him.

"Well, look at you. Proper dandy."

Julius blushed. The woman was always too interested in his comings and goings, but she didn't mind his practicing and he didn't want to antagonize her.

"It's my sister's dance." The doorbell rang again, more insistently.

"Off you go and enjoy yourself, then." She watched him as he went down the stairs, admiring his height and the nape of his neck above his starched collar.

Julius's friend Armstrong was standing on the step, and there were two other music students, Vaughan and Zuckerman, waiting in Zuckerman's car. Zuckerman gave an impatient hee-haw on the car's bulb horn when he saw Julius emerge. Julius and Armstrong scrambled into the back seat, and they bowled away toward Belgrave Square.

There was a short line of taxicabs and chauffeured private cars outside the house. Julius caught a glimpse of Hugo limping up the steps with his friend Farmiloe, and an ancient Earley aunt moving like a tortoise in their wake. Her Victorian tiara was slightly askew on her thin white hair. He marshaled his own trio of guests with a sense of duty rather than anticipation.

Armstrong was his friend, a thin, studious, and very young man with a weak chest, but he didn't know the other two particularly well. Vaughan was much older, wore a black moustache, and had a mysterious private life. Zuckerman was a talented flautist. He had a rich father and an enigmatic expression heightened by spectacles so thick-lensed, they were almost opaque. Julius had invited the three of them to his sister's dance because Eleanor had begged him to.

"It will be a disaster," she had sighed. "There are no young men, none at all. Whom will the girls dance with?"

"I don't know. Is it important?" It seemed to Julius that a shortage of dancing partners for Clio and Grace was hardly the most serious consequence of the war.

"Of course it is important. When your Aunt Blanche and I came out, we danced with everyone, even the old Prince of Wales."

"Yes, of course." Julius had heard the story enough times.

"Then be a lamb, and ask some of your student friends, won't you? You must know lots of nice young men."

He had done his best, but the forlorn group in Belgrave Square now seemed hardly adequate. Zuckerman had pulled a silver flask out of his pocket and swallowed a long gulp. He winked at Julius as he screwed the cap on again. "Over the top and into the fray, then."

Blanche's butler opened the door to them. "Good evening, gentlemen," he muttered with the utmost gloom. Julius gave a silent prayer of thanks that he had resisted all Blanche's invitations to bring his friends to the family dinner before the dance, and let himself be carried forward into the ball.

As soon as they entered the ballroom, Julius hesitated in the doorway and quartered the room with his eyes. He always looked for Grace first. Only then, when he had caught a brief glimpse of her, could he turn his attention to other people.

Tonight, peering through the crowd, he could only see men with red faces, dowdy chaperones, and girls in white dresses anxious with their dance cards, none of them Grace. The room was already hot, and the dancing had only just begun. Julius could feel Zuckerman and Vaughan crowding up behind him. Armstrong stood to one side, hooking his index finger down inside his stiff collar, a sure sign that he was nervous and uncomfortable. Julius couldn't see Grace anywhere.

"Come and meet my mother and my aunt," Julius said, reluctantly abandoning his search. The music students trooped after him.

Eleanor and Blanche were receiving their guests in front of the vast rust-colored marble chimneypiece that dominated the room. Nathaniel on one side of them looked hot and rumpled, with his beard spreading over his white tie, while John Leominster on the other made an almost comical contrast in his stiffly immaculate evening clothes.

Their wives looked as alike as the men were different. Although they both had fine threads of silver in their dark hair and their figures were now unfashionably full, they still looked the Victorian belles that Sargent had painted. Blanche was in sea-green with the Stretton diamonds glittering on her bosom and in her hair. Eleanor wore dark blue shot silk, with the more modest jewels left to her by her mother the previous year. The dance for Clio and Grace was the first big family celebration to be held since Lady Holborough's death.

As Julius kissed them in turn, he saw that Eleanor and Blanche both had the same eager, faintly anxious expression. It made them look even more the reflection of each other. He breathed in their old-fashioned flowery scents, white lilac and stephanotis.

"Aunt Blanche, may I introduce my friends from the College?"

"Thank you, my darling," Eleanor whispered while the others shook hands with Nathaniel and John. "Such nice-looking boys. Won't you take them now to meet Clio and Grace? I was so afraid that there would be no young men. But now I think it will be all right." Her anxious expression lightened a little.

"Of course it will be all right." Julius smiled at her. He saw Clio, standing to one side of John Leominster. Her rolled-up hair showed her white neck, and the bodice of her dress revealed the childish knobs of bone at the base of her throat. Her head was bent, and she was reading the little tasseled booklet in which she wrote her partners' names as if it interested her.

"Clio, may I introduce my friend Victor Zuckerman?"

It was then that an avenue opened through the dancers and he saw Grace. She was waltzing with a man he didn't know. Her head was back, and she was laughing. The wide skirts of her ball dress made white waves over the polished floor. There were white flowers in her hair.

Clio was thinking that it was a shame that so much hope and effort and anticipation should have been put into planning an evening that was so dull. She was aware of the apparent ingratitude of the thought; but then she decided that she was not being ungrateful, simply realistic.

A good deal of money had been spent. Uncle John Leominster probably had the money to spare, although he counted every penny that his wife was spending on Grace's Season. Clio knew that her own father didn't even really have the money and wouldn't have been able to give her a Season at all if Grandmother Hirsh had not helped him. And then, once he had consented to Clio's coming out in the year before beginning to study for her degree, he had been generous to the limit of his means. It was Nathaniel who had insisted that Clio must have three ball dresses, and new tea gowns and suits and a visit to Blanche's London *coiffeuse*, just like Grace. Nathaniel's view was that if the job was to be done at all, it must be done properly.

Clio felt a rush of love for her father. It was only a pity, she reflected, that his determination that she should be fairly treated and the collaboration between the two families should have resulted in the choice of the same band, the same food, the same flowers, and apparently the same guests as at every other girl's dance. The only difference, as she surveyed the room, seemed to be that here the faces were redder, the band more lackluster, the air more stifling and the yawns behind the white gloves less well concealed than at any of the other dances she had been to.

There had been a number of other dances. The first Season after the war was well under way, with a determination from everyone concerned that it should be as glittering as any Season had ever been. There had been tea parties too, and ladies' luncheons, and

Clio had dutifully met and talked to the other girls of her year, and their mothers, and their surviving male relatives, and had invited the same girls under their mothers' chaperonage to meet her own brothers and cousins this evening.

There were far too many ancient Stretton and Earley and Holborough uncles, gallantly but creakily waltzing, and a severe shortage of the handsome young men that even Clio had allowed herself to dream of at her coming-out dance. In fact, if it were not for some medical student friends of Jake's, some boisterous Oxford men that Hugo had brought, and the odd-looking trio that had just appeared in Julius's wake, there would be almost no young men at all.

Clio missed Peter Dennis, as she had missed him every day for more than a year.

She missed other things too: the calm routine of Oxford, her books and the garden, and the conversation of rational human beings. She thought she had never met so many empty-headed and snobbish people as she had done in the last month, nor wasted so much time in changing her clothes, eating food she did not want, and exchanging pointless small talk with girls she did not wish to talk seriously to.

Clio was priggishly dismissing her Season as frivolous nonsense. She was only enduring it because it pleased her mother to see her, and because what pleased Eleanor also pleased Nathaniel. She would have been reluctant to admit to her dreams of meeting an interesting man. Clio was sure that she was still in love with Captain Dennis.

Victor Zuckerman was asking her to dance.

"Thank you," Clio said meekly, and let him take her hand.

"Jolly good band." Victor tried, not quite managing a convincing imitation of Hugo or one of his friends. He smelled strongly of whiskey. Clio looked at him, trying to gauge his expression behind the thick lenses of his spectacles. His hand felt burningly hot in the small of her back. But at least he danced in time to the music. He might not trample on the toes of her satin slippers.

"Do you think so? It is the third time I've heard them this week. Familiarity must be breeding contempt."

Over Mr. Zuckerman's shoulder she saw Grace's partner leading her back to her place. Grace was still laughing, with her head close to his. Grace would always find something to enjoy, however dismal and predictable the occasion, Clio knew that. And yet she had been sent to finishing school in Switzerland as soon as the war ended. She had made new friends, traveled to Italy, had her horizons enviably broadened. Clio could not understand her pleasure in this boring ritual.

"That's a jolly pretty dress," Mr. Zuckerman offered.

"Thank you." Clio couldn't help smiling at him, he was trying so hard. Her dress had been made by Eleanor's Oxford dressmaker. It was paper-white taffeta, with a tendency to collapse into concave panels instead of standing out in a stiff bell. The same dressmaker had made her two other ballgowns, one shell pink and one powder blue with darker blue bows. Clio had wanted rippling gold satin and ink-blue velvet, but Eleanor had insisted that neither was suitable.

Grace had been taken to Reville & Rossiter for her ballgowns. The London couture house was not quite Paris, of course, but it was good enough. Her dress tonight was oyster-white silk, tight-bodiced and pannier-skirted, with a hooped overskirt of the finest white net that made her look as if she were dancing in a halo of light. It was a romantic denial of all the sensible plain tunics of the war years.

Clio looked away from where Grace was being led back into the dancing by a different partner. She tried to ignore the bitterness that she felt, telling herself that she should rise loftily above it. But it was difficult not to be aware of the gulf between the two of them, just because the whole evening seemed to emphasize it.

The dance itself was being held in the Strettons' house, whereas Clio and her family had traveled up from the increasingly battered and down-at-heel household in the Woodstock Road. Even the stiff engraved invitations declared the difference between Lady Grace Stretton and Miss Clio Hirsh.

Clio was not ashamed of her Jewish name. She was fiercely proud of her father and his academic reputation. But she was sensitive enough to have noticed in the past weeks that other people spoke her name in a certain way, looked at her in another certain way, with a flicker of speculation. "The father is Jewish, of course," she had once overheard one matron whisper to another.

Clio frowned, anger stiffening her spine a little. She looked across to where Dora Hirsh was sitting on a gilt chair. Levi Hirsh was dead, but Nathaniel's mother was alert and straight-backed, a tiny figure in a shiny black dress with her black and gold net purse clasped on her lap. It was Dora's money, mostly, that was paying for the band and the wilting flowers, and the bland chicken and dryish trifle that they would be eating later. Clio tried to convey love and pride and solidarity across the room to her grandmother. She was glad to see that Jake was sitting beside Dora on another gilt chair, volubly talking.

"Are you all right?" Victor Zuckerman asked. He must have felt Clio's stiffness. "Didn't tread on you, did I?"

It came to Clio that her partner was almost certainly Jewish too. She smiled at him with real warmth. "Of course not. You're a good dancer."

Victor beamed. He had just noticed that Hirsh's rather prim and silent sister was extremely pretty when she smiled. Instinctively he held her closer, letting himself imagine her legs under the swaths of taffeta.

The room grew hotter. Clio danced with Jake, and then with one of the medical students who told her he was her brother's dissection partner. They shared a cadaver between them, he said proudly. Clio thought she could detect a faint smell of formalin clinging about him, reminding her of the Pitt-Rivers.

The more elderly relatives were beginning to make their way to the supper tables in the library when Blanche tapped Clio on the arm. "I don't think you have met Mr. Brock, Clio, have you? His mother was a cousin of your mother's and mine on the Earley side."

It was the man Grace had been laughing with. Clio saw that his evening clothes and his fairish hair were as conventionally cut as John Leominster's, but his long, humorous face and a gap between his front teeth made him look immediately interesting, even rakish.

"Anthony Brock," he said, taking her hand. Blanche had already moved away, having done her duty with yet another introduction. Clio had a momentary impression of a sea of polite pink faces, drifting away from her into oblivion, before she focused on Anthony's.

"I saw you dancing with my cousin Grace," she said, and, before she could stop herself, "What were you both laughing at so much?"

Anthony grinned. His well-dressed-brigand look intensified. "Ah, about the rituals and rigors of doing the Season. About all this, I suppose."

One small movement of his forefinger took in the crowd, and everything that had seemed dismal about it to Clio at once became less depressing.

"I was going to ask if I might have the honor of escorting you into supper?"

No one else had asked her. She answered with the same ironic formality. "With pleasure."

The supper room was only half full, and it looked pretty with shaded candles on the little round tables. Clio's spirits lifted further. Anthony Brock brought her a plate of the inevitable sauced chicken and poured hock into her glass. Clio learned that he worked in the City, in his father's stockbroking company, but had ambitions to enter Parliament. He had fought in France, but it wasn't until later that she heard from elsewhere that he had been awarded the MC.

"And you?" he asked.

Clio blushed. "I'm going up to Oxford. Modern languages."

"Are you, now?" Anthony drank his wine reflectively. "You look very like your cousin," he told her.

"I know." She was aware that he was studying her face. His head was a little on one side, as if he were making some decision. He put his glass down on the white cloth, matching up the foot to the faint circle left by its own weight. Then he said softly, "I told Grace that I was going to marry her. I don't think she believed me."

Clio felt her small, presumptuous glow of happiness dwindle and fade. Nothing changed, the half-eaten chicken on her plate retained the same consistency and the candles under their shades threw the same soft light, but the supper room was ordinary again, and the faces around them once more in focus, pink and solid.

She lifted her head. She was glad that he was so direct. It was a relief not to have been left to cherish an illusion, a pointless illusion.

"I don't suppose she disbelieved the intention. It isn't quite unique." Clio couldn't keep all the sharpness out of her voice. It was true, in any case. Grace had accumulated several admirers and more than one proposal in the course of the Season. Clio herself had had her share, although she couldn't imagine herself accepting any one of the offers. She thought they were oddly flippant. There was a desperation under the gaiety of it all that made her think that the men who had survived wanted nothing more than to turn their backs on what they had experienced, with any woman, the first to hand.

She hadn't talked about this to Grace, although she wondered if she felt the same. For all their present enforced intimacy, the two of them spoke only in superficialities. They were still wary, after their year's separation.

She went on, trying to sound kind. "It's just that I don't think Grace wants to marry anyone at all. Not yet."

Anthony was perfectly composed. "I can wait," he said. "But I will marry her, in the end."

Clio laughed then in spite of herself, liking him, and at the same time remembering how she had seen Grace laughing too. "I shall enjoy watching the chase. I wish you the best of luck." She meant the good wishes, and Anthony saw that she did. He put out his hand again.

"Shall we be friends?" he asked her.

"By all means," Clio said, shaking it. And so Anthony Brock became her friend as she became his ally in the pursuit of Grace.

The evening was far from over. There were more introductions and more small talk, and yet more dances contracted for, entered on the card, and limply undertaken. Clio took her turn with the swarthy Mr. Vaughan, the chronically nervous Mr. Armstrong, her brothers, and Hugo's friend Farmiloe. Hugo could not dance, but he was not short of company on his sofa to one side of the hideous chimneypiece. Hugo represented a catch, of course, and all the mothers were interested in him. Even Clio understood and accepted as much, even though it was plain that her own brothers were far cleverer and more handsome than the Viscount.

At last, when it seemed that there was not another lungful of air left in the ballroom, the trickle of girls and chaperones making their thanks to Blanche and Eleanor became a steady stream. Eleanor was leaning on Nathaniel's arm, with Blanche on his other side. John was in the card room, where most of the remaining men had retired to play bridge and smoke cigars. The sisters were weary but satisfied. They had achieved an evening neither more nor less remarkable than a hundred others. Their daughters had looked prettier than most of their competitors, they had danced every dance, and all the requirements of the occasion had been met.

"Did you enjoy yourself, darling?" Eleanor asked Clio when they found themselves looking at an empty floor littered with the bruised petals from corsages and tassels dropped from dance cards.

"It was wonderful, thank you," Clio said dutifully. "I'll always remember it."

Grace had been patting a cloud of net into place around her white shoulders, but now she lifted her head and caught Clio's eye. Her expression was one of such wicked mockery and humor and conspiracy that Clio had to look away quickly to suppress a snort of laughter. It came to her that Grace was her partner in all of this, her fellow and contemporary. Eleanor and Blanche, even Nathaniel, belonged to a remote generation. *They are Victorians*, Clio thought. She found herself wishing that she and Grace were better friends.

Upstairs in the faintly chilly bedroom, Clio took off the paper taffeta dress and hung it up. She stood in her petticoats in front of the looking glass to unpin her hair. The house was quiet at last. The bulbous mahogany bedroom suite gleamed faintly in the dim light of one electric bulb. The bed had been turned down ready for her, and there was tepid water in the ewer on the washstand, left for her by the maid. Clio splashed some of it into the white china bowl with the Leominster crest and carefully washed her face.

She was pulling her nightdress over her head, shivering as she thought of the cold, stiff linen sheets waiting for her, when there was a knock at the door. A moment later Grace slid into the room. Her hair was in a plait over the shoulder, and she was wrapped in a flame-colored silk robe with a golden dragon embroidered on the back. She was giggling, and Clio thought immediately that Grace had managed to put away more of the innocuous white wine than she had done herself. Sober or tipsy, Clio was surprised to see her. Late-night visits to each other's bedrooms were not a feature of their present relationship.

"Oh God," Grace was whispering, "Oh *God*, I thought it would never end. I told myself, if *one* more young man praises the band or asks me how I'm enjoying it all, I shall scream until they send for the *fire brigade*."

"You looked as if you were enjoying yourself well enough," Clio said reasonably. "You were laughing so much with Anthony Brock, I thought you might be on the point of creating a frisson of interest."

Grace sighed. "Oh, Anthony Brock." She flung herself down on Clio's bed and patted the pocket of her robe. Then she extracted a flat cigarette case and a small gold lighter. She selected a cigarette and snapped her lighter. The flame lit one side of her face with a brief coppery glow, transforming her instantly into a woman of the world.

"*Grace.*" Clio was shocked.

Grace held out the case. "Want one? No?" She breathed out a long, efficient plume of smoke and leaned back against Clio's pillows. "It's so bloody cold in here. Get in under the covers, for God's sake."

Clio did as she was told. They pulled the heavy blankets up around their shoulders. The cigarette smoke wreathed their heads.

"Anthony Brock said he's going to marry me. Didn't ask me, *told* me."

"I know."

Grace's eyebrows went up. "How?"

"He said so. At supper. We also agreed to be friends, and shook hands on it."

"Cozy."

"It was, rather. And so what did you say in response to this news?"

"Told him I wasn't going to marry anyone." She sighed again, tilting her chin to stare up at the plaster fruit and flowers wreathing the cornice. "Oh, Clio. Darling Clio. Why is it always marriage? Is that all there is for us?"

"Not for me," Clio said, with a touch of smugness.

Grace turned on one side then, so that she could see her cousin's face. "You're right. Not for you. How lucky you are, how very lucky. All there is for me is an extension of tonight. Politeness, and good form, and utter tedium."

Clio was surprised by her vehemence. "You always look happy. I thought you were. Tonight, for instance."

Grace shrugged. "I try to. One has to do that much."

"You are very good at it. Much better than I'll ever be. Listen, Grace. You don't have to be conventional and do the right thing and marry whoever it is Blanche and John single out for you. Anthony Brock or anyone else."

There was a voice within Clio whispering that Grace was lucky, as always, and that she would not reject Anthony as readily herself. But she ignored it and went on, "Five years ago you might have had to, but the war has changed all that. Women can live their own lives now. They have proved it, by doing men's work. Look at all the women in shops and factories. I'm going to get my degree and then work as a translator. Live abroad." She began to be fired by her own fantasy. "Be what I want to be, not just a wife and mother. It was right for Eleanor and Blanche, Victorian ladies. But it's not right for me. Not for us, Grace."

Grace stabbed out her cigarette and sat upright, wrapping her arms around her knees. "Yes. You're right, of course you are." She looked down at Clio with shining eyes. "Have you forgiven me?"

There was a moment's silence. *No,* the voice whispered within Clio's head.

She said, "Yes."

A year seemed a long time.

Grace laughed, a little wildly. "Good. That's very good. Let's make a pact, Clio. Let's promise each other that we won't submit to the yoke. Let's do what we do only because we want to do it, not because we think we ought to. We must be determined to enjoy ourselves. We must be *free*."

Clio thought that Grace's resolution was grandiose, but typically vague. She wasn't quite sure what freedom from the yoke would mean in detail, and she didn't think Grace did either. But she was beguiled by the passion of her declaration.

"Modern women," she said, and Grace echoed her fiercely.

"Modern women."

If they had had wine, they would have drunk a toast. Instead Grace proffered her cigarette case again. Clio took one now and inexpertly lit it with the gold *briquet*. She inhaled and coughed out a puff of swirling smoke.

Jake and Julius walked out into Belgrave Square together. The June night air was sweet and cool, and they lingered under the trees opposite the house.

"Duty done," Julius said, with some satisfaction. "It was an adequate evening, I think, as such evenings go."

It had even been more enjoyable than he had expected. Armstrong and the others had apparently met his mother's requirements, and his friends in their turn seemed to have had plenty to eat and drink. They had gone off a little earlier in Zuckerman's car. And for Julius himself, there had been the bonus of two dances with Grace. He put his hands in his pockets and looked up through the black fretwork of leaves over his head, into the sky where he could see a dusting of stars. He let himself remember the scent of her skin and hair, and the way that she reached up, putting her mouth close to his ear, so that he could hear what she said over the dance music. He found that he was smiling.

Jake was moody and restless. He had undone his white tie and the ends hung unevenly over his shirt studs. He wanted some more to drink, something stronger than hock or his uncle's third-best claret. He had not wished to penetrate the card room where whiskey, brandy, and port were on offer to John Leominster's friends.

"Adequate is a compliment," he grumbled. "Did you ever see such insipid girls? Were you introduced to the lisping Miss Beauchamp? Complexion like orange crêpe paper?"

"I can't remember," Julius said cheerfully. His Grace-induced good humor was unshakable.

Jake put a heavy arm around his shoulder. "Well then, we've done our filial duty. Where shall we go to finish the evening off? Nightclub, d'you think?"

"Not me," Julius answered without hesitation. "I've got work to do tomorrow."

"Come on."

"No, thanks. I'm going to walk quietly home up Park Lane." Julius's rented rooms were behind Marble Arch. It was late enough, he was thinking, for his neighbor to have been in bed for hours. There was no chance that she would be lying in wait for him as he came up the stairs.

Jake scowled at him. He was on the point of protesting when he saw the door of the house open and close behind Hugo and Farmiloe. Hugo walked stiffly now, on a wooden leg, with the aid of a stick.

"All right, Julius. I shall have to fling myself on the mercy of Hugo and his brother officer. They will certainly have a plan of action."

Julius knew that Jake was half drunk. "Don't do anything reckless."

Jake shouted, "If *you* would just do something reckless, for once. Something other than play the violin and moon after Grace."

Julius glanced sharply across the road at Hugo. "That's enough, Jake. Go on to your nightclub, if that's what you enjoy. No doubt Hugo will be Culmington and keep an eye on you." He wrapped his white silk scarf around his neck and strolled away toward Park Lane.

Jake swore under his breath, and then called after him, "Wait, Julius, can't you?"

But a taxi was noisily drawing up on Hugo's side of the street, and Julius seemed not to hear him.

"Want a cab, gents?" the driver asked.

Hugo waved his arm. "Come on, Jake, come with us. We're going somewhere lively."

The inside of the cab smelled of gardenias and stale cigars. Farmiloe leaned forward between Jake and Hugo. "Dalton's, Leicester Square," he told the driver.

The nightclub was entirely underground. Past the huge doorman who took Hugo's money and waved them inside without another word, there was a narrow flight of steps leading down to a long, stale-smelling corridor. Farmiloe tried to take Hugo's arm to help him, but Hugo impatiently shook him off and climbed down sideways, like a crab. Through the double doors at the distant end of the corridor, they came to an enormous low-ceilinged room packed with people. A band was playing on a platform at the far side, and everyone was dancing.

Jake stared at the jostling crowd and at the naked powdered back of the woman closest to him, and then he smiled. Here, it seemed, was everything that had been missing at his sister's dance. The thick air itself seemed to taste of sin.

They found a table against the wall, and Farmiloe beckoned to a waiter. "A bottle of brandy." There were bottles on every table, as far into the distance as they could see.

"I'm very sorry, sir. It's after ten o'clock." Ten o'clock was closing time, according to DORA. It was so much after ten that the three of them laughed uproariously. Farmiloe took out a five-pound note and smoothed it on the tabletop. A moment later the note was gone, and brandy and three glasses had materialized in its place.

Jake drank, and felt benign anticipation replacing his earlier restlessness. Hugo and Farmiloe were good fellows, and good company. They knew what they liked, and where to find it. This was where he wanted to be, listening to Farmiloe's stories through the throb of the music, and watching Hugo lean back to squint past his cigar smoke at the women on the dance floor.

The bottle emptied itself, and they called for another. The room was pounding with noise, making even their rudimentary conversation difficult to sustain. Jake had been watching a black-haired girl at the next table. Their eyes met, and a moment later she stood up, sinuous in a slip of satin dress, and came to lean over the back of his chair. Her mouth brushed his ear. "Won't you ask me to dance?"

Jake rose to his feet. Hugo and Farmiloe didn't appear to notice as he steered the girl away into the hot mass of dancers.

It was too noisy to talk, too crowded to perform more than a shuffle. Jake saw that the girl's eyes were closed and she was dreamily smiling. Tentatively he drew her closer, and then closer so that she bent against him, pliant and slippery under the thin satin. When he looked down at her face, he saw that her powder was creased with sweat and caked at the corners of her eyes, and that she was no longer young, not a girl at all, nor even pretty. He didn't care in the least. He felt that he loved her, and everyone else in the nightclub. Jake bent his head and kissed her lipsticked mouth. He heard her give a small, sweet sigh.

The woman looked up at him, a coquettish glance under her thin eyelashes. "Do you want to come home with me, dear?"

Jake had seen enough death. He had seen more men dead and dying than there were people packed into this room, but he had survived and he had brought home from the field hospital the discovery that he was not after all a coward, whatever the men who had fought more conventionally might think of him. He had seen the terrible things, and he had worked to alleviate some fraction of the suffering. Somehow he managed to contain the memory and the dreams of the war within himself, without letting anyone else know how they shadowed him. But it did seem that even now he could not escape from death. He had spent today hunched over a corpse, teasing out the strands of dead muscle tissue under their flaps of gray skin. He could smell decay as if it were embedded in his own nasal cavities, and now he wanted the scents of life. He wanted warm, living flesh under his hands and to taste the complicated flavors of skin and sweat.

Jake left Hugo and his friend at their table. He didn't care if they wondered why he had disappeared, or if they were too far gone even to remember he had been there. He followed the black-haired woman out into Leicester Square, and into the warren of streets around Shaftesbury Avenue. They came to an upstairs room with a brass bedstead and a jug and basin on the table behind a painted screen.

There was a brief financial transaction. It didn't worry Jake. He had enough money on him for her requirements, that was all that mattered. When she had folded it away, the woman smiled at him.

"How old are you, dear?"

He told her the truth. "Twenty-one. My name is Jake."

She undid his waistcoat and took out his shirt studs. "Well then, Jake. Are you going to make me happy? A big, tall, beautiful boy like you?"

He said, "As happy as you will make me."

He loved the deft, businesslike way she undressed him and herself, as if nakedness were normal and natural. He loved this room, with its bare walls and minimal furniture, the big bed. She settled back on it now, one arm behind her head, so that he could look at her. Her breasts rolled apart to expose the ridges of her breastbone.

She had heavy thighs, dimpled and very white. They were scented and powdery, reminding Jake of some childhood sweet. Turkish Delight, he thought. He remembered how the sweets came

tightly packed in frills of paper, jelly ridges pressed close together
to yield under his fingers. He lowered himself on top of her. Her
skin seemed to give off little puffs of her sugary scent mixed with a
salty, alluvial smell much closer to the earth.

She was very soft, soft everywhere, deliciously so. He wanted to
bury himself in the rolls of melting flesh, deeper and deeper, until
he silenced the endless commentary within his own head.

She spread her legs for him, exposing liver-colored lips lapped
with fur. Jake's breath whistled in his throat. Without any prelimi-
naries he pushed himself up inside her, as far as he could reach,
amazed by the slippery heat. He forgot that he was supposed to be
making her happy, but that did not seem to matter particularly. He
forgot everything except his own scalding pleasure.

When he ejaculated a minute later, he knew that what he had
guessed was right, that none of his dreams or fantasies or masturba-
tory experiments could ever be as good as this reality. They gave
only the faintest intimation of the heat and pressure and urgency of
real love-making with a real woman.

The sensation was so intense, he thought that his heart might
stop, or that he would faint, or that the blood vessels within his
skull would burst. For a moment he would have been happy to die
there on the brass bedstead.

He didn't die, or even faint. He lay with his face against the
woman's neck until his gasping breaths subsided. Then he opened
his eyes. She seemed hardly to have moved; her head was still
resting against her arm. There was a bluish patch of close-shaved
stubble in the exposed armpit, where the salty smell was particularly strong.

Living and breathing, Jake thought. Full of life. Her various
emanations mixed with his own seemed to affirm the vitality he
longed for. He nuzzled his face into the cup of blue-white flesh.

The woman extracted her arm from beneath him and nudged him
aside, not unkindly. She sat up and swung her legs over the side of
the bed, sitting slumped for a moment with her back to him.

"Can I see you again? Can I meet you?" Jake asked, understanding that their present encounter was at an end.

"If you like, dear. You know where to find me." She stood up
and went behind the screen in the corner. He heard water splashing
and the faint squeak of wet rubber.

"I know," he said happily.

He parted with her at the street door downstairs. She was back in
her satin dress, in a hurry to be off. He wanted to kiss her good-bye,

like a lover, but the gesture seemed inappropriate. He let her go with regret and walked back through the empty streets to his student digs in Bloomsbury.

Quintus Prynne woke up late, with a headache that made him feel as if he had been clubbed. He opened his eyes and saw that he had fallen asleep on the divan of his studio, instead of in his bed at home. The litter of empty bottles and dirty glasses scattered between the paints and canvases and jars of brushes reminded him of some of the events of the night before.

He tried closing his eyes again in order to dodge back into sleep, but it was too late. He was awake, with a mouth that felt full of sand and a vague sense of some obligation waiting to be fulfilled. Groaning softly in sympathy with himself, he crawled out of bed and picked his black and white tweed suit out of a heap on the floor. After a careful search he found his pocket watch, and examined its accusing face.

It was eleven-twenty in the morning, and he remembered what he was supposed to be doing. Calling on Lady Leominster in Belgrave Square, to discuss a portrait of her damned dough-faced daughters, that was it. He staggered across the room, groaning still. At the sink he splashed cold water over his head and face and then, in the absence of a towel, rubbed himself dry with yesterday's shirt.

The lack of a dry shirt, let alone a clean one, presented the next problem. The painter rummaged behind a curtain where he kept a small stock of old clothes in which to dress up his models. He found a grubby white cambric smock, and pulled his tweed trousers and coat on top of it. The addition of a piece of black silk foulard, extravagantly knotted around his neck, hid most of the smock front. He crammed his big black hat on his head and picked up a piece of stale bread and cheese left over from the night before for his breakfast.

Quintus Prynne was humming as he sauntered down Charlotte Street, his headache almost forgotten.

In the first-floor drawing room at Belgrave Square, Blanche was working at her embroidery and Eleanor had been reading the morning paper. She put it aside and looked over the top of her spectacles at the little gilt and porcelain clock on the mantelpiece.

"This young man is very late, Blanche. I don't believe he can be coming."

"Perhaps artists are less fettered by notions of punctuality than ordinary people? I think we should wait. Mary Twickenham was saying that Pilgrim is the most admired painter of the young generation, and that we will be lucky to get him. His designs for the ballet were the most beautiful, Eleanor, I wish you had been with us. I'm not even sure why he agreed to come this morning. Perhaps John's name impressed him?"

Eleanor smiled. "Perhaps. But I think your Pilgrim is much more likely to have been impressed by the size of the fee."

Blanche answered with a touch of irritation, "If one wants the best, then of course one must pay for it. John agrees with me, we must have a portrait marking the girls' year that is as fine as our Sargent. It should be a picture worthy to be hung next to ours at Stretton. Don't you think so, Eleanor?"

"Of course, if that is what you both want. And if you say that Pilgrim is the finest portrait painter of his generation, then I can only accept that too."

"He is very modern," Blanche added, as if that clinched the matter.

"That will make the girls happy," Eleanor said, taking up the newspaper again.

The painter was almost an hour late when the maid finally showed him into the drawing room. He had refused to part with his big black hat, and from the doorway he flourished it and swept a theatrical bow.

"Ladies, I can but apologize. May I be forgiven?"

"Come and sit down, Mr. Prynne. Or is it Mr. Pilgrim?"

He bent over each of their hands in turn. Eyeing his clothes, Eleanor and Blanche felt that they were at least being repaid for their long wait with a full measure of artistic eccentricity.

"For all my professional affairs, my name is Pilgrim. Just that, neither Mister nor anything else."

"I very much admired your designs for the ballet, Mr., ah, Pilgrim."

"*La Nuit et la Rose?* Thank you, Lady Leominster. Now, won't you tell me exactly what sort of commission you have in mind?"

While Blanche told the story of *The Misses Holborough* and explained her wish to have another double portrait, this time of Clio and Grace, to hang alongside it, Pilgrim sat comfortably in his red silk-upholstered chair and looked around him. Eleanor saw that he examined the pictures on the walls, his expressionless stare shifting from the English watercolors to the dark oils of long-dead Stretton dogs, horses, and ancestors.

When Eleanor finished, Pilgrim sighed.

"I see. You had not thought of discussing this second portrait with Mr. Sargent himself?" Pilgrim needed the fee that Lord Leominster had mentioned, but even the size of the fee failed to persuade him that it would be interesting to paint the debutante daughters of these ladies. This room had already told him more than he wanted to know about their opinions and attitudes.

There had been some discussion between Blanche and John about the possibility of Sargent painting the new portrait, and John had very quickly concluded that he would be too expensive. "Get the best of the young fellows, the next Sargent," he had advised Blanche, and Blanche had done her best.

"We would prefer a more modern approach," Blanche told Pilgrim.

A glint of amusement appeared in the painter's reddened eyes. "You are interested in the modern movements? In Fauvism? The Cubists, perhaps?"

Blanche and Eleanor looked at each other. For a moment, it seemed that they might laugh. But then Blanche met Pilgrim's eyes and answered valiantly, "Of course."

Malice took hold of Pilgrim, a sensation he always enjoyed. "I commend your interest, Lady Leominster, Mrs. Hirsh. I think, then, that I should meet the two young ladies?"

Blanche rang for the maid, and a moment later Grace and Clio came in together. They looked faintly sulky for having been kept waiting upstairs. Pilgrim stood up. He shook each hand in turn, and then walked slowly in a circle around the two girls. He rubbed his stubbled jaw, as if thinking.

He had seen, of course, that the mothers were twins, but that had not interested him particularly. What was more intriguing was the physical similarity between these daughters, spiced with the differences in expression and manner. They looked far less dull than he had feared, less conventional than their mothers had led him to expect. One of them in particular, the Lady Grace, appealed to him strongly. There was a challenge in her eyes when she looked at him. Her face was plumper than her cousin's, and her mouth made a more sensual curve. The other one, Miss Hirsh, was more defensive. She didn't pout, but held her chin up, turning her face a little aside.

Pilgrim held out one finger to her jaw and turned her to look full at him. He put his head on one side, as if appraising what he saw. He enjoyed the suppressed whisper of protest from the mothers.

Pilgrim decided that the girls were pretty enough, and that it would be amusing to launch a leisurely, elaborate tease on the parents. He was also, he reminded himself, in serious need of their money. They would get their portrait, but it would be the picture that he chose to paint.

"Very well," he snapped. "I accept the commission. For the first sitting, my studio at number twenty-two Charlotte Street, next Wednesday at three o'clock sharp, if you please."

Afterward, Clio said to Grace, "Well. What did you make of that?"

Grace yawned, pretending lazy indifference. "Of those clothes, and that hat? And was it my imagination, or did he smell, rather?"

"He smelled."

"But he did have quite wonderful eyes," Grace added. They were coal black, under thick black brows that met over the bridge of his nose.

"He did, didn't he? Do you suppose anyone has ever before appeared in Aunt Blanche's drawing room looking so unshaven, so disreputable?"

"Never. Wasn't it delicious? They took it like lambs. He must be very clever or sought-after, or something."

"What do you think it will be like having our portrait painted?"

"Less boring than I had feared," Grace answered.

The first sitting took place as Pilgrim had commanded. Grace and Clio presented themselves at his studio in their white dresses, with Blanche as chaperone. Pilgrim found her a hard chair in a corner, and then turned his back on her. Blanche noted that the high room under its glass skylight was clean, if bare, and that Pilgrim himself was clean-shaven and tidily dressed in a blue painter's smock over flannel trousers.

He spent a long time positioning the girls, prowling around them and lifting an arm or turning a shoulder. At length, he had them sitting side by side, but so close together that Clio's shoulder was in front of Grace's. They looked as if they were leaning together for support, but their heads were turned in opposite directions, away from each other. Pilgrim was satisfied. He retreated behind his easel and began to work, making quick flicks with his wrist. The only sounds in the studio were his cuff brushing over the canvas, and the dim popping of the gas fire. Blanche was only too aware that she had been sitting still for an hour and a half without so much as a cup of tea. The painter took regular sips from a cup at his elbow, but he didn't offer anything to the sitters or their chaperone.

At last, he stood back from his work.

"That is enough for today," he announced.

Blanche stood up with relief and strolled over to look at what he had done. She was surprised to see that there was a sheet of coarse paper pinned over the canvas, and the only marks on it were a series of rectangles, thick charcoal lines, boxes within boxes, receding within themselves like a Chinese puzzle.

Pilgrim removed the paper. "I prefer not to have my work in progress inspected in ignorance," he said.

"I'm very sorry," Blanche said humbly. Grace and Clio looked at each other with awed expressions.

At dinner that evening, Blanche told John that she had found the portrait sitting very boring and uncomfortable, and that she did not intend to stay for the next. "There are two of them, after all," she reasoned. "I would not leave one of them alone with him, but they can look after each other. I'm sure Eleanor would agree, if she were here." Eleanor had gone back to Nathaniel and her younger children in Oxford. "Don't you think so, John?"

"If you say so, my dear," John Leominster answered, without much interest.

For their next sitting, Blanche's chauffeur drove the girls to Charlotte Street, and was instructed to call back for them in two hours' time. Pilgrim met them at the door.

"No Mama today?" he inquired.

"I'm afraid that Mama found your studio drafty and dull," Grace answered.

"Is that so?" Pilgrim was all innocent surprise.

This time they found that the room under the skylights was much warmer, almost cozy, that tea had been assembled on a little table near the fire, and that the bench on which he had originally posed them had metamorphosed into a divan covered with shawls.

"Shall we have some tea first?" the painter invited. "Tea and conversation?" He handed cups and plates as decorously as if he were in a Belgravia drawing room. Clio and Grace drew their chairs up, lulled by the normality.

"I can't paint you in those terrible clothes," Pilgrim announced after a few minutes.

"Why not?" Grace was indignant. She was pleased with her Reville & Rossiter silk.

"They make you look like virgin sacrifices."

"Isn't that the idea of debutante dresses?" Clio retaliated.

Pilgrim was delighted. "Oh yes, of course. But I still can't paint you in them. What have you got on underneath?"

The teacups and iced cake were suddenly incongruous. Grace rose to the challenge, determined not to reveal that she was not constantly answering such questions.

She recited, "Underskirt, with panniers stitched into it to give extra fullness to the skirt. Two petticoats beneath that, one stiffened, one not. Silk stockings. Silk chemise and knickers."

Clio said, when Pilgrim looked at her in turn, "The same, in less luxurious versions."

"Good. We'll try the chemises, then. You can go behind the screen, if you wish."

They didn't dare look at each other. A moment ago they had been sipping tea. Evidently Pilgrim thought nothing of leaping straight from conventional to alarming behavior. They felt embarrassed by their own inexperience, and unwilling to reveal that they were shocked.

Pilgrim read every scruple in their faces. He was lazily excited by their similarity, and by the small shades of difference. He saw their rivalry, too, and counted it out for himself like currency. He would use it later, to make his purchases.

"I am a painter," he told them patiently. "I am used to working with female models, clothed and unclothed. I am also a designer of theater sets and costumes, and I have dressed ballerinas and actresses. I have seen women's legs before this afternoon."

They went behind the screen and emerged again with their heads up, daring him and each other. Pilgrim's interest quickened.

He studied them, sitting side by side on the divan. "Good skin," he said at last. "I like the light and the dark." He touched Clio's white shoulder and stroked Grace's hair. They shivered, although it was warm in the studio.

"The hair is too formal."

As deftly as a ladies' maid, he took out the pins and combs. Hair fell down in thick, dark waves over the pale skin.

"Good. Much better."

He twisted Clio's hair loosely again to reveal her neck and jaw and secured it with a single comb. He left Grace's luxuriantly loose, blurring the family likeness. A pleasing series of opposites and contrasts was beginning to present itself. He found that he was surprisingly eager to begin work on the portrait.

"Lean against each other," he commanded. Their shoulders

touched. He put his finger to each cheek and turned their heads away. He liked the dynamic contradiction of the pose. With a casual gesture, almost an afterthought, he pulled the strap of Grace's camisole off her shoulder to reveal the top of one of her breasts. At once the memory of her mother's innocent portrait came back to her, and her nervous apprehension forced its way out of her as a choked giggle.

Pilgrim ignored her. He went to his easel and began.

Clio felt the warmth of Grace's body behind hers. It was odd, the smoothness of skin against skin, the touch without seeing. As she grew accustomed to it, they seemed to flow together, almost as if the two of them became part of the same, larger frame. And yet she felt the sharpness of their differentiation. When she moved, Grace did not. There was a little sound, almost a kiss, as they peeled apart. Clio's fingers curled into her palms. She tried to concentrate on keeping still, on holding the pose.

Pilgrim was frowning, working quickly.

The minutes passed. The girls had no idea how long they had been sitting, there was no clock visible in the studio.

Pilgrim looked up when he heard someone coming up the stairs. He waited, with his hand poised, and then a woman appeared. It was raining outside; they had heard the sharp rattle of rain on the glass roof. The woman was swathed in a voluminous olive-green waterproof. She discarded the coat in a shower of drops and pulled off her hat. Her hair was dark red, wound up anyhow and piled on top of her head. Underneath the waterproof she was wearing frowsy layers of shawls and torn ruffles, almost a gypsy fancy dress.

She grinned at the painter, ignoring the two half-naked girls. "I'm sorry, Quint, didn't know you'd still be busy."

"Make some tea, will you?" was his only response. He worked for a few minutes longer. The woman clattered to and fro with the kettle, glancing at the sitters now and again without much curiosity. Once she went behind the easel to see what he had done. They heard her sniff. At last Pilgrim put down his brush.

"That will do. You can rest now." Clio and Grace stretched gratefully, turning to look at each other, and then at the redheaded woman. Pilgrim introduced her.

"This is Jeannie. She's a regular model of mine, a very good model. Jeannie, this is Lady Grace Stretton and Miss Clio Hirsh. I'm painting a Society portrait."

Jeannie sniggered, but she held her hand out. "Pleased to meet you." Then she looked more interested. "Hirsh? Any relation to Julius Hirsh?"

Clio was startled. "He's my brother."

The model chuckled. "It's a small world, isn't it? We live in the same digs, just across the landing. You remember, Quint, I told you about the musician? Such a lovely friendly boy. Has he ever talked about me?"

This was an entirely new perspective on Julius. Clio managed to say, "I can't remember if he has or not."

Jeannie was unperturbed. "Well, I suppose he wouldn't. Listen here, Quintus, why are we messing about with tea? Why don't you take your friends and me across to the Eiffel for a drink and a bite of supper? I see there's no cake left, even though it was me that bought it."

Pilgrim hesitated, then seemed to come to a decision. "Would you like to do that?" he asked the girls.

Without consulting each other, without looking, Clio and Grace both knew that they would like it very much. They wanted to know more about Jeannie and Julius and about Pilgrim himself. They were ready to take on the Eiffel, whatever that might be.

"But the car is coming for us at seven," Grace said with regret.

"Tell the driver he can wait. That's the point of having a chauffeur, isn't it?"

"Can we go like this?" Clio asked.

"Well, perhaps better to put your dresses on again. Even for the Eiffel." Pilgrim and Jeannie were laughing noisily.

"That's what I *meant*. . . ."

"I am not proposing some louche dive, madam. Your evening gowns will be quite acceptable."

When they emerged from behind the screen again, Jeannie said, "Shown you any of his pictures of me, has he?"

There were canvases stacked all around the studio, but every one of them was turned face to the wall. Pilgrim shrugged, and she went over to the deepest stack and began to turn the pictures outward, one by one.

They were all of Jeannie, some clothed, some naked. Pilgrim had painted her body as blocks of solid flesh, geometric shapes outlined in heavy black lines, as massive and immobile as slabs of rock. Her russet hair provided the only movement, painted in intricate and regular waves, like water pouring over the rocks. When she was clothed the fabrics were strong greens and violets and ochres, and she lay against plain sheets of thick earth colors.

Her face, full on or in profile, was calm, brooding. Her eyelids were rounded like pebbles.

Pilgrim had made her an odalisque, carved out of stone.

The girls looked, impressed by the power of the Jeannie portraits, trying to imagine how Pilgrim was painting them. They had not dared to glance at the canvas on the easel.

"Struck dumb, eh?" Jeannie scoffed.

"They're wonderful," Clio said at last, meaning it. The pictures made her feel insipid, milky and insubstantial, when she wanted to be strong and elemental as they were. Pilgrim bowed to her. He had already put on his black hat, and a long black cape.

"Shall we go, now?"

As they descended to the street Grace whispered to Clio, "God knows what Blanche and John will make of it all."

"Who cares?" Clio answered, with sudden fervor.

They found the chauffeur waiting with the car. Pilgrim waved him away. "I will see the young ladies home myself, thank you." He offered an arm to each of the girls and swept them off. Jeannie marched in front of them, her gypsy drapes blowing like flags.

The Eiffel turned out to be the Eiffel Tower, a restaurant a few yards away on the corner of Percy Street. Grace and Clio saw with faint relief that Pilgrim was right, this was no low dive.

There were wide, well-lit windows half curtained in warm crimson. Inside was a big room with tables set against the walls, each with a red-shaded lamp. In the center was a brass construction sprouting parlor palms and ferns, flowers and newspapers, with a small table beside it laden with exotic fruit and shellfish, plovers' eggs, caviar and asparagus. There was a feeling of coziness, but also of comfortable space and order.

The girls had time for only the briefest first impression. Pilgrim and Jeannie were flinging off their hats and coats as if they had come home. A portly man with a moustache came surging forward to greet them.

"Stulik, Stulik," Pilgrim cried, patting him on the back. The man kissed Jeannie on both cheeks and bowed to Clio and Grace. Pilgrim introduced him. Rudolf Stulik was the Eiffel Tower's proprietor.

"Welcome, welcome guests, and friends," the man crooned. His accent was foreign, fractured. "See, I have a table for you here." He led them to it.

Grace and Clio saw that the tables were crowded with people, a diverse collection of people in street clothes and theater clothes and half-fancy dress like Jeannie's. There were thin-faced women with cigarettes and eccentric jewelry, and there was even a sprinkling of young men and women in evening dress. They were all busy eating and talking and gesticulating and laughing, but they looked up when Pilgrim's party swept by. Clio felt exhilaratingly certain that they were looking not to see what she was wearing, but who she was.

Pilgrim enjoyed the attention given to their entrance. He returned it with lordly waves and smiles, then settled his three companions into their comfortable, plush-seated chairs. A waiter in a black coat brought them menus, but Pilgrim commanded, "We will have the *plat du jour*. And a bottle of burgundy, to begin with."

The food, when it came, was a *poulet rôti au beurre* that reminded the girls of the Normandy holidays of their childhood. But before they even began to eat, the first of a stream of visitors to their table arrived. He was a huge man with a curling brown beard and gold earrings who thrust his glass down on the tablecloth and waved to a waiter to bring him a chair. He and Pilgrim began to argue at once, with Jeannie mildly interceding as she filled up their glasses. The man with the beard was followed by a woman in black draperies, her hair as red as Jeannie's. She brought her own bottle across with her, and clung tenaciously to it. After the woman came a brace of poets, and another painter or two, and a shifting retinue of art students from the Slade School.

Grace and Clio were introduced to more interesting people during that one rambling meal at the Eiffel Tower than they had encountered in the whole of their debutante season. They drank in the arguments and the gossip and the jokes, understanding almost none of them, but impressed by the liveliness and the wit and the casual intimacy.

At first they were shy and almost silent, but the wine and the conviviality worked on them and they began to talk themselves, and then to laugh. Daringly, they lit cigarettes and waved them about like the red-haired Nina. Little subgroups formed and broke away from the center, drawing Clio and Grace with them. They forgot that they had begun by needing Pilgrim's protection. Clio cupped her chin in her hands and talked in her accurate school French to a Parisian dancer. Grace sat between the two poets, laughing uproariously at each development in a lengthy doggerel-verse account of the evening that they batted between them. More bottles of burgundy were brought and emptied.

When the *poulet* was replaced by plates of *gâteau St. Honoré*, the big man with the beard leaned over to Grace and Clio. His huge fingers pinched at their earlobes, and then rubbed the pearls of their matching necklaces.

"Where did you find these charming English rosebuds, Pilgrim? One would be fine, but a *pair* is magnificent."

Pilgrim was pleased. He grinned, showing his white teeth. "In Belgrave Square, John, where else? I am painting their portrait for Lady Grace's mama. She wants to hang it alongside the portrait of herself by Sir John Singer Sargent."

John bellowed with laughter. "You are a lucky man. And I am sure her ladyship will be delighted to have a Pilgrim to hang in her drawing room."

The evening roared on. To Grace and Clio it was new and entirely magical, but for the rest of them it was no more than a familiar night in their usual haunt. The girls were to discover that Pilgrim held a kind of court at the Eiffel. He used it as his club, where he ran up bills and drank coffee at all hours, read the newspapers, and wrote his letters. It was also his office and unofficial labor market. He trawled for commissions amongst the Society sprigs who daringly penetrated this outpost of Bohemia. It was from just such an infiltrator in evening dress that Blanche's friend Mary Twickenham had heard that Pilgrim was the very best and absolutely the *most* fashionable of all the young artists in London. Somehow the other half of his reputation had not been recounted.

It was eleven o'clock when it occurred to Clio to ask the time. She gave a little shriek of dismay, causing the French dancer to raise his eyebrows in comical peaks.

"We have to go home. Now, at once. Grace, Aunt Blanche will have called the police. We were supposed to be home at seven."

Grace was equally astonished, but she reassured her. "They have gone to a musical soirée. They might not be back, yet, please God, if we hurry. It's just Broddy who'll be worried, and I can square it with her."

They were on their feet, gathering up their wraps. The talk swirled around them, unstoppable.

"Pilgrim, won't you take us home? Please, *now*? Or find us a cab, at least?"

Pilgrim was comfortably ensconced, and had no intention of being dislodged just to make the round trip to Belgrave Square. But he did detach himself for long enough to bustle them into Percy

Street. As they left the overflowing table, Jeannie called after Clio, "Next time, bring that brother of yours, won't you?"

Pilgrim flagged down a cab. Then in full view of the restaurant's lighted window he kissed each of the girls on the mouth. His kisses were thorough, tasting importantly of burgundy and garlic and maize-papered French cigarettes. Then he opened the door of the taxi and bundled the two of them inside. He gave the address to the driver, slammed the door, and disappeared back into the red glow of the Eiffel.

Clio and Grace had no money on them. To pay their fare, they had to borrow five shillings from John Leominster's valet when he opened the door. Blanche and John were not yet back. The girls fled upstairs to Nanny Brodribb and their beds.

Clio lay awake, thinking. She was remembering how Pilgrim and Jeannie had entered the Eiffel as if they were coming home. She had not felt at home herself. It was more like hovering on the threshold of some infinitely attractive household, eavesdropping on the family and longing to be invited in to join them. She felt happy, almost breathless with relief, to discover that there were such interesting people, and full of apprehension that she would not be considered amusing enough herself. "Next time bring that brother of yours," Jeannie had said. At least it seemed to be understood that there would be a next time. She was pleased to think that Julius might be her passport to it.

Then it occurred to her that the world of the Eiffel might not yet feel like home, but it could be a vastly expanded and sophisticated version of the life she had known in the Woodstock Road before the war changed everything. People had come to Nathaniel's house to talk and eat, and Eleanor had complained sometimes that she felt she was running an unexclusive club. Perhaps the image of a family was more apt than she had realized.

Whatever the truth was, Clio knew that she wanted to be able to take off her coat and belong in this stimulating new world as comfortably as Pilgrim and Jeannie did.

She wanted the people she met there to be her friends. She could only hope that she could offer them something of interest in return.

Seven

THE LEAVES WERE CHANGING COLOR under a porcelain-white sky. There was a smoky, wintry bite in the air that whipped Grace's blood. It was hunting weather, making her wish for the woods and hills around Stretton. She thought of the visceral pleasure of a hard gallop and the exhilarating rush of the wind in her face. To be limited to a decorous walk in the Park with Anthony Brock made her feel irritable, and the knowledge that it was her own choice did not improve her mood.

Hugo had gone back to Stretton, to oversee the estate and complete the reopening of the house, and if Grace had insisted on going too, Blanche would have given way to her. But in London there was Pilgrim and the circle that had the Charlotte Street studio and the Eiffel as its center. She would not have retreated and left them exclusively to Clio, however much she might otherwise long for the country.

Anthony strolled beside her in his dark City clothes. He was quiet because Grace seemed to prefer not to talk, and the absence of anything to complain of in his company chafed her further. Grace would have liked an argument, anything to provide an outlet for her energy.

They came to a junction in the path they were following. They had the choice of walking on, toward the Serpentine, or taking a shorter route that would lead them back the way they had come.

"Which would you like?" Anthony asked. "Backward or forward?"

"Anthony, why are you always so gentlemanly? Why are you so implacably good and reasonable and considerate?"

"Perhaps I'm not. Perhaps that is just how I would like you to perceive me." He was looking sideways at her, his long face expressionless. She couldn't tell whether he was making fun of her or not.

"Don't be. Be brutal and intransigent."

"Instead of you? All right, then. We will walk on to the water, because that is what I would like to do."

"Is that the best brutality you can manage?"

"Yes, for the moment."

They turned toward the Serpentine, a flat sheet of silver visible through the trees. Grace sighed. "I'm so bored with the Park and Belgrave Square and shopping and dinners."

"How is the portrait progressing?"

She faltered. It was like Anthony to make the immediate connection between her proclaimed boredom and the reason why she was prepared to suffer it.

"Pilgrim seems satisfied. I haven't been granted a viewing yet."

That was almost a relief. As long as it was unseen, they could hope that it would somehow turn out to be the innocent celebration of their debut that Blanche expected.

Pilgrim did not show any anxiety to finish the portrait. Twice now he had invited the girls for separate sittings, claiming that he felt outnumbered by the two of them together. They had not felt it necessary to mention this new arrangement to Blanche.

For the first of Grace's solo sessions he had worked in frowning silence, making her wonder if she had said or done something wrong. But at the second he had been jovial, and had made only a brief dab at his easel before throwing its calico shroud back over the canvas. Grace was relieved to find that he was in good humor, and happy not to have to hold the familiar pose for another hour.

"I can't work every day." Pilgrim smiled at her. He came and sat beside her on the divan, briefly rubbing her cheek with his forefinger. Grace was beginning to be used to the way that Pilgrim and his friends touched each other. They kissed and embraced the way her parents shook hands.

Pilgrim brought them a glass of wine, and they smoked his yellow French cigarettes while they talked. Grace had met enough of the people who frequented the Eiffel to enjoy Pilgrim's gossip about their affairs.

The pictures of Jeannie still faced into the room. When she looked away from Pilgrim and saw them confronting her, she felt uncomfortable, aware of a prickle beneath her skin. The pictures were erotic. There was a majestic calm in Jeannie's nakedness that mocked her own fiddly attention to her shreds of covering. With part of herself, Grace wished for the simplicity of bare skin. It would be easier to be naked. And Pilgrim had painted Jeannie's flesh with such attention, with such a heavy impasto of cream and coral and bronze that Grace wanted to reach out and touch the crusts of paint. But another part of her flushed at the mere thought and dragged her eyes back to Pilgrim's face.

She saw that he was watching her. His lips were very red, shiny with wine, and his eyes glittered.

"I'm sorry to say," he whispered, "that it is time for my next sitting." He leaned forward and kissed the hollow at the side of her throat.

Grace leaped like a rabbit, relieved and disappointed.

Yet for all her confusion, she had not wanted her sitting to end with Pilgrim at an advantage. When she was dressed in her street clothes she had crossed back to where he was still sitting, smoking. She reached down, until her eyes were level with his. She liked his aroma of paint and tobacco overlying another musky scent that she could only identify as the natural smell of his skin. He examined her, at these close quarters, with frank approval.

"When can I see the picture?" Grace asked.

"When I have finished it."

"Are you pleased with it?"

He was silent for a second. Then he said, "I believe it is my masterpiece."

Grace felt her skin prickle for the second time. Slowly, as if his stare had hypnotized her, she leaned closer until her top lip grazed his. Pilgrim smiled. His face was so near to hers that she couldn't see the expression in his eyes, only the granulation of color in his irises. "Your masterpiece," she whispered back.

Their mouths were still touching when Pilgrim repeated, "It's time for my next sitting."

Grace stood up and drew on her kid gloves. Blanche's chauffeur was waiting for her downstairs with the car.

When Grace asked Clio what happened at her corresponding sittings, Clio only said, "He talks a great deal. About art, mostly."

Grace wondered if that was the truth.

Remembering all this, Grace's impatience with Anthony and their stately progress swelled until she was sure that it would choke her. Her arms swung stiffly, and her feet clapped on the dusty path.

"Shall we walk a little faster?" Anthony asked mildly. Grace lengthened her stride and he matched it, then Grace walked faster still, and faster, recognizing her own contrariness and taking perverse pride in it. Anthony kept pace with her until at last Grace was running, with her head down and the silver foxtails of her wrap flying behind her.

Grace ran, the uncomfortable drumming of her blood finding an echo at last in her thudding feet. She was oblivious to the stares of the other walkers with their dogs and their sticks, and their heads turning to follow her as she passed. Anthony loped beside her. He could outrun her; she would never shake him off.

They came to the water's edge. The Serpentine lay in front of them, the gray surface broken now by ripples licked up by the wind. In the distance Grace could hear another echo, the hoofbeats of horses cantering in the Row. She was gasping for breath, and there were tears in her eyes from the cold.

"You don't want to sprint on to Oxford Street?" Anthony inquired. His breathing was quite even. He held out his handkerchief so that she could wipe her eyes. Grace took it without a word. He watched her, seeing how the silver-tipped fox hairs stuck to her damp cheeks. She was looking away from him, across the grass to some benches under the trees. A group of nannies was gathered there with their high perambulators. There was one toddler with them, buttoned into leggings and leading reins. He strained at the end of the padded leash, and the bells on the leather front of it jingled as he tried to lurch toward the moving water. But his nanny would never let him out of the corral of perambulators. At last he flopped down onto the grass and let out a howl of frustration.

Grace screwed Anthony's handkerchief up into a ball and thrust it back at him. She turned away and began to walk again. "Don't you ever feel that you want to run away? All the way away, out of sight of everyone?"

Anthony said, "Of course I do. We can run away together, you know. Grace, why don't you marry me?"

He loved her, he knew that. He also understood her bewildered boredom. If they were married, he thought, he could divert her. They would work together. They would make a political partnership.

Pityingly, Grace shook her head. "Marrying you wouldn't be running away. It would be running *into* it all. Full tilt."

She was thinking about Charlotte Street and the Eiffel Tower and the merry, unplanned, Bohemian lives that Pilgrim and his friends lived. She did not share Clio's half-awed esteem for their art, and the endless discussions of theories and ideals bored her as much as they fascinated Clio. What Grace liked was the vivid, reckless manner of life in the studios and pubs, and she wanted to be a freelance part of it. She wanted to slip into it, and out of Belgrave Square, whenever it suited her. It was partly that duality that attracted her. She was drawn to the same quality in Pilgrim himself. Part of her knew that her painter was devious, lazy, and probably a liar. But he was also new, and different, and power-fully exciting.

Grace liked to be Lady Grace Stretton of Leominster House, Belgrave Square, and at the same time she liked to submerge herself in the brew of the Eiffel. It was like being two people, at once significant and anonymous.

The thought reminded her of Peter Dennis. It all seemed very long ago. How babyish she had been, with her unsureness of herself and her envy of Clio.

"I can't marry you, Anthony. I can't marry anyone for a long time yet."

There would be a time for all that, in the end, in a distant future she couldn't even be bothered to imagine.

"I'll wait," Anthony repeated.

Grace put her arm through his. The running had burned away some of her gnawing energy and made her forget her ill-humor. "Better not," she said kindly. "Why don't you marry Clio? She likes you, and she would make a good wife."

Freedom, they had pledged each other on the night of their dance. Modern women. But Grace did not believe that Clio was truly dedicated to independence. Grace guessed that for all her bluestocking pretensions, Clio would be happy enough to marry and to have a brood of children just as Eleanor had done.

"I like Clio. And she will be an excellent wife, but not for me."

Anthony believed that Clio was too much like himself. She was reasonable and prudent and conscientious, whereas Grace was none of those things. "It's you I intend to marry."

"Poor Anthony," was all Grace would say.

The light was fading. They retraced their steps across the Park and back to Leominster House. Anthony was to stay to dine and then to accompany the Stretton family party to the opera. Blanche had adopted him as her daughter's unofficial suitor, a suitable temporary holder of the post until the right duke or marquis should present himself. She was always inviting Anthony to dine, or to accompany them here and there.

"But darling, he is a kind of cousin of ours," she murmured when Grace protested. "Of course we must invite him. You can't possibly mind that." And Grace, whose main objection to Anthony was that he was unobjectionable, could only sigh and submit to his company.

The opera was *The Magic Flute*, supposedly a favorite of John Leominster's. Clio sat in the Strettons' box, leaning her chin on her white glove, and looked down into the colored sea of the stalls. She was thinking of her own father's passion for Wagner, played on the wind-up gramophone in the cluttered room overlooking the garden in the Woodstock Road. Music had been one of the languages of her late childhood. Nathaniel would never allow whispering while music was being played, even a recording. Tonight, from the overture onward, the Strettons would murmur to each other and point out their friends and acquaintances in the other boxes.

Clio jumped when someone touched her shoulder. She looked up to see Julius, handsome in his evening clothes. Blanche had invited him to join the party. She had not extended the invitation to Jake, knowing that he would not come.

"I was just thinking about Pappy," Clio said.

"Wagner." Julius smiled. They were fond of their aunt and uncle, particularly of Blanche, but they made their quiet affirmation to each other that they were Hirshes, not Strettons.

Julius shook hands with Anthony and then sat down in the sixth red-brocaded chair just behind Clio's shoulder. Clio resumed her inspection of the crowd beneath.

"Look," Grace said, and pointed with her gloved finger.

There was a disturbance in the center of the stalls. A quartet of people had come noisily in and were threading their way to their seats. Heads turned to look at them and craned in their wake. There was an impression of odd clothes and raised voices.

"Pilgrim."

It was Pilgrim in an immense rusty-black opera cape, and John with his curling beard spread over a crimson velvet coat and his gold earrings glinting in the lights. Their companions were Jeannie, in some outlandish collection of purple drapes, and a young girl. The girl had bizarrely cropped silvery-gilt hair, and she was wearing what looked like a man's frock coat. Clio and Grace recognized simultaneously that she was extremely beautiful. They had no objection to Jeannie, she was part of the retinue, always present, but as soon as they saw the stranger they were jealous. Pilgrim was theirs. He did not belong in the stalls at the opera with somebody else. They did not look at each other. They leaned forward, on either side of Blanche, for a better view.

John Leominster raised his opera glasses. "That's your painter? Good God. What an extraordinary-looking fellow."

Pilgrim had been examining the occupants of the boxes ranged above him. He saw the Strettons now, and his companions followed his gaze. The painters bowed extravagantly in the confined space of the stalls, making a swirl of capes and hair and setting up new ripples of interest all around them. Blanche gave a stiff nod in return.

Jeannie had caught sight of Julius. She lifted both her hands to her lips, kissed them, and blew. Her purple robes and raised arms made her look like the high priestess of some religious cult.

Grace was laughing. She admired the careless spectacle that Pilgrim made, and she was happy to receive his public tribute. She was also happy to be sitting up in her father's box, the focus of attention of all the stalls and the boxes opposite. She waved back at Pilgrim, an elegant flutter of her gloved hand.

Clio ducked her head. She didn't smile because she was mortified to be exposed in the gilt and plush box. She felt the stiff arrangement of their family party, all of them in a row on their red and gold chairs, pinned in their places like butterflies in a case. It was as if they were specimens of their class and position, pleased with their niche and happy to have it spotlit for the audience. They were frozen in their time and place, unchangeable, chloroformed by convention. She longed to be able to creep out of the little door behind her and vanish, but she couldn't move, any more than a dead butterfly could. She could almost feel the jab of the pin through her thorax.

Anthony leaned toward Julius. "Who is the astonishing redhead, Hirsh?"

Julius looked uncomfortable. "I hardly know her. She has digs in the same house as me, just across the landing."

"And the silvery one? Is she one of your girls too?"

Grace was giggling.

Julius said, "I've never seen her before. And Jeannie isn't one of my girls."

John turned around, rigid with disapproval. "What a vile-looking crew of people they are. Can't you find any decent friends among your own kind? I thought you were a violinist, Julius."

"I am a violinist."

Grace and Clio did exchange glances then. Their jealousy of the new girl divided rather than united them, with their rivalrous claims on Pilgrim and his world. But they felt the same response to

Lord Leominster's blinkered condemnation. Pilgrim and his friends were not vile at all. They were rebellious and anarchic and everything that was attractive. At that moment Grace and Clio would willingly have changed places with Jeannie and the silver girl, if only they could.

The conductor emerged from the wings. With more flourishes and gestures the painters subsided into their seats amidst the applause. The lights dimmed, as if all the theater had only been waiting for them to settle themselves. Under cover of the blackness, Clio found that she could smile.

As soon as the lights came up again for the first interval, all four of them left their places. They swept out and they didn't come back again. Clio's eyes kept coming back to the empty seats.

"And so, my little Clio, what shall we talk about this afternoon?"

The gas fire was popping companionably. Pilgrim stood in his painting clothes, peering at her over the top of his canvas.

"I am a shade taller than Grace, as it happens," Clio said coolly. Pilgrim only laughed at her.

"Your height is quite irrelevant. You all looked remarkably fine at the opera."

"I was embarrassed. I felt like an exhibit." If Pilgrim realized that he had made the Strettons' box the focus of attention, he seemed quite unashamed of it. Clio bit the corner of her lip. "I would rather have been sitting with you and Jeannie and John."

"Yes," Pilgrim agreed. "You would have found it livelier."

"Why didn't you come back after the interval?"

He shrugged. "The sets looked as if they had been painted in some village hall by a committee of farmhands. The costumes as if they had been improvised for charades at your uncle's country seat."

"They don't play charades at Stretton. Didn't you enjoy the music?"

"How could I listen to the music, with such eyesores confronting me?" He looked at her again, and then stared for a long time at his canvas. Clio waited, concentrating on holding her pose. She loved Pilgrim's rambling disquisitions on art and music and literature.

"What did you think of the pictures?" he demanded at length. Under Pilgrim's offhand guidance, Clio had ventured into a dusty gallery in Fitzroy Street to examine the ranks of canvases stacked haphazardly against the walls. She had even bought a picture for herself, nervously parting with eight pounds of the money that

Nathaniel had given her "for handkerchiefs or stockings, whatever it is young women need."

It was a small canvas by Harold Gilman, titled *The Bedsitter*. It showed a cold blue-painted room with a half-dressed girl lying on an unmade bed. Her exposed thigh made a gleam of stark white in the surrounding dimness.

Clio took her purchase home and propped it on the mahogany tallboy in her bedroom at Belgrave Square. The picture seemed to sum up all the romantic, spartan life of the Slade students and the poets she met with Pilgrim. It looked highly incongruous in the overstuffed Victorian setting of Leominster House, and Clio liked it all the more for that.

"I thought some of them were wonderful," Clio said carefully. "I bought one."

"Gilman?" Pilgrim scoffed when she told him. "I expect you admire Sickert as well, don't you?"

"Who should I admire, then?" Clio asked.

"Van Gogh."

He worked in silence for another minute, and then he put the brush down. He stood back from the easel. "So. I suppose you had better tell me what you think of this."

Clio thought she might have misheard. But he was waiting, with his black eyebrows raised. He was offering her the first glimpse of his painting.

She stood up and stretched out her hand for the dingy wrap he had given her to wear while she was resting. She put it around her shoulders and fastened it at the waist. Then she walked slowly across the studio to the easel. Pilgrim stood aside, to allow her a clear sight.

Clio looked.

She had thought that she was prepared for anything. But when she saw the portrait she gasped.

The figures seemed to swell to fill the big canvas. They were massive, half-clad Amazons, with profiles framed by geometric ripples of dark hair. Their shoulders were great slabs, and their breasts looked as round and hard as apples. But it was not the sheer size or the uncompromising style of the painting that was surprising. She had seen enough of Pilgrim's work, and that of the other painters in his circle.

It was the interpretation of the pose, and the expressions in the two faces, that shocked her.

Pilgrim had painted them facing away from each other, seeming to strain in opposite directions, and the tension was almost unbearably heightened by their twin torsos appearing to sprout like flowers from the same bud of flesh. He had joined them at the hips. They were two women struggling to wrench themselves apart from a single root.

As Clio stared she saw that the features were just recognizably their own. They were Grace and Clio, but with their wide staring eyes and their lips drawn back from their teeth they were also savages, or feral creatures. The sense of wildness trapped within such ramparts of solid flesh gave the violent picture an odd poignancy.

Clio breathed out, a long ragged breath.

"So what do you say?" he asked.

The picture unnerved her. She went on staring at it, at her own bared teeth and straining muscles.

Pilgrim came to stand beside her. He put his arm around her shoulders and held her against him. The embrace was comforting.

At length Clio said, "Is that how we look, Grace and I?"

"It is how I chose to paint you. It is called *The Janus Face*. Do you know who Janus is?"

"Of course. The Roman god. His head faces both ways, so he looks into the past and the future. He gave his name to January, between the old year and the new one."

"Yes. I like the idea of beginnings and endings, don't you? And I like polarity, too. Similarity and dissimilarity, repelling and attracting, never in stasis."

Clio shivered. She felt the touch of cold premonition, and she tried to shake it off with humor. "*The Janus Face* is a livelier title than *Lady Grace Stretton and Miss Clio Hirsh at Their Debut*."

"You haven't told me what you think of it."

Clio said quietly, "I think it is magnificent." She couldn't deny that it was. It was oppressive and alarming, but it had unmistakable power. "I also think that it will cause a lot of trouble. When the Leominsters see it."

Pilgrim put his head back and roared with laughter. Clio could see his tongue and his strong teeth and the springy growth of long thick hair over his ears. She could sense the mischief in him like a charge of electricity.

"Of course it will. That is part of the fun of it. Did you think I was painting a simpering toffee-tin lid like one of Sargent's?" He was in an excellent humor now. He began wiping his brushes and thrusting them back into bristling jars. He was looking forward to a drink, to taking this thoughtful half of his Janus to the pub, where she would listen attentively to whatever he had to say.

"I didn't want to paint you and your cousin. I accepted the commission for the money. But there's something between the two of you, and as I worked I got interested. It's a fine picture, I'm pleased with it. I don't give *a fuck* what your aunt and uncle make of it. Or rather, their disapprobation will only add to my pleasure."

Clio couldn't help but laugh. "I hope I'm here when you unveil it for them."

"You shall be. Put your clothes on now, we're going to the pub. And *don't* tell me that you are forbidden to go to the pub."

"I've never been to one in my life. And no one has thought it worth forbidding it for when the opportunity should arise."

Pilgrim wound a long, erratically knitted scarf around his throat. "My poor little English rose. Come out and I will educate you."

The invitation was irresistible. Clio knew that she was more than a little in love with Pilgrim. They went to the pub together, and Clio listened while he talked.

To her disappointment, their tête-à-tête was short lived. A group of Pilgrim's friends came to claim him, clustering around him at the bar, jostling and spilling pools of beer, hailing further acquaintances with invitations to join them and wedging themselves up against the brass footrail with the clear intention of staying all night.

Pilgrim began to tell one of his stories but a woman shouted him down, claiming that her own version was better. A heated argument broke out. A soft-lipped boy with curly hair began drunkenly to declaim his own poetry. Clio sipped her half-pint of bitter beer in wide-eyed silence.

"I'm Max Erdmann," a voice next to her announced. "Who might you be?"

She saw a small, slope-shouldered person in a corduroy coat. "I'm Clio Hirsh."

The man held out a packet of cigarettes. Clio took one, and he lit it for her with the last match from a battered box. He grinned his approval to her through the flame, revealing small brownish teeth with gaps between them.

"I'm a friend of Pilgrim's," Clio added, feeling the need to explain herself.

"Isn't everyone? Me, I've known Pilgrim since he was Quintus Prynne, penny odd-jobber and bicycle thief." Max sniffed, unimpressed by Pilgrim's celebrity.

"Are you a painter too?"

"Writer. And editor." After a moment's rummaging he produced a dog-eared card. Under Max's name Clio read the words "Editor-in-Chief. *Fathom*." Max took the card back again.

"What is *Fathom*?"

"Don't you know? It is a magazine. A monthly forum for all that is best in modern writing and criticism. A mouthpiece for the avant-garde."

"That sounds very interesting," Clio said politely.

"It is. And what are you? Art student?"

"No. I've been sitting for Pilgrim. With my cousin."

Max's lips curved knowingly. "Ah yes. I've heard about that."

Clio knew about gossip and Charlotte Street. "I shall be a student next," she offered. "Modern languages, at Oxford. One of the first women to be admitted as full members of the University, actually."

Max studied her face. "Pity," he said. "I was going to ask you if you wanted a job. We need someone to help out on *Fathom*."

"I don't think I could take a job," Clio said, with some regret.

The boy poet had begun to weep. Glassy tears rolled out of his eyes and down his round cheeks.

"Give him another bloody drink, for God's sake," somebody shouted.

Across the bar, Clio saw the silver-haired girl from the opera stalls. She had her arm around a man's shoulder. She looked very young, younger than Clio herself.

"Who's she?" Clio asked Max.

"Her? That's Isolde," he told her. "Would you like to meet her?"

Clio felt envious of the girl's acceptance here, and shy. "No. Another time perhaps."

The Earl and Countess of Leominster climbed the stairs to the Charlotte Street studio. Clio led the way and Grace followed behind them. The stairs were steep, and as they ascended Grace's eyes were on a level with the beaded hem of her mother's jacket. Nathaniel came last. They were filing upward in silence, and Grace could hear her uncle puffing slightly through the mat of his beard.

When they reached the confined space of the top landing, they crowded together, and then the studio door was flung open and Pilgrim confronted them. He was wearing one of his unpressed suits and a collarless shirt. His hair looked even longer than usual.

"Please, won't you come in? My lord? Your ladyship?"

Clio and Grace did not look at each other. Clio had warned Grace that the unveiling of the portrait was likely to cause a disturbance, and even the warning had created difficulty. Grace had not been invited to look at it in advance, and her resentment had flowered into anger. The girls had quarreled, their submerged rivalry breaking the calm surface of their summer's truce.

The studio was littered and smelly. Mingled with the usual painterly odors there was a strong element of fried bacon and a suggestion of stale beer. John Leominster wrinkled his nose as he strode across the room to the shrouded easel. He was wearing country tweeds, the pepper-and-salt color exactly the same shade as his gloomy moustache. He was on the point of leaving for Stretton, where he would disagree with the decisions that Hugo had made regarding the estate's management, and from Stretton he would progress to Melton for a few days' hunting. He was impatient to be on his way, and Blanche's insistence on the tiresome chore of viewing the portrait had made him irritable. He stood in silence, fingering his watch chain.

Nathaniel looked around him. The portrait was finished, and Clio no longer had any reason to stay in London. He had come to escort her back to Oxford, and while he would not normally have been any more than mildly interested in a portrait of the two girls commissioned by John and Blanche, something in Clio's wary manner when it was discussed had sparked his curiosity. He was thinking that this studio was defiantly squalid, and that Pilgrim himself looked a rogue, but an attractive rogue. It would be interesting to see what representation he had made of Clio and Grace in their white dance dresses. There were dozens of other canvases in the studio, but every one of them was turned to face the wall.

Pilgrim was smiling. John slipped his gold hunter out of his pocket and snapped it open.

"May we see this picture now, Mr. Pilgrim?" he asked in his wintry manner. "I have a long drive ahead of me."

Pilgrim's smile broadened. "By all means, Lord Leominster. That is what you are all here for."

Clio felt the blood humming in her ears. Pilgrim twitched the shroud off the easel. A little noise, like a mouse's squeak, came out of Blanche's mouth. After that there was silence.

Clio couldn't recall afterward who had spoken first, or what the exact words had been. She only remembered that the silence was suddenly filled with words, tremulous whispers from Blanche and sharp barks from John. *Not what we expected*, Blanche murmured, *not suitable at all.* And John snapped *filthy,* and *disgusting daub,* and *travesty of the respectable art of portraiture.* Grace stood between them, red-faced and round-eyed, looking as if she wished that her parents could be swallowed up by the paint-splattered floorboards. At that moment she didn't care what the portrait looked like, only that her parents would not humiliate her in front of Pilgrim.

Clio edged closer to Nathaniel. She saw that her father was looking carefully at *The Janus Face,* rubbing his beard with the palm of his hand as he did when he was giving something his critical attention.

"I won't pay for it," John said at last. "Not a penny. You'll be lucky if I don't sue."

"We couldn't hang it, you see," Blanche fluttered beside him. "Not at Stretton. Not alongside the Sargent."

Pilgrim's smile had vanished. "The Sargent," he snarled. "The bloody chocolate-box Sargent. Well, my lord and lady, I tell you that I wouldn't sell my picture to you. I wouldn't sell it to you if it were the last thing between me and starvation. I wouldn't take your mothball-stinking, blind-eyed, miserable money to save myself from the gallows."

He was shouting now. Grace imagined that the words boomed down the stairs and swirled up through the glass skylights to echo over Charlotte Street for all the world to hear. She wanted to hide her face in her hands. "*The Janus Face* is not for sale. Not to you, my lord. Go and buy yourself another Sargent, if that is what you want."

John Leominster pulled his tweeds more closely around him, as if Pilgrim might touch and contaminate him. Then he gripped Blanche by the elbow, jerked his head at Clio and Grace, and steered them all to the door without a backward glance. He made an ostentatious detour around the easel.

Nathaniel lingered. He was still examining the canvas. Pilgrim rubbed his mouth with the back of his hand and scowled at him.

Nathaniel said, "I would like to buy the picture. It is a portrait of *my* daughter, as well as Lord Leominster's."

"I told you. It's not for sale."

Nathaniel inclined his head courteously. "That is for you to decide, of course. If you should change your mind, I would be glad to hear of it." He took out one of his cards and placed it on the corner of the table. Then he followed the rest of the family down-stairs to the waiting car.

Pilgrim snatched the picture from the easel. He held it up, twisting the wooden stretcher, glowering as if he were about to fling it to the ground. But then he seemed to think better of it. He replaced the portrait and stood for a long moment looking at the two figures. At last, he gave a snort of laughter.

"Filthy daub," he said affectionately. He found a half-empty bottle of whiskey in the clutter, took it up by the neck and drank deeply.

Grace missed Clio's company. It was five days since Nathaniel had taken her back to Oxford.

She stood up from the writing desk in her bedroom and walked across to the window. A gale in the night had stripped the leaves from the trees in the square. There was nothing to see.

If Clio were here, there would be someone to talk to. To Grace, their quarrels were no more than enjoyable sparring matches. Clio irritated her sometimes, with her accuracy and circumspection, but Grace thought of her as an ally. Especially so now that Jake and Julius were busy with their own lives. Grace remembered the red-haired, actressy-looking woman who had blown kisses to Julius at the opera, and the way Julius had blushed when Anthony asked him about her. Grace had been just a little shocked. Julius had always been her own unquestioning admirer.

She turned back across the room and sat down at her table again, resting her chin in her hands. She thought nostalgically of the days when they had been the magic circle, Clio and herself and Jake and Julius.

If only there were someone to talk to.

She had begun a letter to Clio, but she had broken off after only a few lines. She wanted to write about Pilgrim and the anger and shame she had felt when John rejected the portrait. But Clio had become her rival for Pilgrim's attention. They had stopped talking about him and had set out to make their separate claims on Char-lotte Street.

Grace picked up her pen and turned it over in her fingers before putting it down with a sigh. The house was empty. John and Hugo were in the country, Blanche was out at a luncheon party, and Phoebe was a baby in the schoolroom. Thomas was away at Eton.

There would be plenty of talk in the Eiffel, Grace thought. She could see Pilgrim sitting at his table with a bottle in front of him, papers spread all around. There would be Stulik, surging forward in welcome, and the regular traffic of friends.

It came to Grace with sudden clarity that she could be part of that traffic, simply by walking into the Eiffel herself. She was a modern woman, and needed no one's permission.

She went straight to the nursery and told Nanny Brodribb that if her mother should come home and happen to ask where she was, she had gone shopping. To Selfridges. To buy some handkerchiefs. She walked out into Belgrave Square and hailed a taxi.

The restaurant was almost empty in the late afternoon lull, but Pilgrim was in his usual place. Grace looked through the red curtains and saw him, and she felt a moment's shyness. But then she straightened her shoulders. She only wanted someone to talk to, she told herself, and Pilgrim was always happy to talk. Clio had gone and left her on her own, but that also meant that the field was clear. She had Bohemia all to herself.

Pilgrim looked up as she came in. A shadow of impatience was replaced by a welcoming smile. He stood up and took her hands. They had not seen each other since the unveiling of the portrait.

"Grace, Grace. This is a pleasure. Sit down here with me. You look very pretty, but you know that, don't you? Shall I have Giovanni bring you some tea?"

One of the waiters loitered near the brass centerpiece. Grace shook her head. "No tea, thank you." She peeled off her gloves and laid them on the cloth in front of her. The white linen was spotted with wine and gravy. Pilgrim had been having a long lunch, and she wondered with whom.

"I came to say I was sorry," she improvised.

Pilgrim lit a yellow cigarette and handed it to her, and took another for himself. They contemplated each other through the smoke.

"You don't have to apologize for your father's philistinism."

A spark of tension licked between them. Grace breathed in sharply. She had never heard her father spoken of with open disrespect.

But Pilgrim was right, she thought. John Leominster had revealed his rude ignorance.

"What will you do with the portrait now?" Pilgrim had not asked her for her opinion of *The Janus Face*, she noticed, although he had been eager to hear Clio's.

"I shall keep it. I'm pleased with it. I may loan it, if a suitable place for it to hang presents itself." Pilgrim watched her expectantly, but Grace did not know how she was supposed to respond.

"I hope it does," she said calmly. She had seen that his eyes were bloodshot and the skin was gray below them. Bluish stubble emphasized the hollows under his cheekbones. Pilgrim had evidently been enjoying himself since she had last seen him, and she wondered again who his companion could have been. Perhaps the silver-haired girl from the opera, she thought. Possessiveness together with an absurd wish to protect and care for him overtook her. Pilgrim's weariness made him seem vulnerable, and less awe-inspiring than he had before.

Remembering the afternoon in the studio a week ago, Grace felt an angry distaste for Belgrave Square and a consequent sense of her own isolation. She was not sure now where she belonged, or where her allegiance lay. But out of the confusion of her feelings came one certainty, that she was powerfully drawn to Pilgrim, and that the attraction was adult, no longer anything to do with the childish subterfuges she had practiced with Jake and Julius, and with Peter Dennis. She raised her eyes and looked into his.

Grace wondered if this moment was the first of real adulthood. The sense of its importance created a pressure in her chest.

"And so, what now?" Pilgrim asked softly.

Color rose in Grace's cheeks. "I was lonely," she said. "I wanted to talk to you."

The honesty of the admission touched him. It had not occurred to Pilgrim that Grace Stretton might feel anything of the kind. He had supposed that her days would be too full of shopping and lunching. He put out his hand and rested it over hers. Her bones felt small and brittle, like a bird's. She was, he was thinking, so . . . *ordered*. Her shining hair was coiled under her little hat and secured with a pearl hatpin. Her single-strand pearl necklace showed at her throat under the collar of her shell-pink blouse. Her dove-gray suit fitted her, must have been made for her, and it was brushed and pressed, and the empty fingers of her pale gray gloves were neither stained nor darned. She smelled sweet, and her lips were slightly parted, and her breath stirred the hair of her fur wrap.

Jeannie was not ordered. She carried her own grubbiness and disarray with her. And Isolde . . .

Isolde could not be categorized, but Pilgrim knew that he would never see her in a pearl necklace. The recollection of her, and the juxtaposition of that image with Grace, made him feel suddenly, distinctly aroused. He had thought that he was much too tired, but now he knew that he was not.

"We can't talk here," he said. "Come with me."

He held on to Grace's willing hand and led her out of the restaurant. Giovanni watched them with an impassive face, but when the door had closed behind them, he clicked his tongue. He turned the card that hung against the glass so that it read in its French script "FERME." They could all wait now, he told himself, until the proper time to open for dinner.

Pilgrim locked the door of his studio behind them.

Grace looked around her, suppressing a shiver, although she was not cold. It was all familiar, but she was seeing it differently. She had no reason to be here alone with Pilgrim, no social alibi. *The Janus Face* might be one of any of the dozens of canvases turned with their faces to the wall, and it was finished.

She was on new territory. Modern women, she reminded herself. She thought fleetingly of Clio, and as Pilgrim came toward her she felt a little, indecent flicker of triumph.

He undid the clasp of her pearls and let the strand run through his fingers into the palm of his hand, a nacreous snake. With an answering gesture she drew the pin out of her hat and lifted off the shell of veiled felt. Her hair fell around her shoulders.

Grace was not embarrassed to find herself undressed. She had sat for hours in her silk underclothes on the shawled divan, with Pilgrim's eyes on her. He led her back to her old place now, and slipped the silk straps down. His hand felt large and rough on her skin, on her breast.

Grace was exhilarated and afraid, as well as triumphant, but as Pilgrim touched her she felt another sensation. It was a surprising and strident physical urgency all of her own.

She put up her arms, wrapped them around Pilgrim's neck. She drew him down to her, closer, until his unkempt head obliterated the light. Then there was nothing to see but his eyes, and the dark bar of his eyebrows, and the puckers and creases of his skin, suddenly revealed to her in all their intricacy.

He pushed her backward until she lay flat, and he hung over her, magnified in the field of her vision. He kissed her, reaching his tongue into her mouth, and she opened it to admit him, wanting to offer no barriers. He tasted faintly of onions, much more strongly of tobacco, and the bristles of his beard scraped her face. He was breathing heavily, with a tiny rasp of mucus deep in his chest.

His fingers probed her flesh. Grace found that she was holding her breath, and then gasping in a lungful of the thick studio air.

Pilgrim fumbled with the last of the tiny pearl buttons.

"Let me," she whispered. She wriggled out of the last wisps of her clothes, and then lay back again. He looked at her, his eyebrows drawn together and his lower lip jutting. His hand ran over her ribcage, the curve of her hip, as if she were a piece of sculpture. Grace found herself thinking of the pictures of Jeannie.

"Won't you take your clothes off too?" she asked him. "I'm not your model today." The lightness and steadiness of her own voice surprised her, and she saw that he looked with a kind of admiration.

"It's your first time," he said, not asking a question.

"There always has to be a first time."

Pilgrim was very hairy. His arms and shoulders and chest were covered in dark hair. Peter Dennis had had smooth, very pale skin, and Julius and Jake had only been boys. Long ago, long ago. Pilgrim lay down beside her and took her in his arms. Grace knew there would be no running away now, no slipping back into the noisy currents of the Woodstock Road house or escaping across the water-meadows to where the other children called out for her in their game.

She knew what was supposed to happen now. She knew, but she had no idea.

He began to rub and stroke her. The vague, smothering feeling of wanting him that she had felt at the beginning had all disappeared, but now she felt a different, stronger, but imperfectly localized sensation that made her want to wriggle and roll her head. It was like glimpsing a face that ought to be perfectly familiar but was hidden by a thick veil, and so was tantalizingly obscured. She frowned, trying to identify it.

The feeling did not last long. Pilgrim rolled above her, and then nudged between her thighs. The smell of onions, tobacco, and sweat intensified.

"You'll learn," he was mumbling. "You'll soon learn, the goodness of it."

It was painful, but not unbearably so. After a moment of stillness in which he grunted and nuzzled against her neck, Pilgrim began to move. Grace lay for a moment and then twitched her hips, willingly trying to echo what he did. His mouth curved into a smile against hers, and their teeth grated together. His breath was very hot in the back of her throat as he murmured to her.

"That's right. Oh, you're a natural little chippy you are, my lady, my love, I could tell that from your mouth, that first day in your mama's drawing room. Like a tiny red pillow, all soft, for a man to lie on.

"Lift yourself up to me, like that.

"Sweet, sweet, isn't it? Like nothing in the world. They call it a little death, you know. To die a little . . ."

It was as if Grace's head had been severed from her body. Her body with all the friction and pressure and stickiness belonged to someone else, and only her head was her own. She kept repeating to herself, I'm doing it, here and now, with this man. This hairy body. On this divan with the musty shawls. Is this what it is? Does it mean this, all the business of men and women?

Pilgrim was tired. He had had almost no sleep the night before, and he was barely sober now. The girl was lovely, but she was sexually naïve. Of course she was, he told himself, how could she be otherwise? And this was not the time to begin her education. There would be other times, he decided. More leisurely times, he would teach her what to do. . . .

He stopped thinking and gave himself up to enjoying her.

Grace held him in her arms, wondering if his groans meant that she was doing something wrong. She tightened her hold when he gave a defeated bellow and collapsed on top of her.

The movements stopped, and from that she knew it was over. She felt a small but definite pang of regret. That was it, she told herself. She had irrevocably crossed the divide from childhood into womanhood. The portentousness of the thought made her wish for a grander setting than the divan and a louder fanfare than Pilgrim's shout.

Pilgrim moved sleepily, and then hauled himself up to look at her. He cupped one hand under her chin, and the tenderness of the gesture consoled her.

"That's the first time out of the way," he excused himself. "The best thing about it is that it leads to the second and third."

Grace allowed herself to be reassured. This was only a beginning, then. The impatient sensation that he had stirred in her slowly faded away, and she felt ordinary again.

Pilgrim lit a cigarette, and she settled in the crook of his arm. It was comfortable to lie with her cheek on his chest, listening to the muffled drum of his heartbeat. She rested one leg across his, looking down at the whiteness of her thigh against the black fur of his. It came to her that she was comfortable with her nakedness, calm and pensive, as Jeannie had looked in the pictures.

Grace smiled. She was here now, and she and Pilgrim were a part of each other. She loved him. She was glad to have crossed the divide.

He slid his hand over her ribs, to rest in the hollow of her waist. "Are you hungry?" he asked her.

To her surprise, Grace discovered that she was.

"Let's go to the Eiffel, then," Pilgrim said briskly.

He watched her putting on her clothes. "If we are going to do this again . . ."

"I want to," Grace said. She was determined to be honest in her new maturity.

". . . If we are, you need to fix yourself up. Perhaps you could talk to Jeannie." Pilgrim was vague, leaving the suggestion hanging between them.

Grace nodded, having only a faint idea that he was referring to something women did, and knowing that she couldn't possibly discuss anything of the kind with Jeannie. She presented her back to Pilgrim, so that he could do up her buttons for her.

The Eiffel was crowded.

Grace saw a quartet in evening dress at a table near the door and recognized them as acquaintances from Belgrave Square. They must be having an early supper before seeing some dull show, she thought, and congratulating themselves on their daring in venturing into the raffish Eiffel Tower. She waved at them, and airily passed by on Pilgrim's arm.

Pilgrim's friend Nina and a crowd of others were sitting at his table. There was a chorus of greetings as chairs were moved up to make room for them. Grace looked around, and was faintly disappointed to see that there was no sign of Jeannie or the silver girl. But there were half a dozen others she recognized, and she saw that they all looked back at her.

Did they know? Grace wondered. Could they see it in her eyes?

Her face glowed above her crumpled collar, and the men in the group shifted in the hope that she might sit next to them.

On the other side of Pilgrim, Max Erdmann muttered, "So it's the other one tonight, is it?"

Pilgrim grinned, making no attempt to hide his pleasure and satisfaction. "What is a man supposed to do? Beat them off with a stick?"

"I have no idea. My problems tend in the opposite direction. But do you really need two of them?"

Pilgrim half closed his eyes, still smiling. "Is it not your experi-

ence, Max, that every woman is invariably lacking in some depart-
ment? This arrangement is perfection itself. There is one for conversation and company, and one for bed, according to their natural
aptitudes. It is like having one woman, with twice the variety and
none of the drawbacks. The female Janus. I've painted her, and
now I'm enjoying her."

"How fortunate you are," Max said, with noticeable dislike.
Pilgrim returned his attention to Grace.

"Grace, would you like the *plat du jour*?" he invited, mindful as
always of his bill. Grace smiled her acquiescence. She knew that
this evening, in her happiness, whatever she ate would taste like
ambrosia.

Nathaniel and Eleanor always liked to give a party at Christmas,
although for the years of the war it had been a muted affair. Now, at
the end of 1919, they had decided that they must compensate with a
bigger and much more splendid event. It would be their own
celebration of the first year of peace, of Jake's and Julius's proper
emergence into the world, and of Clio's coming out.

The party would also celebrate the hanging, in the drawing room
overlooking the garden at Woodstock Road, of Pilgrim's double
portrait.

Pilgrim had declined to sell *The Janus Face* to Nathaniel, to
Nathaniel's private relief because he suspected he couldn't possibly have afforded to pay for it, even for the sake of teasing his
brother-in-law. It had been Pilgrim's own suggestion that he
should bring the picture to Oxford, and leave it there on indefinite
loan.

The painter had been a lively and welcome guest. Pilgrim had
obviously enjoyed the comfortable informality of Eleanor's household and his planned overnight stay to supervise the hanging had
somehow stretched to a week.

"It's just like home," he said expansively, although he never
offered any more information about his own domestic life. Clio
knew that according to Charlotte Street gossip, Pilgrim lived in
some bleak rooms in Tottenham, and only ever returned to them
when in dire need of some refinement like clean clothes or hot
water that was unavailable either in his studio or someone else's
more conveniently situated residence.

Nathaniel liked him. The two men sat underneath the portrait in
its place of honor on the long wall facing the garden, and argued
about politics, pictures, and Wagner. Pilgrim was gallant to Elea-

nor, insisting that she was by far the ripest and loveliest of the quartet of women, until she blushed and protested.

And Clio fell deeper in love with him. Pilgrim occupied the tower room that had been Peter Dennis's, and his robust presence exorcised the paler ghost. Pilgrim's behavior toward Clio was impeccable, to her slight regret. He took her to tea at Tripps', not counting the cost of chocolate cakes, then marched her around the pictures in the Ashmolean Museum. They were familiar to her, but he made her see them with different eyes. He made her walk around the circumference of the Radcliffe Camera and lift her head to examine the lines of the Bodleian and the Sheldonian Theater. All of these things had been familiar to her from childhood, but in Pilgrim's company they were new and fascinating.

Over their tea in Tripps' he also warned her not to waste too much of her life in learning instead of doing.

"What do you mean?" she had asked him.

"Do you really want to spend years buried in some library here, or chaperoned by women dons whenever you set foot outside the College walls? You've seen Oxford now. What about the rest of the world?"

"It isn't quite like that," she had protested, but she had begun to think, much more seriously than his casual remark had warranted.

All the Hirshes missed him when he went back to London. Tabby and Alice begged him to come back soon and draw more animal pictures for them. Nathaniel and Eleanor told him that he was welcome to visit the Woodstock Road whenever he wanted to.

"Won't you come to our Christmas party, to celebrate the portrait?" Eleanor begged. Eleanor had calmly accepted the defiant, seminaked representation of her daughter and niece. Nathaniel admired the portrait, and that was good enough for Eleanor.

Pilgrim bent over to kiss her hand. "If only I could," he lamented. "But I must go to Paris. Work, work."

The truth was that he had promised Isolde a holiday trip. The use of an apartment on the Cité had been promised to him by two painters he knew. He felt well fed and well rested from his week in Oxford, and after Clio's receptive intelligence and thoughtful questions he was more than ready to divert himself with Isolde in Paris.

Clio came with him to the gate, where a taxi was waiting to take him to Oxford station. He took off his big black hat with a sweep of his arm and kissed her on the mouth. Clio saw that he was glitter-eyed, looking forward to his next adventure.

"I shall miss you," she said in a small voice.

"I hope so. But not too much."

Pilgrim clapped his hat on his head again and subsided into the taxi. Clio wandered back into the house, wondering if it was her permanent fate to be in love and lonely all at the same time.

The party was to be held three days before Christmas.

Nathaniel loved making the excuse of his Gentile family for decorating the house before the festival. A huge fir tree was always stationed in the hall and decorated with carved wooden ornaments and silver stars and gingerbread figures suspended on scarlet ribbons. Holly garlands were made for the mantelshelves, and Nathaniel always led a children's excursion to Port Meadow, where mistletoe grew among the branches of one of the trees. Tabitha and Alice hung paper streamers and lanterns from the cornices, and Clio helped them to set out the beautifully detailed and painted Nativity scene that Eleanor had inherited from Holborough.

Nathaniel regarded all this, and the singing of carols and hanging-up of stockings, with impartial pleasure.

"A feast is a feast," he said, "whatever religion it belongs to."

This year the decoration was done earlier than usual so that the house would look festive for the party. Eleanor and Mrs. Doyle, assisted by Clio, embarked on a marathon of cooking. There would be more than sixty people for dinner, and afterward Julius and his friends would play music for dancing. The worn Persian rugs in the drawing room were taken up in readiness, laying bare the fine oak parquet floor. Eleanor's housemaid spent a whole day waxing and polishing it. The Janus portrait gazed down at the preparations. It had looked perfectly comfortable in the Woodstock Road from the moment it had been hung amongst the books and music stands and manuscripts.

Clio had a new dress for the occasion. At last she had achieved the ink-blue velvet she had dreamed of for her coming out. She went to Elliston's and bought the material herself, and Nanny Cooper helped her to cut and sew it into a narrow column that rippled when she moved. She was pleased with the effect, and told herself that she would look just as elegant as Grace in her Reville & Rossiter. If only Pilgrim were coming, she thought wistfully. She would not have minded at all letting Grace see that they were such good friends after a whole week spent together.

The Stretton party arrived from London on the afternoon of the party. They would stay overnight, and then travel on to Stretton for the Christmas holidays. John was not with them. He had no wish to join in any celebration of Pilgrim's notorious picture, and had instructed Blanche and the four children to ignore the painting as far as possible. Blanche told Eleanor, and Eleanor told Nathaniel, who roared with delighted laughter at the absurdity of it all.

"I am looking forward to seeing Hugo doing his duty and standing with his back to it all the evening," he said gleefully. As a tease, the whole business of the portrait hanging had exceeded his best expectations.

Grace was quiet when the family party reached the Woodstock Road. She barely spoke to Clio, and hardly seemed to notice Jake and Julius. She announced that the journey had been tiring and that she was going to lie down. No one saw her again until the evening began.

At seven o'clock, everyone was assembling downstairs ready to meet the guests. All the children were to be allowed to stay up for dinner, even Alice, who ran up and down the hallway between Phoebe and Tabitha in a state of wild overexcitement. The Oswald Harrises had already arrived and were greeting Nathaniel and Eleanor when Grace finally came down the stairs. She was wearing an ivory lace dress, with Blanche's magnificent pearl and diamond choker at her throat and an ivory fillet in her hair. Her eyes were very wide, and there was an unusual flush of color high on her cheekbones.

Clio heard Julius draw in his breath when he looked up and saw Grace at the head of the stairs.

Julius went forward and took Grace's hand as she came down.

"You look very beautiful," he said. She turned her head, meeting his eyes, but she did not smile.

The Hirshes' guests flooded in, neighbors and Nathaniel's colleagues, past and present students who were still near enough to Oxford to reach it in the middle of the Christmas vacation, musicians and clergymen and philosophers. Hugo hobbled about on his stick, nobly making conversation as if he were at a tenants' ball, with Thomas doing his best to imitate him. The younger children carried plates, and the smell of food mingled with the scents of pine branches and mulled wine. Grace's high color faded, and she began to look as ivory pale as her dress. Julius never took his eyes off her. Once, seeing her pallor, Jake asked her if she felt all right. She fixed him with a wide-eyed stare. "Never better," she answered.

After dinner the dancing began. Nathaniel smiled to see the Strettons carefully not looking at the portrait. All except Grace. She stared at it, her pale face quite expressionless. From across the room, Clio watched her. She felt less pleased with her blue velvet dress, less than satisfied with the whole evening. A dull feeling of apprehension gnawed at her innards, although she had no idea why she should feel apprehensive.

Julius played the fiddle for the dancers, waltzes and foxtrots and one-steps, but he longed to leave the other musicians to play and step through the crowd to Grace. He knew that her cheek would feel cool against his, and that she would bend with him like a reed in the dance.

At last, Alice fell asleep on the sofa with her best dress rucked up to reveal her white stockings. Eleanor was serving coffee, and the dancing slowed and then stopped. Julius and the others put down their instruments.

Grace was standing alone at one side of the room, under *The Janus Face*. Jake and Julius both went to her, both of them glancing up at the seminaked figures above them with their straining muscles emerging from the common bud of flesh. Clio was drawn closer too, unwillingly, but by some inescapable compulsion. Grace waited until they made a ring around her.

"The magic circle," she said slowly. "Let's go upstairs to the old nursery. It's so noisy down here."

She led the way, and the others followed her. Clio's feet were heavier than lead. What self-dramatizing instinct, she wondered, was prompting Grace to draw them all out of the heart of the party?

The old nursery belonged to Tabby and Alice now. The paper remains of streamer- and garland-making still spread out on the deal table. Grace sat on the old-fashioned high fender and looked down into the embers of the fire.

"We should have brought up some wine," Jake said cheerfully. "We could have had our own party." He had enjoyed the evening. Several of Nathaniel's old colleagues had pretty daughters, and the dancing had given him plenty of opportunities for whispered flirtation.

Grace did not look up. She was still staring down into the glowing coals when she made her flat-voiced announcement.

"I think I am going to have a baby."

The words seemed to echo in the corners of the room.

Julius sat still, frozen into silence. Clio could only think, stupidly, *But you can't. You have to be married first.*

It was Jake who went to her. He bent down on one knee and took both her hands in his. When he looked up at her, it was as if he were parodying a proposal.

"How many days late are you?" he asked gently.

To his shame, Julius found that he was blushing scarlet at the mention of such things to his cousin and his sister.

"Fifteen," Grace said, in the same flat voice.

"That isn't so long," Jake told her. "It might not be what you're afraid of. There could be all kinds of other reasons. Overtiredness, or anemia, or anxiety."

"No. I know what it is. I can feel it."

There had only been half a dozen times in all. Perhaps six afternoons in Pilgrim's studio, with the warmth of the gas fire and the musty shawls to wrap themselves in. There had been sufficient time for Grace to learn to enjoy what they did, even to feel eager for it, and more than enough for the damage to be done. She had never talked to Jeannie about "fixing herself up," whatever that was supposed to mean, and Pilgrim had never mentioned it again.

Clio licked her dry lips and asked the question. "Who is it? Grace, whose baby?" She heard the hostility in her own voice, and felt Julius's eyes flick toward her.

"Pilgrim's, of course." Grace hardly turned her head. She was as white as paper now, even her lips were colorless. The pearls looked dirty yellow against her neck. She said to Jake, "I thought you might know somebody who could help me. A doctor. If not a proper doctor, then whoever it is who does these things." She spoke as if they were discussing some unpleasant but necessary domestic chore.

Jake's horrified reaction showed clearly in his face. "I don't know anyone who would contemplate performing an abortion, if you mean a medically acceptable operation. And I have seen women die after going to back-street abortionists. I have *seen* them, Grace." He was still kneeling in front of her, holding her hands, almost as white in the face as she was herself. "You can't butcher yourself."

Grace was stonily calm. She had already done her thinking. "I was afraid you would say that," she said. She disengaged her hands from Jake's, spread out her ringless fingers, and stared at them. "It seems that there is no alternative but to get married as quickly as possible."

Clio stumbled to her feet, almost knocking over her chair.

"To *Pilgrim*?"

She knew that there was as much envy as disbelief in her voice. The idea of marriage seemed so safe and simple. If she were married to Pilgrim, Clio thought, and a mother, her life would be settled. There would be no more uncertainty, and no need to answer questions for herself about what to do with her time and what goals to aim for. She would know what to believe in, because it would be her husband and his work and their children.

Grace was laughing. It was an uncomfortable, jagged laugh that was full of bitterness. "Not to Pilgrim. I wouldn't marry him, any more than he would marry me. No, I shall marry Anthony Brock. Our baby will be born a little early, but it will turn out to be as good a little Brock as anyone could wish for."

Julius moved then, stiffly, as if his limbs hurt him, across the room to where Grace sat. He crouched down beside his brother, but he was oblivious of Jake, and of Clio too. There might have been no one else in the house but Grace and himself.

"I love you," he whispered to her. "I'll marry you. Marry me, not Anthony Brock."

With burning face and eyes, Clio watched her brothers as they knelt at Grace's feet. A tidal wave of anger and bitterness was sweeping through her.

All the time Pilgrim had been lecturing her on Cubism and Christopher Wren and Samuel Palmer, all the time she had been meekly listening to him, he had been making love to Grace. While she had been childishly dreaming, Grace had taken the real thing for herself, just as she had always done, all through their childhood and growing up. While she had been standing to one side waiting for life to begin, Grace had helped herself to it. Clio thought savagely that now, not even to be pregnant with Pilgrim's baby would be a punishment for Grace.

She would simply marry Anthony, wry and ironic Anthony whom Clio had come to look upon as her friend, taking him as she had always taken everything else. She would be the focus of attention, with her wedding and her baby, and Anthony would love her, and she would never have to suffer for any of the damage she caused.

And here were Jake and Julius, like the rival suitors in some stupid Victorian tableau, kneeling at her feet. Even after her confession they were still ready to support and comfort her. Julius had told her that he loved her and would marry her. And still, Grace was ready to turn on loyal Anthony and use him to father another man's child, to enter into a lifelong lie and expect Clio herself and her brothers to keep her secret for her. . . .

Clio could taste her own sour jealousy in her mouth. She felt how it pinched her lips and dug premature lines in her cheeks. A childish refrain like one of Alice's hammered in her head. *It isn't fair. Grace, it isn't fair, I hate you for it.* . . .

Grace had Pilgrim, and Anthony, and Jake and Julius. Clio felt that she was left with nobody. Grace had even taken Peter Dennis, although Clio knew in her heart that he had loved her, not Grace.

The taste in her mouth was so strong that she wondered if it would make her sick. She forced herself to take deep breaths of air into her churning stomach.

Grace put out her hand and stroked Julius's hair. She said very quietly, "Thank you. I'll remember that you offered that, Julius. I wish I could marry you, but I can't. It would be like marrying Clio."

Julius's head was bent under her hand, and she couldn't see his face.

"You could do much worse than marry Anthony Brock," Jake said. He felt that it was his role to be practical. He was thinking that Anthony would make an excellent husband for Grace, and a devoted father when the time came. Grace would be lucky to have him, and in the end she would probably come to love him exactly as her mother had learned to love John Leominster. A well-disguised accident of paternity would soon be forgotten.

Grace nodded wearily. "I'm sure you are right," she said.

She had been clinging to the hope that somehow, against all rational principles, to lay her problem in front of the magic circle would be to find a solution. But there was no solution, of course. There was no such thing as magic, and the circle was broken open. She had snapped the link between Clio and herself. She could see it in her cousin's face; she had made an enemy of Clio now.

The knowledge made Grace long for her support and friendship. She knew that she had brought herself to the edge of disaster and humiliation, and her only resort was to trap herself in a marriage with a man she didn't love. All the bright future was extinguished, and in her loss she was crying out for Clio's love and sympathy.

She looked over Julius's head to where Clio leaned in her dark blue velvet against the scarred old table.

"Help me," she begged.

Clio had been utterly silent, but now a convulsion jarred her. In a single movement she flung herself across to the fender and leaped at Grace with her fingers hooked like claws, ready to tear her face.

"Clio, Clio . . ." Jake and Julius caught her and pinned her arms, dragging her away from Grace, who never stirred from her perch on the fender.

Clio found that she was gasping for breath, and she wrenched incoherent words out between her sobs. "Help you? I hate you. I despise you, do you hear me?"

Grace's expression was stiff and controlled. "Yes, I can hear you."

As he looked from one to the other, Julius was horrified to see the wild eyes and wrenching strain of the Janus portrait.

Then Grace stood up, smoothing the pleated front of her lace dress. In her ordinary conversational voice she said, "Anthony is coming to spend Christmas at Stretton, you know. I think in a day or so it will be in order for you to congratulate us on our engagement." As she walked to the door she was thinking that if it was all a mistake, if there was no baby, she could break off the engagement and all would be well again. But with dull certainty she knew that there was no mistake. It would be better for the baby to be born a Brock than a bastard. It would be better for her to be Mrs. Anthony Brock than nobody at all.

"Goodnight," Grace said quietly. "Thank you, Jake. Thank you, Julius."

Eight

CLIO UNWRAPPED A POTTERY PLATE and smiled at the sight of its decorations of flowers and fruit. She had bought it and its fellows from Omega Workshops, sometime after her acquisition of the Gilman painting. The plates and the picture were her first extravagances, the first expressions of her own taste rather than her parents', and she was very fond of them. They were still almost her only personal possessions apart from books and clothes.

She held the plate up for Jake to see. "Where shall we put this?"

Jake was unpacking medical textbooks and stacking them on shelves. He glanced perfunctorily at Clio.

"It's a plate, isn't it? Put it in the kitchen."

She smiled. Jake was uninterested in aesthetics. Still holding the plate she picked her way through the heaps of their separate belongings to the kitchen at the back of the house.

There was one tall window here, looking out over the chimneys and rooflines of Bloomsbury. Clio saw the roosting places of pigeons amongst iron gutters and soot-stained windowsills, and the dusty windows of the mews opposite, and by craning her neck to the left she could see the tops of the plane trees in Bedford Square. It seemed to her the most satisfactory vista she could possibly imagine. It had taken months of argument and persuasion to achieve it.

In front of the window was a stone sink and a wooden drainer with a zinc dish containing a sliver of soap. Clio turned on the tap and rinsed off the smears left by newspaper wrapping on the Omega plate. She dried it carefully, admiring the colors under the glaze, and put it on the bare pine table at the other side of the kitchen. When she ran her hand over the tabletop, she found a film of dust and ancient crumbs, and even that made her happy because she knew that she would wash it down and it would be part of making a home for herself and Jake, here in four partly furnished rooms overlooking Gower Street.

"Home," she said, trying the word for effect. She pulled out one of the ladder-back chairs from the table and sat down, swinging her feet up onto the seat of another. She could hear Jake in the next room, still arranging his books on the shelves. Jake was about to begin his clinical practice, the last stage on his way to becoming a doctor, at University College Hospital. The hospital was only a few yards farther up Gower Street. It was Jake who had found this flat and who had made her see that, by putting together the small amount of Holborough money they had both inherited, they could afford to buy the lease.

But, Clio thought proudly, she had done the rest, the infinitely more difficult part, entirely by herself. She had secured herself a job. She was to start work on Monday morning at nine o'clock.

The thought of it was immediately exciting. She stood up and walked the nine paces from one end of the kitchen to the other, wrapping her arms around herself in pleasure. She was a professional woman, responsible for herself and answerable to nobody. The realization seemed both momentous and deeply romantic.

Two months ago, just after Jake had first mentioned the possibility of her sharing his Gower Street purchase, in the middle of confusion and indecision about her future and without giving herself time to think twice, she had taken the train from Oxford to London to see Max Erdmann in the *Fathom* offices in Doughty Street. She had found Max unusually sober, busy, and without any idea who she was. He had no recollection at all of having offered her a job months before, and his only aim had been to get her out of his chaotic office as quickly as possible in order to get on with compiling his overdue September issue.

To her surprise, Clio found herself standing her ground. "I need a job, Mr. Erdmann. I can make myself useful."

Max had barely lifted his head from a sheaf of galley proofs. "How do you know that? Can you type, for instance?"

Clio looked around at the drifts of paper, the overflowing wastebins and dusty boxes of *Fathom* back issues and subscription forms.

"I'm very neat, very methodical. I can keep records and do filing and correct proofs."

"Can you *type*?" Max sighed.

"I can learn."

"Do that. Then come back and talk to me again. I won't have a job for you, but talk is free."

"You need me," Clio had said boldly. "You should give me a job."

And to her amazement she had found that employing insistent Grace-tactics worked. She had embarked on the latest in a series of arguments with Eleanor and Nathaniel, and enrolled herself in a Pitman's course. Six weeks later, she had emerged as a competent typist with a rudimentary grasp of shorthand. She presented herself again at the *Fathom* offices on the day that Max's editorial assistant announced that she was going to have a baby.

"I told you you needed me." Clio smiled.

"Start in two weeks," Max responded with the best grace he could manage. "You will be on a week's trial."

"Thank you." Clio's smile shone at him.

Whatever the job was like, she thought now, it couldn't present anything like the difficulties she had already overcome to convey herself here, to Gower Street, to the beginning of her independent life.

The worst of it had been telling Nathaniel and Eleanor that she was giving up Oxford.

"You want to work in some office, as a stenographer?" Eleanor had murmured, fanning herself with a copy of *Fathom* that Clio had brought home to show them. "Whatever for? I can understand that for some young women a job may be a necessity, but not for people of our sort. You can study your languages, and then you will marry and have your own children, just like Grace. . . ."

"No," Clio had said, as gently as she could. "I don't want to do that. I need to live in the proper world. Jake and Julius do, don't they?"

"That is quite different."

"Because they're men?"

Eleanor was shocked and distressed. "I don't want you to turn into one of these strident suffragette women, Clio. Women are not the same as men, thank God. I have brought you up to be a lady, and a wife and mother."

"In that order?" Clio demanded with sudden bitterness. "Is that all? What about to be a person, an individual, with my own rights?"

"*I* am an individual. But I have never felt ashamed of having devoted my life to my husband and children. How can you imagine that you will assert your individuality by sitting in some office addressing envelopes for a complete stranger who could hardly compare with your father or your brothers, or your own future husband?"

Clio had never seen her mother so angry, nor guessed that out of her anger would come articulate pride. She thought that she hardly knew Eleanor at all, not as herself rather than just Mother, and that there was a distance between them that she had never noticed.

Grace was her nearest female kin, and now Grace was removed from her too.

The sudden sense of her own isolation seemed significant and possessed of a kind of glamour. It strengthened her resolve, and at the same time she felt a quiver of laughter at Eleanor's idea of her entirely abstract future husband like a knight in armor outshining poor, disheveled Max Erdmann. *Perhaps I'll marry Max,* she thought, and had to swallow her smile before Eleanor could see and misinterpret it.

Humbly she said, "I didn't mean to belittle what you have done. You are the best mother. I love you." She put her cheek against Eleanor's, but Eleanor sat stiff and straight. "The war came between your childhood and mine. I don't believe that we can go back to the way we were before. None of us can. But it won't be so very much different for me, you know. I would have studied for three years and then found a job. I just want to begin a little earlier."

Eleanor only said, in exactly the same way as she had concluded every lost argument throughout their childhoods, "You must talk to your father about it."

It was much harder for Clio to attempt an explanation for Nathaniel. To Nathaniel, scholarship was the most important matter in the world, second only to his family. He could not comprehend Clio deliberately turning her back on it. She tried to make him understand the appetite and impatience that had grown within her following Pilgrim's casual warning and Grace's marriage, but she knew she was only rearranging words that her father did not want to hear.

"I want to begin properly, not to go on making ready for my life. I want to leave home, and Oxford, and start to fend for myself."

Nathaniel watched her face. He had grown heavier, and he laced his fingers over his stomach in a gesture that was becoming characteristic. His beard spread over his chest.

"Have you been so unhappy here?"

"No, I didn't mean that, of course I didn't. I just want to . . ."

"To go?" His fingers spread, and he shrugged. The gesture and his disappointment hurt her, but she kept her determination. "Go by all means, if that is what you want. But why turn your back on everything you have worked for? There is nothing wrong with London University, for example."

"I want to work at *Fathom*. I like the work they publish."

It was inadequate, she knew that it was, but she couldn't convey to Nathaniel the pull of a world that was so opposite to everything she had known. The regulars of Charlotte Street and the Eiffel were more interesting than female versions of the dons she had known all her life. Even the dust and litter of Max Erdmann's office seemed preferable to the book dust of the Bodleian.

Nathaniel's face was somber. "It's your life, Clio. I can't force you to do anything against your will. I hope you will remember that your mother and I are always here to help you, if you need us."

"Thank you, Pappy."

She had knelt down by his chair, ready to hug him, but he had only patted her shoulder. And then he had asked her, "Does this have anything to do with Grace's sudden marriage?"

"No," Clio said, almost truthfully. "Nothing."

That was all. The only concession she had had to make was to agree with the Senior Tutor that her place would be held open for her for another year. But she knew that she would not be coming back.

Blanche had asked her to come and live at Belgrave Square, and Eleanor had been determined that she should accept. Clio had told both of them, firmly, that she would be living in Gower Street with Jake. Eleanor had reacted as if she were planning to move into barracks with a division of the Life Guards.

"Who will chaperone you?" she quavered.

Clio smiled at her. "Girls don't need to be chaperoned anymore. They catch buses and go to tea shops and have bank accounts. Jake and I will look after each other."

"Who will *marry* you?"

As Grace had been married. Legitimized, placed in her niche in the world. Grace had an ambitious husband, a pretty little house, and soon she would be a mother. Clio did not want what had happened to Grace to happen to her. She couldn't make her mother understand that she was not made anxious by there being so few men left to meet the needs of all the women of her generation. She smiled again.

"Somebody will. Someday."

And so she had reached Gower Street, and freedom. With Jake's help she had borrowed or bargained for the minimum of domestic comforts, and they had moved in with their few possessions. Her Gilman picture hung over the narrow cast-iron grate in her bedroom, and her clothes were hidden behind a white curtain drawn across one of the corners of the room. The scenery was very like the bedsitting room in the picture. Clio thought that she might increase the likeness by painting the dingy walls blue, or maybe stencil them with borders of flowers and fruit. She could go out now, to Tottenham Court Road, to buy the colors.

She could do whatever she liked.

She called to Jake, "Do you want some tea?"

His face appeared around the door. "There isn't any."

Capably, smoothly, Clio told him, "I'm going out to buy some paint. I'll shop for us on my way back." She was domestic, the commander of her own kitchen, as well as a woman of the world.

"Get some muffins, or a cake or something, then, will you? A friend of mine is coming to tea, a girl. And Julius said he might look in too."

Anxiety assailed her at once. Jake was generally accompanied by some woman, rarely the same one, but this would be the first guest to be entertained at Gower Street. Everything must be done perfectly. Clio abandoned the paint scheme and tottered back from the shops with enough food to entertain the entire hospital to tea.

Julius arrived, and teased her about the feast spread out on the hastily scrubbed kitchen table.

"Be careful that you haven't exchanged the yoke of scholarship for the treadmill of catering for Jake's appetite."

"I'm happy to do it," Clio protested. "I like to see people eat."

"You sound like Grandmother Hirsh."

"I'm happy about that, too."

Jake's friend was a nurse from the hospital. She was Jewish, small and dark with wide, bright eyes. Clio guessed that she was a little older than Jake. Her name was Ruth Sherman. She shook Clio's hand warmly, but her glance was appraising, only softening when she turned to Jake. His eyes followed her wherever she moved.

Ruth was hungry. She explained to Clio that she was working a night shift and had only woken up an hour before. She would have to be on the ward at six and work until midnight before her break.

"And she does voluntary work in a free clinic, in her off-duty time," Jake said with pride. "We don't have enough nurses like Ruth."

"Please, eat as much as you can," Clio begged her. "Julius has teased me enough about there being far too much."

"But there are two kinds of cake. If you only saw the food in the nurses' hostel. This is wonderful."

Clio turned pink with pleasure. This was how it should be, she thought, this was what she wanted. To have friends and family gathered informally around the table, eating and talking.

Jake and Ruth told hospital stories, completing each other's sentences, smiling at each other. Clio began to understand that Ruth Sherman was more important to Jake than any of the other girls she had met with him. When the conversation turned serious, she listened attentively to what Ruth was saying, and saw that Julius did the same.

Ruth was an only child, born late to elderly parents who had wished for a boy. When they found they were the parents of a girl, they had set out to prove to themselves and to Ruth that she was as good as a boy. They had never put anything out of reach because of her sex. Ruth had been brought up to believe herself the equal of any man. When she emerged into the world, she was shocked to discover that her beliefs were not universally held. She had become a suffragette and a campaigner for women's rights. After qualifying as a nurse she spent her spare time working in a clinic for the women who lived in the back streets beyond Euston.

"They take care of everyone. Husbands, children. No one takes care of them," Ruth said. Her eyes glittered with indignation. "When women can vote, *all* women, we shall have a proper body of women MPs, not just Lady Astor in her furs. Then we shall be able to legislate for equality, for proper pay and benefits and medical care for mothers."

Listening, Clio was impressed. She had thought it an amazing advance that married women over thirty had achieved the vote, and that two women had been elected to Parliament and one had taken her seat. But to Ruth, so much was clearly only an inadequate beginning. Clio felt herself warming to her, liking her after an initial wariness. "One of those strident suffragette women," Eleanor had said. Ruth was not strident at all, she was small and low-voiced, but she had the air of invincibility.

"Will you achieve all that?" Clio asked her.

"Of course we will," Ruth said. "If you came to one of our clinics, you would see the strength that women have."

Jake took her hand. "I know your strength," he said.

"It's the same as your sister's. And your cousin Grace's. Jake has told me about her," Ruth added to Clio.

"Grace is married now. She's going to have a baby soon," Clio said.

Julius said nothing, but his expression changed. He rarely spoke of Grace these days.

"Married or single, old or young, rich or poor, Jewish or otherwise, it makes no difference," Ruth pronounced. "We have our strength and we must use it together."

It's a pretty idea, Clio thought, *but how, together? Grace and I? Our mothers and ourselves? Ruth and the Euston women?*

There were too many faces, all turned in different directions.

"I would like to come and see one of your clinics," Clio said aloud.

"We don't encourage sightseers."

"You could find something useful for me to do." Clio felt that she was always begging for something useful to do, as if all her life up until now had equipped her for nothing.

"Perhaps," Ruth agreed. She had finished her tea. She must have been very hungry, because there was very little left of all the food that Julius had laughed at. With Julius's help Clio cleared the table, and when they had finished, they found that Jake and Ruth had wandered away into his bedroom and closed the door.

"Let's go out, for a walk somewhere," Julius said.

Clio was glad to leave the flat. They walked down Gower Street, with the river of traffic, until they reached Bedford Square. The air was stale and motionless, and there was a veil of dirt suspended in it that needed rain to wash it away, but a breath of freshness still lingered under the trees in the square.

It was the beginning of August, the time when everyone Clio knew from her debutante days had left for the country, or for Scotland, or for the sea. Even Pilgrim had gone away, to paint in the south of France. That she was still unseasonably here, settled and about to start work, made Clio feel properly a Londoner. She looked affectionately at the homegoing office workers on the top decks of the buses, and the tide of summer dresses and business suits flowing toward the tube station. Max Erdmann had told her that he would be going on holiday himself in a few days' time, leaving her in charge at the *Fathom* office. Now that he had accepted her imminent arrival, there was no more talk of a week's trial.

"Give you a chance to prove yourself," Max had mumbled.

Clio was looking forward to the challenge.

They strolled under the trees, enjoying the shade. Julius was wearing a linen jacket and a panama hat, and he tipped the hat back on his head to look down at Clio.

"What did you think?" he asked.

"I was impressed."

"Did you like her?"

"Yes, I did. Didn't you?"

After a moment, Julius answered, "She is the kind of woman who is liked better by women than by men."

"Except for Jake, obviously." Clio was thinking that Julius would not be drawn to her. No one could be less like Grace.

"I think Jake has met his match this time," Julius observed.

"He looks happy enough."

"Yes, he does." They stopped walking and faced each other. Julius put his arm around Clio's waist. "You've still got me," he said.

Clio loved his knobbed shoulders and the elongated fingers of his bony hands. Julius had always been there, all her life, like the better half of herself. She kissed his warm, dry cheek. A woman passing by thought they were lovers and turned her head away, pursing her lips.

"What about you, Julius?" she asked gently.

"Falling in love?" He shook his head. "I play music. That's good enough for me." Neither of them mentioned Grace. After a moment they walked on, with their arms linked.

After surveying the contents of her wardrobe for a long time, Grace lifted out a narrow gray crêpe dress on its padded hanger. It was November now, three months after Cressida's birth, and she was thin enough again to wear her dressmaker's clever copies of Mme. Chanel's chic tunics. Anthony was not yet rich enough to buy her the real thing, although she was determined that he soon would be.

Grace lifted her white arms and let the folds of fluid crêpe drop over her head. Then she sat down at her dressing table and brushed her hair. She had just had it bobbed, and was still aware of the strange sensation of lightness around her bare neck and shoulders. She powdered her face with white powder and blackened her eyes with kohl. Then she leaned forward to the glass and with careful concentration drew in her mouth with bright red lipstick.

Grace liked the ritual of dressing more now that it was a private affair between herself and her wardrobe and cosmetics. Her clothes and underclothes and her hair were much simpler than they had been, although her maquillage had become more elaborate. She did not need or want a lady's maid, even if she could have afforded to employ one. To run the house in South Audley Street, she had only a cook-housekeeper and a housemaid, a nurse for the baby, a charwoman and an odd-job man for the heavy work, and Anthony's valet-driver, who doubled as a butler when they entertained. Even with this fraction of her mother's indoor staff, she was regarded with envy by most of her young married friends. They telephoned each other with invitations for cocktails mixed by the husbands, or for pot-luck suppers, or for parties where the rugs were pushed back ready for dancing at any time of the day or night.

It was all supposed to be informal and impromptu and the greatest fun. *Great fun* was a phrase they used a lot. "It was great fun, darling," they told one another, all the new young married couples.

Grace picked up a crystal bottle and puffed a cloud of scent around her head. Then she snapped a heavy silver bracelet like a cuff onto each wrist and turned to look back over her own shoulder into the glass. Her back was bare almost to the waist, and the lines of her uncorseted body showed clearly under the gray crêpe. Her cropped hair made her neck look like a long, fragile stalk. She was glad to be thin again. She had hated the swollen balloon shape of her pregnancy.

Behind her own satisfying reflection she saw the door open as her husband came into her bedroom.

"Darling, you're home."

He came to her, dropping a kiss onto her shoulder and then holding her close to him.

"I'm home, thank God. I've had enough of the City for today. The pound's down below three dollars fifty."

"Poor old baby. How boring."

Anthony breathed in her scent with a luxurious sigh, and then let his hands fall to his sides. He knew that Grace was not interested in the minutiae of his business. He didn't expect it, and he didn't love her any the less for it.

"How about you, my darling? Have you had a busy day?"

Grace made a pretty face. "Frantic." She had shopped and had lunch with a girlfriend, and then spent an hour arranging the flowers in the drawing room. She felt jittery with unused energy rather than tired, but *frantic* was what one always admitted to, on the telephone or kissing cheeks at parties.

"How's Cressida today?"

It was Anthony's invariable question. He was deeply devoted to his baby daughter.

"Utterly perfect. Nurse will bring her downstairs when you're dressed."

Anthony took off his jacket and removed the gold links from his shirt cuffs. "Who is it this evening?"

"Family, darling. Mine. Jake and his girl, and Julius and Clio. Just some cocktails and a little supper. Does that suit?"

"Of course it does." Anthony was always pleased to see Grace's cousins. Clio especially. "Do I have time for a bath?"

"The very quickest one. I'll bring you a drink, shall I?"

Anthony walked through the adjoining dressing room and into his bedroom where his valet had laid out his evening clothes. He strolled into his bathroom, whistling, and ran his own bath. He could hear the jazz music that Grace had put on the gramophone downstairs. Steam silvered the mirrors and clouded the tortoiseshell backs of his brushes. When Grace came in with a Sidecar, the frosted glass dripped cold tears of condensation. He wanted her to perch on the side of the bath and talk to him, but she laughed at the suggestion.

"And let your steam make my hair as lank as pondweed? Do hurry up and come downstairs."

He watched her sinuous bare back recede, and then lay in the seductive warmth. He tipped his glass and drank, relishing the jolt of alcohol in his empty stomach. He was thinking that he was happy; happy rather than content, because contentment implied a lack of ambition, and Anthony was very ambitious. He intended to make a great deal of money, and then to take over as senior partner in the stockbrokers Brock & Cowper when his father retired to play golf in the country. After that, when he was securely established, he aimed to be adopted for a safe Conservative seat. Then, once elected, he would campaign for economic reform; there would be plenty of opportunities for young men when the Conservatives were returned to power.

There was a great deal to be done.

But he was happy now, in this isolated moment. There was nothing he wished to change. He had a momentary sense that his life was like an oriental rug, the largest expanse of it still tightly rolled but a small strip unfurled, so that the beginning of the intricate pattern was revealed. He had Grace, best of all he had Grace, but he also had Cressida. Anthony still counted it as a miracle that everything had come to him so quickly and easily. At one minute there had seemed no hope that Grace would ever agree to marry him, and then all at once she had accepted him and there had been the mercifully simple wedding.

"If you love me, just marry me," Grace had said. "I can't bear all the fuss and trousseaux and dressing up like a doll."

He had been dazed, but he was also so happy that he would have agreed to anything. His wife-to-be was capricious, Anthony knew that. He loved her no less for it.

Then, almost as soon as they were married, Grace was pregnant. The baby's prematurity had been an anxiety, but Cressida was born quickly and easily and she was a robust little creature. Anthony adored his daughter.

Soon, he thought, as he relaxed in the hot water, there would be more children—sons—and the continuation of their comfortable family life. They had their pretty house, admirably arranged by Grace, and they had amusing friends and more invitations than they could respond to.

Anthony finished his drink. If Grace did not seem especially happy, it was because happiness was unfashionable. It was necessary to be frantic, or excited, or languid, or dismissive. Not plainly, sturdily happy. He did not mind being unfashionable himself. Grace had more than enough style for the two of them. He loved her very much, and all the variety of her quicksilver moods.

Downstairs, in her first-floor drawing room, Grace was standing at one of the windows with her cocktail glass and a cigarette in her hand. Looking down into the wintry street she saw a car drive up and a group of people scrambling out of it. She recognized Clio, in a little hat and a short fur cape over a pleated skirt. The man with her was Julius, looking serious and formal in evening clothes. Grace's red lips curved with affection at the sight of him.

But there were more people. There was a short man in a greasy-looking overcoat. With an effort of memory, Grace placed him as Max Erdmann, Clio's boss at the little literary magazine, whatever its name was. And then two others, one in a man's dinner suit although she was plainly a woman with a mass of reddish hair, and the other tall and muffled in an opera cloak, his face hidden by a black hat.

Grace leaned forward, stiff with dismay, until her forehead

touched the cold glass. There was no mistake. It was Jeannie and Pilgrim.

She tried to tell herself that Clio must have offered them a lift, that they would set off now in some different direction, but the thought had hardly formed before they crossed the pavement in front of the house in a phalanx, with only Clio hanging back a little. Grace lost sight of them beneath her, and at once the doorbell sounded. The butler would come up the stairs from the basement and let them in, then show them upstairs to the drawing room.

Grace looked wildly around. There was nowhere to go, of course, and Anthony would be down in a moment. She would have to brazen it out, whatever it was that Clio was plotting.

A second later they were in the room, all five of them. Pilgrim and Jeannie and Max brought a distinct smell of the saloon bar. Clio came across the rug to Grace with both hands outstretched to take hers.

"Max brought Jeannie and Pilgrim into the office just as I was leaving. They both said they would so much like to see you and your house, and everything. . . ." Her voice trailed away, betraying her helplessness. Grace took hold of her cold hands for a moment, and then let go. Not Clio's plot, then.

"Lady Grace." It was Erdmann's voice. "They would admit *no* denial."

And you? Grace thought. *I don't recall inviting you, either.* But she only said, silkily, "Pilgrim and Jeannie are old friends of mine. I couldn't be more thrilled to have them drop in like this. Thank you for bringing everyone, Clio darling."

Pilgrim enveloped her in his cloak, and, like some made-up old stage-door roué, Jeannie mouthed exaggerated kisses at her. Grace guessed that they must have been doing some steady drinking. She felt sympathy for Clio, even in the midst of her anxiety about what might happen next.

Julius had said nothing. He stood still, looking at Grace, as if trying to absorb her into himself. She went to him now and hugged him, and let herself feel reassured by his protection.

She managed to say, "Now, shall we all have a cocktail? Jeannie, Pilgrim, do you need any more to drink?"

If she had been hoping they would say no, she was disappointed.

"Most certainly we do," Pilgrim boomed. Jeannie arranged herself on a sofa and patted the cushion next to her to indicate that Julius should sit down.

Anthony came in. He was much too well mannered to betray any surprise at the unexpected addition to the company. After shaking hands he went to the silver tray of bottles and glasses and busied himself with mixing drinks. When everyone was holding a fresh cocktail, he told Grace, "I went along to see Cressida. Nurse says she will bring her down, just for five minutes." He was proud of his baby. He wanted everyone to admire her.

There was no time for Grace to forbid it on the grounds of the room being too smoky or there being too many people. The butler was showing Jake and Ruth into the drawing room, and behind Jake's shoulder Grace could already see the nurse's white starched headdress. The bundle of baby was in her arms.

Pilgrim was not so drunk as to be unaware of what was happening. Rather, he was at the stage of intoxication where the action around him seemed slowed and artificially highlighted. He saw Grace standing in the middle of the room. Like a snapshot frozen out of the surrounding commotion, she was very still and there was fear in her eyes as she looked at him.

With a leap of drunken intuition, Pilgrim understood everything. He had lazily speculated, and it was mostly mischievous curiosity that had drawn him here this evening, but now he knew for sure.

He had fathered the baby that the nurse was tenderly putting into Anthony Brock's arms.

Grace had found herself pregnant. That was the reason for her hasty marriage to her stockbroker admirer, that was the secret that frightened her, and that was why her cousins were staring at him like rabbits hypnotized by a snake. That was why the pliant Clio had been so unwilling to bring him to South Audley Street. Even Max and the little Jewess seemed to smell the threat in the air. Only Mr. Brock and the nurse were oblivious to it. They were adjusting the baby's dress, smiling down on her, making little reassuring murmurs.

Pilgrim stood up.

Watching him sweep across the room Grace thought that he looked like a great black bat. She found that her hands were shaking so much that the contents of her glass slopped on her dress. Pilgrim stopped at Anthony's shoulder and hung over Cressida. The nurse stepped respectfully backward to stand against the wall with her hands folded over her apron.

Pilgrim saw a round, rosy face and a pair of unblinking eyes. A fringe of dark, spiky hair protruded under the frill of a bonnet, and a small fist had escaped from the swaddle of white blanket. A tiny whitish bubble swelled between the miniature lips.

It was a baby, that was all, a routine assemblage of limbs and powdered buttocks and oversized cranium. He felt nothing, no wish to touch it and no prompting of curiosity. What he did feel was admiration for Grace, and a touch of gratitude. She had rescued herself from disaster, without reference to him. She had conveyed herself here, to this elegant drawing room and the protection of a husband and eager father. Grace had done well, and he knew what he owed her.

He felt all the eyes fastened on him. He waited, furling his cloak, and then he unleashed his widest smile.

"Why is the young of the human species so *extravagantly* ugly?"

The silence was broken by a clockwork chorus of protests and exclamations.

Jeannie left Julius and swayed across to examine the baby herself. "Pilgrim, you're full of beer and wind. She's a beautiful baby. Look at her darling little fingernails, will you?"

Pilgrim affected to take a closer look. "Mmm. Your chin, Brock, I think. But she'll probably turn out to be a beauty when called upon."

The conversation around them broke out in relieved bursts. Ruth went deliberately to the nurse and began to ask her about her training. Jeannie sidled back to Julius, and Clio and Jake fell on each other as if they had not met for weeks. Pilgrim felt the talk like bubbles, buoying them all up. He wanted another drink, but he went to Grace, who was still standing alone in the middle of the room.

She handed him her half-empty glass. "Hold this for me, would you? I've made a stupid stain on my frock." She had taken out a lace handkerchief and began to scrub at the wet mark.

He saw how her hands trembled. "I should congratulate you," he murmured.

Her head jerked up. She was fierce, ready to attack or defend, and she was so beautiful that he wanted to kiss her. He drank the remains of her cocktail instead, and dabbed his mouth with the back of his hand. Grace's distaste showed in her glance, but it only made him feel even more affectionate approval. Grace was no milky girl. She was a survivor.

"I wish you every happiness in the world," he mumbled, waving the now-empty glass. The last shot of alcohol seemed to have taken him over the edge. "I mean that. You *deserve* every happiness."

Suddenly, confronting the lurching painter who had seemed to hold all her security in his grimy hands, Grace felt her fears dropping away. Pilgrim's eyes were barely focusing. He was on the point of becoming hilariously drunk. He knew nothing, and evidently cared even less. He couldn't give her away, and the magic circle never would. She was sure of that, even sure of Clio, after seeing her distress tonight. Clio loved Anthony, of course. She wouldn't wish to see him hurt.

Relief and elation propelled her across to extricate the flattered nurse from Ruth's attention. "Cressida should go back to the nursery now. She mustn't be excited by too many people."

At once, Anthony surrendered his daughter, and she was swept away. Grace held up her arms. "I must go upstairs to change my frock. *Look* what a silly mess I've made. But I want you all to stay to supper. Yes, you absolutely must, I won't hear you say anything about going anywhere else. We can forage in the kitchen and scratch some things together. It'll be the greatest fun. Anthony, darling, what about some more drinks for the troops?"

They were all smiling, even Jake's dour little girlfriend. Grace felt the winning effect of her own sparkle. She was in control, she could defend her redoubt, such as it was. As she passed by him, she lightly kissed the top of Anthony's head.

She was beguiling enough, Ruth thought. With her gaiety she wound up something inside you that made you want to laugh and joke and be frivolous. There was nothing wrong with that, if you had the time. She glanced at Clio. It was odd that Clio and Grace looked so alike, but were so different. It wasn't that Clio wasn't good company, and funny when she wanted to be, but Clio also had her thoughtful and responsible side. Clio understood that there was work to be done, but Ruth didn't suppose that Lady Grace had ever done a stroke of work in her life.

Ruth didn't make friends very easily, but she counted Clio as a friend now. She knew, for example, that Clio understood, without ever having referred to it, that Ruth did not feel at home in the muted luxury of this rose-pink and gray drawing room. She knew because when they came to South Audley Street, Clio took the trouble to draw her into the talk and to give a clear lead through the maze of etiquette.

For a household that took pride in its informality, there were a surprising number of rules to be observed compared with, say, Gower Street. Grace would have insisted that there were no rules, that this was Liberty Hall, darling, but of course that was not the truth. If any one of her guests had made the wrong move with a table placing, or a servant's attention, or any other move in the dance, then there would be a brief stare, and then the quick, fluent, and well-mannered move to cover up the solecism.

Ruth was far too proud to risk making a mistake. She watched Clio carefully, and was grateful to her.

Ruth was suspicious of Society. Not the cozy society of her parents and their friends, of quiet card evenings and fork suppers, and wedding and anniversary and bar mitzvah celebrations in their distant suburb, but this cocktail-drinking Society that was written about in the gossip pages of the newspapers and was governed by arcane laws that Ruth knew she would never understand. It was populated by diamond-brilliant creatures like Grace, and Clio and Julius and Jake seemed to move in and out of it at will, perfectly at ease.

It was odd, Ruth found herself thinking, that even though she felt awkward in it, and for all her sensible resolution not to care whether she did or not, she was still fascinated by this other world. She knew that it was part of Jake's attraction for her. He had an air of ease and natural authority that made him quite unlike the eager, anxious, and hard-working Jewish boys she had known before. She approved of Jake's pacifism and his wartime work, and she believed that by listening to him talking and talking about them with him, she had helped him to overcome some of the terrible experiences of the field hospital. She was secretly proud that he refused to discuss those experiences with anyone but her. She approved of Jake's dedication to medicine, too, and his cleverness, but she had fallen in love with his glamour.

All the nurses had.

And yet he had chosen her. It was the right choice; Ruth had not been brought up to underestimate herself, and she had no quavering fears that she was in some way not good enough for Jake. She was hopelessly in love and was satisfied by his devotion in return. She intended to marry him. They would make a valuable life together.

It was quite simple, as Ruth believed most things to be if they were properly handled. The clear certainty of her future made her dark face shine. From across the room where he was talking to Anthony Brock, Jake looked at her admiringly.

Grace was back again. She had exchanged her gray for peacock blue, and now there was a peacock's feather in a bandeau around her head. The feather dipped and nodded as she moved around the circle.

Ruth smoothed the folds of her good dress over her lap. She knew that if she tried to wear a feather in her own hair, she would look like a Red Indian, and the knowledge made her reluctantly the more admiring of Grace.

Grace was saying gaily, "I have been down to talk to Cook, and she says there is more than enough dinner for all of us. She will certainly give notice tomorrow, but for tonight we are safe. Shall we move downstairs?"

With the smallest of gestures, she indicated that Anthony was to offer Ruth his arm down to dinner, and that Julius was to take Jeannie. She held out her own hand to Pilgrim, and left Clio to Jake. Max Erdmann brought up the rear, alone. They all followed Grace in their ordered file, even Jeannie, as meek as Victorian children.

The dining room was decorated in chalk white and black. A suite of starkly black-and-white modern architectural photographs hung on the walls. The only color was provided by heavy wicker baskets filled with hothouse flowers, scented and luxurious in late November. Anthony and Grace took opposite ends of the table and disposed their guests between them. Pilgrim and Max seized their glasses of Anthony's good claret as soon as they were filled, and Ruth took covert note of the files of knives and forks laid out in front of her.

Grace surveyed her table. "Clio," she began. "What have you been doing all this age? How are things at *Depths*?"

"*Fathom.*"

"*Fathom.*"

"Stimulating." Clio smiled. "Hard work, of course."

"You are only saying so for my benefit," Max interrupted. He leaned across to Grace. "Miss Hirsh has nothing to do but lunch with her admirers from amongst our contributors and to take telephone calls from the remainder who have not been able to achieve a luncheon. When there is a letter to be typed, I ask *very* politely, to make sure I am not treading on the toes of a love-sick Georgian poet or a swooning Vorticist."

"Max," Clio protested.

Grace's expression of polite interest never wavered.

"Quite true," Pilgrim boomed. "When did I see you in the Fitz, Clio? Wednesday or Thursday? You were surrounded by adoring men of letters, all weeping tears of frustration into their halves of bitter. No time even to speak to poor old Pilgrim."

"You exaggerate, Pilgrim, as usual. I was talking to one poor man who can't get his work published, and another who has a wife and two children in Fulham. And I always have time to speak to you."

Under the table, out of sight, Grace's fingers pleated and repleated the hem of her napkin.

Jeannie cocked her head toward Clio, as if estimating the level of threat in what she said. Then she seemed to shrug it off, and leaned closer to Julius. Her hand rested on his arm, and she put her red mouth to his ear, whispering.

"There are two poems by Mr. Eliot in the new issue," Clio primly told Grace.

"They are profoundly brilliant," and "They are unmitigated balls," Max and Pilgrim said simultaneously. A fist-thumping argument broke out at once, with Clio in the thick of it. Grace watched them, her expression still unreadable.

What a crew, Ruth thought. There was no need to worry about her own demeanor this evening. No one would remark on it if she danced on the table. She turned back with relief to her conversation with Anthony. They had been talking about the miners' strike. To her surprise, Anthony was agreeing that the miners had a just cause.

Daringly she asked, "Why do you hope to stand as a Conservative?"

"Because the Conservatives are the only party who can achieve anything now. The Liberals are finished."

The conversation eddied on.

They were all drinking steadily, even Julius and Clio.

Grace felt that she was adrift, even though she was sitting at the head of her own table, surrounded by the presents from her marriage in a room that she had designed herself and with her husband opposite her.

Sometimes, like now, when she looked at Anthony, she could hardly convince herself that she knew him at all. He was a pleasant stranger, surely, not her husband and Cressida's father?

Grace frightened herself by almost letting out a wild laugh. She lifted her napkin, the hem ribbed with pleat marks, and dabbed her mouth.

That alarming moment was past, at least. Pilgrim didn't know, couldn't know, and the secret was safe. All she had to do was to live with it, day by day. She could do that. She was sitting here now, wasn't she, with Pilgrim and Anthony at the same table?

Pilgrim had spilled red wine on his necktie. He was waving his hands about, big heavy hands with uncleaned fingernails.

Part of her recoiled from him, with fear as well as distaste. But there was another part of herself, unburied, that remembered the afternoons in the studio with the rain needling the glass roof and the lazy hissing of the gas fire. She had stretched herself out on the divan, comfortable in the fetid warmth, relishing the freedom of nakedness. And then Pilgrim had covered her, prickling with hair and smelling of French tobacco and garlic. She had not recoiled then.

Grace stared at the tablecloth, not trusting herself to look anywhere else.

She didn't think that she would recoil now, in the same place. What Pilgrim had done was so different from Anthony's gentlemanly approach from his dressing room and into her bed.

"Grace?"

It was Anthony's voice. She looked up, and realized that she had forgotten to signal for the removal of the plates.

"Isn't this fun?" she heard her own bright voice responding.

It was not just Pilgrim who attracted her; in a sense it was not even Pilgrim, but his milieu. It was grubby and sluttish and immediate, governed by appetites and their gratification.

Not like mine, Grace thought. *What governs me, apart from fear of losing face?*

It was Clio who had achieved the life she wanted for herself. Grace watched her as she sparred with Max and Jake. She looked happy and animated.

The taste of jealousy was becoming familiar in Grace's mouth.

Jeannie was growing soulful in drink. She rested her head against Julius's shoulder, and tears made tracks in the black paint around her eyes. There were red lipstick marks on Julius's cheek. Max Erdmann was blinking like an owl, and Pilgrim had taken to refilling his own glass in the intervals in his monologue. He was a good talker when he was drunk. Anthony and Jake were listening and laughing.

Grace knew that she should have brought the evening to an end. But some perverse instinct possessed her. She wanted to wring some satisfaction for herself out of the party; she wanted to stake her claim on these people who slipped away from her like beads of mercury. While they were here, they were at least partly hers, even if she couldn't stop them rolling together and agglomerating, little silver beads into bigger ones.

She didn't want them to go noisily into the night without her. She didn't want them to go and leave her alone with her husband.

"Upstairs!" she called out. "Let's go upstairs and dance."

"It's getting late," Anthony murmured, although everyone else seemed to want to dance.

Grace kissed him on the nose. "Darling, don't be stuffy."

There was a big pile of shiny black records beside the gramophone in the drawing room. She picked one out, and Jake and Julius rolled back the rug.

Anthony came to claim her, and Max Erdmann almost fell over in his rush to Clio. Jake and Ruth moved together, and Pilgrim turned his attention to the whiskey decanter. Jeannie lay at full stretch on a sofa and tried to pull Julius down beside her. Grace and Anthony tangoed past, and Grace saw that Julius was blushing like a schoolboy. She slipped away from Anthony and went to rescue him.

"Dance with me, Julius, won't you?" Gratefully he took her in his arms.

They danced in silence. They were both reminded of the lessons of their childhood, when they had been one of the pairs of children circling under a teacher's scrutiny in the ballroom of somebody's London house. Julius had always been the better dancer. He had listened to the music, serious-faced, when Grace wanted to run away and hide behind the chairs. He bent his head close to hers now.

"Don't be unhappy," he said softly.

Two spots of color showed beneath Grace's white face-powder. "I'm not in the least unhappy. I'm having the very best time."

She would have repeated her protestation, but her attention was diverted. Jeannie had staggered to her feet and in doing so had caught at a spindly tripod table placed beside the sofa. The table overbalanced, and a fluted glass vase smashed on the parquet floor.

"Steady," Anthony said, catching at her elbow.

Jeannie rounded on him. She frowned in the attempt to focus. Then she shook his hand off and tossed her head, almost falling again.

"Bourgeoisie," she yelled at the room. "Bloody silver salvers and decanters and napkin rings. How d'ye do and old boy and kiss my backside. Think I'm not good enough, don't you?"

"I don't think anything," Anthony murmured.

Jeannie was gathering her strength. She swung her fist and connected with Anthony's cheekbone. There was a sharp smacking sound. Anthony hardly flinched, but he stared at her, his face turning a dull red. Ruth left Jake and went to put her arm around Jeannie's waist.

"Stop it," she said clearly. "Stop it now, there's a good girl."

With a sigh, Pilgrim put his glass down. "Jeannie. It's time to go home."

He could hardly walk straight, but he went to support her other side. They leaned onto Ruth like a house of cards about to topple. Jeannie gave a sidelong, cunning smile and then pointed.

"Julius can take me home. Lives just across the passage. Lovely. Convenient."

"We'll go together, all of us," Julius said. He looked around with a touch of desperation. "Clio will see you to bed."

"Don't want *Clio.*"

Embarrassment galvanized them all into a rush of activity. Pilgrim and Jeannie were half carried, half hurried down the stairs. Taxis were hailed, and Jeannie was levered into one with Clio and Julius. Jake and Ruth took charge of Pilgrim and Max. Once the cabs had turned the corner Grace and Anthony went inside and trailed slowly back up the stairs to the disordered drawing room.

Grace stood with her arms hanging at her sides. With the toe of her shoe, she poked at the broken glass on the floor. There was a knuckle mark on Anthony's cheekbone.

"I'm sorry," she said flatly.

He was going to touch her, but she held up her hand, fending him off. Their eyes met in silence. There was the chance to commiserate with each other about their evening and then to laugh about it, but Grace would not take it. She wouldn't put herself on Anthony's side against Pilgrim and his friends. They both knew that the refusal was significant.

"There's nothing to be sorry about," Anthony said at length. He bent down and began to pick up the tiny fragments of glass.

"Violet can do that in the morning," she told him, but he ignored her. Grace left him and went upstairs to her bedroom.

Clio sat in front of the gas fire in the sitting room at Gower Street. The wine she had drunk had made her feel dazed and thirsty but not at all sleepy. She had made a pot of tea and put on the Chinese silk robe that she had bought in imitation of Grace's, although she never felt as dashing in it as Grace looked in hers. Now she was trying to read the manuscript of a long story that Max had passed on to her for an opinion. It was about a pig and a monkey, and was probably clever and allegorical, but the significance of it evaded her tonight.

She shuffled the typed pages together and let them lie in her lap.

Max would want her comments, but she knew from experience that he wouldn't be looking for them tomorrow morning. Max wouldn't appear in the Doughty Street office until after lunch, and then he would spend most of the afternoon groaning and resting his head in his hands. In peaceful solitude she would open and arrange the post, answer the telephone, and chat to anyone who called in person. She liked being on her own at *Fathom,* and the illusion of being in charge.

It was only an illusion, of course. Max was far too careful of his paper baby to give her any real, threatening responsibility.

Clio stared at the opening paragraph again. She was beginning to form the heretical opinion that Max's latest enthusiasm was for several thousand words of pretentious nonsense. She twitched the end of the plait that hung over her shoulder and laid it over her top lip, moustache-fashion, as she had done as a schoolgirl concentrating over an essay.

She heard the front door open and close downstairs. Jake was passing the solicitors' offices that occupied the ground floor. He had been to take Ruth back to the nurses' hostel.

They had deposited Pilgrim and Max on the corner of Charlotte Street and gone on to Julius's digs. Between them Clio and Ruth had put Jeannie to bed, not very gently.

"How can anyone live like this?" Ruth had wondered, wrinkling her nose as she looked at the mess in the room. Clio had only laughed. They left Jeannie lying on her side—"In case she vomits in her sleep," Ruth explained—and snoring loudly. Julius was clearly relieved.

Jake came in and stood in front of Clio, his back to the fire. When she saw his face she put the manuscript aside.

"What's happened?" she asked. His expression reminded her of the way he had looked when he was given a bicycle for his fourteenth birthday. He was dazzled, and at the same time afraid that the prize might be snatched away again.

"I asked Ruth to marry me. She said yes."

Clio leaped up and wrapped her arms around his neck. "I'm so pleased. I'm so happy for you both. Oh, Jake, I truly am pleased." There were tears in her eyes. "When? When will it be?"

"Next year, after I qualify."

Evidence of Ruth's prudent common sense in that. Nothing hurried, nothing impulsive. Clio held both Jake's hands, looking into his face. His happiness was plain to see.

"Grace, and now you. Only me and Julius left."

"Your turn will come," Jake told her. "You'll see. If that's what you want."

"I don't think I know what I want," Clio said, almost to herself. She felt that the words struck an inappropriate, melancholy note. In a different voice she said, "There's some tea, is that celebratory enough? There isn't anything to drink."

"I never want to see another drink. This evening was so awful." They laughed at the recollection of it.

Grace's engagement diary was lying on the table beside her bed, and she looked at it before she turned off the light.

Tomorrow she would have lunch with another friend, a young married woman like herself. They would eat very little and smoke at the table, in defiance of custom. They would gossip desultorily about the people they knew in common. In the evening Grace had accepted an invitation for Anthony and herself to dine with one of the couples in their set. There would be cocktails, more gossip, and perhaps a sortie to a nightclub. She would dance with the husbands of the other women, and flirt with them if she could summon the energy.

She hadn't bothered to look at the arrangements for the day after that. She closed the little book and reached up for the light switch.

Grace lay and looked up into the darkness. She had locked the door that led into Anthony's dressing room and bedroom. She waited to hear him turn the handle, wanting to know that he had tried to come in to her. She listened hard, straining into the silence with such intensity that she felt the pain in her temples. After all the drinking she had done, she felt that the bones of her skull might collapse into the deeper darkness within her head. She didn't hear anything.

Nine

ELIZABETH'S VISITS TO THE HOUSE in Little Venice were sometimes fruitless. On the bad days Clio sat in her chair, outwardly the same small, upright figure, but her memory had slipped out of focus, and she asked her visitor querulously why her tea was late, and where her usual nurse had gone. And then on other days her mind was clearer, and she seemed to welcome the opportunity to relive her memories.

On these days Elizabeth let her talk, interested in the links and connections of reminiscence although the threads were often buried too deeply for her to follow. She had a sense of the older woman's recollections forming a fragile web, and her mind traveling out and along the filaments like the spider darting from its still place at the center.

"What was she like, when she was a little girl?" Elizabeth asked once.

Clio had been rambling. One minute she was recalling the scent of the roses that Eleanor had grown in the Oxford garden, and in the next she was disparaging the upbringing of modern children.

"We were taught to hold up our heads, speak when spoken to. We did the same for our own children. Cressida, Romy . . ."

Clio did not like to be interrupted in the unraveling of her memories. She waved her knotted hand impatiently. "Who? What was *who* like?"

"Cressida. My mother. When she was small."

There were photographs, of course. It had been one of Grace's patient occupations to mount them in albums, each snapshot cornered with triangular hinges and captioned with names and dates. Elizabeth had been through all the big, heavy volumes, pursuing and reidentifying the faces that smiled out of groups on lawns, on beaches, or around tables. The thick, dark gray pages were brittle but well preserved, and still interleaved with whitish tissue that covered the hundreds of captured smiles like so many shrouds.

Amongst them there were pictures of Cressida in the elaborate baby clothes of the time, propped up against cushions or held by a uniformed nurse. There were more informal snapshots of her toddling in the sunshine with her hand in Anthony's, or at Stretton perched on a tiny pony, or dressed up as Little Miss Muffet for some village fête with a mob cap on her head and a huge spider made from pipe cleaners crouching on her shoulder.

There were almost none of her alone with Grace. Elizabeth could only recall one. There was no caption beneath it, unusually, not even a date, but it was clearly Cressida's christening. The baby was dressed in the Leominster christening robe, a waterfall of antique lace. Her mother seemed to hold her inexpertly, in a bundle, instead of showing her off. Only her round head and one small fist were visible. Grace was wearing a black-and-white organdy dress, trimmed with inset bands of ribbon. She gazed into the eye of the camera from beneath the brim of a black ciré hat decorated with osprey feathers. Her face was expressionless.

"She was well behaved. A good, quiet little girl."

Grace's photograph albums were revealing, but only to a superficial level. It was most noticeable that for the years following the Brocks' marriage until sometime in 1927, almost all the photographs that Grace had chosen were of parties. There were the startled eyes and half-turned heads of flashbulb pictures snatched through a veil of cigarette smoke in nightclubs and restaurants, where the men had white ties and brilliantined hair and the women held glasses to lips painted a plum red that looked black in the flash. Everyone seemed always to be laughing, or drinking, or tilting languidly back in a chair to squint through the smoke.

Other pictures were taken on country-house lawns, where terraces or open French doors provided the backdrop for informal groups in deck chairs or crowded hilariously onto sunbeds. The men wore flannels and the women sundresses, and they cuddled together on the beds and on the rugs spread out on the grass, husbands with other men's wives, and the wives with anyone but their own husbands. Their mouths were often open because they were calling out to the photographer, and there were waving arms and bare feet and open-necked shirts. There was usually a portable gramophone, tucked beside one of the deck chairs, and a tray of glasses, and someone at the front striking a theatrical pose.

There were more pictures of parties on beaches in the south of France, and some of the Venice Lido, with men and women in almost identical bathing suits that covered their shoulders and thighs. In these photographs there was more horseplay, with the women riding on the men's shoulders and the men wrestling in the sand, and tanned arms draped over shoulders as they crowded together into the frame, all of them laughing in the sun.

There were photographs of two or three couples squeezed into big shiny cars, waving; of barely recognizable faces at fancy-dress parties; frowning through boot-blacking or beneath turbans; of tennis parties and race-meetings and Christmases.

Elizabeth noted that all these gatherings seemed to leave little room for the family. There were no pictures of Grace and Anthony alone together. When they did appear in the same photograph, it was at opposite ends of some group, over a caption in Grace's erratic handwriting that would read, "Reggie, Ivor, Viola, Katharine, self, Diana, St. John, Duff, Anthony. Deauville, 1926."

After the baby pictures Cressida hardly appeared at all. Sometimes she was there to one side, almost like a shadow, her pale face half turned from the camera or hidden by a hank of dark hair. She was in the very few family groups that Grace had recorded. There was one at Stretton, where she was a five-year-old standing solemnly in front of her Uncle Thomas, and another at Oxford, taken a year or so later at a birthday party for Nathaniel. She was holding Tabby's hand and looking over her shoulder, as if searching for Anthony in the row of men at the back. Grace was near the center, giving the camera her expressionless stare.

Cressida was smiling in only two of her photographs, and in both of them she was alone with Anthony. In one of them he was swinging her in the air, and in the other he was on horseback. Cressida was perched in front of him, holding tightly to the pommel of the saddle, and her face was suffused with happiness.

Elizabeth had gone back to that picture again and again. All her prospecting through Grace's albums of the Twenties brought her back to the same place. Cressida had adored Anthony. And Grace had never been a mother. She had been many things, but not a mother to her only child.

Clio stopped talking, perhaps out of weariness, more probably because she had seen that Elizabeth was not listening.

"Have you had enough for today?" Elizabeth asked, as gently as she could.

She was often relieved when their interviews came to an end, but the relief was tinged with disappointment. She came away with the feeling that Clio could tell more, if she wanted to. Perhaps there was one story or one small detail that would illuminate Grace for her, but the old woman wouldn't part with it.

"Have *you*?" Clio snapped back.

"No. If I'm not tiring you." Elizabeth gazed around the room, looking for something neutral to remark on, to set their talk going again.

There were no photographs here. None of her husband or child, as if Clio's happiness in the long years of her marriage were a matter to be kept private from visitors. There was only the portrait, *The Janus Face,* behind Clio's chair. Elizabeth wondered yet again why she kept it there. Pilgrim's reputation had risen and fallen, and then fallen further still. But he was still representative of the avant-garde of his period. There were three or four of his pictures in the Tate collection, although not currently on display. A major portrait of his was worth money, and Clio was not a rich woman. Elizabeth examined the streaming hair and the Amazonian shoulders, and the staring, straining faces.

"You don't like it, do you?" Clio remarked. "You sit there, frowning at it."

"Does it matter whether I like it or not? I find it oppressive. The size of it, the weight, in a room this size . . ."

Surprisingly, Clio laughed. It was a thin, high sound, like the winding down of a mechanical toy. "It was once considered rather fine. I stopped asking myself long ago whether I really liked it or not. Here it is, and here it stays. Pilgrim gave it to me, you know, after my father died in 1942. For all those years it hung in the Woodstock Road. In the same place, facing the garden. Pilgrim only took it back once. For his big retrospective." When her memories took hold of her, Clio's voice grew stronger, and the swooping accent of the Twenties debutante more noticeable. The laugh came again, louder, a clockwork rattle.

"Retrospective, dear, if you please. That was very Pilgrim. When was it, now? Nineteen twenty-six. Or 1927, perhaps. He must have been somewhere in his late thirties, no older than that. At the very peak of his popularity. There was a big party, a private view, in the gallery in Albemarle Street. I remember it so clearly. Everyone was there. Everyone."

Clio grinned, it could only be described as a grin, showing the pink superstructure of her upper false teeth.

"Grace and Anthony were there."

"Tell me about it," Elizabeth said.

"I nearly didn't go. I was working at the Mothers' Clinic." She broke off and glared at Elizabeth. "Do you know about that? Do you know who Dr. Stopes is?"

"Yes, of course. The birth-control pioneer."

"I worked there with Jake, and Ruth. Ruth wouldn't go on to the party, she didn't care for that sort of thing. She went home to Lucas and the baby, and Jake and I drove to the gallery in my car. I had one of those little Austins, do you know about them?"

"From *Punch* cartoons," Elizabeth said.

It was the beginning of 1927.

Clio had been working as an afternoon and evening volunteer at Dr. Stopes's clinic for almost two years. Ruth had taken her there the first time, as a visitor, when Ruth herself had just started work as a part-time nurse.

The Mothers' Clinic occupied a small house in Marlborough Road, Holloway, two miles away from the almost identical terraced house that Jake had bought for Ruth and their two children in Islington.

Jake was a general practitioner, and his patients were drawn from the working-class population of the area. When Ruth was at home with Lucas, the first baby, and then Rachel, Jake would come in at night to find her with Lucas on her lap and the rosy-faced baby asleep in the bassinet beside them. He would sit down, unlacing his shoes, sometimes too tired and dispirited even to speak. More often than not he would be called out again, urgently summoned by some dirty barefoot urchin thumping on their front door.

Ruth knew what they always said, even though Jake was at the door before her.

"It's me mam, sir. She's bin took bad. Me dad says can yer come?"

Or it was Grandad, or the baby. Or it was our Ruby, who had been up a back street or had resorted to one of her own knitting needles, and was lying bleeding on wadded newspapers with a towel between her teeth to stop her screaming.

"If there weren't so many of them," Jake would say when he came back. Ruth would watch him, washing his hands at the stone sink in the pantry and rinsing the soap out of the thick, dark hairs on his forearms. "If there weren't too many children and too little money and food and affection to go around."

Jake sometimes tried to remember exactly how it was that he had felt at the beginning, when he had decided to become a doctor. There had been a fiery idealism, he could recall that much, but the exact way that he had been driven on in his wish to help others now entirely escaped him. He supposed he must have believed he could improve the world for other people, his needy patients, through his own skill and dedication. The thought of the priggish boy, long vanished, made him turn down the corners of his mouth where there were lines deepening behind his thick beard.

It seemed now that the neediness far exceeded his small abilities, to the point where the vast sea of sickness and decay threatened to drown him. He longed to remember how it had been to feel confident of his own value. That would have been a comfort, as he had once found a comfort in clinging to pacifist beliefs in the midst of carnage. But the confidence had faded as he grew older, together with his pacifism. It no longer seemed to matter particularly how hard he worked, or how skillfully, since there was much more suffering in his practice alone than he could ever hope to put right. There seemed no particular reason to push himself any harder, because it would not achieve any significant result, any more than his most fervent denial of violence had saved the life of one single infantryman.

Jake wondered if this was how it was to be a grown man. There was a fading of intensity, that was all it was. Even the war and its aftermath receded, so there was a compensation for this dulling of his senses. He still dreamed of the field hospital, in vivid and nauseating detail, but his fury at the waste had all but gone.

He didn't even tell Ruth when he had a dream now, although when they were first together she had held him and murmured to him until the sweating and shivering had stopped.

When he was tired and depressed, as he often was these days, Ruth would put her arms around his waist and rest her cheek against his shoulder. Ruth was still optimistic. She would say something to try to rally him, something like, "There's the Clinic. It's a beginning."

The first birth-control clinic in London, the first in the entire Empire as Dr. Stopes enthusiastically proclaimed, had opened in 1921. Jake worked there for two sessions a week, giving his services for nothing. Every married woman who made her way to it was carefully examined, in comfort and privacy, and then instructed by doctors and nurses how to use the method of birth control that suited her best. All the advice was given free; only the supplies had to be paid for.

The women crowded in. Most of them already had more children than they knew how to look after, and many of them were poor enough to have had to save for their fares across London.

Jake and Ruth were friends and admirers of Marie Stopes. They kept her notorious books *Married Love* and *Wise Parenthood* on their shelves, and talked openly about their theories and advice. They practiced as they preached. After Rachel's birth, Ruth had attended the clinic as a patient, and had been fitted with a domed rubber cap. The Hirshes did not intend to increase the size of their family.

As soon as her children were old enough to be left with a local woman for a few hours a day, Ruth joined the Clinic's nursing staff.

"I'm trained, I can't waste that," she explained to Clio. "And the work is as important as anything I could do. One of the ways that women can take control of their own lives is by limiting the number of children they have to bear. If they are not worn down by constant pregnancies or disabled by abortions, they will have energy to spare for themselves."

Ruth herself had plenty of energy. She ran her small household and looked after her children and her husband with capable ease, and then she rode off on her bicycle to the Mothers' Clinic and dispensed the same friendly common sense there as well. Marriage and motherhood had not changed her very much. She was still the same mixture of feminism, strong opinions, and suspicion of anything that was outside her own knowledge or experience. Clio regarded her sister-in-law with affection and admiration. She also knew that Jake loved his wife and was proud of her. But sometimes, just occasionally, she caught him looking at her with an expression that she could only describe as cold, and judgmental.

Ruth took Clio to the Clinic because Clio asked to see it.

Clio sat in the waiting room with all the other women, watching and listening. The women lined up on hard benches, shoulder to shoulder, patiently waiting. Some of them had brought babies or small children who cried and wriggled on their laps, or stared at each other with round eyes in small faces. There was a sour smell of dirt and poverty and—more disturbing, Clio found, because she had never encountered it before—an atmosphere of absolute resignation, as if disappointment and the absence of hope were inevitable. She felt aware of her own neat clothes and clean hair and skin. But no one looked at her with any curiosity.

Most of the women sat in silence, only whispering commands to their children. There was just one who talked. She was enormously fat, shrouded rather than dressed in a shapeless garment of unsuitable polka dots. She talked to the room in general in a wheezy Cockney monologue.

"Eleven kids I've 'ad, seven of 'em still living. Been knocked up eighteen times in all"—there was a burst of rasping laughter—"before and after getting the ring on me finger. I'm not ashamed of that. Why should I be? Not much else to do down our way, is there, my duck?"

No one laughed with her, but there was no current of disapproval either. It was simply familiar truth to all of them. *Except to me,* Clio thought.

The voice went on. "I've come 'ere, see what they can do. I've been bad since I fell with the youngest, and they said to me then there shouldn't be no more. But I'm married, aren't I? We've all got 'usbands, all of us, else we wouldn't be 'ere."

Clio's ringless hands were folded under her gloves.

"Mine's a good man, I wouldn't complain. Works down the docks in the day, goes on the beer at night, comes 'ome and 'e wants it. Well, that's a man, innit? Stands to reason."

There was a gusty sigh. The fat woman spread her hands, purplish slabs, and the white flesh all up her arms quivered.

"So 'ere we all are," she said, as if pronouncing a valediction on each of them, all of the silent women ranged on benches around her.

Ruth came out of one of the consulting rooms, small and straight in her white nurse's uniform. "Mrs. Miller?" she asked, smiling at her. The polka-dot mountain heaved itself up and was shepherded in to see Jake.

Clio watched the women coming out again. They carried brown paper bags containing the contraceptive supplies that the doctors had fitted them with and the nurses had explained how to use. Every time, she noticed, there was a change in the woman's expression. There was a suggestion of daring, a curious glance to each side, as if from now on there might be time to look at the world. Then came a movement to hold the paper bag closer. Every single woman looked younger, and taller. Clio was moved by the sight of them.

"There must be something I could do to help," she said later to Ruth and Jake, reiterating her old plea.

"We need a supplies clerk, just for a few hours a week," Jake said. "You could do that easily enough."

And so Clio added her voluntary work at the Mothers' Clinic to her responsibilities at *Fathom.*

She had plenty of time, because *Fathom* did not occupy more than half of her attention. She still read whatever Max asked her to read, and gave him her punctilious views that he had come to trust, and she typed for him and dealt with the subscriptions and the galley proofs and the printers. She also acted as an informal confidante to all the aspiring poets and writers and critics who drifted into her office in search of Max and acclaim in the pages of *Fathom*. She listened to their grievances, made them tea, and consoled or congratulated where it was appropriate.

"How would I manage without you?" Max sometimes asked when he was in a better than average humor. Clio knew perfectly well that he would manage by replacing her with another eager, literature-struck, overimpressed late schoolgirl.

It was still Max who chose the contributions, and made up the issues, and decided who was to be included in the magazine's favored circle and who was not. Clio had learned quite early on that he did not welcome her separate suggestions, and if she discovered a promising writer of her own and put his work forward to Max, it was guaranteed that Max would turn it down, and so the discovery would be lost to one of the other quarterlies. She had her role at *Fathom,* a useful role that was quite clearly defined, and although she enjoyed her work and the people who revolved around it, she knew that she had fallen into a comfortable rut. The Mothers' Clinic provided her with a new focus, and the sense that she was useful, instead of a fixture.

Clio took charge of the Clinic stores, and became responsible for monitoring and reordering the stocks of rubber caps and contraceptive pessaries, sponges, and sheaths. She also kept the records, filing the case-sheets after the nurses had completed them, and she set up a simple appointments system to help the doctors and reduce the waiting time for the patients. It gave her satisfaction to see the women coming in, and leaving again, looking around them as they went, with their brown paper bags in their arms.

There was a good deal of open talk amongst the staff. It was part of the Clinic's philosophy, inherited directly from Marie Stopes, that sexual matters could be freely discussed between adults and professionals. Clio read the books and listened to what was said. Along with her growing expertise on methods of contraception, she absorbed the theory that sex was natural, and beneficial, and even desirable for healthy adults. She knew, because she had heard the assurance made often enough, that nothing a married couple did together could be regarded as wrong or shameful, provided that it gave pleasure to both of them. She knew about sexual stimuli and erogeneity and the female orgasm.

Sometimes, with a slight sense of shame, she looked speculatively at Jake and Ruth, and found herself envying them.

Clio was fully aware of the irony of her position. She was a sexually knowledgeable virgin. Peter Dennis's feverish embraces and Pilgrim's mild philandering seemed a long time in her past, and there had been no one else since then. She began to understand, with dry regret, that Eleanor's fears for her had been justified. There were few eligible men of her age, and there were very many eager women. Of the writers and artists she met in Soho and Bloomsbury, most were married, or at least attached. Those who were not were drunk, or hopelessly disreputable, or not interested in women. In the last years, dividing her time between Max Erdmann and the Clinic, Clio had almost accepted the external image of herself. She was a spinster of almost twenty-six.

Even the Babies were grown up. Phoebe Stretton was nineteen, a jazz-mad flapper who had adopted the knowing manners of her generation. "How's your sex life, darling?" she and her friends would greet each other. At seventeen Tabby Hirsh was shy and quiet, but she had cut her hair like Phoebe's and was going to dances with her cousins. Alice was fifteen. She was not out yet, but she watched everything the others did with greedy curiosity. All the Babies thought that Grace was an old married lady, and that Clio was simply old.

On the evening of the party for Pilgrim's retrospective, it happened that Jake and Ruth and Clio had all been at the Clinic. Their various shifts did not usually coincide, but tonight Clio met them outside as she locked the front door of the Holloway house.

"I don't want to go," Ruth was saying briskly. "It will be all drink and arty talk, the usual nonsense."

"I would like to go. I would welcome a drink, and art and nonsense are welcome diversions these days. Clio, you're coming to Pilgrim's party, aren't you?"

"Yes, I'm coming. I'd like to see Pilgrim, and Max will expect me to be there." It would be the same familiar faces and arty talk, just as Ruth predicted, but Clio thought with a touch of weariness that that was not a reason either for going or for staying away. She would go because she had nothing else in particular to do. "I'll drive you," she told Jake.

Ruth was already wheeling her bicycle to the curb. "Don't

expect a hot dinner when you get back," she called in Jake's direction, and pedaled away. Jake didn't watch her departure. He bent himself double and folded his long arms and legs into Clio's tiny car.

Clio drove for a little distance in silence. Then she asked, "Is everything all right?"

Jake had grown fleshier since his marriage. He was clean-shaven lately, but even without the curling black beard, his resemblance to Nathaniel was growing stronger and stronger.

He said in a flat voice, "Everything? Yes, Clio, thank you. Everything is quite all right."

The Albemarle Street gallery was already crowded when they reached it. Clio and Jake were carried away from each other at once by the cross-currents of people. Clio saw Pilgrim's head in the middle of the room, and she fought her way across to him, ducking between raised glasses and gesticulating hands and the choppy waters of conversation.

"A purely materialistic functionalism . . ."

"Rapacious bloody agents . . ."

There were familiar faces everywhere, but the familiarity seemed stale rather than comfortable. Pilgrim put his arm around her and kissed her on the mouth. He was wearing a white silk shirt with a yoke and full sleeves that made him look even more like a prosperous gypsy.

"Clio, my Clio, here you are. What do you think of the hang?" He waved over the milling heads in the direction of the gallery walls.

"I'm sure I would admire it if I could only see it."

"Oh, they'll all bugger off before long. Your picture is over there, at the end. Pride of place. And look who's standing in front of it."

She looked, and saw Anthony and Grace. They were turned away from *The Janus Face* and they were talking intently. Even in the crush they gave the impression of being a little apart. Pilgrim winked at Clio.

Clio left him and battled on across the room. She saw Grace and Anthony hardly at all nowadays. The last time had been in Oxford, a few months ago, at Nathaniel's fifty-fifth birthday party. She knew that Anthony devoted himself to his business and the beginnings of a political career, and that Grace spent her time with a Society set whose doings were regularly written up in the gossip columns. Grace was "Party-going Lady Grace," or

"Lovely and vivacious wife of that bright young man Anthony Brock."

Sometimes, very rarely, Clio's social path intersected hers. They had met at Duff and Lady Diana Cooper's, who were neighbors of Clio's in Gower Street, and once at a Twelfth Night party in Gordon Square where Lydia Lopokova had danced for the company. But Clio's life centered on Bloomsbury and Fitzrovia, and she almost never crossed over into Mayfair.

Anthony and Grace greeted her warmly. Anthony looked tired and there were frown marks between his eyebrows, but his gappy smile and humorous manner were unchanged. Grace was unerringly chic in a black satin tunic dress with long ropes of pearls. The cousins kissed each other, and as they separated a flashbulb popped in front of them. The photographer ducked and was reabsorbed by the crowd as rapidly as he had emerged.

Grace shrugged nonchalantly. "Too good a chance for him to miss. The picture'll be in tomorrow's *Daily Mail* captioned 'Kiss and make up for Pilgrim's Janus' or something equally rubbishy."

" 'Vivacious Lady Grace's Janus kiss,' more likely," Clio could not help saying. She looked up at the picture. It no longer told the truth, even if it once had done. All the tension trapped in it seemed incongruous now. It had dissipated itself in reality, fading away into indifference. Grace and she were grown up, grown away. It was only a portrait, a self-consciously deliberate flouting of convention that looked less outrageous than it once had done.

"What are you doing here?" Clio asked. Grace usually took care to avoid Pilgrim.

"Anthony wanted to come," Grace said, as if that were sufficient explanation. Another flashbulb went off in their faces, leaving a white dazzle burning in their eyes.

Grace put her hand to Clio's arm. "Let's move away. We're striking altogether too much of a pose."

They moved into a corner, hemmed in by two of Pilgrim's still lifes. Clio took a glass of red wine off a passing tray. It was better than the usual vinegar, and she drank it gratefully, then replaced the empty glass with another full one. The three of them exchanged family information, trading assurances that Cressida was well for the latest news from Julius. Julius had taken Jake's place in Gower Street for a time, then had gone to live in Paris. He was beginning to be in demand on the European concert circuit and found Paris a more congenial base than London.

"I miss him," Grace said.

"Yes," Clio conceded. She drank some more wine. The room was very hot, but the crowd was beginning to thin out. "But what about you two?"

Grace looked at Anthony, then put her hand on his arm. Her nails were painted to match her lips. "We've just come back from Swansea. We've heard that Anthony has been adopted as the candidate. You know he was up for selection? Meetings, platforms, speeches. It's as if he were born for it, Clio. He's a natural politician."

There was a resonance in Grace's voice that Clio had never heard before. She tried to define for herself exactly what it was that was new, and then she realized it was simply that Grace was excited. The possibility of Anthony becoming an MP *excited* her.

It was good news, and Clio's pleasure in it was unaffected. "Anthony, I'm so glad. Congratulations, and congratulations."

It was a by-election, following the death of the sitting member in a solid Labour constituency. Anthony accepted Clio's good wishes with characteristic modesty. "It's not an easy one. There's a majority of fifteen thousand. But I think we can dent it, a significant dent." He put his hand over Grace's, covering hers where it rested on his arm.

They talked for a little while longer, and Clio saw how Grace bent her head toward her husband, and how she listened to what he said. The cold pressure of her own loneliness seemed more evident in the overheated room.

Pilgrim passed by them, with Jeannie and two young men. Jeannie had aged noticeably. Her hennaed hair had thinned to reveal patches of scalp, and she had teased the remainder into defiant puffs. The skin of her face was invisible under a layer of white powder patched with rouge, and her eyes squinted out of a delta of cracks. She was wearing an elaborate brocaded coat with a dirty lace collar. She was also quite drunk.

"Grace and Anthony, this is a *great* honor," Pilgrim called out, swooping back toward them. His little retinue stopped short and regrouped around him. "You all know Gloriana, of course?"

The comparison was cruelly accurate, like the best of Pilgrim's malicious wit. Jeannie looked exactly like the ancient Queen Elizabeth, still imagining herself the majestic beauty.

"And this is Tony Hardy. And Miles Lennox."

Clio had met Tony Hardy before. He was a publisher with an interest in experimental fiction. And she had heard of Miles Lennox. He had been medically unfit for combat, but he had written some acclaimed war poetry and a year or so after the end of the war had published a highly praised collection of stories. She had heard someone saying, somewhere, that Miles Lennox would write the great postwar novel. She looked at him with interest and saw a fair-haired man with neat features and clear, light-olive skin. He held out his hand and she shook it.

Conversations began around her. She heard Jeannie making some incoherent overture to Grace, and Anthony complimenting Pilgrim on his work. Tony Hardy said something to her about *Fathom,* and she made a sensible response and then found herself listening to the words as though they issued from someone else's mouth.

Too much wine, she told herself, and then, with surprising defiance, Why not?

Miles Lennox smiled at her. "You're Clio Hirsh. I've heard about you."

Jake was in the opposite corner of the room. He was talking to silver-haired Isolde, who seemed only to grow taller, and slimmer, and younger-looking as time passed. Isolde had replaced Jeannie as Pilgrim's official girl, but it was not an exclusive commitment for either of them.

Jake had drunk several glasses of the good wine. He was thinking sentimentally that Isolde was like a silver birch tree. She had tiny breasts, and hips like a boy's. She stood very close to him, with her wide-apart pale green eyes fixed on his, and uttered a stream of nonsense in a soft, low voice. She was very unlike Ruth. She was the exact opposite of Ruth, Jake thought, because Ruth was small and buxom with a bloom of dark hair on her upper lip. Ruth was brisk, and sturdy, and she never talked nonsense or stared at him with unfocused lust. Even in bed, Ruth was businesslike.

Jake felt exactly as he had done long ago with Grace in the hawthorn corner of the meadow. He wanted to pull this Isolde down into the long grass and cover the sappy length of her with his black bulk.

It seemed to Clio that when she looked around again, the room was empty. Grace and Anthony had gone, and Jeannie had been helped away by Tony Hardy and, presumably, Miles Lennox. Jake was nowhere to be seen.

She walked slowly past the pictures, examining each one in turn. Pilgrim materialized beside her. "What do you think?"

"I think, I think . . ." She started to laugh, realizing that she had no idea what she thought. "I think you are *magnificent.*"

"Thank you, dear Clio. I'm glad of that." He sighed theatrically. "It seems that we are both abandoned."

Clio squinted. Evidently Isolde had disappeared too. Mustering some dignity she said, "*I* haven't been abandoned. I am just myself."

Pilgrim put his hands on her shoulders. "Yes, you are, aren't you? Now, I am going to take you out to dinner. Don't say no, or make some dull objection."

"I don't have any objection. I would like some dinner, thank you."

Anthony and Grace had gone home to South Audley Street.

There was a cold supper laid out in the dining room, so they took their plates and sat in armchairs beside the fire. Grace kicked off her shoes and put her feet up on a stool.

"We could have looked in at the Ritz, or the Café de Paris," Anthony said, handing her her filled glass.

"We could have done. And we would have joined some people, and then gone on with them to the Bat or the Slipspin. Then you would have said that you had an early start in the morning and should come home, and I would want to dance some more, so in order not to start a quarrel you would have come home in a taxi and somebody or other would have seen me back here later on. By which time you would be in bed asleep, and when I woke up in the morning you would already have gone out, and so I would not see you until tomorrow night."

Grace felt that she was describing the pattern of almost every night of their married life. She knew the grooves of their social circuit too well.

"I would much rather be here, with you."

"Would you? Is that the truth?"

His pleased surprise touched her. She swung her legs down and went to stand beside his chair, bending down so that her cheek rested on the top of his head. His hair was thinning. It came to her that she had wasted so much of their time.

"Yes, it's the truth," she whispered.

She had told Clio the truth, too. Watching Anthony in South Wales had made her see a different man, a man who was not just her husband, who was not just involved in a business world that did not interest her. For the first time in their years together she had admired him. She had also felt that they were jointly concerned.

The Conservative grandees liked her. Anthony needed her on the platform beside him, as the candidate's wife.

The selection and the work they had done together, and the prospect of the by-election itself, had had a powerful effect on her. Clio had correctly recognized the current of excitement.

Grace had fallen in love with her own husband.

Contemplating the possibility of her own happiness, Grace felt it like a weight in the depth of her stomach, resting between the bony crests of her hips. It was comforting ballast that would help her to hold her course after years of drifting.

But she was superstitious about happiness. It was an accessory to other people's lives, not her own. *If it is not already too late,* she warned herself. *If I have not wasted too much of our time.*

Anthony put his hands up, to hold her. "Grace?"

"I'm here."

"We didn't go to the Ritz, or anywhere else. We came home together, instead. Let's go to bed."

Anthony wanted another child, and Grace longed to give him one. She hoped that it might compensate for Cressida. It was harder still for Grace to look at Cressida now, to be reminded of the lie she told Anthony every day of their lives.

They went upstairs together. At the foot of the second flight that led on up to the nursery, Anthony said, "I'm going up to see her."

He liked to lean over her bed and listen to the soft breathing, and to inhale the scent of soap and clean skin. Grace knew that he wanted her to go with him and bend over the white bed, so they could share their parental pride, pooling their love for the child. She smiled at him, feeling that it was like a crack in her face. There Pilgrim had been at his party, dressed up in a foolish shirt like some third-rate actor in a repertory *Hamlet*.

"Go on, then. I will go and get ready for bed."

Anthony's visit to Cressida only took a moment. Almost at once, as Grace was unwinding the ropes of pearls from around her neck, he was knocking at the door that separated his dressing room from her bedroom.

"Come in," Grace said softly.

Pilgrim and Clio had dinner together in Soho. The Eiffel Tower had not, just lately, played quite such a central role in everyone's lives. There were other restaurants and retreats, and there was the Fitzroy Tavern. They ate well and wandered rather unsteadily through the rain-wet streets to Charlotte Street. They did not discuss where to end their evening, or how. The studio drew them back.

The glass roof was dark overhead, reflecting first the yellow spark when Pilgrim struck a match, and then the wider bloom of the lamps. When Clio looked up, she saw that the reflections fractured at the margins into blurred webs of color.

She wandered through the big room, smelling the oil paint and turpentine, and the mustiness of old clothes, and dust worked into folds of matting and the creases of an ancient velvet armchair. She sat down in the chair, rubbing her hands over the greasy scalp of the velvet, and looked at the canvases around the walls. The old nude studies of Jeannie had gone long ago. Pilgrim's work had lately become more abstract. There were wells of primary pigment now, and slabs of flat ochre and sienna and umber like rocks in some desert. But there was no real change. Pilgrim's work did not tease with sly, rhetorical questions. It came straight out and shouted.

Then she looked at Pilgrim himself. He was standing at his table on which cups and glasses were jumbled together with jars and brushes and tubes of paint. He was polishing the fingerprints off a whiskey glass for her, using an oily rag marked with indigo paint. The dim light hooded his eyes and deepened the hollows in his cheeks, emphasizing his piratical appearance.

Clio pondered for a moment on Pilgrim's secondary reputation. She knew how many women he was rumored to have had. She also knew that the reality was probably less startling, but even so, many women found him attractive. She heard enough of the talk in the Fitzroy and elsewhere.

She was attracted to him herself, and always had been.

Yet somehow, they had mutually overlooked that. They had slipped past the point of possibility and moved on into friendship, without Pilgrim ever having made a serious overture to her. Clio felt impatient with the pallor of her own history. If she was not careful, she thought, the pattern of her life would become set, with her own existence forever on the margins of other people's. Or rather, if she did not give up her circumspection. If she did not stop being careful.

Pilgrim had shone the glass to his own satisfaction. He stuffed the rag into his pocket and from amongst the bottles produced an unlabeled version of Scotch. He poured out, generously. Clio stood up. She insinuated herself between him and the table, settling herself on the edge of it, so that she could look up at him. Their faces were close together, so close that she could see the reflection of herself in his eyes. She arched her neck back a little, widening the focus, to see his expression. She saw that he was surprised, but not displeased.

Clio lifted her hands and cupped them around his face. Then she drew down his head and kissed him on the mouth.

It was a liberating gesture. As soon as she had made it, she felt that she had taken some small measure of her fate into her own hands, instead of always waiting for it to creep up and take possession of her by default. She was smiling, and panting a little.

Pilgrim was quick enough to respond. His heavy arm came around her and he kissed her back, pushing her backward until she felt the prodding fingers of bottles and brushes beneath her. Her experience elsewhere was limited, but Clio liked the way he kissed her. His mouth and tongue were gentle, almost playful. But she didn't want him just to be playing with her.

After a moment he lifted his head, studying her. "Clio, is it possible that you might be slightly drunk?"

She shook her head. "No. I'm not drunk." It was the truth. She felt quite clear-headed. She supposed that she must have drunk herself sober again. In a steady voice she asked him, "Don't you want . . . to?"

Pilgrim was too rigorous for that. "Want to what?"

"Want to make love to me."

As soon as she had said it, from the sharp inhalation of breath and the twist of his mouth, she knew that he did want to. The recognition gave her a sense of power. Not simply over Pilgrim, but over herself as well.

She had the sudden sense of her virginity as a piece of luggage, too heavy, that would be easy to put down. Or as a skin to be sloughed off, leaving a shinier, more knowing skin beneath. Had Grace felt this?

Pilgrim turned in the air, like a cat, concealing his surprise and the stab of lust. He did not like to find himself the prey rather than the predator, and his counterquestion was crueler than it need have been.

"Are you not afraid that I might make you pregnant? Or have you got an obliging stockbroker standing by, ready to repair the damage?"

"I've no idea what you mean," Clio said. She stuck fast to the convention that none of them knew anything, that Cressida was Anthony's, that there was no secret to keep. Neither she nor Jake nor Julius had mentioned it, even to one another, since Cressida's birth. It frightened her that it should raise its head now, and angered her that she had not thought this far ahead. It was inevitable that the comparison, the old comparison with Grace, would disinter the roots of memory for Pilgrim.

But she wasn't like Grace. They were not alike even then, eight years ago, and they were utterly different now. She would not let him compare them.

"You won't make me pregnant," Clio said. "You can be sure of that." She wriggled away from him and bent down to pick up her handbag from where she had left it with her coat. She opened her bag. "Look," she said.

Pilgrim looked, then gave a roar of laughter. Inside Clio's bag, in their own neat inner bag, lay a flat sponge and a small phial of olive oil.

Primly she said, "At the Clinic we have recommended a contraceptive sponge soaked in ordinary domestic olive oil as the most suitable method of protection for approximately one thousand nine hundred patients. That was the total the last time I went through the case-sheets and counted."

It was the simplest method. For that reason Clio had extracted a sponge for herself from the supply cupboard, and repaid the exact amount of money into the petty cash account. She had provided herself with olive oil from her own kitchen, and folded the two items away out of sight in her handbag. Her conscious intention had been to be responsible, according to the Clinic's teaching. She heard so much discussion of sexual practices and handled such a volume of contraceptive devices that it seemed quite normal and natural to be making her own arrangements, even though she had no lover present or past.

Subconsciously, she now realized, she had probably been preparing for exactly the situation in which she now found herself.

The subconscious, Clio thought cheerfully, had a great deal to answer for.

Pilgrim was still laughing. "I had forgotten about Dr. Stopes and her Clinic. I only think of you behind your typewriter in Max's office, pounding away at rejection slips."

A fixture. Dear Clio, always there, never obtruding. That hurt her, but she knew that he had not intended it. "A bad mistake," she told him, pouting a little. She was reminded of Jeannie being coquettish, but this was not Jeannie. *This is me,* Clio warned herself. But she had come too far, now, to think of any retreat. Pilgrim had stopped laughing. He had come very close again. His hand was resting on her bare neck.

"You are lovely, and original, and clever," he whispered. *Original,* that was what mattered. Herself, not a shadow of anyone else. "Come here, with me."

He took her hand and led her. There was the divan with its knots of paisley shawls and discarded clothes. She felt the edge of it against the backs of her knees, threatening to unbalance her. Pilgrim undid the fastenings of her dress and lifted it over her head.

Clio remembered the complicated petticoats and underpinnings that she and Grace had worn beneath their dance dresses only eight years ago. Now, under her thin dress, she was almost naked.

Pilgrim unrolled her rayon stockings from the tight garters and put his mouth to each of the red bracelet marks left on the pale skin.

"Lovely Clio," he murmured. She wound her fingers in his wiry hair and let him wrap his arm around her haunches and tilt her backward on to the divan.

She watched as Pilgrim emerged from his clothes. There was a lot more curly black hair, matted over white skin. There was everything else she had expected to encounter from her reading and associated helpful diagrams. She could have put labels to the various parts. The thought made her want to laugh.

Pilgrim lay down beside her. His skin was warmer than hers, and the springy hair prickled her. He put his arms around her and held her close to his chest. His erection (that was what it was, of course. "Under the influence of sexual excitement the penis of the male becomes engorged with blood . . .") prodded against her belly. Clio reached down and encircled it with her thumb and forefinger. She did not feel either alarmed or aroused. She felt a kind of detached interest.

But Pilgrim propped himself on one elbow and with an unhurried calm began to explore her body. He ran his tongue in small circles around her nipples and reached his hand between her legs. Clio heard her own moist flesh make a small sound, *tac,* under his fingers. A shiver ran from the base of her spine through the pit of her stomach and up to her breasts. *Tac.* She stretched against him, and his fingers probed more insistently.

She forgot her academic interest. The edges of her consciousness seemed to blur and fade. She began to concentrate fiercely on what Pilgrim was doing to her. When he kissed her, she opened her mouth to his tongue. Tastes and smells became mingled, whiskey and tobacco, cleanish sweat and salt. He lay between her legs now. She looked down at the way their bodies cleaved together, pale and smooth, black and white.

He whispered in her ear, "Clio, where's your sponge?"

She considered for a moment. "I think you have to effect complete penetration first. Before I can insert it, you see. Is that all right?" She found that she could only command the lecture and textbook language.

Pilgrim gave a series of small grunts, then rolled away from her. He lay flat on his back and looked up at the glass roof.

"This is the first time? For God's sake, I've just realized. This is the first time, isn't it?"

"Yes."

It must have been the first time with Grace too. *I'm not still trying to draw level with her.*

"Why are you so surprised?"

"I imagined something else, that's all."

From her age, and from all her confidantes in the *Fathom* offices and the Fitzroy, she supposed.

"Clio, is this what you want? Here with me, like this?"

As if she were not, after all, old enough to know her own mind, having reached her advanced age and having come this far.

She said, "Yes, I do."

When he did not turn back to her, but went on lying on his back and staring up at the roof, she looked to see what had happened. And she saw that there was no longer any erection, but a series of small cushions of puckered flesh, pinky-gray and entirely vulnerable.

"Why?" she asked.

There was a shrug.

She had confronted him with the unexpected. She was the taker, to suit herself, and that was Pilgrim's own self-appointed role. His expression reminded her of Lucas, Jake's little boy. She felt immediately protective, and sorry that she had disconcerted him. She leaned over him and rested her head on his chest. She remembered, "No action that a loving and considerate man and wife can perform together is wrong, so long as it is agreeable to both of them."

She moved her head, so that her hair brushed over his belly, and then took him in her mouth. The soft pouches stirred and stiffened, and she had to lift her head so that he did not choke her.

"You surprising girl," he said, with clear satisfaction.

Pilgrim pressed her back into the nest of bedding and spread her legs. He pushed himself into her, and she felt a brief shock of pain, only very brief. Then he began to move up and down, slowly, sighing a little.

"Wait," Clio said.

"The famous sponge?"

She slid away from him and stood up. He lay back, in command again now, lazily grinning. She went behind the screen, the old model's dressing screen behind which she and Grace had daringly taken off their dance dresses. She remembered just how she had felt, emerging from the shelter of it in her silk chemise to Pilgrim's scrutiny. Her hand was shaking a little as she spilled the drops of oil onto the sponge and watched it soak in, darkening and softening the pocked surface.

She put one foot up on a three-legged stool and took the sponge in her fingers. She was surprised by the muscularity of her own interior. When she looked down, she saw that there was a thin thread of blood on her inner thigh.

Clio emerged from behind the screen again. She walked back to the divan and Pilgrim.

There was not much more, after that. He came greedily back inside her, prodding and bucking. He muttered incoherently into her ear as he reared up and down, and she tried to listen and to find the rhythm that would match his and also, as a kind of afterthought, to discover how to satisfy her own needs. Women did have needs, the reading she had done assured her of that. She had a sense that if there had only been more time, more care, she would have been able to pinpoint her own pleasure. She would have been able to peel back the layers of it and reveal the mysterious bud, whatever it was, at the center of herself.

Was that what Grace had felt?

As it was, Pilgrim ejaculated with a roar that diminished into a groan.

When it was over, he lay on top of her in a heavy heap, his breath fanning the damp skin beneath her jaw. Clio stroked his hair. She found herself smiling over his shoulder into the skin of glass that held back the friendly night. She lay quite still. Dr. Stopes had written somewhere that it was physically beneficial for men and women to absorb each other's secretions.

At last Pilgrim gave a gusty sigh. He sat up, mopping at their thighs with one of his supply of painting rags. Then he settled back, unaffectedly cross-legged, and lit a pungent cigarette.

Clio studied him. With his broad shoulders and white, slabby nakedness and his solemn face wreathed in smoke, he looked like one of his own portraits. *Naked Man II,* perhaps, or *Omnium Tristum Est.* The urge to laugh came back to her.

"Well?" Pilgrim asked.

"Quite well, thank you," she responded. It was less flippant than it sounded. All was well, or quite well. She did feel exactly as if she had put down some heavy piece of luggage or wriggled out of some old, constricting skin. She had taken a lover, but she was comfortably sure that she would not be left with a painful passion for Pilgrim. She would feel the same about him tomorrow as she had done yesterday. It was about herself that she felt differently. She had her own power, and the ability to control, after all.

She also knew that Pilgrim was eyeing her with a shade of guilt and anxiety. Would she weep or complain or make further demands?

Clio held out her hand, rested it on the inelastic skin of his thigh.

"May I ask you for something?"

"Of course," he told her, meaning, "Of course not, if it will cost me anything to give it." Clio had observed his malicious teasing over the years, and it pleased her to extract a momentary revenge.

"For one of your cigarettes?" she said sweetly. The relief in his face was so clear to see that she was reminded of Lucas again. She did laugh now, out loud. He took a cigarette out and lit it for her, and put it between her lips. Then he reached for their whiskey glasses.

"Here's to the next time," he proposed, glad to see that she was happy.

Clio drank before amending the toast. "The future," she said, over the rim of her glass that tasted strongly of the polishing rag.

When they had drunk the whiskey he made her lie down again, and settled beside her, covering them both up with the paisley shawls. With her face close to his and her wide eyes unblinkingly watching him, he felt suddenly tender and grateful. He almost said *I love you.*

"My lovely Clio. You are unique."

"Of course," Clio said, with calm conviction.

"The party for Pilgrim's retrospective was early in 1927," Elizabeth said in her knowing way. "It must have been, if it was just before the first by-election."

Clio inclined her head. "It must, if you say so."

Her vagueness was deliberate. Silly things, unimportant things, she sometimes couldn't recall, but others she had never forgotten. February 17, 1927. The day she had lost—no, not lost but divested herself of—her virginity with Pilgrim, on the musty divan in the Charlotte Street studio. Afterward he had walked her home through the rain to Gower Street because she had left her car outside the gallery. They had sung to each other, only she couldn't remember what the songs were.

She was not going to tell this inquisitive girl the significance of the date, of course. It was only a party, one of hundreds.

Grace and Anthony had been there, but they had not stayed for long.

A few weeks later, Anthony had been defeated in the South Wales by-election. He had not been expected to win the seat. He had been put up to contest it in order to show what he could do, and he had done well. He had reduced the Labour majority by several thousand.

In the same year Grace had had a miscarriage, a late one, and had been ill for some months. After Grace lost the baby, Anthony and she had dropped out of their set of bright young people. They seemed to prefer each other's company to anyone else's. Clio had hardly seen them.

She had been busy herself.

Pilgrim's retrospective, she remembered. The portrait, hanging at the end of the gallery. Pride of place, someone had said. Was it Pilgrim?

On that evening, in the crush of the party, she had first met Miles Lennox.

Ten

Shropshire, May 30, 1929

THE BLACK CAR WITH ITS curved mudguards like fastidiously raised eyebrows was incongruous at the bottom of the village street. The sleek, shiny length of it crept up the hill a few paces and then stopped. Blue ribbons fluttered from the bright chrome of the door handles, and the bumpers glittered in the May sunshine.

The women hesitated in the shadows of their doorways, and the children stopped playing and stared with their mouths hanging open. Anthony Brock's driver climbed out and skirted the long bonnet, trying not to wince at the sight of the whitish dust from the unmade road that filmed his polished coachwork.

He opened the passenger door, and Grace stepped out.

She crossed the street at once, gaily heading for the nearest pair of cottages. She held out her hand to the aproned woman hovering on her step and said, "It's Mrs. Fletcher, isn't it?"

The woman was amazed, and delighted, as Grace had intended her to be. But it was not such a great feat of memory. The district electoral roll lay on the warm leather seat in the car. Grace had studied it as they drove from village to village between the high hedges of West Shropshire. During the last few days, canvassing with Anthony, she had visited almost every hamlet in the rural constituency and now, on polling day itself, she felt as if she knew every lane and farm and every cottager and laborer who inhabited them. It was, in any case, almost her home ground. Stretton lay only twenty miles north of this village, within the constituency borders.

The woman shook the offered fingers, nodding vigorously, brushing her wispy hair back from her red face with her unoccupied hand. One knee folded behind the other as if they might collapse together into a curtsey, but reached a compromise in a parlormaid's bob.

"Yes, mum, my lady, that is."

"Mrs. Fletcher, are you coming out to vote?"

Mrs. Fletcher looked embarrassed. She glanced from side to side, hoping to find an answer reflected in the craning faces of her neighbors.

"I don't know, mum. I don't know as my husband . . ."

Grace said gently, "Your vote is your own, you know. Don't you remember the Franchise Act? We women have won the right to a vote, and we owe it to one another to use that right."

She was smiling and her smile was warm and genuine, even after more than half a day's constant employment. The words *we women* seemed to hang in the still air.

Mrs. Fletcher looked her in the eye now. The gulf between the laborer's wife in her apron and the candidate's in her pearls and her navy-and-white-spotted silk seemed to have narrowed a little. On the doorsteps, that was Grace's talent. It was impossible to forget that she was Lady Grace, daughter of the Lord Lieutenant of the county and the Conservative candidate's wife, yet at the same time her manner was friendly and direct. The women thought that she was easy to talk to. "No airs and graces on her," they told one another. The men looked sidelong at her with grudging admiration.

Mrs. Fletcher folded her arms. "Maybe so," she conceded. "Maybe so. But if I come out and vote for your husband, what will he do for me and mine? Tell me that, now." She looked around triumphantly at her neighbors, surprised and pleased by her own daring. There was a murmur of agreement, although no one else was quite brave enough to echo her words.

Grace turned to face the little crowd that had gathered. There were women and old men and grimy-faced children, all mutely staring at her.

"You know me, all of you, don't you? You know my father and my brother, and what this part of England means to us? My husband is a young man, a good man. He is proud to have been selected as your candidate. A vote for him is a vote for peace in the world for your children, for work for your menfolk, but it is also a vote for West Shropshire, for *yourselves*."

Her voice was ringing. There was a moment's silence and then, not exactly a cheer, but a ragged chorus of assent. " 'Er's right," someone said from the back of the group. " 'Er's one of our own, like old Wardle."

Mr. Wardle was the previous Conservative member, a local landowner, retiring after a long silent career on the back benches.

"What'ud we be doing with one of them Liberal lot, or one of MacDonald's pack of Bolshies?" Grace's supporter demanded.

"Quite right, sir," Grace called cheerfully. "Now then, who's coming to the polls with me?" She tucked a strand of dark hair back under the brim of her navy-blue cloche and bent down to the level of the children. She selected the smallest girl with the least matted hair and an almost clean jersey and hoisted her up in her arms. "You'll come, won't you? You'd like a ride in my car, I expect, and you can bring your mother and whoever else would like to come. And those we can't fit in, we'll come back for. That's fair, isn't it?"

The child nodded, solemn-faced, her eyes on Grace's lustrous pearls.

The other children swarmed over the car. Anthony's chauffeur thought longingly of his chamois leather, but Grace only laughed and let them clamber in their boots over the upholstery. The mothers and grandparents followed behind, leaning unaccustomedly back in the plush interior. When the car was packed full, Grace waved at those left in the dusty road. "We'll be back for you," she called gaily, and the car rolled away.

The polling station was two miles away, in another village, in the school that served all the outlying hamlets. As they drove, a boy leaned over the back of Grace's seat and shouted in her ear, "Usually us has to walk all this way to school."

"Today is special. Election day," she said. "Today you ride."

The road was almost a tunnel, winding between green hedges laced with may blossom. Grace knew that in the grass along the high banks there would be the white stars of wild strawberry flowers, and the pale freckle of wood violets. She felt a kind of rooted affection for this home countryside, although in the same instant she could have laughed at her own sentimentality. It would not matter if Anthony were standing for some East End constituency or a Midlands manufacturing town or anywhere else, so long as he won it. But at the same time it gave her satisfaction to think that he was here, on the other side of the county, ferrying the voters back and forth along the familiar lanes, and that Hugo and Thomas were out too, all the big shiny cars festooned with blue ribbons and rosettes, bringing their people in.

Anthony had done well in his unwinnable South Wales by-election. The party had rewarded him with West Shropshire, a safe seat, his own ground at least by marriage. He had worked hard, from the beginning of the campaign, and he deserved to hold the solid majority.

If we don't, Grace thought, *it won't be for want of trying.*

But Mr. Baldwin's reelection battle-cry of "Safety First" had hardly set the electorate on fire. There was a feeling that after five years of Conservative government a change would be welcome. And even in the rural depths of West Shropshire both Liberals and Labour were fielding strong candidates. Nothing would be certain until after the last votes had been counted.

The packed car smelled strongly of bodies, and two or three of the children had begun to sing. There was a holiday atmosphere. "As good as the Church outing," someone was saying. "Vicar took us in a charabanc all the way to Shrewsbury."

At the polling station the car disgorged Grace's cargo of voters. They filed into the Victorian schoolhouse and the children hung around in the yard, peering at the officials and the placards tied with string to the iron railings. The familiar building was different for a day.

The women and old people came out again, looking solemn and important. Grace shepherded them back into the car. "Home we go. Thank you for coming, thank you for your support."

As they motored back through the lanes, she was wondering, How many more villages did they have time for, how many more of their people could she bring out to vote for Anthony? She was tired now, and thirsty, and her face felt stiff with smiling.

Anthony Brock, MP. Grace was superstitious. Even now, she quenched the flicker of pleasure the thought gave her. Last night at Stretton, Anthony had said, "I think we have done all we can," and she had corrected him fiercely, "Not until the polls close tomorrow night."

Alice sat on the window seat in her bedroom at Stretton, looking down the curve of the carriage drive between the great trees. She was waiting for the cars to come back. She had decided that as soon as she saw Grace and Anthony arrive, she would run downstairs to meet them. She would be first to hear the news, whatever stupid Cressida chose to do.

There was a book on her lap, but she hadn't opened it. Her legs were stiff with sitting, and the wall felt cold against her back. If her cousins' old nanny came in, she would fuss and scold her about getting chilled and probably hustle her into an armchair with a hot-water bottle. But Alice would not change her position. She stayed huddled in the narrow window slot, her back numb and her eyes smarting with the effort of keeping watch.

Alice had had a bad bout of measles. The illness had affected her eyes, and she had spent a long time lying in her darkened bedroom in the Woodstock Road, with the boundaries between sleep and waking blurred by fever. She had dreamed of prisons and confinement, and when she woke up the old room had seemed like a cell. By the time the fever receded and reality had become a matter of certainty again, she was thin and weak, but filled with the need to escape from the room, and from the house that enclosed it.

Blanche had kindly invited her to Stretton to convalesce.

"Cressida will be here," she had told Eleanor on the telephone. "They can be company for each other while Grace and Anthony are out electioneering. Although I can't think why Anthony wants to involve himself in politics at all. Every politician I have ever met talks nothing but inflated nonsense. But John says that Anthony may be some use, and Grace is as keen as mustard on the idea. That's a blessing, of course, anything that occupies her attention. There won't be another b-a-b-y until she's forgotten the last time, I'm sure of that."

"Grace is still only a young woman," Eleanor had said firmly, only too well aware that Clio was not even married yet. "There's plenty of time for a dozen more babies."

So Alice had been transported to Stretton wrapped in traveling rugs, and ensconced in a bedroom on the second floor under the care of Nanny Brodribb. It was a few days before the Brocks arrived. She spent the time that Nanny allowed her out of bed wandering through the vast house, listening to its private language of creaks and sighs. It was interesting to have so much space after the confinement of illness, and she found that there was a melancholy satisfaction in solitude after the hubbub of her parents' ever-open household. She avoided her uncle John Leominster and cousin Hugo, but found it restful to sit in the saloon with her aunt for an hour at tea time.

While Blanche sewed or wrote letters, Alice sat dutifully with her own work but rarely looked at it. She had always been strong, and now she felt unmade by sickness, as if there were a new shape to her within the old one, not yet dry or set, waiting for experience to cut its marks into it. She let her thoughts wander, without direction.

The sofa she sat on was opposite the Sargent portrait of her mother and aunt. Alice decided that she much preferred this romantic vision of two fresh young girls to the later image that hung in the drawing room at home. In this one she liked to look at the pearly tones of the skin and the warm coils of hair, and the light and shadow in the intricate pleats and folds of the Victorian dresses. The Pilgrim picture was ugly, for all Nathaniel's admiration of it.

It was interesting that no one had suggested that Phoebe or Tabitha should sit for anyone when they came out. There would be no thought of it when her own turn came next year. Alice shivered at the very idea of having to expose herself to some painter's scrutiny. She pulled the loose ends of her hair to hide her cheeks and wrapped her thin arms around herself.

"Are you warm enough, darling?" Blanche asked.

"Yes, thank you, Aunt Blanche," Alice answered.

After a few days the Brocks arrived, Anthony driving Grace and Cressida in the big black car and the chauffeur following on in a smaller saloon. Alice went shyly out with Blanche to meet them. It was a long time since she had seen her older cousin, and when she came laughing and exclaiming into the great hallway, with her high heels tapping a brittle rhythm, she seemed as modern to Alice as the latest dance tune. With her perfectly made-up face and tiny butterfly of a hat, she was also as exotic as a hothouse orchid. Alice stared at her in fascinated admiration.

"*Alice*. Is this really you?" Grace kissed her on both cheeks and then held her away so that she could examine her. "So grown up. And so beautiful and *slim*. Not at all a fat baby anymore."

Alice had always hated being the baby of the Babies. She said sharply, "I'm seventeen and two months." And then, afraid that she might have offended this vision of elegance with her brusqueness, she added in an awkward mumble, "I'm awfully scraggy. But I've been ill, I can't help it. I expect I'll grow bonny again, like Nanny says."

Grace laughed. "Don't think of it. Everyone longs to be thin, you know. Ferocious diets, suffering for every single chocolate, all that. You keep your lovely narrow hips and count yourself lucky."

Alice flushed with pleasure. Compliments on her appearance did not often come her way in the Woodstock Road. Grace was thin, too. The bones of her hips seemed to jut through the silk jersey she wore belted over a pleated skirt. But at the same time, Alice could not help noticing Cressida standing half hidden behind her father. Her eyes were fixed on the floor, as if she were fascinated by the veining in the marble.

Cressida was plump. She seemed to be made of cushions of plumpness riding on big bones. Her tweed coat was tightly belted around her middle, making her torso look like a pair of solid pillows. She was holding on to her father's hand.

"I used to be huge," Alice offered into the thin air. No one said anything, and she found her voice trailing away. "Before I got the measles."

Grace was already tapping away, peeling off her long gloves and lifting her hat from her short, waved hair. "Oh yes, some tea, please. You wouldn't believe the traffic on the A1. Where can they all be going? In the saloon, Mummy?"

Anthony said to Cressida, "You remember Alice, Cressida, don't you?"

But Cressida wouldn't look at her.

Alice thought that Anthony Brock was rather nice, too. He had a funny, attractive gap between his front teeth and an expression that seemed to indicate that he always saw the amusing side of what went on around him. Alice admired the way that he opened doors for Grace and settled her in the chair and clicked his gold lighter for her cigarettes, without ever acting like her appendage. He seemed very capable and strong and masculine. He was quite unlike her own brothers, or her mild, shambling, quizzical father. She decided that she would like just such a husband for herself when the time came, although the thought made her blush even in the privacy of her bedroom. Alice was prudish for her age, although she had spent years trying to be as knowing as Tabby and Phoebe.

She hadn't understood, until the Brocks arrived, just how lonely she had been. Grace's feminine camaraderie and Anthony's friendliness were like a warm wind in spring. Alice opened to them like a flower.

It was a sign of Blanche's optimistic vagueness that she had assumed that Alice and Cressida would be company for one another. Cressida was not quite nine. The girls regarded each other across a divide in years that was widened even further by Cressida's hostility.

Alice tried to be friendly at first. Her eyes had just been opened to this new, glamorous phenomenon of Grace and Anthony, and she wanted to talk about them. She imagined, wrongly, that Cressida would be willing to share, not exactly secrets, but snippets of gossip that would enable Alice to feel that she was remotely part of their family.

"I do think your mother is pretty," she said. "I can't believe she's my first cousin. I mean, she's practically Clio's *twin*."

Clio wore serviceable clothes and talked about art and literature and worked in her spare time in one of Jake's peculiar clinics.

"Where does she get her hair done like that? Does she go to a smart salon in Mayfair, or does her—um—maid do it or something?"

"I don't know," Cressida said, staring out of the window.

Alice tried again. "Do you think your father will win the seat?"

"I don't know." But then, with surprising animation, "I hope *not,* if it means he's going to be away and busy all the time."

Alice was shocked. "How can you hope that?"

"I can hope whatever I like. He's *my* father."

"Yes, but he'd be a fine MP. Don't you think?"

"I hate politics," Cressida muttered. "And I wouldn't tell you what I think." She stood up, still not looking at Alice, and walked away. Her wool plaid dress was tight on her and decorated with a dainty white piqué collar and cuffs edged with lace, as if Grace bought clothes for a child who in her mind's eye was small and slender.

At last, Alice saw the two cars coming up the driveway. She threw her book aside and ran.

Grace and Anthony came in together, laughing. There were several men with them wearing dark clothes and big blue rosettes, and there was Hugo leaning on his stick. Alice was so anxious for news of the polling that she slipped through the cheery group and went straight to Grace.

"What happened? Will we win?"

The men in the dark suits all looked at her. Hugo made an irritable movement as if to brush her aside, but Grace swung around, her smile like a beacon.

"Oh, darling, what a day. All the gaffers and grannies and the women and children. In and out of the cars, up hill and down dale, out you come and vote for us, vote for Anthony Brock. It was such fun, you would have *adored* it." Grace waved her gloves in the air, like a flag.

I would have done, Alice thought. She could smell and almost taste Grace's exhilaration, and the glittering force of it drew her like a magnet. The cars, and the men, and stuffy Hugo and even the gaffers and grannies and constituency politics were bathed in the Brocks' glamour. She ached to be part of it all. The blue rosettes were like the membership insignia of some grand order. The order was to do with old England and country tradition and the proper way of doing things, but it was also spiced with pearls and perfume and wafted in fast cars.

"Grace was marvelous," Anthony said kindly to Alice. "She got all the people out, charmed them to the polling stations and back again. If we win, it will be more thanks to her than to me."

Grace put her arm through his and kissed him on the cheek. "No, it won't. It will be because they want you."

A jovial man rubbed his hands. "The signs are good, either way. No counting any chickens yet, mind you."

Hugo said impatiently, "Gentlemen, come through and have a drink. We have all earned one."

"I wouldn't say no to a whiskey and soda," said another red-faced man who held a round bowler hat by the brim.

"Where's Cress?" Anthony asked.

"Upstairs, I think," Alice said. She knew that he was going to ask her to fetch her down, but Grace put her hand on his arm.

"Have a drink first," she murmured.

The group moved off, with Grace at its heart, toward the small drawing room. Alice watched them, wistfully. Grace looked back over her shoulder, and winked at her. Alice would have died for her.

Cressida was stupid. Why wasn't she here, why hadn't she come down to see her marvelous parents?

"She's sweet, Alice, isn't she?" Grace was saying to Hugo as they went through. "She reminds me so much of Clio at that age, and me too, I suppose. So eager, and hungry for something to happen, any old thing."

The polls were closed. There was a large party for dinner at Stretton that evening. The agent was there and his wife, and some of the other party officials, and the local Tory grandees with their wives in old-fashioned jewels and stiff gowns with capes and tiers that released the smell of mothballs. Hugo and Thomas, bachelor sons, were gallant to the ladies, and the candidate moved smoothly amongst their menfolk, thanking them for their hard work and a good, clean, well-fought campaign. Blanche wore her emeralds with blue velvet and tried to interest herself in the conversations about Mr. Baldwin and the free market and the League of Nations. John Leominster was almost genial. It was the kind of gathering he liked best, outside the hunting season. He was amongst his own people, who knew their place, and his. He was pleased with his son-in-law, who would make a decent Member, and with Grace's support of him. The evening went well.

Cressida went to bed early, after having drunk the cup of hot milk that Nanny Brodribb considered essential to a good night's rest. She had won a precious twenty minutes with her father before he changed for dinner, and she had heard the news of the day. Grace had looked in for a moment on her way down, and waved a kiss at her.

Cressida pulled the covers up over her head. She liked her bed, and the comfort of sleep.

Alice sat up, watching the guests arrive from her bedroom window. Later she went out onto the stairs to listen, but she could hear only a confused hum of voices, and there was nothing to see but the heads of the footmen passing to and fro beneath her.

Downstairs in the dining room the candles were lit. The glow reflected off the massively ugly silver epergne in the center of the table and softened the faces drawn up on either side of it.

Grace looked down to Anthony, sitting on Blanche's left hand. His hair was watered smooth. He looked handsome and happy. Then he glanced up and caught her eye. There was a flicker of amused complicity between them that acknowledged the frowsy company, the tedium of the talk, and the sense of their duty being soundly done. Then Grace bent her head smilingly to her dinner companion, the man with the red face. She still felt the chord vibrating between her husband and herself. They were together, working in unison. She loved him; she was very nearly content.

The gentlemen came out to rejoin the ladies almost as soon as Blanche withdrew. It was time for Anthony and his party workers to drive to Ludlow, where the count was taking place, for the declaration.

"Are you ready?" Anthony whispered as he draped Grace's wrap around her shoulders.

"For anything," she responded. She meant that if they lost this time, well then, they would try again, and again. But she did not think they would lose.

They drove back through the winding lanes, the cars' headlamps cutting yellow wedges through the early summer dark. They found a press of people waiting at the hall, with photographers from the national as well as the local papers amongst them.

"Lady Grace spotters." Anthony laughed, but Grace insisted that they were there to see Anthony, not her.

The other two candidates and their supporters were waiting in a stuffy room at the back of the hall. When Grace and Anthony joined them, there was some handshaking and self-conscious joking, and then a tedious wait before the result could be declared. At last they were shepherded in an awkward group out onto the platform where the Mayor was presiding as returning officer. They stood with their heads bent while he recited the preamble in a sonorous voice.

The names came, with Anthony Patrick Earley Brock first in the alphabetical order, and the number of votes cast. Grace was listening so hard that she heard only a meaningless jumble of recited thousands, half drowned by cheering. She looked around in bewilderment and saw Anthony step forward with his arm raised, acknowledging the cheers. He had won. Not handsomely, but he had won.

Anthony Brock, MP.

Grace went to stand beside him, smiling into the flashbulbs. Her heart sang. The dull dinner and the round of provincial pleasantries that had led to this moment were forgotten. It had all been worthwhile. She was thinking of Westminster, and of Anthony's coming rapid rise through the Parliamentary party. She was dreaming of the Cabinet, and the possibility of Number Ten itself, and of her own role at his side. They stood proudly together on the platform, receiving their due congratulations at the beginning of it all.

Tomorrow, there would be photographs in the later editions. They would no longer be captioned "That bright young man Mr. Anthony Brock and lovely, party-going Lady Grace." They would be "The new Member for West Shropshire and his wife, political hostess Lady Grace Brock." Grace smiled. Not yet, maybe. But soon, soon enough.

The two girls heard the news in the early morning, when they came down to breakfast and found Anthony sitting alone at the table with the newspapers.

"Oh, how *utterly* wonderful, hooray," Alice cried. "I knew you were going to win it, I just knew." She ran around the table and flung her arms around him, forgetting in her rejoicing to be shy or in awe.

"Are you pleased, Daddy?" Cressida asked, muted in the face of Alice's enthusiasm.

"You know, I am, rather."

"Then I am, too, of course. Congratulations," Cressida said

gamely. Her plump cheeks looked pinched, as if invisible thumbs pressed into them, leaving white hollows in the flesh.

Clio read the result in the newspaper. She folded the paper and propped it against her coffee cup so that she could study the photograph more closely. She decided that Anthony looked satisfied, in his modest and undramatic way, and that Grace, with her small neat head rising out of a cloud of furs, looked indecently exultant.

"It sounds like a Labour government, then. I don't see how Baldwin can hope to carry on, do you?" Julius said, glancing up from *The Times*. "Is there any more of that coffee?"

"I'll make some." She smiled at him. "Is this in yours?" She passed the *Mail* across the table and went into the kitchen with the coffee pot.

Julius looked at Grace. It was more than a year since he had seen her, much longer than that since they had exchanged more than superficial family talk. He couldn't even remember when they had last been alone together. But the unexpected thought of her could still dislocate the steady, colorless structure of his life. It was as if he suddenly lost his balance on familiar ground, slipped and had to grasp at the displaced features of the landscape as they whistled past him and he fell. He was a successful violinist, in London for a series of recitals. He was staying in the old flat, with Clio. He had a routine; it was a little anemic and lonely, it was true, but he was not uncomfortable.

And he was still in love with Grace, as he had always been.

The difference was that simply to love her had once been enough. He had been calm and content, taking pleasure in the knowledge that she existed, and that there was time, and a world of opportunity. But now Julius felt the beginnings of disappointment. He considered his life, and recognized that there was nothing in it but his music. There had been one drunken night, long ago, with that red-haired model of Pilgrim's. Jeannie. He did not want to remember what had happened. There had been two girls, at different times, in Paris, both of them only briefly. For a long time now there had been no one at all.

I am not yet thirty, Julius thought. *And I already feel dried up, as if my bones are rubbing together inside me.*

He studied the picture. Even through the blur of newsprint, through the coarse dots that swam together to make an approximation of her features, he could see that Grace was growing more beautiful. The fact that he loved her seemed irrelevant, pathetic even. It was the weary obsession of a lonely man, doomed through his own weakness to worship the icon left over from his adolescence.

Julius smiled, his mouth making a thin curve. He knew all this, and he loved her none the less.

Clio came back with the coffee pot and leaned over his shoulder to pour. Julius tossed the folded paper back across the table. "They look pleased with themselves," he said.

"Anthony deserved to win. And I'm sure he'll make a good, solid, Tory MP. Pity for him it will have to be in opposition."

"Unless there's a Liberal coalition."

They began to talk about the election result. They were circumspect with each other when Grace was mentioned.

They had finished their coffee when Clio heard the rattle of the morning's post falling into the wire basket behind the letterbox. She left the table and ran to collect it.

When she came back, she was sorting a sheaf of letters.

"Two for you," she announced, holding them out. "Bills and boring things for me."

Julius saw that there was a blue envelope in the pocket of her Chinese robe—the same bright silk robe copied long ago from Grace's wardrobe. And a moment or two later, she slipped away from the breakfast table and went to her room, to read the letter in private.

Julius watched her go. He had already guessed that Clio was in love. Her increasingly habitual wryness had suddenly softened into a more gentle hesitancy, and the lines of her face had softened with it. She looked younger and prettier, sometimes almost girlish. She also, he noticed, took much more trouble over her appearance. Her stockings and gloves were carefully mended instead of being allowed to run into holes, and she had begun to wear colored scarves at the necks of her jumpers, and smart little head-hugging hats. On her dressing table, when he had looked into her bedroom in search of aspirins, he had caught a glimpse of Elizabeth Arden's foundation cream, and a pot of the Vaseline that she rubbed onto her eyelids.

Julius was pleased for her. He wondered who the man could be.

Clio sat down on her bed, breathless with anticipation, and carefully slit open the blue envelope. She had only seen Miles yesterday, when they had lunched rather unsatisfactorily together. He had been preoccupied over his escalope Milanese, although she had tried hard to divert him with *Fathom* gossip, and he had left quite abruptly before the waiter had brought the pudding menu. But Miles often wrote a letter immediately after they had met, especially if it had not been one of their happiest encounters, and his letters were invariably delightful.

She unfolded the thin sheet of blue paper and read: "How is the dear little piglet this morning? Has she brushed her bristles and buffed her trotters ready for the day?" There was a drawing of a piglet beside the words, with a corkscrew tail and a broad smile. "But perhaps she thinks that her big bad pig was altogether too bad and piggified yesterday, to run off when she was being so sweet and good in trying to cheer him up?" Another piglet, this time with a ferocious scowl.

If she does she is quite right, and he sends her herewith a penitent kiss and plea that she will not bother her pretty piglet head with his vain moods. He is worried about his work and his bad debts and 1,000 other boring and unpigwig details that he would not dream of whispering to her, only hoping that she will forgive him his ill humor and let him take her out for a slap-up piggy dinner just as soon as his ship comes in.

(A check any day now, Tony Hardy has sworn on his life.)

In the meantime, shall he slip into the office just for the briefest of minutes this afternoon, perhaps to persuade the princess of piglets to dip her snout into a glass of beer with him?

There was no signature, only a drawing of a rather larger pig, sitting disconsolately beside a milestone bearing the words "Too many miles from Clio."

Clio read the letter twice, then smiled. "Idiot," she said aloud. Then she folded it and replaced it in the envelope and put it carefully with a thin sheaf of identical envelopes in the top drawer of her dressing table.

She would have lunch with Miles again today, of course, if he did turn up at *Fathom*. She had tried before now to pretend that she was busy, in the wake of some disagreement or show of bad humor, but he always persuaded her. The truth was that she never wanted to resist him. Sometimes she had to hold on to her chair, or on to the beery mahogany curve of the bar, physically to restrain herself from leaping at him, snatching him to her, because she wanted him so much. And all the time she had to make herself light, and whimsical, because that was what he liked, and never to hint at the dark possessiveness that gnawed at her like a cancer. Sometimes all the nerves in her body screamed with the effort of it.

Well then, she thought. She would see him today because she couldn't bear not to see him. But she would ask Julius to meet her too, and when Miles appeared she would ask him to join them, and the three of them could go along to the Fitzroy or the Hope or somewhere. She could listen to the two men talking, and try to see Miles through her brother's eyes. It would be a relief, a respite for her from her own anxiety and jealousy and Miles's pressure on her to be a happy piglet.

"Have lunch with me today?" she asked Julius when she re-emerged from her bedroom dressed for work.

"Of course I will," he said, so happily that she felt guilty.

The *Fathom* offices looked the same as they had always done. Clio's desk was heaped with orderly piles of manuscripts and proofs, with her big black typewriter set in the middle of them. Her desk was an oasis of order in the usual chaos of boxes of back issues, review copies, files, and dirty teacups. The door to Max's inner office stood open, revealing his empty chair and overflowing ashtray. Max had already gone out.

Julius looked around with distaste. His own domestic habits were spinsterish in their precision. "How can you bear to work in here?" he asked, but Clio only laughed at him.

"Shall we go?"

"Um, in a minute," Clio answered. "Just let me do something quickly for the post."

While he was waiting for her, Julius stood looking out of the dust-veiled window into the street. He saw a taxi draw up and a man step out of it. He was wearing a creased linen jacket and dark blue trousers like a French workman's. He turned and strolled toward the front door, and then pushed it open without knocking. He stood in the doorway, gazing in at them and smiling, as if he belonged there and they were the visitors. He was wearing a red handkerchief knotted around his throat, and he had large hazel eyes and warm-colored skin. Julius knew immediately that this was the man who had written Clio's letter.

"Miles? I wasn't expecting to see you," Clio lied. She tried to make her voice light and teasing, but it stuck in her throat. She knew that Julius was watching her, and cursed herself for the stupidity of bringing them both here.

Miles's eyes widened. "*Weren't* you? I'm sorry, and now you're busy, so I'll just go away again. But won't you introduce us first?"

"This is my twin brother, Julius Hirsh. Julius, this is Miles Lennox."

"The violinist?"

Miles held out his hand. He had an attractive voice and he spoke clearly, enunciating each word as if it were important. It had the effect of making people listen to what he said, even if it was nonsense.

"Yes." Julius shook the hand.

"This is wonderful." When he smiled, the naturally pensive lines of his face became sunny. "But now, I'm interrupting. Perhaps we'll have a chance to meet again?"

"Miles, I don't think Julius will mind if you join us for lunch. Will you, Julius?"

"Not at all," Julius answered, as if he had any choice in the matter.

Clio's urgent job for the post seemed to be forgotten. She put on her hat, and the three of them went out into the early summer sunshine. They walked westward, through the Bloomsbury streets and spring-green squares, to the Fitzroy Tavern. Miles talked, sometimes dashing a few steps ahead and then turning to face them, running backward in little half-strides so that he could see them as they walked. He was in one of his buoyant moods, and Clio began to relax. Julius would like him, he could hardly help it, and it was plain that Miles already liked Julius.

The bar seemed dark after the brilliant day outside. When Julius's eyes accustomed themselves to the murk, he saw walls and ceiling browned by decades of cigarette smoke, small brass-ringed tables and upright chairs arranged on the bare floor, and a long brown bar. There were quite a lot of people standing and leaning down the length of the bar, and the air was thick with smoke and the malty stench of beer.

Julius's companions were clearly regulars here.

"Miles and Clio," someone called out, and another lugubrious voice murmured, "Greetings, you two. How your bright faces do enliven the dull day."

Julius looked at Clio, and saw that her cheeks were pink with a kind of meek happiness that he had never seen in her before. Her eyes shone as she watched Miles.

The owner of the lugubrious voice, a man in corduroys and a walrus moustache silvered with beer froth, was offering drinks. Julius let himself be introduced and drawn into the circle. He had never much liked London pubs compared with the cosmopolitan bustle of cafés in Paris or Berlin, but he accepted a half of warm bitter and prepared to enjoy himself for Clio's sake.

Clio glowed. She had done the right thing in bringing her brother here after all. She had heard the greetings through his ears as they came in, "Miles and Clio" and "you two." They were a couple, of course, and her anxiety was only bred from her knowledge that she was twenty-eight, and had been a little lonely, and was now so consumingly in love. She knew that if she couldn't have Miles, she didn't want anyone else. She seemed to have been waiting for him ever since they had been introduced at the party for Pilgrim's exhibition, and for long before that in her imagination. Even going to bed with Pilgrim that night in his studio now seemed a preparation for Miles, discharging herself of her virginity in order not to embarrass him with it.

Only Clio and Miles did not sleep together, not yet. He kissed her playfully, and sometimes he held her close to him with a kind of wistful intensity. She was ashamed of the sharp currents of sexual longing that these episodes set off in her. She wondered if she was abnormal, then remembered the Marie Stopes teaching that it was right and natural for women as well as men to feel physical desire. Miles must feel exactly as she did, she reasoned, only Miles was a gentleman whereas Pilgrim wasn't.

Clio worried about how they might progress beyond their present expressions of mutual affection. Just once, she had tried to show him that he could do more than kiss her. But it had only been once. He had shivered with an involuntary *moue* of shock and distaste, and she had felt crass and unladylike. She warned herself that she must let Miles set his own pace. Only time went on, and he seemed quite content, and she had to tread around the circle of her suppressed anxiety and appetite without ever seeing the way out.

Julius and Clio stood for a few minutes with the writers and painters and publishers at the bar, listening to a vehement argument about the outcome of the General Election and Mr. Baldwin's chances of forming a coalition with the Liberals. Miles seemed to drift through the group, acknowledging it and at the same time suggesting his distance from the clamor. At length, smiling faintly, he raised his eyebrows at Julius and Clio.

"Shall we sit down over there?"

They took their drinks and went, with relief. Julius noticed that Miles guided Clio's arm and drew out a chair for her to sit down. He was pleased to see her taken care of, and to hear from their acquaintances that they were accepted as a regular partnership. It was better than he had hoped at his first sight of Miles Lennox.

More drinks were brought from the bar. Miles was drinking whiskey to follow his beer, and no one seemed disposed to eat anything. Julius nursed his half of bitter and dreamed of a melting *omelette aux fines herbes,* or the *plat du jour* at La Coupole. Tomorrow night he was playing a Bach concert at the Wigmore Hall. He needed food, and sleep, and no disturbances. He began to regret having accepted Clio's invitation to this place full of unkempt, vociferous people.

"I see that your smart cousin won his seat in the shires," Miles was saying.

"My cousin's husband," Clio corrected him.

The corners of Miles's long mouth curled humorously as he turned to Julius. "Clio doesn't like me to tease her about her grand relations."

"They aren't so very grand," Julius said. He didn't want to talk about Grace here, and to change the subject he asked, "Are you a writer, Miles?"

At once, both Clio and Miles looked pleased.

"A very good one," Clio told him, firing up with pride. "He published a wonderful collection of stories, *After Image.* You must read it, Julius. And some war poetry, and several very much admired pieces for *Fathom* and *The Calendar of Modern Letters.* . . ."

Miles leaned across to her and put his hand over hers, indulgently. "Darling, that's enough. What will Julius think? It's all juvenile stuff," he told him. "What I am working on now is much more significant. It's a big novel, very experimental in form, an exploration of the modern condition unconfined by traditional narrative techniques. I want to break away from the idea that a story must begin and end, even that it must have recognizable characters.

"I'm trying to capture and distill the generality of human thought and experience, give it expression through a series of disembodied voices, if you like, each one crying out of darkness. Even *Ulysses,* you know, is quite conventional. We know who Bloom and Molly are, so all our perceptions of them are precolored by that knowledge—"

Miles broke off and looked modestly down into his whiskey glass. Clio slipped out of her chair and took the empty glasses to the bar.

"How interesting. How far have you got?" Julius asked, suppressing the tremors of skepticism.

"It goes very slowly. I have to break off to do hack work in order to live, of course. More steadily in the last few months, mostly thanks to Clio. But it's bad luck to be too optimistic. . . . As a matter of fact, I'm meeting my publisher one evening next week. I'll show him some of the early sections. If he likes it, I shall breathe more easily."

Clio came back and set the fresh drinks on the puddled table. "Really? You're ready to let Tony read it? That's marvelous. You didn't tell me."

Miles took her hand again. "I know. Superstitious, or something. Anyway, that's quite enough about that. Thanks for the drink, darling. Now, Julius, are there any tickets left for tomorrow evening?"

They talked about music, and then about new films, and at last the conversation slipped back into literary gossip. Miles was good company, but Julius began to feel very conscious that he had had two drinks on an empty stomach. At half past two, Clio looked at her watch.

"Oh, God. Back to work for me."

Miles showed no inclination to move. Someone at the bar had sent over another whiskey for him. He put his long fingers up to Clio's chin and drew her face down to his so that he could kiss her on the lips. "Mmm. Let's go together to hear Julius's lovely music tomorrow night, shall we?"

"Yes, let's do that. Don't sit too long in here drinking whiskey, will you?"

"Would I?"

As she left with Julius, Clio looked back to see that Miles had already been reabsorbed. He was listening intently to what someone was saying, with his fingertips pressed together and his smooth, symmetrical features composed like a brooding saint in a pre-Raphaelite painting.

Julius and Clio retraced the way through the sunny streets, blinking at first in the great slices of light that cut across their path. The city had settled into the yellow daze of a hot afternoon. Julius felt the beginnings of a headache vibrate between his eyes.

"Thank you for coming. I wanted you to meet him," Clio said simply.

"Do you always drink so much? Don't you eat anything, even a sandwich?"

Clio stopped, immediately contrite. She put her hand on his arm. "Oh, I'm so sorry. I'd completely forgotten you need to eat regularly. Look, there's a Jewish café on the next corner. You can get salt beef on rye bread." The delicacies of Nathaniel's childhood. Julius's irritation dwindled a little.

"I was asking about *you*. I can make myself a sandwich at home."

Clio shrugged. "I don't usually bother. It saves money. And it makes me at least feel thinner, even if I don't look it. If you think that's drinking a lot, just go in there this evening. Any evening."

"How serious is it?" Julius asked abruptly.

Her voice was so low that he could hardly hear it. "It's serious. I would marry him tomorrow, if he asked me."

I don't think it will come to that, Julius almost said. He didn't know whether to feel relieved or pained for her. "Does he make you happy?"

There was a moment while she thought about it. He saw the soft, girlish look that had transformed her. The innocent surface of her expression seemed to shiver with anxiety.

"Oh, yes. Yes."

"Well, then." He kissed her forehead. "Bless you."

Clio smiled at him. "Thank you. You are the first person in the family to meet him. I wanted it to be you first."

"It's your life, Clio. Not ours. It doesn't matter what any of us think."

"It does. You all matter to me. Mummy, Pappy, Aunt Blanche, the Babies. Even Grace," she finished, oddly.

Julius stayed in London for five more days, then left for Paris. He told Clio that he planned to move soon to Berlin. In Germany, Hindemith and Schönberg and the other pioneers of atonal music were revitalizing the orchestral repertoire, and he wanted to work at the heart of the new movement.

"I wish you weren't so far away," Clio said.

"Berlin isn't far, and Paris is close. Come and see me. You can speak the languages, why not use them?"

"Perhaps I will." Clio smiled at him, knowing that she wouldn't leave London while Miles was still there.

She missed Julius after he had gone, but she was happy to have the Gower Street flat to herself again. Miles liked to visit her in the evenings after his day's writing, and these were Clio's happiest times, but he had not called at Gower Street at all while Julius was staying with her.

On their evenings alone together Miles would sit beside the gas fire with his long fingers curled around a whiskey glass and gossip to her about books and publishers and their friends from the Soho pubs. Miles was an excellent talker, and he was a clever mimic and a waspish but accurate observer of Soho people and their pretensions and calamities. He could make Clio laugh until her eyes ran with tears, and make the frowsy world of literature seem wild and funny and glamorous.

"It's all perfectly true," Miles would protest, peering sideways and shaking his smooth head at her, after recounting the latest scandal or rejection or lover's quarrel with a full repertoire of voices. "You don't think I would make it up, do you?"

Clio loved to be alone with him, in the little flat, while he made her feel part of a cosmopolitan conspiracy of two. She cooked him ambitious dinners, of which he was always appreciative, and kept his glass filled with wine or whiskey. And then after they had eaten and Clio had removed the dishes and made a pot of coffee for him, Miles often read to her. He liked Housman and Kipling and Browning and he read well, with humor as well as passion. Clio would sit on the floor with her head resting against his knee, half listening and half dreaming, while his warm hand smoothed her hair.

One night, after even more whiskey than usual, Miles had fallen asleep in his chair. She had hoisted him up while he mumbled and protested and steered him through into her bedroom. Then she had let him fall sideways onto the bed and had loosened his collar and taken off his shoes, and covered him with her blankets. She lay down beside him, in the warmth that he had generated, and listened to his thick breathing until she fell asleep herself.

In the morning she had brought him tea and aspirins, and he groaned and pretended to hide his head. But then he caught hold of her hand and looked straight at her, and said, "I wish we could always look after each other, just like this, without any piglet play."

Somehow Clio had stopped herself from answering triumphantly, "But we can. It's what I want. Just that."

She had smiled at him, and adjusted the curtains halfway across the window so that the morning light was not too bright for his headache. It was one of the best of all their times together.

A week after the Wigmore Hall concert, Clio spent the evening alone at home. She made herself an omelette, and when she had cleared it away, she sat down to read a sheaf of submissions for Max. There was nothing she could admire amongst them, and she was left with the dry taste of boredom and disappointment. At eleven o'clock she got undressed and put on her Chinese robe. She washed some stockings and hung them to dry over the bath, and stood for a few minutes looking blankly out of the tiny window at the black rooflines and pasty-lit rooms of Bloomsbury. A nauseous sense of futility and apprehension weighed in the pit of her stomach, but she made herself ignore it and went wearily to bed.

The sudden drill of the doorbell made her start and shiver. The ringing went on and on, as if whoever was doing it was pressing the button with the last of his strength. She pulled on her robe and groped to the door.

"Miles."

He was leaning against the jamb, white-faced, with blood dried on his puffed mouth.

"Oh, God." She put her arms under his, took the weight of him. "Come here, let me help you."

Somehow she found the strength to haul him inside and up the stairs. She let him fall into an armchair and tilted his head back against a velvet cushion to look at his chin. Miles's eyes were closed and his face was waxy. She brought a bowl of warm water and a cloth, and knelt beside him to sponge the blood away. There was dirt in his hair, and his hands were bruised and filthy. He stank of whiskey.

Clio concentrated on the practicalities of what must be done, not letting herself speculate on what could have happened to bring him to this. The gash in his mouth was not deep, and she did not think the jaw was broken. He was so white that she thought he might be about to vomit. She tipped out the bloody water and left the empty basin on the floor beside him.

Miles opened his eyes. He saw Clio's concerned face hovering over him. She looked a picture of rosy sanctity, roused from her blameless bed. Rage and bitterness rose up, swelling inside him like nausea, and focused on Clio. He lurched out of his chair and swayed across the Turkish rug, scattering manuscripts and books and a bowl of potpourri with one sweep of his arm. Clio had to spring out of his way.

Miles howled at her. "Don't look at me like that. Don't look. Sheep's eyes, drowning sheep. What do you want, damn you?"

"I'm sorry . . ."

"Sorry? What do you know about sorrow, bloody"—he thumped himself in the chest, and staggered again—"stupid bitch."

Clio faced him. She was angry now too, with the quick childish anger that sprang up in their quarrels. She said coldly, "I thought *you* might want something. Ringing my doorbell. It's the middle of the night. If you don't want anything except to insult me, you can go away again. Sleep it off somewhere else. You are disgusting."

He swung at her. His hand clipped the side of her face, and she recoiled, shocked rather than hurt, almost spitting her fury at him. Then her arm came up, and she struck back at him with her sober strength, the flat of her hand against his bruised jaw.

For a second he hung in front of her, his face changing, contracting with pain. Then he seemed to shrink, growing physically smaller as if she had punctured him. His arms wrapped around his chest, and he sank down to his knees. He looked up at her, reflecting her own posture when she knelt to bathe his broken mouth. The whites of his eyes were yellow and bleary with hurt.

"Miles . . ."

There was a rug in front of the gas fire. He lay down on it, drawing his knees up to his chest. With a sound like tearing cloth he began to cry. His face was a child's, in the grip of a nightmare.

"*Don't,* Miles . . ."

Clio lay down beside him. She curled her body against his back, trying to warm him with her own warmth. His sobbing shook her.

"What has happened? You must tell me. Miles, I'm here. It's Clio, I love you. Just tell me what's happened." The words became a murmur of comfort while she held him, waiting for the storm to be over. "I'm here. It's all right. Don't cry anymore."

At last he lay quietly. She made him turn to her, and she smoothed his hair and held his face between her hands.

"Your hands, so cool," he said. The weeping fit seemed to have sobered him, a faint glow of color was creeping back into his face. They lay looking into each other's eyes.

At last Clio said gently, "What happened? You must tell me, you know. Whatever it was." She made herself ready for the worst. For violence, murder even.

"Fight in a pub."

"Why?"

"I was drunk. Still am. Sorry. Drunk because I was angry."

She soothed him, with little movements of her hands, with her soft voice. He felt the viciousness subsiding.

"Didn't mean to hit you. Say . . . what I said. Sorry."

"It doesn't matter. Why were you angry?"

"Oh, Christ. Because I gave the first draft of my book to Tony Hardy."

Clio knew how important that was. "What did he say?"

"He said it was no good. 'I can't offer you any encouragement, Miles, I wish I could,' were his actual words." Miles's face contorted, and his grazed fists clenched. "The smug little bastard. I could have . . . I wanted to *kill* him. With my hands. I could have done it, while he was sitting there smirking at me. But I didn't, did I? I left him to it and I went to the Swiss, and there was a crowd of people in there. Then an argument about something or other, can't even remember what it was, now. Hit someone, then someone hit me back."

He tried to smile at her and then winced, reaching up to touch his face. "Sorry about everything. You are the only good thing I could think of."

Clio's whole body relaxed, as if a wire had been cut. She could have shouted out her relief. He hadn't run away from anything, there was no dreadful scene of violence outside in the dark. Only rejection, temporary rejection. She wanted to laugh and hold him tighter, but the laugh would have been too wild with the release of tension. She said calmly, "That was very short-sighted of Tony. But you are stronger than that, Miles, aren't you? You know the importance of what you are doing. There are other publishers, other publishing houses, dozens of them. What does one opinion matter? It's a small setback, that's all."

She felt strong now, all her fears gone. She knew what had to be done. Miles was vulnerable, and she could defend him. "Listen, you can finish the book. Complete it, and then we'll show them. Think of all the people who admire your work. Max, Leonard, Peter and Cyril, Nina . . . Everyone *knows* you will write the great novel. Remember the success of *After Image*. Tony Hardy and Randle and Cates are not the sole arbiters of what is good and valuable. . . ."

Anger flared up in Miles again. "Tony Hardy's a liar, a *charlatan*. That list at Randles is the last refuge for . . . the written-out and washed-up. I wouldn't publish my laundry lists with them, I wouldn't pick him up if he was begging in the gutter. . . ."

Clio let him rage. The depth of his bitterness startled her but she waited, holding him close to her.

At last, exhaustion overcame him. He shrank into passivity, and turned his face against her breast. Clio was weary too, but the old circuit of anxiety and longing had been broken. Miles had turned to her when he needed her, and in the security of knowing that, she felt capable enough to make the decisions for both of them. Miles must be left in peace to work, that was all that mattered.

"Your book will be published," she whispered. "It will have the acclaim it deserves." She had not read a word of it, but she felt fiercely protective and proud of it.

Miles nodded obediently. "Yes. Clio, I . . ."

She put her fingers over his mouth. "That's enough. Come to bed now."

She stood up and helped him to his feet. He almost fell, and she had to catch him and support him.

"Still drunk," he mumbled. "Bad pig behavior."

Clio's bedroom was lit by small shaded lamps. There was a crochetwork bedspread and framed family photographs, and a jumble of feminine paraphernalia on the dressing table. Miles looked around him in momentary bewilderment and then gave a wild hoot of laughter.

"Beddy-byes, is it?"

Tenderly, patiently, Clio undressed him. He was unsteady but quite compliant. She folded his stained clothes and laid them on her Regency chair. His skin was very white and smooth, and his penis hung like a limp candle against a bush of reddish hair. She folded back the covers for him, and he lay down. When he was safely under the blankets, his face sagged, and she thought that he would cry again.

"Everything is all right now," she told him.

Clio undressed herself, folding her own clothes and placing them on the chair opposite Miles's. Then she slipped into bed beside him, stretching her body alongside his. When she looked into his face she couldn't fathom his expression, but he lifted his hand, as if his arm were stiff, and laid it on her breast. She waited, expectantly, but there was no sign of his arousal.

Clio had read the textbooks and the medical notes. Very gently she reached out and began to stroke him.

His face changed. The disconcerting laughter welled up in him again. "Turn over," he ordered her. "With your back to me."

His hand descended to her buttocks. He cupped them, and then parted them. At once, she felt him harden. A moment later he was inside her.

It was the briefest love-making, but they had achieved it.

When it was over Miles slid away, rolling over to lie on his back with his eyes closed now. Clio saw that there were tears under his eyelids. She felt unformed with love and tenderness. She whispered to him, "Miles? Don't worry anymore. I'll look after you, if you will let me. I have this place, a little money of my own. You can move in here with me, it's quiet here. You can work in peace, you needn't think about anything else, no other work until your novel is written. I'll always be here, if you want me to be."

His eyes opened, focusing on hers. "Will you?"

"Yes. Always."

Miles's fists clenched, then loosened again. He had the sense of a line being thrown to him, out of a heavy sea. "I . . . wish . . . you . . . would be."

Clio said, "We will get married as soon as we can, and then we'll belong to each other forever."

He repeated with a kind of wondering docility, "Forever."

He lay still, then, listening to the last ebb of traffic in the street and the creaks and sighs of an unfamiliar room. His breathing grew more even, rising and falling against Clio's, opposite and then in harmony. She clicked a switch and the room went dark, and she settled herself against him. He felt the scented weight of her.

"Piglet," Miles said.

Eleven

"YOUR FATHER AND I WOULD have liked to give you a party at home." Eleanor sighed, not for the first time. "A real party for all our friends, like in the old days."

Clio watched her fussing around the bedroom, in which all traces of Miles's occupancy had been carefully hidden. Her mother was already dressed for the evening. The old-fashioned and favorite dress she had chosen was cut to show off her bosom and hide her thickened waist, and the dark red shot silk flattered her coloring. Eleanor made no concession to the modern fashion for women to look as much like boys as possible. Her long, thick hair was still piled on top of her head, and her heavy figure was tightly corseted. She looked handsome but distinctly of another era, like some ornate mahogany sideboard placed four-square in a mirrored Deco salon.

The thought stirred a protective tenderness in Clio. She knew how much Eleanor wanted to be maternally involved in her first daughter's marriage preparations, and the sighing and fussing were only expressions of her frustration because Clio could find nothing for her to do.

The wedding itself was to be small and quiet, in St. Pancras registry office, with a lunch in the Eiffel Tower afterward. Ruth and Jake were giving the party this evening, and in her capable way Ruth had refused all offers of help. Clio understood that tonight her mother would like to be arranging her hair and making last-minute needle-and-thread adjustments to some frivolous frock for her, but she could not offer her even that much. Her hair was cut in a short bob, because Miles liked it that way, and could be brushed into waves in ten seconds, and her simple blue dress was already ironed and waiting on its hanger on the back of the wardrobe door. And she was afraid that Eleanor's fiddling would at any minute expose some evidence of Miles that she could not explain away.

"Why don't you go into the other room and ask Pappy to pour you a drink, to calm you down before we go to Jake's?"

Her mother turned on her, the magnificently prominent bosom heaving. "I *am* calm. Why should I not be? I was only saying I wish you had let us give a party for you at home. You only marry once, Clio. There are so many people in Oxford, in your own world, who have known you since you were tiny. . . ."

Piano teachers, Clio thought, and French mistresses, and one-time undergraduates who were slowly metamorphosing into portly dons. She felt no particular nostalgia for the rotation of the academic year in the Woodstock Road.

"*This* is our world, mine and Miles's," she said, as gently as she could. "And everyone in the world I care most about will be at Jake and Ruth's this evening, except for Julius."

Julius was in Berlin. Clio said hastily before Eleanor could begin to bewail his long absence, "This is what Miles and I both wanted. And it's not as if I'm the only daughter. Tabby and Alice will probably both demand huge weddings in the same year, and Pappy will be driven to the verge of bankruptcy to provide them with orange blossom and white tulle, and you will both be thanking your stars that I chose St. Pancras and a tailored costume from Selfridges."

Eleanor sighed yet again. "Tabby is more interested in teaching her Sunday-school classes than in meeting a suitable young man. I have tried to encourage her since she came out, believe me, but she's not like Phoebe. I suppose Phoebe might be accused of overenthusiasm in the other direction, but then I suppose most of the young behave like that nowadays. And Alice . . . who can possibly predict what Alice will want when the time comes?"

Alice was stubborn and moody, given to unpredictable enthusiasms and sometimes seemingly at the mercy of her own unfocused intelligence, but when she wanted to be, she could also be funny and charming and affectionate. She was her father's delight, as she had been ever since babyhood.

While they were talking, Clio had put on the blue dress and fastened it without more than a glance in the wardrobe mirror. Now she went to Eleanor and put her hands on her shoulders. She bent slightly and kissed her mother on the forehead, where two vertical lines showed between her eyebrows.

"Everything will be all right," she promised her.

She guided Eleanor out of the bedroom with relief. If any rumpled male vest or stray cut-throat razor should happen to present itself in one of the other rooms, she could dismiss it as left behind by Julius.

Nathaniel was sitting beside the gas fire, reading the current issue of *Fathom* and smoking his pipe. He had lit and relit it with matches from a box belonging to Miles, absently picked up from the table beside him. As soon as Eleanor and Clio came in, he laid the quarterly aside, with a touch of regret, and stood up.

"How beautiful you both look. I shall be able to claim the two belles of the ball as my own."

"It isn't a ball, Pappy. What can you be expecting, in Jake and Ruth's little house? It's a small party, for family and a few friends. Nothing formal or elaborate."

Eleanor rustled to his side. "Do you see what I mean? No music or dancing. No flowers, not even a corsage for her dress, and the plainest dress for a bride-to-be, as if she wants to disappear into the wallpaper instead of shining, as it is her right to do. And it's *not* as if it were a question of money, although she keeps talking about how poor she and Miles will be, because I have told her we could quite well afford—"

Nathaniel put his hand on her arm. "Eleanor, this is Clio's wedding, and she must have it as she wants. If she wanted massed bands and twenty attendants, she would have said as much. If she prefers beer and a chicken sandwich in Islington, then she has my blessing also." His eyes were crinkling over the gray and black wool of his beard.

"I don't think it will be quite as grim even as you paint it," Clio told him before she kissed him. Although in her heart she felt a shiver of doubt as to whether the party was such a festive idea as it had seemed a month ago, when Miles had agreed to set a day for their wedding. She saw her mother and father glance at each other, and then the loving determination of their smiles.

There was an extravagant bottle of champagne keeping cool on the sill outside the kitchen window. Clio had intended to bring it in with a flourish and drink a toast to Eleanor and Nathaniel and to her own future, but the moment suddenly seemed too brittle with their separate anxieties. The champagne had better stay where it was while they attended soberly to whatever the evening required of them.

Perhaps Eleanor was right after all, she thought sadly. Perhaps there should be music and flowers, and a dress that would swirl in the scented air as she danced with her lover.

But Clio only said, "If we are all ready, perhaps we should drive over to Islington now in case Ruth does need any help at the last minute?"

Her little car was parked in the nearby mews. As Nathaniel squeezed into the back seat and Eleanor settled alongside her, Clio was thinking that the Austin was becoming a luxury that she and Miles could no longer properly afford. Since Miles had stopped doing hack work in order to concentrate on his book, they had had to make a series of economies so as to be able to exist on Clio's money alone. She had a small income from her Holborough grandparents, as well as what she earned at *Fathom*, enough for one person to live modestly on but hardly enough for two. She had made the necessary sacrifices joyfully, for Miles's sake, and for the great novel.

But her car gave her a sense of independence, and she still loved the mechanical business of driving it. Perhaps they could manage as they were for a few more months, she decided. Until Miles's book was completed. Or perhaps she should look for another part-time job, one that would pay, instead of giving her time voluntarily to the Mothers' Clinic. She would have to talk it over with Jake and Ruth. She had hardly seen them, except at the Clinic, since Miles had moved in, whereas the three of them had once been almost inseparable.

The weight of her anxieties seemed to depress the bones of her skull, but when she tried to single them out and confront them, they shifted and slid, leaving only the sickly reminder of their pressure. *I am getting married,* she told herself. *We shall be poor for a time, but this is what we have chosen.*

The car bumped gently over the cobbles in the mews, then turned out into Gower Street.

Ruth was in the kitchen with an apron tied over her best dress. She pulled out a drawer and gathered a handful of silver forks, then laid them in a rattling sheaf on the tray to be carried upstairs. She could hear Tabby with Dorcas in the dining room overhead. Perhaps between them they would be able to make a half-decent job of laying the buffet. Dorcas was willing enough, but she was only the daily cleaner and couldn't be expected to have much idea about waiting at table, and Jake's sister was a good-natured girl who couldn't keep an idea in her head for five minutes at a time. Ruth assumed that she would have to go up in the end and redo every-thing, but before then there was still the best cutlery to be sorted and the cream to be piped onto the sherry trifles.

She wiped her fingers on her apron and turned to the table where the dishes were waiting. They were heavy; Jake would have to carry them upstairs.

Where was Jake? He was late back from surgery, and he had promised faithfully that he would be home in time to help her.

Tabby put her head around the door at the top of the narrow stairs that led down to the kitchen and shouted, "Do you want us to use the big white tablecloth?"

Ruth winced. Tabitha had been staying in the house for two days, and she still hadn't understood that once the children were in bed, the house must be kept quiet until they were properly asleep. Now Lucas would probably be out of bed and running up and down the stairs, and Rachel would start calling for another drink.

She went to the foot of the stairs. "Of course I do, that's why I put it out. Don't shout, Tabby, please."

The forcing bag was in the drawer of the table. Ruth found a metal nozzle and fitted it in place, and spooned whipped cream into the mouth of the bag. The basement kitchen was dark, lit only by an overhead bulb, and she stood in her own light and frowned at the bland yellow faces of the trifles. The custard looked rubbery and was shrinking away from the sides of the bowls, but she could pipe the cream to disguise that. The cream came out of the nozzle a fat corrugated worm, following the impatient movement of her fist.

The front door opened, and Jake's medical bag thumped on the hall floor. Ruth heard him greeting Tabby and Dorcas, then coming down to the kitchen. His bulk in the doorway seemed to darken the room further.

"Big surgery?" Ruth asked, not looking up from her piping.

"Interminable. Winter's coming." He came to the table, prod-ding a finger into a dish of potato salad, then putting his arms around her from behind. He kissed the back of her neck under the coil of dark hair. The weight of him pressed her up against the table edge, and he slid his hand down over her hip.

"Jake." Ruth moved to one side and went on working. He surveyed the laden table good-humoredly.

"It looks good, all of it." Jake had a hearty appetite. "The fish especially."

He had been down to Billingsgate Market to buy the pair of fat sea bass. Ruth had poached them in a borrowed fish kettle, and now they lay nose to tail on a big oval platter, an astrological sign in hammered silver decorated with cucumber rings. The fish had been expensive, but in a private conversation Nathaniel had assured Jake that he would pay.

"It's what fathers do," he had said jovially. "Foot the bills." He was pleased that Clio was marrying at last, and believed that she was old enough to make her own decisions. Miles Lennox did not seem particularly hardy, but Clio had strength enough for the two of them.

Jake was wondering how he would feel when the time came for him to give Rachel to another man. He did not want to imagine her wriggling eel's body transformed into a woman's.

"Are you going to stand there all evening, or might you go upstairs to change and then come and help me?" Ruth asked.

"Five minutes," Jake told her. He went upstairs whistling.

Don't wake the children, Ruth wanted to scream after him.

At last the puddings were finished and the table was ready, laid out to Ruth's satisfaction. She was still in her apron, directing Dorcas and Tabby to move chairs against the wall, when Clio arrived with the senior Hirshes. The small rooms seemed full as soon as they crowded in.

Jake accepted the praise for the buffet as if he had done all the work himself. But Clio took Ruth to one side, undoing the strings and pulling off her apron for her. "There." She smiled. She brushed the loose strands of hair from Ruth's damp cheeks. "Thank you for everything."

Ruth's shoulders lost a little of their stiffness. "Well. I hope you'll be happy. I wish you every happiness."

"Thank you," Clio said again. They kissed, and over her sister-in-law's head, Clio saw Miles arriving with Max Erdmann. Miles was wearing his good tweed jacket and a presentable shirt, even a proper tie. He was early, as he promised he would be, and he was rather pale but obviously sober. Clio's face brightened, and the sharper lines dissolved as she looked at him. She felt some of her anxiety lifting. The party would be a success, why should it not be?

They met in the middle of the room and embraced each other, to the satisfaction of all the onlookers.

"Are you all right?" Clio murmured. She could see the pale fuzz of hair on the rim of his ear, and a shaving nick under his cheekbone. She tried not to think of putting her mouth against it.

Miles studied her in return. She wanted to put her hands up to her hair, to pinch color into her own cheeks to bloom for him.

"A little tired of hiding out in Max's sordid den."

Max had offered to put Miles up while Nathaniel and Eleanor were staying in Gower Street.

"Only a few more nights," Clio consoled him. She drew his arm around her waist and turned to face the room.

Ruth's parents were arriving with her unmarried sister, and some writer friends of Miles followed behind them. Clio saw the Fitzroy regulars glance curiously at the table with its cargo of sea bass and fish balls, potato salads and heavy cream puddings, before herding into a corner with Max.

The doorbell rang continuously. Colleagues from the Mothers' Clinic came in bearing wrapped presents under their arms, making Clio think hilariously of the brown paper bags of contraceptive supplies. More *Fathom* regulars appeared, apparently the closest family Miles could claim. He seemed to have no relatives of his own, but there were more than enough Hirshes and Shermans to make up for that. The noise level rose, and Jake and Nathaniel pushed through the crowd, filling glasses and exhorting everyone to eat and drink and enjoy themselves.

The silver fish were already shredded, and there were craters dug in the bowls of salad when Grace arrived, an hour after everyone else.

She stood poised in the doorway, looking in at the red-faced guests on their upright chairs with mounded plates and napkins spread on their knees. Clio knew that she was seeing Nathaniel and Jake holding their bottles aloft, and Ruth with her hands full of dirty cutlery, and wire-haired Dorcas shrinking behind the table as if she would be happier hiding beneath it. Miles lounged with one shoulder against the wall and a cigarette in his mouth, squinting through a plume of smoke at Clio's grand relations.

Thomas was with Grace. He came in resplendent in his cavalry officer's uniform, his head seemingly almost touching the ceiling, and behind him were Phoebe and Cressida and Alice.

Because she had begged and pleaded to be allowed to, Alice was staying with the Brocks instead of being billeted on Jake and Ruth. She hovered on the dividing line now, not sure whether to rush across and put her arms around Nathaniel or to linger in Grace's scented orbit. Cressida hung back even farther behind, peering around Phoebe, curious to see this first adult party but embarrassed by her own lavender ribbons and buttoned patent-leather shoes.

Grace sailed across the room. She was wearing ivory silk and her ropes of pearls, and all the men in the room turned to look at her.

She held two hands out to Clio. "I'm so sorry we're all so late for your party. Will you forgive, darling?"

"Where is Anthony?" Nathaniel boomed.

Grace turned to him, smiling, with Thomas and Phoebe beside her like a pair of lieutenants.

She's so secure, Clio thought. *So certain of everything.*

"Uncle Nathaniel, Aunt Eleanor, darling, how marvelous you look. *Don't* stand up. Anthony is partly the reason why we're late. He's not very well, the poor boy. He wanted so much to come, but I wouldn't let him. He sends all his love, and apologizes, and wishes us all a wonderful time."

"What's the matter?" Clio asked. Her voice showed her concern.

"Oh, just a feverish cold, I think. But I sent him to bed."

Grace was a little piqued. Tom and Cim Mosley had been coming for drinks, and she had had to cancel them, and then she had had to drive all the way out to nowhere on her own, with a carload of babies, to come to this impossible party. It was not Anthony's fault that he was ill, of course. It was simply that she did not much enjoy even their own circle without him beside her.

Clio said, "What a shame. But I'm glad *you* could come. Miles, here's Grace."

With a round of introductions and greetings, the ripples that the new arrivals had made spread outward to the walls and became part of the choppy waters of the party. Alice rushed to tell Eleanor and Nathaniel the latest elegant details of life in South Audley Street, and Clio took Cressida by the hand and led her to the buffet. Ruth continued to clear plates with her lips slightly pursed.

Grace was able to look quickly around her and establish that Pilgrim was not there. Relief lightened her mood at once. Jake made his way through the crowd. He put his heavy hands on her shoulders and looked down at her. With his height and girth he was an imposing figure, but Grace could no longer see the handsome boy in him. It was Julius who seemed always unchanged.

"Anthony is all right, is he?"

"I think so, doctor, thank you. He's been overworking, rather. He gave a big speech last week on national relief schemes. He's made an impression from the back benches already, you know."

"I'm sure he has. Look after him."

"Jakie, who are all these people?"

Jake laughed. "Family, and medical and literary folk, of course. Who would you like to meet?"

"Are there any of Anthony's constituents?"

"I doubt it very much."

"Wait, then. Which are Mr. Lennox's family?"

"Oh, I think he sprang into the world unaided."

"And remained unclaimed thereafter?"

"So it seems. Until now, that is. Now he has all of us."

They were quiet for a moment before Grace asked, "Do you like him?"

Jake considered. "I don't dislike him. Our interests don't coincide, but I can hardly blame him for that. I believe he's good for Clio. Her face shines when she looks at him."

Jake knew that look. It was the dazed impatience of sexual obsession, and he envied her. Miles was less easy to read, but then Jake did not consider it necessary to analyze his sister's fiancé. Clio was grown-up enough to judge for herself. He simply wished the best of luck to both of them.

"Really?" Grace murmured. Privately she thought that Clio seemed nervous in a way that could not be explained just by the imminence of her marriage.

Cressida was sitting on the other side of the room, doggedly eating trifle. Grace thought back to her own wedding, and her anxiety to become Mrs. Brock as quickly as possible while all the time lamenting the loss of her precious Bohemian freedom. What would that freedom have amounted to, she wondered now? The chance to drink in pubs and go to bed with characters like Miles Lennox's friends?

A wash of love for Anthony poured through her. *Lucky,* she thought. *So lucky.*

Would Clio be as fortunate? It was just possible that she was pregnant, but somehow Grace did not think so.

"Why don't you talk to Miles yourself?" Jake was saying.

"I will."

The room was overheated and the noise level rose steadily. Ruth's own efforts and her chivvying of Dorcas seemed to have no effect on the rising tide of dirty plates and filled ashtrays and clouded glasses. Grace picked her way through the detritus to the corner where Miles and his friends were talking. They were beginning to be tired of drinking without a congenial bar to lean on, and were wondering how soon they might slip away. Miles stood up when he saw Grace coming and cut off the rest of the group with a hitch of his shoulder.

"*Lady* Grace."

"Anthony is very sorry not to be here. He wanted to wish you both well. Clio's a great favorite of his."

"Is she?"

The sneer in his voice was unmistakable. Miles picked a shred of tobacco from his lower lip. Grace determined that he would not rebuff her.

"How is your novel?"

"Quite well, thank you."

The careless insolence almost took her breath away. She thought, There is so much *hate* in him. Which of us does he hate, and why? Is it all women, or only women like me?

Clio can't be going to marry this man . . .

He was waiting, one eyebrow lifted, for her to say something else. But in the middle of the room Nathaniel had risen to his feet.

"Friends, family," Nathaniel called. He spread his hands, enjoining them all to make a circle around him. Miles strolled away from Grace with his hands in his pockets and took his place at Clio's side.

Nathaniel made a graceful little speech. He welcomed Miles and wished the engaged couple every happiness, and paid a generous tribute to Ruth for her food and hospitality. He thanked all the guests for coming, and the natural warmth and affection that radiated from him made them feel that they had indeed been part of a convivial and successful evening.

Nathaniel raised his glass. "Miles and Clio," he proposed.

"Miles and Clio," they answered, and drank from the glasses that Ruth had not managed to clear away. Clio blushed, and Miles turned his head and touched his lips to her face.

Grace watched, feeling cold in the hot room.

An overenthusiastic nurse from the Clinic began to sing, "For They Are Jolly Good Fellows," and a thin chorus of voices joined in. When the cheering was over Grace looked away in relief, and found Cressida beside her.

"I think we should go home to see how Daddy is," Cressida said.

"I think we should too," Grace agreed. "Let me first have a quick talk to Clio."

Clio had left the room. She had seen Ruth shouldering her way downstairs with a tray of leftovers.

Grace found them in the basement kitchen. They were standing side by side at the sink, and Clio's arm was around Ruth's shoulders.

"It's your wedding. I don't *want* you to help," Ruth was insisting. She looked as if she might be about to cry. They both turned to stare at Grace.

"Lovely party, Ruth," Grace said.

Ruth picked up the empty tray and pushed past Grace. They heard her feet clumping up the stairs behind them.

Clio turned her back again. She slowly rolled up her sleeves and plunged her arms into the sink.

Grace was suddenly exasperated by the smell of fish, the harsh shadows thrown by the single lightbulb under its glass coolie shade, and the grease-filmed water that left a scaly tidemark around Clio's elbows.

She asked, "Clio, are you really going to marry that little queer?"

Clio stood very still. Then she raised her head. Above her, through the dark window, she could just see the basement area and the railings above. Feet and legs shuffled beyond the railings. Some people were leaving, and she had not said good-bye to them.

Almost absently, she said, "Miles isn't a queer. And even if he were, I would still be in love with him."

Grace opened her beaded bag with a snap. She took out a cigarette and clicked her lighter, then inhaled sharply. "Clio."

Clio spun around. Water splashed on the bodice of her dress. She had to make an effort not to shout, *Go home, will you, please, Grace? You don't belong here. We don't want you here.*

They confronted each other. Grace wanted to go back, to begin again, softly this time, but Clio gave her no chance. Her eyes were like stones. It was Grace who looked away first.

She shrugged, waving her cigarette in its own smoke, then butting it out amongst the dirty dishes on the table.

"You know where I am if you need me," she said. As she climbed the stairs she was surprised to find that her legs were shaking.

The door to Anthony's dressing room stood ajar and the light was on. Grace let her fur wrap drop over the back of a chair and stooped briefly to glance at her face and her hair in the triple mirror. The cut-glass bottles and silver accessories on her dressing table caught the light and glittered back at her. It was reassuring to come home.

She crossed quickly to the dressing room. The door leading to Anthony's bedroom was also open, and she could see the shaded lamp burning beside his bed. He must be still awake, waiting for her to come in.

"Darling, I'm back at last," she called. She would sit beside him and talk for a few minutes, and forget the evening.

She reached the bedside before she saw for sure that he was asleep. He was lying on his back with his mouth open, one arm crooked over his eyes. His skin was flushed and damp, and his cheek when she put her hand to it was burning hot. As soon as she touched him, he flung out his arm, muttered something, and rolled away as if her touch had hurt him. Grace saw that there was a darker patch on the pillow where his head had rested. A single wheezing snore escaped from deep in his chest.

She hesitated, and then told herself that sleep was the best thing for him. She drew the covers up around his shoulders and turned off the bedside lamp, then tiptoed back to her own bedroom.

"It's seven-forty-five, Lady Grace."

The housemaid brought in Grace's tea early the next morning, as she had been instructed to do. Grace had a nine o'clock fitting, followed by a charity committee meeting. As soon as the maid had put the tray down, Grace got up and pulled on her silk robe. She went through to Anthony's bedroom and found him still asleep. Only she saw that he must have been up in the night, because some books and papers had been moved off his table and the little shaded lamp had been knocked over. She set it upright again, frowning.

She watched him for a moment and saw that at least he seemed to breathe more easily. If he was not much better by the afternoon, she decided, she would call in Dr. Boothe.

Grace gave instructions that Mr. Brock's tray was to be taken up at nine-thirty, if he did not ring for it before, and left the house.

Cressida stood at the drawing-room window, looking into the street. She held a fold of the dove-gray curtain in her fingers, pleating and repleating it into a series of concertina creases that would have earned a sharp rebuke from Grace if she had been there to see. But in her anxiety Cressida did not even think of that.

Please come, she breathed.

At last, at midday, a taxi drew up. Grace stepped out with a milliner's box and some other packages. Cressida ran.

She reached the foot of the stairs as the front door opened. "Mummy, where've you been? You've got to ring the doctor. Daddy looks strange. Nanny says the doctor should see him."

Standing with her arms full of parcels Grace stared at Cressida.

Her daughter's round black eyes were accusing. The sight of her was an irritation until the words sank in.

"What is all this, Cressida? Where's Nanny?"

There was the sound of running feet, and Cressida's nanny appeared at the head of the stairs.

"It's Mr. Brock, my lady. His temperature is very high. I think the doctor . . ."

"Mummy, oh quickly, Mummy . . ." There was panicky fear in Cressida's voice.

"Calm down, Nanny, for goodness sake." Grace dropped her packages and hurried to the stairs. Cressida wriggled in front of her and would have darted up ahead, but Grace seized her arm. "Go downstairs and sit with Cook, please, Cressida."

For a moment it seemed that the child might refuse to do as she was told, but then she bent her head and melted away. Grace followed the nanny, keeping her eyes on the white starched triangle of her headdress as it receded ahead of her.

Anthony was lying on his side with his eyes open. Grace stooped beside him. His face looked congested, and he was breathing noisily through his mouth. At first he stared without seeming to see her, but then he licked his cracked lips and muttered, "Hello, old thing. We must look at the portfolio."

Grace stood up. Anxiety tightened in her throat. "Stay here with him, Nanny. I'll go and telephone."

Cressida hovered as silent as a shadow in the passage outside the drawing room. She heard her mother talking to the doctor's receptionist in a high, tight voice.

". . . I don't care who he is seeing. This is an emergency, do you understand? Put me through to him at once."

Usually her mother's imperious ways made Cressida shrink with embarrassment, but now she dipped her head in two sharp nods of encouragement. The palms of her hands felt cold and clammy spread against the beige-painted dado of the corridor wall. Grace talked briskly to the doctor. Cressida shrank out of sight again when her mother came out of the drawing room, then listened to the door of her father's room opening and closing, and the low murmur of voices.

Cressida closed her eyes and resigned herself to waiting. The house felt quite different from normal. It was unnaturally still and the air seemed heavy, she had felt it as soon as she woke up. Before she had even looked into her father's room. She tried a prayer but could only manage *Please God, please God,* over and over.

The doctor came quite quickly. He was a pink man in a pin-striped suit with a watch-chain. Grace had been sitting in a chair beside Anthony's bed, holding one of his hands between both of hers, but she jumped up as soon as he was shown in.

"Dr. Boothe . . ."

"If I might just look at the patient first, Lady Grace."

She felt herself dismissed. She wrapped her arms around herself and stood at the window, willing herself to be calm as the doctor made his examination. Anthony was quiet at first, but then he began to talk in a low, hoarse voice about stocks and dividends. He wanted to get up and sort out some papers. That was what he must have been trying to do in the night, Grace realized.

"That's right, old chap, but not to worry about that now," the doctor soothed him. "The thing is to get over this little bout before you do anything else."

The doctor's face was somber when he finally motioned Grace to one side. "Do you have someone you can send out to have this prescription made up?"

"Of course."

Anthony's man was dispatched, and the nanny was recalled to watch by the bed. The doctor washed his hands, rinsed and dried them with meticulous care.

"Please tell me what it is, Dr. Boothe." Grace was even meek in her fear now.

The doctor led her into the next room. Grace allowed herself to be stationed on her own day-bed to receive the news. "I believe he has a form of influenza. That in itself would not be threatening to a healthy man of his age, but there is now a secondary, pulmonary infection. An infection of the lung, that is. His temperature is high, there is some delirium, and some cardiac irregularity. How long has he been unwell, Lady Grace?"

"A day. No, two days. He—we thought it was a feverish cold."

"I understand. Is he worried, in any way out of the normal?"

"He gave a major speech to the House, just last week. His father's business, he is a stockbroker, and there was the Hatry crash last month, of course. I believe there were . . . clients who suffered losses. I don't think it damaged Anthony personally, financially, that is."

"I see. It doesn't help that he has political or business anxieties, naturally."

"What will happen?"

"I can't say, yet."

Grace stared at him. His pink face seemed to hang in front of her like some jack-o'-lantern.

"What do you mean?"

"The infection must run its course. But it is a virulent one, threatening, to have taken hold so quickly. The question is if his system can hold up against it."

Grace did not move. If, he had said, *if*. An hour, two hours ago she had been concerned about the fit of a winter costume. Now this man was saying there was a chance that Anthony might die. She knew he was saying that, although the words were fuzzy, the darkness of them inadequately bleached by euphemism.

Sudden fear drained the blood and heat out of her, and she felt that she could not raise her arm, or move her fingers, to save Anthony or herself. She sat on the day-bed looking toward the dressing-room door. She could see his face, distorted with the pain of drawing breath, as if the walls were glass. The life they had constructed together had seemed invincible, like a stone tower, and now the difference of a few hours threatened to bring it down.

"If you had called me in earlier . . ."

"He was asleep when I came in last night, and this morning. He was feverish, but I saw no reason to call."

"I see, of course."

Grace realized that the doctor was watching her. He was judging her, and her capacity to deal with the crisis. Her back stiffened at once. She could move her fingers, all of her body now. She would not let Anthony die.

"Anthony is very strong, very determined. He will recover."

"There is a good chance." The doctor was relieved. They would work as a team, at least.

"What must be done for him? Will you remove him to hospital?"

"I would not like to take the risk of moving him now. He will need professional nursing: I can arrange that for you. He must be given the medication I have prescribed; we will do what we can to bring his temperature down."

"Thank you," Grace said. She stood up, wanting to get away from the man's amorphous predictions, back to Anthony.

He was lying as they had left him, his eyes half closed. Occasionally his lips moved, forming words they could not hear. Cressida's nanny looked frightened.

Dr. Boothe said, "The nurses will do everything that needs to be done for him, Lady Grace. It would be better for you to have some company. Your mother, or a sister, perhaps?"

Grace was thinking of the tower of her marriage, square blocks of stone years, defying its shaky foundation. The ground beneath it had begun to ripple as if in an earthquake, mocking the jaunty little structure. She didn't want anyone here now.

"Perhaps," Grace said.

"I will be back at five," the doctor told her.

Cressida drew back into the shadows at the end of the corridor as he passed by. She waited with her anxiety for Grace to come out and tell her what the doctor had said, but Grace did not emerge.

The house became possessed by a kind of grim bustle. From her vantage point next to the drawing-room curtains, Cressida saw two nurses arriving. They had white caps tied with strings under their chins, and dark capes that made her think of the folded wings of birds of prey. Footsteps passed up and down the stairs, and voices murmured urgently.

After the nurses came a van, and two men with a railway porter's upright trolley. The trolley was painted cream with big chips knocked out of the paint to show the bare metal ribs beneath. There was a tall gray cylinder mounted on it, with a sinister apparatus of silver taps and black rubbery tubes on the top. The men dragged the trolley and its cargo backward into the house, and Cressida heard it bumping up the stairs.

The telephone began to ring. Someone answered it, not Grace, and almost at once it rang again. There was the sound of opening and closing doors, but beneath it all there was the same ominous silence of the day that crept into Cressida's head and hammered with the dull pulse of her blood.

She waited, willing Grace to come and find her, until she could bear it no longer. She slipped up the stairs and saw one of the nurses hurrying with a covered bowl. The door to her father's room opened and closed again, shutting her out. She tiptoed to the door and pressed her ear against it. The door was heavy, and she could hear nothing.

If he . . . *he mustn't.* She could not bear that. But they must not keep her here on the outside any longer. She should be with him too, as well as Grace.

Cressida lifted her chin. She was about to give a timid knock, but then changed her mind. She twisted the handle and the door swung open.

She saw the bed and the high white pillows. The porter's trolley had been wheeled up close to the bed and the rubber tubes snaked over the covers. There was a black mask covering her father's face. One of the nurses held it there.

Cressida ran forward, with some thought of snatching it away. *"Cressida."*

Grace jumped up from the chair beside the bed. The nurse lifted the mask, and Cressida saw her father's face. He was white, and his lips were blue. His eyelashes seemed very dark. He opened his eyes and looked at her.

Grace caught her, pulled her back from the bed. "What are you doing in here? Where's Nanny?"

The arm around Cressida's shoulder seemed a restraint, not offering any comfort. She said in a slow voice, "I want to see Daddy. I need to. Daddy, I—"

The other nurse, the one without the suffocation mask, came to her other side. "Not now, dear. Best not now. Come and see your daddy tomorrow."

They were dragging her away, Grace and the nurse between them. They were almost at the door when she heard it. Anthony said distinctly, "Cressida."

"I'm here," she shouted, twisting and trying to duck out of their hands. She could hear him gasping, and then the mask descended again. She was out in the corridor once more, with Grace. The door closed on them. Cressida saw that her mother did not look like herself. Her face seemed to have been peeled and left raw. It frightened Cressida to realize that for once Grace did not have the time or the strength to be angry with her.

"I want you to stay with Nanny. Just stay downstairs with Nanny and Cook."

Cressida found the courage to confront her. "Is Daddy going to die?"

"Of course not."

"Why are they putting that *thing* on his face?"

"It's an oxygen mask. They are giving him oxygen to help him to breathe."

Nanny appeared on the landing. "There you are. Where have you been? I've searched everywhere. Your tea is ready, Cressida. Come on with me, now, there's a good girl." Nanny didn't scold, either.

Cressida thought of refusing, of making some effort to cling on to the door handle, so that they would have to pry away her fingers one by one. But then if she went and ate her tea and seemed to be good and normal as on any other day, then everything might somehow become normal again, and the ordinary, dull, blessed routines of every day would descend. Cressida bent her head. "I'm coming," she said.

She allowed Nanny to lead her away. Grace went back into the bedroom, and Cressida plodded downstairs. She sat at the kitchen table and ate a boiled egg and bread and butter. After the bread and butter Cook gave her some iced biscuits, as if in some way she deserved a special treat. Cressida ate them in silence, staring at the black-leaded range and the line of polished pans suspended above it.

"All right, ducky?" Cook asked, exchanging glances with Nanny over her head.

"Yes." Cressida contained her anxiety with weary economy.

"That's a good girl," Nanny said.

A tray was laid for Grace, linen cloth and napkin, china and silver and tiny morsels of food, but it was sent back almost untouched. The doctor came back again, and this time he stayed. The telephone rang and was answered. More food was prepared and sent up for the bird-of-prey nurses.

Cressida's neck and shoulders began to ache with the effort of sitting still, listening to muffled sounds and trying to decipher them. There was no sign of ordinariness descending again. She felt rather than saw the semaphoring of the servants above her head.

"I want to see Daddy," Cressida said, when Nanny told her that it was bedtime. "Just to kiss him goodnight."

"No," they answered, "you can't see him tonight, dear. Perhaps in the morning."

"Do you promise?"

"We'll see. Time for bed now, Cressida."

She went and lay in her bedroom with the night-light burning. Grace did not come. The same disturbed silence weighted the house, a heavy and monotonous silence broken only on its surface by hurrying feet and opening doors. Once, before she fell asleep, Cressida heard Jake's booming voice, cut short as yet another door closed. She dreamed of her father's blue-lipped face and the black mask, grown huge and soft and shapeless, descending on it.

Anthony lay in the ramparts of pillows. His mother and father came, tiptoeing beside the bed, but he did not know them. He did not know Jake either when Jake bent his dark head over him. His eyes were turned inward, beneath closed lids, to a restless landscape of burning rocks and seething water pictured in the hot coals banked around his heart.

Grace sat in the chair next to the bed, listening to the battles he fought for his breath. Sometimes the forces were regrouped and the attack remounted, and it seemed that they might win. She leaned forward in her seat to look at his face, willing her own strength into him. But each time the attacks were beaten back and dispersed, and the gasps grew shallower, and wider spaced.

For the last hour each breath that he took was a shudder, a sigh of pain. At the end Grace was praying that it would finish. Jake's face was a black mask.

Anthony died at twenty to four in the morning.

It was October 28, 1929, the day before Wall Street crashed.

"Leave me now," Grace said to them.

Her voice was clear and high. There had been no tears yet. Jake made as if to stay behind, but she motioned him away with the others. When they had gone, she sat down again, in the chair she had occupied all night, and took hold of Anthony's hand. She felt as if their square tower had been reduced by some cruel alchemy to powder, dust, and now the tower slowly collapsed, falling inward within itself, the dust whispering, until only a cold and meaningless heap of it was left.

She looked at his face. It had closed up to her so quickly. He had been there, and now he had gone, and she was left behind.

She let her head fall forward so that it rested against his cold hand. She wanted to cry, to rail and moan and howl, but she could not.

Cressida was screaming.

"You wouldn't let me. I wanted to see him. He called me, I heard him. I never said good-bye, and now I can't because he's dead. I only wanted to see him."

"I couldn't let you into that room, Cressida. It was no place for a child."

Cressida's face contorted. The terrible, obvious pressure of her grief threatened to crack it open. *"I hate you. I loved Daddy."*

The rage and venom were the more shocking because she had been such a silent, biddable child. Grace tried to hold her, but Cressida tore herself away. Grace did not know what to do, could think of nothing but removing her so that she could be alone again. She murmured to Jake, "Perhaps a sedative . . . ?"

"Let her grieve," Jake said.

Nanny came and led her away, still sobbing and howling out her misery.

Clio had come at once, but Grace would only see her briefly. They spoke on the telephone, when Grace finally accepted one of her calls.

"We are postponing the wedding, of course."

"Why?" Grace asked with detached curiosity. "Anthony wouldn't want you to do that. What difference could it possibly make, if you marry next week or next month?"

"I just thought—with the funeral only two days before—"

"Go ahead with your wedding, Clio. I don't want you to postpone it."

Clio was embarrassed and disconcerted to find that the square face of death was hung about with the little veils of her own social anxiety.

"If that is what you want," she said, a little harshly.

Grace seemed not to hear her. "It's an odd irony, don't you think, that I should lose my husband in the very week that you gain yours? We are like a pair of scales, perpetually unbalanced. A heavy weight in one pan, mysterious air in the other. Up and down, forever flying past each other."

"It is a cruel coincidence, yes," Clio said, unable to offer anything more.

Grace was sitting in her gray and rose-pink drawing room. She had been intending to write letters, the first replies to the flood of condolences, but she had not even picked up her pen. She stared down at the morocco edge of the blotter, at her wrist emerging from the cuff of her black dress. The physical world was unchanged. It was lewdly overfull of rustling and clattering *things*, of photographs in silver frames and crystal decanters and fur coats and sugar tongs, and yet in the face of such overpopulation she had to learn to take account of a vacancy so complete that it defied nature.

She could not measure the emptiness. When she tried to define it for herself, the space ahead of her was trackless, unbroken by even a point of light. But yet it had to be measured, day by day. She had to travel through it because she was still alive. There was no objective, and no motive for traveling on except that she could not stop. Anthony had stopped. He had simply gone away, silently in the night, and this was the terrifying void in which he had left her.

The old world, the real world, was equally fearsome. It was the crowded detail of it that frightened her. The trays of food and the engraved cards and the jewelry in velvet boxes had once been familiar but were now hideously distorted by her sudden recognition of their irrelevance.

Grace ran her fingers over the leather blotter, picked up her gold-nibbed pen and stared at it, then squared a sheet of her headed writing paper in front of her. None of these objects seemed related. Their pointless solidity was chilling.

She rested her forehead in her hand for a moment, wondering if she was unhinged.

Then she gripped the pen and made herself write, "My dear Tom." She heard the bell ring downstairs, and the front door open and close. She had given orders that she was not to be disturbed. My dear Tom. What next, what did people say?

The drawing-room door opened.

Grace looked, then dropped her pen.

"Julius."

He was unshaven and tired. He was carrying a canvas grip in one hand. "I've come straight from the boat train. I set off as soon as I heard."

Uncertainly, she stood up. Julius put down his bag and came to her. His arms fitted around her, but he was gentle, as if he knew that her bones felt brittle beneath her skin.

She stood quietly with her eyes closed.

Julius was solid, and he was a part of the old, real world, but he did not baffle or frighten her. He was simply there, seeming to fill a small corner of the windy space. She held on to him, her fingers curling in the thick stuff of his traveling clothes.

"I am so pleased you are here," she whispered.

"I am always here."

He guided her to a sofa and made her sit down. He held her cold hands, rubbing them between his own. He did not know what he had been expecting to find, had not even allowed himself to imagine what manifestations of grief. He saw now that she was composed. Her hair was drawn tidily back from her white face, and her dark dress was elegant, with a pearl pin at the throat.

Of course, Grace would contain her sorrow. She would not let it spill out, like the viscera of some dismembered hunt quarry after the kill, for all the huntsmen to see. She would have her vulnerable and hidden face, but only Anthony would have seen that.

Julius felt a stab of jealousy, and the persistence of it sickened him.

Grace shivered. "Are you cold?" he asked her. "Shall I ring to have the fire made up?"

"No. Don't move, I don't want you to move."

He went on rubbing her hands, feeling the fine bones move under his fingertips.

"How are you?" he asked. He couldn't think of any way to dress up the threadbare conventionality of the question.

In a small, thin voice she said, "It was very sudden, you know. Just a day, really. If I had had more time to make myself ready, I might have been able to bear it better." Then she added, "But that isn't true. Nothing would make it easy to bear the death of the person you love most in the world."

He looked down at her hands, at the diamonds and the plain gold wedding ring.

"Do you want to talk now?" he asked gently.

"Do I? I don't know. I don't know anything." She was shivering again. Julius got up and went to the tray of drinks on the table between the windows. He poured whiskey into a glass and gave it to her. She sipped at it, and he heard the rim of the glass rattling against her teeth.

"The funeral is tomorrow, you know."

"Yes."

"Oh, Julius, the vulgar, meaningless *refinement* of it all. The order of service. The flowers. The casket. Like some—like some horrible padded box of chocolates, like a tart's present, to *put him in.*"

She raised her head and saw Julius's face. It was softened, blurred with his concern.

"Couldn't someone else have dealt with that? Your father? Hugo, or Jake? What have they bloody well been doing, damn them all?"

"No, I had to deal with it myself."

But his tenderness and his quick anger had unstopped something inside her, at last. She felt the tears sharp behind her eyes, and then they began to burn on her face, running down her cheeks.

"Cry. Go on, cry," he ordered her.

She did cry, and he held her, and then he refilled her glass and listened while she talked.

Grace talked for a long time. She realized that since Anthony died she had hardly spoken, and now words spilled out with the tears. The happiest memories of Anthony came out mixed up with her horror of the formal arrangements that had to be made after his death. She talked about how much she had loved him, and then her face contorted with anger at him for deserting her. She said that Cressida was angry too, but with her, not her father. "She thinks it is my fault."

"Poor Grace. Poor Cressida, too."

She told Julius about her fear of the void she had stepped into, and her feeling of disgust with the irrelevant material world.

"You are shocked," he told her. He was relieved to hear her talking. The iron mask of composure was not so firmly set, at least. "Shock is disorienting. Didn't Jake tell you that?"

"Yes. Probably. I didn't hear."

"Talk to me some more."

"Give me another whiskey, then. Isn't it strange that we should be drinking and talking here, with everything the same, while Anthony is dead?"

"Yes. But it only looks the same. The truth is that it is all different, because he is dead."

Grace frowned. The whiskey was beginning to affect her. "How will I learn that? Sometimes I forget, you know, that it has happened. And then, the pain of remembering it again. Do you know, there probably isn't any money?"

"What?"

"I saw the solicitor and Anthony's father. Only briefly. They were treading very carefully. Something about the will. It seems Anthony might have transferred funds to New York. After the Hatry crash, he must have thought it would be safer to be in American stocks and bonds. I don't know for sure yet." She shrugged at the opulent room. "So many *things.*"

"Don't worry about it now." Julius had seen enough, in Berlin, of the absence of money. The lack of it seemed inconceivable here in South Audley Street.

"I'm tired," Grace said. "But I can't sleep. Tell me about Berlin."

"Such a city. Such a bizarre, startling, diverse place. You must come with me someday."

"Perhaps I will."

Julius knew that she could conceive of nothing beyond her loss, and he did not try to press her.

The whiskey decanter was almost empty.

"What are you going to do?" he whispered, when she had drained the last of it. He meant, sleep or sit up, but she chose to look further.

"I don't know what to do. Find out how to go on living without him, I suppose." It was like taking a breath of air without oxygen.

Julius saw her gasp, but he saw something else too, as clearly as if a bright light had flicked on in a pitch-black room. His certainty gave everything a hard-edged, polished clarity.

"You must stand in his place. You must take Anthony's seat in Parliament."

Grace's sudden laugh broke in her throat. "I hadn't thought of that one." She stood up, and staggered a little. "You'll have to help me up to bed, Julius. I'm half drunk."

He led her upstairs, helped her off with her dress as gently as a lady's maid, and left her under the covers with her arm protectively crooked over her eyes.

Clio was married two days after Anthony's funeral.

In the last few days Miles alternated between bouts of morbid depression, in which he claimed repeatedly that he was not good enough for her, and fits of optimism when he promised her the moon and the stars as soon as his book was finished and his fortune was made.

"I don't want the moon or the stars," Clio said. "I just want you." She told herself that he was nervous, that they were both shocked by Anthony's death. She wished that she could be alone to mourn her friend, but she did not want to let Miles out of her sight. Once they were married, she thought, there would be calm enough. There would be time then to console each other.

"If you want me, you shall have me, most precious piglet. Princess of piglets."

"Please, Miles." She was going to say, *No piglets, not now,* but she caught his eye and the words stopped in her throat. Sometimes he was angry, and the anger alarmed her.

Miles said, "Come on, let's go out. I have had enough of sitting here watching you weep."

Clio knew that he was drinking too much, but she went, because it was better than letting him go alone.

It was a subdued wedding ceremony. They were married as planned at St. Pancras registry office, with Jake and Max Erdmann as their witnesses. Clio said "I do" almost inaudibly, and accepted the narrow gold band that Miles gave her. She emerged, blinking in the thin sunlight of a cold November morning, as Mrs. Miles Lennox.

Twelve

IT WAS A LONG TIME since Clio had last visited Stretton. She was startled by her first sight of it from the window of the station taxi. She had expected that it would seem somehow smaller than it had done to her childish eyes, but when it appeared out of the fold of landscape, the great bulk of the house was undiminished. It sat between the bone-white sky and the dun ridges of the park and seemed to play brazen tricks with perspective. It was closer than it looked, or it was a giant's mansion, or it was two-dimensional and at any moment the canvas it was painted on might ripple in the wind.

The taxi stopped on the sweep in front of the great doors, and Clio looked up. There was no trick; the house was solid and as big as she remembered. Dozens of windows blankly reflected the winter light.

She paid the taxi driver and carried her own suitcase up the steps. It was much colder here than in London. The wind stung her cheeks.

The Strettons' butler opened one half of the double doors. It was the same butler they had always had, but he looked noticeably bent and feeble now. Long ago he had found Grace and Julius and herself stealing beer from the big barrel in his still room to bait a slug trap, or for some similar childish project that she had forgotten, and he had chased them through the kitchens and out into the dairy yard.

"Good afternoon, Mrs. Lennox." The name was still new enough to catch her unawares. For a moment she had been a little girl running across the slippery cobbles.

"Hello, Hodges. How are you?"

"As well as can be expected, thank you, Mrs. Lennox. Lady Grace is with her ladyship in the small drawing room."

"I'll make my own way," Clio said quickly.

"Very good. I will get one of the maids to attend to your luggage."

Clio knew that she would come to her bedroom and find her skirts and blouses unpacked and hung forlornly behind the doors of some vast armoire. She would hunt for her underwear through a dozen drawers empty except for yellowing newspaper and shreds of lavender that had long ago lost their scent, and find it at last in the least likely corner. There would be a well-laundered linen cover with the Leominster crest worked on it neatly laid on top of the pile. She would fold her underthings in it at the end of the day, and they would be discreetly borne away for laundering.

She was thinking as she made her way under the dome that nothing had changed at Stretton. There was the same faint, churchy smell of candle wax and evergreens and damp, and the same ambivalent treatment of daylight. There were so many tall windows, but they were all screened with dusty curtains and holland blinds in case too much sunshine should strike the brocades and gilding of previous generations. At three o'clock in the early December afternoon the high rooms were almost dark.

But by the time she reached the door of the small drawing room, Clio had already changed her mind. The house was different, because the cold seemed more intense than usual and the silence less penetrable. When she opened the door and looked into the room, she had the feeling that the occupants had withdrawn here, into the last redoubt of warmth and comfort in the entire rambling, deserted pile. It was as if the house were laying siege to its owners.

Blanche and Grace were sitting one on either side of a stone fireplace. A log fire was burning in the iron basket, and one of John Leominster's springer spaniels was asleep almost on top of the flames. A pair of lamps had been lit, making the room seem cozy in contrast with the view of blue-gray mist and damp-black branches visible through the windows.

Blanche was on her feet at once. "Clio, dear child. We never heard the car. What a joy that you are here." They hugged each other with mutual pleasure. Clio smelled her familiar scent, old-fashioned white lilac.

At Anthony's funeral Blanche had looked old and bewildered, but now in her country tweeds with the firelight warming her face, she was herself again.

"Aunt Blanche, you look well."

Grace had stood up too. She was wearing a navy-blue cardigan jacket and pleated skirt. She was very thin, and the way that the flesh had shrunk over her long nose and hollowed beneath her cheekbones made her no longer pretty. But when she smiled, as she did now, the bones seemed to soften and her face took on a handsomeness that Clio had not seen before.

"I'm so glad you came," Grace said.

"I don't know why you wanted me so much. I've no idea what I can possibly do," Clio protested.

But Grace had begged her to come, and she had not been able to refuse. Now that she was here, she was glad. Stretton enclosed her with a thousand memories. From this vantage point, in the firelight, they seemed all to be happy ones. Julius and Jake, Clio and Grace. Running away from the Babies. Teasing Hugo for being so Culmington.

"You can keep me company, at least," Hugo called.

"Hugo, are you here?"

Clio hadn't seen him at first, because he was sitting on a sofa in the shadows beyond the fire. He heaved himself to his feet now, reaching for his stick, and the dog lifted its head to watch him as he hobbled across to kiss his cousin.

"Not that that will be much of an entertainment. And you only married five minutes ago."

"A month now," Clio said. And so a little more than a month since Anthony's death. Each one of them thought it, and knew that the others were thinking the same.

"Miles can easily spare me," she said quickly. "He's come to a difficult point in his work, and some peace and quiet in the flat will be a help."

She had chosen the moment for telling him very carefully. He had had a good day, and had been buoyant and lively when she came in from work. Not every day was like that, by any means.

They had gone out to the pub together and had two or three drinks, no more. Miles had sat with her hand tucked under his arm, and they surveyed the coming and going at the bar in gossipy good humor. Even so, when she had made her tentative suggestion, he had rounded on her with only a thin veil of pleasantness masking his hostility.

"Why do you want to go all the way up there? Those people aren't our people. What do they have to do with us, or you with them?"

"They are my family," Clio said. "I want to go because Grace has asked me. I'm glad there is something I can do for her."

"Don't put yourself at her beck and call," Miles said coldly.

"Why not? But it isn't like that. I'd like to go, Miles, just for a few days. If you don't need me."

"But I do need you. A man needs his little wife." He had pouted and looked mock-sulky, and Clio laughed with relief. It would be all right, she could go.

"A man shall have his little wife. He will appreciate her all the more after a few days of having to fend for himself again."

"Nasty shopping and cooking, do you mean?" He had pretended to recoil in horror. Clio laughed again and kissed his forehead, then went to the bar and bought them both another drink.

The flat had begun to seem rather small now Miles had spread himself and his possessions through the rooms. There were always piles of books and papers everywhere that she was not allowed to touch or tidy. She tried to be as quiet as she could when she came in from *Fathom* or the Clinic, but it seemed that Miles was distracted by the slightest sound. Being disturbed when he was writing made him angry, and she was the butt of his anger.

A few days in the somber expanse of Stretton had begun to seem inviting, and it would be good for Miles to have some time for uninterrupted work.

The grand relations, as Miles sneeringly named them, were clearly pleased to see her. They fussed around her as if she had traveled much farther than by train from London, and Clio gave herself up to it with guilty enjoyment.

"Darling, come and sit by the fire. You look half dead with cold. Is it too early to ring for tea, do you think?"

"Tea would be heavenly."

Tea was rung for, and brought in by the butler and a housemaid. Clio had provided herself with a potted meat sandwich for the train, the bread cut from the heel of a stale loaf because she did not want to broach the fresh one left for Miles, and now she was hungry. There were wedges of anchovy toast, and hot muffins in the folds of snowy-white napkins, as well as scones and dark fruitcake laid out on the low table beside her. The tea came in a wide shallow cup, the porcelain so fragile that it was translucent.

Clio sat back in her chair and let the food and the fire warm her. The Stretton family might be under siege in the vast space of their own house, but after Gower Street this was still the height of luxury. Clio had not realized, until this moment, that she was tired of shopping, and cooking, and washing-up. In her single days she might have gone out to a café or skipped meals altogether, but now she felt that Miles must be properly looked after while he worked. It just seemed that it was more difficult to look after two people than one.

"John is out today," Blanche told her, "but he will be back for dinner, of course."

"Don't know what kind of a run they'll be getting. The meet was over at Stinchford," Hugo said.

John Leominster had recently sold his hunting box at Melton Mowbray, claiming that he could no longer afford to keep it. Now he had to content himself with the local hunt and with complaining about its inferiority to the Leicestershire packs. Hugo could not ride, and Thomas kept his hunters stabled with his regiment. The stableyard at Stretton was almost empty.

"Your father had a good day last time they were over there," Blanche said. "I remember they killed in old Garnett's woods."

Grace rolled her eyes at Clio. "Have you seen your room yet?"

"No, I came straight in here."

"If you've had enough tea, I'll take you up."

Clio would have liked at least one slab of fruitcake, but Grace made it clear that she wanted to escape the hunting talk.

"I expect you girls want to chat," Blanche said, as if she had forgotten that they were no longer eighteen. "We do still dress, Clio. . . ." Her voice trailed away in vague apology. Clio wondered if her aunt was so suspicious of her unimaginably Bohemian lifestyle that she was afraid she might shock Uncle John into an apoplexy by coming down to dinner in trousers.

As she closed the door, Clio saw Blanche pick up some sewing. In his corner Hugo stretched his artificial leg out in front of him and stared silently into the fire.

The corridor outside was dark. The cold smelled acrid.

"God, this bloody house," Grace muttered.

"How are you?" Clio asked.

"Let's get upstairs first."

The bedroom was just as Clio remembered it. There was a high half-tester bed and a tallboy and a writing desk, and any number of drawers where her underclothes might have been hidden. A small fire had recently been lit in the grate, and the chilly air was tinged with smoke. The bathroom was several doors away. Clio recalled it as a cavernous place of green paint and chipped enamel. John Leominster was not the man to squander capital on modern plumbing.

Grace stood at the window, looking down into the trees. Her hands massaged her thin arms. Clio located her outer clothes and put on her warm coat.

"Cold," Grace said. It wasn't a question.

"I'd forgotten. If I ever felt it. Perhaps children don't?"

"Cressida is always complaining about it. And she has enough flesh to cover her bones."

"Where is she?"

"In the old schoolroom probably. With Nanny, anyway."

Grace's profile was dark against the clouded glass. Clio balanced on the arm of a chair, watching her. "Is she getting better?"

"She cries a lot. Terrible, salty, soaking outbursts. She believes it was my fault, that if the doctor had come sooner, he might have saved him. She says that she loves her father, not me." The dark head tilted, rested sideways against the musty velvet of the curtains. "If it were not so sad, it would be funny, wouldn't it? But at least Anthony never knew. At least there's that."

"Grace." Clio stood up, went to her. She put her arm around Grace's shoulders, but Grace did not bend or yield. Clio could feel the concentration in her, vibrating like a wire.

"Thank you for coming up here," Grace whispered. "You, and Julius and Jake, I don't know what I would do without you."

Clio was unnerved by the tautness. She felt that Grace could not let go of herself, because if she did she might break into a hundred pieces. "Come and sit, tell me about the election," she pleaded.

Grace sat down, but on the edge of a chair, ready to spring up again. She smiled at Clio. "They don't want me to stand, you know. Ma and Pa. They think it isn't suitable. A recent widow. A mother. A *woman* in Parliament."

"There have been women in Parliament for ten years."

"Pa doesn't count Lady Astor. 'Damn Yankee divorcée,' of course."

"Yes. Well then, the Duchess of Atholl. Who else is there? Mrs. Wintringham and your friend Lady Cynthia Mosley."

"Those two are your side of the House, darling." Grace grinned at her, a flash of the old Grace.

"That doesn't matter. Are you really going to stand?"

"*Yes.*" It was as if Clio had plucked the wire in her. Grace leaned forward, her eyes wide. "Anthony would want it. I can continue what he began."

Clio began to say that the intention was admirable, but was hardly a political platform. Grace brushed the interruption aside.

"Not just for that. I want to do it for Anthony's memory, of course, I need that, but for myself too. For the sake of women, because I can, because the constituency is here for me. It isn't for Hugo, or even Thomas, with their horses and land and their old values, but for *me*. A woman, a widow. Don't you see how it has all changed?"

She jumped up again, turning so that the pleats of her skirt fanned around her calves.

"Look at Blanche and Eleanor, Clio, and now look at us." A log fell in the hearth, sending up a shower of soft red sparks. Grace spoke in a low voice, but her hands danced, smoothing and chopping the air, building edifices of her own reasoning. "Our mothers had to marry. What else was there for them? Marriage or Holborough Hall, lifelong subservience to Grandmother. They had so much youth and energy, you can reach out and almost touch it in the Sargent picture downstairs."

You can in our picture too, Clio thought. *Where has it gone? Or do you still have all that vitality, while I have lost mine?*

There had been an evening long ago; when, exactly? After their coming-out dance, that was it. They had smoked Grace's cigarettes and saluted each other as modern women, free agents who would not be yoked by convention as their mothers had been. Clio almost smiled. *So much for our girlish idealism, then. I have no more real freedom than Eleanor did.*

The fine threads of association wove around them both. Clio thought they would surely trip her, but Grace swept on. "It must have seemed an act of rebellion for Eleanor to marry Nathaniel. But she was only doing the same thing as Blanche. They gave themselves up to exist through husbands and children because their world didn't permit them to do anything else.

"It has changed now, Clio. It's different for you and me. Women went to war, they drove ambulances in France and nursed on the Russian Front."

What did you and I do, Grace? We were only children. We stayed at home and hurt each other over poor Captain Dennis.

"Now women can live their own lives. London is full of stenographers and nurses and shop assistants, independent in their digs, not daughters or mothers or wives."

"And in West Shropshire?"

"I can represent the constituents here as well as Anthony did. Once I am in Parliament, I can represent a wider constituency of women too. I will be adopted for the seat, and I will win it, because

I know I can. I'm a woman and a mother. I had to marry, didn't I? I tried to be a cipher-wife, and I was so unhappy, did you know that? It wasn't until Anthony came into politics that I fell in love with him properly. We had a common project, and I will not abandon it now, not for Anthony's sake nor my own."

"I see that," Clio said slowly. Out of the wash of Grace's words, she did pick out that much, that Grace and Anthony had loved each other.

The fire had warmed the room at last, or some of Grace's alarming energy had radiated off her and thawed the air. It was dark outside now. The window had become a grid of black squares that swallowed the room's reddish light. Grace came and half knelt in front of Clio, smiling at her.

"And you. Look at you, Clio. You did what you wanted to do, poetry magazines and birth-control clinics; and you married on your own terms, didn't you? You were always free, you still are."

Grace had taken her hands. Their hands lay in Clio's lap, linked together. Clio was thinking that she was not free, she belonged to Miles. She sheered away in her mind from what Grace had called him on the evening of the party.

Somehow, without quite understanding how it had happened or why, she had made herself his appendage. She had imagined a partnership, envisaged herself reading his manuscript and making discerning comments, but the dreary truth was that Miles did not want her help. She was no wiser about his work than she had ever been. He wanted warmth and security and domestic comfort, and she was glad to give him those, to the limited extent that she was able to provide. He had not married her for sex, she understood that already.

And for herself, she had wanted warmth and security too, she had wanted to be married. She had had enough of being bravely single, and now that she was no longer, she supposed she ought to be happy. She was not modern; she was the opposite face of Grace's postwar woman. As always, as ever, they misunderstood each other. They slid by, meeting but never touching. Clio's mouth curled and Grace saw it. She sat back on her heels to look at her.

"I was so envious of you when I was first married and Cressida was born, and you were reigning in Pilgrim's set in the Eiffel. Did you know that?"

"I can't imagine you ever being jealous of anyone," Clio said truthfully.

"I was. It wasn't until much later that I realized my good fortune. In being married to Anthony."

The shape of her face seemed to change. The muscles beneath the thin skin drew her mouth into a line and flattened her cheeks into waxy slabs. Her eyes filmed. Clio looked into them and saw her grief.

"Oh, Grace . . ."

"Don't say anything." Grace was fierce and hard. "I don't want to blub all the time. It was Julius's idea, you know. He told me I must stand. He's so clever, isn't he? If I hadn't had this, I think I would have died of sorrow."

Clio leaned forward to her, and their cheeks touched.

To one side of the room there was a tall glass on a stand. Clio looked into it and saw their reflection. The difference in their clothes seemed only to emphasize their physical likeness. As in Pilgrim's portrait, they might have been twins. For now, they faced each other.

"Will you come to the adoption meeting? To support me?"

Clio said, "Of course I will. That's why I'm here."

Grace nodded. "It's important to me. You all are, you and Julius and Jake."

"I know."

But somewhere within Clio, the old worm of mistrust still coiled itself. She pinched down on it, wishing that she could cut it in half, as they had done as cruel children. But then perhaps it would grow a new head and tail, and multiply.

Grace stood up. She smoothed her beautiful pleats and touched one hand to her hair. "Are you happy with your Miles, Clio?"

"Yes," Clio said.

After a moment Grace told her, "You were right to marry him. I'm sorry for what I said on that horrible evening at Jake's."

It wasn't easy for Grace to apologize. It never had been, Clio remembered that from the earliest times. For some reason she thought of the rowing boat, the *Mabel,* and the time that Grace had almost drowned.

"It's forgotten," she said stiffly.

"Good."

They were both looking away, into the fire. It had burned down to a few red embers.

"Shall I ring to have it made up for you?"

"No, I can do it myself," Clio said. She took a log from the neat stack in the basket beside the hearth and threw it onto the ashes. A wisp of smoke rose. There was an outdoor smell from it of bonfires and leaf mold, and Grace shivered.

"Time to change for dinner, I suppose." Abruptly she added, "They'll try to talk you over, you know. Enlist you to support them against my going into Parliament."

"Don't worry."

Grace lifted her hand, then let it fall again. "Thank you."

Clio went down at exactly half past seven, but she found that John and Blanche and Hugo were already waiting for her. Blanche was wearing her jewels and one of her mist-colored gowns made of panels of floating net that disguised her stoutness, and on either side of her her son and husband were stiff in their white ties. Hugo leaned on his stick, but otherwise his stance was identical to his father's. Clio found herself longing suddenly for Julius and Jake. She chewed at the corners of her mouth and pretended to shake out the folds of her trusty old dress.

"We keep country hours," John announced, after he had greeted her. He took his pocket watch out and frowned at it. "Where is Grace?"

"She will be down in a minute, I'm sure," Blanche murmured.

But it was a quarter to eight before Grace finally swept down the stairs and into the drawing room. She was wearing a column of plain black satin and her throat was bare. She gave her father a dazzling smile.

"I think we'll go straight in," John said.

They took their places at one end of the immense table.

There was a silent interval broken only by the clink of cutlery and china before John raised his head and said to Clio, "What is your opinion of this Parliament notion of Grace's?"

After they had handed the plates the footmen stood, as ever, against the walls with their white-gloved hands folded in front of them. Clio could not stop herself from glancing at the man directly opposite her, because she had never grown used to talking in front of the servants as if they were carved out of wood. The man's face was utterly impassive.

"What?" John demanded. Clio saw that Grace and Hugo and Blanche were all looking expectantly at her.

"I think it is a good idea."

"It is not." John Leominster was not used to being given answers he did not like.

"Why is it not?" Clio asked, very gently.

"Self-evident. Not a woman's job, politics. If anyone from this family were to stand, it should be Thomas. I would have no objection to that."

"But Grace can represent West Shropshire just as well as Thomas. And for the very reason that she is a woman, she can represent a wider constituency too. Women need voices in the House."

"Thomas has no desire to . . ." Hugo began.

"Bravo," Grace interrupted him. Turning to her father, she said cheerfully, "There you are. I told you that Clio would agree with me. There's no going back, women are in Parliament to stay. There are fourteen now, next time there will be forty. And I shall be one of them."

The Earl's face was turning the same color as the burgundy in his glass. Hugo frowned, and Blanche unhappily crumbled her bread. Clio had only been repeating Grace's arguments, but it came to her now that they reflected her own beliefs. Forty women members, she thought, and then four hundred, why not? Her admiration for Grace was reluctant, but genuine. She had found herself a supporter.

"I shall be one of them, whatever you have to say about it, Papa," Grace concluded. She was smiling, but there was no question of her determination. Clio suddenly understood the meaning of Grace's independence. She had left her father's house. She had been married and widowed, and now she was alone. If she wanted to become a Member of Parliament, if the constituency party of West Shropshire adopted her and if the people voted for her, there was nothing John Leominster could do to prevent it. The recognition of something so obvious and simple almost took Clio's breath away. She felt like cheering.

John threw down his spoon. Tiny droplets of soup splashed and lay like murky gems on the polished table.

"Damned nonsense. Damned feminists and suffragettes, meddling in what they don't understand."

He was shouting, a surprisingly loud shout from his thin frame. Clio remembered Eleanor once telling her that he had been nicknamed Sticks, long ago, for his skinny legs. The footmen went on staring at the opposite walls.

Grace sat forward a little in her chair. Her thin wrists with their prominent knobs of bone rested on the table on either side of the ranks of ivory and silver cutlery still waiting to be used.

"Who are you to imagine that you understand the world any better than feminists and suffragettes?"

Clio thought that her uncle might choke. "I am who I am. A member of the Upper House." The Leominster crest winked back at them all from the silver and the napkins. "And I am also a man, and your father. I will thank you to remember that, madam."

"John . . ." Blanche faltered.

"Oh, I don't forget it," Grace said. "But you don't make the smallest difference, you know." She dabbed her mouth with her napkin. Her lipstick left a crimson print on the linen. She stood up, and a footman moved to draw back her chair for her. She crossed the room, straight-backed, and the door was opened for her by white-gloved hands. It was closed again silently behind her.

After a moment Hugo said, "Grace will do what Grace wants to do. We all know that." He was looking at Clio, trying to draw her back to them. But Clio felt as if she had just seen the grandeur of Stretton, the heritage that had awed her all her life, crumbling down into a pile of stones. Grace had done that, with her singularity. She felt utterly disoriented.

The Earl's face was still dark red. He picked up his spoon and then dropped it again. "Are we going to get any damned dinner this evening?" he demanded.

Blanche inclined her head to the butler, the signal to remove the plates.

The conversation for the rest of the miserable meal was between John and Hugo, entirely about estate business and hunting.

When Blanche and Clio withdrew and left them to it, they found Grace in the small drawing room sitting in an armchair to one side of the fire with her feet up on a stool. She was eating an apple and flipping through *Vogue,* evidently quite comfortable. Clio wished that she could have exchanged her own experience of dinner for a picnic and a magazine.

"Grace, how could you?" Blanche said.

Grace threw her magazine aside and stood up. She went to her mother and put her arms around her. "I had to."

Blanche was not appeased. "In front of Clio, too."

Clio knew that she must align herself. She said tentatively, "In a way, Aunt Blanche, Grace is right."

Blanche pushed Grace away. She went to her chair and sat in it with her head up and her back stiff, as if the seat were a throne. To Clio's eyes she suddenly looked smaller, a plump little woman with graying hair and too many heavy jewels. She was stranded in a corner of her great cold house, defended by the aging rump of an army of footmen, an anachronism. Immediately Clio thought of her own mother. Eleanor was getting old too, and Nathaniel, and the tide was beginning to flow away from the Woodstock Road. She had seen it without recognizing it, but now as she looked at Blanche it was clear.

Her mother and father had always been pillars in Clio's life, and in their own way so had her aunt and uncle. To see this diminishment was painful, and it left her feeling cold and exposed. She found herself wanting to cry, and she blinked angrily.

It was Grace who had been widowed, and Grace who was striking out. For herself, she was newly married and at the beginning of a partnership. She had not yet discovered what kind of partnership it might be, but there was no need for tears. Old age came to everyone, if they were lucky, luckier than Anthony had been.

"What will you do about money?" Blanche was asking in a cold voice.

Grace sighed, and sat down again. To Clio she said, "There is some problem about Anthony's estate. Did Julius tell you?"

"No."

Julius had said nothing at all. As always, he was secretive where Grace was concerned.

"Anthony lost a lot of money in the American crash. Cressida and I are his beneficiaries, of course, but as it happens there doesn't seem to be much left. The disentangling isn't quite finished, but it looks as if we shall be quite poor."

"I'm sorry, I didn't know." Clio doubted that Grace's notion of poverty would quite correspond with her own. "What will you do?"

Grace shrugged. "Whatever I have to do. Sell South Audley Street and buy somewhere much smaller, perhaps nearer to Westminster. Practice stringent economies, that sort of thing. Might even be rather fun, don't you think?"

"Don't be so ridiculous. Think of Cressida." Blanche was angry. Grace had been almost teasingly calm all through the evening, but now she showed an answering spark of anger.

"There is nothing ridiculous about my intentions. I have thought of Cressida. Being a Member of Parliament is paid work, you know. Would you rather see me selling tea gowns in Selfridges?"

Blanche had never been good at arguments. Her cheeks wobbled, and the soft creases deepened at the sides of her mouth.

She's a bewildered old lady, Clio thought. *She doesn't understand any of this.*

"You know it would never come to that. If you would only listen to your father, if you would come home with Cressida for good . . ."

Grace turned to Clio. She looked tired now. "If I do what is expected of me, Papa will provide. If I do not, then Cressida and I can't expect any financial assistance from his lordship. That's it, stripped of the polite verbiage, isn't it?"

Blanche put her hand over her mouth. "You are so hard, Grace. What have we done that you should have become so hard?"

Grace went to her again, and took her hands. She turned them over in her own, and her red-varnished nails tapped against her mother's rings.

"What would you really like me to do?" she asked softly.

"I would like you to come home again, to live with us." Blanche gestured with their linked hands, and all three of them looked upward, as if into the dark and drafty recesses of the great house. "And then, after a decent interval, I would like to see you marry again, some good man who will look after you and Cressida."

Grace shook her head. "I can't come back here, you know. I'm not a girl any longer, and you can't wish me back into one. And Anthony was my husband. I shan't marry again."

Clio shivered at the flat certainty in her voice.

Grace stood up, laying her mother's hands back in her lap. Then she bent over and kissed her cheek. "Don't worry. You never know, you might even end up feeling proud of me." She had recovered her calmness, but she made it clear that there was no more to say.

"Clio, we are neglecting you. Would you prefer tea or coffee? Mummy, shall I ring for the tray?" Then she laughed, apparently with real amusement. "One might as well command while there are still those to be commanded, don't you think? Or would you rather have a proper drink, Clio?"

"I will have a large whiskey and soda. Very large." Clio smiled, choosing not to see Blanche's shocked expression.

"And I shall join you." Grace strolled to the decanter that had been placed ready for the men.

When they had their drinks Grace lifted her glass to Clio.

"To the adoption meeting," she proposed, and Clio took a deep gulp.

The adoption meeting was in Ludlow. Grace drove them there, with Hugo sitting stiffly beside her and Clio and Cressida in the back. John had refused to mention the meeting at all, and Blanche had miserably divided herself between supporting him and recognizing the inevitability of Grace's progress toward Parliament. But at the last minute, as they were preparing to leave, Hugo appeared in his hat and coat.

"I can't sit here and let the two of you and the child go on your own," he grumbled.

"We won't be on our own, Hugo." Grace smiled. "There will be the Conservative Party Association of West Shropshire. But thank you. I would like it very much if you were there."

The hall where they met was dusty and wooden floored, with rows of seats lined up in front of a low dais. A Union flag and a picture of the King and Queen hung above the platform. Grace was ushered in by her campaign manager, the red-faced man with the bowler hat who had also worked for Anthony. She stepped up onto the dais in her silvery furs and then turned to survey the crowd.

As soon as she came in, the dingy room seemed to lighten. People leaned forward in their seats and the buzz of conversation grew louder. Grace evidently knew many of the members. She nodded and smiled to them as she took her seat in the middle of the row of officials, apparently completely at ease. Clio and Hugo were placed to one side, with Cressida a little in front. Clio took a quick sideways glance at her. The child sat still, with her feet and gloved hands pressed together, looking straight ahead into nowhere. She was wearing a felt hat that even Grace's dexterity had failed to tweak to a flattering angle, and a mushroom-colored coat with a big blue rosette pinned to the brown velvet collar.

The chairman of the local party called the meeting to order. Clio felt her stomach suddenly pitch with anxiety. She focused on the faces in front of her. There were women as well as men, most of them with reddened farming complexions, people of all ages, sitting quietly on their wooden chairs and looking at Grace.

Grace's campaign manager made a short speech. There was no need, he said, for him to make any introduction. Lady Grace Brock was known to them all as a staunch party supporter, as her late husband's loyal champion, and as a friend.

Grace stood up. Her hands holding her notes were steady, and her smile was warm, but inside herself she was afraid. Platforms and speeches had been easy when she was only expected to sit at Anthony's side, in the safety of his limelight. Now she was here alone. The room seemed huge; she was conscious of Hugo with his leg stretched out at an awkward angle, and Clio's intent face, but they seemed a long way away. She could feel Cressida watching her back.

Her adoption speech had been carefully worked out with her manager and supporters. She looked down at the notes and saw a series of hieroglyphics. Then she raised her head and saw a woman sitting in the back row, a little woman in a hat like a bun. She remembered that she had talked to her at some party function, and the woman had patted her arm and confided, "I'll vote for you. A vote for your husband is a vote for you, isn't it?"

Grace abandoned her notes and began to extemporize.

Once she had begun, it was easy. The sentences seemed to unroll before her eyes, like tickertape, and she had only to read them off.

"Don't look at me as a woman," she ordered them in her ringing voice. "Don't look at me as Lady Grace Stretton, or as Mrs. Anthony Brock. Look at me as a candidate first. Look at me as a worker, who will work for you and the constituency. I will represent each of you, every one of you, to the best of my ability. Let me go forward to fight this by-election for you; and as my husband did, so will I do. You have my word."

There was a single cheer, and then a ragged chorus of cheering that gained strength and confidence.

Clio listened, amazed. Her anxiety evaporated. This was Grace, standing up in front of her in her furs and Chanel, but it was also not Grace at all. She saw, for the first time, a politician.

"I have heard it said that mothers of young children should not put themselves forward in the political world. That a woman who has children should stay at home to care for them."

From somewhere, a man's voice called, "Hear! Hear!"

Grace swung in his direction. "I believe that to be true, sir, wherever you are. This is *my* daughter, here on the platform with me, and I believe that it is my responsibility to care for her. But I feel that someone ought also to be looking after the less fortunate children. My child is one of the lucky ones, and because I know that, I want to go to the House of Commons to fight. To fight not only for the men, not only for this constituency, but also for the women and children of England. *That* is my care and my responsibility."

The cheering became a roar.

Cressida's heavy face burned a dull red. Even her ears were alight under the felt brim. She dropped her eyes to her lap and pulled sharply at the cuff button of one of her gloves. *Luck.* The word reverberated as if a cracked bell had been struck. She did not know how to manage the welter of shame and disbelief and rancor rising inside her.

Grace called out, "Adopt me as your candidate. I will serve you, each and every one of you, to the best of my ability."

Cressida sat mute, trying to hide her boiled cheeks. Clio was applauding with everyone else. Beside her, Hugo's face showed his startled and embarrassed pride.

"Bravo," he muttered, as if afraid that he might be overheard.

The meeting belonged to Grace. There was another candidate for the nomination, but even before he stood up to speak, it was clear what the outcome would be.

Grace was unanimously adopted as the Conservative candidate for West Shropshire. She would fight her campaign against the same candidates who had opposed Anthony. Polling day was to be December 18, just a few days before the House retired for the Christmas recess.

Clio stayed at Stretton for four more days, accompanying Grace as she threw herself into her campaigning. The big black car with its blue ribbons and rosettes went everywhere. Clio heard Grace speak in village halls to Mothers' Unions and working men's groups, and to clusters of people gathered in the windswept cold of market squares.

Sometimes Cressida came with them. Grace had given her a jaunty little pennant with "Vote for Mummy" printed on it. She held it in the back of the car, and on the makeshift platforms, but she would not wave it.

Each time, everywhere they went, Clio was impressed by Grace's freshness, her willingness to answer questions if she knew the answers, and her adroitness in deflecting them if she did not. She handled hecklers with wit and good humor.

"I didn't vote for your husband, and I won't vote for his wife," a man yelled.

"More fool you not to vote for my husband," Grace shouted back. "He was the best MP you'll ever have. And I don't want your vote if you don't want a woman to fight for you."

Grace crackled and shone with vigor. Every day she was up early, eagerly waiting for the car to be brought around. She never flagged or complained of the cold or the bad roads or a hostile reception. Watching her, Clio thought she looked not like a widow but a bride.

When it was time for Clio to go home, Grace herself took her to Shrewsbury station. She swept through the ticket hall and booking office, shaking hands with porters and passengers and clerks. When the train came in, they kissed each other with genuine affection.

"Thank you for coming," Grace said.

"You didn't need me," Clio answered.

"Yes, I did. Wish me luck."

"Good luck, Grace. But you don't need that either."

Back at Gower Street, Clio found Miles sitting in an armchair, like some hibernating creature in a nest of manuscript pages and cigarette ends and unwashed plates. He was wearing braces over a dirty gray flannel shirt, and his hair stood up in a crest as if he had slept too long on it. The small rooms had a musty, vegetable smell.

"How's the work?" Clio asked.

Miles shuffled some manuscript pages into a heap. An ashtray rocked on the arm of his chair and then overbalanced, spreading its contents on the floor.

"All right. Just starting to get somewhere, actually."

Clio did not miss the implication. If she had not come home to interrupt him, he might have made progress.

"That's good," she said neutrally. When she passed behind his chair and leaned over to kiss the top of his head, he made a defensive clutch at his papers. Clio said nothing more. She opened the windows, letting in the traffic noise from the street, and began to collect up the dishes and cups. She scraped the food debris onto one plate and removed it to the kitchen, where the smell was even stronger. The sink was a mess of tea leaves and eggshells. She took a brush back into the next room and began to sweep up the spilled contents of the ashtray.

"For Christ's sake," Miles snapped. "Do you have to start doing this the minute you step in through the door?"

"I wouldn't have to clear up if you hadn't made such a mess in the first place, no."

"What in God's name is the matter with you? I've been writing, not working as a bloody housemaid. Is the state of a couple of rooms in Gower Street really so important in the great scheme of life?"

Clio faced him. Miles shrank back into his chair with his manuscript held back against his chest. She saw that the whites of his eyes were yellowish and his unshaven cheeks were gray. The fingers of his right hand were nicotine-stained. It came to her that he looked miserable. His eyes didn't meet hers. Concern for him replaced her irritation.

"Miles, you don't look good. Do you feel ill?"

His head fell against the back of the chair. He glanced up at her, under his eyelids, then closed his eyes. "Yes. It's a headache."

She put her hand on his forehead. His fingers fastened around her wrist.

"Lovely cool hand," he murmured.

"How long have you been sitting here?"

"I don't know. Ages."

Clio sighed. She stroked his hair, and he murmured, "That makes it much better."

"Would you like me to make you a cup of tea?"

"Yes, please."

She made him his tea and sent him into the bedroom to lie down while she cleaned up the cluttered rooms. She worked with a kind of patient exasperation. When she had finished, she looked into the bedroom and found him sitting up in bed waiting for her. He patted the covers beside him, and when she sat down, he took her hand.

"Dear Clio," he said. "I missed you, you know."

She seized on the words, her heart lifting. "Did you?"

"Of course."

She was looking at her Gilman painting of the bedsitting room, hanging on the opposite wall. The bareness of the little blue room made her think of the spare routines of her life before Miles came, and this solid presence now in the bed warmed her out of her irritation. She did not think that she would exchange now for then. Clio stretched out beside her husband and kissed his cheek.

"I'm glad to be home. Don't you want to hear about Grace and the election?"

"Not very much," he answered, but he said it pleasantly, and she laughed at him.

"I'm going to tell you, whether you like it or not. She was adopted, of course. I went out to see her campaigning. She was very good, you know. I was surprised by just how good."

Miles lay back against the pillows while she told him about the village halls and the market squares. She even coaxed him into reluctant laughter with her descriptions of the rustic hecklers and pompous party officials.

When she had finished, he looked at her, the same sly glance from under his eyelids.

"You are impressed by your cousin Grace, aren't you? Do you know how often you talk about her?"

After a minute Clio said, "She has just always been there, that's all. She is a part of my life. I don't know if impressed is the right word." She tried to sift through the words stacked inside her head, to pin down which the right one might be, but words that had always been her allies faded and crumbled, evading her grasp, and she was left with only a series of images, bright as snapshots.

Grace in her Chinese robe. Grace walking on the riverbank at Oxford with Jake. Grace in her wedding dress, her ballgown, her chemise in Pilgrim's studio. Grace under the sea, with her face turned up and her eyes and mouth like black holes.

Clio shivered.

"Are you feeling better now?" she asked Miles quickly.

He yawned and stretched. "I am, rather. I think I might go and have a bath. I said I might meet some people later on, as a matter of fact."

"Oh? Anybody I know?"

"No, I don't think so."

Blue light from the Gilman picture seemed to filter into the room, cooling the precarious intimacy that had sprung up between them.

"Shall I come with you?"

He gave a little laugh. "Do you want to? Would you enjoy yourself, piglet?"

Something pinched inside Clio. In a bright voice she answered, "No, you go. It will do you good to go out after working so hard all the time I've been away."

A little while later, bathed and shaved and dressed in a clean shirt that she had ironed for him, Miles put on his coat and went out.

Clio looked in the kitchen cupboards, but she couldn't find anything left to eat. Miles seemed to have consumed everything. She went back into the tidy living room and stood at the window looking down into Gower Street. She toyed with the idea of going out to see Jake and Ruth, or calling in at the Fitzroy to see who might be there, but the business of going anywhere at all seemed to call for more energy than she possessed. In the end she went to bed with a book, and fell asleep over it long before Miles came home.

The Parliamentary and political history was well documented. Elizabeth had researched it thoroughly from contemporary reports and family papers.

Lady Grace Brock was elected to her late husband's seat by a narrow majority of eighteen hundred votes over her Labour rival.

She was introduced into Parliament just two days before the Christmas recess of 1929, to take her seat with the fourteen other women MPs of all parties. Grace's sponsors were the Duchess of Atholl and Winston Churchill. Anthony had been Churchill's friend, and Churchill had agreed to present his widow to the House even though he disliked the presence of women there in principle.

Women in the House of Commons were no longer a novelty, but there was interest in Grace's arrival because she was Anthony's widow and because she had the reputation of a Society butterfly. The House was full after Question Time, and the Press Gallery was crowded.

John Leominster only rarely took his seat in the House of Lords. He had even less interest in the proceedings of the Commons except when they affected his lands or the old order, and he nourished a profound dislike for Ramsay MacDonald and his government. Today, looking as if he wished he could be anywhere else in the world, he sat in the Distinguished Strangers' Gallery with Nathaniel beside him. Blanche and Eleanor were with Clio in the Ladies' Gallery.

"I remember it clearly," Clio said. "I can see it all." Her ivory claw hands massaged the velvet arms of her chair in slow circles.

Elizabeth waited patiently. She knew that Grace had arrived in the Chamber at a quarter to four and stood under the gallery at the far end while her sponsors took their places on either side of her. She knew that she was wearing a somber but elegant dark blue coat and skirt, a plain white blouse, and a tiny cocked hat, and she carried her election writ. Elizabeth had pored over the photographs and read every description because she prided herself on her conscientious research. She knew what had happened, but she let Clio tell her again.

"After Question Time there was a silence," Clio said. "A whispering silence when we all leaned forward, trying to see her. Then the Speaker looked down the Chamber. He called out, 'Members desirous of taking their seats will come to the table.' I looked to one side, and I saw my mother and my aunt, one profile seemingly superimposed on the other. They were so alike, even when they were old women. Then I saw Grace, walking down the aisle between Winston and the Duchess, and she looked like Blanche and Eleanor too, and I could see my own face in theirs, and I felt the ties between us all as strong as ropes. I loved her, then. I loved her, and I was proud of her."

Clio darted a glance at Cressida's daughter to see what she made of that.

"I'm sure you were," Elizabeth murmured.

"She bowed to the House, and then she took the oath and read out the declaration, all in a wonderful strong voice. I remember thinking, if only Anthony could see her. I knew at that minute she was right to have stood, even ... even before the work she did afterward on improving conditions for women in prison and introducing nursery education for needy children and all the rest of it."

The old woman's head sank forward, and one of the bird claws came up to support it. The effort of talking seemed to have exhausted her.

"You are tired," Elizabeth said.

The head lifted again at once, in determined contradiction.

"There was a dinner party in the House that evening. Winston was there, and Tom and Cim Mosley, and some other friends of Grace's, but I remember it best as a family party. Uncle John and Aunt Blanche, my mother and father, Hugo and Jake, we were like one family. I can't remember any other time quite like that. We were all proud of her, you see. Whichever side we were on."

It was odd, Elizabeth thought, that the old lady should use just that phrase.

Grace waited until the next sitting of Parliament to make her maiden speech. When she did speak, it was with Mr. Baldwin's permission in defense of the government's Widows, Orphans and Old Age Pensions Bill. It was a good speech, and well received, and it was the beginning of her association with women's and children's interests.

She began to make her mark. As her reputation grew, little by little the old criticisms were forgotten. She was not just Anthony Brock's wife, or a frivolous socialite. She was a politician.

Thirteen

ON THE FACE OF IT, the next years were tranquil ones. Clio went patiently to work, and from *Fathom* to the Mothers' Clinic, and from the Clinic home again to Gower Street and Miles. Anyone who saw her, even Jake and Ruth, might comfortably have assumed that she was happy.

It was only Clio herself who knew otherwise.

Sometimes she felt that she had no reason to be less than content and so, by the forces of logic, she should actually be content. It must be that her recollection of the exact quality of happiness was imprecise, that her memory tricked her, by favoring what was in the past and was no longer accessible over what she knew now and could not escape from. There was nothing wrong with her life, she told herself, except her own perverse nature.

While these moods lasted, she made herself take the slow steps through her routine with a sort of faltering optimism. If all was not well now, then someday it would be. Miles's book would be finished and published to the proper acclaim; they would find a tune to their life together; she might even have a child.

At other times she knew that she was deeply unhappy. The sickening inevitability of it clogged all her movements and made her weary and dull.

Miles was the cause of her unhappiness, but he also provided the reason for continuing the unappetizing business of her life. She could think of no other explanation for her persistence in it. She no longer went to her job at *Fathom* for the pleasure or the interest of it, but to earn money. She apportioned the money very carefully, weighing every expenditure with miserly reluctance, so that it would stretch to support them both. She went out to the Clinic not because she wanted to give her help any longer, but in order to allow Miles peace and space to do his work. She did all this to hold on to their life together, but it was the life itself that was extinguishing her.

However often her thoughts traveled the same circuit, she could never reach any conclusion. Everything she did was done for Miles; Miles did not repay her. She did not relish the life she had; she could not bear to think of changing it, for what would she do otherwise?

But Clio's sickened indecision was only a faint echo of Miles's own.

His changes of mood were terrifying because of their violence and unpredictability. For days, sometimes weeks at a time, he was subdued. He would work, sitting in his armchair with a lined notepad on his lap, scribbling feverishly and then tearing the sheets from the pad and crushing them as if he wanted to wring blood out of them. When he was not scribbling, he would stare ahead into some invisible universe, glassy-eyed with desperation, and then he would drop his head into his hands and his whole body would seem to shrink into the shelter of the chair.

At the lowest point he would turn to Clio, letting his head fall against her as she knelt beside him. "I can't do it," he would whisper to her.

"Yes, you can," she soothed him. It became an effort to put enough conviction into her voice. "Please, Miles. Won't you let me read what there is, so I can reassure you?"

He hissed at her, "*No. I can't.* It's like pulling out your own viscera for public show. You don't understand anything, do you?"

"I try to," Clio said humbly. "But I am not just the public. And you let Tony Hardy read it, didn't you?"

"That sordid little money-grubber? Commerce is his only criterion. I don't give a monkey's fart for his ideas or his critical opinions. What does he know? Anyhow, that was long ago. I've rewritten every word since then, everything in it is new."

A terrible fear and suspicion were beginning to burn in Clio. She tried to pinch them out, but they always started to smolder again. She was afraid that there was no *everything,* that there was no great novel at all.

After Miles's moods of depression, floods after drought, came the bursts of wild elation.

He would gather up his notepads and lock them away, and burn every crumpled, discarded sheet. He would swell up out of his chair until he seemed to fill the untidy little rooms. He would eat all the food that Clio had laid in, destroying her thrifty menus for a week, and laugh at her for her bourgeois anxiety.

"The Lord will provide," he would exult. "Inspiration and macaroni and cheese together."

He would pull her close, kissing her with deliberate thoroughness until she felt herself unpeeling, like some bitter-skinned fruit, to reveal the pulp within her. She clung to him in her eagerness for his affection, but then Miles would stop what he was doing and look down at her. He would unwind his arms, very slowly, and then pat her shoulder, as if he had caught her in some act of indecency but was ready to forgive her.

"Dear piglet," he would murmur, and then he would wander away with his hands in his trouser pockets, or pick up a magazine and immediately become absorbed in it.

Clio would be left feeling cold and deflated. She had no doubt that he enjoyed exercising his power over her, and she understood that he used it because he felt powerless in so many other directions. What she did not know was whether he tried deliberately to hurt her, and so to localize his general anger with an unfair world, or whether he simply did not understand that she loved him and needed his love in return.

And then, in his moods of elation, Miles seemed to grow too large to be contained by the shabby walls of the flat.

At best he would call to Clio, "Come on, haven't we been cooped up in this place long enough? Let's go out. Let's go and have a few drinks and talk to people. I'm tired of long faces and tap water."

He would seize her by the arm and march her off to Charlotte Street. They would join the group at the bar, any bar, standing rounds of drinks and accepting them in their turn, finding themselves sucked back into the tiny, greedy world of literary gossip. Clio would remember the old days and tell herself that nothing had changed except her own humor.

At worst, and it was much more often, Miles would go out without her. Once or twice, he emptied her purse before he left. When he came back, he would be drunk, either melancholy-drunk or violent-drunk, and shouting out his resentment of Fitzrovia, other men's successes, and his shrinking wife.

One night, looking for something on which to vent his rage, he blacked her eye. Clio told Jake that she had had one drink too many in the Fitzroy and had walked into the door in the ladies' cloakroom. Her dissembling was so practiced, had become so much

second nature to her, that Jake believed her. She was vaguely
surprised that her brother should be taken in by such a perfunctory
lie.

"You drink too much," Jake told her.

Clio knew that there was a brandy bottle in the drawer of Jake's
surgery desk, because she had seen it once when Jake opened the
drawer to look for something else.

In the beginning, when his children were smaller and Ruth was
too busy with them and with her work at the Mothers' Clinic to
have much attention to spare for him, Jake had bought the brandy
and drunk a small tot after a long and more than usually disheart-
ening surgery. The spirit had warmed him, and he had enjoyed the
moment of calm and solitude, with the waiting room empty at last
and his nurse gone home. He drank the measure and poured
himself another. When he eventually went back to Islington, a
little muzzy and vague in the head, the house had seemed untidy
and unappealing. Ruth was banging plates in the kitchen and
shouting at Lucas, but she did not seem to have noticed that Jake
was late. Ruth was always busy and irritable. Jake knew that she
had too much to do, but he saw that as her own choice. He
resented her brusqueness, and the way that she turned heavily
away from him in their bed at night and fell instantly into a deep
sleep.

The first bottle emptied itself and was replaced. The thought of
his quiet moment with it at the end of the day became a comfort for
Jake.

Clio retorted, "You drink too much too. It's the age we live in."

They looked somberly at each other, where once they might have
made a joke about their habits. The times were changing. The
frivolity and youthful optimism of the Twenties seemed to have
receded with their own youth, and much further than just over the
arbitrary cusp that separated them from the new decade.

In the early years of the Thirties, London seemed full of gaunt-
faced men holding up placards that read, "I served my King and
Country. All I ask is a Job." There were no jobs, and there appeared
to be no policies that could create any. And in the pubs and studios,
when conversation moved beyond the parochial concerns of publishing and painting, there had begun to be anxious talk of German
rearmament. London had become a grim place, and life in it
seemed beset by dreariness.

In the memory the postwar years seemed quaint and much more
remote in history than the real passage of time indicated. Clio's

feelings exactly matched her sense of the period. She could hardly believe that she had once been the bright-eyed ingenue who had followed Pilgrim to the Eiffel Tower and had begged Max Erdmann for a job. Had she once believed that to sit behind a typewriter in Doughty Street or to lift a half-pint beer glass in the Fitzroy was to allow herself the dizzy freedom of the wide world?

The bitterness of her reflections brought her back to contemplation of her marriage. The cycle was unbreakable, a treadmill that went on through the days and into her dreams at night. Had she truly imagined that marriage to Miles would bring her the safety and calm, the fruitful and mutually rewarding literary partnership that she had longed for?

More and more, the truth became plain to her. She could not, any longer, pervert it with optimism or excuses.

Miles had married her to acquire a meal ticket, a free bed with the drawback that it also contained her body, and an unpaid cook, cleaner, and washerwoman. There was the added advantage, in his black fits, that she was unfailingly there to stroke his hair like a mother and to shore up his weak and wandering ego.

All this Clio came to understand perfectly well, in the years between 1929 and 1932. She also understood that Miles was all she had, and that however miserable she might be, to be without him would be worse. She had learned to devote herself to him, and she could not, now, think of anything else she might do with herself.

Clio was vulnerable, but she had her pride. She had wanted to marry Miles, had even insisted upon it, and now that she found herself in this position, she could not have borne to admit it to anyone. There were also a few occasions, very few but she clung to the thought of them with great tenacity, when Miles treated her with tenderness. She could not stop the old optimism from surging up, then.

As the months passed, to all outward appearances Clio was a happy wife, and a busy and useful contributor to her world. Eleanor's veiled hints about the possibility of more grandchildren were obscure enough for Clio to pretend she did not hear them.

Grace sold the house in South Audley Street and moved with Cressida to a much smaller establishment near the river in Westminster. The little house was decorated and furnished with Grace's usual flair, but once the work was done and they were installed, Grace seemed to feel that the place required no more of her attention. She entertained her new political allies in the upstairs drawing room and gave occasional small dinners, but Vincent Street served her more as an extension of the House than as a home.

It was Blanche's suggestion that Nanny Brodribb should come down from Stretton to look after Cressida in the simplified household, and Grace agreed at once. Thereafter Cressida saw much more of Nanny than she did of Grace herself.

Grace devoted her time and energy to politics. She was often in the House until late at night; she spoke regularly on her pet topics; and she sat on the numerous committees that dealt with women's and children's rights. There were regular trips north to the constituency, where she was popular with the local party and with the voters. She held her seat, with an increased majority, in the General Election of 1931, and under the National Government headed by MacDonald and Stanley Baldwin, she began to be spoken of as a coming young woman. Her energy and stamina were apparently boundless.

Grace had discovered that work was an effective pain-killer. She had never done any before now, except for carrying trays up to Eleanor's convalescents during the war, and she was surprised by her own ability to concentrate on what she was doing. If she kept the Indian Women's Franchise Bill in the front of her mind, then she could make herself forget, for quite long stretches of time, that Anthony was dead and she was alone.

The Vincent Street house contained few reminders of him, except in Cressida's room, where photographs lined the bureau and shelves, but its very smallness and silence made her remember how different the other house had been. She was glad to leave it behind in the morning, and she never hurried back to it at night.

Cressida was eleven. Grace had found a small private school for her in Pimlico, where the fees were reasonable and most of the other girls were the daughters of Army widows or disabled officers.

Nanny walked her there in the mornings and met her at the end of the day. Cressida was not exactly unpopular with her fellows, but she simply preferred not to enter into the intense friendships that the others enjoyed. They stopped asking her to tea at their houses because Cressida never accepted, and she did not invite anyone to come back to Vincent Street. She was happier to eat her tea in the kitchen alone with Nanny and Cook, who ran the house between them with the help of a daily, and then to go upstairs to read, or draw, or write stories for herself. The stories were always written in lined exercise books, bought with her pocket money from a corner newsagent on the way home from school. The stories were almost always about tiny domestic crises befalling happy, loving families. The crises were easily resolved. Cressida knew that her stories were dull, and she preferred them that way.

When they sat down to breakfast together, Grace and Cressida dutifully asked each other about their respective days, but they did not talk very much otherwise. They very rarely spoke about Anthony.

If anyone had asked her whether she was happy, Grace would have said that she was content. She did not have any expectation of happiness. But as it happened, nobody did ask her. Her busyness was an effective screen. Even Jake, who worried that she never allowed herself to cry or to be weak, did not presume to mention the fact of her prickly defensiveness to the coming young woman of the Conservative party.

Clio and Grace saw each other only rarely. The main link between their two households in these early years of the 1930s was Alice.

Alice was twenty in 1932. She had inherited her father's height and her mother's statuesque figure. She was neither graceful nor particularly pretty, but her large, oval face with regular features and wide, clear eyes that rarely blinked gave the impression that somehow she saw more than was apparent to other people. Her blunt manner made an odd contradiction to this impression of sensitivity.

Alice's hair had always sprung off her broad forehead into thick curls, and in defiance of fashion she wore it long, in a pre-Raphaelite cascade, or braided into thick coils over her ears. Phoebe Stretton called her the Dear Old Ox, or Patient Griselda, but the nicknames were not very apt. Alice was full of uncomfortable passions. She was clever but her cleverness lacked focus; she was affectionate but touchy; and she loved company, especially the company of good-looking young men, but was too shy to take much advantage of it when it presented itself.

Alice had come out two years earlier. Her Season had been a halfhearted affair because she was the last of the daughters, and even Blanche and Eleanor no longer had much appetite for the ritual. There had been her own dance in Oxford, shared with another girl, and the usual round of London dances in reciprocation. Alice had twice fallen desperately in love in the course of her year, but neither young man had quite come to the point of proposing marriage.

After that, Alice tried hard to find something to do. Tabitha was still living at home in the Woodstock Road. Tabby was quietly religious, and she was content with her Church and with her job as a teacher in a local kindergarten. There had been some talk of Alice training as a teacher too, but that plan had come to nothing. She did a secretarial course instead and for a few months worked as a secretary to a London publisher, a friend of Max Erdmann. During the week she stayed with Clio and Miles in Gower Street, sleeping in the bedroom that had once been Julius's. Miles mostly ignored her, but he did not object to her being there, only remarking that the rent was useful. Clio was glad of her company.

But before she had been in the job very long, Alice gave in her notice, for no particular reason. She went back to Oxford for a little while, where she worried Nathaniel and annoyed Eleanor with her lumpish indecision, then made her surprise announcement.

"I'm going to live with Grace," she said to Clio.

Alice had never lost the puppyish admiration for her older cousin that had sprung into focus when Anthony was electioneering at Stretton. Now that Grace was a Member of Parliament herself, she was Alice's heroine. Alice interested herself in economic affairs and unemployment and measures for the restoration of world trade, just so that she could talk intelligently to Grace about them. And Grace responded to her with a kind of absent-minded affection that occasionally kindled into direct if amused encouragement, making the flame of Alice's devotion burn up even more brightly.

"Why are you going to live with Grace?" Clio asked.

Alice's broad cheeks were hot with happiness. "I'm going to work for her. I'm going to be a kind of assistant. In her political work, you know. I shall deal with some of her correspondence, arrange her appointments diary, travel up to the constituency with her. There will be plenty to do."

She was so proud that Clio had to swallow her instinctively doubting response. "I'm sure there will. It sounds very interesting."

"Grace can't pay me very much, of course, but that doesn't matter at all. I'll have my bed and board, and I don't need much else."

Alice had a small income of her own, just as Clio did. It was like her, in the grip of one of her passions, to deny that she had any requirements beyond food and somewhere to sleep.

"What does Pappy say?" Clio asked.

Alice looked surprised. "He wants me to do whatever will make me happy."

Clio nodded. Nathaniel had never been able to deny Alice anything that she wanted.

"And what does Cressida think?"

Alice only shrugged. "You know what Cress is like. No one ever knows what she thinks. And Grace still imagines that we will be jolly company for each other."

Clio said sharply, "Alice, you will be kind to her, won't you? Cressida doesn't have a very easy time."

Alice only looked back at her out of her clear eyes. "What? Oh, yes, of course I will."

So Alice moved into Vincent Street to become Grace's willing lieutenant. When anyone telephoned the house, it was usually Alice who answered, and it was Alice who was the guardian of Grace's engagements diary, her correspondence, even her wardrobe. Alice had little interest in her own clothes, but she made painstaking lists of which outfit Grace had worn to which engagement, and with which accessories, so that she could rotate them efficiently for her.

Grace accepted the devotion lightly. She said that Alice was making herself very useful, that she seemed to be enjoying herself, and there was not much else that the family needed to know about the arrangement.

Eleanor fretted a little to Clio. "Why does Alice want to act as some sort of unpaid secretary-companion to Grace?"

"She needs to devote herself," Clio answered. "Alice needs a cause."

"And what about the people she meets there?"

Eleanor meant Grace's political friends, of some of whom she and Nathaniel disapproved.

"Alice isn't a little girl anymore. She can make her own judgments."

"You are all grown up," Eleanor said sadly. Clio saw the soft lines of regret in her face.

"Aren't you happy to see us all launched in the world?"

"I wish you were babies again."

Once, Eleanor remembered, long ago, she had gone into a bedroom where Jake and Julius were asleep. There had been the sound of the sea beyond the curtained window, so it must have been at one of the summer holiday houses. She had bent over Jake and he had stirred in his sleep, then reached up to put his hand in hers. She had held it, noticing the size of it, almost as big as her own where it had once been a tiny curl of fingers. She had leaned over to kiss him, and the scent of his head had been the same as his baby smell.

She was still young then, still the mother of young babies, but she was overwhelmed with the sense of loss of that one babyhood, and also by the awareness of time passing, declining, running away from her.

The feeling came back to her now. She made an effort to dispel it.

"I suppose all women yearn for babies. And there are always the grandchildren."

"Yes," Clio said stiffly. "Always the grandchildren."

Grace had told Cressida that Alice was coming to live in the house with them, and that Alice would be company for her because she was so busy herself.

"I don't need company," Cressida said. "I'm quite all right with Nanny and Cook."

"Company of our own kind, darling. Be a good girl, won't you?"

That was all. Cressida withdrew further into her reading and her story-writing, and let Alice eagerly scoop up whatever crumbs of Grace's life fell her way. She made it clear that she didn't welcome Alice's company, any more than Alice wanted to bestow it on her.

Early in 1932 there was a party at Vincent Street.

It was not a large, lavish party of the South Audley Street kind because Grace no longer had the money or the space to entertain on a grand scale, but still she liked things to be done properly, as she expressed it. She would give a little shrug as if to say: These are not *my* requirements, but it is what one must do.

"Will you arrange some of your lovely flowers, darling?" she asked Alice, and Alice brought in armfuls of striped lilies and arranged them in tall vases on the console tables in the drawing room. Streaks of tigerish pollen daubed her nose when she looked in the glass in her bedroom. They made her look interestingly pagan. She smiled at the thought as she rubbed them away, and changed into her best dress with a puff-sleeved bolero to cover her shoulders. As an afterthought she wound a tiger-print scarf in her curls.

"You look splendid," Grace called over her shoulder. She was filling one of Anthony's monogrammed silver boxes with Turkish cigarettes.

"I wish I could look like *you*."

Grace laughed. "Don't be silly. My looks are no longer an issue

of any significance. Whereas you have everything ahead of you."
Downstairs the bell rang. "Oh God, right on the *dot*, of course."

Alice had addressed and posted the cards of invitation so she
knew all the guests by name, if not by sight. But she did not
immediately recognize the tall man who came in alone when the
party was at its height. He stood in the doorway, waiting with lazy
expectancy as if he knew the company would come to him, rather
than being under any obligation to make a foray into it.

Alice saw Grace detach herself from a group of people and go to
greet him. He took both her hands and kissed her on the mouth.
Alice was near enough to them to overhear what he said. The man's
voice was low, but his proximity seemed to sharpen her ears.

"Ah, Grace. I wish you had come with us. We could have
achieved so much, with the right blood."

"You may yet achieve it. But I must stay where I am, you know."
Then she turned, still holding his hand. In a different voice she said,
"Look, everyone is here. Won't you come and meet?"

It happened that Alice was part of the group Grace drew him
into. He seemed to know everyone but her. When Grace came to
introduce him and he held out his hand to shake hers, she looked up
at him. He was dark, with black horizontal brows and sharp, bright
eyes. He had a dark moustache and a mouth that crooked at one
corner.

"Alice, this is Sir Oswald Mosley. My cousin, Alice Hirsh."

"Tom," the man said. He had a firm grip.

Alice knew who he was before Grace told her his name. Sir
Oswald Mosley had been a Labour politician, a Cabinet member,
until the year before. He had left the party and with five other MPs
had founded his own New Party. There had been much talk, and
more promises. Yet for some reason, the New Party had failed to
attract the membership its founders had hoped for. Left-wing newspapers were beginning to describe the new organization as "fascist," and Mosley had just returned from a visit to Mussolini in
Rome.

But still, Oswald Mosley's brilliance was widely admired. People even now spoke of him as a future Prime Minister.

Alice felt her mouth drying and a red flush spreading over her
collarbones beneath the bolero jacket.

"You are Grace's cousin," he said. He was examining her, still
smiling. Alice wanted to keep his attention, but at the same time
she wished he would move on and leave her to shrink back into
anonymity.

"Yes. Our mothers are twin sisters."

"Of course. I remember now."

Did he? she thought wildly. Why should he remember something as trivial as that?

"Tell me your name again."

She was almost whispering. "Alice. Alice Hirsh."

"Hirsh?" Mosley nodded. He pushed his lips out under the soft bristle of his moustache as if committing the syllables of her name to memory. Then he drew his heels together and made a small, precise bow. He was swept away at once by a dozen other people competing for his attention.

Alice stepped backward. She folded her hands behind her. The palms were damp, and they made a tiny kissing sound when she pressed them against Grace's cream-painted wall. From her corner Alice watched Tom Mosley moving through the current of the party. He was like a river pike, she thought, in the shoals of minnows.

She was still watching as he left, escorted to the door by Grace. When he had gone, the room seemed dimmer. Alice looked up to see if one of the little electric bulbs had failed under its cream silk shade.

The party was a success, as Grace's parties always were. The last group of guests bore Grace away with them, to dine at the Savoy Grill.

"Will you be all right, darling?" she called to Alice.

"Yes. Of course I will. Have a lovely time."

When she was alone, she made a slow circuit of the room. The ashtrays were filled with reddened butts, and the tables were ringed with the interlocking prints of cocktail glasses. The air was heavy with smoke and the final musk notes of a dozen different perfumes.

There had been other parties, similar in almost every respect, but even the stale air of this one seemed to contain a new and significant scent. Alice lifted her head, like one of the foxhounds in the Stretton coverts. She picked up the discarded glasses and examined each one before placing it on a tray. Was this the one the man had used?

It took her a long time to clear the drawing room. Cressida did not appear at any point. Alice took the glasses and ashtrays down to the kitchen and helped Mabel and Nanny to wash them up.

It was the end of the following day before Alice encountered Grace again. Cressida had already gone to bed when Grace came home from the House and dropped her fur wrap on one chair, her bag and gloves on another, her papers on a third.

"Dear Lord, what a day. Anything in the post, darling?"

"Nothing important. Lots of thank-you notes. Shall I fix you a drink?"

"Whiskey and water, very weak." Grace kicked off her suede shoes and rested her feet on the sofa cushions. She took the glass that Alice gave her and watched her over the rim of it.

"The evening went off well," Alice said.

"*Mar*velous clearing up job, lamb, I do appreciate."

"I'm happy to do it. I enjoyed it all," Alice answered truthfully. And then after a minute, "I . . . thought he was rather impressive."

"Who's that?" Grace murmured.

"Sir Oswald. Um, Tom." She wanted to talk, like Phoebe and Tabitha when they were giggling girls, but part of her also wanted to keep this new scent to herself, hoarding it, lest it should evaporate. She pretended to be busy with the coal scuttle. Grace said nothing, waiting until Alice had to look around at her again.

After a moment their eyes met.

"I shouldn't fall in love with Tom Mosley, if I were you," Grace drawled.

"I hadn't thought of doing anything of the kind." Alice went stiff with indignation. "I said I thought he was interesting. His ideas interest me, that's all."

"Do you know what his ideas are?"

Alice knew something. She knew that his New Party had been formed less than a year before in contempt of the old men of politics. Its goals were an ending to class warfare and the introduction of radical economic measures to bring prosperity back to the nation. She knew that Mosley believed in government by a small, strong executive without much accountability to an enfeebled Parliament, and she had heard the same principles described as fascist.

But somewhere, she remembered, she had heard or read a claim of Mosley's. He had said that, given a quarter of a million pounds and the support of a press baron, he could "sweep the country."

The words had stirred her then, that was why she remembered them. Now they came back to her, and affected her more deeply. The country needed to be swept. All the stifling ills of stale government by timid old men, the economic cowardice and unemployment and the miasma of failure that gripped them now, they all needed to be bundled up and swept away.

The man with the black moustache and the bright, penetrating eyes was the one to do it. Alice was suddenly certain of that. He was brave enough, and he had the determination. It was the raw potential of his power that she had scented last night, through the smoke and the lilies and the women's perfume.

The New Party had failed, but Mosley's bearing seemed to indicate that that did not matter. Alice felt within herself that it did not matter either. There was a way forward, she was sure of that, and she knew that Tom Mosley could find it. The country would be swept.

If I could be part of that, she thought. She held the idea within herself, protecting the flare of it as if she cupped her hands around a flame.

Grace was lying back against the cushions. One silk-stockinged foot drew apparently idle circles, but she was watching Alice intently.

"He asked you to join his party, didn't he?" Alice demanded.

"Yes. I thought hard about it. I admire him personally, like all sorts of other people, from Bob Boothby to Aneurin Bevan. I also think that his economic ideas are very sound. But in the end I decided I could be more useful by staying where I am, within our own party."

You were afraid to risk your own seat, Alice silently translated. *Oh, if I had been in your place, I would have gone.*

"In the end he only recruited five Labour MPs and one Conservative. I think subsequent events, catastrophic election results, and the pitched battles and the violence that seem to follow him wherever he goes, have proved me right."

"What will he do now?" Alice asked.

"I should still like to see him doing something splendid. Heading some force for change that would be clear-cut and strong and incontrovertible."

"Like Hitler in Germany?"

"Perhaps," Grace mused. "But I don't think that anything as modern and coherent as Hitler's movement will ever be possible in this poor, damp, vacillating country of ours."

"I would like to go and hear Mosley speak. I would like to offer to help him. I could do that, couldn't I?"

Grace swung her feet down onto the floor. Her glass was empty now. "Yes, you could do that. Only what will Nathaniel say if he discovers you marching in uniform with the fascist youth bands?"

"I don't wear a uniform, and I shan't march." Alice frowned and her solemn face went red. "Anyway, Nathaniel isn't a Bolshevist, you know."

"Of course he isn't. But I don't believe he is a great admirer of Hitler or Mussolini either."

"I know that. But I must find out what I believe in myself, mustn't I? Pappy would defend my right to do that, he would defend anyone's."

"Yes, he would. And so would I," Grace said softly.

Alice went to hear Mosley speak.

The first time was in Trafalgar Square, and she walked there from Vincent Street through the mild London sunshine. There was only a small crowd; Sir Oswald Mosley stood on the plinth at the foot of Nelson's Column and a little corps of eight young men wearing black shirts and gray flannels surrounded him. Alice was able to come close to him, and he seemed to speak directly to her. She found that she could not take her eyes off his face.

"We must be the movement of youth," he told the crowd. He had an orator's voice, rising and falling as rhythmically as music. "We must gladly accept discipline, and the effort, and the sacrifice, because only by accepting these can great purposes be achieved. By these alone can the modern state be built."

His words seemed to enter Alice's blood.

After the rally was over, she walked home again alone, wishing that she could have followed Mosley and his young men. The streets she passed along seemed to glimmer with a light as hard and bright as diamonds, and all the soot-stained buildings were cleaner and sharper and seemed to stand higher against the colorless sky.

It came to her suddenly that she did have something to be proud of in being British, and that she was ready to defend it against apathy and degeneracy and the creeping tide of Bolshevism. She lifted her head and swung her arms as she walked.

Grace was, as usual, not at home, but Alice met Cressida on the landing outside her bedroom.

"How was the great rally?" Cressida asked.

In the flush of her excitement Alice said warmly, "It was marvelous, utterly marvelous. You should have come, I wish you had heard what he had to say."

Cressida blinked. Her pale, short eyelashes gave her a myopic appearance, although she saw perfectly well. "You wish *I* had been there? *I* wouldn't go anywhere near muck like that. I am a socialist."

Cressida had recently adopted a left-wing stance. Grace was amusedly tolerant of her political posturing—when she took any notice of it at all—but Alice found it deeply irritating. Alice was too serious and too literal-minded to be amused by the notion of a twelve-year-old socialist.

"You only claim to be one because you want to oppose Grace." Opposing Grace was the most incomprehensible aim, to Alice.

"Not just Mummy. Grandfather and good old Uncle Hugo, with their feudal notions, and military-minded Uncle Thomas as well, actually."

"What do you know about anything?"

"As much as you, dear Alice. I can read, can't I? And listen and make up my own mind."

"You're just a stupid little girl."

"I'm not stupid, stupid." Cressida lashed out with a clenched fist. With all her weight behind it, the blow connected with Alice's arm, and Alice gasped with pain. She was ready to hit back, but then with an effort she regained control of herself. She was always conscious of her own dignity, and she didn't want Grace, or even Nanny or Mabel, to hear that she had been fighting with Cressida like an infant in the schoolroom. She turned and walked away, still quivering with anger.

Cressida watched her go. Her fists were still clenched, and her stolid face was mottled with hatred.

Alice learned to be circumspect about her new-found zeal. There were more meetings and rallies to be attended as the British Union of Fascists slowly emerged under Mosley's leadership, and Alice slipped away to join the swelling, uneasy crowds whenever she was able. Her work for Grace didn't fill all her time, and she was often able to absent herself from Vincent Street. But she did not talk much about what she saw and heard. She kept the fire of her devotion well shielded, away from the crass misjudgments of those who would not understand it.

There began to be scuffles and then full-blown fights at some of the meetings, between Mosley's supporters and bands of hostile antifascists. Alice watched the battles indignantly, but she was proud when hecklers and communists were thrown out by the Blackshirts.

At one meeting there were persistent interruptions from a trio of men up in the gallery of the hall. Mosley raised his arm and pointed his finger. Alice shivered, as if he pointed at her instead.

His accusation rang out. "There you see three warriors of class war, all from Jerusalem."

It was the first time Alice had heard him single out the Jews as a target. He said afterward, to qualify his words, "Fascist hostility to Jews is directed against those who finance communists and those who are pursuing an anti-British policy."

Alice believed what he said. Of course, anyone who gave money to support communism or worked against the national good should be a target, whatever his faith or nationality. If any Jews did such things, then they must be prevented from doing so.

After that meeting there was a march. Mosley and seventy of his young men marched along Fleet Street and down Whitehall to their headquarters. The men wore their black shirts, and they strode along without coats or hats, singing and calling out the Union's rallying cries. There were no women with them, but Alice slipped along in their wake, almost a part of the rabble of antifascists that scuffled at the tail of the march.

The singing and the sound of marching feet and the sight of Tom's handsome head held high at the front of the column were almost unbearably stirring. There were tears in Alice's eyes. She would have done anything for the cause at that minute.

The pain was in the reality that there was nothing she could do except run along behind the men.

Perhaps her chance would come. She watched the bareheaded young men swarming into the party headquarters in a great burst of cheering before she turned away and made her way back home.

Clio and Jake saw what was happening, but they also did not see.

Alice had discovered a vein of secrecy within herself. When she met her brother or sister, it was easy to convince them that she cared about nothing but being Grace's secretary-assistant, eagerly hanging on at the outer fringe of her cousin's political life. The pretense that it was not important, did not even exist, made the flame of her new devotion burn brighter and sweeter inside her.

There was sly excitement in coming back from a Blackshirt rally with the Leader's oratory like a bell in her head, to Gower Street or Islington or just to Vincent Street, and seeming to be the same Alice that she had always been.

The knowledge that she was not the same nourished her more richly than any food could have done.

She had always been the baby of the Babies, the youngest one of all the brothers and sisters and cousins, the last to arrive at the table when all the knowledge and wisdom and experience were being dished out, but now she felt herself growing big and strong. She alone knew where the future must lie. She was superior to all of them. Superior even to Grace. Alice thought that in her heart Grace understood and believed in the right way, but she was weak enough to let political expediency dilute her intentions.

As it happened, Alice underestimated what Clio and Jake did know. Separately, they were aware of their sister's growing fanaticism, but for different reasons they were unwilling to admit it to each other, or even to themselves.

To Jake, Alice was still partly a little girl. He cherished the memory of her as an innocently demanding toddler in the last summer before the war. Alice had slept on a rug with her curls damp against her flushed face while he was importuning his cousin Grace in the angle of a hawthorn hedge. Alice belonged in those prewar days, when the world had seemed to Jake to be a sunny and equable place. That was before the trenches and the stretchers, and the rare quiet times between bombardments when he had sat reading Donne by the light of a paraffin lamp.

> *He ruined me, and I am re-begot*
> *Of absence, darkness, death; things which are not.*

The words came back to Jake with peculiar resonance now. The world had not regained its sunniness for long, and darkness and death had become overfamiliar presences in his medical practice. There was a particular bitterness in the possibility that Alice might be affected by this darker world, and so he chose to convince himself that she was not.

Jake was repelled by the anti-Semitism of the Blackshirt movement. There was a bad evening at Islington, when Alice was sitting down to a family supper with him and Ruth and the children, Rachel and Lucas. Out of nowhere, out of nothing more than the small currency of exchanged news and domestic opinions, had come a disparagement of Hitler's treatment of the Jews in Germany.

Alice had laid down her knife and fork. She lifted her head, and Jake saw that her eyes were wide, and very bright, the pupils like black glass.

She began to parrot the old propaganda. There were good Jews, like Nathaniel. Like Levi and Dora Hirsh and Ruth's mother and father. And there were bad Jews, corrupt financiers who embezzled and stole and who undermined the economy and gave money to the communists. The bad Jews must be punished. They must repay what they had stolen. *Stolen from us,* Alice said.

Ruth had gasped. For once, she was at a loss for words.

Looking from his Jewish wife to the round, smooth faces of his Jewish children, Jake had felt sick. He had felt as if the ground shivered along some fault under the floorboards, under the folds of the cloth that covered his dining table, and that at any moment the fault might crack open and they would be pitched in different directions, some of them landing on one side of the chasm and some on the other, and some of them vanishing into the blackness itself.

And yet . . . Alice was his sister, and he loved her as he loved all of his family. He felt that they were all bound together by threads that spun out of the Woodstock Road and held them tight forever. It was because he loved his mother and father that he couldn't tell them that their beloved Alice had joined the Women's Movement of the British Union of Fascists. It hurt him that he did not know for certain that she had, that she left him to guess and to imagine the worst. And it cut him that she could come to his house and say such things in front of Ruth and the children. Yet he loved her as much as he loved the children. More, perhaps, than he loved their sharp and combative mother these days. Jake was not sure how the gulf had opened between Ruth and himself, or how long ago, but now that it was there, he had no idea how to bridge it again. They went through all the rituals of living a domestic life together, but the sharp pleasure that they had once known in being together had now entirely faded. They existed side by side, and curbed their irritation with each other as best they could.

He found some inadequate words. "That is enough of that talk at my table, Alice."

Ruth had glanced at him, a hard look that seemed to say, *Is that all?*

And Jake had looked away from her to his sister, who coolly met his eye. Then she had smiled. Her top lip lifted, showing her white teeth and her gums, making her look like some healthy and utterly unquestioning farm animal.

The excuse that Jake chose to make to himself for his sister's sudden and frightening allegiance was male, and doctorly. He knew that Mosley was a handsome and charismatic man, and that the youths who marched behind him were mostly well set-up and shown off to their best advantage by the buttoned-up black shirts and fascist insignia of their uniforms. He decided that Alice was in the grip of a sexual fixation, intensified by the charged atmosphere of rallies and marches. Her ill-informed fascist enthusiasms would soon pass, he told himself, once she was safely married.

There was the risk that she might be carried off by one of the young thugs of the movement, but almost none of them were of her class or background. Jake reasoned that she was much more likely to be claimed by one of the scions of Tory families who passed through Grace's drawing room. He thought that would answer her real inclinations. And once she was properly bedded, this dangerous phase would be over.

It was a reassuring line of thought, but the pursuit of it stirred other ideas within Jake. He sat in his surgery after the last patient had gone home. He took the brandy bottle out of the bottom drawer of his desk and poured a measure into the medicine glass kept for the purpose. He tipped the spirit into his mouth and thought about Ruth, tracing in his mind's eye the creases that ran under her belly and the mottled veins that had begun to spread over her thighs. He could hear her remonstrative voice in his head.

Then he began to consider other possibilities. Moving slowly, heavily, he stood up and went to his coat that hung from the hatstand in the corner. He took a notebook from his pocket and referred to it before he lifted the telephone receiver.

Clio knew, or guessed, how deeply Alice was being drawn into the net of fascism. But she did not discuss her fears with Jake and Ruth out of a kind of delicacy, a respect for the Jewish solidity of their family life and shame for Alice. She also had the idea that it was not Alice who was finally to blame, but Grace.

It was Grace who allowed, or even encouraged, Alice's allegiance to Mosley. Grace had introduced her to him, in her own drawing room. It was Clio's belief that Grace was drawn to the movement herself, but was too careful of her own position to admit it openly. But through Alice's membership she could experience it vicariously, in perfect safety. Through her silly, adolescent devotion to her cousin, Alice had become a pawn in Grace's game.

Clio had hardly seen Grace since Alice had gone to live in Vincent Street, but she felt the old, dissonant chords of mistrust and suspicion begin their deep vibrations all over again.

However, the main reason for Clio's failing properly to stand guard over her sister was nothing to do with Grace, or even with

Alice herself. As the winter of 1932 came, and Clio's third wedding anniversary passed, she was increasingly preoccupied with the tightening spiral of her own life.

It was a cold winter, and fog-bound, murky chill descended on London and settled in the dingy Gower Street rooms. Miles was drinking heavily and seemed lately to have given up all pretense of working. They had very little money. Resentment against him flared up in Clio when he wasted what they did have, but she smothered it rather than allowing it to erupt into one of the vicious arguments that her husband seemed almost to enjoy.

Clio was weary, and the weariness oozed out of her in a series of small illnesses. There was a cold, and then a gastric infection, and then another cold that she could not shake off. She had almost never been ill in her life before, and the experience made her feel even weaker and more helpless than ever. The days spent lying in the disordered bedroom, wondering when Miles would slam out of the house or come banging back again, were the dreariest she had ever spent. Her sense of a lost, parallel life that they might have lived together if only an elusive detail or two could have been changed was heightened by his occasional kindnesses.

Sometimes he brought her a tray, with invalid food invitingly prepared and a nonsensical poem rolled in her napkin ring.

"I'm sorry to be such a wet blanket," Clio said, trying not to cry as she twisted the scroll of paper in her fingers.

"Poor old blanket," Miles said lightly. He bent over to kiss the top of her head and then slid away, out to the Fitzroy, or Soho, or wherever it was he spent his time.

Jake came to see her and pronounced that she was run-down and anemic and needed a change of scene.

"Can't you get Miles to take you away somewhere? You've got no children, no real ties. You could go away for the rest of the winter, to the south of France, or Morocco, even. There's no reason to stay here."

"And there's no money to take us anywhere else." She tried to smile, and Jake did not seem to see the bitterness in it. "I shall have to make do with Christmas in the Woodstock Road."

That year, Miles would consent to leave London with her only for two days. Nathaniel and Eleanor did their best to make it a happy family Christmas, but it was a gloomy festival. Alice came home, filled with a glittering, unfocused brightness that seemed to strike at an awkward angle off all of them. Ruth could barely speak to her.

Ruth had only ever come to spend Christmas holidays with her husband's parents out of a belief in family solidarity. She always disapproved of Nathaniel's secular enjoyment of a Christian festival, and this year with the specter of Alice's fascism gliding between them all, she had tried to refuse Eleanor's invitation.

Eleanor had begged her. "The children love it so. It isn't Christmas without children, Ruthie."

In the end, they came. Luke and Rachel were duly spoiled with stockings and too many presents beneath the tree and too much to eat. Overexcitement turned to bad temper and then tears, and Ruth darted her sharp, hard glance at Jake to say, *I told you so.*

Miles ate as much as he could of Eleanor's good food, and drank volumes of Nathaniel's College claret and nineteenth-century port. He was charming and amusing, as he always could be when it suited him.

Clio sat coughing and snuffling on a sagging sofa in the room that overlooked the frozen garden. Staring up at *The Janus Face,* it came to her that she hated the portrait.

"Why do you keep that horrible thing hanging there?" she asked Nathaniel.

Nathaniel was surprised. "It's a fine painting. He's caught the look of both of you." The old tease of John Leominster was long forgotten. "Besides, I'm fond of the man. What's become of him?"

"Pilgrim?" Clio had recently met Jeannie in Charlotte Street. The artist's model looked fifteen years older than her real age. Jeannie's news was that Pilgrim and Isolde were in Berlin together.

"He likes it. Says it is divinely decadent. Don't know why he wants to be there, with Hitler and all the rest of them," Jeannie told Clio, and coughed derisively through the smoke of her cigarette. "How's that lovely brother of yours?"

"Pilgrim has probably seen him more recently than I have."

Julius had not come home for Christmas. He sent imaginative presents for all of them, and a long letter mostly concerned with his work.

"Pilgrim is in Berlin too, I believe," Clio answered her father.

Nathaniel's face turned somber. "I wish Julius would come back. It is time he came home."

Clio tried to be light. "Perhaps there's a reason for him to stay. Perhaps there's a girl." Only it was more likely that Julius stayed in Berlin because it was easier not to see the only girl he wanted, than to see her and be unable to have her.

"Perhaps," was all Nathaniel would admit, without a smile.

• • •

New Year came and went. Clio and Miles did not stay up to see in 1933. Miles was in the grip of one of his depressive fits, and Clio did not believe that the new year would bring anything different from the old one, so had no reason to celebrate it.

January was cold and fog-bound, and the blackened facades of the very buildings seemed to exude a miasma of soot and ice as Clio plodded past them on her path between *Fathom* and Gower Street. On the thirtieth of the month Adolf Hitler became Chancellor of Germany, and torchlight parades of brownshirts marched through Berlin to the cheers of the crowds.

Clio fell ill again. On the last day of January she got up and went to the office, to finish work on the proofs of the next issue. But by lunchtime she was coughing so much that Max Erdmann came out of his office.

"Go home, Clio, for God's sake. Go to bed, and don't let me see you again until you are fit company."

Max was being kind to her. It made Clio think that she must be really ill. She put the cover on her typewriter and took her coat off its peg. She walked back through the Bloomsbury squares, where the dripping branches of the plane trees made frayed black lacework against the yellowish sky.

She collected the morning's post from where it lay on the mat inside the front door and went up the stairs. Her feet felt heavy, and she tried to suppress the need to cough that sawed in her chest.

She put the key in the lock of their door, turned it, and pushed the door open. She saw at once that the gas fire was burning under its little domed hood, but the sitting room was empty. Miles had gone out and left it on. The thought of the shillings ticking away in the meter made her angry. She coughed, and threw the sheaf of letters down on the table.

Then she stopped. The flat was very still, filled with an odd silence that seemed to press outward on the walls and windows. The sounds she made were amplified beyond their proper value.

Clio walked through to the door of her bedroom and opened it.

Miles and another man were lying in the bed together.

There was a rush of sensations, seeming to make a great noise and confusion in her head. She saw that her husband was lying on his back, with one arm crooked behind his head. The sheet had fallen back to expose his naked chest and the marble-white roll of flesh below his ribcage. She saw that the other man was black-haired, and that he looked as rough and dirty and dispirited as the husbands of any of the women who came to Jake's clinic.

Was this what people would do for money? Clio thought.

She had no doubt that this was a commercial transaction.

Miles did not move. He only looked back at her, in defiance, or a kind of relief.

Clio knew that she would remember his exact expression. She would remember the other man's coarse features, the way his fingers on her bedsheet were rimmed with black. She would remember each detail, even through the tumultuous confusion of horror, and revulsion, and shame that threatened to overpower her now. She would not be able to forget.

The tableau was like some terrible caricature of her marriage, with this man lying prone in her place. Whenever she thought of her marriage she would see this, the two faces staring at her.

She took two steps backward, with her hand cupped over her mouth. Her fingers were shaking. With the other hand she groped for the door handle. She found it, smooth and hard, and jerked sharply at it. The door closed, and she was left staring at the wooden panels. There was dust in the moldings and in one spot a rash of tiny splinters, like the stubble of a man's beard.

The unopened post was still lying on the table where she had left it no more than a minute before, aeons ago. Outside in the street it already seemed to be growing dark. She could hear the traffic swishing past.

Clio left the flat and went back down the stairs and into the freezing afternoon.

With no idea of where she wanted to go or what she might do, she began to walk. She walked a long way, through the streams of shoppers in Oxford Street and then down the shining wet arteries of Hyde Park. It was intensely cold, and she walked quickly, trying to keep the blood moving inside her. The briskness of her movements contradicted her sense of having come up against a blank wall, at the end of a mean cul-de-sac that her life had become. The route did not offer any way forward or any escape to either side, and she did not see how she could go backward and undo what had already been done.

On the other side of the Park the trickle of homegoing office workers became a steadier flow. She had no idea where she had been, and could not have retraced her steps. She went into a workmen's café and sat at a zinc-topped table warming her fingers around a thick white mug of tea. She ordered pasty slices of white bread and butter and then sat staring out through the steamy glass without touching them. She paid for what she had ordered with fumbling fingers, staring at the coins as if they were some unfamiliar currency, and then left the shelter of the café to walk on again.

She had not intended it, and had given no thought to the direction her feet took her, but in the early darkness she found herself standing at the end of Vincent Street. She looked at the lights of Grace's house, and then saw that there was a taxicab waiting outside. The motor was running and the cabbie had wound down his window. Clio could see the plump cloud of his breath.

The front door opened, and Grace bobbed down the steps. She was wearing her furs and carried a leather portfolio under her arm.

Clio took a few steps, uncertain whether to turn forward or back, and then she began to run. Her feet were pinched and blistered in her office shoes and her legs and her chest ached.

She called out, "Grace! Grace, wait for me. . . ."

It reminded her of when they were children, running over the sand after the boys, each of them determined not to be left behind, not to come panting and last to the latest discovery.

Grace heard the uneven clatter of Clio's heels. She turned and saw her running, then put out her arm to catch her. They swayed together for an instant, as if they both might fall. Then Grace steadied them. There was a streetlamp in its bluish nimbus over their heads, and by the light of it Grace looked into her cousin's face.

"Come with me," Grace ordered her.

The cab rumbled along the Embankment. Inside it Clio felt placid in her exhaustion, with the lights outside swimming in the river mist and the driver's broad back insulated beyond the thick panel of glass. She was conscious of Grace's profile rising out of the silver-tipped swath of fur. In the regular slices of light, before the darkness claimed her in its turn, she could see the sheen on her silk-covered calves and the neat Louis heels of her shoes. Her kid-gloved hands were folded on the leather portfolio.

There did not seem to be any need to recite what had happened.

Are you really going to marry that little queer?

Clio could hear the words as if Grace had only just uttered them.

They were almost at the House of Commons before Grace broke the silence. Her kid forefinger tapped the leather in her lap. "I'm speaking in the House tonight. The debate is on women in prison, you know. Will you sit in the gallery to hear me?"

"Yes." Clio's voice cracked. She said more loudly, "Yes. I would like to hear you."

She found herself in the Visitors' Gallery. It was almost deserted. She leaned over the balcony and looked down into the Chamber of the House, thinking how small it was. There were men's bald heads and red faces, and so few women amongst the men. Grace came in, having removed her furs and her hat. She looked up at Clio as she took her seat.

Clio listened to the debate, and at the same time her mind slipped and looped through the nets of memory. Distant events, childhood times, all rose up and haphazardly jumbled with the sharp details of today, and the dreary planes of the last months. She felt rudderless, able to swing with the currents, and her random meditations threw up at one minute an image of children's initials carved in a desktop, at the next the black fingernails of the male prostitute lying in her bed.

The debate went on. There was so much rhetoric, Clio thought. So many flying words and unpinned ideas that would all drift together in the end, into random heaps, like dead leaves to be stirred up by the wind. She felt cold, and she wrapped her arms around herself and tried to concentrate on the speeches. She knew that she was feverish and that she should go home to bed, only she had already tried to do that, and now she could never get into that bed again.

Grace was on her feet. She had taken notes out of her folder, but she did not look at them. She spoke in her natural voice, calm and fluent. She began to describe the plight of women prisoners, their enforced separation from their babies and small children, mistreatment by prison warders and brutal conditions.

Poor women, Clio thought. She gazed down on the rows of men, but she began to see the faces of the women who had swirled past her in the streets that afternoon. With her feverish sharpness of recall, she could see individual sets of features, young and old, preoccupied or vacant, hopeful or desperate or dull. Amongst them she began to see herself, as a child and then a young woman, and Eleanor was with her, and there were other women she knew around them, from each of the different strata of her life.

Pity for all of them warmed inside her. She was sorry for Eleanor and Blanche, left behind by the unrolling of time, and for Ruth who could not make Jake happy, and for Alice and Cressida, and desperately merry Phoebe and poor, sodden Jeannie, and

Isolde who wasted her brightness on Pilgrim; and she was sorry for herself.

Down on the floor of the House, Grace began to wind up her speech. She quoted statistics on repeated offenders and the effect on them of a more liberal prison regime. Her arguments for penal reform for women were cogent, persuasive.

Clio did not feel sorry for Grace. Somehow, as always, Grace seemed to stand apart from her, and to be ungoverned by the common rules. Grace was so strong, and Clio knew that she needed that strength now. She had come for it, seemingly unwittingly, walking blindly through the streets on the darkest day she had ever known.

Grace's speech was well received. A confused rumble of "Hear! Hear!" rose up to the Gallery as she sat down.

The debate wandered on. So many words, Clio thought again. The confusion of memories claimed her.

When she looked down to Grace's seat once more, she saw that it was vacant, and a moment later Grace appeared beside her. "Come home with me now," she commanded.

They took a cab, driven by a different man in a frieze coat, back through the foggy streets. The house in Vincent Street was quiet and warm. Nanny and Mabel the cook must already have retired to bed, because when Grace led Clio downstairs, the kitchen was empty. Grace made Clio sit in the chair beside the stove while she heated milk and found a tin of cocoa, and it came to Clio that she had not seen her perform any domestic task since the days of carrying trays up to Peter Dennis.

How long ago.

Grace looked at her and read her mind. She laughed.

"What a great fuss, wasn't it? Poor Captain Dennis." She gave Clio the hot drink, then hunted in the dresser cupboard. She found a bottle of brandy and poured some into two glasses.

She settled herself at the table next to Clio. "You had better tell me," Grace said.

She listened, saying nothing. And then at the end she took Clio's hands between her own. She rubbed them, looking down at the blue veins and sinews under the thin skin.

"I'm sorry. I'm so sorry, Clio. What are you going to do?"

"I can't go back."

"Stay here with me."

"Not just tonight, I don't mean that. I can't ever go back. I feel as if everything ended today. Have you ever had that feeling?"

"When Anthony died."

Clio bent her head. Their clasped hands lay on her knees. "I'm sorry," she whispered in her turn.

"Don't be. I can tell you this, everything hasn't ended. That's the bloody point. It goes on, and you have to find a way to manage it. It's the going *on*, day after day, when it should all have ended, when the lining of your skull and the soles of your feet and your bruised skin all tell you it should have finished for you, that is what is really difficult. But you have to do something just because you are alive."

"Is that how you felt?"

"More or less."

"But you went off and got yourself elected to Parliament."

"Yes, I did."

Clio looked at her. There was Grace's strength, defined and incomprehensible. She had allowed Clio a brief insight into her grief, and she had felt it under her own skin and in her skull so that Grace had almost become one of the company of women. But then she had shifted her position and the chink had closed, and Grace was apart again. *I wish we were closer,* Clio thought. *I wish we could ever have been close to each other.*

"What will you do?" Grace asked.

I can't become an MP. I can't go back to Fathom, *or my own home, or to Oxford. . . .*

Hectically, feeling Grace's eyes on her, she began to improvise. "I'm going to go away. Right away, from London and everywhere else I know. There are all these paths I've been treading, around and around, for so long. I'm going to walk clear away from them."

"And so where will you go?"

Don't press me. I don't know. I don't know anything. "Abroad, probably. I speak French and German. I've never been anywhere, much. I don't have any money, now I come to think of it, so it will have to be done on a shoestring, not the Grand Tour or anything like that. . . ." An immensity of problems seemed to crowd in on her. Where to go, how to convey herself through the maze of ticket halls and cheap hotels and restaurants? She felt her weakness like an affliction.

Grace said coolly, "You own your flat, don't you?"

"Yes."

"Sell it. You don't want to leave it for him to live in, do you? You can borrow some money against it in the meantime."

"I could do that." A step, appearing as if the tide ebbed against a flight of steps in a sea-wall to reveal first the shiny ledge, suggesting the others still submerged.

"I have an idea," Grace said.

"What is it?"

"I'm going to Germany soon, on a political visit, to Munich and Berlin. I want to see this *Volkwerdung* with my own eyes."

"Volkwerdung," Clio repeated, giving it the correct pronunciation. "Awakening of the people."

Grace laughed merrily. "Come with me. Come and be my interpreter. Just for two weeks, it can be a holiday. We can see Julius in Berlin."

Miraculously, another step appeared from the sea. It was slippery and shrouded in weed, but it was still a step.

"I despise fascism," Clio said stiffly, "and all that Hitler stands for."

"How can you despise what you have never seen?"

"But I would so much like to see Julius." It came to her that she wanted her twin more than anything or anyone in the world.

"Come, then. It's quite simple."

"Shall I?"

Grace unclasped their hands and held out her right, palm sideways. "Shake on it?"

The old formula of schoolroom pacts, often broken.

"All right then, I will."

They shook hands, solemnly.

Fourteen

CLIO'S FIRST IMPRESSION OF BERLIN from the window of her sleeping car in the dim early morning was of a city that turned within itself, denying the daylight. As the train crept into the heart of it, she glimpsed the ends of brown streets and the corners of squares lying in shadow under brick and iron arches and hidden between the angles of tall brown buildings.

The little light that did penetrate seemed to have filtered first through peat, or tobacco, or coffee, and so become thickened and stained. It did no more than lick the upsides of the ponderous buildings here and there with washes of paler umber and khaki, intensifying the depths of shadows alongside. Sometimes there were stretches of water visible through the gloom, a canal like a ribbon made of the dun sky and then a wider expanse, a lake the color of chocolate, fringed with the skeletons of trees.

Then the train rattled over a viaduct and a level crossing, and she found herself looking up the great open curve of a broad, deserted street, with tramrails fading away in a silvered arc and gas lights still burning as bronze haloes in the ochre fog of the air.

The sleeping car was unheated. As she stood with her face pressed close to the glass, her breath made another fine layer of mist, and she rubbed it away with her gloved fingers. The train had slowed almost to walking pace. She saw the ends of apartment blocks with uncurtained windows and yellow lights showing in the murk, a baker's shop with the mud-brown shutters coming down ready for the day, and an old man with a metal drum on wheels into which he swept the night's debris from the gutter.

Grace came back from the tiny washroom at the end of the car. She was fully dressed, down to her furs and ankle boots.

"Aren't you cold?" she asked Clio rhetorically. Clio had been awake most of the night, shivering under a layer of clothes, listening to Grace's even breathing. She had been cold for so long that it seemed hardly worth remarking on it.

"And don't you mind everyone peering in at you?"

There were crowds of people waiting at the crossings now, patient-looking people in ugly dark clothes, and more people in the brown streets beyond. Grace reached out and twitched down the green waxed blind to cover the window. Clio put on her coat and sat on the lower berth, watching as Grace nested silver brushes and crystal bottles in her dressing case and snapped the locks. Her initials GEACB were embossed on the lid.

"We'll be in in a minute," Grace said, looking at her wristwatch. And as she spoke the train slowed again, and steam hissed through the cracks in the wood paneling to fill the compartment with the smell of damp bedclothes.

Anxious to see, Clio flicked the blind. She blinked at the smoky yellow light outside. The train slid into the Bahnhof Zoo and stopped under a great glass canopy. She could see over the heads of hurrying crowds to little green-painted iron kiosks stocked with newspapers, flowers, and glinting bottles. There were posters everywhere, pasted on top of one another, torn and peeling beneath and patched with later additions, headed in thick black Gothic script that competed for her attention. She read slowly, piecing the demands together: "Action for a Pure Germany," "Victory to the National Socialists," *"Gleichschaltung"*—what was that, Integration? The words were vaguely puzzling, as if they were not quite German but some dialect that she had never learned in her Oxford classroom.

"Plenty of porters, at least," Grace said.

They were lined up along the platform in high-crowned peaked caps, waiting with their trolleys. Grace rapped on the window and pointed to one man. A moment later he was at the compartment door, scooping their bags into his thick arms.

Clio stepped down onto the platform. City commuters jostled past her, men in homburgs and women in headscarves, berets, ratty furs, all indistinguishably muffled against the February cold. The air smelled of smoke, and frying onions, and sweat.

The porter rattled ahead of them, shoving a passage with his trolley. At the other end of the platform Clio noticed two loitering men in brown uniforms with thick leather belts. They wore red, white, and black swastika armbands. Hitler's SA.

A moment later Clio and Grace were in a taxi. "Adlon Hotel," Grace ordered briskly.

Clio was thinking, *Grace doesn't speak a word of German, but she has still taken charge. She knows how to command things, while I just follow on behind.*

She leaned back in the seamed leather seat while the old Opel bumped over the tramlines. There were gaunt trees overhead and a street paved in square setts, black and shiny in the wet morning. She saw great buildings with dark domes and wreaths of classical detailing and black statues, and all the buildings and spires and heavy baroque ornamentation and even the streets themselves seemed to be made from the same cocoa-colored stone, everywhere darkened with a layer of soot.

Grace asked, "Are you tired?"

Clio turned to her. Grace's eyes were bright, and she was sitting forward, her arm looped through the leather strap beside the seat to steady herself against the jolting. *She is excited,* Clio thought. *All ready for whatever's coming.*

"No, I'm not tired," Clio answered. She remembered the posters with their black, staring lettering and the SA men at the station. There was another group of them here, in a little cobbled *Platz.* They were laughing, and their breath vaporized in a cloud about their capped heads.

"What is it exactly that you are going to do here, Grace?"

Grace held on to the leather strap and stared ahead, through the driver's window. "Oh, there's plenty to do," she said. "People to see."

They came along a broad avenue that ran between a dense mass of trees. Ahead of them, Clio recognized the silhouetted arches of the Brandenburger Tor, the Brandenburg Gate. The taxi rolled beneath it, dwarfed by the immense pillars, and came to Pariser Platz beyond, and the Adlon Hotel.

The Adlon was a high building with tall narrow windows in a wide, dignified street of similarly grandiose edifices. Uniformed flunkeys waited at the doors, and Clio and Grace were swept under a canopy on a tide of bowing and saluting into a marble foyer. They stood under the diamond waterfall of a vast chandelier to sign the hotel register. There was no whiff of onions or bodies here, only French perfume and hothouse flowers.

Clio was pleased to see her bedroom. There was a high white bed with a hard bolster, a feather bag in a white cover instead of blankets and sheets, and a large quantity of ornate, shiny, and bulbous mahogany furniture. It reminded her faintly of one of the guest bedrooms of Leominster House in Belgrave Square, the difference being that this room led into its own bathroom. Here she found a vast iron bath, a basin as big as a washtub, and a lavatory with a dripping cistern so high up that she had to tilt her head to look at it.

Clio splashed water on her face and retraced her steps across the expanse of black and white tiles to the bedroom. She was hanging up her clothes in the cavernous wardrobe when she heard someone knock at the door.

She called, "Come in," without looking around, assuming that it must be Grace.

A man's voice said, "Well, I call this the lap of luxury."

"*Julius.*"

Clio ran to him. She was filled with happiness at the sight of him, but there was a darker edge of sadness that cut into her as she hid her face against his shoulder. It was a long time since she had seen her twin, and his thinness made him seem taller than she remembered. There was a new streak of gray in the dark hair over his temple. The last time she had seen him, she had still been Miles's wife, with her defined place, and everything had changed since then. There was a darker veil over her world, like the dun-colored shadow that muffled the city outside the windows of the Adlon Hotel. She clung to Julius, foolishly smiling, aware of the vacuum that disappointment had made inside her.

"I meant to come to the station," he said.

"We didn't expect you. I wasn't expecting you here, not yet. Oh, Julius. I'm so happy to see you. You've no idea how happy. I've missed you so much in London. In London . . ."

She had been meaning to say something light, something to convey the sense of changing times, like, *The old crew has all sailed away, forsaken the Fitzroy and gone forever,* but the words failed her. She knew that the pubs and the restaurants would still be crowded and the gossip would buzz in Charlotte Street and Blooms-bury, but it was not for her. That was Miles's territory, and she was still running from it. She could feel the empty spaces at her back.

There was a silence before she whispered, "There's nothing in London. I couldn't stay there any longer."

Julius took her face between his hands. He looked at her, and then he kissed her cheeks.

"It's all right. I'm here. You'll be all right." With the same words he had comforted her when they were both little children, when some imaginary terror had threatened her and he had squared up in her defense. They stood still, both of them remembering the whispering huge grassy hollows of the garden in the Woodstock Road, and the immeasurable uncharted territory of Stretton's park.

They glanced around them, comparing that recollection with this reality of fanciful yellowing plasterwork, these stuffy drapes framing the window, and the bulging knobs and rigid carvings protruding from every piece of furniture. The distance between the two seemed so great, and the collapse of time that had protected them from that to this so inexplicable, that they could only laugh again. Laughter took possession of them, and they shook with it, rocking in each other's arms like the children they had recalled.

"And so welcome to Berlin," Julius gasped. He took a handkerchief out of his pocket and dried her eyes. Clio did not know for sure whether she was shedding tears of mirth or otherwise.

"I'm glad to be here," she told him, truthfully.

He nodded, smiling at her, the old Julius. Then he let go of her and walked slowly across to the window. He stood looking down into Pariser Platz.

"There is a lot to talk about," he said.

"Shall we go and have a drink somewhere?" Clio asked.

She had written to Julius about Miles, but she had only told him the bare details. She had dreaded the recital of the rest. Yet now that she was here, and after their laughter, she felt her repugnance begin to fade. Her marriage was in the past, it belonged in a place she no longer occupied. There were other things: her brother, the city she had glimpsed from the train window. She felt her curiosity begin to revive, the beginnings of appetite when she had thought that she would never feel hungry for experience again.

Julius was right. There was a lot to talk about. She understood that he meant Germany and what was happening here and now. The weight of her own concerns lifted from her shoulders.

"A drink, at this time of the morning?" He smiled at her.

"I'm thoroughly disoriented. Breakfast, then. I haven't had any yet."

"Not in this place."

"Why not?"

"I'll tell you, you'll understand why, but not now. There's a little café I go to sometimes, a couple of streets from here."

"Let's go there, then."

Clio put on her coat, but Julius hesitated. They hadn't mentioned Grace, and the silent omission was like a false note ringing between them.

He was afraid to betray his eagerness. The thought that she was here, somewhere close at hand, made him shiver as if he had a fever. The sight of Clio after so many months' separation sharpened all his senses for Grace. Clio did not look as much like her as she once had done, but the resemblance was still striking enough. It was not quite a reflection but an echo, and it intensified his longing for the reality.

"Julius?" Clio said softly.

But she was standing at the door, and she heard the whisper of footsteps on the other side before the knock came. There was nothing to do but open it. Grace stood there with her hand still raised. She was smiling, her head on one side, with color in her cheeks and the light of anticipation in her eyes.

"Julius, how wonderful."

He stepped forward to her, his hands on her arms, kissed her warm cheek.

Clio watched. *I have lost him,* she thought. The words sprang into her head from nowhere.

She was witnessing the affectionate greeting of cousins, there was nothing more to see in the kiss than that. They had already separated, smiling, and Grace was fingering the rows of pearls around her smooth throat as she looked around the hotel room. But Clio's eyes were fixed on Julius. His longing seemed so intense that there was something craven in it. It was as if he wanted to kneel in front of Grace and lift her foot in its crocodile-skin shoe and press his mouth against the silky instep.

"We were just going out, for some breakfast," Clio said in a flat voice.

"What a marvelous idea. I'm starving hungry. But why can't we just go downstairs?"

"Julius says not."

We *have already conferred, before you came, so there.*

Clio could hear the retort in her own voice from years ago, with all the hard-won maturity instantly thinned out of it. It was like when they were children . . . *I was here first, he's* my *brother.* The glint of her optimism faded and left her dull again. The very pettiness of her response seemed dim compared with the incandescence of Julius's devotion.

Grace was apparently deaf and blind. "Why not, Julius?" she demanded cheerfully. "This is the Adlon, isn't it? I thought it was the best place in Berlin."

"So it is. And frequented by the highest class of hoodlum. SA,

SS, informers, top Nazis of all kinds. The Führer himself is seen here when he is in Berlin."

Grace picked delicately at her ropes of pearls. "Hoodlums? But you say the Führer . . ."

"Exactly so. I would prefer not to drink my coffee in their midst."

She gave the smallest shrug. "We shall have to submit to your superior local knowledge, Clio, shan't we? But I should have thought that whatever is good enough for the Chancellor of Germany ought to be good enough for us."

Julius paused for a moment. Then he repeated very softly, "There is a lot to talk about."

Clio did not think that Grace heard him. She gave no sign of having done so.

They descended to the ground floor in the ornate gold lift cage and crossed the marble foyer. A group of men in uniforms emblazoned with red and black swastika badges were being ushered in, to be greeted by more uniforms, and heels clicking on the shiny floor. They raised their arms in the Nazi salute.

Heil Hitler.

Heil Hitler.

Grace and Julius and Clio were caught up as they tried to pass by. The officers glanced at them, then stared at Grace. Her red lips and her furs and her cool expression were immediately striking.

Julius slipped aside. He seemed to melt away in the direction of the great doors that led out to the street. Clio followed him, but no one was looking at her.

The officers clicked their heels and bowed to Grace. "Heil Hitler."

She lifted her arm and held it, palm downward and fingertips outstretched. "Heil Hitler," she responded courteously.

Clio and Julius were waiting for her in the street. Julius said nothing, but Grace squared herself in front of him.

"You don't think I should have done that, do you?"

"No. I don't think you should give the Nazi salute."

"Listen, Julius. I am an elected member of the British Government. This is not an official visit, but I still have a specific part to play. I'm here to observe, and to report where I can. I have to remember that I am a guest, and this is their country."

It was intensely cold. An icy wind blew the sodden remains of torn pamphlets and handbills around their ankles. Clio could see clearly in Julius's face the conflict between surprised distaste and the old, unquestioning devotion. She did not have any doubt which would win out.

Julius said fiercely, "Grace, you can't have any idea what fascism really means, or you wouldn't salute it. These people are brutal and corrupt. They stand for the very opposite of democracy and freedom. Their rule is fear."

Grace's eyes were bright, and her cheeks glowed in the cold air. "Perhaps their instruments are brutal, I don't know. It is an unfortunate truth that powerful movements attract violence, at the lowest level. I do know that great political advances are rarely achieved without some social upheaval, even suffering. I also believe that Herr Hitler might be capable of a political and economic progression that will affect us all, not just Germany. I have come to see for myself, at first hand. That's all."

Clio saw how the scent of debate fired Grace. She seemed to grow brighter and stronger with the reminder of it. Clio also knew her cousin's determination and tenacity. She would defend her standpoint to the last, even if the reasoning beneath it was crumbling away.

Julius hesitated. He knew Grace too. Then he rubbed his mouth slowly with the back of his hand. "It's too cold to stand here in the street," he said at length.

He took Grace's arm in his, and held out the other to Clio. They began to walk, their heads ducked against the wind.

Grace shrugged off Julius's rebuke, and she talked cheerfully about the news from London. They passed a dozen cafés, but Julius ignored them all. Clio tried to read the news placards and political posters as they passed them. There was one poster that faced her everywhere. It read *"Hitler—Arbeit und Brot."* Work and Bread. The syllables began to beat a refrain in her head. She counted the different uniforms that thronged the streets and attempted to look into the faces of the ordinary people. It struck her that no one would look straight at anyone else. The Berliners hurried past with their eyes turned away, a shabby and derelict-looking flood of humanity.

They came into a narrow street lined with tall thin houses. Three steps led down from each dingy front door straight onto the littered road. The Café Josef was at the far end. It was no more than a window obscured by a thick lacework curtain, let into a flat green-painted facade.

Grace looked curiously at it. "Do you live near here?" she asked Julius.

"Not far away." He pushed open the door for them, and an old-fashioned bell at the end of a spring pealed over their heads.

It was warm inside, steamy with warmth. The women saw a line of rickety tables set around with bentwood chairs, smoke-yellowed walls hung with photographs, a floor of bare wooden boards, and a cramped bar at the far end laden with unfamiliar bottles. A handful of customers sat at the tables. These Berliners did look. Every one of them turned to see who the newcomers were.

"Julius!" someone called in greeting. Stares gave way to smiles and nods, and then curious but not unfriendly glances at the two women. Clearly, if they were with Julius, then they were accepted. He led them to a table, and they sat down.

Clio looked around her. A sense of something familiar about the Café Josef tugged at her until she realized that it reminded her of the Eiffel Tower as it had been when she had first visited it, long ago, with Pilgrim and Grace at the time of *The Janus Face*. There was no decorative resemblance; the Eiffel was luxurious to the point of decadence compared with this bare room. The similarity was in the atmosphere. This was a place frequented by people with a common outlook. There would be no outsiders here. If inimical strangers did happen on the café by chance, they would not be given a warm enough welcome to make them eager to come back again.

A swarthy, grubby-looking man wrapped in a blue apron appeared from behind the bar. He slapped Julius on the back. "Good day, my friend," he said in heavily accented English.

"Hello, Josef."

Clio smiled involuntarily at the man. The café proprietor even looked like an unshaven, disheveled version of old Stulik.

"Josef, may I introduce my twin sister? Mrs. Lennox. And my cousin, Lady Grace Brock. Clio, Grace, this is my friend Josef Frankel."

Josef took their hands, in turn, and bowed low over them. "Madam, my lady, I am delighted to make your acquaintance."

There was a music-hall orotundity about his English, his whole demeanor, that appealed greatly to Clio. She liked Josef instinctively, and his café too. She looked at the pictures on the dingy walls. They appeared to be photographs of nightclub artistes. There were chanteuses in slippery satin gowns with smoke wreathing their hair, and odd-looking men in evening clothes with heavily painted eyes and lips.

"You are just to Berlin?" Josef asked.

"We arrived not much more than an hour ago," Grace told him.

"I wish you welcome." His eyes flicked to the door. "I wish you could make your visit in more happy times."

Clio was aware of the heads around them lifting again, and eyes turning to the street in case there might be anyone to overhear what was said within the café.

"My cousin is a Member of the British Parliament," Julius said dryly.

Josef widened his eyes and blew out the ends of his ragged moustache. "Then we are honored indeed. I hope you will look carefully to see how we must be living now, all of us here in Berlin, and tell your important friends what you have noticed when you are once more home again."

There was a little pause, and then Grace said, "That is what I hope to do, Herr Frankel."

"So. Tell me, what can I bring these distinguished guests of ours?"

Clio and Grace were hungry. The food, when it came, was piled high on thick white plates, and it was excellent. They ate their eggs and ham and heavy German sausage while Julius drank coffee and told them about the concerts he had been playing.

"There are problems, of course," he said. "But everyone has problems now."

"What kind of problems?" Grace asked. Her voice had taken on a sharp, interrogative note.

"Jewish ones," Julius said simply. The quiet that followed amplified the click of forks and chink of coffee spoons. Clio sat very still, knowing that Oswald Mosley was now a regular guest in Vincent Street, remembering how only yesterday she had seen Alice leaving the house with a pile of anti-Semitic fascist pamphlets to be handed out in the streets. Alice had taken to wearing a black shirt on her political expeditions.

Grace's doing, she thought.

"But you are not Jewish, are you?" Grace countered. "I thought it was necessary for a Jew to have a Jewish mother. And your mother is no more a Jewess than mine is."

"To be considered a Jew nowadays, in Germany, it is only necessary to have one Jewish grandparent. My score is two, I am proud to say. But I am a foreigner; I have a British passport. It is easier for me than it is for other people."

With an almost imperceptible tilt of his chin, Julius indicated the other people in the café. Clio looked at them again, and realized what she had blithely failed to notice before. She pushed her plate away from her. Her appetite had gone. There was a little cold finger of apprehension pressing at the base of her spine.

"What is this place?" she asked Julius. "Who comes here?"

"Jews." That was what Clio had belatedly seen. "Socialists. Even a few communists. Dissidents of various other kinds, who do not wish to follow the line marked out for them by the Führer or his brownshirts. We are comfortable here, together, thanks to Josef."

Clio said, "It reminded me of the Eiffel when we first came in."

Julius nodded. In a voice so low that they had to lean closer across the table to catch his words, he said, "The sense of *in here* against out there. But it isn't the same. In the Eiffel we felt our superiority, didn't we? The rest, the outsiders, were philistines, the unknowing. We could smile gently in our superiority as artists and intellectuals. But here we are beleaguered. This place is a refuge first, and a meeting place for the like-minded only a long way second. Don't you feel that?"

Clio looked around at the men, sitting singly at their tables or in quiet groups of two or three. They held their newspapers folded so that the mastheads were not visible, and they watched the street door.

"Yes," Clio said. The Café Josef felt like home, but it also made a knot of apprehension tighten in her stomach.

Grace extracted a cigarette and her gold lighter from her handbag. Julius took the lighter from her hand and clicked it so that the flame spurted. Their fingers touched. Grace bent her head, and when she looked up again at Julius, twin yellow plumes of light were reflected in her pupils.

"Why are you beleaguered?" she asked.

"Oh, come. Even straight from England you must know what it means to be a Jew or a dissident in Germany today. You walked here through the streets with me not an hour ago."

There was the flash of animation again at the prospect of a debate. Grace's head came up as she answered the challenge.

"I saw people on their way to work. I know that in 1930 a third of the labor force of this country was on the scrap heap, and the wages of the rest had dropped by thirty-three percent. Since Hitler has been in power the Nazis have resuscitated industry and introduced a public works program that will halve unemployment figures. If we could do that at home, it would be something to be proud of. The Germans can be proud. Perhaps some unpalatable measures are necessary in the process of achieving an economic miracle."

"You sound like a speech in the House of Commons, Grace. Are random violence and persecution of the innocent and helpless as a matter of routine merely *unpalatable*?"

"Perhaps some of Hitler's agents employ the wrong tactics. Perhaps there are isolated incidents. I am sure the leadership, Hitler himself, knows nothing about them."

"You are sure, are you?"

"Julius, you are a musician. A fine violinist. I am a politician."

Can't you see? Clio was thinking. *You must see now what she's like.* But all she could see in Julius's face was concern, and the old, ravenous glitter of his love.

"Listen," he said. "I will ask Heinrich there to tell you a story."

He lifted his hand, and a man who had been sitting at one of the other tables stood up and came across to them. Julius introduced him, but only by his first name. Heinrich had a thin, lined face, and his clothes and his manner were as colorless as his unmemorable features. Clio understood that his anonymity was deliberate.

"My sister and my cousin," Julius assured him. "They are friends. Will you tell them what happened to Herr Keller?"

Heinrich spread his hands on the table, palms down. Josef brought him a blue-gray pottery mug of beer, but he left it untouched at his elbow.

"I worked for Herr Keller," Heinrich said. "He was a Jew. He was an excellent lawyer and a good employer. I was his . . . what would you call it?" he appealed to Julius.

"His clerk."

"Exactly so. It happened that Herr Keller was often called upon to defend political prisoners."

"Enemies of the Reich, you understand," Julius said softly.

"And then one morning, no more than a month ago, Herr Keller did not come to our office at the usual time. I waited for him. He was a punctual man, and I had never known him to be late before."

The bell over the door jangled on the end of its metal strip. Clio and Grace looked up with the others, and they saw a man and a woman come in. The man was tall, as tall as Julius, and he stooped a little as if he were used to living under low ceilings. He wore a sheepskin-lined coat, like a farmer's, and a knitted cap that he pulled off to uncover a head of thick fair hair. The girl with him was hatless. She was also blond, and her hair was plaited and the plaits were wound around her head like a crown.

The newcomers were obviously familiars. They came straight to Julius's table, drawing up chairs to join the circle. The table was not large, and now the six of them found their shoulders rubbing together, making conspirators of them. Josef leaned over with more tankards of beer, and coffee for the girl with the crown of hair.

"Heinrich was just telling us a story," Julius said. "About Herr Keller and the Brothers Sass."

"Go on, Heinrich," the blond man said. He looked coolly at Clio and Grace. "After the story we can introduce ourselves." His English was almost accentless.

"I waited for Herr Keller all that morning, but he did not come. In the end I left the office and went to his flat, in the Wedding district. From the window of every apartment in his building, there was hanging a swastika flag."

Clio had seen the flags from the train, through the brown mist, bloodred squares enclosing white circles with the black swastika. There had been dozens of others in the streets between Pariser Platz and the Café Josef. They lent the city an air of ominous gaiety, as if it were decked out for a fete planned on some inappropriate date.

"Except that there was no flag in Herr Keller's window. I knocked on his door, hammered on it, but no one came. Herr Keller was a bachelor who lived alone. If he was not there to answer the door, no one could let me in. In the end I went down and found the caretaker of the building, an old woman, who said she had seen nothing. But she let me into the apartment with her key. It was empty, and quite as usual. A chair had been overturned, that was all."

They sat in silence around the table. Heinrich took a drink of his beer and wiped the froth from his lips. Grace clicked her lighter, just once, but the shade of her impatience was unmistakable.

"I telephoned Herr Keller's relatives, but none of them knew where he had gone. The police denied any knowledge of his whereabouts. A whole week passed.

"And then his sister came to see me. A political detainee, a friend of Herr Keller's, had called on her. Her brother had been seen, he could not reveal by whom, lying in the cellar of an SA barracks near Alexanderplatz. He had been too badly injured to move, even to recognize anyone.

"Then, a day later, we were notified that Herr Keller had been brought to police headquarters. But none of his friends were to be allowed to see him. He was being kept under arrest for his own protection, that is what they called it, in the hospital of the prison.

"But almost at once, we heard another rumor. A gang of SA men had gone to the police hospital and insisted that Herr Keller be returned to them for questioning. The police informed his sister that he had been handed over to the Nazis, who wished to investigate further his serious crimes against the Reich.

"What could we do? I had to tell his sister that I was afraid there was an end to it. I did not think we would see him again.

"But then, after two more days, Herr Keller was found. He was lying in an alleyway behind a cinema, no more than a few hundred meters from his own home. A shopkeeper, a man who owned a little dairy, had found him when he went to open up in the early morning. He told Herr Keller's sister there was so much blood that he thought for a moment a drum of oil had been spilt by someone trying to set light to a bundle of rags in the gutter.

"He was still alive. The shopkeeper carried him in, and Fräulein Keller and I went to him. We took one of our own doctors"—here Heinrich glanced at the blond man—"and between the three of us we managed to get him back to his own apartment. His tongue had been cut out and his ears had been sliced away. One of his eyes was gouged from the socket, and his sex organs had been severely mutilated. The doctor did what he could, which was almost nothing. Herr Keller died before the morning was over."

Grace's gold lighter was clenched in her fist now. Julius moved an inch forward, leaning toward her as if he wished he could have protected her from the necessity of hearing Heinrich's story. Clio moved her lips. Her mouth and throat were dry, painfully so.

"Who are the Brothers Sass?" she whispered.

The new man surprised her with a smile. It acknowledged humor, even absurdity, without diminishing the horror and the pity of what Heinrich had described.

"SA and SS," he said. "We call them the Brothers. For their good fellowship, and compassion to all men."

Julius said to Grace, "These things happen every day. Innocent ordinary men simply vanish, and never come home again. Or there are attacks in the streets, when half a dozen brownshirts with truncheons turn on a single man. And even when there is no violence, there is the steady persecution of socialists, communists, and non-Aryans. Jewish shopkeepers are made to display signs in their windows, telling their old customers that Germans may only buy from other Germans. There are demands to stop Jewish pupils from attending schools and universities, and Jewish doctors and lawyers are boycotted. How can these people live, if they can't work?"

The girl with the crown of hair said, "It extends even to the smallest things. I have taken my washing, for two years, ever since I came to Berlin, to the same laundress. Just this morning she refused to take it, saying that she is too busy now. I know that it is because someone has told her that I am Jewish, and probably a communist also. Now I must look around and try to find a Jewish laundry."

Clio gazed at her. With her pale hair and light-colored eyes, the girl looked a perfect Nordic type, the Aryan ideal. Her husband, or lover, whatever he was, looked just the same. They might have appeared on a poster advocating racial purity.

"We are all Jews," the man said, smiling at Clio. "We can't help our coloring. And we are also Germans. I come from Thuringia, my father kept a small farm-machinery business."

He held out his hand to her, across the small table with its clutter of beer steins and cups and cutlery.

"My name is Rafael Wolf."

"I am Clio . . . Hirsh." Her real name here, Nathaniel's name and Grandfather Levi's before that. Levi and Dora had come to England two generations ago, but they would have left behind them a village not very different from Rafael Wolf's. In Berlin, in the Café Josef, there was no need for her to admit to Miles Lennox. The realization cheered her.

Rafael laughed. "Of course. Julius's twin sister. That's not difficult to see."

"And I am Grete."

The girl held out her hand too, and Clio and Grace took it in turn. Watching Grete's face Clio thought how lovely she was, with her broad, smooth forehead and clear eyes. Clio tried to make sense of the impressions of the morning: the story of Herr Keller, the sight of the flags hanging in the streets and the men in uniform and the people with their averted eyes, and this beautiful girl's claim that a laundress had refused her custom because of her race. Berlin seemed a terrible and threatening place, but it drew her too—because of the Café Josef, and Julius and these people.

She listened to Rafael talking to Grace. She wanted to turn her head to look at him, but she did not. She looked at Grete instead, and at Julius lounging over another cup of Josef's coffee.

Grace did look as well as listen. She had put her gold lighter away, and her hands were clasped on the table in front of her. She had seen Rafael Wolf glance at the rings she wore, and then the corners of his mouth had tucked in. There was a judgmental quality about him that she did not like very much.

Heinrich's story had shocked Grace. She had no doubt that the substance of it was true, and everything else she had heard probably also had at least a basis of truth in it. The brutality disgusted her, even if it was exaggerated in the telling. But as she had rationalized to Julius, was it not also true that small pockets of shameful behavior at the end of the chain of command were an inevitable part of otherwise admirable movements?

Grace knew well enough that even in London there was viciousness between her friend Tom Mosley's Blackshirts and the young Bolshevik boys who followed the tail of the marches, and between the hecklers at his meetings and his official marshals. When strong opinions and strong emotions were unleashed, it was not always easy to control the people; Tom had told her that much, with deep concern. It must be the same here in Berlin; that much she could establish for herself by watching and listening.

In her heart, for all her provocative defense of them, Grace was neither in favor of nor opposed to the Nazis. She was intrigued by what was happening in Berlin, and all the rest of Germany, and she was impressed by the power that Hitler had accumulated. The Café Josef, and Julius's friends and their testimonies, would be weighed against the rest of her observations in good time.

"Is this happening to the Jews and political dissidents only here in Berlin?" Grace asked Rafael.

"Not just here, no. In Munich, under the eyes of the Führer, and everywhere else too. Jewish families are emigrating from all over Germany, especially from the Rhineland and Saxony. Some of them have come to Berlin because they believe that they are safer and less conspicuous as strangers in a big city than in the villages where they have lived all their lives."

"They have that option, then," Grace said quietly.

Rafael was calm, seemingly imperturbable. "Yes, no one has yet tried to deny them the right to leave. But they are also Germans, you see. They consider themselves to be Germans of the Jewish faith. Why should they leave their homes and their livelihoods for Hitler and his bully-boys like Streicher?"

Grace did not try to frame the answer that came immediately to her, Because Hitler is creating a new Germany, for the German people, and there is no room in it for profiteering, for capitalist corruption, for the perversion of the national resources by a small minority.

The small minority of bad Jews, of course. She made the old distinction still.

With Rafael Wolf's eyes resting meditatively on her, she only said, "I don't know why."

"Perhaps you will have found out some more before you go back to London and the House of Commons?"

Julius came to her defense. "Rafael? Grace has only been in Berlin for a few hours. She has made the effort to come here, at least, instead of giving vent to ignorant and noisy speeches to the House like a dozen other MPs."

Rafael's expression changed at once. "Yes, of course. Forgive me, Grace. These are not comfortable times for any of us, but there is no excuse for bad manners."

"I forgive you." Grace suddenly smiled back at him. It seemed to Clio that Rafael Wolf's charm worked instantly on Grace to make her as coquettish as a debutante in a ballroom. She kept her own eyes turned downward, but still she saw his long hands and wrists protruding from the shaggy cuffs of his farmer's coat.

The conspirators' group around the table was breaking up. Heinrich nodded abruptly to Clio and Grace and went back to his own table. Grete took her woollen mittens from her pocket and thrust her hands into them.

"I must go and search for a Jewish laundry."

She was smiling, as if at some outlandish joke. Rafael stood up to accompany her. He said good-bye gravely to Julius and the two women.

"I'm sure we shall meet again." He bowed. Clio watched the two of them until the door closed behind them with a mournful *ting* of the bell.

"Back to the Adlon," Grace announced. "I feel that Herr Wolf has given me a responsibility to discharge."

"I'll walk with you," Julius said.

Josef came out from behind his bar to say good-bye. "We are all friends, here," he reminded them. "And I have no need of any more customers. Please don't trouble to recommend me to anyone, will you?"

It was an assurance of hospitality and a warning together. The contradiction seemed to be the very essence of Berlin.

They left the cinnamon-scented steamy warmth of the café and began the walk back to Pariser Platz. Brown rain had started to fall in dismal spurts. The wind drove icy darts of it into their faces.

Grace walked quickly, looking straight ahead of her, with her hands folded into the sleeves of her fur. Clio matched her steps to Julius's.

"Are they good friends of yours, Rafael and Grete?"

"Yes, I think they are."

"What do they do in Berlin?"

"Grete gives music lessons. Piano. I met her because we teach the children of the same family, sons of an industrialist who live in a hideous house out at Grünewald. Rafael is, or was, a lawyer rather like Herr Keller."

Clio could suddenly hear her own footsteps clipping on the cobbles. The note of fear seemed as loud and clear within her. It was strange to feel such terror for the safety of someone she had only just met.

"I think he is also involved in some political propaganda work. We don't ask each other questions of that sort."

She said quickly, for the sake of saying something, "I didn't know you gave lessons."

"We do what we have to, nowadays. I don't mind it. Some pupils are interesting and talented. They are not all like the Bayer boys out at Grünewald." Julius laughed. He seemed happy in this cold, monumental, dislocated city. Clio wondered if it was because Grace was here at last.

"They make a wonderfully striking couple," Clio said in a low voice, as if it were a valediction.

Julius stopped walking, turned to stare at her, and then took her arm. He swung it with his and began to laugh again, tipping his head back with pure pleasure. The sound of it made Clio think that Nathaniel was here with them.

Grace glanced back with a touch of irritation, then resumed her brisk march.

"Oh, Clio, my Clio. I never believed in love at first sight until this morning."

"I don't know what you mean," Clio said stiffly.

"Yes, you do. Take off that stricken face. Rafael and Grete aren't a couple, you idiot, any more than you and I are."

Even in the hopeful confusion that began to hammer inside her, she made the silent response, *Any more than you and Grace are*.

"They are brother and sister, children of a farm-machinery dealer in Thuringia. So be happy, darling. I saw you look at Rafael, and I saw him look at you. If *that* wasn't love at first sight, I can't whistle 'The Blue Danube.'"

He was still swinging her arm, and now he skipped and began to run, pulling her with him, so that they galloped after Grace.

"Wait," Clio gasped.

"What for? Berlin isn't all Nazis and violence and falling in behind the Führer, you know. There's another side to it. I'll show you, we'll see it together."

They came up behind Grace, panting a little, and now they were in Unter den Linden and the arches of the great gate loomed ahead of them, with the Adlon Hotel to one side.

"Come out with me this evening," Julius ordered both of them. "Surprise party. I'll come for you at eight."

"Won't you let me stand you dinner here first?" Grace asked, pointing to the canopy and the flunkeys.

"Not a chance." Julius grinned at them both. He looked like a boy planning a birthday surprise. "Just be ready, that's all."

He left them at the margin of the canopy, turned back once to wave, and disappeared back the way they had come.

There were two messages waiting at the desk for Grace. She opened the first envelope, and Clio glimpsed the paper headed with an ornate eagle crest. She also saw that even Grace could flush with surprised pleasure. The letter was quickly folded again.

"A welcome to Berlin from the Führer's own office in the Chancellory," she said, with an attempt at offhandedness. "Isn't that rather marvelous, just to a humble English MP when there must be so many millions of other things to think of? Unfortunately, Hitler himself is in Munich now, but I am going to meet Herr Goebbels and some of his staff."

"I *say*." But Clio's irony went unregarded. "And the other?"

"Oh, an invitation for us both. Just to drinks at our Embassy."

"Just? These are elevated circles for me, remember."

Grace was not listening. "Darling, I've got to go out now. I'll see you later, shall I?"

There was no more talk of Clio acting as her interpreter. Bright-eyed with anticipation, Grace whirled away to do her own business.

Clio ate lunch alone at a table in the corner of the hotel dining room and watched the flood tide of Berlin's *haut monde* swirling past her. There were women in the latest Paris fashions, powerful-looking men in business clothes, high-ranking Wehrmacht officers, a prosperous-looking and cosmopolitan parade. The faces here were different from those of the street people. They were rosy with optimism. It was less than a month since Hitler had seized power, but there was solid satisfaction in the air. Clio had the impression that she could almost taste it, and it gave an unwelcome flavor to her dish of calves' liver in the Berlin style.

In the afternoon, she walked under the bare trees in the Tiergarten.

The rain had stopped and the sky had cleared. It was colder still, and silent filaments of frost crept over the dead ground.

She tried not to think back to London and the dismantling of her life there, and an odd, superstitious streak in her made her reluctant to think of the coming evening. She had no idea what Julius was planning, but she felt that she was on the edge of some new territory where the ground might be steep or icy, or might vanish altogether from beneath her feet.

She held herself carefully, not wanting to slip, but not wanting either to damage the fragile eggshell of hope that Julius had given her. Her thoughts skidded away from Rafael Wolf himself. To consider him directly would be to put too much weight on the first steps of this adventure into Berlin.

"Surprise!" a voice called behind them.

Julius and Clio and Grace were sitting at a restaurant table protected from the door and part of the room by a thick curtain of worn crimson plush. They could see the band on a small platform opposite, and some of the other tables that were already crowded with drinkers and diners. A new kind of Berliner seemed to have emerged with the fall of darkness. These people were determined to enjoy this evening to the full, whatever might happen tomorrow.

"Surprise!"

There was a second, louder shout as the three of them looked around.

Pilgrim and Isolde were fighting their way across the floor toward the table.

Grace's mouth set in a thin, angry red line. She looked furious. Her head twisted toward Julius, but it was clear from his expression that he had not been expecting this apparition either.

"Don't look *too* thrilled, dear ones, will you?" Pilgrim demanded. "After we have come all the way through this vile night to welcome you?"

Clio had already drunk two glasses of wine. She discovered that she was delighted to see familiar faces in this place. She stood up and flung her arms around Pilgrim.

"I am glad. I'm just so amazed. Why are you here?"

Pilgrim was wearing a long black cloak that might well have

been the same one he had always worn. Isolde was thinner in the face, her eyes were ringed with black paint, and the roots of her silvery hair were dark, but she was no less beautiful. Clio had been aware that the two of them were perhaps here or somewhere not far away, but she had had no idea that they would show up so soon.

Pilgrim twirled a chair out for himself, leaving Isolde to squeeze past him and settle herself next to Grace.

"Why am I here? Because I telephoned Julius's landlady, of course. Frau Buss? Bat? Bum?"

"Baum," Julius said with dry resignation.

"Exactly. And she told me where to find you. *Voilà*. Darling Grace. So chic you look. What are we drinking? *Sekt?* Waiter, more *Sekt*. We have some celebrating to do."

Evidently, Pilgrim had had a small celebration already. Grace unbent just enough to let him kiss her cheek. She found herself unwillingly smiling. There was a force in Pilgrim that was not quite resistible. And there was no real threat in him.

No threat, now that Anthony was gone. Cressida was in London, a long way away.

A shadow fell across Grace like a bird swooping across the sun, but she was used to the shadows, and a second later it was gone.

"If you say so, Pilgrim," she murmured. "Hello, Isolde. You are looking very artistic."

"Bugger art, and all the rest of that shit as well," Isolde shouted, altogether missing the delicacy of Grace's snub. "I'm bored to death with it. Give me a huge drink and a plateful of dinner instead, and I'll be as happy as a nigger with a saxophone."

Pilgrim raised his eyebrows. "Isn't she a peach? You don't mind us gatecrashing your party, Julius? Couldn't resist, you know, once I'd chatted to Frau Bum. Lovely Janus, tell me all the hottest gossip from London."

Clio put her glass firmly down on the table. "I left Miles, you know. Does that count as gossip?"

"Did you? Can't see how you put up with him so long, myself. What else?"

That was all. Clio could have hugged him again.

The talk began to drift around the table. It was lazy at first, and then it gathered momentum. They were happy to see one another, after all. The restaurant grew noisier and more crowded, and the sweating waiters ran to and fro with plates heaped with food. The musicians sawed at their instruments, and people began to jump up to dance.

Clio gazed at everything. She felt hazy with happiness. From the familiar patterns of gossip circulating around her, they might all have been in the Fitzroy, but it was the Fitzroy set free from the malign chill of Miles's influence. In London everything had been constrained, fixed in rigid grooves of hopelessness. Here there was nothing at all, an empty space, still to be defined.

Clio thought of Miles and his pick-up, reclining in her own bed. She saw the black-rimmed fingernails once again. But for the first time, she felt no repeating shock of nausea.

Good luck to them, she found herself murmuring.

Clio realized that she must be very slightly drunk. It was an attractive idea, a very *good* idea, and someone had kindly, thoughtfully, refilled her glass. She couldn't remember when she had last felt so ready to enjoy herself.

She caught Julius's eye, and lifted the glass to him. "I'm glad I came," she said.

"Wait a little," he answered.

Pilgrim leaned over and asked her to dance. Clio gave him her hand. They edged out onto the floor together. It was wonderful to dance. The rhythm of it swept through her. Pilgrim was grinning like a pirate as he spun her around. Julius had led Grace out too. His face wore the expression of unbelieving gratitude it always had when he was close enough to her to touch. His hand spanned her back, where the white skin was left exposed by the deep V of her dress.

Across at their table a man in a striped jersey had slid into the chair next to Isolde.

Over Pilgrim's shoulder, Clio noticed that more people were arriving. There were lights slowly revolving above the dancers, and the beams raked over the heads of the newcomers. A flicker of brightness lit one head, momentarily turning the fair hair butter yellow.

She saw that it was Rafael. He was still wearing the same shepherd's coat, but Grete beside him had changed into a low-necked blouse of some shiny greeny-black stuff with her hair worn loose over her shoulders. They were peering into the dense crowd, looking for someone. Then they came down the steps and vanished into the mass.

Clio lost the rhythm and stumbled, and Pilgrim trampled on her feet. "Let's have another drink," he bawled.

When they came in sight of their table, Rafael and Grete were already there, sitting with Julius and Grace.

"Here she is," Clio heard Julius say.

She knew with complete conviction that he was answering Rafael's question. For an instant the din in the restaurant became silence. All the noise and confusion surrounding her fell away. She moved along a channel, through the wonderful stillness, with no fear about which direction to take. She felt warm and light, and although her expression was solemn, there was happiness radiating through her bones and lighting her face. She had forgotten how it felt to smile from inside herself, with no forcing of the inarticulate muscles and frozen mouth. She was gliding toward the table, drawn by a thread of certainty that was as simple and as beautiful as pure gold.

Rafael stood up again and held out his hand. "I was asking where you were," he said.

"I know." It was wonderful to Clio, but she felt no surprise. She had been sure since she had first seen him that he would change everything, but she had been too superstitious to admit it to herself. All day she had been nudging and shaking the idea, as if it were a present wrapped up and not yet to be opened.

"I wanted to see you again."

"I'm glad," Clio said simply.

He held out a chair for her, and she sat down beside him. It was as if she were unfolding the tissue-paper wrapping of her present, but the outline of whatever lay inside was not yet discernible.

At the same time, and slowly, rather jerkily, the restaurant began to come to life once more.

Clio became aware of Isolde performing some complicated dance step with the stripy man, of a waiter arriving with another ice bucket, Grete putting her hand over Julius's to reassure him of something. Introductions were being performed: Pilgrim to Grete, Pilgrim to Rafael. No one had noticed anything unusual. The extraordinary rhythm of her own heartbeat was inaudible. She sat back in her chair, turning her head, hiding her hands under the folds of the tablecloth because she was suddenly aware that they were shaking.

Clio was not aware of it, but Grace had seen.

Grace thought, *I never knew what it meant, to say that someone looks radiant. Clio does. She is beautiful. Why have I never, ever noticed that before?*

Grace's eyes and lips were perfectly made up, and her skin was creamed and powdered to peachy smoothness, but her mouth hardened now and she looked older, no longer Clio's twin.

Pilgrim stumbled into the place next to her. "Why so gloomy, goddess?"

She looked at him from beneath her eyelids, *rapprochement* forgotten, drawing back by the smallest fraction of an inch as if to suggest that he might contaminate her.

"Gloomy? How could you imagine, on such a delightful evening? Maybe slightly fatigued by such a crush and so much noise, that's all."

Pilgrim twirled the *Sekt* bottle in its bucket and then snatched it out in a spangle of icy water.

"Don't worry, darling. We'll finish this, and we'll all move on to a little *Stube* I know. They have a floorshow there that you will hardly believe."

Clio was sitting quite still. She felt no compulsion to try to impose herself on the cross-currents of conversation. Grace was leaning forward, saying something to Grete, with her back elegantly but positively turned on Pilgrim. Julius was talking too, and Rafael's head was inclined as he listened.

Clio examined his profile. Now that she was close to him, she saw that there was a fine net of wrinkles at the corner of his eye, and the skin beneath the lower lid was soft and darkened, as if he were tired. His Nordic, outdoor looks were deceptive. Clio guessed that he was a few years older than she, perhaps in his late thirties. She liked the way he had casually shrugged off his coat, and the well-worn blue-and-gray-checked shirt that emerged from underneath it. She also liked the way that he gave his whole attention to what Julius was saying. He didn't twiddle his glass or touch his chin or gesture with a cigarette in the way that everyone else did. The movements that he did make were calm and economical.

"You should play, I think," he was saying seriously to Julius. "What reasons can you give for not doing so, except their own reasons?"

"Maybe you are right," Julius said quietly.

Isolde had fought her way back to the table with her admirer in pursuit. She wriggled and squirmed to get out of his amorous clutches. "Go away, there's a darling boy. Pilgrim, tell him."

Pilgrim yawned. "You tell him."

There was some pushing and gesturing and a rapid dispute in shouted German. Grace and Clio were startled, but everyone else seemed to take the disturbance completely for granted. By the end of it, Pilgrim had clearly lost interest.

"Oh, let's shove off, shall we? Otherwise we'll have Hansi here pestering us all evening. Come on, the Balalaika, what do you say?"

There was a general movement. Clearly, with Pilgrim in charge of the evening, there was no thought of going home yet.

"I quite like the Balalaika," Julius was saying.

"So long as it isn't one of the Russian nights." Grete laughed.

Rafael turned to Clio. His eyes were dark gray, she noticed, not blue. "Would you like to go?"

Clio laughed too. "Yes, I think I would, rather."

"Then we shall."

Clio would happily have gone anywhere, the Balalaika or the Russian steppes themselves.

"Only just the other side of the Ku'damm," Pilgrim told Grace, who did not look pleased. "I feel it's just the spot for all of us tonight. And 'goodnight to you,' " he crooned to Isolde's disappointed suitor as they bundled past him.

The Balalaika was, indeed, only around the corner. It was much smaller and more dimly lit than the restaurant, and what was visible of the decor was not noticeably Russian.

All of them except Grace and Clio were clearly Balalaika regulars. When they arrived and settled at a table, there was a good deal of greeting and waving to people at the neighboring tables. The clientele was an exotic mix of young and old, with every variety of dress and appearance. Some people were in evening clothes, while others looked as if they had just wandered in off the streets. The visitors had a new sense of Berlin as a rambling village populated by animated and interconnected groups, in odd contrast with the oversized baroque formality of its public exterior.

"Do you know everyone here?" Grace asked Julius.

"Not quite. But I've noticed that since the Nazis came to power, people seem to need to hold together. Not that we actually talk to one another very much, you understand. It's more as if we are all saying, 'Here we are, still. What will happen now?' There's an air of apprehension, but there is also that rather sickened excitement that goes with uncertainty. It leads to a lot of evenings like this. Groups of people determined to enjoy tonight, in case it turns out to be the last."

"It reminds me a little of London in the Twenties, when we were young things," Grace said. "All those desperate parties, because none of us could think what else to do."

"There is more desperation here."

"I suppose that depends on your political outlook," Grace said. There was a steady stream of visitors to the table.

Clio couldn't remember ever having met so many people in such a short space of time. There were students and musicians, actors and painters and professors and teachers. The preferred drink in the Balalaika was vodka, presumably in acknowledgment of the Russian theme, taken ice cold in a single gulp. After two shots Clio felt as if all her veins had melted. She gave up trying to remember names. She nodded and smiled, sitting next to Rafael but separated from him by a tiny space that seemed to hum and buzz with a current of its own.

In a little while the floorshow began. There was a lot of laughter and repartee between the performers and the audience. The high point of the show was a beautiful blonde who came on and sang sentimental German songs in a tiny, breathy, little-girl's voice. The applause was rapturous.

Clio whispered to Rafael, "Is she really that good?"

"He."

After that, the floor was cleared for dancing.

Rafael touched the back of Clio's hand with his forefinger. "Would you like to dance with me?"

"Yes."

On the floor, he held her lightly. There was no room to do more than sway a little.

After a moment Rafael said, "Julius asked Grete and me to come tonight, you know. But if he hadn't done, I would have found a way to meet you again."

"I know," Clio answered. Everything seemed very clear and shiny, but as brittle as spun glass. She was afraid that if she moved too fast or clumsily, all this happiness would break. "If I hadn't found you first."

They moved closer, an infinitely small distance.

"Does this evening seem very long?" Rafael asked.

"Yes. And very short too, much too short because it has to end."

His mouth was almost touching her hair. "Don't worry about the end," Rafael said.

Julius was dancing with Grete now. Under the lights her hair looked metallic, like threads of gold. Grace sat at the table, watching them, with Pilgrim sprawled beside her. Isolde had disappeared again.

As Grace looked on, Julius turned Grete in his arms, whispering something to her, and their eyes met. Grace sat slowly upright, leaning forward to observe more closely. She was surprised by a sudden, ugly twist of jealousy. Pilgrim, as ever, missed nothing that might be of interest to him. It was amusing to see that Lady Grace could be jealous of a Berlin Fräulein in a home-sewn blouse. Nor had he failed to see that Clio and Rafael were hemmed in by the press of dancers and yet seemed to move apart, in a circle of their own creation.

"Ah, my Janus Face," he drawled provocatively. "Forever staring in opposite directions."

"Shut up, Pilgrim," Grace almost spat at him.

"I don't think I will shut up," he mused, pretending to be equable. The spirit of mischief burned up in him, fueled by vodka. "I think I feel like a good old heart to heart. Here I am, after all, away from London and cut off from all I belong to."

"You don't belong to anywhere or anything. You are an opportunist."

Pilgrim pretended not to have heard. "My daughter, for instance. How is my daughter? She must be quite a beautiful creature by now. Let me see. Thirteen in August, isn't she?"

Grace had gone white. There was an interval of two or three seconds. Then she drew back her arm. With all the strength she could find, she slapped her hand against Pilgrim's face. He grunted, and sagged back in his chair. Grace leaned across to him. Her heavily made-up eyes seemed to sink into black holes in her face. Her voice came out as a hoarse whisper.

"She is not your daughter. She is my daughter, and Anthony's. You are never, ever to speak of her again. I don't want her or him contaminated with your dirt. With your . . ." Her politician's ease with words had deserted her. She gasped and then managed, "*Filth*."

Pilgrim began to recover himself. He tried to taunt her. "I think you do protest too much, my lady."

Grace would have struck out at him again. But Julius reached the table, with Grete bewildered behind him.

"What is it? Pilgrim, what in Christ's name are you doing?"

"What am I doing? I merely inquired about my daughter's progress. . . ."

Julius caught his wrist and twisted his arm. Two waiters put down their trays and began to edge toward them.

"I don't believe you have a daughter," he said softly. "And even if you did, how could Grace know anything about it? I think you should go home now, Pilgrim."

"I want to go," Grace whispered. She was still white. "Julius?"

"I'll take you," he said. "We'll go now."

Pilgrim was not done yet. "See? He'll always come running. There's no need for you to be jealous, darling."

"Shut your evil mouth," Julius hissed.

"People keep telling me to shut up. But I'm only telling the truth, so why is it, I wonder? Are you all so anxious about your secrets?"

Julius took hold of Grace's arm. "We'll go. There's no need to stay here. Rafael will look after Clio. Grete?"

Grete smiled at him. "Go. I will stay with Pilgrim here and keep him company until his Isolde comes back."

Pilgrim shrugged. "That sounds a fair exchange. Go on, Grace. Run away. Leave golden Grete to me."

The waiters folded their napkins over their arms again. When Rafael and Clio came back to the table, they found Pilgrim with one arm draped around Isolde and the other holding Grete. There was a fresh supply of icy vodka, but Pilgrim was silent at last. He looked ready to slide into a deep sleep.

"I'll get him home." Isolde sighed. "Don't worry, I've had years of bloody practice. Come on, you stupid arse."

"Gold and silver," Pilgrim muttered, "silver and gold. Goodnight, sweet ladies."

"I am going to talk to Madeleine and Georg," Grete said when they had staggered off. "I will take a taxi home." She kissed her brother quickly on the cheek, and then kissed Clio too. "Goodnight to you both," she murmured, then turned away.

They sat down at the emptied table and drank one more shot of vodka each. The pure spirit tasted as cold as a Christmas sky.

"I will walk you back to the Adlon," Rafael said at last.

In the empty street he put his arm in the sheepskin coat around her shoulder. Clio turned her face a little toward the warmth of him, and they began to walk. They passed a great illuminated clock-tower, and she saw that it was half past three.

Rafael said, "In an hour, the first people will be going to work. The U-bahn will open, and the first trams will start up. It will be morning, another day with everything that must be faced in that day. But now it is still the middle of the night. The quietest hour."

Now that they were alone, in the deserted night streets, they found that they were not sure what to say to each other. Clio felt that there were great jams of words piling up within her, torrents of explanation and description, all her history waiting to be related in exchange for Rafael's. She felt greedy for his, and impatient, and uncertain about where they would make the beginning.

"I think once we start to talk, we shall never be able to stop," she told him.

"I know that. There is this quiet hour, and then there is tomorrow."

"Do you promise?" Suddenly she felt like a child. She wanted to seize his lapels and twist them, pummel his chest with her fists, extract a promise from him that could never be broken.

Rafael began to laugh. The sound of his laughter was wonderful in the silent city street. They stopped walking, and when she looked into his face, she read the happiness in it, a reflection of her own, as if in some magical mirror.

"I promise," he said. "I promise there will be tomorrow, and all the days after that."

"Thank you," she said, now like the child who had unwrapped her present and found it was what she had hoped for, and more than she had dared to hope for.

They reached Pariser Platz and stood under the canopy that ran from the street to the great doors of the hotel. Rafael bent forward and kissed her on the mouth. His mouth was warm, and she could feel the curve of a smile in it.

"Until tomorrow," he said.

"Don't forget."

Clio walked on under the canopy and up to the shining doors where the Adlon night porter in his buttons and braid was waiting to let her in.

Fifteen

BERLIN WAS A DIVIDED CITY, and the cold split in it ran invisibly beneath the prosperous streets crowded with shoppers and under the cosmopolitan restaurants and cafés and outlandish nightclubs just as surely as the straight line of Unter den Linden ran up to the Brandenburg Gate and on into the Tiergarten.

Within just a few hours of their arrival, Clio and Grace found themselves set on either side of the divide. There had been no chance of bridging it, even at the beginning, and soon they felt that there was no possibility even of calling out to each other from a safe distance beyond the icy edge.

Clio went back to the Café Josef with Rafael Wolf, and Grace received an invitation to take tea with Adolf Hitler at the Reichskanzler-Palais in Wilhelmstrasse.

"Are you going to meet him?" Clio asked when the invitation came, delivered to the Adlon Hotel by one of the Führer's bodyguard. Grace stared at her in utter disbelief.

"Of course. Did you imagine that I would refuse?" Her movements were made jerky by excitement. There was unusual color in her face.

"I don't know what I imagined," Clio said. She was amazed at Grace's susceptibility, her willingness to associate herself with the Nazis after what they had seen and half heard. "Not this, anyway."

"Then you can't have imagined very much at all," Grace answered coldly.

There was no suggestion that Clio might accompany her to the Führer's palace, any more than there was further mention of her assisting as Grace's translator. They stood on opposing sides of some conflict that they didn't even fully understand, without having taken a single step.

As Clio watched her, Grace took a dress on its hanger out of the wardrobe and laid it on the bed. Grace was remembering something that Pilgrim had said in that dismal nightclub, what was it, the Balalaika?

My Janus Face, forever staring in different directions.

Well then, so be it, she thought with sudden savagery.

There was a milkiness about Clio, a soft and sentimental lack of direction that blurred her judgments. Grace realized that she found it profoundly irritating. She wished that she had come to Germany on her own, because she did not want to have Clio's dim misgivings clouding her perception of this new regime.

"I have to get changed now," she said.

Clio went, leaving her to her own affairs.

Grace was escorted with due ceremony from her hotel by two SS men. The palace was only a few steps away, beyond the British Embassy.

The building formed three sides of a square. It was restrained by Berlin architectural standards, a double row of windows with decorative detailing above and a third row of simple dormers in the roof. There were only four classical statues on the top of the central pediment, and the Nazi flag flying from the flagpole in the center. The fourth side of the square was marked by high railings and pillars that separated it from the street. There were storm troopers guarding the gates, and they gave the Nazi salute as Grace passed by.

In the middle of the courtyard there was a circle of frostbitten grass and a stone fountain with nymphs supporting a shallow basin. Grace walked around the circumference of the grass and approached the main door. There was a shallow flight of steps and a glass canopy to protect them. A man in uniform was waiting for her on the top step. Through a flurry of salutes and Heil Hitlers, Grace recognized Bruckner, Hitler's adjutant.

He bowed over her hand, murmuring a welcome, then led her inside.

They walked down marble-floored corridors and through anterooms hung with gloomy portraits and Nazi insignia. Finally they came to a set of double doors guarded by yet more armed and uniformed men. Grace had a momentary impression of swastikas dancing everywhere. And then the doors were opened, and she found herself looking into a light, bright room. It was a drawing room, disconcertingly feminine. There was gilt and cream furniture, spindly legged, and small tables decorated with fine porcelain.

A group of people was arranged in the middle of the room taking afternoon tea. The Führer was sitting amongst them with a cup and saucer balanced on his knee.

It would have seemed funny to Grace, this domestic tableau, if she had not suddenly found herself awed to be in his presence at all. All the way across the courtyard of the Reichskanzler-Palais and along the booming corridors, she had not quite believed that at the end of the march she would come face to face with him. And now Adolf Hitler stood up, a small man in a neat civilian suit, and came to meet her with his hands outstretched. She saw very clearly his highly polished shoes and manicured fingernails, and the indoor pallor of his skin.

He greeted her in German. "Lady Grace, may we welcome you to Berlin?" He clasped her hand in both of his. His grip was firm and surprisingly warm.

Grace's poise deserted her. She could think of no word of German, no words at all, not even the conventional murmurs of drawing-room exchanges. She stood with her feet fixed to the carpet, looking at him, with red patches of color flaring in her cheeks and her right hand still held between Hitler's.

"Wilkommen," he said again, smiling at her.

Then he let go of her hand and touched her elbow, to guide her forward. She was taller than he was. Grace took a step, beside him, then another. She heard a tiny sound within her head, *click,* and movement seemed to start up once again around her. Color seeped back into the room, bleeding inward from the edges of her field of vision. She became aware of the Führer's other guests, also standing up to greet her. She could even recognize some of the faces: Dr. Dietrich, the controller of Hitler's press and publicity, and his architect, Albert Speer.

Grace shook hands around the circle. There was a director of Mercedes-Benz and his lively wife; the Führer's personal physician; one or two senior SS and SA men; a handful of others.

Her moment of paralysis was past. She smiled into each pair of eyes and made the appropriate responses. One of the SS men at her shoulder became her interpreter.

Lady Grace Brock, British Member of Parliament visiting Berlin in an unofficial capacity but as a warm friend of the Reich . . .

"How do you do?" Grace murmured. "I am very pleased to meet you, very pleased to be here."

And then she was sitting in the place of honor, beside Hitler, on a straight-backed Empire sofa upholstered in cream- and gold-figured silk. A white and gold teacup was put into her hand, and she gravely declined the offer of chocolate cake layered with cream, then quickly accepted it when she saw the disappointed expression on her host's face.

The tea party resumed its mild course.

The conversation was about opera. Hitler was talking about Bayreuth, Grace picked out that much. She sat stiffly beside him, trying to decipher what was being said. After a moment the Führer turned courteously to her and asked her if she was an opera-lover and if she had ever visited Bayreuth herself. The interpreter translated while Hitler watched her. Grace found his stare hypnotic. It became difficult to know where to look, and what to do with her hands, which felt overlarge and clumsy in her lap.

"I have never had the opportunity to hear opera in Germany. But I love Mozart, and Wagner."

The translator relayed her banal response, and Hitler nodded solemnly.

Grace thought of Julius and his Mozart, and of Nathaniel listening to *The Ring* on the gramophone in the Oxford drawing room.

"Perhaps you will have the opportunity to hear some music while you are in Berlin, Lady Grace."

"I hope so, very much."

There was the polite and stilted interpretation again. Grace had imagined before she was admitted to the cream and gilt room that there would be some serious talk, but now she understood that she would be disappointed. This tea-party conversation circled and led nowhere, while Hitler and his aides listened intently to her uninteresting answers. They all nodded at one another and cocked their heads to the interpreter, and their solemnity seemed only to underline the meaninglessness of their exchanges.

A sense of *déjà vu* stirred in Grace. She realized that in spite of the splendor of the drawing room, she was reminded of afternoon visits that she had been obliged to make as a young girl, with Blanche, to country neighbors and hunting families a little less grand than themselves, or to the upper strata of tenant farmers who lived on the Stretton estate. There had been the same polite constraint, and the same edge-of-the-seat attention to formal etiquette.

Only the difference was that here she was sitting beside Hitler, and this small, neat, and vaguely unhealthy-looking man was the focus of all their covert attention. She found that she could not look away from him for more than a few seconds at a stretch, and then her eyes were drawn back again. From her quick glances at them she thought that his staff and the small circle of friends felt the same compulsion.

The men waited for him to speak, and leaned forward a fraction when he did so. The Mercedes-Benz director and the doctor in their beautifully cut suits were as deferential as the officers in their uniforms and medal ribbons. The two women were more talkative, especially the wife of the Mercedes man who tossed her head and turned it from side to side to show her pretty throat, but like all the others she almost never took her eyes off the Führer's face.

Of all of them in the room, only the Führer seemed completely at his ease, watching them and smiling and listening to their banalities as if they were gems of wisdom.

Grace was sure that the gatherings of Hitler's intimates could not always be so insipid. Then, with a sudden clarity that almost winded her, she realized why this one was so determinedly neutral. Of course, they were suspicious of her. She had not been given a privileged invitation into the inner circle at all, and it had been vain to imagine that she had. These people imagined that she was a spy or at the very least some kind of eavesdropper for the British Government, a subtle choice for the very reason of being a too-obvious choice.

Was that what it was?

Once they had occurred to her, the possibilities of pretense and counterpretense multiplied in her imagination until she felt dizzy. She also felt sick. The room with its draped curtains and spindly Empire furniture and gilt-framed mirrors reflecting their tense faces was overheated, and the chocolate cake much too sweet and rich.

She had let it be known that she would welcome an opportunity to meet the Führer out of admiration and friendship. Was this vicarage tea a rebuff, or merely a baffling ritual that she was too much of an outsider, or too stupid, or too British even to understand? She shook her head in a tiny gesture of bewilderment, and at once Hitler leaned forward in solicitous concern. His hand rested for an instant on her arm. He did not mistrust her, Grace was sure of that.

At the same moment one of his aides came forward and murmured to him. There was a general movement, and Grace looked at her wristwatch. The audience was clearly over.

Hitler escorted her to the door himself. In English, after he had bowed over her hand, he said, "We meet again, perhaps."

"I do hope so," Grace said. Her disappointment melted away at once, like spring snow in a west wind.

Then there was another escort, in the reverse direction, past the portraits and insignia and out into the cold courtyard. When they reached the gates and Unter den Linden, Grace turned to the SS man, who evidently intended to accompany her back to the doors of the Adlon.

"Thank you so much," she said clearly. "I am going to walk a little way on my own."

There was an immediate straightening, then the Nazi salute. "Heil Hitler."

"Heil Hitler," Grace responded.

She turned right, out of the gates, and began to walk through the crowds toward Friedrichstrasse. The people flowed past her, no longer looking curiously at her once she had left the palace gates and the guards.

The feelings of confusion and faint nausea left her at once.

She was thinking, *I have been there. I sat and talked about Wagner to Hitler himself.*

She looked at the faces of the people as they passed by her. Their expressions were stolid or sour or satisfied or anxious, like a parade of human fallibility. It struck her that they were lucky to be here, now, of all times, even if they did not seem to know it.

And what would they think, she wondered in her strange exhilaration, if they knew where I have been?

She came to the corner of Friedrichstrasse and stood under a lamppost to look through the stream of cars and lumbering cream buses across to the Café Kranzler and the Café Linden on their opposite sides of the street. There were balconies of iron lace at the first-floor windows, and yellow lights blossoming behind them. She thought of going to sit at one of the white-colored tables to smoke a cigarette and stare out through fogged glass at Berlin going by. She felt an affection for it, this brown and pungent city as it went through the shuddering pangs of rebirth.

Grace had no doubt that it would be reborn. Not after this afternoon, after the cream and gold drawing room and the man sitting at the center of it.

But in the end, she did not cross over through the traffic. She could see that the café tables were crowded with after-work Berliners, and she knew that the rooms would be hot, and ripe with smoke and the smell of packed bodies and damp clothes. She turned back instead and walked the way she had come, past the

Reichskanzler-Palais to the Adlon Hotel. Grace walked quickly, no longer looking at the people who passed her, with her own face turned up to the cold air.

Clio and Rafael had left the Café Josef. There had been an afternoon of talk, and heads drawn close over the puddled tables. Clio had sat listening, only half understanding the rapid colloquial German, content that Rafael trusted her enough to bring her here again. The men had eyed her at first, but her association with Rafael had seemed to be enough of a testament to her trustworthiness. They had soon forgotten her presence.

At length, the gathering had broken up. The men left separately, slipping one by one into the gloom outside, until only Clio and Rafael were left. Clio understood that the Café Josef was the headquarters of some kind of communist cell, and that Rafael was tangentially involved in the movement. The muttered plans and the secrecy and the very shabbiness of the conspirators themselves seemed to Clio to offer a pathetically small opposition to the Nazi ostentation of the brown city beyond the café window.

When they were alone Josef brought them coffee, hot in an earthenware jug, and they drank it quickly.

"Are you a communist?" Clio had asked Rafael.

"No."

"What, then?"

"A Jew. A humanist, I suppose."

She had smiled then. "Like my father."

Their eyes met. "I would like to meet him."

"I am sure you will, someday," Clio said softly. There seemed to be no point in a modest pretense that she did not know what was happening to them. The thought of Miles swam into her head like a fish in cloudy water, but she dismissed it again.

When they left the café, Josef had come with them to the door, nodding and smiling like some benevolent Pandarus. They had started to walk, without any destination in mind beyond being alone in the anonymous streets. After a little way Rafael took Clio's arm and held it against the warmth of his farmer's coat.

They were in the oldest part of the city, Alt-Berlin, in a network of narrow side streets spreading away from the bank of the Spree. There were few people about, and the old houses had an old-fashioned provincial aspect that Clio found reassuring. The last light was fading out of the strip of sky overhead, and gas lamps flared at the corners with street signs lettered in Gothic script projecting from them like accusing fingers. They turned at random, left and then right, watching their own breath as it condensed in clouds ahead of them.

They began the talking.

It was as if they had been holding their breath until now. They used a mixture of German and English, a hybrid language whose absurdities they were too engrossed to notice. All that mattered was to find out about each other, and in their greed for discovery, they forgot the cold and the thickening darkness. Clio felt warmth radiating from Rafael as they fitted their steps together, moving hip to hip.

Rafael told her about growing up in the village in Thuringia. He described his schoolfriends and his mother and his father's business, and the village festivals and the rituals of the farmer's year.

"It sounds very happy," Clio said.

"It was. Until our mother died, when Grete was twelve and I was fifteen."

"I'm sorry."

"How do you think it sounds if I say I am glad, now, that she has gone? I would not want her to be here to see what is happening to Germany."

"I understand that."

His hand gripped her arm more tightly. "Do you?"

"A little, I think. My father's family are Jews, from Czechoslovakia originally. My grandparents are both dead now. They were remarkable people. I loved them very much."

"Tell me about when you were small."

Clio told him about the house in the Woodstock Road, and the influxes of eager undergraduates, and Eleanor's housekeeping, and about her brothers and sisters.

"It sounds very happy," he echoed her, smiling. "So many of you children."

"I was always closest to Julius."

"And your cousin, the Member of Parliament? The twin who is not a twin?"

"Grace. Grace and I are like ... weight and counterweight. Equal but needing opposition to balance us. Or like the two people in those little weather houses, one in and the other out, fair moods or foul. Or just oil and water in a bottle, our faces forever reflecting each other, but our souls immiscible."

"But Julius loves her." It was a statement, not a question.

"Yes. He always has done, ever since we were children."

"And you are jealous of that." Again, there was no questioning inflection. Clio considered a denial, and then she made herself tell the truth.

"Yes."

Rafael stopped walking. They were in the angle of two houses, where the street turned a sharp corner and one frontage projected beyond the other. The building nearest to them housed a little shop; Clio could see the wooden shutters over the window and faint gilt-colored lettering on the fascia over the door. Behind Rafael's head there was the spire of a church, a slender point of thicker blackness against the evening sky.

"I was jealous of Grete when I first met you both," she said helplessly. "It is my failing."

"Don't be jealous," Rafael whispered.

He leaned forward, until his mouth touched hers. His hands came up and rested on her shoulders, and then he took her face and held it so that he could look down into her eyes. When he kissed her again his cheeks were cold, but his mouth and tongue seemed to burn.

Clio closed her eyes, and when she opened them the rooftops behind him and the church spire and the weight of the black clouded sky seemed to recede, shrinking away from them until they seemed to float together in some empty space. She was giddy and clung to him because she was afraid that she might fall. But still she could feel reality in the cold of the stone paving striking up through the soles of her thin shoes, and she knew that a wind had begun to blow, bringing a spattering of rain with it.

"You are shivering," Rafael said. He wrapped his arms around her, pulling her closer to him inside the sheepskin until she felt the contours of his body. He was much taller than Miles, and thin, without the soft pouches of flesh that Miles's body had put on in the years of their marriage.

"I'm not cold." She wanted to cling to this moment, without anything changing, for as long as she could. "Let's walk some more. What happened when you grew up, when you left the village?"

"I went to university, in Jena, to study law, and then to Dresden. Grete went to music college. The good children of bourgeois parents that we were. Then I practiced for a time near Dresden, and Grete came to Berlin. I followed her here about eight years ago." He shrugged, and for the first time Clio sensed some bitterness in him. "There were good times. But I am a Jew, of course. Since the

Nazis came to power, we can only do what little we can. I have to learn now to help people in other ways, instead of through the law."

Clio remembered again how fragile the resistance had seemed, in the Café Josef, against the machine of the Reich. She had no sympathy with the Bolsheviks, any more than with the Nazis. It was the brutality of the division itself that seemed too sad to contemplate.

She stumbled out with some words. "Why did you never marry?"

Rafael thought, and then he answered, "I don't believe I ever gave myself the time. And then, afterward, when there was time, it seemed that it was already too late. I was used to being alone. Is that a reason?"

"I think so."

The cold fish swam more insistently now, until she could no longer ignore it. The threat of it glittered at her. She was afraid that what she must say was going to alter everything, but she knew that she must say it. Clio looked ahead along the empty, murky street. She had the feeling that she was submerged, deep under water.

"Rafael . . . I was, I *am* married. I married the wrong man at the wrong time, everything about our partnership was wrong, but I am still his wife."

Rafael went on walking. The rhythm of his steps continued, and his hold on her arm did not loosen. "Why are you here in Berlin?"

"I . . . ran away. I can't go back. I came here with Grace because she was planning the trip anyway and I so much wanted to see Julius. I thought it would be far enough away, and strange enough, for me to be able to submerge myself. . . ."

"Why can't you go back?" His voice sounded even, the essence of reason and logic.

"Because I came home early one afternoon and found my husband in our bed with a man."

He did stop then. They faced each other, and Clio made a small gesture of resignation. "I should have known all along what he was, but I managed to convince myself otherwise. I remember my cousin Grace asking at the pre-wedding party, 'You're not going to marry that little queer, are you?' I can't recall what I said to her. It doesn't matter now."

Rafael took her hands. He rubbed them between his own to coax some warmth back into them. She loved him because he didn't try to offer her any misplaced sympathy, or any retrospective wisdom. His silence left her free of obligation to describe any more of the mess of her life that she had left behind in London.

"Clio." She also loved the way that he said her name, separating and drawing out the syllables as if he were unwilling to let them go. "Where do you want to go now?"

He was inviting her to look forward, instead of into the past.

"I want to go with you."

"Not back to the Adlon Hotel?"

"No, not back there."

"If you do come with me, can you accept the other things that I am, also?"

Clio knew that he meant not only his race, but his political work, whatever that might really be, and his precarious foothold amongst the unmapped sands of Nazi Berlin. She felt no doubt, only a swift contraction of fear for him.

"Yes," she said.

Rafael's laugh startled her. He put his head back and laughed in pleasure like a noisy boy. "Come on, then," he ordered her, and she followed him.

There was a busier street running at right angles to theirs. They rounded the corner into it, and Clio saw a U-bahn station ahead. Rafael drew her on, and they descended into the turquoise-tiled depths that to Clio's heightened senses echoed like a swimming bath.

The train when it came was crowded, and they stood close together in a press of people. Rafael put his arm around her shoulders to shield her. It could have been London in the rush hour, but for the Berlin smell and the faces surrounding them. Close up against Clio there was an old woman with a black scarf covering her head, and a man with seamed, brown skin who might have been a Turk or an island Greek, and a pale, exhausted boy who stared down at his own soaking shoes. Clio remembered each of them for a long time afterward, as if they had been old friends.

At the end of the journey they emerged in Wilmersdorf, on the west side of the city. The seemingly identical residential streets were lined with rows of apartment houses, many of them with Nazi flags at the windows. Rafael lived in one of the blank-faced buildings. He led her up the shallow stairs to the first floor and unlocked the door.

"Do you really live here?" she asked.

"What did you expect?" He smiled at her. "Something a little more Bohemian? I am a respectable Jewish lawyer, not a person like your friend the painter."

Clio thought for a moment of the old studio in Charlotte Street, and the mess of paint and empty bottles and dirty clothes; the divan where they had posed for *The Janus Face,* and of Pilgrim and Grace.

"I am very glad that you are a respectable Jewish lawyer," she said primly.

He closed the door behind them.

There was a large room, the walls lined with books, and between the columns of books there were primitive paintings of mountains and forests that made splashes of intense green and blue amongst the brown leather bindings.

"The paintings are Grete's," Rafael said. "They are of our home. I will take you there, someday."

"I would like that," Clio said.

"And now." He took her coat and hat and put them neatly to one side. She saw that the room was full of papers and journals as well as books, but that everything was tidily arranged. The careful order of it all reminded her of Julius, except that wherever Julius lived was always barer than this, as if he wanted to be ready to move on at a moment's notice.

"Would you like some tea?" he asked her. "Or something to drink?"

"Nothing. Thank you."

Now that they were here, she felt suddenly awkward, and unsure even of how to hold herself, like some gauche schoolgirl. The years with Miles had made her feel that her body was in some way objectionable, a mildly embarrassing mistake to be overlooked wherever possible. She had to resist an impulse to cross her arms over her chest as Rafael looked at her.

"Well then," he said gently. With one hand he reached out and undid the buttons at the neck of her blouse. Clio almost sprang backward away from him.

"Come here," he said in the same mild voice.

She stood still now, and he undid more buttons to leave her shoulder exposed. He touched the skin with his mouth and she shivered.

"Are you afraid?" he asked, lifting his head again to look at her.

"Not of you." It was so inconceivable that she smiled, and she saw the taut lines in his face relax at once. "Only of what happened before."

"Before is not now. Now is where we begin. You must forget before."

His certainty was so simple that it disarmed her. She took a breath, and then she undid the last button herself. Her blouse fell in a heap at her feet, and as he watched her she stepped out of her skirt, and then discarded the crêpe-de-Chine folds of her underclothes.

There was another brief flicker of recollection. Grace and herself behind the screen in Pilgrim's studio, peeling off their debutante dresses. But then the image swam away again, and she was thirty-one years old, in Rafael Wolf's apartment in a house in Wilmersdorf.

Rafael put his hand up to touch her cheek, then the swell of her breast. Looking down, she saw that he had big hands, with broad tips to the fingers. They were working hands, not like Miles's.

"Come here with me," he said.

The room was L-shaped, and in the toe of it there was a bed covered with a dark blanket. Rafael bent and pulled back the covers, and she lay down with her head propped on one arm to look at him. He took off his own clothes, unhurriedly and without a shadow of self-consciousness. He seemed so clean and natural that Clio thought she could catch the scent of the mountains off his skin, and she turned her head to glance at Grete's paintings.

Rafael sat down on the edge of the bed and put his big, warm hand on her belly, then slid it through the tongue of dark hair and between her legs.

"You are very beautiful," he told her.

"No. I'm ordinary, I'm . . ."

His touch made her draw in her breath in the back of her throat. She forgot what she was saying and lifted one arm instead to draw him down beside her.

They looked at each other. Rafael's skin was white and clear, and the hair on his body was dark gold, darker than on his head. It curled into points in his armpits, making Clio think of the barley-sugar twists she and Julius had bought as children out of big jars off the shelf of a sweetshop in North Parade.

She felt suddenly hungry for him, as she had never dared to be with Miles, not after the very beginning. She dipped her head and nuzzled the curls of hair, breathing in the clean scent.

He began to stroke her, making long smooth movements with his hands, over her ribs and into the hollow of her waist and then down over her flanks. His face was half in shadow, and then as he bent forward, light from the single lamp licked over his cheeks, and she saw his intent expression. He made small inarticulate sounds as he concentrated on her, as if she were some wild animal that needed to be calmed.

Slowly the stroking became more focused. His fingers moved over the insides of her thighs and worked in the soft place between them. Clio gave a long sigh that was partly astonishment and partly an acknowledgment of her pleasure. Her knees fell apart, and Rafael moved to kneel between them, bending over her until his mouth touched her damp hair and his tongue probed and rubbed the sliver of scalding flesh against the hard bone underlying it.

Clio's arms stretched out, and her fingers clawed as she lifted her hips to the pressure of him. She was too amazed to feel awkward, or exposed, or to wonder what she should do next.

Miles had never done anything like this.

On the rare occasions when he had wanted to touch her at all, Miles had preferred to make love to her from behind, with short jabbing movements that seemed expressive of frustration or even anger, and he had kneaded and pinched her backside until it hurt, and when he came, he had yelled Christ, and then he had rolled over and apparently fallen instantly asleep. Sometimes, lying in the dark afterward and listening to his breathing, Clio had touched herself where Rafael's tongue was teasing her now.

There was nothing wrong, she had told herself. She knew Dr. Stopes's theories and had read the earnest, wholesome manuals at the Clinic. But even in the darkness of her own bedroom, her cheeks had begun to burn and her body had lost its dull tingle and begun to feel like cold meat, and she had withdrawn her hand and turned over to try to sleep. It was a continuing irony that she knew everything on paper and nothing in the reality of warm flesh and blood.

"Rafael."

Clio clenched her fists, and her fingernails made red half-moon weals in the palms of her hands.

She was afraid that she would scream out loud, and she was even more afraid that this imperative goal would still elude her.

"Rafael."

He lifted his head to look at her. She saw the glint of her own juices on his lips. Clio began to shudder, long shaking waves that came from inside her, from nowhere.

Rafael's blond head bent again. His tongue flicked delicately, and then he drew the point of flesh and the seaweed fronds into the warmth of his mouth and sucked on them.

Without warning, a bolt of white light split Clio's body. It ran through her as all the muscles in her body contracted into a single shivering knot and then burst in scalding ripples, then knotted and burst again, over and over, spilling the light out of her, so that the light fell in showers of sparks, a thousand rockets contained in the extraordinary envelope of her own flesh, and then the sparks that were released drifted slowly, exquisitely downward and away into powdery blackness.

She never knew whether she screamed out or not.

When she opened her eyes again, Rafael was looking down at her, and she read the tenderness in his face like a blessing.

"I never have—" she began, but he put his fingers over her mouth. She wanted to lick the broad ends of them; to kiss each of the knuckles in turn.

"This is now," he said. "Not before."

Clio sighed with happiness. Her limbs felt warm and supple, as if they could reach and stretch any way she wanted. The lamplight made the room cozy and turned the piles of books and papers into mysterious crooked towers. She lay in the crook of his arm, looking around her. It seemed odd to feel secure in this place she had never seen before, with a man she hardly knew, but that was what she did feel.

After a little while she turned her attention back to Rafael. Sweat had darkened the curls of barley sugar on his chest so that they looked as if they had been licked into sugary spirals. She leaned forward and rubbed her cheek against them.

Even his penis looked different from Miles's. Her husband's had prodded bluntly out of the undulations of flesh beneath his belly. Rafael's was longer, and it stood clear of the triangle of crisp golden hair at the base of his flat stomach. In her innocence Clio had imagined that all men looked like the diagrams in the Clinic's manuals, or the same as Miles, a matter of gray and purple pouches and an angry red eye.

But now that she looked at him, she saw that Rafael was beautiful.

She lazily touched him with the tips of her fingers, then closed her fingers around him.

"Like this," he murmured, meaning to show her.

The exhortations in the manuals danced in front of her again.

"I know what to do," she told him firmly, then surprised him with her laughter.

Rafael lay back against the pillows, watching her. To Clio, he seemed to be offering himself up to her with an unaffected generosity that was the opposite of all Miles's delicately wounding snubs and puzzling subterfuges.

It was all quite simple, she suddenly understood.

All the mystery required was for two people to be equal and honest with each other, so that what one of them wanted gave the other pleasure to perform.

In a matter of minutes, Rafael had taught her more about love-making than she had learned from thousands of dutiful hours at Dr. Stopes's Clinic, and from the whole of her married life.

Clio bent her head. Very carefully, she took him in her mouth. She traced the contours from the shaft to the head with the tip of her tongue, and she heard his sharp indrawn breath. The sound of it gave her as much satisfaction as her own startling climax had done.

At length it was Rafael who slipped away from her. He turned her so that she lay on her back, and he knelt between her legs again.

"May I?" he asked, with serious formality.

The smile she gave him was luminous, hazy with tenderness. "Yes," Clio said.

He came inside her, joining their bodies, but the communication was all in their eyes as Clio lifted her arms and drew him down to her. This was more familiar now, and the familiarity troubled her. She held him as tightly as she could, denying the chilly memories of Miles and the sudden fear that came with them of what would happen tomorrow, and the day after, to Rafael and herself. She felt the thin shreds of her momentary security torn and whisked away by her own anxiety. For all the closeness of their bodies, she was removed from him, even as he reared up over her and then blindly called out her name.

Afterward, he lay still with his eyes closed and his head against her heart.

"I'm sorry," Clio whispered. "Other things came crowding in. I didn't want them to."

"It is all right," he told her. "You don't have to give all of yourself at once. This is only the first time."

"What will happen?" she asked, hearing herself like a plaintive child.

Wait, don't ask too much, don't try to take too much.

"When?"

Humbly she said, "Tomorrow. The next day."

Rafael laughed at her, but she could hear that he understood her question. "We shall go to Julius's concert, of course. To the Balalaika for some more drinks. I shall take you out to the Havel for some walking by the lakes. What else?"

Clio was ashamed of her importunity. She lay more comfortably against him. "Grace will be going back to London in three days' time."

"Do you want to go with her?"

"No."

"Then stay here with me," Rafael said.

His simple certainty dispelled her fear again.

The Philharmonic Hall was almost full. Clio and Rafael took their seats with Grete and Grace, and as they settled themselves, they saw that Pilgrim and Isolde were already in their places in the row in front. Pilgrim swung around with an extravagant wave, and Isolde rolled her eyes and twitched her red lips into a kiss.

Grace looked away and frowningly studied her program. Julius would be playing a popular selection of Mozart and Richard Strauss. She was grateful to see that it was at least music that she could comprehend, even though it would not have been her own choice to spend her last evening in Berlin in a concert hall in close proximity to Pilgrim and Isolde, as well as to Clio and her rural Bolshevist friends.

But she was here for Julius's sake, Grace thought, because he had so evidently wanted her to come. There were not many things she could have refused him. The realization made her cheeks feel warm, and she straightened her back against the uncomfortable seat until the moment had passed.

While she waited for Julius to appear on the platform, she craned her neck, very discreetly, to see who was occupying the VIP seats at the front of the hall. She had heard a rumor that Goering would be in the audience, but she could see no sign of him.

Clio was looking around her too. The audience was composed of the prosperous Berlin bourgeoisie. There were plenty of jewels on powdered bosoms, and tight waistcoats stretched over comfortable stomachs. There was also a preponderance of brown uniforms. She was conscious of Rafael beside her, a little unfamiliar in a dark suit, and of the pearl-gray silk folds of Grace's skirt fanning over her own woollen one. Rafael shifted a little in his place, as if he were uncomfortable or apprehensive.

The hum of conversation in the hall modulated suddenly into an expectant aria of coughing and whispering. Clio lifted her head. She saw the conductor emerge from the wings and bow to the surge of applause that swept up to greet him, then turn to repeat the bow to his orchestra.

The space at the center of the platform was empty.

She felt the pluck of empathetic stage fright that she always experienced before Julius's performances. She knew that he would be waiting, out of sight behind the red plush drape of the curtain, with the music beating in his head.

Then, to another burst of clapping, Julius came out onto the platform. He walked quickly to his place at center front with his violin tucked under his arm and his bow swinging in one hand. His movements were so perfectly characteristic, and so familiar to her, that for a vertiginous instant Clio could have believed that they were not his but her own, and that she had passed from one body into the other, and now would have to play Mozart's Concerto No. 4 in D major to an audience of *hauts* Berliners. Absurd fear gripped at her bowels, so that she turned to Rafael to try to smile it away. Only she saw that Rafael was staring at the stage, leaning forward as if to detect some sign that was both invisible and inaudible.

Julius bowed his dark head. When he lifted his eyes again, Grace thought he was scanning the rows of seats in search of her. His face was very white, as white as his starched collar and the butterfly wings of his tie. She found that she wanted to stand up, to signal to him *I'm here with you,* and she curled her fingers around the edge of her seat to anchor herself.

Then he turned aside, so sharply that the black tails of his coat flipped behind him. There were the formal bows exchanged between soloist and conductor, soloist and the orchestra.

The audience was silent now, fully expectant. Clio noticed only subliminally in the split second before Julius lifted his violin that there was none of the usual coughing and fidgeting before the music burst out.

Julius began to play. At first he seemed tense, but after a few bars his face cleared, and then settled into the expression of remote concentration that it always wore when he became absorbed in his music.

Clio's breath came more easily. She sank back by small degrees until her shoulder blades connected with the plush padding of her seat. Rafael eased his long legs into a more comfortable position in the cramped space. The music rose around them and up into the gilded vaults over their heads.

The whistling was the more shocking just because Julius's playing had taken hold of all of them.

There was one long, sharp blast that cut across the sweetness of the music like an obscenity, and then three or four more that came and went and then united in a single harsh shriek.

A collective gasp seemed to stir like a wind in the concert hall, and then the old seats creaked and groaned as people turned to gape at the source of the noise. The whistling went on, raucous and defiant. Isolde leaped to her feet and shook her fist at the back of the hall, but neither Clio nor Grace looked around. Their eyes were fixed on Julius. At his back the conductor let his baton fall, and the orchestra struggled on and then raggedly faltered into silence, section by section.

Julius continued to play. The notes rose thinly, sliced into fragments by the whistles.

"Julius," Grace whispered. She covered her mouth with her fingers.

Isolde was shouting something while Pilgrim jerked at her arm. There were more shouts, and a banging of seats, and then the stamping began.

Clio looked sideways at Rafael. He was hunched forward, with Grete's hand on his. Slowly, moving her head as if her neck were painfully stiff, Clio turned to see what was happening behind her. All the time she could hear Julius's unaccompanied playing and see the image of his death-pale face.

A group of young SA men had occupied the last row of seats. They were standing up, as stiff as if they had been called to attention, and they were holding shiny silver whistles to their lips. The blasts were synchronized now into sharp, short volleys of noise, and the stamping and handclapping from the body of the hall fell into the same vicious rhythm.

"Stop it," Isolde was tearfully screaming. "Damn you, stop it."

Grace bit into her own knuckles as the noise swelled up like the sea.

A man's full-throated voice roared out, *"Jude! Jude!"*

Clio felt rather than heard Julius stop playing.

She turned again to face forward and saw him lower his violin until it rested at his side. The conductor had already left the stage, and the players in the orchestra sat in a silent phalanx, looking nowhere.

Julius bowed again, with ironic grace, into the storm of his audience. Then he walked away, straight-backed, and disappeared into the wings.

Clio caught at Rafael's arm. The chorus had been taken up in other sections of the hall.

"Jew! Jew!"

"What can we do?" she whispered.

"We must get him away from here."

He was already pushing away from her, over the feet and knees of their neighbors, toward the end of the row and the aisle. Grete was ahead of him. Clio and Grace stumbled in their wake, clutching at their evening handbags and trailing wraps. "Excuse me," Clio heard Grace muttering as she trampled on the feet of Berlin matrons. *Excuse me,* as if they were making an unscheduled exit from a Shaftesbury Avenue matinee.

They ran the length of the concert hall, past the young men in their brown uniforms, and out through the double doors into the foyer. A group of ushers was peering into the hall around an opposite set of doors. They seemed merely curious, rather than surprised or shocked by the disturbance. Rafael leaped down the shallow steps that led from the main doors into the street with Pilgrim at his shoulder.

The performers' entrance was in a side street overshadowed by the dark bulk of the hall. The door was open, and they saw Julius standing in a dingy entry. He was wearing his old black overcoat buttoned to his chin, and he held his violin in its case close against his chest, as if it were a child.

"Come with us," Rafael ordered.

Julius hesitated. "If they decide to restart the concert . . ."

"Come *now.*"

Clio had a vision of the brownshirts in the hall realizing that they had been deprived of their sport and spilling out into the street in search of their Jewish violinist. Heinrich's story of Herr Keller the lawyer came back to her.

"Please, Julius. There isn't going to be any more music tonight. Do what Rafael says."

Still he did not move. He drew his violin case to him and looked back over his shoulder into the light, as if he could not believe they would not call for him again, that there had not been some administrative mistake that could all be explained away. He had played other concerts in Berlin; sometimes the posters bearing his name were defaced, or there were the gaping spaces of empty seats in the prominent front rows, even catcalls when he took his bow, but he had never dreamed of being driven from the stage. Clio and the others saw that he was numb with shock.

It was Grace who broke through to him. She seized the violin case in both hands and wrenched it away from him, and then she took hold of the lapels of his black coat and shook him until he looked down into her face. His expression changed at once. Grace wrapped her arms around him and leaned her cheek against his shoulder.

"Come home," she whispered. "We can't stay here, all of us."

"I'm coming," Julius said.

Pilgrim picked up the violin, and they closed around him, with Clio and Grace on either side. The side street was empty, and the wider street beyond. There had been no exodus yet from the Philharmonic Hall.

"Perhaps they have found another soloist," Julius said softly. "Perhaps one of those boys can stand up and play the violin as well as the tin whistle."

"Where can we go?" Clio asked Rafael. Her head was filled with images of dark alleyways and bundles of rags left lying in the gutter.

"He cannot go back to his own place," Rafael said. "Not for a day or so until they have forgotten him and fixed on someone else."

"My studio is nearest," Pilgrim offered. "Two stops only on the U-bahn."

Even Isolde was silent on the short journey. To Clio, the divided city seemed to have become universally hostile. Every young man out with his girl looked like SA or SS, ready to pounce on Julius and drag him away out of reach to the terror of some shuttered brown house.

Pilgrim's studio occupied part of an old warehouse. It was reached by an internal spiral staircase of flaking ironwork rising through a hole in the floorboards into a shadowy space beneath the iron girders that supported the warehouse roof. They climbed the tight spiral and stood in an awkward group at the opening of the stairwell while Pilgrim swore and fumbled at the lights.

When the lights did come on, the sudden antiseptic glare threw into prominence all the clutter of canvases and empty bottles and paint jars jammed with brushes. There was a screen for models to change behind, and a divan heaped with discarded clothes. The roof was pierced with glass skylights, black shiny strips now in the darkness. Even the smell was the same. It was like stepping back into Charlotte Street.

"Welcome, Janus," Pilgrim said slyly.

Grace and Clio did not look at each other.

"It's not exactly the Adlon Hotel, Julius, or the Reichskanzler-Palais, but perhaps you won't mind that for a day or so. May I offer anyone a drink? There's some schnapps, Isolde, isn't there? Maybe even a drop or two of Scotch."

"I'll get it," Isolde said wearily. She kicked aside a heap of grubby clothes and went to the stone sink in the corner of the studio. The glasses that she distributed were sticky and filmed with dust, but Julius took his and drank the whiskey in a grateful gulp. He sat on the divan with his hands hanging loosely between his knees, staring at the floor in front of him.

A silence swelled in the thick air.

At length Rafael put his glass aside. There were gray lines at the corners of his mouth. "I am sorry, Julius," he said. "I am ashamed of Germany and the German people."

"No, Rafael, it is not a matter of *shame* for you. . . ."

Grete moved closer to his side, but Julius held up his hand before she could say any more. He seemed dazed, still, but his eyes were fixed on Grace.

"I was warned. But I was sure that music transcended everything. I thought my playing determined what they thought of me, and that everything else was incidental. A political matter, not my concern." Rafael shifted impatiently, and Julius glanced at him before his gaze returned to Grace. "I misunderstood, that is all. I failed to see what should have been obvious to me. It was my own mistake.

"I shall not make the mistake now of pretending that it is not going to grow worse every day. Jewish violinists will not be allowed to play Mozart any longer, any more than Jewish doctors will be allowed to look after the sick or Jewish lawyers to practice the law."

The bewilderment in him was so evident that Clio felt a rush of anger clotted with tears burning at the base of her throat. She jumped up and sent a bottle of linseed oil skidding across the floorboards.

"You have to go *home*. You have to leave this place, while you are still able to go." Her voice sounded sharp and hollow. There was a slight echo in the high-roofed studio. "Can you *hear*, Julius?"

Julius did not take his eyes off Grace's profile. "Go home? Are you going to go home, Clio, because of what has happened tonight?"

Rafael did not move. He sat with his big hands cupped, as if they still held the whiskey glass.

"No," Clio answered. The certainty came to her as she spoke. Her voice was clearer now, more like her own. "I don't want to leave Berlin. But it isn't the same for me, is it? I'm not Julius Hirsh, the violinist. Nobody knows who I am."

"They will do," Rafael shouted. "They will know us all, by the end. We shall have to creep, and dissemble, and lie about who we are and where we come from, or else we will have to run away."

There was no contradiction. No one tried to say anything to soften or deflect the words.

After the echo of Rafael's prediction, the silence deepened around them. The rattle of raindrops on the skylight over their heads sounded unnaturally loud. Clio was reminded of the afternoons in Charlotte Street when Pilgrim had invited her to sit alone, and she had listened greedily to the disquisitions on art and spouts of Fitzrovian gossip while he dabbed at *The Janus Face*.

And of course there had been the other afternoons, opposite but not equal, when he would have made love to Grace on the sleazy divan. Then there had been Cressida, and Anthony for convenience.

Clio's anger burned up like a clear, bright flame. She could see Grace, dancing in her debutante dress, a little figure at the very heart of the flame. She turned deliberately, to see where Grace sat beside Julius. Grace held her back very straight, with her knees and ankles together, the folds of her silk skirt falling elegantly to the dirty floor. She seemed to claim Julius for her own just by sitting at his side. She absorbed all his devotion, as a bolt of perfect black velvet absorbed the light, and reflected nothing back for him.

Clio whispered, "Do you see what they have done, your Nazis? Do you see what they are going to do, to Julius and Rafael and Grete and all of us, with their uniforms and their whistles and their violence and hatred?"

Grace never flinched. Her manner was at its most coldly patrician. "They are not *my* Nazis. It would be presumptuous to claim them for myself. I expressed my admiration of the Führer, and sympathy with their economic and cultural ideals."

"With anti-Semitism, with murder and the pogrom as cultural ideals?"

"I am not anti-Semitic, Clio. How could I be?" Grace's fingers, still wearing Anthony's rings, made a small, disdainful movement. "This evening's display was ugly and disturbing. If the Führer were to hear of it, I am sure there would be an investigation and proper punishment. But it is the sad truth that at the tail end of any great political movement, there are always thugs. Left or right. Communist or National Socialist. Is that not true, Rafael?"

Julius made a sudden movement. He leaned over to Grace and put his arm around her shoulders. Then he kissed the side of her head, where the dark hair waved over her temple.

"Don't, Grace. Don't talk about this anymore. I said that it was my own mistake, and I would rather it was forgotten."

Grace closed her eyes for a second. When she opened them again, they looked very deep and brilliant. She smiled at Julius.

"Of course, if that is what you want. But I think you will see that I am right, just the same."

Clio waited for him to contradict her, but Julius said nothing. She would have shouted herself, refining the flame of her anger toward Grace like a gas jet turning from smoky yellow to blue, but Rafael warningly touched the back of her hand.

Pilgrim was slouched against his screen, watching them all in sour amusement.

"There's no more whiskey," Isolde announced. "You can have the schnapps, if you want."

"Is Julius safe here?" Grace demanded of Rafael.

"Yes, safe enough. If he's willing to stay for a few days, until the Nazis find themselves another target."

Grace's expression softened when she looked at Julius. Some of the stiffness seemed to melt out of her rigid back. "Will you do what they say? If you won't leave Berlin? Pilgrim and Isolde will look after you."

"I shall be here," Clio said coldly, but Grace ignored her.

"I have to go back to London tomorrow, Julius. I want to know that you are not in any danger."

"From Hitler and Streicher and the Jew-hating bully-boys," Clio hissed. Rafael took her hand and drew it toward him, restraining her.

"Will you do what Rafael tells you?" Grace insisted.

Wearily, Julius nodded his head. "Yes."

It was agreed that Pilgrim and Isolde would bring him food and books and newspapers, and whatever else he might need. There was no more discussion.

When the others were preparing to leave, Grace said, "I am going to stay here for a while with Julius."

Clio saw his face. It was as if the evening's humiliation had never happened.

After they had gone, Grace half knelt in front of Julius. He was still sitting in the same position, with his head bent. Grace put her hands on his shoulders, then leaned slowly forward until their foreheads touched. Their profiles seemed to reflect one another, like the Victorian paper silhouettes Grace had cut out as a girl.

"I'm sorry for this evening," Grace whispered. She could not have borne for all the rest of them to know how much it had disgusted her, but it was important to make the confession to Julius.

"It doesn't matter," Julius answered. At that moment it was the truth.

He put his fingers under her chin and tilted her face upward. Then he kissed her on the mouth, but so lightly that his lips only brushed against hers.

Grete and Rafael took Clio back to the Adlon Hotel. She was crying as they crossed Pariser Platz, and the tears left icy trails on her cheeks in the cold wind. The three of them kissed goodnight, clinging together for an instant, before the Wolfs melted away into the darkness. The concierge in his buttons and braid handed Clio in through the heavy doors. As she crossed the ornate foyer under the chandelier, she told herself, *This is the last time. Tomorrow I will find lodgings.*

The decision seemed to commit her to Berlin.

On the evening of February 27, 1933, Clio prepared dinner for Rafael in her new room. Behind a curtain in the deepest recess of the room, there was a tiny kitchen cubicle with a cold-water sink. Frau Kleber, the landlady, had drawn back the curtain with a flourish when she showed off the bedsitter to Clio.

"See! Your own cooking place. You will not have to prepare your food with Kleber and me in the kitchen downstairs, and you will be able to entertain just who you like in fine style."

Clio had ignored the broad wink, but she had taken the room. It was expensive, eighteen marks a week without board, but it was in a tranquil street in Wilmersdorf not far from Rafael's apartment. She had arranged her clothes in the creaking wardrobe and placed a few books on the shelf over the narrow bed. It was an odd place to call home, she thought, but after three days she felt more comfortable in the room than she had ever done in Gower Street with Miles.

This was the first time she had entertained Rafael. She had enjoyed an afternoon trip to the local street market to buy food and flowers, and she had spent an hour chopping vegetables and braising meat in the blistered aluminum pan provided by Frau Kleber.

When Rafael arrived, they had made love and then, laughing at his protests, Clio had climbed out of bed to heat up the dinner and set knives and forks on her rickety table. For a little while Rafael lay and watched her, but then he grew restless and turned on the new wireless that stood on the table beside the bed.

The wireless had been his housewarming present to her.

"So you will always know what is happening," he had said. "Or at least, what is happening that they want you to know about."

Clio remembered that she was polishing chipped plates when she heard the wireless announcer's report.

"The Reichstag building is on fire."

They listened to the bulletin in silence. Clio put the plates down, very carefully, in their respective places.

"We should go and look," Rafael said when the announcement was over.

"What about the dinner?" The disruption of their evening dismayed her. She felt as if huge outside events were thrusting clumsy fingers into their small world.

"We can come back and eat dinner later," he told her.

They took the U-bahn together to Potsdamer Platz, and then walked down Friedrich Ebert Strasse in the direction of the Reichstag. The street would normally have been almost deserted, but now it was crowded with people, all moving in the same direction, with their faces turned up to the night sky.

It was a dismal, rainy evening. They should have been walking in near darkness, but instead of the dark there was an ugly red glow licking the undersides of the clouds and reflecting back from the puddles. When they came closer, they saw that the whole sky above the Tiergarten was like a curtain of flames.

Clio and Rafael stopped in front of the Brandenburg Gate. The crowds were very dense, held back by cordons of police. Clio's first, startled impression was of how quiet the mass of people was. They whispered to one another, but no one shouted or waved or drew attention to himself.

She looked up at the burning building.

The great, heavy dome stood out against the dull red sky, a powerful two-dimensional black silhouette in a veil of coquettish sparks. From the windows in the square towers on the eastern side, columns of flame suddenly leaped upward, and clouds of smoke poured upward into the pall that hung over the old trees of the Tiergarten. The Reichstag on fire was beautiful, and monstrous.

Firemen had run ladders up against the wings of the building.

Their tiny black figures danced among the intricate ornaments of the roofline. In the crimson light, even the jets of water from their fire hoses looked like spurts of liquid fire.

Rafael began to shoulder his way through the crowd. Clio wormed her way behind him until they reached the ropes of the cordon. There was a man standing at the very front, staring impassively at the flames as they reached higher. Rafael shook his arm, and when the man turned, Clio recognized one of the *habitués* of the Café Josef.

"How did it start?" Rafael asked.

The man grinned sardonically, his eyebrows reaching into reddish peaks. "Arson. Marvelously well prepared, so I hear. Dozens of bottles of petrol and bundles of rags soaked in it, all stowed in strategic places, everywhere in the building. And then the man responsible ran right around and set light to them all."

"*One* man?"

"How could one man have done it?" Clio asked, bewildered.

The man's demonic smile faded. "Ask Goering how," he snapped. Then he elbowed his way past them and was swallowed up in the crowd.

Clio and Rafael stood pressed together, shifted from side to side by the movements of the mass like stones rolled by the tide. The roar of the fire was like a deep voice, and the whispers of the people sounded puny and inconsequential against it. Clio strained to hear what they were saying.

"A man has been arrested. A communist. He has confessed everything."

"They will pay for this. They must be made to pay."

Clio looked up at Rafael. She saw that his eyes glittered, reflecting the red light like everything around them.

They stood at the cordon for a long time. They were too far away to hear what he promised, or even see him inside the protection of the cordon and the ranks of his SA, but Goering had come to look at the fire. His words were, "We will show no mercy. Every communist must be shot on the spot."

At last, the fire burned lower. The ribs of the building still glowed crimson, but there were no more jets of fire.

Rafael and Clio turned away with the other onlookers and their whispers, and made their way back to Wilmersdorf.

Neither of them wanted the food that Clio had prepared. They drank the bottle of wine that she had bought and listened to the account of the burning of the Reichstag as it was broadcast.

The fire was reported as having been started by a Dutch communist named Van Der Lubbe. He had been arrested in one of the corridors of the Reichstag with a lighted torch in his hand. Although he had lost his coat and shirt, he was carrying his Party membership card in the pocket of his trousers.

Rafael leaned across and twisted the brown knob. Silence flooded back into Clio's room.

"What did your friend mean when he said, 'Ask Goering'?"

"He meant Goering is the man who will know how and why it was done."

It was very late when Rafael went home to his own apartment, but Clio knew that she would not sleep. She took a cheap exercise book out of the drawer of her table and began to write a description of what she had seen and heard.

Sixteen

THE BOUND VOLUMES OF *The Times* from 1931 to 1940 were shelved together at the far end of the room. Elizabeth took off her knitted jacket and draped it over the back of her chair, then set out her pad and pencils ready for work. She ran her forefinger along the row of tall red spines with their gilt lettering and took out the volume marked January–June 1933.

Elizabeth turned the brittle pages with great care. The library was transferring its newspaper collection to microfiche, but for the time being she could derive an almost sensual pleasure from handling the real thing. It was like holding a taut thread that stretched directly between Grace and herself.

She settled in her place, propped her chin on her hand, and began to read.

The dry, sober language of *The Times*'s reports and leaders unrolled in her head. She read the accounts of the Reichstag fire and then of the Enabling Bill that allowed Chancellor Adolf Hitler rather than President Hindenburg to rule Germany by decree. There were magisterially disapproving descriptions of the violence and intimidation practiced by the Nazis during the March 1933 election campaign, and of the persecution of Jews and boycotting of Jewish businesses throughout Germany.

Elizabeth turned forward, and backward again. Grace's name suddenly leaped out at her from the columns of newsprint. There was a report of a speech that she had made to the House in defense of freedom of opinion. She had been referring to a violent confrontation in Piccadilly Circus in which a handful of Mosley's Blackshirts, peddling anti-Semitic pamphlets, had been mobbed and threatened by an angry crowd.

Grace had been careful to disassociate herself from any taint of anti-Semitism on her part. But the newspaper had quoted her words. "I would defend to the death the right of British men, and women, to hold their own opinions, if those opinions are neither treasonable nor directly threatening to the common good."

Elizabeth's mouth curved in a smile. She picked up one of her sharp pencils and copied the report word for word on a file-index card. Her methods were slow, but they suited her well enough. She added the newspaper reference and date and slotted the card into her box. There was another bonus, too. On the very next page she discovered a Society reporter's description of a Mayfair luncheon party. Amongst the guests was "Lady Grace Brock, MP, chic as always in a taupe double-breasted jacket, finished with white piqué collar and cuffs, and a black velvet hat trimmed with a fine mesh veil."

The contrast between the two manifestations of Grace was deeply pleasing. Elizabeth hummed under her breath as she copied out the second and filed it alongside the first.

She didn't know what impulse made her turn back to the page carrying the report of Grace's speech. There was a photograph of the Piccadilly Circus incident next to the column, and she bent over it now, idly examining the faces. The Blackshirts looked very young, and surprisingly vulnerable as the wave of the crowd pressed in on them. Elizabeth was about to move on when something else caught her attention.

One of the faces belonged to a girl. She was standing a little to one side of the group, but there was no doubt of her identification with it. She was wearing a black shirt and a dark, close-fitting beret. There was even a glint of white at her throat, the photographer's flash reflecting off her party badge. Elizabeth stared at the uneasy, defiant expression. It was the expression, rather than the features themselves, that was familiar. She had seen it in the family albums that Cressida had carefully preserved. The Blackshirt girl was Alice Hirsh.

Had no one made the connection, Elizabeth wondered, between Lady Grace Brock and her cousin? There was nothing in the caption to suggest it.

She touched the girl's face with one fingertip, as if the mere contact might provide an answer. She stared at the photograph so hard that it began to dissolve into its component dots, the code becoming more impenetrable instead of offering up its secret.

There was a swimming sensation in her head. It was a familiar feeling: It came when one of the parts of her painstaking picture was dissolving, and it meant that she would have to switch the fragments around and refocus them.

Elizabeth knew the bones of Alice Hirsh's story, but that was all. But she had never heard Clio mention her. Nor, it came to her now, could she remember Cressida ever having talked much about Alice as an adult. Like the photographs in the albums, all the stories, except for the last one, had been connected with Oxford, or Stretton, when they were children.

She was suddenly certain that there was something here, some significant relationship between Grace and Alice, that she would have to pursue.

Not for the first time, Elizabeth reflected that Clio certainly knew much more than she was prepared to tell. She wondered with a touch of weariness whether it was worth making another trip to Little Venice to try to talk to the old lady again. Sometimes it was worth the effort, and then at other times Clio retreated behind a veil of almost willful senility.

"She's a very old lady," the nurses would whisper. "You can't expect too much."

Yet still Elizabeth felt suspicion stir like a twitching nerve behind her eyes. Clio seemed able to draw down the veil at will, so that the ghost of her sharp intelligence taunted Elizabeth from within its gauzy protection.

She looked for a minute longer at the newspaper picture. Alice's unhappy eyes seemed to stare directly up into her own instead of into the photographer's lens. Then she shook her head. She began to turn the pages again, once more following the thin trail of Grace's political career.

Elizabeth made another discovery on that same day.

She had been out to buy herself a sandwich and a cup of tea at the coffee bar in the next street, and had settled back into the drowsy afternoon hum of the library. She had worked her patient way through several of the other big red volumes of *The Times,* but something—perhaps Alice's mute stare—had drawn her back to January–June 1933.

This time she came across an item she had missed before. It was headed "An Eye-Witness's Account." The byline was Clio Hirsh's.

Elizabeth knew all about Clio's reports from Berlin. She knew that she had written several articles from the viewpoint of an "ordinary British observer," brief descriptions of aspects of life in the city as the Nazi grip on it tightened, all of which had been published in *The Times* over a period of a few months in 1933.

Clio had told her, in the course of one of their more lucid conversations, how it had all come about. The newspaper's editor, Geoffrey Dawson, was an old friend of Nathaniel's. He had been a frequent visitor to the Woodstock Road in the old days, and he remembered Clio as a child, then as a schoolgirl with an interest in journalism. After she had begun to work for *Fathom*, she had even met him, once or twice, within the turning circles of Fitzrovia. After some hesitation Clio had sent her Berlin stories to Mr. Dawson, and he had printed them.

Elizabeth had read the articles. They had been collected, once Clio began to make a name for herself as a writer, and published in a small volume with some others of her nonfiction pieces. There was even a copy of the book in the London Library collection, and Elizabeth had taken it down from its place on the shelf upstairs, noting that she was the first borrower in more than two years. She had read it carefully, making notes of whatever material related directly or indirectly to Grace.

But she had never seen the very first article in its original form. She read it again now, reluctantly admiring the elegance of Clio's writing. There was scope for elegance in the newspapers of those days, Elizabeth thought.

Then she closed the big volume, and sat for a moment with her wrists resting against the edge of it. The afternoon was almost over, and the other readers were beginning to drift out of the doors of the library and away across the square. It was the time of day Elizabeth liked best, when the light was fading and windows were beginning to show as cozy yellow squares.

Her discoveries were not particularly surprising; they added up to much less than a coincidence. She was unraveling the threads of Grace's career in the House, and she had known that Clio's article was there somewhere, even though she would not have bothered to search it out. It was only the sudden juxtaposition of Alice alongside the two of them that was interesting.

Elizabeth pressed the palms of her hands flat on the smooth binding. It seemed to vibrate beneath her fingers.

It was Julius who had told Clio that she must send her article to Geoffrey Dawson.

She gave it to Julius to read because he had asked her what it had been like, watching the Reichstag burn. There was no wireless in Pilgrim's studio, and Julius had spent the evening of February 27 alone, lying on the musty divan and reading *The Small House at Allington.*

"It was like this," Clio said. She took out the exercise book and handed it to him. "I couldn't sleep afterward. I kept seeing the flames against the sky and hearing the people whispering. Not shouting, or even talking, but *whispering.* I wanted to write it down not to remember it, but to . . . exorcise it."

Julius read, and then read it again. Then he had looked up at his twin with an odd expression on his face. "Now I feel as though I did see it," he said softly.

Clio blushed.

"What are you going to do with this?" Julius asked her.

"Nothing. I wrote it because I felt I needed to, that's all. Why?"

"It deserves to be published."

Clio had demurred, but in the end Julius had persuaded her.

She borrowed a typewriter from a friend of Rafael's and copied her piece out of the exercise book. Editing and retyping a manuscript brought back memories of *Fathom,* but the other world seemed very distant from Berlin. She wondered what Miles was doing and made the discovery that although she knew he had hurt her, she could no longer recall exactly what the pain had been like, as if a severe headache had melted away to leave only a raw, peeled sensation behind her eyes.

Clio had written a diffident letter to her father's old friend and sent it off with her manuscript. The response reached her with surprising speed. Her eyewitness account would appear in the newspaper, and a check for five guineas was enclosed. Mr. Dawson sent her his kind regards and indicated that if Miss Hirsh were to write any other firsthand accounts of life and events in Nazi Berlin, *The Times* would be glad to consider them.

"What did I tell you?" Julius proudly demanded.

"This is wonderful." Rafael beamed. "Now you have a proper reason to stay in Berlin. You had better take the typewriter on a more permanent loan."

"I don't need any other reason to stay in Berlin," she had protested, meaning *other than you,* but he had put his fingers to her lips.

Rafael would not make any promises or even talk about the future beyond tomorrow or perhaps the day after that. Clio understood that it was not because he would not commit himself, but simply that he could not. He did not know, any more than the other prominent Jews and political dissidents knew, whether tomorrow might be the day when the men in brown shirts would knock at his door. There were many unexplained disappearances in those days. They lived with the threat, as they lived with the beer restaurants and the Balalaika and the burned-out shell of the Reichstag, as a fact of life in Berlin.

Clio bought a ream of paper and squared it on her table beside the borrowed typewriter.

She wrote an account of election day, of the Hitler flags hanging from the windows of all the houses and the polling stations occupied by Nazis in uniform who greeted every voter wearing a swastika emblem with Heil Hitler. She also wrote about the April 1 boycott of Jewish businesses and shops, when Jewish professors were prevented from entering their lecture rooms and the windows of Jewish shops were smashed or plastered with posters reading, "Germans, defend yourselves against Jewish atrocity propaganda. Buy only at German shops!"

Mr. Dawson printed both stories, and asked for more.

Clio learned to discuss nothing but trivialities with anyone except Julius and Rafael and Grete. She fell into the habit of keeping her door locked, and of slipping out to call on Rafael only when the streets were temporarily empty of the roaming bands of Nazi auxiliary police. She learned to keep quiet, even in the company of the seemingly friendly Klebers, but to watch and listen as closely as she could to everything that went on around her.

Berlin's late spring crept up and then slowly became established. The trees in the Tiergarten came into leaf, and tables were put outside the cafés in the Kurfürstendamm and Leipziger Strasse. Julius no longer performed in public, but he continued to teach his pupils and to play in private for Clio and the Wolfs and Pilgrim. Grete introduced Clio to a Jewish laundress, laughing with such genuine amusement at the necessity to distinguish between Aryan and non-Aryan washing that Clio could only admire her generous spirit. She showed Clio the best street markets, and the dozens of little shops where Jewish retailers struggled to make a living through the Nazi boycotts, and the two women slowly became friends.

Rafael spent what time he could spare with Clio, but she knew that he had other work to do. He defended his clients within the law where it was possible, and where it was not he provided advice, whatever money he had, and sometimes a sanctuary under his own roof. Often Clio met haunted-looking men or terrified mothers with bewildered children hiding in the book-lined room. She learned to be ready to see Rafael whenever he appeared, not before, and tried not to wish for anything more.

Sometimes she saw Pilgrim and Isolde, but she was often alone. When she was not writing she listened to the wireless, or to the talk of ordinary Berliners in the streets or on the U-bahn. Her German improved by great leaps. Under Rafael's direction, she began to read Goethe and Schiller and Rilke.

The summer came.

For all the daily diet of fear and anxiety, even through the news of shootings and street violence and the rumors emanating from the Oranienburg camp not far from the city, Clio was happy. She was almost ashamed of the resonant depth of her happiness, in everyday contrast as it was with so much misery and loss. But she was deeply in love for the first time in her life, and the miracle of that overcame anything that Hitler and his people could do.

And even as life around them became increasingly extraordinary, Clio and Rafael still managed to enjoy ordinary pleasures.

They went back to the Balalaika, and soon Clio was able to understand the innuendoes and allusions in the lyrics of the cabaret songs. Rafael introduced her to his friends, beyond the shadowy clique who frequented the Café Josef, and with this group of teachers and doctors and artists they went to other nightclubs, to beer halls and to noisy little restaurants, and to one another's rooms to listen to music and to talk, endless talk that covered every topic except politics.

Nobody discussed politics. The omission shivered between them all like ice filming the surface of still water. Some but by no means all of Rafael's friends were Jews. Some of the others, Clio silently noted, had swastika flags hanging from their windows. On some evenings forbidden topics seemed to loom at the end of every avenue of talk, and on such evenings there was no choice but to make neutral conversation and to go home early to Wilmersdorf. But then, on other evenings when the beer or the schnapps flowed and Rafael smiled as he talked, with one long arm hooked over her shoulder, it seemed to Clio that there could be no better or more sympathetic company in the world than this riven group of Berliners.

They were not always surrounded by other people. There were evenings when Rafael played Mozart and Beethoven on his gramophone and held Clio in his arms under Grete's mountain pictures.

They made love tenderly, and violently, and with every nuance of expression in between. Clio learned to listen to her body as well as to her mind's dictates, and she could almost feel herself growing sleeker and more luminous with the warmth of sexual satisfaction.

This is what it is like, she told herself. She had seen the same satisfaction in Jake and Ruth at the beginning of their marriage, and in Grace and Anthony not long before Anthony's death, and she had imagined that she would always be a hungry spectator at the feast. But now, in her happiness, she felt that she was sitting at the head of the banquet table.

Clio yawned and stretched her body like a cat, covertly admiring the litheness of it. She began to look in the spotted mirror of her wardrobe as she dressed and undressed, narrowing her eyes and turning to look at the curves of her own waist and hips.

In all her hours of talk with Rafael she rarely mentioned Miles, but she did tell him about Captain Dennis and how she had imagined that she was in love with him. He laughed at the story.

"How could any man have confused your cousin Grace with you?" he wondered, lazily spanning her belly with his hand.

Clio felt a spasm of pure delight. She leaned over to kiss him, tangling her fingers in his hair to hold him where she wanted him.

"I don't know," she whispered. "It was a terrible mistake."

On warm Sunday afternoons they took to traveling by tram from Potsdamer Platz out to the Grünewald. They walked for hours through the pine trees that fringed the lakes, watching the pleasure steamers and the families picnicking beside the water. Once they took the Stadtbahn to Potsdam and admired the formal gardens of Frederick the Great's palace. Clio poked mild fun at the architectural excesses of the vast Neues Palais, and Rafael pretended to be patriotically offended.

And then, when the full heat of summer arrived, they would travel to the Wannsee to sit on a ribbon of beach with the weekend crowds of Berlin boys—who looked so harmless out of their uniforms and in their woollen bathing shorts—and their pouting girls, and the old grandmothers with rolled-down stockings showing their mottled legs, and the eddies of shrill little children. Clio was enchanted by the double beach chairs with their huge wicker hoods, and always insisted that they hire one in which to create their own private kingdom within the wide, benevolent territory of the Sunday beach.

The shade under the chair's hood made her think of the canvas pavilion that Blanche's chauffeur used to erect to protect her ladyship and her sister from the mild Norfolk sun, and of the red pennant fluttering over it, and then of the rowing boat, the *Mabel*, sawing through the North Sea swell.

In August it grew very hot. The sky turned the color of an ugly bruise and seemed to hang too low over the sweltering city. The small rented rooms and apartments were stuffy and collected the smells of mice, of food cooked in stale fat and the puddles of urine left in the doorways of Jewish shops. As she dragged herself to and fro, Clio found that she almost longed for the bone-chilling brown cold of a Berlin winter.

Rafael was tired and low-spirited. As a Jew he was now debarred from practicing the law in any public capacity, but he still worked long hours preparing cases for those of his clients who could persuade a German lawyer to act for them. He was always available to anyone who wished to consult him, and he worked endlessly on appeals against the Nazi appropriation of Jewish property and goods.

For two weeks Clio saw almost nothing of him, and then one evening he came to visit her in her room. He lay on her bed with his shirt unbuttoned in the heat, too listless even to eat the food she had prepared for him. She saw that there were gray circles under his eyes, and that the skin of his cheeks was unhealthily dry and flaky.

She sat on the edge of the bed and took his hand. "You need a holiday," she said. "Can't we go on holiday?"

Rafael frowned. He began to list the reasons why he couldn't leave Berlin, but then he looked up into her face and stopped himself.

He lifted his hand to touch the corner of her mouth, and rubbed a fingertip to smooth the anxious line that ran beside it. He was trying to memorize the planes and angles of her features, and the exact pull of elastic muscles under the smooth skin that composed her expression now, in this moment. He wanted to be able to recall her face when they were separated, when he could no longer look at her and touch her.

"What is it? What's wrong?" Clio asked, her voice sharp with sudden anxiety.

Rafael found a way to smile, to reassure her. "Nothing is wrong. Of course we can go away for a few days, if you would like that." When he thought about it, he knew that it was exactly what they must do, while they were still able. He seized on the idea now, polishing it in his mind so that it shone back at him.

"Would you like to come home with me? To Waltersroda?"

"Yes," Clio whispered.

Rafael's village was in a clearing in the Thuringian Forest. They reached it in the early evening, after a long train journey from Berlin and a bus ride through small country roads. They climbed down in the village square and watched the bus rumble away from them in a cloud of whitish dust. When it had disappeared, Clio took a deep breath of air. It tasted pure and cool, and as sweet as milk after the sour heat of the city.

The little houses around the square were built of rough stone blocks and great beams of wood. They had small windows and shutters with decorative shapes cut in the center, a different one for each house. A cluster of children played in one corner, under the eye of a brown-faced grandmother who sat on a bench with her sewing. Clio gazed around in pleasure. She realized how accustomed she had become to the massive, florid architecture of Berlin.

"It's like a picture in a storybook," she said.

There was a familiar banner draped from the gable of one of the houses. It read "*Hitler—Arbeit und Brot.*" Work and Bread.

Rafael lifted their bag onto his shoulder, carrying it like a peasant moving a bundle of wood. "My father's house is this way," he said quietly.

They took the road out of the square, down a little street lined with more of the picturesque houses. They passed groups of children, girls with blond pigtails and colored ribbons and boys in shorts and neat checked shirts, and rosy-cheeked young women wearing aprons over their print dresses. There were men coming home from the woods and fields, with knapsacks on their backs and shirtsleeves rolled up to show brawny arms.

They were fair-haired, healthy-looking people, exemplars of the Nazis' Aryan ideal.

Clio began to see Rafael in this clear rural light. He was as tall and strong and blond as any of these villagers, and she had seen at the very beginning, in the Café Josef, that he and Grete had a glow of health that made them look different from the Berliners.

She understood that he belonged here in the forest clearing, amongst the people with whom he had grown up—and yet he did not.

Some of the people who passed them greeted him. They shook

hands and smiled at Clio, and one or two of them clapped Rafael on the back, and claimed that he had deserted Waltersroda for the big city.

"Heil Hitler," they all called out as they went on their way again, and Rafael nodded courteously in return.

The last house in the village street was a cottage, with red geraniums in the window boxes. A woman came out into the garden at the side and began to throw grain to a flock of Buff Orpingtons.

"That used to be my friend Peter's house," Rafael said. "He is a Wehrmacht officer now."

The street became a little road, curving between high banks toward the edge of the forest. The fringe of trees looked dark and solid in the fading light. The roadsides were milky with Queen Anne's lace and the white tufts of old man's beard. After a little way Rafael pointed. "There," he said.

Clio saw a square house standing back from the road behind a tidy garden. The forest margin lay just beyond. There was one light showing, in a downstairs window. It seemed a lonely place.

The front door opened before they could reach it. Herr Wolf must have been watching for his son. He held out his arms as they came up the path.

"Welcome home, son," he said. "Welcome, miss."

The room was lit by paraffin lamps with sparkling glass mantles. Clio sat back in her chair to look around, now that the greetings were over.

It seemed a more prosperous home than the glimpses she had caught of the village houses. There was a mahogany sideboard with a polished silver urn standing on it, and a series of photographs in carved frames that she longed to look at more closely. Against the far wall was an upright piano, with sheet music arranged in a painted wooden box beside it. There was a woollen cloth embroidered with flowers decorating the simple wooden mantel, and a painted bookcase housing matching editions of what looked like German classics. A long-case clock with a brass pendulum ticked sonorously in the corner.

Everything was neat and well dusted, but the room felt faded, as if the furniture and the knickknacks had all been set in their places long ago and no one had had the heart or the interest to rearrange them. Leopold Wolf sat beside the tiled stove in a chair with frayed cushions. Evidently he sat in the same place every evening; the seat seemed to hold the imprint of his body. Clio and Rafael perched opposite him on a wooden-backed bench.

"And so you are English, from Oxford?" Herr Wolf asked Clio.

"Yes. My father teaches linguistics at the University."

"You must inherit from him your skill in languages. Your German is truly excellent."

Rafael's father had an old-fashioned, rather courtly manner. He spoke very quietly, as if it cost him an effort to utter even a simple sentence.

"Thank you. Rafael has been helping me."

The old man nodded. He had white hair, sparse enough on the top of his head to reveal the papery scalp beneath, and a gray-white beard trimmed to a point. He was smaller than his son and much more slightly built, and his shoulders were stooped. While Rafael talked and Clio contributed what she could, he leaned forward, listening greedily but with an air of faint bewilderment that puzzled Clio. She kept looking around, trying to imagine Rafael and Grete as boisterous children playing in this desiccated room.

It was a little time before the explanation came to her. She realized that Herr Wolf was simply unused to hearing so much talk. The house was shrouded and muffled with his loneliness. It was the old man's solitude that had bled the life out of the house, like summer's drought sucking the sap out of a felled tree.

The contrast between this house nudged against the forest wall and the memory of the Woodstock Road seemed unbearably sad. Clio suffered a pang of pity and of homesickness together that brought tears to the corners of her eyes. She blinked and stared at the dim colors of the rag rug in front of the stove.

They had been talking for an hour, or Rafael had talked while his father listened, when the old man looked at the clock.

"See the time," he said. "I must go and look to the *Abendbrot.* You will be hungry, both of you."

Rafael stood up too, stretching half a head taller than his father. He put his arm around him. "How is it here?" he asked suddenly, as if their change of position had freed him to ask the question that he had avoided before.

Herr Wolf lifted one hand, then let it fall again. *"Still, sprich durch die Blume,"* he answered.

Hush, speak through a flower.

Clio had heard the expression before. It meant, Say nothing

about the Government, or the members of the party, unless you can praise them.

"Suitable flowers are not so easy to find, these days," he added. "It is easier to say nothing at all. It is not so bad. Mostly they leave me alone."

The weight of his loneliness seemed to stifle even the monotonous ticking of the clock.

"And in Berlin?"

Rafael said, "The same."

Clio knew that in Berlin it was not the same because Jews were not left alone, but she kept her eyes on the framed photographs on the sideboard and did not speak.

Rafael's father sighed. "Some food, then," he said.

In the kitchen there were plates and cutlery laid on the scrubbed table, and a small bunch of garden flowers beside two of the place settings, but even these welcoming preparations could not dispel the impression that this room, and the other, and all the house had been frozen years and years ago, and that nothing would happen now to thaw the ice and set warm life in motion again.

They sat down at the table and ate thick soup and cold ham and pickled cabbage, and salty local cheese.

"This is good," Clio said, and Herr Wolf smiled at her. She saw Rafael in him, then.

"My wife was a fine cook," he told her. "Known beyond Waltersroda, in the old days. I learned from her, but I have only one hundredth of her skill."

Rafael laughed. "As much as a hundredth?" Then the glow from the yellow lamps seemed to catch their faces, and they were all smiling at one another, and Herr Wolf lifted his glass.

"To happier times," he said.

They drank, but Clio knew that they were celebrating times that had gone, without the hope that they could ever come again.

Rafael put his glass down. He reached across the table and rested his hand on his father's arm. "Won't you come to Berlin?" he asked gently. "To stay with Grete or me, not to live if you don't want that, but to let us look after you for a while?"

Clio felt that it was a question that had been put often enough before.

"I need looking after? Miss here says that my food is good. What could you do better in Berlin?"

"You know what I mean."

Leopold Wolf inclined his head. "I know what you mean. I can't leave here. Not now, to go to a city I am too old to understand. This is where I belong."

The forest stretched behind its dark margin only a few yards beyond the house wall, and in this clearing in the trees lived the healthy, fair-haired country people who were Herr Wolf's neighbors, with their banners and their cheerful Heil Hitlers. This place with its mild, sweet air was a long way from the huge brown city of uniforms and swastika flags, but it wore the same German face. Rafael's father was alone here; she did not know whether he was any safer than he would be in Berlin.

Clio wanted to press herself closer to Rafael, to hold him and never to let him go. The strength of the impulse alarmed her, and to subdue it she stood up and began quietly to gather up the dirty plates.

When they were washed and dried and stacked in their places on the wooden shelf, Rafael's father lit his pipe and sat down at the table to smoke it. Clio left the two men alone, and slipped back into the other room. She stood at the sideboard and looked down at the framed photographs. There was one of Grete and Rafael as children, sitting on a felled tree trunk in a woodland clearing, and another of a woman with a calm, pale face. She looked like Grete, with the same high forehead and a crown of hair piled on top of her head.

In the center, in pride of place, was a sepia-tinted print of a straight-backed young couple. The girl was wearing a full-skirted dress and a laced bodice, and there were wreaths of flowers in her hands and in her long hair. The man wore an embroidered shirt and held a broad-brimmed hat with flowers tucked into the band. It was the Wolfs' wedding picture. Clio turned away and began to study the titles of the books ranged on their shelf instead. She was sitting on the cushioned bench, reading, when Rafael and his father came to find her.

At bedtime, carrying her candle for her, Herr Wolf himself escorted Clio up the stairs to her bedroom door. He opened it courteously and put the candlestick down on the night table.

"I am glad that Rafael brought you here," he said. "I see few people nowadays. I hope you will sleep comfortably, Miss Hirsh."

"I shall, in this quiet place."

The room had been Grete's. There was a wooden-framed bed, painted with flowers that had been almost rubbed away, and covered with a patchwork quilt. The sheets were linen, fragrant-smelling but worn thin with many years of use.

Clio lay down and listened to the sounds of the house. Beyond these bare walls Rafael was lying too, in his boyhood bedroom. As she drifted into sleep she thought of him, wrapped in the familiarity of the house as if in a quilt made of a patchwork of memories.

That night Clio dreamed of flowers and trees, and columns of marching men.

They stayed in Waltersroda for three days. They walked in the forest, following ancient footpaths through the huge groves of oak and beech, where the smallest rustle of a bird in the undergrowth was amplified in the cathedral silence and the thick felt of dead leaves muffled the sound of their footsteps. Rafael knew every path, and the glass-clear streams where they refilled their leather water bottle, and the names of the birds and the unambitious creeping plants of the forest floor.

They saw no one, except in the distance the foresters in their gray-green clothes.

Clio loved the great smooth gray pillars of the trees and the canopy of shifting green knitted over their heads. The sunlight slanted obliquely across their path, with the impatient heat filtered out of it, always directing her eyes to some different miniature landscape of moss and leaf. She felt calm and strong in the forest, as if some of its endurance had entered into her soul.

It also made her happy to see Rafael here. She began to understand how the quiet but implacable power of the place had shaped him and had given him and Grete the distinction that she sensed when she saw them for the very first time in the Café Josef.

Once they came out into a swath of open space where the woodsmen had cut a stand of trees. Clio turned her face up, closing her eyes in the sudden warmth and brightness. Then a shadow blocked the sun again, and when she looked, she saw that it was Rafael, standing close. He came closer still, putting his hands on the lapels of her jacket and drawing her against him. When he kissed her, she felt a white shaft of happiness passing through her like the blade of a sword.

Clio said, "I love your woodlands."

Rafael smiled at her, and she was too dazzled to see the sadness in him. "Who could be happy for long anywhere it is not possible to enjoy the rest and comfort of trees?"

She saw then that the clearing was not empty. It had been replanted, and the saplings stood in neat, straight lines, reaching up to the sun. The little trees seemed to offer the most potent symbol of hope for the future.

"All will be well again, someday," she whispered.

"I hope so," was all he could offer her in return.

They walked on, out of the clearing and into the holy dimness of the forest once again.

At night, after they came home to Waltersroda, they would sit with Rafael's father over a simple meal. Clio listened to the two men talking. Most of their talk was concerned with reminiscences, of Rafael's boyhood and then further back to Leopold's own childhood, and the slow country rituals of another century. His voice lost its unused timbre as he told them about the harvests and wedding parties and festivals of fifty years ago, and he filled their glasses with more beer and the atmosphere in the little house became almost celebratory. Clio loved the stories. She took them away inside her head and used them to piece together her own picture of Rafael and the people he had come from. She felt closer to him, as if they fitted more nearly, than she had done in all their time in Berlin.

"This is dull for you, miss," Leopold said once.

"No. I want to hear everything," she answered.

The old man turned to Rafael. "You are lucky," he said. He lifted his glass to them both.

On their last morning in Waltersroda, Clio knew that the muffling silence was descending on the house again. It lay in the corners of the rooms whence their talk had driven it for a few hours.

Leopold came to the front door with them and opened it cautiously, but he did not step onto the path. He kissed Rafael, and took Clio's hand between both of his. "You will come again," he told her, as a simple prediction.

"Won't you come to Berlin instead?" she begged. "For their sake?"

He shook his head. "I am too old to go anywhere now," he answered.

They were going to catch the bus again from the village square. Rafael picked up their bag and hoisted it onto his shoulder, and his father stood in the doorway, half shielded by the door itself, to watch them go. As he had watched for their arrival, Clio remembered.

They stopped at the bend to wave, but he had already retreated into the cover of his house. She felt the silence, pressing inward in her head. They waved in any case, feeling his eyes on them from behind the sun-streaked curtains.

"Couldn't you come home to him, then?" she asked Rafael

when they passed the house with the Buff Orpingtons, where his friend had once lived.

"I am more use in Berlin," Rafael said quietly. "There are worse evils for Jews now than the solitude of old age."

"He is your *father.*"

Rafael looked at her, but he didn't slacken his pace. "Do you think I don't remember that?"

He was as implacable, she thought, as one of his forest oaks. There would be no dissuading him, once he had fixed his intention.

It was not until they were in the motorbus and on the winding road that he turned to her. "Don't be angry with me," he said. "We still have two days."

"I'm not angry," Clio answered. She let her head rest against his shoulder. She was thinking about the healthy, strong people in Waltersroda and the warning, speak through a flower. "There is so much fear. Even in this beautiful place."

"There will be more, too. More than we can even begin to comprehend, before this is over."

Her own happiness and the threat of what was to come seemed to shiver in the balance on an edge between light and dark.

"What can we do?"

Rafael touched her cheek and her hair. "Be happy while we can. What else?"

He took her to the wooded ridge of mountains called the Thüringer Wald, rising steeply from Thuringia and then falling away in a series of gentle foothills toward Franconia. They stayed in a wooden-floored room in a quiet inn, with a brass bed and a feather mattress to envelop them.

Their three nights apart seemed a long time, now, when they reached for each other again.

Clio had never felt so greedy for him, even at the beginning of their time together. They made love over and over again, reaching and stretching to come closer, for the satisfaction of possessing each other more completely. She sat astride him under the white-washed beams of the little bedroom, leaning down to kiss his mouth until her own felt bruised, like damaged fruit, then twisting above him until he reached up to grip her waist, and held her, and drove up into her as she gasped and gave a sudden, sharp cry like one of the invisible animals in the wood.

Afterward they lay hip to hip, silent except for the rasp of their own breath, looking into each other's eyes as if they could climb into the depths inside and make them their own.

"I love you," Clio said on the last night. "I want to stay with you forever."

"I love you," he told her. "Take a day, and a night, and then the next day, and the night after that, if it should come. Don't look any further than that, because it is impossible to see."

She was comfortable in his arms, and already beginning to drift into sleep. She smiled, and he kissed the corner of her mouth.

"I am happy just with tonight," she murmured.

In the morning they ate the last country breakfast at a table in the inn garden. There were eggs and brown bread and smoked sausage and cheese, honey and jam, set out on flat pieces of scoured white wood instead of plates. Afterward they walked to the bus in the yellow sunlight. They caught the Berlin express from Blankenburg, and by the evening they were in Wilmersdorf again. When they turned into Clio's street, they saw that Hitler flags were hanging from the upper windows of the Klebers' house.

Fear squeezed Clio's heart, twisting it in her chest, and she knew that she was right to be afraid of this violent blush of Nazism that colored Berlin with its insignia and shone in the bright faces of the villagers of Waltersroda.

"Rafael, can't we leave Berlin? Leave Germany? You could come to London, or to Oxford, and bring Grete and your father, while there is still time. . . ."

As she had known he would, Rafael answered, "No. I am needed here. But perhaps you should go home, to your mother and father, where you will be safe."

"I can't leave you," Clio said.

Rafael was still looking up at the flags, hanging limp against the dusty glass.

Two nights after their return, Clio was sitting alone at the wobbly table in her room writing about Waltersroda when Frau Kleber called up the stairs to her.

"Fräulein Hirsh? You are at home? There is a visitor here to see you."

She stopped typing at once. She pushed her chair back and ran to open the door, smiling with the anticipation of seeing Rafael. She had not been expecting him, but his appearances were often unpredictable. The stairs outside her room were dark and descended steeply, but Rafael knew the way. She leaned happily on the smooth wooden rail of the banister, looking down for the first sight of his blond head as he climbed up to her. But there was no one there.

"Fräulein Hirsh!" Frau Kleber was not particularly patient. She must be waiting down by the street door.

Clio clicked on the landing light. It was harsh and bright under a white glass shade. She ran down the angle of the stairs, from where she would be able to see Frau Kleber in the hallway with her visitor.

She swung around the corner, still smiling, looking forward to seeing who it could be.

At the first glimpse, Miles's upturned face was so familiar that she felt no surprise. It was only a minute afterward that shock spread up from her stomach, cold and clammy like a sickness.

He was wearing his greenish tweed coat, as if he had just stepped out to the Fitzroy, but there was a portmanteau beside him that she did not recognize.

Clio began to shake. As she descended toward him, she wondered if her knees would support her. She was aware of Frau Kleber's eyes, sharp with malicious curiosity.

"Hello, darling," Miles said, using his boyishly charming manner that now seemed as false as the female impersonator in the Balalaika. "There was some confusion with your landlady here, who insisted that she didn't know any Mrs. Lennox. You don't look very happy to see me, by the way."

"Miles."

He kissed her, and she had to fight the impulse to break away from him and run away into the street.

"Frau Kleber, this is my husband."

"I did not know you were a married lady, Frau Hirsh." Clio did not like the Frau's expression.

"No." She turned to Miles and said in English, "I suppose you had better come up, now you are here."

As they climbed the stairs Frau Kleber called after her, "This is a house for single ladies, Frau Hirsh. That is how Herr Kleber prefers it. Gentlemen visitors once in a while he perhaps does not notice, but we cannot have husbands taking residence."

Clio said in a cold voice, "That is quite all right. He is only making a short call."

When they reached her room she closed the door and leaned against it, as if she could keep the malign effect of her husband contained within four walls. The sight of Miles in his green coat brought back the memory of Gower Street, his chair with the ashtray on the arm, the spread-out manuscript pages, their table and bed and all the accretions of their married life together. The flat had been sold and her own possessions packed and stored— kind and capable Tabby had overseen that for her—but Miles's presence carried the unhappy images of those years like a pene- trating smell.

He had put down his bag in the middle of her floor, and now he hung his coat over the back of a chair and coolly examined the room. He flicked the sheet of paper rolled into the typewriter, and cocked his head to read the titles of the handful of books on the shelf.

"Quite the artist's garret." He could not resist sneering at her.

"What do you want, Miles?"

"I've seen some of your stuff in *The Times*. It's quite good."

"How did you find me?"

Miles was grinning. "What did the old bat downstairs say? Gentlemen callers, was it? Is that what's keeping you here in Berlin?"

She hadn't known he understood so much German. Clio found the steel to confront him. "So what if it is?"

He retreated then, lifting one hand in a warding-off gesture. "Just a question. I met Partridge in Old Compton Street, and he gave me Pilgrim's forwarding address." Partridge was Pilgrim's London agent. "When I got off the train I called in at that studio of his. Pilgrim was busy daubing at some filthy canvas, and he was happy to send me on here."

That sounded like Pilgrim.

"And so what do you want?" Clio asked again.

"Do you have anything to drink?"

"No. Or yes, there's some beer." She gave it to him and sat down at the table, waiting. Miles perched on the edge of her bed, rolling the glass between his hands, and then he began to talk.

Clio listened to the words of his story, quicksilver little words that were polished in the telling in Miles's droll way, but she could also hear the dull and unpleasant weight of reality behind them. He had found a room to live in after he had been obliged to leave Gower Street, but he had managed to borrow money from his landlord and then failed to pay any rent, and the trickle of writing commissions had temporarily dried up. There had been no more money, and then there had been an incident.

Miles wiggled his fingers in the air, as if the incident had been comical, but Clio knew that it was not. There would have been drink and some violent outburst, and an aftermath that made her scalp tighten across her skull with the effort not to imagine it. Miles would have decided, or perhaps it had been decided for him, that it was a good idea to leave London. He had cast around for a suitable refuge, and had come up with Berlin, and Clio.

At the end of the story he smiled at her. It was a whimsical smile that she remembered very clearly. It made her sick to realize that she had once found it so charming. In that minute she saw her husband complete and whole, as she had never been able to see him before, and understood that he was helpless.

"How much do you want?" she asked.

Miles looked wounded. "It isn't money. Well, actually it is, but I wouldn't ask you for that. It's you I need."

He let the fey mask slip a little, or tried to give her the impression that it slipped. In either case, she knew it was no less than the truth. He did need her. He needed her as a shield, and a cushion.

Clio remembered the pendulum swings of his mood between elation and depression, and the blackness that had engulfed him at the lowest points. He had wept and clung to her. After one of those black fits, he had first made love to her, and she had held him in her arms and convinced herself that she could take care of him. As she had done, for more than four years. Miles had been much cleverer than she, and was no less clever now.

"You are my wife," he said. There was a threatening edge in the wheedling tone that made her pity him less.

"I want to divorce you."

"Divorce? My darling, I have *never* believed in divorce. I couldn't agree to it." And now there was triumph, suppressed but still glinting in the corners of his eyes.

Clio kept her voice steady. She had found him in her bed, lying beside a male whore with black fingernails. There was no cause for the mush of pity or sympathy.

"Then don't agree to it. But I am not your wife any longer."

There was a little silence. "That is very harsh."

"What did you expect?"

Miles hunched his shoulders. His beer glass was empty. "I know. I haven't the right to expect anything. But do you think I'm happy to be the way I am? Pleased, or proud?"

He was playing a role, of course, as he always was, wheedling for her sympathy now, yet Clio understood that there was a seam of honesty in the sham.

"No, I don't suppose you are. What can I do?"

He took her intended disclaimer and deftly flipped it. "You can let me stay for a little while, now that I'm here."

"You can't stay. You heard Frau Kleber."

"I didn't mean in this room. I wouldn't expect that, after what you saw. But I could find somewhere nearby, couldn't I? Or even a hotel, a cheap one?"

Clio summoned all the brutality she could muster. "It would have to be cheap. Since I'll be paying for it, I suppose."

"I can stay, then?"

Wearily she answered, "Do I have a choice?"

It was hateful to think of Miles in Berlin, weaving himself like a discolored thread into her life here. But he had come, and he had been her husband for three years, and she couldn't unpick that. Looking back at the past months, she felt that she had been covering over the wound that she had left behind in London, and now it was time to open it up and cauterize it.

Miles stood up and poured more beer into his glass. He was pleased to have insinuated himself. "Some for you?"

"No, thank you."

He strolled to the window and looked down into the suburban street, as if gauging its potential for him. Then he turned back and leaned against the corner of the table so that he could look down at her.

"Who are the gentlemen callers? Am I allowed to know?"

Clio took a breath before she answered. "There is one caller, as you put it. He is a friend of Julius's. And my lover, now." There, the truth. It was easier than she had imagined.

Miles's eyebrows made inquiring peaks. He looked amused, even indulgent. "A German?"

"Of course."

"Not a *Nazi,* I hope."

"I will introduce you. Then you can judge for yourself."

They would have to meet. She couldn't hope to hide Miles from Rafael, nor would she want to try. *Cauterization,* she reminded herself.

"I shall look forward to it," Miles said.

"I think you should go now," Clio told him. The beer was all gone; she wanted her room to herself, so she could think.

Miles had got his own way, and was prepared to be amenable in everything else. Clio gave him some marks, and directions to a hotel in a nearby street.

"Until tomorrow," he promised. He kissed her, and she held herself very still until he had removed his hands again. When she opened the downstairs door to let him out into the street, she knew that Frau Kleber was watching from her lair.

Rafael and Miles met at a pavement-café table. It was not one of the big cafés on the Kurfürstendamm or Friedrichstrasse, because Jews no longer frequented the main thoroughfares in case of attracting the attention of the SA or auxiliary police. The café was a small, ordinary place on a corner in the Altstadt, with a handful of tables placed outside under a faded awning.

Miles was sitting reading an English newspaper, but he looked up as Clio and Rafael crossed the street. It was the beginning of September, and noticeably cooler. A slight breeze lifted Miles's fine hair and ruffled it over his forehead.

"Rafael Wolf, Miles Lennox," Clio said, and they shook hands.

Rafael had listened carefully when Clio told him that Miles was in Berlin.

"I am still his wife," she finished. "In law, if nothing else. And he is so helpless. It is his helplessness, at the root of everything, that means I have to help him."

"What do you want to do?" he asked her.

Clio considered. "I . . . know how clever and how devious Miles can be. He likes to manipulate people, and it might amuse him or suit him to manipulate us. Or me, rather. To make me feel that I should in some way conceal him from you, or pretend about him in some other way, and so create an untruth between us. He is inquisitive about you. I want you to come with me to meet Miles, so that it is you and I who are one, and not Miles and I. So that there are no secrets. Would you mind that very much?"

Rafael had laughed. "Why should I mind? Of course I will meet him, if that is what you want. Only don't expect me to like him. From what you have told me, I don't think I shall."

It was as simple as that. Clio was still amazed by how clear and simple Rafael could make matters that seemed to her to be shadowed and complicated. He was neither jealous nor possessive, and she loved him for it. It was only the perversity of her own nature that made her long to be possessed, and to be able to look into the future beyond tomorrow, or the day after that.

And so Clio and Rafael sat down at the little metal-topped table, and Miles signaled to the waiter. He brought them coffee and schnapps, and Clio was amused by the thought that they looked like any trio of friends meeting for a drink and an exchange of the wary talk that passed for gossip in Berlin now.

The sun was bright on the opposite windows, and it was pleasant under the shelter of the awning. A little tongue of happiness licked up inside Clio. Even Miles couldn't affect her here. She watched him, as he leaned back with his foot on the opposite chair. He looked rested and cheerful, just a neat-featured man in a shirt with a worn soft collar.

There was nothing to be afraid of, because she was with Rafael and Miles couldn't hurt her any longer.

They drank their coffee and listened to Miles's tourist's impressions of Berlin. Clio leaned closer to Rafael, and he took her hand and folded it under his arm. That was all. Love welled up inside her like spring water.

"What are your plans?" Rafael asked Miles.

"To stay here for a little while. To have a rest, perhaps. I have been working on a book for a long time, and it's almost completed now." Miles's manner was confiding, almost flirtatious.

"Clio told me about your book."

Miles darted a look at her. "Clio has been very kind to me."

"And to me also," Rafael said.

"Kindness is a fine attribute in a wife." He was as delicate as a cat, but the implication was plain. *My wife.*

"And in a husband too, I imagine."

Miles inclined his head. He turned his coffee cup a half-circle on its saucer, then asked, "Do you think I should take a trip out to Grünewald? For a steamer ride?"

"If you like lakes and steamers and pine trees, why not?"

Clio saw sunlight dancing all the way along Garnisonstrasse. She wasn't afraid of Miles. The wound would be cauterized, and then it would heal over completely.

They sat under the awning for perhaps an hour, until Rafael announced that he must take Clio away because they were expected somewhere else. There was nothing left for Miles to do but to stand up, shake hands, and peck Clio on the cheek.

"I'll look in to see you tomorrow," he called after her.

"If I'm at home."

She turned the corner with Rafael, and they walked on arm in arm.

"Thank you," she said at length.

He smiled. "I am glad to have met him."

"What did you think?"

"I thought he was like a butterfly. One of those velvety-brown ones with pretty markings. And about as substantial."

They came to the Spree and turned to stroll beside it. The water was gray flecked with blue, and there were dabs of foam on it that made Clio think of waves in the sea.

"He says that he won't divorce me."

Rafael stopped walking. He took her face between his hands and looked down into it.

"I want to marry you."

Clio stood still.

"But if I can't, it doesn't make any difference. I love you as much and in the same way. Your poor butterfly doesn't stand in the way of that."

"Do you really want to marry me?" She was minutely conscious of the river and the stone walls, the little bridges with their high backs to accommodate the barge traffic beneath, and the tall brown buildings with their blank eyes.

"Yes, I do. I would marry you tomorrow, if I could."

The simplicity of it. The intricate, breathtaking mesh of loving and being loved. Clio took his hands and gripped them until her fingernails dug into his flesh. The intensity of her sudden determination made her voice harsh.

"Rafael, I want us to leave Berlin. I want us to go away from here, to England, or to France, to anywhere you like, but away from Germany. I have never been happy in my life like this and I won't let it go. If we stay here . . ."

He loosened his hand from her grasp and put his arm around her shoulder, drawing her face closer to his.

Rafael knew what would happen to him if he stayed in Berlin. It could only be a matter of time before the men in uniform came for him as they had come for the others, those he knew and the hundreds more that he did not. There was still work for him to do here and now amongst those who were robbed of their homes and their livelihoods by the Nazis, but he would be no more use to anyone once he was in prison or in a camp.

For days, Rafael had been debating with himself whether to leave Berlin or to stay until the inevitable happened. To leave would be to run away, he had no doubt of that, but if he did leave, there would be some hope for himself and Clio, and the possibility that he could make himself useful elsewhere. The argument went around and around in his head, but he had come no closer to resolving it.

He had said very little to Clio about his anti-Nazi work, because he believed that the less she knew, the safer she would be. But it was hard not to be able to share his dilemma with her. He saw her intent face now, and her struggle with herself not to exert too much selfish pressure on him, and he knew how much he loved her.

For an instant, then, the decision seemed simple.

"We'll go," he whispered, before the moment of clarity deserted him. "If you want it so much."

The sun seemed to swing over Clio's head, making a dizzy arc in the slot of sky as they held each other.

"I want to go home, to your apartment. Now, this minute. Please, Rafael."

"There is the U-bahn," Rafael said.

A handful of days went by. In a blaze of happiness Clio told Julius, and Pilgrim and Isolde, and Miles himself that she would be leaving Berlin soon, with Rafael.

"That is the best news," Julius said. "The best possible news." Clio shone with a kind of delight that he had never seen in her before. It made him feel dry and brittle by comparison.

"Come too. Come back to London," she begged him.

"I might, soon. Not just yet." The effort of removing himself from Berlin seemed too great. He had his familiar routines of practice and teaching—even if he could no longer perform in public—and the seclusion of his rooms, and the solitude of his life in the wary city suited him. He could think of nowhere else he particularly wanted to be.

Clio noticed his lethargy, and worried about it, but she knew that Julius was not to be persuaded against his will.

"You should come home," she repeated, but Julius only nodded and smiled absently.

Pilgrim told her, "You are right to get out of Germany. It begins to be oppressive, as well as dangerous. I don't mind a little danger, but I can't bear gloom. Isolde and I have been talking about Paris."

"Paris, why not?" she agreed absently.

Clio was ashamed of their desertion. She knew that she was making Rafael leave the place where he was needed, but she was also certain that there was nothing else they could do. Almost every day they heard news of Jews who were leaving or had already left.

The reports of arrests for "fighting with storm troopers" or "consorting with German girls" and the unexplained disappearances were so common that they no longer remarked on them. Now that the decision was made, she felt a feverish anxiety to be away that she had to struggle to suppress. Rafael was making his own arrangements, and she tried not to hurry him. He was worried about Grete and his father, and about the vulnerable people he would be leaving behind.

At the Klebers' house she packed her books into a box, addressed it to the Woodstock Road, and took it to the Parcel Post Office in Oranienburg Strasse. She put the cover on the borrowed typewriter and returned the machine to Rafael's friend.

"You are leaving Berlin?" Frau Kleber asked her.

There was no point in denying it. "Not yet, but soon. I'm not sure when. Please don't worry. I shall be quite happy to pay extra rent if you think the notice is too short."

"I have heard about many people who are going away," Frau Kleber said. Clio felt her sly, appraising glance. There was none of the friendliness that there had been when Clio first moved in. Frau Kleber was trying to gauge exactly what she was harboring under her roof and just how un-German, how Jewish, the foreign girl might be.

"You are going back to London with your husband?"

"Back to London," Clio answered, and slipped away into the street rather than stay in the house under the woman's scrutiny.

"So you will be in London, and I shall be here." Miles only laughed when she told him. Berlin had done him good. His veneer of charm and capability seemed to be intact again. "What about your handsome Jewish boyfriend?"

Clio met his eyes. "Lover. Let's not be euphemistic. Rafael will come too. Are you going to stay on?"

"If you could lend me a little money. I feel that I can write here."

That was the price, then.

"How much money?"

Miles named a sum, and she offered him half of it, as though they were haggling over a carpet in a bazaar. *That was my marriage,* she thought. They reached an agreement without much difficulty.

"I wish you luck," Miles said, after he had taken her marks.

Clio focused her thoughts on England. She had begun to feel that she had been away for a very long time. She planned how she would take Rafael home to Nathaniel and Eleanor in Oxford, and then how they would find another flat in London. She would work;

perhaps there would be something else she could do for Geoffrey Dawson, or maybe she could go back to Max Erdmann at *Fathom*. Rafael could do some legal work; they would live an ordinary life together, ordinary people.

It was the middle of September. On the last morning she was still asleep, for some reason sleeping much later and more heavily than she usually did, when Frau Kleber rapped at her door.

"Someone downstairs for you," the woman called out. Even through the thick confusion of sudden waking, Clio could hear her displeasure. She crept out of bed and put on her robe, rubbing out a yawn with the back of her hand.

There was a man standing in the brown hallway, looking up, in exactly the same spot where Miles had waited for her before. Frau Kleber policed him, with her arms folded.

It took Clio a moment to recognize him. Even then, she couldn't remember his name. He was just one of the shadowy men from the Café Josef.

Slowly a kind of realization dawned in her. She stood still, shivering, on the bottom stair. The realization was so terrible that she couldn't meet it. The warmth of her bed drew her back. She must hide in it, retreat into sleep again.

"Please come," the man said. "It is important you come."

The linoleum under her bare feet felt like ice.

Without a word, Clio turned and ran up the stairs. She fought her way into her clothes, tearing her nails and jerking her hair in her haste.

When she came down, the man was waiting for her in the street. There was a thin mist under the whitish sky, and the leaves of the suburban trees were beginning to brown and curl. It would soon be winter again.

They began to walk, so fast that it was almost a run. Clio waited until they had turned the corner out of sight of the Klebers' house. Then she snatched at the man's arm. "What is it? Where is he?"

The man looked at her, pitying and fearful. He had a thin, undernourished face. "They came for him."

Grete was already at the apartment. She was sitting on the end of the bed, wrapped in an old coat, with her hair loose over her shoulders. She was crying.

Clio looked around her. She saw that Rafael had begun to take his books off the shelves, ready to be packed up. Two of Grete's blue and green forest landscapes were propped up against the wall, leaving dusty rectangles where they had once hung. This place that had once been warm and safe had never felt so empty and cold.

One of the chairs had been pushed aside; there were no other signs of a struggle. The memory came back to Clio of the first time in the Café Josef, and Heinrich's story of Herr Keller the lawyer. Grete and Rafael had come in as he was telling it.

A terrible panic washed through her. She stumbled, and knelt beside Grete at the foot of the bed. "Where have they taken him? *Where?*"

Grete shook her head. Her mouth was distorted with her sobbing. "I don't know. It could be Alexanderplatz. Or one of the brown houses. Or Oranienburg, or Dachau."

Anywhere.

"What can we do?"

There was no answer. The room was utterly silent except for Grete's weeping.

Very slowly, Clio reached up and put her arms around her. They clung together, motionless, in the silence.

Seventeen

IN THE FIRST-FLOOR DRAWING ROOM of Grace's house in Vincent Street, Alice replaced the telephone receiver in its cradle. She stood for a moment looking intently at her reflection in a gilt-framed looking glass that hung over the console table. Then she shrugged and went downstairs to the small room off the hall that Grace used as her study. Alice sat down in her chair and drew a message pad toward her. There were flowers on the desk, arranged yesterday in a little malachite vase by Alice herself. She wrote quickly, setting out the gist of the message that Clio had given her. Then she tore the sheet of paper off the pad and set it neatly in the center of the blotter. Grace was at a committee meeting and could not be disturbed, but she would see the note on her desk as soon as she came in.

Cressida was downstairs in the kitchen, sitting with one of her story notebooks open in front of her. "Who telephoned?" she asked, as soon as Alice appeared.

"It was Clio," Alice answered briefly. Cressida's eternal questions made her impatient, and she was in a hurry.

"From Berlin?"

"No, not from Berlin. From Jake's house. She's back in London, and she wants to speak to Grace urgently."

"What about?"

"*I* don't know. I didn't ask. Is there anything else you want to know? Because I have to go in a minute."

"Got to polish your badge? Or hand out some anti-Jew leaflets?"

"It's none of your business," Alice said sourly. She gathered up her handbag and gloves and banged out of the room. To live with Grace was important, even essential, but being close enough to Grace meant existing in the same proximity with Cressida.

The two girls didn't like each other any the better for the amount of time they had to spend together.

Alice let herself out of the front door. She was not going far, only to the party headquarters in the King's Road. It was not always comfortable, being there, because the other party workers were wary of her, and there was sometimes nothing for her to do. But Alice was very determined. If she waited long enough, she was usually given some sort of task, and however menial it was, she did it with great care and attention. And there was always the chance that she would see the Leader, even that he would stop to talk to her. That made any amount of tedious clerical work worthwhile.

As soon as Alice was gone, Cressida slipped into the study and read the note. It told her no more than Alice herself had done, but she had wanted to make sure. Cressida liked all her Hirsh cousins except for Alice, and she was particularly fond of Clio. It was good news that she was back in London.

Nanny was in the kitchen, looking for her. "There you are, dear. Have you had enough breakfast? Would you like me to make you some toast?"

Cressida thought longingly of hot buttered toast and jam, but she said firmly that she was not hungry. Cressida had turned thirteen a month before, and she was determined to get thin. Not for reasons of vanity, she assured herself; there was enough vanity in the house with Alice forever fiddling with her face-powder and her hair and her black beret. But Grace set great store by slimness, and Cressida wanted to achieve it just to prove to her mother that she could.

"You'll waste away," Nanny said comfortably. "Give me a hand with these plates, ducky, will you? Miss Alice has gone and left everything, as usual."

Across London, in Jake's house in Islington, Clio was also sitting in the kitchen. She was nursing a cup of cold coffee and talking to Ruth. Ruth was still in her dressing gown, a dark blue woollen one that she wore tightly belted over her nightgown and that showed the accumulation of weight on her stomach and buttocks. Her dark springy hair was streaked with gray.

Ruth clattered the breakfast dishes in the stone sink. Jake had gone to his surgery, and the two children were at Hebrew class. Ruth had become defiantly more orthodox of late.

"You look terrible," Ruth said in her old, blunt way.

"It's that sleeper," Clio said. "I never do sleep."

She had arrived from Berlin the previous afternoon. It was true that she had not slept on the train journey, but she had hardly slept either on any of the nights since Rafael had disappeared.

"What did milady Grace have to say?" Ruth asked.

"She wasn't there. I left a message with Alice."

Clio rested her head in her hands. She was overwhelmed by the weight of her own helplessness. In Berlin, in the terrible days after Rafael had gone, she had circled from the Café Josef to every one of the friends that Rafael had introduced her to, around and around, begging for any information or advice that might give her a crumb of hope. All she knew was that "a friend" had telephoned Josef to say that Rafael had been seen in the first light of that morning, being led away by the brownshirts. He had been coatless and bareheaded. She could find out nothing else. No one knew or no one would say, and she couldn't fathom which. The utter blankness terrified her. It was as if he had never existed.

With Grete and Julius she had waited, in desperation at first and then as the days passed with the cold beginnings of understanding. They could ask what they liked, but there would be no answers. Questions did no more than draw attention to themselves.

"I don't know," Josef said. He looked less like the expansive Stulik of the Eiffel nowadays. "Who knows anything? He could be anywhere. We can only wait, Fräulein."

After a week, Clio could bear it no longer.

"I'm going back to London," she told Grete. "I know people, important people. If I can't do anything for him here, I might be able to do it in London."

She had packed and removed her belongings under the eye of Frau Kleber. Grete and Julius had come with her to the Bahnhof Zoo to see her off. They had hugged one another on the platform.

"If you hear anything," Clio begged, with tears running down her cheeks. "Promise me?"

"I promise," Grete said.

Julius stood and waved, a tall, gaunt man in clothes that were too loose for him. Clio watched, leaning from her window until she could no longer see them.

Ruth sat down opposite her now. There were crumbs on the front of her dressing gown. She took Clio's hand and held it. "What do you think Grace can do for your friend?"

"Rafael is an innocent citizen. He can't be arrested and held for nothing, for no reason. I want Grace to ask a question in the House."

Ruth half-smiled. "Grace admires Hitler. Do you think she will put herself out politically on behalf of some German Jewish lawyer, even though you are in love with him? Particularly if you are in love with him?" Ruth's tongue was no less sharp than it had ever been.

"I don't know," Clio whispered. "I have to try everything, don't I?"

She stood up abruptly and walked around the table. Grace was too close, she could feel the painful chafing of all the links between them, buried in their history further back than she could remember. They had parted in Berlin on dangerous ground. Clio would have to cross the ground again now, finding some stepping stones to reconciliation, to make Grace help her.

What else was there to do?

"I'll ask whoever else I can. There's the editor of *The Times*. Uncle John Leominster, the House of Lords. But Uncle John is ill, so it will have to be Hugo. And Hugo's just an old Tory, who cares about nothing but death duties and the Milk Marketing Board. Nathaniel's an Oxford don, the other people I know are literary journalists, critics, artists—"

Clio stopped. All the solid weight of British Society she had felt she could command in Berlin seemed to be dissolving around her. These were individuals, that was all, well-meaning but without collective power. How could she have imagined that she could command anything here? It came to her that she should have stayed in Berlin instead of removing herself, and she had to resist the immediate impulse to run out of Ruth's house and away, back to the boat train.

She walked around the table again. There was a pile of Jake's shirts on a sagging chair in a corner, Luke's flute in its case, one of Rachel's paintings pinned to the wall. These evidences of a family life sharpened her sense of disconnection. She thought of Waltersroda and the forest, her room at Frau Kleber's and the apartment with the blue and green paintings on the walls. Desperation closed around her throat like a noose.

"Grace is my best hope," she said. "Grace went to tea with Hitler."

"*Ach,*" was all Ruth would say, with her mouth twisting. She went back to the sink and the breakfast dishes.

Later the children came home from their Hebrew lesson. Luke was diffident and almost silent in front of Clio, but the little girl was more confident and sat down with her aunt to talk. She was pretty, with a look of Eleanor about her. Clio noticed that Ruth was faintly disapproving toward her daughter, whereas she rubbed Luke's hair and praised him for the work he had done at the class. Luke flushed uncomfortably and slipped away as soon as he could.

It was late in the afternoon when Jake came in, although it had only been a morning surgery. Ruth shot a fierce glance at him, then went on peeling potatoes.

"Too many people, and the same old, unresolvable problems of poverty and ignorance," Jake said to Clio, evidently feeling that some explanation was called for. "Have you spoken to Grace?"

"Not yet. I'm waiting for her to call back."

Jake sat down heavily at the end of the table. The Hirshes clearly lived their life in the dim basement kitchen.

"I'm going to have a drink. Clio? Ruth?"

The women shook their heads, but Jake took the whiskey bottle out of a cupboard and poured himself a measure. The telephone rang above the stairs, and Ruth went to answer it.

"If it's a patient, I'm still out on calls," Jake shouted after her. He raised his glass to Clio with an ironic tilt of his wrist and drank a gulp. It was Grace on the telephone.

When Clio came back Jake had refilled his glass.

"I'm bidden to Vincent Street this evening," she told him.

"I'll come with you," Jake offered.

"Will you really?" Clio was relieved at not having to go alone. And the old childhood deference to Jake as the leader of the magic circle and arbiter of all they did still lingered on. Grace felt it too, she suspected, even if she would never admit it. It would be easier to ask for Grace's help if Jake was there.

Ruth said nothing. She only scooped half of the unpeeled potatoes into the pouch of her apron and returned them to the sack in the pantry.

Grace was waiting for them, with Alice, in the Vincent Street drawing room. There were great sheaves of copper and russet chrysanthemums in all the vases, glowing like autumn bonfires against the pale cream of the walls. The siblings and cousins kissed, in pairs, as if following the movements of some formal dance. Grace was friendly to Clio, in her cool way. She did not offer or seem to expect any overt gesture of reconciliation. There was no sign of Cressida.

Alice was wearing her improvised uniform of black shirt and mannish serge trousers, but Grace was dressed for dinner in an ivy-green satin dress with a wide, rustling skirt. She sat down on one of the cream-covered sofas and crossed her legs. Clio saw the sheen of silk on her smooth calves, and knew that Jake was watching it too. Her own lisle stockings were snagged, and she was wearing the same tweed suit that she had traveled in.

The pettiness of the jealous irritation that she felt dismayed her, but it could not be denied. It was the relatively innocent white peak of an iceberg, protruding above submerged depths of darker resentment.

Poor us, Clio thought, in a giddy moment. *How could we ever have expected to be friends?*

The pointed toe of Grace's suede shoe drew a circle in the air as she leaned back against the cushions and sighed. "What a day. If I was cherishing any lingering illusions about the glamour of politics, the Nutrition Committee has dispelled them for good. Alice, darling, are you going to mix the drinks?"

Alice sprang up and went to the tray. She made cocktails for them all, displaying considerable expertise with the silver shaker. Clio and Jake glanced at each other. Alice had never been noted for her willingness to help out in the Woodstock Road.

"And so, what is it all about?" Grace asked. "Jake?"

"Not me," he answered. "Clio, and Berlin."

Grace listened while Clio told her story. Alice had begun by feigning lack of interest, yawning and glancing sideways at a magazine, but after a few minutes she sat up straighter and stared unblinkingly at Clio.

"Nobody has any idea where they might have him," Clio said at the end. "I think it can only be one of the camps."

"I'm sorry. Believe me, I am," Grace told her. She remembered how happiness had made Clio look beautiful in Berlin. That had faded now. Clio looked her old self again, but there were tight, white lines around her mouth. Grace was tired after the minutiae of the Committee. She wanted to close her eyes in some silent and empty room, instead of confronting Clio and the prospect of a political dinner.

"What can I do?" she asked. Her rings glinted as she made a little dismissive gesture.

"Ask a question in the House," Clio answered. Her anxiety blew at Grace like a hot, stale wind.

There was a moment's silence, then Grace sighed. "A question? Do you know what the likely time lag is between a question and any kind of answer, even with a sympathetic Government? No, you don't. Well then, it's more likely to be months than weeks."

"What about a direct appeal to the Foreign Office?" Jake said.

"Rafael Wolf is a German national. He is also a single individual. I do know that in small matters, the FO will give due weight and consideration, and the weighing and considering can go on and on until the original case is all but forgotten."

"Or dead," Clio said. "You were in Berlin, Grace. You sat at Josef's with us and heard what happened to the lawyer who was taken away. He was beaten and tortured by your friends the Nazis, and left to die in a gutter. Do you remember that, or do you prefer not to? The same thing happens to Jews every day, only mostly no one ever sees or hears of them again. I don't know what has happened to Rafael. I'm asking you to help us."

Grace turned to her, and their eyes met. Clio thought she saw the glint of satisfaction now. Grace had power, positive power that was no longer anything to do with brothers and cousins and childish rivalry, and she was pleased with it.

"You won't do anything, then," Clio said. In the warm and comfortable room, her words fell like pellets of ice.

"I didn't say that." Grace was thinking of her dinner engagement. There was an opportunity to show what she could do, much more immediate than tabling a question or following the proper tortuous diplomatic procedures. "You will have to let me see what I can do in my own way."

In her corner Alice suddenly made an impatient noise. "He is a Jew, for goodness' sake. The Führer is right, they should all be rounded up and shot."

No one spoke.

Alice had made her pronouncement as if she were a child announcing that she would no longer eat green vegetables, or say her prayers at bedtime. Clio and Jake had heard the same defiant tone a thousand times before, and they remembered Nathaniel's amused and indulgent responses. *"Your hair will fall out, Alice, and who will dance with you then? If you don't say your prayers, how can they be answered?"*

They looked at her now as they always had done, at the overindulged child who struck absurd attitudes to gain the attention of her elders. It was hard for them to believe that the little girl had changed into this political fanatic.

Jake frowned at her. "That's enough of that, Alice."

It was the wrong response. Alice did not want to be dismissed as if she were still the baby of the Babies.

She sprang out of her chair and went to stand on the hearth rug, with her arms folded. She wore her party badge at the throat of her blouse. To Clio, she looked as heartbreakingly young as the Berlin boys in their woollen swimming costumes on the beach at Wannsee.

"Mosley says that the Jews are responsible for all the economic ills and half of the crime in this country today," Alice parroted. "Not the good Jews like Pappy, but the greedy and crooked ones."

Jake leaped to his feet. He was a head taller than Alice, and she shrank a little as he loomed over her.

"What you need, Alice, is a damned good hiding. I've half a mind to give it to you as well."

Alice wriggled past him, scarlet in the face with anger and injured pride. "Grace—"

Grace frowned at her. "Don't be unnecessarily provocative, Alice."

Alice drew herself up. "What do any of you know? Or really believe in? Even you, Grace. Nothing can be put right in this country without *provocation*. Without purging what is rotten and reinforcing what is strong and right."

Jake advanced on her. His open hand looked meaty and heavy. *"Don't you touch me."*

Alice's own hand flew to her throat, covering her pin. She ducked away and ran to the door. The slam of it behind her reverberated through the house.

The three of them left behind waited uncomfortably, without looking at one another. Clio felt accusations rising inside her— *your influence, your political friends*—but she bit them back, and stared at the fiery mass of the flowers. There was a faint echo of the first slam from somewhere higher up, and then silence.

Jake said, "Alice needs to grow up."

Grace answered with relief, "That's exactly. She is only half formed, full of undigested ideas. Most of the things she says she doesn't mean. She's confused, but very loving. Passionate, really. I'm very fond of her, you know."

"Perhaps this isn't the best place for her to be living," Clio said, "passionate and unformed as she is."

Grace looked steadily back at her. "Why not? She is happy here."

"And she is twenty-one," Jake reminded them. The tone of his own voice as he had reprimanded her came back to him. "We still treat her as if she is a baby, all of us. Pappy especially. She has to keep demonstrating that she isn't, with her absurd ideas."

Alice had been a plump, toddling creature once, with corkscrew curls and a smile that threatened to split her fat cheeks. He remembered her in the hot, still summer before the war. She had seemed to him then to be the symbol of innocence that was threatened by the coming violence. That was the summer of the picnic, and the corner of the field hidden in the angle of the hawthorn hedge.

They had all been so innocent then. Grace and Clio were hardly out of their school pinafores. His own tortured lust for Grace seemed inconceivable now that they were adults with their different fears and preoccupations, but he knew how that early longing had affected him. It had left him with a fascination for the mystery of women; the need for different conquests and the melancholy sweet triumph of each discovery.

Jake felt a shiver of apprehension, and at the same time the strong and enduring beat of love for his siblings and cousins.

Grace stood up, sweeping the folds of her ivy-green skirt behind her. Jake watched her, and Clio watched Jake.

"I am dining with the Astors this evening," Grace said. "There may be someone there I can talk to about Rafael."

They were dismissed.

Grace came down with them. At the door they kissed again, making the formal exchange of cousinly affection, but Grace kept her hand on Clio's arm afterward.

"I will do whatever I can," she promised. "I could see in Berlin that . . . you loved him. You are lucky in that, at least."

Jake drove Clio back across London. Jake had a car now, a dusty black Riley with creased brown leather seats that gave off a rich tobaccoey smell.

"Do you love him?" Jake asked.

Clio's head was turned away in the dark shelter of the car. She was watching the sooty, familiar streets. She said, very softly, "Yes. I couldn't have imagined, before, how loving him would change everything. Even inanimate things, chairs and tables, ugly city corners, take on a kind of importance. As if they are painted with a layer of fresh light, different colors. Every dull detail takes on a new significance, just because he exists."

"I remember that," Jake said.

Clio hunched forward in her seat. She thought of Rafael all the time, in every waking minute, and inseparable from the thoughts was the speculation about where he might be, what he might be suffering now, at this same minute. At night, when she was asleep, the dreams were worse. Fear and loss ballooned suddenly and crazily inside her, making a churning hollow of nausea beneath her diaphragm. What had once seemed simple was now a nexus of pain, fracturing and spinning away to form new constellations of terror and bewilderment.

"I don't even know if he is still alive," she whispered.

The longing to move, to whirl out of the car in search of Grace, the Foreign Secretary, the King himself, possessed her again. But her limbs felt leaden, so heavy that she couldn't even lift her arms.

"He's alive. He'll come back again." Jake spoke without the resonance of conviction.

They came to the end of Oxford Street, and Jake turned northward, up Tottenham Court Road, and then swung left again. They passed Pilgrim's old studio in Charlotte Street.

"There's not much point in going home," Jake said. "Ruth won't exactly be keeping dinner hot for us. We might as well go to the pub."

He took her to the Hope, around the corner from the Fitzroy. There was a little supper bar in one corner, and Jake came back to Clio at the table with glasses of beer and two plates of sausages and peas.

It was utterly familiar, from hundreds of other evenings spent here and in similar places, but at the same time Clio felt that it was strange, as if it belonged to another part of her life that she had left sealed, in some remote and irrelevant past. She wondered what she could do, tomorrow and all the time after that, if Rafael never came back. The smell of sausages and beer was making her feel sick.

"Clio? Are you all right?"

"Yes." To deflect Jake's concerned gaze she said quickly, "What do you think about Alice?"

Jake took a long pull at his beer, and then wiped the froth from his beard with the back of his hand. Clio found that she needed to concentrate hard on the framed picture of the King and Queen hanging over the bar.

"Alice should arrange to fall in love with some robust and available young man as soon as possible. All this obsession with fascism and Mosley and uniforms is a clear and simple case of thwarted sex drive."

Clio pushed the plate of food as far away as she could. "Jake, do you believe that everything in life is to do with sex?"

He laughed, but there was not much humor in the laughter. "If only it were. How simple life would be."

Grace was shown into the dining room of Lord and Lady Astor's house in St. James's Square. In the group of guests closest to hand, before Nancy came forward to greet her, she saw Lord Lothian, the Chancellor of the Duchy of Lancaster, and Sir John Simon, the Foreign Secretary. Both men bowed to her, their chins dipping over their white ties. It was evidently to be a political evening of the most serious kind.

Lady Astor swept across the room. She was in her midfifties now, but she had lost none of her strong American good looks. She was wearing ropes of enormous pearls, and a black velvet high-necked gown. Her sharp blue eyes fixed on Grace.

"Grace, my dear gel, here you are at last."

"I'm so sorry," Grace said with surprising meekness. "I had to receive a deputation."

"Come with me at once. There is someone you must meet. Not you, Philip."

Grace put her hand on her hostess's arm. "First of all, may I ask you a favor?"

Nancy cocked her head. "Yes, darlin', you may. Anythin' you like, so long as it's legal."

Grace murmured to her.

"Now, you do realize that will destroy my *placement,* don't you?"

"If it were possible, Nancy, I'd be more than grateful."

"Hmm. I'll see. Let me introduce you to this charmin' man, first."

Grace allowed herself to be propelled forward. Lady Astor would have denied it vehemently, but she was an ardent matchmaker.

When the time came, Grace went into dinner on the arm of the charming man. The Astors' dining room was laid for forty people, and it was a candlelit blaze of crystal and silver. As soon as she reached her chair, Grace glanced sideways to see the name on the place-card to her right. Then she smiled, looking down the length of the shining table to Nancy sitting as straight as a ruler at the far end.

Lady Astor had done as she asked, and placed her next to the German Ambassador.

Alice had gone up to her bedroom, but she was not yet in bed. She was sitting cross-legged on her counterpane, looking at her pictures and mementoes. Her wiry hair was loose over the shoulders of the pajamas she always wore, striped blue and white ones, like a boy's. Without her face powder and hairpins, she looked much younger than her age.

There were two pictures. One was a photograph of Oswald
Mosley, wearing a black high-necked jersey with a row of medals
pinned to his chest. It was signed *"To Alice, from your friend and
fellow-campaigner."* The other photograph was of Adolf Hitler.
Neatly laid out beside the photographs were Alice's party badge,
presented to her one miraculous evening downstairs in Grace's
drawing room by the Leader himself, and a swastika armband, a
whistle, and a pair of black leather gauntlets. These were the
finishing touches to Alice's home-made Blackshirt regalia.

There was also a folded newspaper clipping, weighted with a
small pebble. Alice moved the stone and unfolded the paper,
careful not to touch the fragile crease. The newspaper picture
showed a group of the boys, and herself, standing a little to one
side, in her black beret.

Most of the time Alice thought most of the boys were stupid and
vulgar, with their loud voices and bad accents, but on that evening
they had been almost brothers. They had been handing out leaflets
about Jewish crimes, and the crowd in Piccadilly Circus had suddenly swollen and begun to heave and murmur around them. There
had been abusive shouts, and a stone had clattered against a lamppost. More stones had followed the first, and Alice and the others
had picked them up and hurled them back again.

They had stood their ground in the shouting and stone-throwing
until the police arrived to disperse them. And even then they had
marched away, with their arms linked, singing as loudly as they
could. It was as if they had won a battle.

Alice was proud of the memory. She had kept one of the stones
and made it part of her shrine.

She swung her legs off the bed now. She looked at the door, to
make sure that it was securely bolted. She had bought the bolt
herself, and screwed it in place. It was unbearable to think of
Cressida looking in here, perhaps catching sight of one of her
rituals.

Alice picked up her photographs and kissed each one in turn.
Then she replaced them, in exactly the right position, and lifted her
arm in the salute. At last she knelt down on the hooked rug beside
her bed and clasped her hands. She kept her eyes fixed on the
pictures.

"Here I am. Here I am."

She whispered the words over and over again. They were her
self-dedication, and she offered herself up more fervently than she
had ever prayed to any other God. Alice wanted nothing more than

to be noticed, and to be allowed to contribute to the Cause whatever it was she might be capable of. And in all the flowing vigor of her youth and strength, Alice believed that she was capable of the greatest things.

After a week in London, Clio went home to Oxford, to the Woodstock Road, because she couldn't wish herself on Jake and Ruth any longer.

Nathaniel was preparing for the new academic year. There were reading lists and sheaves of papers heaped on the desk in his study, and he set off briskly for College every morning with his bag bulging under his arm. In the evenings there were often colleagues or graduate students arguing in the drawing room overlooking the big garden, while Eleanor sat in the lamplight with her head bent over her sewing. Meals appeared as haphazardly as they had ever done, and the housemaids were always on the point of giving notice. Music from Nathaniel's gramophone boomed up the stairs, in place of Julius's practicing, and there was the same family jumble of hats and umbrellas and galoshes rising in the hallway.

To Clio the house was much as it had always been, only emptier and quieter. The emptiness seemed to make the house even bigger and to throw its shabbiness into sharper relief. Dust lay thickly on the oak treads of the staircase, and there were balls of fluff on the old Turkey rugs in the drawing room.

Tabitha was the only one of the children still left at home. At twenty-three she seemed to have settled into an immutable routine that might well continue until she was sixty-three. She taught an infants' class at a church school in Summertown, and on Sundays she went to services at a great red church with a pointed spire in Jericho, where she also led a Bible study group. Tabby had always been religious, even as a small girl, but now her Christianity had become the central point in her life. Clio watched her, and listened to what she said, even though Tabby was no more talkative than she had ever been, and understood that her sister was fulfilled by the work she did, and was also happy. *Happier than any of the rest of us, Jake or Julius or Alice or me,* Clio thought.

Lying on her bed in her old room at the top of the house, Clio began to feel as if she were twelve again. The creaks and whispers of the house were so familiar, even the faint squeaks of the bedsprings when she turned her head. She slept, descending unpredictably into unconsciousness, and dreamed of her childhood. When she woke up, in confusion, she thought she had dreamed of having been a woman. Sometimes, she had to run the tips of her fingers over her body, with its different softened contours, to convince herself that she was grown up, no longer dressed in her school serge tunic.

Only this involuntary retreat into childhood did not offer any illusion of security. Rather it made her feel less able to confront the adult fears that were crowding in on her.

She telephoned Julius in Berlin. She could hear the taut shiver of concern, like a bowstring, in his voice. There was no news to tell her, good or bad. He and Grete had heard nothing. Clio telephoned Grace, too.

"I've done all I can," Grace said. "I made a very strong representation, as directly as I could. To the Ambassador, as it happens. I also wrote to the Führer. Clio, I've stepped a long way beyond what protocol allows."

Clio was impressed, and grateful in spite of herself, but Grace cut short her thanks.

"Wait and see if there are any results."

Clio waited.

She read a good deal, and walked in the University Parks. The trees were turning, in a prodigal display of red and gold, but the flame colors seemed to leap into the air above the branches, making her think of the burning Reichstag. She felt very tired, as if her bones weighed too heavily within her.

If Nathaniel and Eleanor were anxious for her, they didn't show it. Clio had explained to them, as matter-of-factly as she could, that she and Miles had decided to live apart because they no longer made each other happy. Nathaniel, ever liberal-minded, nodded sadly.

"I'm sorry, Clio. Marriages should be made to last. But if this is the path you have to take, then your mother and I will accept it, of course. And your home is here, for as long as you need it. Miles is still in Berlin, is he?"

"Yes."

Eleanor said, after Nathaniel had gone back to his desk, "Perhaps it would have been different if you had had children, the two of you."

"It is much better that we didn't," Clio answered.

She also told them that a Jewish friend of Julius's had been arrested by the Nazis and that they were all fearful for him. Nathaniel read the reports of Hitler's withdrawal from the League of Nations and the Geneva Disarmament Conference with her, and the Nazi threat to Germany and to Europe became an even more fiercely argued subject around Eleanor's dinner table.

That was all. Nathaniel and Eleanor seemed detached and serene within their own world. It came to Clio that her parents had tended and nourished their children, had done for them all that they were capable of, and that now they were releasing them, for better or worse. Her mother and father were getting old, and the next generation were preparing themselves to take their places. She felt a small but distinct twist of apprehension in her belly.

In those autumn days Nathaniel was preoccupied with his work and with University affairs. Eleanor went to Stretton for a few days to keep Blanche company. John Leominster had been ill, with a series of chest infections that obstinately refused to clear, but when Eleanor came home to Oxford again, she reported that he seemed to be on the mend.

"Poor Blanche. John is a terrible patient," she said.

At last, at the end of October, Clio went up to London. She had made an appointment to see one of the doctors from the Mothers' Clinic—but privately, in his own consulting room.

The test took only a few minutes, and the examination afterward was briskly done.

"Feeling sick, are you? More tired than usual? Breasts tender?" the doctor asked cheerfully as he probed inside her. Clio resisted the impulse to wrench herself away and to curl up with her knees drawn against her chest.

The doctor withdrew his fingers and snapped off his surgical gloves. "I can't think what else it might be, in a healthy young woman like you. But call my nurse the day after tomorrow, and she'll confirm the good news for you."

Clio took the train home from Paddington. There was no need to wait for the results of the test, she knew by now that she was pregnant. But she did telephone, at the appropriate time, slipping into Nathaniel's study when he was in College and Eleanor was resting. The test was positive.

"Between two and three months, Doctor says," the woman chirped. And she added, "Congratulations."

Ten weeks, or thereabouts. Clio spread her fingers over her stomach, trying to visualize the shrimp of a fetus within her.

Rafael's baby.

She knew when he had been conceived. It had been on one of the nights in the inn, up in the Thüringer Wald, amongst the great forest trees. She had hoped for it then, with a kind of secret, gluttonous delight. The hope had given their love-making a fluid, interlocking intensity. Then, in the horrible aftermath of Rafael's disappearance, it had seemed too much to expect that she might after all be left with something of him.

And now, with the brisk doctor's confirmation of her pregnancy, Clio felt divided. There was her own body, hard and soft and perfectly familiar, and there was the baby's, undiscovered, nested inside it. There was her happiness at having this much of Rafael, and her fears of solitude, of having to mother this baby alone, and the fact of its illegitimacy cutting her off from the tidy, arranged, and moral world she had always lived in.

For a week, ten days, two weeks, Clio did nothing. She swung giddily between delight and despair. She made elaborate plans for herself and the baby, and then she discarded them. When she lay on her narrow bed and pressed her hands over her belly, she thought she could feel the growing roundness of it.

In the middle of November, the letter arrived. It came one afternoon, in a blue envelope addressed to her in handwriting that she recognized as Grete's, and postmarked Berlin.

Clio tore it open with shaking fingers.

There was a sheet of paper inside, and when she unfolded it, a second sheet fell out. It was a letter from Rafael.

He was in the Oranienburg camp, not far from Berlin. He had been in different places, but he believed that this was where he would stay.

It was difficult, he wrote, but not as bad as it had been. He had been moved to a different section, and there was more food now. And he had been allowed to write this. He was hopeful, and she must be hopeful too. *I love you* were the last words of the brief letter.

He was alive.

She read it again, and a third time. There was no mistake.

Clio gripped the paper so hard that her knuckles whitened as she tried to read the words between the lines. He would not have been allowed to write whatever he wanted. The careful message was too guarded. But she understood enough. It was difficult, but not as bad as it had been. There was more food. He had been allowed to write to his friends. He was hopeful. *I love you.*

A thrill of relief passed through her. She was trembling, and her breath caught in her chest. It was a moment before she remembered to look at the other sheet of paper and see what Grete had written.

"I send you this wonderful news," she said. "It was delivered to me one hour ago. Now we know, and we can hope and pray for him."

Clio whirled around. She was smiling, a brilliant smile that ironed the anxiety out of her face. This house was too quiet, much too somber. The November afternoon was already growing dark. She must share the wonderful news now, immediately.

Nathaniel was teaching. The smooth faces of three undergraduates turned to gaze at her when she burst into his study. She was interrupting their mild pursuit of vowel shifts.

"He's safe, Pappy. He's in Oranienburg, but he's alive and well. I've had a letter. Excuse me," she murmured belatedly to the three boys. She realized that they must be staring at her euphoric smile.

Nathaniel reached up to pat her hand.

"This is your friend Rafael? I'm very glad, my love. This is good news."

"The best news there ever was. Excuse me, again." One of the boys was grinning behind his hand at the apparition of the madwoman.

Eleanor was in the kitchen, and Clio ran down to find her. Clio stood by the old scrubbed table, resting the fingertips of one hand on the smooth wood. Eleanor saw that her eyes were sparkling, and she held the splayed fingers of the other hand over the invisible dome of her stomach. She looked away, and then back to her daughter's face as Clio spilled out the story.

"It's good that he is alive," Eleanor said, although her mouth felt stiff. She wondered, now that she had seen it, how she could have overlooked for so long the obvious truth that Clio was in love. She had been making pastry, and she shifted the floury lump in her hands, and then made a sudden, vicious kneading movement. The dough yielded under her fingers, but the new weight of her anxiety did not move.

"Everything will be all right now," Clio promised her, but Eleanor couldn't find any answer. Caught in the current of her own happiness, Clio didn't even notice as much.

Clio telephoned Grace again. This time Grace could hear the relief, singing in her voice.

"It must have been your doing, Grace. Thank you. It sounds so flat, doesn't it, just *thank you*? But I truly mean it."

"He isn't safe yet."

"I know. But to be sure he is still alive, can you understand what that is like?"

There was a pause. In the humming distance between them was

the memory of Anthony, and all the nodes and connections of the years before and after his death, radiating outward, a web enmeshing them both.

"Yes," Grace said softly.

Clio was thinking of the portrait hanging in its place in the next room. Two faces forever looking in opposite directions, but the figures seeming to sprout from the same root. The web of associations was thickening, supporting her as well as constraining the two of them. It had been at the party to celebrate *The Janus Face* hanging that Grace had confided her secret to the magic circle. If she was going to confide her own secret, fourteen years later, to whom could she tell it but Grace?

"I am going to have Rafael's baby," Clio said.

The silence, again. When Grace did speak, it was in a carefully neutral voice, with all the reactions excluded from it.

"What will you do?"

"What do you think?" Grace had come to Jake, all those years ago, asking if he could find someone to help her. "I'm going to have the baby. I want it more than anything in the world."

"Well, Miles was in Berlin, wasn't he? Surprisingly accommodating of him."

Grace meant that she could claim the baby to be her husband's. Grace had married Anthony Brock, who loved her, just to save her reputation.

"No."

If Clio had been unsure before, the certainty emerged now, as clear as the air of Waltersroda.

"No. I won't pass the baby off as Miles's. I want everyone to know it is Rafael's. I'm not ashamed of him, or of our child. Why should I be?"

"Clio, think." There was color in Grace's voice now.

"I have thought. I want Rafael's baby." *He is not Pilgrim's, conceived out of ignorance or carelessness and then covered over. Poor Anthony, poor Cressida. Such a long-held, shabby secret. But mine is a baby conceived in love, to be born in hope.* "I want him to be acknowledged as his father's son."

"And so. What do you think Eleanor and Nathaniel will say? What kind of life will you have with an illegitimate child? Cut off from your own people? And what if your man doesn't come back again?"

Clio was smiling. To have her doubts removed was like being relieved of toothache after weeks of pain. "He will come back. The

baby and I will have each other. I can make a life anywhere."
Times had changed. She was a grown woman, not a frightened girl.
She could control her own destiny.

The sweeping grandeur of the vision heartened her.

Grace sighed. Clio sounded like a religious convert. There was
the same blind, bell-like conviction in her voice.

"I can't dissuade you, then. But I do warn you."

"Thank you," Clio said.

The web of memory and association held Grace as tightly in its
filaments. Clio had kept her secret. Anthony had never known,
and Grace felt gratitude for that every day, every time she looked
at Cressida. She sat at her tidy desk now, with the picture of her
husband in its silver frame beside her hand, and the silent question repeated itself in her head. *Why did you die? Why did you
leave me?*

"Grace? Are you still there?"

"Yes, I'm here. Listen. I'll try the Ambassador again for you, ask
some more questions. Now we know where he is, it will be easier to
petition for his release. Can you be patient?"

The letter was lying in Clio's lap. She knew it by heart now, and
the loops and slashes that made up every word.

"Yes. You are more generous than I deserve, Grace."

"Oh, who knows what any of us really deserves?"

As Clio went to bed that night, she resolved that tomorrow she
would tell Eleanor and Nathaniel the truth.

She slept much later than usual, after the first untroubled night
since Rafael's disappearance. When she did wake up, it was to find
Nathaniel sitting on the edge of the bed looking down at her. He
had taken hold of her hand to rouse her.

She became fully conscious, at once. Clio struggled to sit upright.

"What is it? *What?*"

"I am afraid it is bad news. Your uncle John died quietly in his
sleep last night."

I thought it was worse. I thought . . .

"Uncle John. Oh, Pappy, poor Aunt Blanche."

The funeral was at Stretton, on a day of thick November drizzle.
John Leominster was buried alongside his parents and grandparents in the family vault at the side of the little estate church. The
pews were filled with neighbors and tenants, and his coffin was
carried by his sons and his estate workers. Blanche sat at the front

of the church, a heavy veil covering her face, with Grace and Phoebe supporting her on either side. She looked smaller than the statuesque woman Clio remembered.

All the Hirshes were at the funeral except for Julius, and Ruth, who stayed at home with the children in Islington. For once, Alice's black shirt and beret did not invite any comments.

When it was over, Jake and Clio and Grace withdrew to the old schoolroom. No one suggested it; they were drawn there as if by gravity. The battered desks with their carved initials were still in place. Clio supposed they were waiting there for Hugo's children, if the new Earl of Leominster were ever to marry and father any.

GBAGH. She remembered the feel of the penknife in her hand, the way the pearl handle had bitten into her palm as she scratched away. GEACS. Grace's initials were more elegantly carved.

The waistband of her black costume skirt felt uncomfortably tight, and she reached under her coat to undo the top button. Clio's mouth curled slightly. She didn't think there was much likelihood that her own son would sit here in his turn, playing and plotting with his Stretton cousins.

Jake was watching her. "You are going to be showing soon," he said.

Clio had told him the news the night before, when Eleanor and Nathaniel were sitting with Blanche. His concern had been medical first, and practical thereafter.

"When is it due?"

"In May."

"Are you getting proper attention?"

"I went to see David Douglas."

"He's good enough. What about everything else?"

"It will be Rafael's baby. Pappy and Mama and Aunt Blanche and Hugo and Miles and everyone else will have to accept that."

Jake and Clio looked at each other. "Hugo doesn't matter a toss, and I don't suppose Aunt Blanche does either. Miles has forfeited the right to any consideration. But it will hurt the parents, you know. Mama especially," Jake said.

"I can't help it," Clio responded, setting her mouth in a straight line. "There isn't any other way to do it."

While they were still talking, the door opened. Cressida materialized in the doorway, but she had clearly been expecting the room to be empty.

"I'm sorry," she said in confusion. "I didn't think anyone ever came up here."

Jake smiled at her. "Is this your retreat too? We used always to think of it as our place, when we were children."

In her black dress Cressida looked taller and thinner, and the moons of flesh that had padded her face were beginning to dissolve, to reveal the bones beneath. She was no longer a dumpy little girl.

"Look," Grace said. She took Cressida's hand and led her to the desks, pointing to the carvings with her red fingernail.

Clio saw something then that she had never noticed before. It was Grace who was the eager one. Grace wanted Cressida to see this evidence of her own girlhood, and she watched her daughter's face for the reflections of her feelings. But Cressida looked closed-in, her newly clear features walled with a kind of stubborn endurance.

"I know. I've seen them." She removed her hand and put it out of reach in the pocket of her dress. Grace shrugged slightly and turned away.

Clio thought of her own child, enclosed within the bands of muscle and mysterious amniotic sea. *It will be different for you and me,* she promised. A silent dialogue had begun between them. The baby answered her with the powerful assertion of his existence and his growth, every hour of every day.

Cressida said with a faint bleat of accusation, "Grandma is crying. Aunt Phoebe and Aunt Eleanor are looking after her."

"I had better go." Grace sighed.

Left alone with Jake, Clio pressed her forehead against the cold glass of the window. The great trees of the park retained only a few flags of leaves, and the grass was already bitten with cold.

"I will tell them," she said.

Jake sighed. "On your own head," he warned her.

It was not easy to find Nathaniel and Eleanor alone, in the great house filled with Stretton children who circled numbly around Blanche and her grief. But in the evening, after dinner, Clio discovered her parents sitting together in the salon. They had withdrawn there with their coffee after Blanche had been put to bed with a sedative.

It was a chill room heavy with gilt and slippery damask, where the Sargent portrait of the Misses Holborough forever confronted the blank panel intended for Pilgrim's picture. Clio sipped from the cup that Eleanor had handed her and studied the Sargent. The innocent girls posed on the love seat in their cream and sky-blue satins and silk belonged to an age so distant that it was almost forgotten. The Misses Holborough of Holborough Hall were Victorians. The recollection gave Clio a shivery premonition that what was coming would be painful for all of them.

She drew up an ottoman that was itself padded and buttoned like a Victorian matron.

"Pappy, Mama, I have to tell you something."

Eleanor's fingers came up to her mouth. Her eyelids were already swollen from weeping with her sister. Clio began, haltingly at first and then with growing fluency, to tell her parents what had happened in Germany.

Her premonition was correct.

Eleanor was frightened and deeply shocked and disappointed, and the confusion of her feelings found its expression in anger. Clio could not remember ever having seen her mother so angry.

"You may not do this. You are *my daughter.*"

"It is already done," Nathaniel said sadly.

Eleanor would listen to no one. "Who is this man? He is a Jewish activist, interned by the Nazis—"

Nathaniel put a warning hand on her arm.

"I am proud of him," Clio said quietly. "And you would be too, if you knew him."

"*Proud?* After he has done this to my daughter? I tell you I would not even spit in his direction."

"Mama, don't say things that you will regret—"

"I have nothing to regret. *I* have been a good wife and a patient mother. And you, you are a married woman also. You have responsibilities, as I have to your father. A marriage is for life, not for a whim, to be thrown off when it gives you a moment's displeasure."

Clio spread her fingers over the clammy, cold stuff of the ottoman. She was searching for the right words to throw a precarious bridge over this chasm of a generation. It seemed vital that there should be some link, even if it was only a thread of honesty, a gossamer filament from a spider's web.

"I made a mistake when I married Miles. I have paid for that mistake, believe me. And now I have fallen in love, and I am expecting this man's baby. I want my child to know his proper antecedents and to be proud of them, as he should be. I want to bring him up to his proper heritage."

Eleanor stared at her. Her mouth hung a little open in her distress, her lower lip shiny with spittle or tears.

"Not under my roof," her mother whispered.

Clio bowed her head. "I believe that women should be free to accept responsibility for themselves. This is my decision. Can you at least allow me the right to decide my own life?"

"Not in this shameful way," Eleanor said.

Clio understood, then, that it was Miss Holborough of Holborough Hall who spoke to her, across the divide of a century. Eleanor was the daughter of a country baronet who had daringly married out of her class and her world, but who yet had lived every day of her life within the strict bounds of her parents' morality. Eleanor had never dreamed or wished to break out of those bounds, and Clio knew that she could not blame her for her anger at her daughter's default.

It will be different for us, she promised the baby. Every minute he was growing, tiny fingers sprouting from budded fists of flesh, fingernails like translucent rosy shells . . .

She edged forward on the hard ottoman. She wanted suddenly to lay her head in her mother's lap, to have her stroke her hair and soothe her, as she had done when she was a little girl.

"I won't shame you," Clio promised in a calm, even voice. "I won't walk down the Woodstock Road with my illegitimate child. I shall go away until after he is born, and stay until the circumstances are forgotten. And if—if Rafael doesn't come back to us, then I shall look after his son as he deserves to be looked after. I shall count myself lucky to have that much of the father."

The note of bravado grew tremulous, at the end. But Eleanor didn't hear it.

"How will you live? Cut off from your family and friends, all the life that you have been brought up and educated to? How will you manage?"

"I will manage," Clio said.

Eleanor saw then that she could, and would. She stood up, stiff-backed, and walked out of the room.

When the door closed, Nathaniel leaned forward very slowly and took Clio's hands between his own. "She will come around, you know," he told her.

"Pappy, I'm sorry to hurt you both." Clio was sobbing now. He put his arms around her and held her against him.

"I think you are very brave, Clio. But I am sorry, too. I can't pretend that I am not."

Clio cried, "But I am glad I am having the baby. If I didn't have Rafael's baby, I would have nothing."

"Where will you go?" he asked gently.

Without thinking, Clio answered, "To Paris. I have always

wanted to live in Paris. Pilgrim and Isolde are there, so I won't be alone. And I have always liked Pilgrim."

Paris was between Berlin and London. Paris was a cosmopolitan city, where she could be anonymous and invisible. The idea took root and began to grow.

"I will help you as much as I can," Nathaniel said.

The apartment was on the Left Bank, up the Boulevard St. Michel, near the Jardins de Luxembourg. It was high up, on the fourth floor, with views from its mansard windows over purplish slate cliffs, and more windows, and the distant peaks of roofs descending toward the river.

There were two rooms, misshapen under the eaves, underfurnished and chilly in cold weather, but full of moving patterns of light. Clio established herself in this place like an animal building her nest. She hung the little blue oil painting of a bedsitting room on one wall, and set out her new typewriter on the table by the window.

She told the concierge that her husband was a Jew who had been interned by the Nazis in Berlin.

"Ma pauvre petite," the woman murmured. *"Et vous êtes enciente, aussi. . . ."*

In this place, half-hypnotized by the swimming light and by the faint butterfly strokes of her baby, Clio began to write.

She started with slow sentences and hesitant paragraphs. Then slowly the paragraphs began to move, dancing under their own momentum, and they shivered and began to knit together, twining more closely and insistently and running faster over the blank pages, until she stood back almost breathless with the speed of it. The story grew out of her and then ballooned away, out of her control as if it were no longer part of her, like a baby being born.

The writing became Clio's novel about herself and Rafael, and the Café Josef and Wilmersdorf and the burning of the Reichstag. It was published, not then but later, as *Berlin Diary,* and of all the books she was to write, it was the best, and the one for which she was remembered.

Winter turned into spring while she was writing it. She saw Pilgrim and Isolde, and went for slow walks beside the river where the willows on the tip of the Île St. Louis grew faintly green. The concierge looked out for her, and she became part of the life in the little cobbled street between the *boulangerie* and the newsstand where she bought her foreign newspapers. The *patron* of the corner café called after her when she passed, and she stopped to talk to her neighbors when she saw them. But mostly Clio was content to be alone.

And then, in March, there was the telephone call.

The concierge called up the stairs to her, as Frau Kleber used to do. Clio climbed awkwardly down. Her pregnancy had made her no longer quite certain of the dimensions of her own body. The old-fashioned black telephone was housed in a dim cubicle at the back of the narrow hall.

"Clio, it is Grete here."

Grete was crying. At first Clio could not distinguish the words. And then her fingers closed around the warm black bakelite with a sharp and pure spasm of joy.

"He is out. They let him out. He wouldn't stay here, even for one hour. He is on his way to you, Clio."

Clio went slowly back up the stairs. Her face was wet, and she could hardly see her way. She sat down on her bed, watching the thin ribbons of sunlight move across the ceiling, waiting for him.

At last, she never knew how many hours later, he knocked at her door. When she opened it, she saw a gaunt man with a speckled gray beard, the hollows in his face like fist marks. But he held out his hands to her, and it was Rafael. He looked, for a long moment, as if he were seeing her for the first time. And then he knelt down and put his arms around her, with his face pressed to her stomach.

"They let me out. They just put me outside the gates, in the early morning, with my papers."

Clio knelt too and touched the sunken contours of his face with the tips of her fingers. "It must have been Grace's doing. It must have been."

They clung to each other then, blind and deaf.

"I love you," Rafael said.

"I love you," she repeated.

Clio's baby was born in Paris, in May 1934. It was a girl, although she had never doubted that she was carrying a boy.

Clio wanted to give her a German name, but Rafael would not let her. In the end they named her Rosemary Ruth, but from the day of her birth she was called Romy.

Eighteen

London, 1936

THE ROUTE OF THE MARCH led along Oxford Street toward Hyde Park. At Hyde Park Corner, the Leader would address the crowd. Alice marched with her head up, swinging her arms to the rhythm of the pounding feet.

Behind the big plate-glass windows they passed were bright displays of summer fashions, but Alice didn't even glance at them. When she did turn her head a little to one side, it was to see if she could catch a glimpse of her own reflection in the shimmering glass. But mostly she stared straight in front of her, at the Union flag and the lightning-flash BUF banners proudly floating at the head of the march. Mosley was there, heading the column, and her thoughts were fixed on him.

She let herself be carried along by the singing and the chanting. The patriotic songs seemed to enter right into her soul, burning her with images of freedom and England. It was no effort to keep on marching, even though they had already come a long way. She was buoyed up by excitement, and her feet seemed to float over the hard road.

Alice loved marches and meetings. She attended them all, or as many as her work for Grace allowed her to. These fascist gatherings were like sharp peaks sticking up out of the monotonous plain of her life. They gave meaning and perspective to what was otherwise dull, and monotonous, and puzzling.

The ordinary business of life did puzzle her. Alice suspected that she was not quite like other girls. She was not like Tabby or Phoebe, for instance, and certainly nothing like the daughters of her parents' friends with whom she had come out, who were interested in nothing but potential husbands and dances and clothes. Alice was interested in her Cause, and she pursued it with greedy anxiety. Because if she did not have that, she thought, what else would there be?

Very occasionally, with a kind of numb and clumsy regret, Alice would feel that it might perhaps be more comfortable after all to be like the other girls. It might be pleasant to have a suitor, then maybe a wedding, and children and a home of her own. But then at once she would feel guilty, as if she had betrayed the beloved Cause and the Leader himself. She would take down her photographs, or her party handbooks, and fix her attention on those.

And on days like today, she had no doubts at all. It was glorious to be here, marching, and she felt sorry for anyone who was not.

They came to Oxford Circus and streamed through the channel that the police created for them. There were shouting and fist-waving protesters behind the shoulders of the police, but Alice was used to that. One of the policemen walking on the flank of the march was keeping pace with her, she noticed. He kept looking at her. He had a very young, pink face under his helmet. She looked ahead, resolutely denying his attention.

At last they came to Hyde Park Corner. The marchers flowed into the park and surrounded a flag-draped podium. Alice dodged and squirmed her way forward, closer and closer to the edge of the platform until she was standing almost directly beneath it. The hecklers had closed in too, and the chanting began to rise between the two factions. The anti-fascists called their taunts:

Hitler and Mosley, what are they for?
Thuggery, buggery, hunger, and war!

and the supporters, in response, set up a drowning roar, "Mos-ley, Mos-ley!" Alice crooned the Leader's name, her eyes closed and her arm raised in the fascist salute. She forgot the policeman, and everything else except what was happening on the platform.

Mosley climbed up the steps ready to speak. He came closer to the microphone until his mouth almost touched it. There was a sigh from the crowd, like a gust of wind rolling through the trees.

His subject was peace, and the terrible threat of war, and the Jews.

"We do not attack Jews on racial or religious grounds. We take up the challenge that they have thrown down, because they fight against fascism, and against Britain. They have striven for the past eighteen months to arouse in this country the feelings and passions of war with a nation with whom we made peace in 1918. . . . We fought Germany once in our British quarrel. We shall not fight Germany again in a Jewish quarrel!"

The cheering was like a storm now. The heckling was all but obliterated by it.

Alice cheered with the others. It took only a small effort of will, she knew from experience, to focus very closely on the words as they boomed over her head.

There must be no war, of course.

It was unthinkable that there could be a war with Hitler's Germany.

It was the organized power of the Jews that was striving for war policies. It was not Nathaniel who was guilty, of course, nor anyone like him. Alice almost smiled at the idea. Nathaniel went quietly on in Oxford, teaching his linguistics to lumpy undergraduates, as he had always done.

But there was a sinister force, separate from her family and the people she knew. It was the weapon of financiers and bankers and industrialists, all of them Jews. It was unseen but no less threatening for that, and it was working against British order and equality and opportunity. It was this force that must be opposed, before it was too late.

This was what Alice knew.

The speeches went on. Alice felt dizzy with exhilaration as she listened and cheered and pressed closer forward.

And then when it was over, when she was right up against the edge of the podium, there was more triumphant singing and chanting. "Britons fight for Britain only! Britons fight!"

She craned her neck up to see the polished boots and black trouser legs of the men on the platform, and their torsos foreshortened by the awkward angle of her head. She felt that they were superior beings, poised so far above her. It would have made her angry, if she had had the strength for it. But she was tired now, and her throat ached.

Then someone came forward and stooped down to her level. She saw his dark moustache and bright eyes.

"Alice, what are you doing down there, all on your own?"

It was Mosley himself. He reached out one hand and took hold of her wrist, and at the same time one of his lieutenants caught her other arm. They swung her up, so that she hung in the air for an instant with the crowd pressing behind and beneath her, and then her feet found the boards of the platform and she stood upright, and the Leader steadied her with an arm around her shoulder.

The view was wonderful, a sudden panorama of upturned faces and bobbing hats and waving hands, and she could see the ribbon of police uniforms at the edge of the crowd, the brown shiny flanks of the police horses, and the protesters excluded beyond them.

There was a ragged, ironic cheer. Alice lifted her hand and grinned, shyly, like a child unexpectedly noticed by the adults.

"What would Grace say?" Tom Mosley was asking her. He was laughing, but she could see that he was concerned.

"She knows I'm here, really she does," Alice earnestly promised.

"Are you sure?" He was teasing now, and it made her feel awkward, but at the same time pleased and excited.

Behind them the crowds were beginning to disperse. Some of the marchers were forming up into ragged columns, still contained by the dark blue markers of police uniforms, and the singing and shouting had become vague and fractured, without the antiphonal chorusing of before the meeting. On the fringes, away from the platform, there were scuffling fights and some stone-throwing.

"Are you going back to Vincent Street now?"

Alice nodded, touched with the invariable feeling of anticlimax that came after meetings.

"I'll give you a lift," he said.

Her face bloomed her delight at him.

"I thought I'd drop in to see Grace," Mosley said when they were ensconced in his car. Alice sank back in the passenger seat of the Bentley, admiring it and the panache of his driving. They seemed to skim along twice as fast as the rest of the mundane traffic in Park Lane.

"She might be at the House," Alice ventured, knowing perfectly well that she was. Cressida would be at school. There was no one at Vincent Street except Nanny and the servants. She held her breath, and her wish was granted.

"Oh, I'll look in anyway," he said.

The house was empty and very quiet. They went up to sit in Grace's creamy drawing room. The Leader seemed perfectly at home there. He leaned back against the sofa cushions, crossing one leg over the other, watching Alice with his bright, penetrating stare.

"Would you like some tea? Or a cocktail?" She found that she didn't know what time it was. The day had slipped into a different perspective that did not seem to be governed by the usual rules and dimensions.

"A drink, perhaps."

She went to the tray and clinked about among the bottles and glasses. Her fingers were trembling, she noticed. When she handed the glass, he touched the cushions beside him.

"Sit down here, Alice."

She sat, and it was as if her arm and the shoulder nearest to him lost a protective layer of skin. The flesh prickled and burned with his proximity.

"You're a faithful girl, aren't you, with your work at headquarters and attendance at all the rallies?"

"Thank you," she said, not knowing what else to say.

He studied her for a moment. Alice held his eyes.

"Wouldn't you like your work to be acknowledged with some more . . . official position, with the Women's Section?"

"No," Alice said fiercely. "No, I'm quite happy just doing what I do."

Alice had no desire to be promoted by relegation to the women's ranks, to type envelopes away from the heady atmosphere and uniforms of the King's Road. She drank her cocktail, without noticing the taste, and stood up to mix them both another.

The familiar room as well as the ordinary rules of time seemed to dissolve around her. The walls and the ceiling were a long way off, but the cream-on-cream figured patterning of the sofa cover was close, intensely vivid and important, as if it were an extension of her sensitized skin. She rubbed the tips of her fingers over it as they sat talking and sipping their drinks. Alice supposed that she had dreamed this scene so often that now it was really happening, it seemed more dream than reality.

"I'm sorry Grace isn't here," she said at last. She was afraid that Cressida might come in, or that he would say he really must leave now, but the Leader showed no inclination to move.

"Are you?" he asked, raising his eyebrows.

"Not really," she whispered. Her throat and the tight patches of skin over her cheekbones suddenly burned with color.

He took her hand, very lightly, and turned it over in his own. He examined her ringless fingers and the blue veins under the transparent skin at her wrist.

"And so what are you going to do with yourself, little Alice?"

The question stung her. It sounded like a tolerant adult asking a small girl about her plans for a summer's day.

"I'm not a child," Alice said.

"Of course you are not." He held on to her hand.

Looking at her, Mosley saw that she was right. She was a little goose, but not an innocent one. There was an intensity of concentration in her face now that made her look almost cross-eyed. Her mouth hung slightly open, and there were tiny beads of perspiration on her upper lip. She was not pretty exactly, but there was a coiled spring of energy in her that he found momentarily intriguing. He leaned forward, still holding her hand, and touched his mouth to hers.

Her fingers flexed and hooked on to his. When he lifted his head, he saw that she was panting slightly. He smiled at her, a famous crooked smile.

"Well," he murmured, in apparent regret, with the intention of disentangling himself. He was still close enough to notice that there were amber flecks in her dark eyes.

Alice did not blush, or look modestly down into her own lap, or lean back against the cushions and begin knowingly to talk about something else. She held herself quite still for a second, fixing him with her wide-set stare that now seemed touched with craziness. Then, in a single fluid movement, she drew closer, and opened her mouth against his.

Her tongue was hot, darting in his mouth. The wild springiness of her hair around them seemed to give off sparks of electricity. There was a moment when they leaned together, and when he might have pressed forward to taste more of her. Her short, ragged breaths sounded unnaturally loud to both of them. Her hands reached convulsively to hold on to him, twisting on the sleeves of his coat. There was a close, singed smell about her skin.

He drew back from her then. It did not take a great effort to remember that this was Lady Grace's drawing room, and this girl was her puppyish cousin. He began to regret his moment of flirtatiousness.

"Forgive me for that," Mosley whispered. He could make his eyes twinkle roguishly, and he did so now.

Alice did not relax her grip on his arms.

He slid forward, preparing to stand up, and her grasp tightened.

"Alice, you must let me go."

"No," she said, in a low voice. "I can't do that."

"Alice . . ." He was still gentle. He was uncomfortable now, but there was also something fascinating and definitely flattering in this urgency of hers. For a brief instant he toyed with the idea. She would have strong white hips and a broad bottom, and her sparky hair would fall over his face when she leaned above him. But he dismissed the thought almost as soon as it came to him.

"You mustn't be so wicked," he told her, with an attempt at playfulness.

"It isn't *wicked*."

"What is it, then?" If he teased her a little, a properly light atmosphere might still be regained.

She was solemn, almost rapt. Her mouth was shiny, and he could see the glint of wetness inside it. He realized that there was something dislocated about Alice Hirsh. Her eyes were opaque, and the minutely unfocused glare of them alarmed him.

She whispered, "It is good and natural. And wonderful, as well. And I *have* been waiting, waiting for such a long time."

She was going to seize him again, he realized. She was breathing in the same short, audible gasps. He glanced at the door, firmly closed, and at the cushions and covers and knickknacks of Grace's drawing room.

"You don't mean any of this," he told her. Very firmly he put her hands back to rest in her lap.

She smiled, drawing back her lips to show her teeth and a crescent of pink gum above them. The smile made her look unhappier than she had done since their tête-à-tête began.

"How can you know what I think or feel? I know about you, yes, I do, but you know nothing of me. Look."

She reached up and undid the top button of her black shirt. He saw the white skin below her flushed neck, and then when more buttons were undone, a strip of wholesome plain underclothing, and the tops of her breasts above it.

It was time to leave, and if Alice was determined not to allow it, he would go without smoothing out this awkward wrinkle.

"You are very fresh and lovely, Alice, and you flatter a man who is far too old and tired for you. But I'm afraid I'm not what you think, or really want, you know."

He was being very patient and gentle with her, more so than she deserved, but she seemed not to recognize it. She went on sitting, with her clothes half undone, watching him as if she were preparing to pounce.

"Thank you for the cocktail, Alice, dear. Will you give my regards to Grace?"

He stood up, and as he straightened his coat, he saw that this lopsided girl was not interested in gestures, or the polite formulae that existed between men and women, or in saving her own face. At the same instant he remembered back to when he had first met her, at some party of Grace's. Had it been in this very room? She had always stared at him, following him with her eyes wherever he moved. She was not unique in that; women were often affected by him. But there was this difference in Alice Hirsh. It came to him that it was desperation.

He said good-bye, politely but without offering any opportunity for contradiction.

Alice jumped to her feet. It was now, she thought, *now* with everything she had to give, or never again. Her heart was pounding arrhythmically, knocking at her ribs so hard that she was afraid that she might choke. All the breath seemed squeezed out of her, to be replaced by suffocating clouds of heat that burned her lungs.

"No," she whispered, somehow finding the oxygen to form the word.

But he was going, just the same. He was very tall and upright; she could see the groove at the nape of his neck, and the dark and surprisingly soft fur of his moustache as he half turned.

"Please."

Alice half fell and half knelt in front of him. Her fists clenched on the hem of his coat, and she looked imploringly up at him. It didn't matter, she thought with a split-second's flare of exultation. It didn't matter; it was now or not at all, something was happening to her at last. She smiled again, showing her teeth and pink gums.

Mosley hesitated, with the girl's hands locked on him. He was afraid that she would make him drag her. Her disordered clothes seemed to spill flesh over him.

"Get up," he ordered coldly.

Alice's face had suddenly turned puffy and vacant. Her eyes didn't fix on him any longer. She whispered, "But I love you. You and the party are the only things I care about in the world."

As she spoke, and with huge relief, he recognized that he would not have to pry her off him.

She was shrinking away from him and down into a small huddle on the white rug. Her hands fell loosely, palms open, in a gesture of defeat.

Alice had given up, almost as soon as she had recklessly offered herself to him, as if she had no high opinion of her own value and therefore no real expectation that he would appreciate her either. She had tried and was not surprised to fail. The pathos of that brushed him lightly, but his relief was far stronger. He glanced down at her bowed head, noticing the whiteness of her scalp along the line of her parting.

"Good girl," he said more kindly. "There must be plenty of things for you to care about, you know, if you did but look out for them. Now, listen to me. After I've gone, go and wash your face and brush your hair, and no one will be any the wiser."

He stopped at the door, holding the knob in his hand, and looked back at her. Alice was still crouching in the middle of the rug, her face hidden under her tumbled hair.

"That's a good girl," he repeated, before he went out. He thought that he had struck the right note of friendliness and detachment.

The Leader went down the stairs and retrieved his hat from the hallstand. A pile of letters neatly stacked on a silver tray waited for Grace. The house was still quiet. He opened the front door and closed it behind him firmly.

Alice stayed where he had left her for what seemed quite a long time. Her muscles grew stiff in the unnatural posture, but she didn't raise her head or unclench her fingers. No one came. It became obvious as the long minutes passed that no one was going to come. He must be back in the King's Road by now. Did they laugh at her there, she wondered, all the young men?

At last she looked up. Her neck and her head were stabbed with needles of pain. She saw their two empty cocktail glasses on the table beside the sofa arm, and the mussed cushions.

This was not, then, some trick of her imagination. She had done what she remembered doing.

She pushed her hair back from her face. Very slowly, reaching out one hand to steady herself in case she fell, she stood upright. The dimensions of the room were still all wrong. The walls were too far away, and the floor rose up against the soles of her feet, ready to tilt and unbalance her.

Alice felt a pressure inside her. She didn't know if it was caused by the swelling up of tears or screams, but she was afraid that some membrane would rupture and let whatever it was spill out of her. She concentrated very hard on containing the pressure in some deep recess. Her jaw and her fists tightened with the effort of it.

No one must know anything else. Not after this afternoon. Was it still afternoon, or was it evening now?

She bent down and plumped up the cushions, one by one. Then she placed the cocktail glasses neatly on the tray. The familiar actions seemed utterly bizarre counterposed with the images in her head. She kept seeing herself as if she were watching someone else, someone she ought to feel very sorry for. This person was leaning forward to kiss a handsome man who did not want to be kissed. She was kneeling down clinging onto the man's coat. She was unbuttoning her clothes.

Alice looked down and saw that her black shirt was undone. Her hand came up to her mouth, and she bit hard into the soft heel of it.

Upstairs. She must go upstairs and hide herself.

She reached her bedroom, somehow, and bolted the door behind her. The photographs in pride of place on the shelf above her bed stared down.

Alice sat down on her bed. The immediate world seemed to be under her control again. This room did not bulge threateningly out of shape, and she could see from the little traveling clock in its case on her bedside table that it was twenty minutes past six in the evening. But she had begun to shiver now, and her teeth chattered. The return to normality only threw the enormity of what had happened into sharper relief. The swamp of humiliation and shame rose up around her.

She could never see the Leader again. She looked up at his picture, and then saw herself in the drawing room downstairs. Alice's knuckles knocked against her teeth with her shudders.

She could never have any more to do with the party, and it had been the center of her grown-up life. She could hear the snickering laughter and see the smothered grins and the gleeful nudges. They would know, somehow, all of them.

She put her head in her hands. The pressure was growing stronger inside her. Alice realized that she was afraid of what might happen. She was afraid of being alone, and afraid of being pitied, and most of all afraid of herself.

The idea of oblivion came to her like a gift.

As soon as she had assimilated the idea, Alice stood up, without allowing herself time to think.

She unbolted her door and slipped along the corridor to Grace's bedroom. There was a faint aura of her perfume in here, and the tiny sounds of the house were muffled by thick carpets and heavy curtains. The white quilted satin of the bedcover shimmered in the dim light.

Alice crossed to the bathroom door. She clicked the string that hung beside it and blinked in the sudden glare of the yellow electric light. This was a place of receding reflections and ranks of glittering glass bottles. There was a mirror with a curved top over the marble washstand, and Alice knew that there was a cupboard let into the wall behind this mirror.

She touched the latch, and the mirror door swung open. Inside there were narrow glass shelves with more bottles and jars ranged neatly upon them. Some of the bottles contained medicine. Alice knew which they were; sometimes she collected prescriptions for Grace from her doctor's receptionist.

She found what she was looking for. It was a small brown vial. She pushed it deep into her pocket and closed the door of the cabinet with a final click.

Down the corridor again in the much smaller and more functional bathroom that she shared with Cressida, Alice filled a toothglass with water. Then she went back into her own bedroom and bolted the door. She tipped the contents of Grace's medicine vial into the palm of her hand and discarded the empty bottle.

Alice put out her tongue. She licked up the first of the small white tablets. The taste was powdery and then bitter. She took a mouthful of water and swallowed the pill.

Soon there was a rhythm. Tongue, bitter taste, sip and swallow.

In a few moments the hollow of her hand was empty except for a trace of whitish dust.

The cocktails had made her thirsty. Frowning now, Alice drank the last of the water from the toothglass. She took the photographs down from her shelf and put them on the floor opposite the bed, propped up against the wall so that she could look at them. Then she let herself fall sideways, to lie down on top of the wrinkled bedcover. She drew her knees up to her chest and eventually closed her eyes.

Cressida went upstairs at ten o'clock. Grace had been dining elsewhere, and so Cressida had eaten her meal down in the kitchen with Nanny.

"Where's Miss Alice?" Nanny had asked over the shepherd's pie.

"At one of her meetings, I expect," Cressida answered, without much thought. Nanny sniffed and took another mouthful.

On her way up to bed, however, Cressida did begin to think. It was not like Alice to miss a meal. And if she had been invited to some fascist feast or gathering, she would have been eager to announce it.

She went along to Alice's door and knocked sharply.

"Alice?"

There was no answer, and she had not expected one. Cressida dropped down on one knee and peered through the keyhole of the solid old door. There was no key in the lock—it must have been lost long ago, Cressida knew that perfectly well. It was not the first time she had spied on Alice.

She could see the bed, and the black hump of Alice lying curled up on it. She was wearing her stupid uniform.

"Alice?" Cressida pounded on the door with the flat of her hand. "*Alice,* for goodness' *sake.*"

Cressida peered through the little hole again. Alice had not even stirred.

"God," she whispered to herself. She straightened up, knowing—without the smallest faltering hope of anything else— that a terrible thing had happened.

She twisted the handle sharply, but the door would not open. She leaned against it and pushed, and it still held. Then Cressida stood back, gathered herself, and launched her shoulder with her full weight behind it against the door panel.

The door was solid enough, but the little bolt that Alice had bought was flimsy. She had impatiently screwed it in place with the socket against the molded frame, and the screws had never bitten properly into the old wood. The bolt sprang out now and wrenched the socket away with it. Cressida catapulted into the room and caught herself against the bureau. A photograph of Adolf Hitler slithered under her feet, and the toe cap of her school lace-up shoe clinked against something else that had fallen to the floor.

Cressida bent down beside the bed and shook Alice by the shoulder. Then she bent closer to look at her face.

Alice's eyelids were blue, and they seemed to have sunk into her head. Her mouth was open, and there were bluish marks around her lips. She was breathing slowly and thickly.

Cressida's hand was still gripping her shoulder. The futility of this rough, friendly attempt at awakening struck her at once. Alice's body felt heavy and solid, but Alice herself within it seemed to be removed, at some great distance. Cressida withdrew her hand, looking down at Alice's face.

A refrain started to pulse in her head. *Oh, God. Oh, God.*

She found a way to scramble to her feet. There was another photograph there, on the floor, but she didn't stop to glance at it. She lurched to the door and gripped the frame with one hand.

"*Nanny,*" she screamed into the corridor. "Nanny, please come. Oh, please, come now."

•   •   •

Nathaniel and Eleanor reached the Westminster Hospital in the early hours of the morning. Grace was there, sitting on an uncomfortable chair in a little waiting room, smoking and staring at the shiny tiled walls. A junior nurse had brought her a cup of thick tea with a biscuit laid in the saucer, gazing in awe at Grace's dress and shoes before scuttling away again.

"Where is she?" Eleanor demanded. "I want to see her."

Nathaniel put his hand on her arm.

Grace's telephone call had woken them both. They went to bed early nowadays, after the news on the wireless. They had dressed with desperate speed in the big, dark house and had driven straight to London. To Grace, her uncle and aunt looked smaller and older than she remembered, with the marks of bewildered anxiety in their faces clear in the overbright hospital lights.

"She will be quite all right," Grace said at once. She had told them as much on the telephone. The doctor had been quite definite about it. "There weren't enough pills left in the bottle to do any real damage."

"Where is she?" Eleanor repeated.

"Next door."

Alice was lying on her back with her arms stretched out on the white sheet. Her eyes were closed. A middle-aged nurse in a complicated starched cap was sitting with her.

"Professor and Mrs. Hirsh?"

"Yes," Nathaniel said. Eleanor ran to the side of the bed.

"She is asleep now. I am afraid we had to pump out her stomach. Doctor explained it all to Lady Grace."

Eleanor looked up. She was holding one of Alice's limp hands. "*I* am her mother. I would like to see the doctor, please."

The young doctor was found. He told them only what they already knew—that the dose had not been large enough to threaten Alice's life, that she would make a full recovery within a few days.

"Thank you," Nathaniel said. "That is a great relief."

"Have you any idea why she might have wanted to take her own life?" the doctor asked gently.

Eleanor looked straight into his face. "No. We cannot think of any reason at all. Alice is a normal, happy, healthy young woman."

"I see," the doctor said.

They left Alice under the nurse's eye and went back to the waiting room. Grace was still sitting, smoking yet another cigarette. Nathaniel put his big hand on her shoulder.

"Thank you for doing what you did, Grace. Your aunt and I are very grateful."

Grace suddenly felt very tired. She had been waiting in the airless room for hours. She knew that Alice, the last-born, had always been Nathaniel's favorite child, and his simple thanks touched her with unexpected force. She looked down at her handbag and gloves, wondering for a moment if she might be going to cry. It would be an inappropriate weakness, she thought.

Eleanor turned on them, as Nathaniel stood at Grace's side. Her face looked bruised with her anxiety, but the concern was overlaid with a harder glaze of suspicion and resentment.

"Why did she do this?"

"I don't know," Grace answered truthfully. Alice had seemed content enough, between her secretarial duties and her political enthusiasms.

Eleanor said, "She is unhappy. It isn't natural, I do know that. All these ideas she has learned." *From you*, they all knew that was what she meant. "Anti-Semitic poison, bigotry, racism. It isn't what we taught her."

Grace regarded her steadily, but said nothing. She did not want to embark on a political argument with Aunt Eleanor in a hospital waiting room at five o'clock in the morning.

"It isn't natural," Eleanor repeated. She suddenly sounded helpless rather than aggressive. Her back had always been straight, but now her spine seemed to curve, diminishing her.

"What is natural?" Grace whispered.

At once, Eleanor stiffened again. "To do what we have brought her up for. To marry some decent man, to have children, to be a wife and mother."

And yet none of Eleanor's daughters had achieved as much. Grace thought fleetingly of Clio, in Paris with Rafael and her illegitimate baby. And of spinsterly Tabby, with her school and church.

"That is not the choice of every woman," Grace said. "And Alice is an adult, capable of her own decisions. We should be grateful that women's lives are no longer as circumscribed as they were when my mother and you were young."

Eleanor's mouth made a hard line that was at odds with the tired folds and curves of her face. "You may be grateful, but I am not."

Nathaniel put his arms around his wife. He held her head against his chest and stroked her hair.

"Alice will be all right," he said. "You will see. There will be a husband and babies, all in good time."

Grace regarded him as he stood holding Eleanor. He was a big, warm man filled with love and affection. But there was also a fatal softness in the core of him, a flaw that had been transmitted to all his children.

She bent down slowly, with aching limbs, and picked up her bag and gloves. She eased the supple glove leather over her fingers and smoothed it over her wrists.

"I think I will go home now," Grace told them. "I have a busy day tomorrow. Today, that is. Uncle Nathaniel is right, Aunt Eleanor, you know."

"I pray as much," Eleanor said, without looking at her.

Cressida had been to bed and had even slept, but she was up again by the time Grace reached home. She was sitting at the kitchen table in her woollen plaid dressing gown. Her face was pale, and there were dark patches under her eyes.

"Is she all right?"

"Yes, quite all right." Grace sighed. She would have liked China tea, after the brown hospital brew, but it was too much trouble to make it. The sight of Cressida with her unbrushed hair and white cheeks was obscurely irritating.

"Why did she do it?"

"The doctor told me it was a way of saying, 'Pay attention to me. Look at me.' "

"Do you think that is true?"

Grace picked up an orange and began to peel it. Cressida watched how neatly she stripped off the peel and white pith and laid the segments in a crescent on a china plate.

"It could be. Who knows, with Alice? Uncle Nathaniel and Aunt Eleanor are with her now."

"Will they take her back to Oxford, when she is better?"

"I suppose so. Cressida, why are you sitting there like that? At least brush your hair, couldn't you?"

Grace picked up her plate and a glass of prune juice. She was going upstairs for a hot bath before the day began. Cressida watched her until the door closed behind her.

Look at me, listen to me, Cressida thought.

In the evening, Jake came to the hospital. He found Eleanor close beside Alice's bed, and Alice herself awake, her hair brushed and coiled to frame her white face. Nathaniel was sitting heavily in the corner of the room with an unopened newspaper beside him. Eleanor and Nathaniel looked expectantly at Jake, as if with his

knowledge of bones and blood he could diagnose his sister's
ailment.

"Poor Alice," Jake murmured. His helplessness presented itself
to him more strongly than usual. He sat down on the high bed and
held her wrist to count her pulse, then angled her chin with his
fingers so that he could look into her eyes.

Alice tried to turn her head aside. She felt the probing of their
concern, glaring through her eyelids like a light that was too bright,
and longed to be asleep again. The family was closing around her,
pressing her up against the wall of her own failure.

All the time she had been lying in this bed, some of the time
pretending to be asleep and for the remainder avoiding her parents'
painful optimism, she had been thinking.

She could not go back to yesterday, that was impossible. The
thought of it made her want to roll away, wadding up the shame and
horror inside her.

But she had no idea which way to go forward. Perhaps, she
thought, there never was any going forward. It was quite possible
that life just went on and on, as messy and flaccid and unformu-
lated as it was now. One needed the party to give all of it some
meaning, and after what she had done, how could there be any
more party?

Yet Alice was sure of one thing. She had not wanted to die, she
had only wanted to live differently. It was a relief to find herself
alive, even in this little room. Even with Eleanor and Nathaniel
bravely not admitting their sorrow and Jake with his doctorly bluff
bedside behavior. The family closed its ranks around her, protecting and containing, as it had always done. And still she was glad to
be here.

She turned and met Jake's scrutiny full in the face, with her old
defiance.

"Why did you take the pills?"

The temptation to tell him, barefaced, rippled through her. It was
so unthinkable that she almost laughed, then felt uneasy with the
spectacle of her own amusement.

"You must know why, Alice," Jake persisted. Nathaniel and
Eleanor watched and waited.

"I felt unhappy," she said at last. "I'm sorry. I'm better now."

It was all she had said, and all she would say.

"Poor Alice," he repeated. She noticed that there were creases in
his cheeks that his full beard no longer hid. Jake would soon be
forty. No longer a young man to whom anything might happen.

Vaguely, she wondered what were the satisfactions that gave Jake his apparent endurance.

"She will be quite all right," he was saying to Eleanor, just as the hospital doctor had done. "Rest is what she needs. Rest and a complete change of scene."

"She must come back home, of course," Eleanor said. "I can look after her there and she will be away, away from . . ." Her voice trailed off, but they knew she meant away from Grace.

Alice's expression did not change.

"Would you like that?" Jake asked her gently.

"To be like Tabby?" Alice asked.

There was a little silence. Nathaniel eased his bulk forward in his chair. His big hands hung between his knees.

"Come for a little while. Keep your old father company through the Long Vac."

The note he struck was wrong, they all heard it. He spoke to her as if she were the adored child, and not white-faced grown-up Alice in her hospital bed.

"I think I am too old to come home," she answered flatly.

The pressure of their concern was in one way almost intolerable. She longed for them to go away, so that she could close her eyes again. But yet her effect on them gave her some sense of power to be used when she had so little strength elsewhere.

Now was the chance, she thought suddenly. Now was the time to seize an opportunity, while they were ready to concede to her. If only she could think of any concession that might be worth the winning.

"I would like to go away somewhere," she announced.

Their faces brightened with the hope of it.

"To see Julius, perhaps. Would he have me for a houseguest, d'you think?"

To Berlin.

No.

Eleanor snatched at her hand.

"You cannot go to Berlin. It is far too dangerous. I only wish that Julius would have the sense to come home."

Alice, why do you want to hurt us?

They were frightened of Nazism, which was so strong and simple and obvious. Alice lay against her pillows as the protests and reasonings and love washed up against her. She felt cut off from them now, family and feelings, within the walls of her own self-interest.

"To Clio then, in Paris."

No.

But the reasons were different now, and the protests only came from Eleanor.

Clio was living with a man who was not her husband, and an illegitimate baby; living on little money and what they could scrape from hand-to-mouth jobs; Clio had set herself apart from their world.

"But Clio is very happy."

It was Jake who said it.

Clio wrote to them all very often, long and affectionate letters that described the apartment in the Marais that she had taken with Rafael and Romy, her writing and the peculiar jobs that she and Rafael took on when money was short, the friends they had made and the city she had grown to love. There were photographs of the tow-haired baby girl, and of Rafael in the park at Versailles, and of herself with a new, shorter hairstyle. These pictures had taken their place, without comment being made, in the family photograph albums.

But Clio had never come home again, and the letters that Eleanor wrote in acknowledgment were short and formal.

"Don't you think that happiness is a good influence?" Jake persisted.

Eleanor bent her head.

"I think we should let Alice go to Paris to have a holiday with her sister, if that is what she wants," Nathaniel said.

When Eleanor would not look at him, he picked her hand off the laundered-thin hospital bedcover and held it between his own. He thought of all the times he had done this, and the progress of the years, and the baby that Alice had once been.

"She can see our granddaughter for us," he said.

Eleanor had begun to cry. She would not raise her head, but she answered, "If you say Alice may go, who am I to say that she may not?"

The apartment in the Marais had only three rooms and a tiny kitchen with a cubicle containing a sit-up bath leading off it. There were interesting views of narrow streets and tall, twisted buildings from the windows, and Clio grew a few flowers in terracotta pots inside the tiny balconies. Grete had packed up some of Rafael's books together with her paintings of Waltersroda and sent them from Berlin. Rafael put up shelves for the books, and hung the pictures. He acquired some carpentry tools of his own and made Romy's rocking cradle, and then a neat little desk-table that held Clio's typewriter.

Clio loved to watch him work. He was deft with his hands, and the logical progression from raw wood to stained and varnished furniture was infinitely pleasing. The rooms were slowly furnished, and became home.

Rafael could not practice the law in France, but he was sometimes able to find legal clerical work, and they both did translations for an academic publisher. They lived on whatever they could earn and on the remains of Clio's Holborough inheritance, and when that was not enough Rafael worked as a porter at Les Halles. Sometimes Clio sold an article to Geoffrey Dawson or to one of the other newspaper editors, and she also began to write short stories. Two or three of these were published in *Fathom,* although Max Erdmann begrudged paying her the minuscule fee.

"You are *family,*" he protested.

Clio retorted in turn, "You would not want family to starve to death, Max, would you?"

Sometimes, in the quiet evenings, she took out the manuscript of her Berlin diary and worked on that.

After Romy was born, they divided the responsibility for her care between them. She was a placid baby who cried only rarely. As soon as she was old enough, there were simple family expeditions to Versailles and Compiègne, and one wonderful summer holiday on the Breton coast.

Their anxieties were for the condition of Germany, and the threat of war when the Nazis entered the Rhineland.

Grete and Julius were still in Berlin and Rafael's father was growing older and weaker in his house at the edge of the Thüringer Forest, and Rafael was often made impatient by his enforced exile. Clio learned to recognize his darker moods, and to sympathize with his fear that he had slipped away from oppression and left others behind to suffer it.

But even so, Clio was to look back on these threadbare Paris years and the beginning of motherhood as the happiest time of her life.

When Nathaniel's letter briefly explaining what had happened reached them, Clio agreed at once that Alice must come to Paris. They made space for her by moving Romy's small bed into their own room, and on one sunny Sunday morning they went to the Gare du Nord to meet the boat train.

Alice held her single small suitcase in her hand and looked down from the high steps of the third-class carriage. She was almost the last person to leave the crowded train. Down at the end of the platform she saw Clio, bareheaded in a blue and white cotton summer dress, holding a plump toddler up in her arms. There was a big, blond-haired man beside her. Porter's work had thickened Rafael's muscles, making him look burlier than he once had done. They looked like a happy family.

Clio saw Alice at the same moment. She was struck by the change in her. Her broad face was blank, as if it had been wiped with a cloth, except for the dark hollows of her eyes. As they advanced to meet each other Clio was reminded of how Nanny used to dab the baby Alice's face with a sponge, after nursery tea, long after the rest of them had grown old enough to use their napkins.

Alice was wearing a black shirt and her British Union of Fascists badge. The last group of passengers looked curiously at her.

"Alice, darling," Clio called, and held open her arms.

Alice hesitated, then glanced around to each side of her as if she were calculating which effect to aim for. Then she lifted her arm in a salute.

"Heil Hitler," she said.

When Rafael held out his hand to shake hers, she took it only after a small hesitation and released it again at once.

They did their best to welcome Alice to Paris. On that first Sunday afternoon, the four of them walked along the quais. Romy ran ahead in little bursts, negotiating the uneven cobbles with her hands stretched out in front of her, then peered back over her shoulder to make sure that her parents were still close by. Strolling French families in good Sunday clothes passed by them, some of them smiling their admiration of the little girl's mass of fair curls.

"*Bateaux*-boats," Romy called, pointing to the river barges. Her first language was an engaging trilingual mixture.

There were flower vendors beside the steps with wicker baskets full of blooms, and cages of tiny birds, and old men selling balloons and paper twists of colored bonbons. Pavement artists made quick charcoal sketches and sold them for a few francs apiece. At one corner, near the Pont Neuf, they came to a little wooden kiosk offering newspapers and magazines.

Alice stopped, her attention caught by a newspaper photograph.

While Clio and Rafael waited for her, holding on to Romy, she dug in her pocket and held out a handful of small coins to the kiosk man. As soon as the paper was in her hands, she spread it out on the smooth stone coping of the river wall. Clio watched her puzzling out the words of the caption with her inadequate French.

"What does it say?" Clio asked at last.

Alice held out the paper. Clio saw a queer, nervous, glazed look in her eyes. Unwillingly, she looked down to see what it was that had captured her attention.

The photograph was of Hitler at the Olympia Stadium in Berlin. He was shown in profile, angrily leaving the tribune from which he had been watching the Games. The story beneath the picture announced that Jesse Owens, the black American athlete, had just won the two hundred meters, and the crowd in the vast stadium had risen to salute him. Only the Führer had not stayed to honor his achievement.

Clio folded the paper again and handed it back.

"I think he is quite right," Alice said in a tight voice. And when Clio did not respond she added, "The Olympic Games should be a proud competition for the Aryan races. They should not be open to black mercenaries like Owens, or to Jews either. The Führer was quite right to leave the stadium."

Clio looked down. The sun was still filtering through the branches of the plane trees and making irregular blots of light on the old cobbles. She saw her daughter's face, turned upward, and suddenly noticed that she looked like Grete under the baby curls. Rafael was standing a little to one side, seemingly watching the barges pass under the arches of the bridge.

"I shall pretend that I didn't hear what you said," Clio said.

"I did say it."

Clio was reminded of childhood arguments: *I did so. No, you did not.* As the youngest Alice had often come off worst in those, except when Nathaniel intervened for her. With the thought came the sudden conviction that what was wrong with Alice was that she had failed to grow up. She was not a little girl any longer, but she had never fully metamorphosed into the twenty-four-year-old woman that her exterior presented to the world. She seemed unhappily frozen into adolescence.

Clio knew that her sister was unhappy. She could feel it seeping out of her. Whatever it was that had caused her to swallow Grace's sleeping tablets in London was still with her, following Alice's faltering tracks.

She made herself reach out and touch Alice's arm, pushing through the prickle of dislike that she felt for her sister's hostility to Rafael. She could ignore her politics, Clio thought, but not her rudeness to her lover. The arm was solid, almost resistant to her touch under the warm black stuff of her blouse.

"I didn't hear," she repeated. "Come on, let's go home and have tea."

They were difficult days.

Sometimes, Alice was like the child she had been in the Woodstock Road. She romped with Romy, rolling her over on the floor or on the bed until the child gasped with excitement, then chased her the little length of the apartment until Romy hid behind a door or behind Clio's legs, shouting in terrified delight, "*Nein!* Mummy, no!"

And then at another time Alice turned to Clio and said seriously, "You must be glad that she is so fair. At least she doesn't look like a Jewess."

"Your own father is a Jew," Clio shouted.

Suddenly they found themselves squared up to each other, like fighting cats, ready to pounce. Clio was shaking so that she could hardly control herself, but Alice was massively calm, even somnolent.

It was Rafael who put his hands on Clio's shoulders and turned her away, sending her into their bedroom until she stopped shuddering with anger and her breath came more easily in her chest.

In bed at night, Clio lay against him. "I am sorry for what Alice says," she whispered. "I am ashamed."

"Don't feel ashamed, and don't be sorry except for Alice herself. What do you think has happened to her?"

At last, Clio answered, "Alice never had anything of her own, I suppose. All the acceptable attitudes had always been used up by the rest of us before she had a chance to try them out. This at least is her own. Except what she has learned or copied from Grace. Alice always adored Grace, especially after she became an MP."

Clio did not try to resist the notion that Alice's attitudes were in some way the result of Grace's influence.

A week went by. Alice seemed determined to test them by seeing how far she could go. At every opportunity she voiced hostility toward all things Jewish. Rafael was quiet and obviously troubled, but he remained outwardly friendly. It was Clio who found it increasingly difficult to be patient and tolerant when her sister was neither of those things. The current of her sympathy slowly dried up and drained away into the sands of disgust.

On the evening of the second Sunday, after Romy had been put to bed, there was a terrible argument.

They had been sitting over supper around the circular table in the window that looked down into the street. Clio made some meaningless remark about the charm of the old houses opposite to them, and Alice leaned across to her with combative determination that seemed also touched with weariness. Perhaps at that moment even Alice was bored by the battle.

But she said, "French manners, French food, French views. Aren't you proud at all to be British?"

Alice had eaten her share of the French *pot au feu*, Clio noted. She only answered, with a shrug, "Does it matter?" London seemed a long way from these warm little rooms.

Alice would not let it go, now she had stirred herself up. She had lately taken to wearing a good deal of makeup, and her cheeks began to burn under the sallow mask of it. Her bright red lipstick seemed to slip askew on her mouth.

"Don't you care about Britain?"

Clio regarded her coldly. "Not in the way that you and your fascist friends pretend to care. Britain will survive. I care far more about Rafael and Romy."

Alice's fist slammed on the table, making the plates and glasses ring.

"There is no pretense. We are being led sideways toward a war with Germany by a conspiracy of Jews. We made peace with Germany in 1918, and the Führer is our friend."

"He is no friend of mine or Rafael, or of Julius or any of our friends in Germany. You have never been there, Alice. What do you know about the misery and the violence and the suffering caused by your precious Führer?"

Clio was shouting now, like Alice.

Out of the corner of her eye she saw Rafael with his head resting on one hand, the broad fingers splayed out in the hair at his temple. He was wearing an old brown jersey with a strand of wool unraveling at the cuff. She thought how much she loved him.

"Rafael spent months in Oranienburg. What do you think that was like?"

"What had he done?" Alice asked.

Clio's hand shot out, but Rafael caught her wrist.

"Don't," he ordered her gently. It was as if there were no one else in the room. He spoke to her alone, for her alone to hear. Alice was completely excluded. "You will wake up the baby."

Alice stood up. She rested her fingers for a moment on the cloth that was still scattered with crumbs from their dinner. Then she walked away and into her bedroom and closed the door. Clio and Rafael heard the key turn in the lock.

They cleared away the dishes and washed up, moving around one another in confined spaces, and made the little rooms tidy again, but Alice did not re-emerge. Later, in the darkness, they made love with Romy breathing evenly in her low bed next to theirs. Clio reached out for Rafael, blindly touching the landmarks of him, aware of the solidity of their happiness.

In the morning, they discovered that Alice was gone.

The door of her room was open, revealing the empty cupboard and the bedclothes roughly pulled up. Romy had woken them early, but Alice must have been up earlier still. She had crept out with her suitcase, leaving them no message.

Romy wandered into her old bedroom and peered around with interest.

"Alice gone?" she said.

"Yes, Romy. Alice has gone, for a little while."

Clio and Rafael waited anxiously for two days.

They had no idea where Alice might have gone, or even how much money she had had with her. Clio's only conviction was that she had not returned home, either to London or to Oxford. On the morning of the third day she was on the point of telephoning Eleanor and Nathaniel when the wire came from Berlin: *Alice here with me. Few days only. Don't worry. Julius.*

It was Alice who had directed him to wire, Clio knew that, and who had not wanted her to worry about her whereabouts. The two faces of her sister, the unstable fanatic and the affectionate child, slipped and slid in her memory, never coalescing.

"She will see now what it is like," Clio said, through her anxiety.

"Perhaps," Rafael answered.

Nineteen

"THE USUAL TABLE, FOR THE English lady."

Alice followed the waiter through the crowded restaurant with her head up. She was becoming used to the glances from the other diners, and to the business of sitting alone at this usual table. She didn't read, although she sometimes brought a newspaper with her, mostly for appearance's sake. She ordered from the semi-comprehensible menu, chewed through whatever it was that was brought to her, and waited, watching the door and the other diners.

On her very first day at the restaurant she had been lucky. She had hardly been able to believe it when it happened, but the Führer himself had come in with a small party, and had been seated in an alcove diagonally across the room. He had not noticed her, of course, but she had been able to look at him from where she sat. Her food had gone cold as she repeated to herself, *The Führer. Sitting across the room, where I could touch him.*

She felt rewarded for everything.

Alice had not stayed for very long in Berlin. She discovered very quickly that there was no opportunity to reach him there. She had seen him once, in the Wilhelmstrasse, being driven in a big black Mercedes car. She had gone to some of the torchlight parades and big outdoor rallies to hear his speeches, but there she had been just one in a crowd of thousands, kept in her place by the police and Hitler's storm troopers. It had been stirring and magnificent to see the torchlights and hear the singing of "Deutschland über Alles," and to be a part of so much conviction after the fighting and heckling that surrounded the fascists in London, but it was not what she wanted. Alice had decided that nothing less would do than to offer her allegiance directly to Hitler himself.

So she had told Julius that now she found herself in Germany, she wanted to travel in order to see more of the country and its people. Julius had tried, but he had been unable to change her mind, or to convince her that it was unsafe to wander around on her own. She had a little money, and she was more than old enough to take responsibility for herself.

Alice had come to Munich, where the Führer was at home. After a few days she had discovered the Osteria Bavaria, and at once, by some miracle, he had materialized with the members of his inner circle, only a few feet away from her.

She had come back every day, to eat her solitary meal.

The hope that he might come in and might even acknowledge her outweighed the discomforts of her cheap *pension*, the emptiness of the days, the suspicion that she was stared at and speculated about. Nothing mattered to Alice except the certainty that her devotion was unique, and her unshakable determination that she was going to bestow it in the right place. Her love and her willingness to serve had gone unrecognized in London, and then had been humiliatingly rejected. Even now, the thought of that made her cheeks sting. But here, at the heart of fascism, she did not believe that she would be rejected again. The Führer would see her, and ask who she was, and then she would be drawn into the circle where she belonged.

It was only a matter of time, Alice told herself.

There was a little stir near the door. There was Captain Rattenhüber, the head of Hitler's bodyguard. The *maître d'hotel* bent attentively to hear what Rattenhüber was saying. Then there was a brief flurry of waiters around the empty alcove table, and a moment later the Führer and his guests appeared. It was a smaller party than usual, Alice saw. She recognized Himmler, Lammers the Reichsnotar, and Hoffman the photographer.

They passed by her table. Alice wanted to stretch out her fingers to touch his coat, but she kept them out of sight, twisted together in her lap. Then, after they were seated, she saw the Führer glance in her direction at last.

His eyes seemed to burn straight into her head.

She longed to jump out of her chair and go to him, to invoke her relationship with Grace, to offer anything that might make him notice her properly. But then, after a moment's examination of her face, he looked away again. He was absorbed in conversation at once.

Alice did not bow her head. She sat upright, with her hands still folded, while the hum of the restaurant went on around her.

Hitler asked Rattenhüber, "Who is that lady?"

The answer came quickly. "It is a young English *Fräulein*. Her name is Hirsh. She is staying alone at the Pension Post near the Mauerkirchstrasse."

"Hirsh."

"That is correct."

Alice sat at her table until the Führer and his party swept by her. Only long after they had gone did she allow herself to wander back to her silent room at the Pension Post. The next day she was in her place once more, and on the day after that. It was only a matter of waiting patiently enough for the attention that she knew was her due to be bestowed on her.

A day came.

There was the now familiar stir at the door of the Osteria and the gavotte of waiters around the table that was always kept empty. He came in, with his guests, and Alice was certain that they all looked at her.

Today, she thought. There was a suffocating flutter in her chest. Her one good leather handbag was on the floor beside her chair. Automatically she reached down for it and slipped it onto her lap. She snapped the gilt clasp open and rummaged amongst the familiar contents. She was searching for the little gold powder compact that had been her twenty-first birthday present from her aunt and uncle Leominster. There was a mirror inside the lid, and she wanted to be sure that her makeup looked just as she wanted it. Before she found the compact, her fingers touched another smooth metal surface, but this was cylindrical, not flat. It was the barrel of a small revolver, a 6.35 Walther.

Alice had paid some attention to the warnings that Julius delivered in Berlin. She had not really believed him when he insisted that it was dangerous to wander around unaccompanied in Hitler's Germany, but she had decided that she might just as well have some kind of protection. And then in a tiny place in the Alt-Kölln, part pawnbroker's and part junk shop, she had seen the little gun. It had a pretty pearl handle, and it was cheap.

"A lady's gun," the shopkeeper had said, smirking a little, when he handed it over.

She found the powder compact. Alice took it out and opened it, glancing at her reflection in the octagon of glass. She frowned and dabbed the pink puff into the well of powder. Then she patted it surreptitiously over her nose until the shine was subdued.

When she looked again, she saw that the Führer was watching her. He was sitting with his back straight and his hands clasped on the white cloth in front of him. And then, with his eyes still on her, he inclined his head in a bow of greeting.

Relief and satisfaction and enchantment flooded in a great wave all through Alice's body. She knew, at last and for certain, that this was her signal. It only remained for her to stand up and cross the restaurant, and to make herself known to him. She had long ago worked out the words she would use.

I have come from England. I am a cousin of Lady Grace Brock, the English Member of Parliament. I have long been an admirer of the Nazi party and, if you will allow me, of Mein Führer. My name is Alice Hirsh. . . .

They were all looking at her now. Alice began to smile, the same smile that Tom Mosley had seen in Grace's drawing room, a long way off in Vincent Street.

She stood up, her hands still vaguely groping with her leather handbag. *Now or never*, ran the flicker of thought before she stepped forward. She was doing something at last, after all the waiting and wishing. . . .

Alice was always physically awkward. As she dashed forward, the dangling strap of her handbag caught over the back of the unoccupied chair facing her own. There was a second while she half turned to tussle with it, but her own forward impetus was too strong. The chair rocked, and Alice stumbled with it. Then the bag seemed to twist itself out of her hands, and the chair fell with a great crash away from her. Alice overbalanced and fell too, and the contents of her handbag leaped and spread themselves over the floor of the Osteria Bavaria at Hitler's feet.

She was trapped on all fours between the tables and the legs of the diners. All around her, it seemed, there were people springing up from their places. She had only one thought, and that was to retrieve the contents of her bag, the cosmetics and the little gun, and her purse containing a few marks and a photograph of Nathaniel and Eleanor in the garden at the Woodstock Road. She tried to scramble forward on her hands and knees.

The moving legs and shiny boots were too quick for her. She was surrounded by them. There was a lot of noise, and a thicket of hands snatching for her gun. One of the big boots trampled on her outstretched fingers, and she gave a small yelp of pain.

The hands descended and caught hold of her arms, wrenching at her shoulders. Alice found that she was suddenly hoisted upright.

Somewhere, beyond her confusion, she was reminded of Hyde Park and the way that the Leader had lifted her to safety onto the podium.

She looked around instinctively for Hitler. But all she could see were SS men, angry faces and brown uniforms.

She tried to say, "I'm sorry, how stupid," but she forgot her few words of German and the English words came out sounding thin and meaningless. Then she saw one of the SS men hand her gun to his captain. And it was only then that she understood how her actions must have appeared. Far too late, the danger of her position struck her like a blow between the eyes.

"I didn't mean any harm," she whispered.

"Be quiet," the captain ordered viciously.

Her hands were pinned behind her back so tightly that they hurt.

"Walk," one of the SS men commanded. She could smell the sausage and beer on his breath, his face was pushed so close to hers.

For the last time Alice looked around for the Führer, but he had been removed by his bodyguards. There was no hope of protection. These people were all her enemies now.

"Help me," Alice called out into the close air. Nobody moved except her captors.

The SS men propelled her forward, past the silent diners. She saw the meaty, red faces of the Munich bourgeoisie gaping at her from behind the barriers of the tables.

Outside the Osteria Bavaria, Alice was pushed into a black car and driven away.

"Where is she?" Eleanor cried.

Nathaniel replaced the telephone receiver in its cradle. "Julius doesn't know," he answered.

Eleanor's face crumpled like paper tissue. She was plump, and her skin was still unlined, and to her husband she looked like one of her own children helplessly weeping. He knew that he should try to protect her from this, but they had always shared everything and he did not know how to keep secrets from her now.

"He is afraid that it may be the worst. After what they say she tried to do."

Julius had been informed by the police in Berlin that Alice had been arrested following an attempt on the Führer's life in a Munich restaurant. She would be detained as an enemy of the Reich.

That was all. There was no more information.

"It's a mistake. Alice wouldn't have done that," Eleanor sobbed. "We both of us know what Alice believes."

"What do we really know?" Nathaniel murmured.

It seemed that with the approach of old age, he had lost the order that had once been the kernel of the old house. With Eleanor, he had been the spine and the skull of the family. Their children had been strong limbs that had once moved independently but as part of the whole body. But now he felt that the limbs were broken off, and they twitched painfully out of reach of the messages that his brain tried to convey. He sat in his old desk chair and watched his wife weeping.

"I shall have to go to Germany," Nathaniel said.

"I'll go back to Berlin and find her," Rafael told Clio.

They were sitting at the round table, watching the last butter-yellow sunlight fading on the roofs of the houses across the street. Romy had fallen asleep on her bed with her thumb in the triangular soft pocket of her mouth.

Clio was frightened. All the dark terrors of the last days in Berlin had dropped around her again like a curtain falling over a window.

"Romy and I will come with you. We must all stay together."

"No."

Rafael never argued, and he rarely denied her anything. But Clio knew that his refusal was absolute. She thought of poor, confused, and unhappy Alice in some prison or camp, and then she looked across to the open door of Romy's bedroom. She felt the dead weight of inevitable misery pressing on her shoulders.

"You don't have to go back to Berlin for Alice's sake," she attempted.

"I think I do."

He would go to do what he could for Alice, although he did not have much hope that he could reach her. But the memory of his own time in the camp was still vivid, and he could not stay comfortably in Paris with the thought that Clio's sister was suffering in the same way.

Alice's capture filled him with fear and with a paradoxical blind determination to help her whatever might come, but in another more rational part of himself it only crystallized a need that he had felt for a long time. Rafael believed that he had slipped away from his people and his country, and left behind responsibilities that he ought to have stayed to share. Perhaps, he thought now, his unwilling return might help to absolve some of the guilt that clung to him.

"When?" Clio made herself ask. It struck her now that this moment had always been lying in wait for them, beyond the precious happiness of their time in Paris. It was for that very reason that it had been so precious to all of them.

"As soon as I can. Tomorrow."

Julius was living in an apartment block in a cocoa-brown street not far from Clio's old place at Frau Kleber's. When the street bell rang up through the murky hall, he went out onto his balcony and looked down into the road. The windows to the left and right of him were showing their Nazi flags, but his own was bare.

Nathaniel was standing with his face turned up to Julius's windows. He looked exhausted after his hurried journey.

Julius turned back into the room. Rafael was sitting reading in the one armchair. They had not spoken to each other in the last hour, because there was nothing at all to say. All their inquiries after Alice had met with silence and—worse than silence—narrow suspicion. The unexpected ringing of the street bell had jerked their heads up and set them sniffing the air like dogs.

"My father is here," Julius said.

He opened the outer door and drew Nathaniel inside the shelter of the building before he opened his arms to him. Then the two men embraced, Julius holding Nathaniel as if he were the father and not the son.

"Is there any news?" were Nathaniel's first words.

"None. Not yet," Julius said. "You should have told me you were arriving today. I would have come to the station to meet you."

Rafael stood up, putting his book down carefully on the arm of his chair. He heard the two men coming heavy-footed up the stairs, and then in the doorway he saw a broad black-and-gray-bearded patriarch with a lined, clever, humorous, and weary face. Clio's father. *Romy's grandfather*, he thought. The generations that had seemed caught between Clio and himself spun away freely, reaching back into the past and on, unseeingly, into the future.

He wished then for a happier meeting ground.

He held out his hand. "Rafael Wolf," he said.

And Nathaniel's great smile when he saw him even wiped away, for a moment, the somber concerns that had led them both to Berlin.

"My son," Nathaniel said.

Julius stood behind him, taller but much thinner and more fragile-seeming than his father, and smiled too.

•   •   •

"We have been doing what we can," Rafael explained later. "It is not very much, I am afraid to say."

The three men had gone out to a workmen's café in the neighborhood. They sat in the back of the room, in the shadow of a high counter, and were served soup and *Würste* by an indifferent girl in a stained apron. Nathaniel saw the faces in the streets and the customers in this shabby bar.

"There are Jews here," he murmured. "Living openly. It cannot be so bad."

Julius dipped his spoon into the soup. "There are perhaps half as many of us left as there were before Hitler came to power. Every day there are fewer. There are streets we can no longer walk in—the Kurfürstendamm, Wilhelmstrasse—and many Jews no longer go to public theaters or concert halls or cinemas for fear of the Nazis. Our children are unable to go to the state schools. I could not guess how many Jewish homes and businesses have been destroyed. Or how many Jews have been rounded up and sent to the camps."

Julius looked at Rafael. "Rafael and I cannot work in Berlin. But life of a kind still goes on. The synagogues are still open. You will find us in places like this, sitting in the darkest corners, not daring to ask one another what will happen."

"Yet you are still here," Nathaniel said.

"I was preparing to leave," Julius told him. "Rafael did right. He left Berlin and went to Paris to be in the open and to live a life with Clio instead of existing in the shadows here."

Rafael put down his spoon. Very courteously he told Julius, "I did not do right. I felt that all the time I was in Paris, I should have been here, where I belong."

He thought of the little rooms in the Marais, and the cradle that he had made for Romy, and of Clio working at her typewriter with her dark head bent and her shorter hair revealing the soft nape of her neck. He wanted to close his eyes, to bring them closer, but he looked steadily at Clio's father and brother instead. He could see the family likeness in the wings of their eyebrows and the mobile lines of their mouths.

But yet, none of them resembled each other as closely as Clio and Grace did. He had never spoken of that to Clio. She was proud of her physical likeness to Julius.

The first twins, the mothers, must reflect each other like images in a glass.

"But you had been in Oranienburg," Nathaniel excused him.

"All the more reason to stay. I survived that. It is survivable."

Rafael suddenly smiled. He reached his hand across the table to cover Nathaniel's, and Nathaniel, who for all his command of languages also believed that physical gestures spoke more eloquently, turned his own palm upward to clasp it.

Rafael told him, "I am glad to be in Berlin now. We will find Alice, and get her back somehow."

For the first time since he had arrived in Berlin, Nathaniel began to believe that it might be possible.

"Can you think of anything you might be able to do, beyond the official channels?"

Nathaniel had already been to see the British Ambassador and the Police Commandant. Their response had been to warn him, as if he had not understood as much, that Alice was accused of a very serious crime.

"Julius and I are doing the best we can through the unofficial connections." Except that, as Rafael had discovered, so many of the old cells and links that had centered on the Café Josef were broken.

It was Julius who answered him, the obvious answer. "There is Grace."

Grace stared into the green glass shade of the reading lamp on her desk. The bulb within made a soft yellowish glow, and her unfocused eyes made a clearing of it, a sunny clearing in a grass-green forest. Realizing that her mind was wandering, Grace sighed and pinched the bridge of her nose. It had been a long day, and she would have liked to let her head fall against the back of her chair so that the weight of sleep could drag her effortlessly downward.

Alice.

The stupidity of what the child had done almost blinded her.

Grace had no doubt that Alice had made some clumsy mistake in her unfathomable double pursuit of admiration and Nazi glory. Tom Mosley had told her enough to enable her to guess what Alice might have been up to. But to drop a revolver at the feet of Hitler and a dozen SS men seemed beyond the bounds of *gaucherie* even for Alice.

And this evening Julius had telephoned from Berlin. It had been a bad connection, and his voice had crackled and faded before suddenly sparking in her ear, as clear as if he had been standing beside her.

"Grace, can you help us again?"

It had given her an odd shock of pleasure to hear him.

She had found herself answering, "If I can, of course I will," while all the time she was listening just to the sound of his words.

The call had been very short. After he was gone she sat thinking, holding the comforting link of the receiver against her throat.

She imagined Julius and Nathaniel, and Rafael whom she disliked, alone together in the thick stew of Berlin. Perhaps they were in the Café Josef, or whatever the place had been called, where Rafael used to go to stir up his communist potions. What would they do, the three of them, to try to secure Alice's release from the Nazis?

When she thought about it, Grace guessed that the Hirshes were probably ready to blame her for what had happened because of her political influence on Alice. But Grace was clear-sighted enough to recognize that whatever effect she had had on the child, it was much less significant than the incoherent longings that came from within Alice herself.

Please help us.

They might secretly blame, but they were also willing to appeal to her. And Grace wanted to respond, not so much for Alice, the little idiot, but for Julius's sake. Only it was much more difficult than the Hirshes in their naïveté imagined.

Grace had been severely reprimanded by the Foreign Office for failing to follow the official channels in her last petition for a German prisoner.

The German Ambassador at Lady Astor's had listened gravely to what she had had to say and had promised to look into the matter as a personal favor. Grace had also written to Hitler himself, and had received a letter from an aide pointing out that the Führer was not directly concerned with such matters, but an investigation of the case would be placed in hand.

That was all. Grace had been as discreet as she thought it was possible to be, but the news of her intervention had traveled. She had been summoned for an interview with the Foreign Secretary and the Chief Whip, and informed that in future she would adhere scrupulously to the proper diplomatic procedures in her dealings with the Reichsführer and his government. She never discovered whether her intervention had anything to do with Rafael's eventual release from Oranienburg.

The green light was hurting her eyes now. Grace reached for the swan neck and clicked off the switch.

She could choose: to do what she could from London for Alice, or to go directly to Berlin. The House was still in recess, although there was enough happening elsewhere in London. Mrs. Simpson had just been granted a divorce from her husband, and it seemed that the entire Government, and every dinner table in Mayfair and Belgravia, was waiting to see what the King would do.

In the dark of her study, Grace listened to Julius's voice within her head. Then she picked up the photograph of Anthony that stood in a silver frame on her desk. Cressida had bought her the frame, for a birthday present, and had placed the snapshot under the glass. The light from the hallway glinted on the silver and glass now as Grace turned it from side to side.

The decision was already made. She would go to Berlin.

Grace flew to Tempelhof. Julius watched her plane approaching out of the whitish autumnal sky and followed it as it touched down and skimmed over the runway to a little patter of applause. There was a festive atmosphere at the Berlin airport. Berliners had taken to coming out for an afternoon excursion, paying fifty pfennigs to watch the planes dipping in and out and listening in the meantime to the band playing on the roof terrace of the excellent restaurant.

Julius saw her as soon as she emerged at the head of the plane's steps. She was wearing a suit in some pale color that made her waist look tiny. He lifted his arm to wave to her, and dropped it again, feeling foolish in the realization that she couldn't possibly distinguish him in the press of so many other people.

But when she came through the arrivals gate, coming straight toward him without any hesitation, she turned her face up in greeting and touched her mouth to the corner of his.

"I saw you as we came in, up there on the terrace," she said.

"Did you?" The idea that she had been watching so closely for him made his breath catch sharply in his chest. To hide it, he stooped down to lift her suitcase, fussing unnecessarily with the straps of it.

They went back to Wilmersdorf, with Julius paying for an unaccustomed taxi instead of returning, as he had come, by tram and bus. Grace was to stay at the Adlon, but she insisted on seeing Nathaniel first of all. He was waiting with Rafael at Julius's apartment.

Grace and Nathaniel embraced each other. Nathaniel held her and cupped her cheek in his big hand as if she were his own daughter. Grace was touched by his warmth, and it made her feel glad that she had come on this chase after Alice.

"Don't worry." She smiled at him with more optimism than she truly felt. "With the four of us to contend with, how can the Nazis fail to release her at once?"

She turned to Rafael. They shook hands with a touch of awkwardness, and then he kissed her cheek. Grace knew that he looked at her so hard for what he could see of Clio in her, and she felt the old prickle of irritation. She thought that Rafael himself looked less hungry than he once had done, a little softened and rounded, as if domestic life with Clio and a baby suited him well.

They were all waiting for her, she realized.

"What do we know?" she asked Nathaniel.

Nathaniel's anxiety swooped down on him again. "Only that she is in custody pending police and SS questioning. The ambassador has made the necessary representations; she is a British citizen, of course, but we are advised that we can only wait. We have no idea even if she is being held in Munich, or in Berlin, or somewhere else altogether. We can't visit her, or discover if she has any legal representation. It is as if there is a wall around her. The diplomats won't press too hard, for fear of upsetting relations here."

Nathaniel spoke coherently, but he could not hide his fear.

"There seems to be no doubt that she did what they say. There were two dozen witnesses in the restaurant."

Grace said sharply, "Whatever Alice did, she didn't attempt to murder the Führer. To marry him, perhaps, but not to kill him."

There was a small sound of protest. She had shocked them. Here, in this place, they would rather contemplate Alice offering violence than devotion. Grace suddenly realized that she knew and understood Alice far better than they did, and her own understanding was imperfect and clouded with impatience. She must do all she could for her, that was clear. Alice was already half condemned by her own family's political bias.

"I will try to see the Führer," Grace said. And to Julius and Nathaniel, "You must persevere with the Embassy and the police. Every day." Julius nodded. He had the strength, she thought.

It was early evening. Julius had bought food and made preparations for a meal, and now he and Nathaniel began to lay it out on the small table. Watching them work in the confined space of Julius's room, Grace was suddenly reminded of the intensity and close-quarters intimacy of family life in the Woodstock Road. It must have been Nathaniel who was responsible for that almost overheated atmosphere, not Eleanor. There had been nothing of the kind introduced by Blanche in the nurseries at Stretton and Belgrave Square.

Rafael was watching too, with his long legs and arms folded out of the way. In a low voice Grace asked him, "Why did you come back?"

He did not turn to look at her. But he did answer. "I had to come."

It had been harder to leave Clio and Romy behind than anything he had ever done, but the awareness of unfinished business had drawn him back to Berlin. And now he was here, he realized that he had not been rational. He was pinioned and immobilized by his own inability to do anything significant either for the destroyed and dwindling Jewish community, which had once been so proud and prosperous, or even for Alice Hirsh. But yet, even though his old contacts were almost all gone, he still knew the names of two men at the Alexanderplatz police headquarters who were not Nazi sympathizers. Maybe there would still be something.

Grace understood that Rafael was not in Berlin for Alice's sake alone. "How is Grete?"

"She is in Waltersroda, with my father. He is an old man now, and he is in poor health."

He thought, as he always thought, *If they would only leave, and come to Paris, or travel to England.* But Rafael knew that his father would never leave Thuringia, and that Grete would insist on staying with him. He felt bitterness wash against him like a cold sea. All his memories of the forest, and Berlin, and Germany itself were tainted with images of decay and corruption.

Seeing him, Nathaniel put a hand on his shoulder. The two men had grown close in the brief time they had known each other.

"Come and eat," he ordered.

The summons to table, as a remedy for all ills, Grace remembered.

They tried hard, over the simple food, all four of them. There was much talk about Clio, and about Romy's achievements, and family news from Oxford and London and Stretton. But none of them could even half dismiss the thoughts of what cell or worse Alice might be confined in, and what her evening meal might be that night, and what her thoughts and fears must be. They ate what they could, and then Grace said that she must go to the Adlon. Nathaniel was staying in a little *pension* nearby, and Rafael was sleeping on the floor of Julius's room.

Julius was to accompany Grace to make sure she reached the hotel safely, and Nathaniel came down to the street door to see her off.

"Thank you for coming out here," he said simply. "It means a great deal to Eleanor and me."

"Whatever little I can do," Grace answered. "Did you know, Cressida is in Oxford with Aunt Eleanor? I didn't want her to stay alone in London without—without Alice or me. It was either Oxford or sending her up to Mama at Stretton. Cressida begged for the Woodstock Road."

"For as long as she wants. Eleanor will be pleased to have her," Nathaniel said, ever hospitable even in his own absence. Julius and Grace smiled at each other.

When they reached the Adlon, Grace said, "Come in and have one drink with me."

Julius hesitated, looking at the uniformed flunkeys and then up at the great facade. "I shouldn't. We avoid places like this, nowadays, because it is easier—"

Grace stood up very straight. "I want you to come in," she said.

The doorman saluted them as Grace swept past.

Up in her room, she produced a bottle of whiskey from amongst the folds of tissue paper and silk in her suitcase. She poured measures into toothglasses and handed one to Julius. They looked at the heavy armchairs bleakly facing one another across the width of the bedroom, and then turned their backs on them to perch on the high white bed. Grace kicked off her shoes and crossed her legs with a sigh of relief. Julius heard the amazing soft rasp of her stockings between her knees.

Grace tilted her glass to him. "Health," she said.

"And happiness. If that is a possibility," he answered.

To be perched on the bed picnicking from toothmugs was irresistibly reminiscent of being children.

Grace laughed softly. "Remember the magic circle?"

"Yes, I remember."

"We thought we were invincible."

Julius lifted her hand from where it had rested splay-fingered on the wrinkled stuff of her skirt. Grace still wore Anthony's rings. He knitted his fingers with hers, looking down at their joined fists.

"No. It was you who believed you were invincible. I don't think the rest of us had any such ideas about ourselves. It was your bravado, your pure high confidence and sureness, that Jake and I were both in love with."

That I still love.

Had he said it? Neither of them could have sworn to it, either way. The words seemed to hang between them, clearly audible whether he had uttered them or not. Grace turned her head, slowly, until she could see his face.

She had always known it, but she had chosen not to know.

Now the bedroom of the Adlon Hotel tilted, throwing heavy wallpaper and ornate furniture out of true until the only thing that was solid and in full focus was Julius's dark profile. It seemed that she had known his features all her life, known them as intimately as she knew her own, and had never looked at them before.

Grace lifted their linked hands and put her mouth against them.

A second later she was in Julius's arms. He moved so quickly, because he was afraid to hesitate. At first he held her as if she might break, or vanish altogether, but then when he felt her solidity and the warmth of her skin, he sighed and with blind eyes pushed her backward until they lay against the massive German pillows and bolster.

He kissed her as if he were starving, and as if she were a feast to which he had long ago given up hope of being invited.

Grace was amazed. Her mouth opened to his, as greedy as he was himself, as she felt the hard weight of him on top of her. She had forgotten it all, the sudden heat and the delight of wanting and discovering that she was wanted in turn. It had been a long time since Anthony went. Her breath was trapped inside her, deep inside, together with some sudden, fierce impulse that she did know and recognize. Julius's hands spanned her body. He undid the buttons at her throat and slid his hands inside. His fingers found her breast and then her nipple, fluttering over it as it hardened.

Julius.

Had it always been so obvious, Grace wondered, drunk with the sensations that assaulted her, so obvious all these years and so carefully ignored?

She opened her eyes to see the dark hair at his temple and a knot of tiny veins that pulsed under the white, vulnerable skin. Julius was close, so close that he was almost part of herself, but his mouth and hands emphasized their differences and set up a need within her that she had believed was all extinct.

Memories stirred in her, unpursued in this instant of urgency but lending their shimmer to it, like fish in a deep tank: Clio and herself, in and out of the wounded soldier's room with their re-flected features and their different intentions, and his bandaged head; Jake in some field, lying on grass that prickled them, scaring her; the rowing boat, the *Mabel*, and the terrible rush of water over her head, the fear of obliteration.

"Your bravado, your pure high confidence"—that was what Julius had said before he took her in his arms.

Sinking, swimming; Grace knew that she was not brave, exactly. Bravery required a due recognition of the risks, and a decision made to disregard them. It occurred to Grace then that perhaps she did not see the world in as much detail as other people—as Clio did, for example. She did not see the dangers, or feel the peaks of satisfaction. She was a little like Alice, in that. Poor Alice.

But all of these thoughts of Grace's were only submerged flickers like muscle tics under the skin of her immediate consciousness. The rest of her, the bulky and urgent business of her arms and legs and mouth, was all concerned with Julius.

His hands moved again. He found the smooth, silky stretch of her stockings above her knees, and then the ribbed band at the top, and the bare flesh above it that was so soft, he thought it might dissolve under his clumsy fingers. Some edge of lace snagged minutely against his fingernail.

Her legs parted a little. It was warm here, and very close and secret, and at the same time immense and primal, drawing him inward. Julius could not think at all. There was a rush of urgency and anxiety in him that made him want to plunge himself into her, grinding her with himself until he had made her his, pounding their separate beings until they were mashed together as one.

"Julius," she whispered. Her back arched toward him, but she was holding him off.

He stopped at once. If she had remained silent, he would have rushed on and into her, but her voice stilled him. Now her hand reached his and held his wrist.

"I would like to wait a little," Grace confessed.

He raised his head, sensing rather than listening to the words, and then he felt a rush of thankfulness. She had said *wait*, not *never*.

Julius sat up immediately, releasing her. He smoothed back his hair, and noticed that his hands were shaking.

Grace sat up too. She straightened her creased skirt and did up the tiny buttons of her blouse, making little adjustments to herself that seemed to him extraordinarily feminine and expressive.

Only when they were both tidied and patted into place did they look into each other's eyes again.

"Do you mind? Waiting a little?" Grace asked anxiously. She knew that she needed time for this, a space to think and recollect and store up the impressions that this evening had thrown at her.

"I don't mind anything about you, anything you do. Now or in the future."

Something about this worried her. Quickly she said, "Don't talk like that. I don't want you to be a slave."

If it was an odd word to choose, Julius seemed to understand what she meant by it. He half smiled. "No more of a slave than I have always been."

Grace slipped off the bed. The white cover was wrinkled and creased. She felt equally disheveled herself, but she did not mind it in front of Julius. There did not seem to be enough space between them for shyness or embarrassment to bloom. Julius stood up too. He picked up his discarded whiskey glass and drank the contents at a gulp. The evening seemed to have traveled in a circle; they smiled at each other then, remembering what the circle enclosed.

At the door Grace reached up and kissed his mouth. She peered at him at this odd angle, her eyes seeming very bright. Julius thought he could see his own happiness reflected in them.

"Until tomorrow," Grace said.

Julius walked all the way back to Wilmersdorf. He might have sung, or danced down the center of the shining-wet streets. He saw two SS patrols, and heard their boot-heels striking the paving stones. There was also one gang of boys who came brawling out of the darkness accompanied by the crystalline ring of breaking glass. Two of them carried the Nazi flag. Instead of singing Julius hid in the shadows until they had gone by, and he reached his own door in safety.

Cressida stood on the narrow, precarious balcony and looked down into her aunt's Oxford garden. In mid-November it was a wispy jungle of colorless stalks and sodden leaves drifting against the old brick walls. The roof-lines and chimneypots of the neighboring houses were clearly visible now that the trees offered only bare branches as screens. Eleanor had not been out this autumn to make her busy sweep of the herringbone-brick paths or to cut back the withering summer growth, and there had been no bonfires of woody debris smoldering in the miniature wilderness at the far-thermost point from the house. There were no children left to clamor for a Guy Fawkes blaze, and Eleanor was too occupied with her anxiety for Alice to wander out into the garden with her pruning shears, or to set about protecting the roots of her tender shrubs with nests of straw.

Cressida turned away from the desolate garden. The knotted strands of an unpruned clematis wound through the rusting wrought-iron lace of the balcony, with a few brittle leaves and tufts of beardlike seedhead still clinging to the shoots. She twisted off a single leaf and let it drift down to settle on the tussocky grass.

Cressida was too much used to her own company to feel bored or neglected. But she would have admitted that the mournful silence of the house had begun to oppress her. Aunt Eleanor did what she could, but her terrible anxiety for Alice was too close to the surface. Sometimes when she was talking about something else, some trivial business to do with running the house or her Oxford voluntary work, she would stop as if she could no longer will herself to make the words, and her eyes would fill up with tears.

"Don't cry, Aunt Eleanor," was all Cressida could say. "They will come home, you'll see they will."

Sometimes Tabby was there. Tabby had an inner strength that seemed to be truly God-given. It shone out of her, in her calmness and mildness, but she was never able to impart even a fraction of it to her mother and cousin.

"We must pray," Tabby told them with her luminous smile.

"I can't pray," Eleanor would wail at her. "Do you think I haven't tried? But I can't do it. I don't know how to."

Her husband and her children had been her religion for almost forty years. It was too late to find another creed now.

"I don't believe in God," Cressida said, with one of her challenging stares.

"God believes in *you*," Tabby murmured, before bicycling away to one of her Bible classes.

Remembering this, Cressida made a small impatient noise and came in from the balcony. Her gloomy survey of the garden had made her feel cold, and she was wondering if, after all, it might not have been a better choice to go up to her grandmother at Stretton. Only since Grandpa Leominster had died, Grandma seemed content to sit in her little drawing room and read an endless supply of novels with her husband's dogs snoring at her feet, and Cressida never knew what to say to her uncle Hugo. The house in the Woodstock Road had always seemed such a fountain of liveliness and warmth in comparison with Stretton. Only now, without Nathaniel and Clio, all the light had gone.

Cressida wondered where Alice was, and what she might be having to endure at this moment. She remembered how she had looked through the keyhole and seen her hunched, motionless shape on the bed.

Shivering a little, Cressida closed the French doors. The drawing room overlooking the garden held the same muddle of books, manuscripts, and sheet music spilling over the unpolished furniture as it always had done. She stepped over the rippled oriental rugs and took her book off the piano where she had left it. She was settling down to read with her knees drawn up as a bookrest, when she heard the front doorbell ring.

From somewhere in the house she heard Aunt Eleanor materializing on her way to answer it. Her heels clicked across the colored stars and diamonds of the Victorian tiles in the hallway. Immediately there was a murmur of voices. Cressida could distinguish a man's low rumble.

A moment later, the drawing-room door opened. There was indeed a man, but it was no one Cressida recognized. He had wiry gray hair, worn long and flowing over his ears. He had a beard too, less luxuriant than Nathaniel's, with yellowish tufts at the corners of his mouth. He was dressed in some kind of long dark cape, and he carried a large hat with a curled brim.

Cressida folded away her book and stood up politely, ready to be introduced to her aunt's guest.

"This is my great-niece, Cressida Brock," Eleanor said. "And Cressida, this is Mr. Pilgrim. The painter, you know."

"How do you do?" Cressida said.

The man swept forward and seemed to loom over her. He had sharp eyes under heavy lids, and his clothes carried the smell that she had sometimes noticed in summertime when the doors of public houses were left open onto the pavement.

"Cressida Brock," he said, with a long, drawn-out theatrical inflection. "As lovely as her mama ever was." He took her hand and lifted it to his whiskery beard.

"Mr. Pilgrim is a friend of your Aunt Clio, and of your mother too. The portrait is his work."

Cressida glanced up at *The Janus Face*.

"What do you think of it?" Pilgrim asked, looking at her intently.

Cressida was used to the violence of the straining limbs and staring eyes, and the lascivious attention given to the naked skin and coiling masses of multicolored hair. She also knew that the artist had an international reputation and that the picture was now worth an enormous amount of money. It was a kind of joke in the

Hirsh household that it was more valuable than the Stretton Sargent and was still left to hang in its old place, on permanent loan from the artist. But she did not much like it as a portrait of her mother and aunt.

"I think it is admirable," she said carefully.

The painter gave a surprising hoot of laughter. "Well done," he said. "That's my girl."

Then he turned his attention back to Eleanor. He had called unexpectedly, hoping to find Nathaniel and an early glass or two of beer. Instead, here was Eleanor wringing her hands over some disaster that had befallen her youngest child in Berlin, and the utterly unexpected apparition of Grace's daughter. The child was practically grown-up. In his imagination she was still a dough-faced infant.

"Eleanor, you must go back to your letters. I have no intention of interrupting your afternoon. I don't need tea, or any attention at all." Then he smiled. "Perhaps Cressida will keep me company for half an hour."

Eleanor looked doubtful. Then Pilgrim twirled around as if he had just had a wonderful idea. "Perhaps I could *draw* her. I would like to so much. The family resemblance, you know."

Eleanor's face cleared as her vague anxieties about chaperonage drifted away. Clio and Grace had been left to sit for Pilgrim, after all, long ago.

"Well, I suppose. If Cressida would like it . . ."

Pilgrim had already produced a flat tin of charcoal sticks from one of his pockets. He was prowling about the room squinting at the light and turning over manuscript sheets in search of a suitable piece of paper.

"I don't mind," Cressida said.

When Eleanor had gone, Pilgrim sat back to look at the child. He had placed her on the piano stool with her face half turned to the light from the tall windows.

He was enchanted. His daughter was a beauty.

Grace had been fiercely protective over the years. Pilgrim had seen Cressida just once, when she was a baby.

He remembered exclaiming, "Why is the young of the human species so *extravagantly* ugly?"

After that, it had been made clear that he was no longer a friend of the Brocks. He had never visited their house after that one time, and on the rare occasions when the separate threads of their London lives had crossed, Grace had ignored him as far as possible.

Pilgrim had not minded particularly. His paternal instincts were not highly developed, and it had never worried him that Anthony Brock had died with his belief intact that Cressida was his own.

But now that he saw Cressida, he felt differently. She was, he calculated, just over sixteen years old. She had a solemn, narrow face with pronounced cheekbones and wide-set eyes. The irises were so dark that they looked plum-colored. She looked like her mother, except for her hands and some of the movements she made. These spoke eloquently to Pilgrim of himself.

"Is this all right?" Cressida asked, nervously gesturing with those broad hands. She found that she was disconcerted by the man's scrutiny.

"Just relax. Find a comfortable position and then hold it," he said briskly, as if she were any other model.

Cressida squared her shoulders. At least she was thin now, she thought. She had willed herself into slimness two years ago, and even now she still ate as little as she could, despite the constant gnawing of hunger. She was pleased with the results of her will-power now. It felt glamorous and adult to be sitting for a famous painter. It was the kind of thing that her mother did.

Pilgrim began to draw. He made strong, black strokes on the blank paper.

"Tell me what has happened to—Alice, is it? In Berlin?"

Cressida told him, and he listened with sympathy.

"And so your mother sent you to Oxford, while she is away?"

"Yes. For Aunt Eleanor to look after me. And for me to keep Aunt Eleanor company."

"An excellent arrangement," Pilgrim said. "You can keep me company too. I have to be in Oxford for a few days, so perhaps I may call in the afternoons, and you can sit for me?"

"I would like that," Cressida said truthfully. The prospect of a visitor of her own, and an important one who was making a drawing of her, was much more interesting than a series of empty afternoons. And she was intrigued by this Pilgrim. He was odd to look at, but she liked the way he talked, and the way he stared at her as if he wanted to see inside her head. She didn't think that anyone had ever paid her such close attention before.

"Go on talking," Pilgrim ordered.

Cressida did as she was told. She talked about Vincent Street, and about Grace's work, and about Alice and the Blackshirts, and about herself.

Later, when Pilgrim had drawn enough, with Eleanor's permis-

sion they went for a walk in the University Parks. The sharp
November air drew color into Cressida's cheeks, and Pilgrim
watched her with deepening fascination as she talked. Once she
had properly begun, and discovered the luxury of an attentive
audience, the words seemed to spill out of her. Cressida was
clever, and the long hours she had spent alone had given her an
original turn of mind. She had opinions on surprising topics, from
politics to Darwinism, and she seemed to have read a great many
books.

Pilgrim listened to everything she said with admiration and the
beginnings of pride.

When he escorted her back to the Woodstock Road, he promised
that he would call again the next afternoon. He came exactly as he
had promised, and spent another hour working on his drawing.
Afterward they walked again, along the banks of the Cherwell
under the lachrymose branches of the willow trees.

There was another day, and the day after that. The little charcoal
drawing was nearly complete, even though Pilgrim worked as
slowly as he could. Cressida opened like a flower under the warmth
of his attention and approval.

"Are we friends?" she asked once, turning to look at him and at
the same time childishly skipping backward so as not to break the
rhythm of their walk.

He made her stop, and took her hands. "Of course," he answered, with what struck her as unusual seriousness. "More than
friends."

Cressida waited, but he did not elaborate.

In Berlin, Grace was granted another audience with the Führer.

She was escorted through the same corridors of the Reichs-
kanzlerei, but this time to a huge office with a great polished desk
set under the red folds of crossed Nazi flags. Storm troopers stood
stiffly to attention beside the doors and between the windows. But
the Führer himself stood up courteously when she was shown in
and even came around his desk to shake her hand.

Grace took the chair that he indicated, folding her hands in her
lap to hide their shaking. He waited, with one eyebrow raised,
polite but cold. For all the formal display of civility, she was not
here as a friend now, she realized. Not like last time. The thought of
the long corridors at her back, closely guarded and separating her
from the light and air, made her shiver as if she were sick. Renewed
fear for Alice gripped her at the same instant.

She began to apologize for whatever it was that Alice had done. Alice was young, a stranger to Germany, inexperienced. She had meant no harm, to the Führer or to anyone else. If she could be released, her imprisonment up until now a sufficient punishment for her foolishness, her family was waiting for her in Berlin. They would take her home at once.

Hitler inclined his head. It was a small matter. A triviality, as far as he was personally concerned. But there were formalities to be observed, and the details were not in his own hands. To emphasize his point, he spread his manicured fingers in front of her.

Lady Grace must rest assured that everything necessary would be done to secure her young cousin's early release and the conclusion of this unfortunate matter.

That was all.

A moment later Grace was outside the heavy doors, steered by the storm troopers toward the daylight.

Nathaniel and Julius and Rafael were waiting for her.

"I don't know," Grace blurted out. "He was polite, he said everything would be done that could be done, and that we must just wait."

There was nothing else she could offer them, when they had clearly hoped for much more. She had half convinced herself, when the summons came, that Alice would be conjured up from wherever she was being held so that Grace could carry her home in triumph. She had a colder vision now.

"It was magnificent that you saw him at all," Nathaniel said, but he was unable to hide his heaviness. It was Julius who came to her and felt her shaking. He guided her to a chair and sat holding her in his arms until the spasm had passed.

"It's all right," he whispered. "You are here with me now."

Rafael and Nathaniel left them. Nathaniel was spending hours of his time at the Embassy, pleading their case with whichever diplomat was available, and Rafael was busy with the legal needs of the shattered families who had belonged to his own circle and with what remained of his Jewish resistance group. Grace let her head fall against Julius's shoulder. She could have wept for crumbling ideals and for her own distorted visions, but she would not let herself.

Julius tilted her chin in his fingers and then outlined the shape of her mouth with one fingertip.

Grace recognized the happiness in his eyes. Julius's old, hesitant manner had gone. He was confident now. At last, after so many years, it was appropriate to acknowledge the feelings he had disguised for so long. It made her look at him quite differently; she read a hundred things in him, as well as the happiness, that she had never seen before. There was something new in herself too. It was inconceivable that they should be happy here and now, but there was the fact of it.

In those hours after they had lain down on Grace's bed in the Adlon Hotel, it was as if they were following the steps of some intricate and glorious dance. They both knew what the final measure of the dance would be, and they let themselves be swept toward it on the imperious beat of the music.

Pilgrim laid down his charcoal stick and blew the last faint traces of dust from the drawing. "There," he said.

Cressida slipped off the piano stool and came around to look at it. She leaned over his shoulder, resting her chin for an instant on the musty corduroy of his coat. Pilgrim resisted the impulse to pull her closer to him, to hold on to her. He was not used to resisting his own impulses.

"It's finished," Cressida said sadly. She gazed at the picture. He had elongated her arms and legs and fingers so that she looked like some timid animal, a gazelle perhaps, ready to take flight. But the face was her own.

"You have made me prettier than I really am," she accused him.

"That is the accepted procedure in portraiture of a certain kind. But you are wrong, in fact. If anything, the picture is less than flattering."

Cressida blushed, he was charmed to see.

"I suppose you have to go back to London."

"Yes," Pilgrim said, because he did.

"Shall we have a last walk?"

"Of course."

They went out into the Parks again. It was a cold day, colorless, with a sharp wind whipping the trees. Cressida strode along in her belted mackintosh with her hair blown back from her face. This sidelong view of her reminded him of Grace, and of the Janus portrait. It was a good piece of work, Pilgrim thought with satisfaction. Better now and better in a hundred years' time than the milk-and-water Sargent it had been intended to complement.

"You are very like Grace," Pilgrim said.

"In looks, perhaps. But more like my father inside, I believe."

"Talk to me about Anthony." With masochistic fascination, Pilgrim wanted to hear about it from the child's own lips.

Cressida said simply, "The day my father died was the worst I will ever know. They put a black mask on his face to help him breathe, but I thought they were trying to suffocate him. His face was so white. I wanted to see him, but the nurses and Mummy sent me away. He died that night. I never said good-bye to him."

Pilgrim tucked her cold hand under his arm, but they went on walking.

"He was a wonderful father. He always seemed to be there, when Mummy was away. He made up games and stories. There was a game we used to play in his study, desert explorers, using a rug to make a tent."

It sounded a banal enough relationship, Pilgrim thought. No doubt most fathers were capable of stories and games. He could probably have performed in the same way himself.

"I miss him still, every day," Cressida said softly. "I still love him."

He was pierced by her devotion then. The pain of it made him want to bend himself double. It felt just as though an arrow were passing through all his accumulated layers of self-interest and self-protectiveness.

Pilgrim had imagined that he was invulnerable, but he was not. If only Grace and he had been different, he was thinking, he might have been able to claim this innocent affection of Cressida's for himself. It would be his, and not poor Anthony Brock's.

He was suddenly burning with jealousy for Cressida's love for her father. And he was angry with Grace for having kept this remarkable child to herself. He felt that he had been fenced out of her young life, like some marauding animal that must be kept beyond the pale of the village settlement. He held on to her arm, feeling the suppleness of her thin wrist, wanting to hold her and keep her as he had never wanted to keep an ordinary woman.

"I used to be afraid of my mother. She always seemed to be so beautiful and busy and clever. And also . . . enameled, difficult to penetrate. She was very good at making me feel that I wasn't quite what she hoped for. She still is, as a matter of fact, but I don't mind that so much anymore. At least I am *thin* now. When I was small, she used to dress me in pretty, babyish clothes that showed off the rolls of fat. Did she do it deliberately, do you think?"

Cressida was smiling. She had grown vivacious in the warmth of Pilgrim's attention.

Pilgrim said, "Your mother is an uncommon creature. You should love her, and admire her too."

They reached the river. It was running high, and crusts of foam rode on the back of it.

"I loved my father best," Cressida said.

Capricious jealousy rose up within him, swirling to the surface of all his other feelings like the river foam. Pilgrim opened his mouth. Coldly and flatly he told her, "Anthony Brock is not your father. I am."

Cressida did not speak for a long moment. Slowly and stiffly, she detached her hand from his arm. She rubbed her elbow briefly with her white fingers, as if it had been bruised.

Afterward she remembered the color of the water, and the fronds of willow branch that seemed to reach out to nip at her hair.

"I don't believe you," she said.

Her denial was so complete and so vehement that there seemed to be nothing that either of them could add. They walked on in silence.

Only inside Cressida's head there was a tumult of noise. It was impossible. The notion was obscene, and horrible. She tried to cling on to the belief that it was impossible, but another much more unpleasant voice asserted that it was not impossible at all. And if it were not the truth, how or why should Pilgrim have suggested such a thing? She thought of the portrait, and the expanses of flesh and waving, wild hair suddenly seemed threatening and significant and nauseatingly erotic. The limbs became her mother's and this man's, coupling. Was she the result of that coupling? Cressida saw her father's face under the black mask, and she remembered the nurses who to her childish eyes had looked like birds of prey.

I never said good-bye to him, she silently repeated, with a terrible wash of bitterness.

Beneath the turbulence of her fear and disgust there was another sensation. It was not quite relief, but it was close to that, like the reverse of a coin. It was as if some mystery had at last been explained to her. Always, for as long as she could remember, she had suspected that there was some detail in her life that was not quite correct. It was a matter of alignment, or shading, perhaps. She could not have expressed it more coherently than that. And if this were the truth, this blurted malice of Pilgrim's, it was more than an explanation. She felt as if some black and filthy pit had opened up at her feet.

But Cressida was Grace's daughter. She had acquired more self-control in her short life than Pilgrim had imagined in all of his. Her white face was the only visible sign of the shock she had suffered.

She walked on, and they turned the familiar circuit of the Parks and came back to the house in the Woodstock Road.

Eleanor was in the drawing room, fussing over giving Pilgrim a proper send-off to London. Cressida sat down on the piano stool, then abruptly jumped up again. She resettled on the sofa with her face turned away from the Janus. Pilgrim slipped past Eleanor and held out the charcoal drawing to his daughter.

"It's yours," he told her.

Cressida glanced down at it, and then laid it aside. "Thank you," she said stiffly.

For appearances' sake she went with her aunt to the front door to say good-bye, but she would not look at Pilgrim, and she only touched his hand with the cold tips of her fingers when he held it out to her.

Pilgrim went back in the train to London. He stared out through the sooty windows at the receding water-meadows, and wished that he had held his tongue.

Twenty

RAFAEL DISCOVERED FROM HIS ALLIES within Alexanderplatz that Alice was being held in a camp near Berlin. For a little while she had been in police custody, first in Munich and afterward in Berlin itself, but then she had been handed over to the SS, who had removed her to Sachsenhausen.

Within two days, the same information came from the British Embassy. Nathaniel was assured that everything possible was being done to bring about her trial and subsequent release, and representations were being made about the conditions of her imprisonment to Himmler and to the Führer himself.

They could only wait, in their anxiety, working over the crumbs of information that they had been given, until the meager facts became greasy and nightmarish from overfamiliarity. For Nathaniel and Rafael, who were needed elsewhere and who could do little except grimly speculate about Alice's whereabouts, the time passed with painful slowness. But for Julius and Grace, the same anxiety was shot with a kind of feverish joy. The days of waiting and listening brought them closer together; the dance-step that they had begun on Grace's first night in Berlin swung them faster and faster.

Nathaniel saw nothing of what was happening. To Nathaniel, they were here for Alice alone, and until she was free and safely on her way home with him, nothing else could have any importance or significance. Rafael did see, but he said nothing, even in the letters that he wrote to Clio. The quickening pulse of attraction between Grace and Julius seemed only to increase his own sense of foreboding.

For Julius and Grace themselves, the beat of longing was amplified by the unsuitability of the time and the place, and by the steady friction of their guilt. In the cold and inhospitable days after Grace's arrival, the pressure of their need grew until they could barely sit in the same room without touching, without blindly reaching for each other. Grace had never known such sharp physical desire, even at the height of her late-kindled love affair with Anthony.

But still they waited. In his new confidence Julius was sure that to wait was all that was necessary, and Grace was stayed by a wish to examine and order and savor this happiness before it devoured her.

She moved out of the Adlon, insisting to Julius that it was for reasons of economy. Both of them knew, however, that it was because he felt uncomfortable as a Jew in the luxurious hotel that was frequented by SS and SA officers, and even ill at ease, in daylight hours, in the surging and prosperous crowds that filled the political center of Berlin itself. She took a room instead in a small, old-fashioned place closer to Wilmersdorf. It was much less comfortable than the Adlon, but Grace was oddly pleased by the creaking floors and fading decor, and by the three generations of an obliging family who ran it. It was a relief to be away from the uniforms and medals and insignia and the Heil Hitlers of the other hotel.

Grace felt that everything was changing, even her once-sure view of the rights and wrongs of the world. She walked in the streets and saw the bright certainty of the faces of the Berliners, and then she saw how Rafael and Julius and Nathaniel moved in the shadows away from the bands of Nazis and their followers, and she wondered how she could ever have believed that this German path was the right one to follow.

December came, bitterly cold, with a wind that penetrated the drafty old buildings and sleet that blew into their faces when they ventured outside.

Julius and Grace became lovers at last in her bedroom in the little hotel.

There were white curtains at the windows, and an ewer and basin patterned with flowers on a marble-topped washstand. Afterward, Julius remembered the details of the room as if he had lived there for many years, as if he had experienced the very central passage of his life within the four dim, yellow-papered walls. He remembered Grace's white limbs, winding around his own, and the intent, almost inward expression of her face when she took him into herself. She held his face between her narrow hands and looked into his eyes, and both of them saw the reflections of each other, and themselves, and between them and behind them was yet another set of features—the still, separate pallor of Clio.

She was like Clio, and yet not Clio. The likenesses multiplied, and fractured between them, and then were overcome and forgotten.

"I love you," Julius whispered.

Grace straddled him, and he reached up to grasp her narrow waist between his hands. Her hair fell forward to hide her face, and then she lifted herself and her head fell back, and he saw her white throat, and the long curve of her flanks above him. He drove upward into her, deeper and harder until her back arched and he longed to reach further, until he touched her heart, until he made her cry out for him.

"I have always loved you," he told her. "Ever since I was a little boy. From the moment I understood what love is, and what it does."

Grace was happy, the warmth of it ticking inside her like a flame, but she was also afraid of what he said. She put her fingers over his mouth as if to seal in the words, but he kissed the hollows of her palms and rolled with her until he lay above her and her skin and her mouth and the warm scent of her were all his, and his alone. The Berlin street outside their window was noisy with the afternoon traffic, but the room was silent except for their ragged breathing.

"*Grace.*"

To say her name while they were so close, with her body wrapped around him, sounded to Julius's ear like a prayer. He moved again, in a slow rhythm, feeling her heat and sweetness enclosing him. Grace smiled in answer now, a smile that made her mouth curve softly in a way he had never seen before. It seemed that she was ready to give herself up to him at last, after all the years, after he had all but despaired.

The room with its yellow walls and flowered jug receded and left them, together with the street noises and the faint squeak of the old bed, until there was only their bodies, one body, given up to each other.

Then Grace's wide eyes flickered, and he read in them the first shiver of her orgasm. He felt the slow kick of his own, gathering within him, irrefutable, finally, question and answer, made and completed and sealed between them.

"Julius," she breathed, her own covenant. *Julius.*

Afterward, when they went back to the Wilmersdorf apartment, Rafael looked up from the chair where he had been sitting reading and saw at once. He ducked his head back over his book, embarrassed by the nakedness of their faces.

"Nathaniel is out," he told them. "Just walking."

Nathaniel had taken to pacing the suburban streets in the shelter of darkness, going nowhere in particular, trying only to work off the frustration of the anxious days.

"Is there any news?" Grace asked.

Rafael shook his head. "Nothing."

He had been thinking of Clio. Something in Grace's look tonight made Clio seem closer, as if she were here in Berlin instead of far off in Paris. He thought suddenly of the little inn in the Thüringer Wald, and the long country nights, and the feather mattress that had enveloped them.

Romy had been conceived at the inn, Clio always said that.

Rafael's face suddenly softened, and he was able to look up at Julius and Grace. There was some joy in Berlin, then, even if it was at odds with everything else that was happening and all the fear that was concentrated inside him.

He stood up and lightly touched Julius's shoulder.

"There is some food," he said. "I went shopping. Shall I lay it out?"

Julius smiled. The taut lines had faded from his face, and the hollows seemed to have filled out. He looked almost like a young boy.

"That would be good," he said simply.

They sat down and ate and talked together. Rafael warmed to Grace a little, because he saw the way that Julius looked at her, and her gentleness to him in return.

When Nathaniel came in, he was tired, and could eat nothing. He drank some of the beer that Rafael had bought, and then went off alone to his *pension*.

Grace knew that she should go back to London. The House was sitting again, and all the speculation was as to whether the King would insist on a morganatic marriage to Mrs. Simpson, or whether he would be forced to abdicate. From the Woodstock Road, she had heard that Cressida was well enough but unusually quiet. According to Eleanor's diagnosis she was probably missing her mother.

Just one or two more days, Grace kept resolving. She could do nothing for Alice. She would allow herself just a few more hours of this strange, sweet, and passionate limbo that Julius had induced, and then she must go home and back to the real world. Neither of them had discussed what must happen when that time came. Julius held on to her, living each moment like a drowning man, and Grace fell under the spell of his intensity.

They moved slowly, as if they were bewitched, from the hotel bedroom to Julius's apartment, out into the cold streets and back into the drafty rooms, entirely lost in each other. Rafael and even Nathaniel were like strangers, on the far periphery of their private world. They talked, almost always about the past, their childhoods and Stretton and Oxford, and the years in between that had brought them here, and they made love, endlessly, with the sharp appetites of the needy.

On December 11 the King abdicated. The four of them heard the news from England on the wireless in Julius's apartment, delivered in solemn, portentous tones by the German news broadcaster.

"Poor devil," Julius said and Grace looked at him, her eyes suddenly bright with tears.

"It is a very great deal to give up, just for a woman," she whispered.

"I would do the same," Julius said.

Nathaniel sat in his corner with his head buried in his hands.

The next day a messenger came to Wilmersdorf from the British Embassy. Nathaniel was required to see the Ambassador at once. He went in a great hurry, pulling on his raincoat and flattening his ancient hat on his head as he emerged into the icy street. Julius went with him, and Grace and Rafael waited at the apartment.

The room they were shown into at the Embassy was small and bare, furnished only with a desk and chairs and a portrait of the King. Julius looked up at it while they waited, wondering if his face would be turned to the wall, or how soon it could be taken down and the new King's image hurried into its place.

Then the Ambassador and one of the Secretaries came into the room, and as soon as he saw them Julius froze with his idle reflections heavy as a stone in his heart. Nathaniel half rose from his place. His bulk seemed awkward and heavy in the confined space, and his knuckles whitened as he struggled to balance by the polished arms of the chair.

"I am afraid I have some very bad news."

The slow, grave words filled the space around them.

There was no air, no light anywhere.

Nathaniel threw his head back, and Julius thought his father was going to howl aloud like a child. He moved quickly, putting his arm under Nathaniel's, having to support what had always seemed a source of power and strength.

Alice was dead.

She had been shot while trying to escape from the Sachsenhausen camp.

The younger diplomat was looking at a single half-sheet of paper held in his hand. "That is all the information we have at the moment. We are doing everything we can to discover how and why this happened. The authorities are being cooperative."

They could not take in what he was saying. Nathaniel had fallen back into the chair. His mouth hung open, and he sucked in one painful breath. Julius knelt beside him and fumbled to loosen his collar stud, and behind him he heard the door opening and the sound of whispered instructions and hurrying feet. A woman with a pearl necklace leaned over his shoulder and held out a glass of brandy. Julius took it and held it up to Nathaniel's mouth.

At last Nathaniel shuddered and leaned forward. He rested one elbow on his knee and pinched the bridge of his nose between his thumb and forefinger. Julius had seen him adopt this pose a thousand times before, discussing some fine point of philology with his graduate students or arbitrating in a family disagreement. It brought back the bookish clutter and the academic preoccupation of the Woodstock Road, sharp as this moment, as the last of his fragile hopes disintegrated. There was no mistake, and no hope. Alice was gone.

He thought of her body, huddled on the ground, and the terrible notion of the bullet hole came unbidden with it. Alice had been a little girl with wiry dark ringlets, running up and down the uneven stairs in the old house. Always behind the rest of them, hurrying to catch up.

Nathaniel seemed to regain some control of himself. Without looking up, he said in a dry voice, "She would not have been trying to escape. She would have known that she would be released soon. That we were all here, working for it."

But she had not been released. They had scratched away at the hard glitter of Nazi Berlin, in all their narrow futility, and they had achieved nothing. Julius thought of the hours they had spent in Grace's little hotel, and the yellow walls that had seemed to make a place of safety.

The Ambassador said, "Our information is that she broke away from her group and ran to the perimeter wire, and kept on running when challenged by the guards. She was warned, but she made no response. A guard fired one shot."

And that was all. There were disappearances every day. Alice was one out of uncounted hundreds or thousands. She was a British citizen, and so there would be questions and official explanations. But it was just one more death, Berlin turning inward, consuming its own flesh. This was not the Germany that Julius had come to years ago, to play the violin and to hear other men's music. He tasted the thickness of disgust on his tongue, disgust with himself for living here for so long, as well as for the regime that had murdered his sister.

The Hirshes could see the diplomats' sympathy and distress, but they could read other truths in the well-bred faces too. There were English girls who came out here and got involved. They made trouble, had affairs with SS men, needed to be bailed out and shipped home. And this was the worst sort of business, the kind they all dreaded. The girl was clearly wide of the mark, and now she was dead. Probably no one would ever know quite how or exactly why. The police and the SS would see to that. It was an incident, a diplomatic embarrassment. It was to be contained, but with the proper degree of dignity and regret. That was what they were thinking.

Julius put his hand over Nathaniel's. The older man's felt cold and boneless. He was still sitting with his head bent, as if he were thinking out some problem in his study at home.

"What will happen now?" Julius asked the blond Englishmen.

After a moment, the younger one said, "We hope that her body will be released to you, for burial here or return to England."

"Thank you," Julius said.

And so Alice would not be huddled into the ground with the other missing, the husbands and fathers and children consumed by Hitler's people. Hitler's people, whom Alice had admired so passionately.

Julius knew that he would cry; he could feel the pain of the unshed tears. But not here, under the Embassy's picture of the displaced King. He must get himself and Nathaniel away from here.

He found a way to stand up, and helped Nathaniel to his feet. They shook hands, listening to the murmurs of sympathy again, and the woman with the pearl necklace opened the door to let them out. They emerged into Wilhelmstrasse. There were cars and buses flooding past them, and people stepping busily and hopefully, and high, shining windows in tiers above their heads.

Nathaniel's head shook, wobbling from side to side like an old man's. Julius guided him to the curb and helped him into a taxi. As they drove past the fashionable cafés and shops and the balconies draped with swastika flags, Julius could only think of Alice lying huddled where she had fallen, and of how she would never see this again, neither these streets nor home, where she belonged.

At Wilmersdorf, Rafael and Grace knew at once that the worst had happened. Julius moved to put his arms around Grace's shoulders and laid his cheek against her hair.

"I am sorry," was all he could say, as if Alice's death were his to apologize for. Grace stood stiffly in his embrace, and her eyes were wide and dry.

"We must tell Eleanor. We must tell her mother," Nathaniel whispered.

It was two days before they were notified that Alice's body had been released. When the message did come, they were taken in a car sent from the Embassy to an anonymous building in the Wedding district of North Berlin. There were two young policemen at the door. They had heavy, uneasy faces, and they stared straight ahead of them as the small group filed past.

Alice's body lay in a plain coffin resting on trestles in a room that looked as if it might once have been a classroom. There were nibbled dents in the dirty walls where maps or posters had been pinned, and the floor was pocked with the marks of desk- and chairlegs. The coffin had been left open, and the lid lay on the floor next to it.

Julius went slowly forward with his arm around his father's shoulders. Grace and Rafael and the doctor that Rafael had brought to examine the body waited beside the door.

In her coffin Alice did not look very much different from the girl who had left London to go to stay with Clio in Paris. Her face was sharpened, and there were hollows under her prominent cheekbones that were like thumbprints in softened wax. But her expression was utterly blank, and as calm as if her eyelids might suddenly spring open and stare unfocused, just for an instant, before life and recollection flooded back into them. Sometimes, Julius remembered, the living face had had that same eerily vacant stare. He would not have remarked on it, in trying to describe Alice to someone who had never known her, but the memory of it struck him now as he looked down into her coffin.

Her hair was loose. It sprang in a wiry mass to cover her forehead and her ears and waved in thick curls around her cheeks.

Nathaniel leaned forward and touched one of her hands. He made a single sound, like a sob that never emerged from his throat. And then he turned and stumbled away. Beside the door, Grace put her hand on his arm. Julius remembered her red nails and the way that the dark-tipped fur of her shako hat seemed to melt into her dark hair.

Julius nodded to the doctor and Rafael. The doctor was a Jew, a middle-aged man with a pale, prematurely lined face. He tiptoed forward and put the tips of his fingers to Alice's chin. He gently turned her head, first to one side and then the other. The hair fell away from the left temple to reveal the bullet hole. There were dark burn-marks in the skin around the black puncture. Julius made himself stand motionless, looking down at where the bullet had entered his sister's brain.

Rafael muttered some words of German and went back to the doorway, to Nathaniel and Grace.

The doctor's fingers moved over Alice's skull. He frowned, as if he were listening to some barely audible instructions. Then he sighed, and his hands dropped to his sides.

Julius lingered for a moment longer. He could think of no blessing or even the gist of a prayer to whisper to Alice. He stooped down instead and picked up the coffin lid. He covered her with it and left her to the darkness.

Outside, when they were away from the young policemen, the doctor told them, "I cannot tell. I can only say that there is a single bullet wound, undoubtedly the cause of death. There are no obvious signs of violence; I think that she may not have been well fed in the days or weeks before her death, but she was not starving." He spread his hands, palms up, showing them his poverty. "I don't know if she was trying to run away or standing still when she died. I am not a forensic specialist."

They did not know and they would never know; Julius was afraid of that.

Rafael said, "I understand."

The doctor added, "You are more fortunate than many. You have her to take back home; you know something, even if it is not enough." And he glanced at them, a sidelong speculative glance that could be quickly deflected, in the way that people in Berlin looked at each other now. "You must have friends somewhere."

Grace stared straight ahead, her dry eyes dark and steady under the cloud of fur. None of the others moved or spoke.

"Is there anything else I may help you with?" the doctor asked. His manner was dignified and professional now; they had a sudden sense of the respected family physician that he must have been before he was denied the right to practice.

"Thank you," Rafael murmured. He paid over some marks, and the doctor took them gratefully, but without looking directly at any of them. He melted away, and the Embassy car slid forward to take them back to Wilmersdorf.

Julius and Rafael made the necessary arrangements. The formalities were completed with surprising speed. All four of them would accompany the coffin back to London; they would travel overnight by train to Paris, and in Paris Clio and Romy would meet them before they moved on again to London and Oxford. Eleanor was waiting in the Woodstock Road. Tabby and Blanche were with her, doing what they could to support her in her grief before Nathaniel came.

It was a good thing that Eleanor needed her husband so much, Julius thought. The need to reach her was the only thing that Nathaniel was able to focus on. He seemed to have shrunk, becoming frail where he had once been as strong as a tree.

Julius was leaving Berlin for good. He packed up his belongings, with Grace's help. He had never taken much interest in material possessions, and so it was not a task that took them very long. Grace remembered the bust of Mozart that had stood on the table in his bare Oxford bedroom when he was a boy. She wrapped it now in a darned jersey and laid it in one of the two suitcases. The apartment was soon stripped bare. Nathaniel's bag had been packed and carried around from the *pension*. Nathaniel himself sat in a chair in the corner. He stared ahead of him, but he seemed to see nothing. Rafael went out, saying that he was going to buy some food for the journey. With all the preparations made, Julius and Grace sat down, close together but not touching, waiting in silence for it to be time to leave.

They were disturbed by the ringing of the downstairs bell. It was the messenger from the Embassy again, and this time he brought a package addressed to Nathaniel.

Inside it there was a letter from the Ambassador, a worn leather-bound notebook, and two sealed envelopes, both of them addressed to Grace. Nathaniel read the letter, and then read it again. He opened the notebook, and slowly turned the thin pages. Then, with a gesture of incomprehension, he held out the book and one of the two envelopes.

"These were returned to the Embassy. He says they are Alice's personal effects." His voice cracked, but he went on. "Not very much, is it? But I suppose we should continue to consider ourselves lucky. It is something of her, at least." Then he held out the second envelope. Grace recognized the Nazi insignia at once. "This is for you, also."

Grace opened the thick, cream-colored envelope first.

It was a personal letter from Hitler.

She puzzled over the high-flown German phrases, understanding only the gist of them.

The Führer deeply regretted the circumstances surrounding the tragic death of Lady Grace's young relative. It was a most disturbing and unfortunate accident, and the Führer wished to assure her that he sincerely mourned the loss of such a life. His sympathy was all for the young lady's bereaved parents, and of course for Lady Grace herself. If there was anything he might be allowed to do, to assist them in any way, then she must not hesitate to indicate it. He remained, and so on.

Grace folded the thick paper and pushed it away from her. Then she took up the leather notebook. The pages were very thin and ruled with faint blue lines. They were covered with drawings, all done with the same soft and very blunt pencil.

Alice had no talent as an artist. But in the camp she had made laborious efforts to draw some of the places she had known, from memory, as if even such inaccurate representations would bring them closer, would somehow bring home nearer to Sachsenhausen. Slowly Grace turned the pages. She recognized the south front of Stretton, although Alice had put in too many windows, and surely this domed building was the Radcliffe Camera? There was an attempt at the garden in the Woodstock Road, and the house itself, with the turret under the witch's hat of purple slate.

Every page had been used. Clearly there would be no more paper, once this was all used up. There were tiny drawings around the edges of the larger ones, faces and figures, not all of them recognizable. Jake and Nathaniel himself were distinguishable by their beards. And these, the faces of two women in profile, looking away in opposite directions, these must be Clio and herself. The pose was the same as *The Janus Face.*

Grace closed the little book and then clumsily handed it over to Julius. She didn't want to have to watch his face as he studied the tiny, incompetent drawings. She stood up instead and walked away to the window. There, with her back to them, she looked at the second envelope.

This one was thin, of the cheapest quality. It was creased and stained, as if it had been written some time ago and then kept hidden.

Alice had addressed the letter very formally, to *Lady Grace Brock.* She had written out the Vincent Street address and added *London, S.W.* There was no stamp, of course. Grace wondered if Alice had planned somehow to send it, or if the writing of it had been just a dream, connecting her back to the old, solid world, like the drawings in her notebook.

She slit open the flimsy envelope. Alice had written in the same blunt pencil, on a sheet of paper torn from the notebook.

Her voice shouted off the page, so clearly audible that Grace had to close her eyes for a second. She had not cried since the news of Alice's death, not even after they had left the coffin in the deserted classroom, but she almost wept now. Alice had written,

> I can imagine what everyone must say, Pappy and Ma and all the others except for you. But I know you know differently, Grace darling, you will understand that I did do wrong and seemed to pull a gun on the Führer, although it was really only a stupid accident. I saw his dear face, through all the confusion, and he seemed only surprised, not angry or afraid. And then when I looked again he was gone and the guards were so red and violent out of fear for him and they marched me away. It is all a sad mistake, but it has not changed the way I feel about anything. There must be rules, and proper punishments, mustn't there? I can bear it quite well, except that there are so many Jews. And I know that soon the mistake will be sorted out, because I am not guilty of anything. I wanted to tell you this, Grace, because you believe in what is Right, as I do. We must never, never give up. I think about you, and Vincent Street, and all the other times, and about coming home soon. I am quite brave, really, you know. Until I see you again, love from your Alice.
> Heil Hitler. God Save the King.

Alice would not have known about the Abdication, Grace remembered. She had always admired Edward. As a little girl, she had kept a scrapbook of his foreign tours.

The thin sheet of paper rustled in her fingers. Grace was stricken by the pathos of the letter. It was so much like Alice herself, such a halting mixture of naïveté and defiance and devotion.

Julius and Nathaniel were both watching her. Grace knew that she could not cry here and now. There was the long journey ahead of them, and Julius and Nathaniel needed her strength.

"What does she say?" Nathaniel asked. "It's odd that she should write to you." Not to her father, or her mother. The words were unspoken, but she heard them.

Awkwardly Grace held out the sheet of paper. It was not odd at all; she wished that it was, so that she might be absolved from the responsibility.

Nathaniel read the letter and then gave it to Julius. Neither of them spoke, but Grace suddenly sensed in Nathaniel the silent and destructive vibration of blame. If Alice had not fallen under her cousin's spell. If she had not adopted Grace's political alignments with such misplaced fervor.

If the world had been a different place, Grace thought bitterly.

But she did not flinch. She put the other letter into Nathaniel's hand. He read it much more quickly than she had done, and then with a hiss of anger he crumpled it sharply into a ball and flung it away.

Julius stood up. Every movement in the still room seemed exaggerated. He paced slowly around the confined space and stopped at the window.

"Where is Rafael?" he said.

Grace realized instantly that he had been away for a long while. Much longer than it should take to walk to the little Jewish-run grocer's shop and back again.

It was almost time for them to leave for the station.

She ran to the window and looked down into the street. It had grown dark, and there were few passers-by. As she craned from side to side, her breath made a foggy cloud on the cold glass, and she rubbed it away with the tips of her fingers. Somewhere in the chambers of her mind a memory stirred.

There was no sign of Rafael.

"He should be back," she said wildly. "He should have been back long ago."

Julius took two steps to the window. The darkness beyond the glass loomed threateningly, and he felt fear tightening like a red-hot wire around his neck.

"Where is he?" he repeated. It seemed terrible now that they had not realized he was so late. He could hear Grace's breathing beside him, and the hollow thumping of his own heart.

"I'm afraid," Grace whispered. "Julius, I'm afraid for him."

He took her hand. They knew too much about the Nazi patrols who roamed the streets. There were policemen and storm troopers and gangs of youths who set upon whoever crossed their path in the wrong direction.

Nathaniel's face was gray. He looked past Grace and Julius to the black square of the window. "We must wait," he said, but his voice was heavy as if he knew already what had happened.

They waited in silence.

The seconds ticked by. The three of them were frozen, aching with the intensity of their waiting. Every sound was magnified, so that they looked at one another with the ballooning of hope and then with its deflation. The scrape of Rafael's key in the lock never came.

Julius looked at his watch. His arm felt heavy, as if his clothes were waterlogged.

"You must go," he told Nathaniel and Grace. The Embassy was arranging for the coffin to be collected from Wedding and placed in the guard's compartment of the Paris train. They had to be on that train with Alice. "You must take her home. I will wait here for Rafael."

"No."

Nathaniel shouted at him. There were wet fronds in the gray beard around his lips and purplish veins stood out on his temples.

"We will all go. Do you understand me?"

Grace was shivering. The darkness outside was full of threats.

In his gentle way Julius said, "I can't go and leave Rafael here, not without knowing what has happened to him."

But they all did know what must have happened. Rafael was a Jew, and a subversive. His efforts on Alice's behalf must have made him too conspicuous in the wrong places. The rest of them were British, and an embarrassment that the Reich would be glad to be rid of. But Rafael could not be allowed to slip away with them to safety, not a second time.

The shock of his absence reverberated in the room. They were all standing now, helpless and afraid. Nathaniel wiped his mouth with the back of his hand. He tried to speak calmly in order to persuade

Julius. There was no time for any subtlety. He must be made to leave now, immediately.

Brutally Nathaniel said, "What do you imagine you can do for him? What have we been able to do for Alice by staying here in Berlin? You are only risking yourself."

"No more than in the last year, or two years."

"No," Nathaniel shouted again.

He looked to Grace for her support. He could blame her indirectly for Alice's death, but he would also take what she could give now. He had no shred of pride left.

Grace tried to take Julius's hand. He withdrew it and held it close against his chest.

"I think your father is right," she said softly. There was no one they could turn to for help for Rafael. She didn't think that she could even find the Café Josef if she went looking for it. And if she did stumble across it, what could she say, and to whom?

A last image of the great brown city swept by marching men and their bloodred banners came to her. There was power and evil in unquantifiable measure. It was absurd to think they could do anything here, except escape from it while escape was still possible.

"Come now," she begged him.

He hesitated, the conflict plainly visible in his haggard face.

"Now," Nathaniel repeated. They could hear the quick minutes ticking away.

With a sudden violent lunge Julius reached and hauled two of their waiting suitcases into his arms. With his head bent, looking nowhere, he shouldered out of the apartment and down the stairs. Grace and Nathaniel followed him with their share of the luggage. The door slammed shut behind them. They stood huddled together, scanning the street, in the hope that Rafael might somehow appear at this very last moment. Then, with a rattle of ancient bodywork, a taxi materialized at the corner.

The Bahnhof Zoo was a hissing cavern of noise and steam under its great arched roof. There was a stink of smoke and grease. The Paris train stood at the platform, and the last passengers were climbing into their compartments. A young man, unmistakably from the British Embassy in his dark overcoat and bowler hat, was waiting beside the closed van at the end of the train. He was anxiously staring along the length of the platform.

As soon as he saw Nathaniel he dashed forward, then remembered why he was there and slowed to a respectful pace again. "I was afraid something had detained you."

None of them could speak.

"The coffin has been put aboard. The papers are all in order." Nathaniel took them and folded them inside his old raincoat.

"The train is about to leave, sir."

A porter opened a door for them, and they climbed into the high carriage next to the goods van. Their luggage was bundled in somehow beside them. The door slammed, and from somewhere along the platform a whistle blew. The young man reached up and shook Nathaniel's hand through the open window. Then he stood back as the train began to move and his arm twitched as if he suppressed a military salute. The last thing they saw of him, through a billow of steam, was the expression of clear relief on his face. He had done his duty and seen his three British subjects, including the Member of Parliament, safely onto the Paris train. There had been no members of the Press to see them go, and no other difficulties had arisen. The absence of the fourth person, the German Jew, was no concern of his.

Grace and Julius and Nathaniel sat upright on the hard seats of the third-class compartment and watched the lights of Berlin slide past the windows. The train gathered speed, and soon they were rolling through the suburbs, where the lights were sparser and the black, empty stretches marked the expanses of forest and water. Then there were no lights at all, and the city lay behind them.

Nathaniel sat silent and unmoving in his corner, just as he had been used to sitting for hours at a time in the apartment. Grace and Julius looked at each other, saw no comfort in each other's faces, and looked away again. Both of them were thinking of Rafael, and where he might be now, and what he might be suffering and would have to suffer. And they knew that in the early morning, in Paris, Clio and their daughter would be waiting to meet him off the train. There was no word that they could offer each other to dispel either their grief for Alice, or their dread of that meeting.

Grace stared unseeingly into the darkness. She recalled the happiness that she and Julius had allowed themselves in Berlin. It seemed separate from her now, a remote and barely conceivable historical emotion that seemed unlikely to survive under the weight of her sadness and guilt. She felt the old constraints of London, of home and the House and Cressida, beginning to lock themselves around her.

Much later, Julius stood up and went to stretch his cramped legs in the corridor. Nathaniel appeared to be asleep; Grace's eyes were wide open, but her head was turned away from him, her gaze fixed on the black window.

The corridor lights were dim. Julius leaned against the murky glass and lit a cigarette, swaying with the motion of the train. Then, as they slowed at a crossing, he glimpsed a streetlight in a halo of rain, and the crossing gates, and a sign alongside them that read *"Passage Interdit."*

For a moment he did not grasp the significance of it. Then he slid open the door of the compartment. Grace turned her white face up to him. "We are in France," he told her.

Germany lay behind them. The train slowed, and lights gathered beyond the windows. When they stopped, it was to let the French customs officials come aboard.

At last, in the dirty light of the very early morning, they reached Paris.

Julius saw Clio and Romy first. They were waiting by the barrier, watching the faces of the disembarking passengers. Clio was wearing a long dark coat and a little hat with a brim that turned back from her face. She was holding Romy up in her arms, and the child reached her fists toward the people that hustled past them. Clio caught sight of Julius at almost the same instant. He felt her catch her breath and then she began to run, pushing her way through the crowds, her head bobbing as she searched for the first glimpse of Rafael.

She reached them, breathless in her haste, with the confusion of eagerness and anxiety and sorrow in her eyes. She counted their three faces, and looked again, still searching, and then her eyes darted to the train and the long line of open doors that disgorged the last few travelers.

Julius and Nathaniel went to her, one to each side. Grace hung back, one hand drawing her furs close around her throat.

"Where is he?" Clio's face had gone gray. Even her lips were colorless.

"Papa?" Romy said, in a bright voice.

"Clio, he—he was taken, last night," Julius said.

Clio's arms involuntarily tightened around the child. She looked dazed, but she was still scanning the faces of the passengers who trickled past them.

"Taken?" She turned to her father. "Taken where?"

"We don't know. He went out to buy some food. Just an errand, two streets away. He didn't come back."

The full meaning of the words stabbed through to Clio at last. She half shook her head, as if to deny them, and then all the muscles of her face seemed to contract in a single spasm. Her eyes screwed up and her mouth opened in a cry, the more terrible because it was silent. Shocking, sudden tears swelled out under the black spikes of her eyelashes and spilled down her cheeks.

"Mama?"

Romy took one look at her mother's face, and then she began to scream. The child's body went stiff, and her screams rose over the station hubbub. Grace came forward and tried to take her out of her mother's arms. But Clio's grip tightened fiercely, and she swung Romy away, out of Grace's reach.

"Pappy," Clio whispered, with the mask of tears covering her face. "Oh, Pappy, what is happening to the world?"

She laid her head against his broad shoulder with the child sandwiched between them, and rocked her, and went on rocking until Nathaniel swayed with them, and the three of them stood on the platform until the first spasm of Clio's grief had worn itself out and Romy's screams had subsided into little muffled sobs and cries.

It was a journey like none of them had ever known. The Channel was rough, and the ferry plowed through the vicious waves that sent sheets of water skidding over the decks. Salt spray rose to blind them as they clung to the plunging rails.

Alice's coffin had been carried into a closed section of the hold. Nathaniel refused to leave her there alone, and he sat through the crossing in the semidarkness in the depths of the ship, willing himself and Alice's body to reach peace in Oxford.

Julius and Grace stood together toward the stern of the ship, where the angle of a rust-browned companionway gave them some protection from the wind and the spray. Grace looked out at the turbulent water, eternally busy like some coiling and recoiling monster, and found herself shivering uncontrollably. Julius moved his body to shield her from the weather, and he leaned down to kiss Grace's mouth. Her skin was cold and tasted of salt. They drew together, feeling the warmth of each other's bodies, and remembered how they had made love in the white-curtained room. Not even this journey could quite obliterate those memories.

"What will we do?" Julius asked, moving his mouth against her. He meant when they had reached England and the funeral was over, and there was somehow light in the sky again. He knew that he should not press her, now of all times, but his fear of losing Grace overcame everything, even his grief and guilt.

"I don't know," Grace said sadly, and her voice was cold, like her face. But she reached up and put her hands to his cheeks.

Clio had been walking the decks. She had found it unbearable to sit in the crowded saloon amongst so many people, and so she had come out into the full force of the wind and stinging spray even though she knew it was too cold for Romy. She carried the child wrapped inside her coat, drawing some comfort from the warmth of her small body. Romy's head in a knitted cap rested against her mother's shoulder, and her thumb had crept into her mouth. She had stopped asking, for the moment at least, when Papa would be coming.

Clio came upon Grace and Julius unexpectedly. They were utterly absorbed in each other, and she was able to watch them for a moment. She saw the weariness and despair in Julius, and the way that Grace held his face cupped between her hands. The thread of visible intimacy that linked them, the very lines of their bodies, told Clio what had happened in Berlin.

She felt a flash of anger burning through her. In that instant it consumed her grief for Alice and her longing for Rafael, and all she could feel was hatred for Grace like an immense pounding wave surging through all the conduits of her body.

It was because of Grace that Alice had fallen in love with fascism.

And so it was because of Grace that Alice had pursued her love to Germany, and it was Grace's fault that she was dead.

Rafael had gone to Berlin for Alice's sake, and the images of what would befall him now had filled Clio's head ever since he had failed to appear on the platform in Paris.

All the threads of disaster ran back to Grace, like the filaments of a spider's web converging on the creature at the center. And in the midst of it, Grace exerted her old, malign influence on Clio's beloved Julius. He loved her more than he had ever done, Clio could see it even in that single brief glimpse.

Only Grace would not make him happy. Grace was incapable of that.

Clio turned abruptly back the way she had come. She walked into the salt wind, bareheaded, like a wild woman. With Romy still

wrapped in her arms, she hunched inward over her hatred for
Grace, containing it, like a live coal smoldering next to her heart.

Alice was buried in the little church of St. Cross. It was a tranquil
place, a green and gray enclosure surrounding the tiny square-
towered church. The ancient stone walls of the graveyard were
softened with green plaits of ivy.

Cressida stood between Grace and Clio. She had looked down
once, over the red-brown earth lip of the grave to the shiny coffin
and its single wreath of lilies, and she had felt giddy with the fear of
what it would be like to fall in there and to lie helpless and hear the
earth tumbling in to cover her. She jerked her head up, fixing her
eyes on the gray strata of the clouds instead. The wind was sharp in
her face, but it smelled of leaf mold and smoke and the rain-marked
petals of flowers. It smelled of life.

Opposite her, Cressida could see that Aunt Eleanor was crying.
She held a handkerchief up to her eyes, and her mouth was twisted.
Julius and Jake stood on one side of her, and Nathaniel on the other.
Jake looked broad and strong, as Cressida remembered Nathaniel
being in her childhood, as if the life had somehow drained and
trickled away from the father into the son. Aunt Ruth stood a little
farther back, in an old-fashioned black costume that was too tight
for her. She was studying the Burial Service in the prayer book with
a tight, closed face, as if it might contain something subversive.
Her plain-faced, clever-looking children were with her. Cressida
did not know them very well.

There were dozens of people at the funeral whom she did not
know. Many of Nathaniel's University friends and colleagues were
here, and neighbors from the big red- and yellow-brick houses of
North Oxford, and teachers and schoolfriends of Alice. Most of the
mourners believed that Alice had been killed in a motor accident
while traveling in Germany. Aunt Eleanor had insisted on that.
Cressida wondered if Alice would have preferred them to know the
truth.

Her scrutiny moved on to Julius. He was looking across the sharp
mouth of the grave and the heaped-up bank of earth waiting beside
it, to Grace. With a shock, Cressida recognized something she had
never seen before. Or if she had seen it, she had never understood it.
It was a man's adult longing, raw and urgent and needy.

Had she suddenly become old enough, then, to notice such
things?

The realization that Julius's longing was directed at her mother made Cressida's throat tighten with dismay and alarm. Her hands were cold, but the palms suddenly felt clammy with sweat. She stole a quick sideways glance.

Beneath the mesh of her black veil, Grace's profile might have been cut in white marble.

The sleeves of the vicar's surplice twisted in the wind like the wings of a sea bird. He stooped to the bank of earth and tossed a handful of it into the grave. The cold crumbs rattled on the coffin lid.

It was then that Cressida saw Pilgrim. He was standing a little distance apart from the other mourners. He held his black coat closely swathed around him against the biting cold and the brim of his big hat was pulled down, but Cressida knew it was him. She had not asked Grace for the truth, although she had thought about it constantly. She was afraid of the question, and the answers.

Cressida made a tiny, involuntary sound in the back of her throat. Her hand lifted, in the beginning to ward off reality, and adulthood, which hung like twin threats over her head. Then her hand dropped again. Clio saw and heard her, and she put an arm around Cressida's shoulder and drew her close against her side.

The vicar had read the last prayer. There was a sigh as they bent their heads, and those of them who were able to pray prayed also, in silence. Tabby's eyes were closed and her lips moved.

When Cressida looked up again, it was to see Aunt Eleanor holding a fistful of earth in her black suede-gloved hand. The fingers straightened one by one, and the dirt fell into the grave. Pilgrim had slipped away.

Julius and Grace found themselves alone together in one of the black cars that were ferrying the mourners back to the Woodstock Road. Julius leaned forward to check that the glass panel separating them from the driver was firmly closed. He wondered if he was mad, or wicked, because the sight of Grace's black silk-covered legs inflamed him even now, on the way home from his sister's funeral.

"Will you let me come to Vincent Street?" he asked her.

Grace turned her marble face. With part of herself she longed to say, *Yes, come home with me and we will hide together.*

Julius would warm her and keep off the cold wind, she knew that.

But she also knew that she could not let him. The hope that had shimmered in Berlin, far from home, before Alice's death, had withered entirely away.

In the wretched aftermath of Rafael's disappearance, she had turned the possibility of marrying Julius over and over in her mind. She had come to the slow and bitter conclusion that it would be a mistake for them to cling together now. It would be out of weakness bred from their mutual sorrow and need.

But there was also another, much older conviction, that came back to her now that they were home. Julius and she were too close. They were more than first cousins, just as Clio and she were too close for cousinhood and yet too separate to be twins. They were the same, siblings and more than siblings deep in their bones, and to marry Julius would be wrong as well as weak.

He had asked her once, long ago, she remembered. On the night when she had announced to the magic circle that she was pregnant.

"Marry me, not Anthony Brock," Julius had begged her.

And Grace had answered that she could not, because it would be like marrying Clio.

There had been a deeper truth in that than she had understood then. There was no future for Grace and Julius together; there had never been, ever since they had been children together.

Grace made herself answer; she had always been able to find the iron within herself.

"I can't," she said at last.

"Is it because of Cressida?"

She owed him the truth, at least.

"No, it isn't because of Cressida. It's because I believe it would be wrong for both of us."

Julius looked down at his hands. They lay in his lap, musician's hands with long, broad-tipped fingers. They seemed meaty and heavy and useless now, for all that they had once stroked Grace's skin and made her turn herself up to him, like a flower opening.

"I love you," he said, because he could think of nothing better to offer her. His voice sounded muffled in his own ears.

Grace knew that she had loved him too, but the last days had severed the love and left it lying like an amputated limb. It was there, a physical fact with its own familiar contours, but it was no longer a part of them.

The thought of Clio came into her head. Clio had hardly been able to bring herself to speak to Grace since they had met on the terrible morning in Paris.

"We can't go back to Berlin," Grace said softly.

They were already in the Woodstock Road. By arrangement, the mourners were returning there for sandwiches and tea and whiskey, the necessary inner fortification after the cold church and windy graveside. Julius knew that he was needed there, to support Eleanor and Nathaniel, but he doubted that he could find the strength within himself.

Grace put her gloved hand over his.

"You must," she said, as if she had read his thoughts.

Elizabeth went back to the family papers after she had seen the photograph of Alice at the Blackshirt rally. She knew that Alice Hirsh had been killed in a motor accident in Germany at the end of 1936, when she was only twenty-four years old. But there was still something that stirred her biographer's curiosity and senses, some deeper connection between Grace and her cousin that she had not fully teased out.

Probably the only person left who could tell her the truth was Clio, and Elizabeth was not anxious to repeat too many of their elliptical conversations that left her feeling confused or—if it was conceivable that a frail ninety-year-old could be capable of it—neatly evaded.

In the end, she made her discovery by accident. She was looking again at Grace's photograph albums. It was the album for 1937, clearly labeled as such in Grace's handwriting on the inside front cover. The great event of the year was the Coronation. Grace had given a party at Vincent Street, and there was a series of photographs of her guests arriving in evening clothes. Amongst them Elizabeth recognized Lord and Lady Astor, Lord Lothian, Sir Oswald Mosley, and Lady Alexandra Metcalf. There was also a formal portrait of Grace herself in Court dress, looking very beautiful with ropes of pearls at her throat and plumes of feathers in her hair.

If there was anything noticeable about the volume, it was the lack of informal and family snapshots. Grace seemed to have had an unusually busy political and social year.

Elizabeth was about to close the heavy leather-bound covers when she noticed that there was a flap pocket at the inside back. She slipped her fingers into it, half hoping that she might discover some photographic negatives, perhaps scenes from some entirely separate and secret portion of Grace's life.

Her fingers encountered something. She drew it out, and saw that it was a piece of lined paper torn from a book. It was covered with pencil writing, faded almost to the point of illegibility.

Holding the paper up to the anglepoise lamp on her desk, squinting at each word, Elizabeth read Alice's letter.

She read it again, and again. The parts of it that she could decipher made no sense. Was it a game, or some overblown girlish code, or simply gibberish? The talk of guards and guns and the Führer surely indicated one of those things. Elizabeth knew the facts: Alice had gone to Munich to learn German, like so many girls of her class and generation, and had died in an accident.

And afterward, as if the grief of her loss had been too much for the rest of them to bear, it was as if she had never lived. The memories of her seemed all to have been locked away and then forgotten.

Elizabeth made a trip to Oxford. She found the old church and the graveyard, surrounded now by modern buildings of yellow brick and plate glass, and after an hour's searching in the wet grass she stumbled across Alice's grave. The simple stone tablet read:

ALICE HIRSH,
born March 1912,
died in Germany,
December 1936.
Ask not for whom
the bell tolls.

And then Elizabeth went to call on Clio again.

The old lady was sitting in her usual place, under the portrait. Her sparse white hair was freshly washed, and one of her nurses had teased it into a halo around her skull.

Elizabeth read the letter to her and explained where she had found it. Clio nodded her head very slowly.

Patiently, Elizabeth said, "I wonder if you could tell me what it might mean. She was only a young girl. *Could* there have been guards and a gun?"

She waited for a long moment until she was convinced that Clio must have forgotten the question. She opened her mouth to repeat it, but Clio darted a look at her. Her watery eyes seemed to peer obliquely outward, then skid away again to the contemplation of some inner mystery. It was this look, in particular, that convinced Elizabeth that Clio knew everything, and was telling nothing.

"What does it mean?" Elizabeth asked again.

"I don't know," Clio said. She closed her eyes. "Alice was very imaginative. You must have found out that much about her."

"I can find out hardly anything. History seems to have swallowed her up. It is almost as if she never was."

"I don't know anything about that," Clio said.

She didn't open her eyes, and Elizabeth closed her notebook on the brittle sheet of paper with a resentful snap.

Twenty-One

London, 1938

JULIUS WAS PLAYING THE D major Mozart Concerto again, but this time there would be no shrill whistling from brownshirts at the back of the hall. The audience at the Wigmore Hall would politely applaud his performance, not too loud or not too long, then disperse to restaurants and supper parties across London.

He put on his tailcoat over his white waistcoat and brushed the lapels out of habit rather than concern for his appearance. He was thinking about the conversations that would be held across those dinner tables; he did not imagine that many of them would touch for too long on the music or his performance. He would play adequately, he was experienced enough to do that, but the need or the hunger—or even the ability—to achieve more had left him. There would be no fire or fury tonight; there had been none for a long while.

Julius looked at his watch. It was almost time. He flexed his wrists and his fingers, and then picked up his violin. With a practiced sweep he tucked it under his chin, closed his eyes, and began to play.

The music did not dispel the heaviness that afflicted his limbs as well as his spirit. There had been a time when it did, but now it seemed that he did not have even that resource left within him.

He lowered his bow, and put the violin down again. He sat in the dressing room's armchair instead and waited for the call.

He came out onstage to the soloist's applause. When he straightened after making his bow, he caught sight of Grace at once. She was sitting in the fourth row, beside Lord and Lady Astor. T. J. Jones, one of the deputy Cabinet Secretaries, was also in the party. Julius was not surprised by the company. Grace had become a regular member of the Cliveden Set.

She was smiling up at him. Her face was like a circle of light in some great, dim space.

Under the cover of the applause that greeted the conductor for the evening, he nodded gravely to her.

The normality of his response was a small achievement.

To see her even now gave him pleasure as well as pain, the fiercest combination of the two that was the only feeling that properly stirred him. Julius had stayed in London because there was always the possibility that their paths might cross somewhere, yet he was afraid of what he might do or say when they did meet. He did not want to weep or to implore her, but he did not want to let her out of his sight, now or ever again.

The conductor raised his baton.

Julius lifted his bow again, and began to play.

Tonight he was better than adequate, far better, because he was playing for Grace.

At the end of the concert when he took his bows, he saw her white-gloved hands clapping in the dim space. He felt that he was being beaten between her palms. His body and his heart ached.

In the dressing room he took off his coat and hung it up, but he did not pull the ends of his white tie and loosen his collar stud, as he would normally have done. He was thinking, *Surely she will come back. Just for a few moments, before she goes on to her political dinner.*

When the tap at the door did come and he reached to open it, he was already smiling. Her name was in his mouth.

When he saw the tall, silver-haired woman standing in the dingy corridor, it took him a few seconds to remember that she was Isolde, Pilgrim's one-time model and girlfriend. She raised a pen-ciled eyebrow at him.

"Is this quite unwelcome?"

"Of course not. No, of course it isn't." He held the door open wider, and Isolde strolled into the dressing room. She inspected it, and then turned to look at him.

"You played wonderfully. Congratulations."

"Thank you." Julius peered vaguely around the small space. He felt confused, and silenced by disappointment that this visitor was not Grace after all.

"Better than the last time I came to a concert of yours, eh?"

Of course, Isolde had been there with Pilgrim that night at the Berlin Philharmonic Hall. They had even taken him back to their studio, wherever it was, and he had stayed there for a few days.

Hiding from the Nazis. It was odd that he had forgotten that. His memory played tricks on him nowadays. It seemed to obliterate large patches of time, and then to highlight apparently trivial events until they loomed enormously in his mind. He was haunted by recollections of meaningless meals and conversations that had taken place years before.

"Yes, it was better than that. Look, I would offer you a drink, but I don't keep anything here. . . ."

Isolde seemed to stare challengingly at him. "We could always go to the pub. After you've changed."

"Yes, we could do that. If you would like to."

There was another knock at the door. This time it was Grace who was standing there. Again, there was the impression of a bright light. Julius found the conventional words, somehow. He realized that he didn't know how long it was since he had last spoken to her.

"Grace, how wonderful. Come in, please come in."

She put her hands on his arms, and he kissed her cheek. The shape and the scent and the feel of her were just the same. The memories of Berlin folded around him, splendid and suffocating.

"Julius, I can see you're busy. I just wanted to say that that was wonderful. The Mozart, especially." She was warm, and easy, and unaffected. "Hello, Isolde."

"We were just off to the boozer," Isolde said. She had never been an admirer of Grace.

"Then I won't keep you. I just wanted to look in and say hello."

Julius thought that if anything, Grace was pleased and relieved by the evidence that he was occupied with another woman, as if it absolved her from the responsibility.

Please stay, he wanted to whisper to her. *Please.*

He could have cursed Isolde. Grace and he were thirty-seven years old, and like an importunate child he still longed to catch hold of her and imprison her. He knew that Grace saw it too. Her face was suddenly shadowed by the nexus of memories and associations.

"I'd better go," she whispered. "They're waiting for me."

Julius said woodenly, "Yes. Of course."

There had been a time, perhaps a year ago—after Alice had died—when he would have begged her. At Vincent Street, or in restaurants, once in a booth at a nightclub, although he could not remember the sequence of events that had led them there, he would plead with her. He had wept, or shouted, or groveled in any other way that might possibly affect her. He had no pride left, and no sense of propriety. It was simply that once he had possessed her, it was unthinkable to be without her.

He understood what until then had seemed an overblown metaphor; after Grace had gone away from him, the world had come to an end.

She had stood firm, from the time of Alice's funeral. Her strength had awed and amazed him.

"We can't go back to Berlin."

They could not go back, nor could she make him understand that the heat of those guilty days had died within her. Once they were back in England, and she had seen Eleanor's grief and Clio doggedly clinging to the hope of news from Rafael, the flame of love and hope inside her had simply flickered and gone out. There was no future for herself and Julius, and it was a weakness to have imagined that there might be.

Only she would have done anything possible to avoid causing him pain, and whatever she did do seemed to hurt him more deeply. In the end there had been nothing for it but to withdraw altogether. For months they had not seen each other at all. Grace had thrown herself back into her political career, in which dedication and ambition stood in almost convincingly for love and intimacy.

"Thank you for the music," she said softly.

She put her hands on his arms again, white gloves against his white shirtsleeves, and kissed his cheek in return.

Outside the corridor the last members of the orchestra were hauling their instruments away. Grace drew her evening cape around her and listened to the echo of her own heels tapping on the cold tiled floor. She was going to dinner with the Astors in St. James's Square. The talk would be about Germany and Austria, and Chamberlain's Anglo-Italian agreement with Mussolini.

"The *pub*, wasn't it?" Isolde reminded Julius.

Obediently he took off his white tie and waistcoat and pulled on an old sweater and tweed coat. He put his violin into its worn leather case and packed away his tailcoat, then went out into the rainy night with Isolde.

They went to the nearest-but-one pub and sat down at a table in the saloon bar. Julius bought a whiskey and lemonade for Isolde and a pint for himself. His head was still full of the sight of Grace with her bare shoulders swathed in fur.

"Cheers," Isolde said brightly, and tipped her glass.

"How is Pilgrim?" Julius attempted.

Isolde shrugged. "You know Quint. The girls get younger, and the drinks go down faster. I don't know how many pictures he's selling nowadays."

Julius nodded. Looking at Isolde, he saw that she was still a beauty of a kind. Her silver hair was dark at the roots and her triangular cat's face was marked with lines, but her manner was still arresting. Several of the pub's customers had glanced over at her. She might be as old as forty, he calculated, but she had kept her model girl's body. He felt no stirring of interest in it.

Isolde was examining his face with her small head held on one side. She leaned forward suddenly and said, "What's wrong? You can talk to me about it if you want, you know. I'm a good listener."

"Nothing is wrong."

Her warmth touched him, however. He had no wish to talk, but he bought her another whiskey and lemonade. Isolde smoked Sobranie cigarettes and chattered to fill the silence. He noticed that she crossed and recrossed her well-shaped legs in front of him and turned in her chair so that the fabric of her skirt stretched over one hip.

"You are not very like your brother," Isolde teased him at last.

"Jake?" Julius was startled.

"Jake would have taken me home and been finished and on his way back to his wife by now." She blew out a long column of smoke, and sighed. "Or there was a time when he would."

Julius knew that Jake had women, but he would not have put Isolde on the list.

"Does that surprise you?" Isolde's ankle rubbed against his.

"A little."

"First time was after some bloody private view of Pilgrim's. Mobs of people, shouting at the tops of their voices, just like always. Albemarle Street, that's where it was. That terrible portrait of her ladyship and your sister was part of the show."

"The Janus Face," Julius said.

"That's right. Bloody stupid. And Pilgrim was being cocky, and revoltingly rude to poor old Jeannie. So I took your black-bearded brother off home with me. Very nice it was too. I saw him a few times more after that." She shrugged her narrow shoulders again. "And then it stopped. Just one of those things. Ten, eleven years ago now. Would you believe it?" Her smile had faded. She was looking down into her empty glass.

"What happened to Jeannie?"

"Didn't you know? She died."

Julius didn't want to hear how.

Jeannie had been the first woman he had ever slept with, in his digs in Bloomsbury. She had been Pilgrim's model and girlfriend also.

There was a symmetry in that, he thought, *Jake and Isolde. Jeannie and me.* He remembered Jeannie's loosening flesh, and the fox-red bush of her pubic hair, and the way that her appetite had disconcerted him, the innocent boy.

He had not wanted to sleep with her again.

It came to him now that he had never wanted anything very much. The blankness of his life confronted him like a rock wall. He felt that he was looking up the cliff and from side to side, in search of a hand- or a toehold, but he could see nothing, only the sheer unbroken expanse, stretching away. It gave him vertigo. He felt sad for the poverty of a life that had slipped by almost unlived, and he was also full of fear.

All his adult life, he understood, he had been waiting for Grace. Even when she was married to Anthony, he had found some queer resistance within himself that had enabled him to go on waiting. Before Berlin he had even been content, in his passive way. He had been able to convince himself that there was ample time, in some stately and inexorable progress that they were making toward each other, and that in the end they would be joined together.

Then she had come to him, like lightning splitting a rock, and he had lost her again.

He had been right in Berlin. The central passage of his life had indeed been acted out within the yellow walls of the little hotel bedroom.

And the futility of everything else, before and after that, glared back at him from the cliff face.

Isolde was staring at him. "Poor Jeannie. She was drunk. Vomited in her sleep, you know, then inhaled it. Drowned in her own mess."

Julius closed his eyes. "I have to go, Isolde."

"One more drink," she said briskly. "I'm buying."

He felt weak, as if standing up and walking to the door presented some great obstacle. The two pints of beer he had drunk were gassy in his stomach. "Whiskey, then," he said.

She came back from the bar with two doubles and put Julius's in front of him.

"Drink it," she ordered.

He did as he was told, like a sleepwalker.

"All right," Isolde said, when the glasses were empty once more. She put her hand under his elbow and helped him to his feet.

Outside in the street she stepped squarely in front of him. Then she swayed forward so that her hips touched his and the length of her body came warmly against him. She took his face between her hands and kissed him on the mouth. Her tongue darted between his lips.

Julius shivered with cold. The feel of her cheek and mouth and her breasts pressing against him was negligible, neither exciting nor disgusting. It was as if both of them were slabs of meat, and he had no more sensation in his own layers of tissue and muscle and bone than he could detect in the woman's.

Isolde's hands fell to her sides. She drew her head back. "I see," she said. "That uninteresting, am I?"

"It isn't that—"

She cut him short. "Never mind. It was worth a try." Julius realized that she must be lonely, just as he was.

"I'm sorry," he said humbly. There was no possibility of anything else.

Isolde was pulling her coat around her. Her hair looked greenish under the streetlights. "Look. I probably shouldn't say this, but I will anyway. I saw you back at the Hall with your cousin. If it isn't any good with you and her, you shouldn't wait about and let it corrode you."

Corrosion was an interesting word, Julius thought.

He felt quite detached from this street scene. He might have just caught a glimpse of two strangers as he hurried past. It wasn't corrosion. That was too hot and vicious. Atrophy, perhaps, or palsy.

"You should go right away and do something else." Isolde was frowning, as if she were delivering advice of considerable complexity.

As he had gone away to Berlin, and stayed far too long, his senses slowly atrophying.

"Thank you for the advice," Julius said. "Maybe I'll take it."

She put her hands in the pockets of her coat and then lifted them away from her sides in an exaggeration of her habitual shrug. "Okay. Thanks for the drinks."

"Thank *you*."

She swung away from him under the streetlight and into the darkness at the corner.

Clio tucked the package of proofs into her bag.

She had spent several evenings correcting the galleys, sitting in the circle of lamplight at her desk after Romy had gone to sleep. The quiet work in the silent house had made her think of the flat in the Marais, and she had deliberately fanned the recollections, as a way of making Rafael seem closer. He was alive, she believed unquestioningly, in a camp somewhere, and he would come back. There was no other possibility to be admitted. She had devised a way of talking to him inside her head, and the long monologues eased her isolation by a fraction.

The little rented house in Paradise Square, Oxford, was empty. Romy had gone to spend the day in the Woodstock Road. Clio didn't often leave her with her grandparents, because a lively four-year-old was too much for Eleanor now. But Cressida was also there, staying with Eleanor while Grace was away on some Parliamentary tour, and Cressida adored the little girl and had more than enough energy to spare for her.

It was time to walk to the station to catch the London train.

Clio checked yet again that the precious proofs of her book were safely stowed away. Then she looked in her purse, to be sure that she had just enough money for her fare and a sandwich. The sight of a folded pound note reassured her. Clio supported herself with odds and ends of journalistic work, and by editing and proofreading for the University Press. There was never much to spare, but she felt richer than she had done when she had been supporting Miles Lennox.

Clio folded her mackintosh over her arm and locked the street door behind her. She waved to the woman next door, who was crossing the square with her baby in its pram, and turned toward the station.

A year ago she had wondered whether it was a regressive step to come back to live in Oxford. But she was comfortable here, if it was possible to be comfortable anywhere without Rafael.

Paradise Square lay at the heart of a run-down working-class area of tiny streets and terraced houses to the west of Carfax in the city center. Clio liked the feeling of a community that looked out for its own, and at the same time kept itself to itself, and Romy had made friends amongst the children who played over the cobbles and unkempt grass in the square. They lived a quiet and uneventful life together. Clio often talked about Rafael to the child, trying to keep the memories of him alive in her.

By twelve o'clock, Clio was in London. She took the tube from Paddington to Chancery Lane, and then walked past the huge plane trees of Gray's Inn to the offices of Randle & Cates, the publishers. She passed close by the old *Fathom* offices, although the little magazine had published its last issue almost two years ago and Max Erdmann had moved on to other ventures.

She looked at her watch as she walked up the steps to the publishers' front door. It was bad timing, she realized with a flush of embarrassment. Tony Hardy would think that she was expecting to be taken out to lunch. He had said any time on Friday morning, and she had taken him at his word. She had had to take Romy to the Woodstock Road and settle her there, or she would have been able to come earlier.

She did not expect lunch. To have her Berlin novel published was more than enough. Tony Hardy's enthusiasm for it was all the food and drink she needed. Perhaps she could pretend that she was expected elsewhere.

But as soon as the receptionist had telephoned up from her desk in the front office, a door was flung open above and Tony Hardy ran down the curving stairs. "Hooray," he shouted over the banister. "You're here in perfect time for me to take you out to celebrate. We'll do the dull bits with the proofs later, shall we?"

He took her by the arm and led her out into the street.

"I'd like to have taken you to the Eiffel, for old times' sake. But Stulik has sold up and gone, did you know that?"

"No, I didn't know," Clio said sadly. She would have liked to have eaten one last *plat du jour* or *gâteau St. Honoré* at one of the little tables with their red-shaded lamps. It was almost twenty years since Pilgrim had first taken her there with Grace, in their debutante dresses.

"The Etoile, then," Tony Hardy said. He waved for a cab.

A taxi was a luxury for Clio nowadays, and she could not remember the last time she had eaten a meal in a restaurant. She settled back into the stuffy interior with a small, unfamiliar ripple of pleasure.

Charlotte Street looked the same as it had always done. Clio found herself glancing toward the old studio for a glimpse of Pilgrim slouching with a sketchbook under his arm to the Wheatsheaf, or the Marquis, or the Fitzroy. She didn't even know where

Pilgrim was nowadays. The last time she had seen him was a brief, surprising glimpse at Alice's funeral.

"What would you like?" Tony smiled at her over the serious menu when they were settled at their table.

Clio was hungry. Randle & Cates were paying; the thought that Pilgrim had always steered her to the *plat du jour* made her smile so that the publisher glanced speculatively at her.

It is a celebration, Clio thought. *I shall be a published novelist.* And then, as inevitable as her own heartbeat, came the wish, *if only Rafael could be here.*

"The lobster, please," Clio said.

"And a bottle of champagne to go with it." Tony Hardy lifted his glass in a toast. "To *Berlin Diary.*"

The proofs were in the bag at her feet. She had made the last corrections with meticulous care. It was hard to believe that her book was passing out of her hands now. After this afternoon it would begin its slow progress into the territory of the autumn list, and the hands of the publishers' reps, and the booksellers and the critics.

She felt a thrill of protective fear for it. The diary of her first days in Berlin had become a novel, but the knotted roots of the story were inextricably buried within herself. Last night she had typed a small slip of paper to be pasted into the front of the galleys.

For Rafael Wolf.

Clio raised her glass. "To the book."

"Thank you for bringing it to us," Tony said.

Clio had never been quite sure why she had done so. She knew plenty of other publishers, from her *Fathom* days.

"I think we shall do well with it," he told her.

"That's why I wanted Randles to publish it."

Clio enjoyed her lunch. Tony Hardy's mild literary gossip and news of shared acquaintances reminded her of other times, and made her realize that the months she had spent living in her little house in Oxford alone with Romy had left her thoroughly out of touch with the world. She felt no particular desire for closer acquaintance, because she had no capacity for wishing for anything beyond Rafael's safety. Her longing for that made other shortages and adversities surprisingly easy to bear.

When they emerged into the midafternoon, Clio found herself blinking in the sharp light after the restful dimness of the restaurant. She rarely drank now, and the champagne and a cognac to follow it had left her feeling sleepy and faintly stupid. They were standing side by side, looking into the traffic for a cab to take them back to Tony's office.

At first, Clio was not even surprised to see Miles Lennox. He was walking toward them, swinging an umbrella with vicious little strokes. He was a part of this world, of Bloomsbury and Fitzrovia and whichever one of the neighboring pubs he had just emerged from. His steps were not quite steady.

"Oh, God," Tony Hardy muttered.

Clio felt the blow of shock then. This was Miles, with his coat and his umbrella and his tie knotted under a frayed collar; her husband. She had not seen him since she had left Berlin for the first time, pregnant with Romy.

"I'm sorry," Tony added. She was not sure if he was apologizing for his own lack of enthusiasm or in advance for the coming encounter.

Miles had seen them too. He stopped, with exaggerated amazement, and put a hand out to the restaurant railings to steady himself. His face looked puffy and congested. The last vestiges of his boyish good looks had disappeared.

Clio thought of the man's black-rimmed fingernails on her bedsheets, and she knew in that minute why she had gone to Tony Hardy with her manuscript. It was because of Miles, of course. Miles admired Tony, and had wanted him to publish the rambling monologue of his own novel. She had done it as a means of stabbing back at him, because he had hurt her. To have Tony Hardy praising her work was like slipping a blade deep into the heart of Miles's vanity and cruelty.

Seeing her husband now, Clio felt ashamed of that impulse.

Miles puckered his lips and raised his eyebrows in a parody of genteel disapproval.

"What a *very* bizarre partnership," he said. "My wife, and Mr. Hardy. Now, Clio darling, I wouldn't have thought that you were at all Tony's type for an afternoon in Charlotte Street. But there, life is full of wonderful surprises."

"Clio is an author of ours," Tony said bluntly. "We are publishing her rather fine first novel in our autumn list."

Miles's mouth twisted. He had drunk too much to be able to disguise his bitterness. It seemed to swell within him like gas in a corpse, puffing out his face and pinching his lips over his discolored teeth. He let go of the railings and stood upright, swaying only a little.

"Life is full of wonderful surprises," he repeated.

Clio wished that Tony had said nothing, or that Miles could have passed this spot five minutes earlier or later. There was nothing but humiliation for both of them in this encounter. She had loved this man, and married him, and spent four years of her life hoping and working in his service. If it seemed inconceivable today, that was her fault as much as Miles's.

But she couldn't let him go by now, wandering off into the desert of the afternoon, without making some acknowledgment.

She put her hand out to him.

"Miles? Tony and I have some work to do now, but it shouldn't take more than an hour. Why don't we meet somewhere afterward? We could have tea, perhaps?"

He seemed to consider. *"Tea?"*

"Or whiskey. Whatever you like."

Tony was waiting.

Miles said at length, "An hour? I will come and get you from Mr Hardy's offices. Four o'clock."

He set off again, swinging his umbrella, without looking at Tony.

"I'm sorry," Tony said again, when they were in a taxi on the way back to his office.

"Why do you have to apologize?" Clio asked. She felt the need to defend Miles, and was exasperated by it and by herself. They sat through the rest of the short journey in silence.

Tony laid the long sheets of the galleys on his desk, and they spent an hour going through the amendments that Clio had made. And then at four o'clock exactly, he escorted her down to the front door. There was no sign of Miles. They shook hands.

"Thank you for the lunch," Clio said.

He looked kindly at her. "Thank you for the book. It will be a success, you know."

Suddenly she realized that it might be. Another small, unfamiliar dart of happiness pierced her.

She had preferred to wait for Miles outside Randle & Cates. For ten minutes she strolled up and down in the sunshine, conscious of the people glancing out at her from the office windows above and opposite. Then she saw him coming around the corner from the direction of Charlotte Street. He lifted his umbrella and brandished it at her.

Clio remembered how long ago, at the beginning, she had been excited and pleased by the sight of him, and how quickly that pleasure had turned to anxiety for what he would do, or how he would treat her.

She waited until he reached her and then smiled as warmly as she could. She could smell the whiskey on his breath.

"There's an Italian café in Queen Square, isn't there? Or there used to be. Shall we try that?"

"Wherever you like," Miles said, without much interest.

It seemed incongruous to be walking along together. Now that they were here, Clio wondered why she had felt the impulse to suggest this meeting.

The café was still there, with the same wooden chairs and rickety tables that she remembered. It had a continental atmosphere, and it made her think of Paris and Rafael. She sat down instead with Miles, and watched him take out a tin of tobacco and fumblingly roll a thin cigarette. There were yellow nicotine burns on his fingers that had not been there before.

The waitress, a fat Italian girl, came to take their order. Clio couldn't think of eating after her lunch, and Miles looked as if he could no longer be bothered to eat at all.

"Won't you have a sandwich? Or cake, or something?" Clio asked.

He drew on his cigarette. Whiskers of smoldering tobacco protruded from the end of it. "I'm not an infant who needs feeding."

"Just tea, for two please."

The waitress shrugged and slopped away.

Miles examined the room and the scattering of shoppers and office workers. "This is cozy."

There was a twist to his mouth again. Clio saw the patina of sneering aggression, and the disappointment that lay beneath it like worm-eaten timber.

It was simpler to be honest in response. "Does it matter what the café is like? Would you have preferred us just to have passed by each other on the pavement outside the Etoile? It seemed appropriate at least to meet somewhere."

"Oh, let us always do what is appropriate."

Clio poured out the tea and handed him his cup. The gesture seemed to parody the domestic life they had once shared.

"Tell me about the rather fine first novel," Miles suggested.

"I'll tell you if you would like to hear. It's about Berlin."

Clio described her book, and the way that her diary of the days after the Reichstag fire had slowly metamorphosed into a novel, a love story.

"Healthy heterosexual sex and a dash of Nazism? I'm sure that will sell."

She was not expecting anything more generous. "Tony Hardy believes so." She recalled again why she had chosen Tony. "And your own work?"

"Ah. Changed, and improved. But I don't believe the climate is right for it. There is a stolidity about fiction now, a rootedness, that is the complete opposite of everything I want to do. One has to be patient."

"How do you live?" Clio wondered if it was patience that had puffed up his face and shriveled the rest of him so that the collar of his shirt stood away from the cords in his neck.

"Some hack work. Other small things. Reviewing and editing. You know how it is."

She did know how narrow the margin was between survival and extinction. It must have been so much more comfortable for Miles, she thought, when he was living in Gower Street with a wife to cook and care and provide for him. He had been so sure of her.

"Yes, I know how it is."

"How is your child?"

"Well, thank you."

They doled out this small currency to each other over the tea-cups.

"I heard that your friend was arrested again."

Miles had been going to add, "Careless, that," but he swallowed the words. Clio's face affected him.

"Yes. He must be in a camp, somewhere. Romy and I pray that he is, anyway."

The alternative was not to be thought of, now or ever.

Clio lifted her head to look straight at Miles. "I would like a divorce," she said.

She had not brought Miles here with the intention in her mind. But it was clear to her now. He laughed so loudly and abruptly that two middle-aged women at a nearby table turned to peer at him.

"What must I do? Take a tart down to Brighton and make sure the chambermaid and a private detective are there to watch?"

"You may divorce me, if you wish. We are equally guilty, I suppose."

Their teacups were empty. The waitress came to clear them away.

"It doesn't matter," Miles answered at length. "Do it any way you like. You want to marry your German Adonis?"

"Yes. When he comes back."

He must come.

"How very romantic."

*More romantic than paid sex with dirty hands in our marriage
bed.*

Clio had an image of her marriage like an inverted pyramid,
narrowing and dwindling away to a speck, and finally vanishing
here and now in the Italian café in Queen Square.

She took out her purse and paid for their tea, then hoisted her
handbag over her shoulder. It was much lighter without the proofs
tucked inside it. With Miles behind her, she went out into the street
again. It was time to head for Paddington and the Oxford train.

Miles was struggling to put on his coat, and automatically she
held one sleeve for him and then turned down the collar at the back.

He seemed frail and irritable, like a much older man. Clio
guessed that he might slide downward now, drinking more and
eating less, until he could no longer detect the boundary between
survival and the opposite.

But then, he might just as easily find his feet again. Miles had the
requisite selfish determination. She was cheered by the optimistic
thought, and he saw the light of it in her eyes. He held out his hand
and she shook it.

They did not attempt a kiss.

They said good-bye, and turned in opposite directions.

"Good luck," he called after her. She looked back, just for a
moment, but Miles was already walking away.

Clio had no doubt of her own ability to survive. It had never been
called into question. She would do it, whatever it cost, for Rafael
and Romy's sake.

It was much later than she had intended when she reached the
Woodstock Road again. She let herself in and at once heard
the sound of Romy's excited laughter. She hesitated, listening to
the voices, and then ran across the hallway with a willful flicker
of hope.

In the drawing room she saw that it was only Jake who was
swinging Romy up into the air. Her chubby legs flailed over her
head as she gasped with pleasurable fear. Cressida was watching
them, laughing too, and Tabby was perched on the piano stool
calling out to Jake to be careful.

Clio was used to the kindling and rapid extinction of hope. Her
face gave nothing away as she went to catch Romy out of Jake's
arms.

"Mummy! Mummy's back! Uncle Jake is *throwing* me."

"I can see that. Jake, this is a surprise."

Romy was set on her feet again, and Clio pressed her cheek against the springy mass of Jake's beard. He kissed her on the forehead.

"I've been at a medical conference. I was going back tonight, but Pappy said you had gone to London to see your publishers and Mama persuaded me to stay to dinner. I'll get the early train back tomorrow. Ruth won't mind, she's got a Jewish Women's Federation evening."

"How nice that you're here," Clio said happily. She saw Jake far less often than she would like. It seemed also that Ruth and Jake were separately busy for much of their time.

"Cress, Tabby, hello too."

The drawing room felt warm and welcoming. Romy was running in circles on the oriental rug. The house might almost have been as it always was, before they all grew up.

"Romy has been good," Cressida said.

"I have. I ate all my lunch, and I had egg for my tea and Cressy took me to the Parks."

"You lucky girl. You haven't missed me, then?"

"Not badly much."

Clio was glad. It worried her that she and Romy lived in too close proximity, and that in Rafael's absence they filled too large a space in each other's lives. She said, "Daddy would be pleased with you."

Behind her, Jake and Tabitha glanced at each other.

"Time for a drink," Jake announced quickly. "Sherry? Has Pappy got any Scotch, Tabby, d'you think?"

"Where are they both, anyway?"

Clio sat down on the sofa beneath Pilgrim's portrait and drew Romy onto her lap. It was a pleasure to come home, to the house that she still thought of as home, and to find Jake filling the thin and overquiet air of the old place with talk.

"Aunt Eleanor is resting and Uncle Nathaniel had a seminar, but he'll be in soon," Cressida answered.

Jake had found the whiskey bottle before they heard Nathaniel's book bag thumping down onto the tiles in the hall.

"Pappy!"

"Grandpappy!" Romy scrambled down from Clio's lap and ran to find him. A moment later, Nathaniel came in with the child in his arms.

Nathaniel seemed physically smaller and less of a dominant

presence than he once had been. His beard was more white than gray, and his shoulders had rounded into a stoop. It was Jake who looked like the tribal leader now. But there was a close link between Romy and her grandfather.

They searched for each other when they came into a room, and they were always happy in each other's company. Nathaniel was whispering in Romy's ear.

"Mummy!" she shrieked. "Grandpappy says I can stay up for proper dinner with him and you if I'm seen and not heard."

"No."

"Oh, Clio, do let her. She had a sleep this afternoon."

"Cressida, you traitor."

"I want to stay up too," Jake shouted. "I shall scream if I'm not allowed to. Pappy, I will."

"Be quiet, Jake."

The noise was like it used to be. Eleanor sailed into the midst of them. She had changed for dinner, as she always did, and her silky skirts rustled around her. She had never cut her hair, and it was wound up in elaborate coils on top of her head and secured with tortoiseshell combs. Out of long-standing habit too, she greeted her husband first, putting her hands on his arms and reaching up to be kissed. Then she made the rounds of her children, and they gathered in a circle around her.

"Can I stay up, Grandma? Can I, can I?"

"Yes, darling, of course you can."

"I am overruled." Clio sighed, without regret. It gave her quiet pleasure to see Romy here with her family.

When Clio had first brought her child home to Oxford, Eleanor had been caught between the need to uphold her Victorian morality and her natural warmth toward all of her family. She had tried to keep her granddaughter at arm's length, but then Clio had begun to notice how her eyes followed Romy's blond head. Romy was growing to look more and more like her father. There was none of the Hirsh darkness about her.

And then, very gradually in the long months after Alice's death, Romy had begun to provide a prop for Eleanor and Nathaniel. Some of her energy and brightness had seemed to pass into them by slow osmosis. She became her grandparents' favorite and their safe focus.

"Shall we go in?" Eleanor said tranquilly. Her husband took her arm, and Jake bent down to offer his to Romy. Clio and Tabby and Cressida followed on behind them.

Romy was given a place of honor at the foot of the table, boosted almost to adult height by three cushions.

Looking across at her, Clio was visited by a memory of Alice sitting in just the same place. She was wearing a white dress and a gold-paper crown on her black wire curls.

It must have been a birthday party; there were jellies and ribbons and fondant sweets on the white linen cloth.

Alice's sixth birthday. The day that Grace had been discovered upstairs in Captain Dennis's bedroom. Alice's sixth birthday.

There had been the terrible quarrel with Grace.

You have to have everything, don't you? Clio could hear her own voice, smothered and small with her anger. *You have to have everything, don't you? I hate you, Grace.*

"Clio, are you all right?" It was Tabby, looking at her with concern. "You've gone white."

"Have I? Yes, I'm all right. I felt dizzy for a minute. Pass me the water jug, could you?"

Family dinner, like so many family dinners before it. Jake and Nathaniel vociferously arguing. Girls with tidied hair and clothes, Alice waving her knife and fork at the end of the table, spilling food on the cloth, and Eleanor rebuking her.

Not Alice, but Romy.

After dinner, there would be the wireless news. They would hear if Hitler had attacked Czechoslovakia and brought the threat of war closer. On her way to the train at Paddington, Clio had seen a woman carrying a new gas mask in its case. She could remember the start of the last war, and the half-heard and half-guessed adult anxieties that had whispered in the house.

Fearfully she looked down the table again, to Romy in her place of honor. What would happen to Rafael, in Germany, if the war came?

"Clio?"

Someone had asked her a question. She smiled and murmured an apology. It had been Eleanor.

"Darling, I only asked about your meeting with your publisher."

Jake was chewing vigorously, showing his red mouth. He pointed his fork at her.

"Mummy's written a book," Romy contributed wisely.

"Yes, how is the famous novelist?"

"Not very famous yet. I went through the proof corrections, and he explained how much it costs nowadays to reset a line of type. It sounds as if I shall end up in debt to Randle and Cates, rather than the other way around. Unless they sell more than a dozen copies, that is."

"We'll buy one each. I'm sure Oswald Harris will take another. There, you are almost in profit already."

Clio joined in the laughter. She wouldn't tell them that she had seen Miles. There was, in any case, nothing to say.

Toward the end of the meal Romy's head began to droop. Nathaniel hoisted her off her chair, leaving Alice's place empty. He held her on his knee, and she fell asleep with her head against her grandfather's shirtfront.

Eleanor rolled up her napkin and put it neatly through its silver ring. "We'll have our coffee in the drawing room, shall we? Mary will have put the tray in there." Eleanor had only a cook and one housemaid to help her run the diminished household.

They went through, with Nathaniel carrying Romy in his arms. He put her on the sofa and covered her with a paisley shawl.

"I'll take her home soon," Clio said, without moving. It was comfortable in the armchair with her coffee cup. Cressida had gone to the piano and was picking out a waltz with Jake humming over her shoulder. Tabby was sitting under the lamp with her sewing.

"Play some more, Cressida," Nathaniel murmured. With his head back against the cushions, he was ready to doze.

In his study the telephone rang.

"I'll go," Eleanor said. "It's Blanche."

Clio and Jake smiled at each other. The telepathic closeness between the twins seemed to strengthen rather than diminish with age.

Eleanor was gone for a long time. Cressida played, and Jake sang a sentimental Victorian ballad, and then Tabby put down her work and joined in a duet. Nathaniel had dropped off to sleep, but Clio laughed and applauded.

"I don't think you can possibly *guess* what the news is."

They looked up to see Eleanor standing in the doorway.

"It isn't the war?" Cressida whispered.

But Eleanor's eyes were bright. "Not bad news, darling. Good news."

"I give up," Tabby sighed. "Tell us at once."

"Hugo is engaged to be married."

The chorus of amazement woke Nathaniel up. Hugo seemed to have settled long ago to a bachelor life, absorbed in the management of his estate and in county affairs. He seldom went beyond the margins of his own land. It had long been assumed in the family that Thomas and Thomas's children were his heirs.

"Who is she?"

"Hugo doesn't *have* women."

"Hugo has farm plans and harvest festival suppers with the farmhands."

"Well, he has a fiancée now, Jake, whatever you might have to say."

"Who is she, Mama, for goodness' sake?"

"She is a Miss Lucy Frobisher."

"Sounds like a nursery rhyme. Or a tale by Beatrix Potter."

"Frobisher? Weren't there some Stretton neighbors called Frobisher?" Clio asked. "I remember Uncle John used to talk about hunting or not hunting over their land."

"Yes. She is the younger daughter of some good Shropshire people. She is twenty-three years old, Blanche says, and very pretty and suitable. Hugo has known her since she was a child, of course, but they have only very recently fallen in love."

"The old devil. He's well over forty."

"Only seven months older than you, Jake, as you perfectly well know. The age difference between them is less than there was between Blanche and John."

"Hugo's a catch for any girl. She'll be the Countess of Leominster."

"He's chosen a good *breeder*, I hope," Jake said seriously. Cressida laughed behind her hand.

Nathaniel laced his fingers across his chest. "I suppose there'll have to be a wedding, now."

"It's the usual procedure, Pappy."

"Blanche says they will be having a big wedding in the New Year. At Stretton, of course. And a ball, and dinners for estate people and tenants. It will be a great deal of work for her, but she is determined that it will be done properly, the way John would have wanted it. It's only a pity that Grace and Phoebe are not at home to help her a little more."

Phoebe had married a banker, with a house in Kensington and two small children of her own.

"A real, old-fashioned county wedding." Clio sighed. She was thinking of Stretton, *en fête*, and the little gray church on the estate filled with flowers and local people and the great families, and the old house decorated and filled with music and dancing to celebrate the marriage of the Earl. She was surprised by how much the idea moved her. It would be an affirmation that not quite everything had changed; it would be England both at its grandest and its simplest.

"I'm very happy for them. I shall dance at their wedding, for one. Well done, Hugo and Miss Lucy Frobisher."

"Quite right, Clio," Nathaniel agreed.

"It *is* very Culmington," Jake said.

Twenty-Two

MISS LUCY FROBISHER BECAME THE Countess of Leominster at a little after four o'clock in the afternoon of March 24, 1939.

Exactly as Clio had imagined it would be, the church on the Stretton estate was filled with family and staff and tenants and neighbors, and hotly scented with the blooms of white carnations and lilies. There was a great garland of apple blossom wreathed over the communion rail, and when they stood up for the last hymn, with a flutter of hats and skirts and service sheets, Clio could just catch the faint, wet-morning scent of that too, and underlying it all the bitter-wood breath of huge trails of plaited ivy.

In the pew in front of her, Eleanor and Blanche were standing side by side, with their profiles matching beneath their hats as if the image of one were reflected from the other. And amongst all the flower scents there was still the faintest trace of their mingled perfumes, white lilac and stephanotis, reminding Clio suddenly of her childhood and the mothers gliding along some seaside promenade in their tight-waisted Edwardian gowns. She thought of Hugo as he had been in those days, amiable and conventional, forever pretending to be aloof from the games that Jake led and she and Julius and Grace unquestioningly followed.

The hymn ended, and they knelt for the Bishop's blessing. In her unpracticed way, Clio tried to offer up a prayer for Hugo's happiness with his Lucy. It seemed that in the vanishing wake of his youth, Hugo deserved some kind of plain fulfillment.

The wedding ceremony had been a simple one, by Hugo's choice, even though it was conducted by the Bishop assisted by three other clergy, including the rector of Lucy's home parish. At its conclusion the bride and groom and their parents and attendants moved away into the vestry for the signing of the register. Clio sat in her place with her hands folded in her lap, looking up into the crimson and magenta lights of the east window. The organist was playing a Bach toccata. It was a fine organ for a small church, installed by Hugo's grandfather eighty years before. The soaring music made Clio think of Julius and wish that he had come to see Hugo married.

Clio glanced sidelong, over the top of Romy's new velvet beret, to Grace. Grace was gazing straight ahead of her, apparently absorbed in her own thoughts, her chin held level above the ivory lace and tucks of her Vionnet jabot blouse. Grace did not seem to age as the rest of them were doing. Clio did not think that their own profiles would match any longer, as they once had done to confuse poor Peter Dennis and to entice Pilgrim.

There was a tumbling fanfare of organ chords, and the bride emerged on her new husband's arm. Lucy's veil had been turned back over the frosty glimmer of the Stretton tiara. Her prettiness was of the regular-featured and unremarkable English variety, set off by a pair of large, pale blue eyes. Clio guessed, from the slightly dazed quality of their smiles as they turned to face the inquisition of the crowded rows of pews, that Hugo and Lucy must be genuinely happy with each other. She had no insight into the workings of Hugo's mind, but she had never seen him look like this. It was as if he had just been given a surprising and wonderful present, but could not quite believe that it might not be just as summarily taken away from him.

The newlyweds walked slowly down the aisle together. Hugo leaned heavily with his free arm on his perpetual stick. He could not move more than a few steps without it, and the twisted stump of his leg gave him almost continual pain. There would be no part in the war for Hugo, Clio thought, if it did come again.

When it came again, as it now seemed that it must.

She turned sideways again, looking back on the congregation, afraid for all of these men with their wedding smiles worn over constricting shirt collars. A cold spasm of fear for Rafael took hold of her and obliterated everything else. Her hands tightened into fists, crumpling the service sheet, and Romy peered up into her face. Clio forced herself to smile her reassurance.

Behind Hugo and Lucy came Thomas, his brother's best man, with Lucy's sister Venetia on his arm. He was splendid in the dress blues of the Household Brigade. Thomas was only thirty-four and a professional soldier. The war would come for him, even if it was no more than a staff war fought from some headquarters well back behind the lines. He winked at Romy as they passed, and Clio wished that she could step out of her place and hug him for it.

Venetia was the chief of the bride's eight attendants. All the bridesmaids wore pale yellow silk with looped panniers of darker gold over their full skirts and crowns of orange blossom in their hair. Cressida was amongst them, thin and solemn-faced, with only the ghost of the plump child she had once been hovering behind her.

Romy rotated her head to watch their stately procession. The youngest bridesmaid was Phoebe's three-year-old, who marched sturdily beside her cousin Cressida with her miniature orange-blossom wreath tipped over her forehead. Romy would have loved to wear a crown of flowers and her own billowing and rustling yellow silk, but she had not been invited to join the company. To Blanche, of course, just as she had once been to Eleanor, Romy was a source of embarrassment. She was to be spoken of in whispers if at all, as the living proof of Clio's unfortunate circumstances.

There was the matter of her name. Even though Clio now called herself Clio Hirsh again, she insisted on describing her daughter as Romy Wolf. No one had said as much, but there was the question—how would the discrepancy be explained for the newspaper reports of the wedding? How, even, was the matter to be discussed with Major and Mrs. Frobisher?

It had been simpler to ignore it, and Romy herself, and to trust to Clio's discretion.

Clio had been discreet, because she understood her aunt and something of her aunt's world, but she was disappointed for Romy. The little girl would have to catch what glimpses she could of the great ball this evening from an upstairs landing, in Nanny's company, but Clio had insisted that she be allowed to put on her best dress and come to the church with everyone else.

Nathaniel gave his arm to Blanche, and they turned to follow the last pair of bridesmaids. Blanche was smiling, happier than she had looked since John's death, at this culmination of her months of planning and weeks of work, and five strenuous days of pre-wedding celebrations. There was still tonight, the Stretton Ball and the climax of the entire grand scheme, but Hugo was safely married now. He had his Lucy, as John had found Blanche herself more than forty years ago, and there would be a new generation of young Strettons to come.

Blanche swept forward with her hand resting on Nathaniel's sleeve, and behind her came Eleanor and Jake and the rest of the families, Clio and Grace side by side, the brothers and sisters and cousins and children. They were all there, all of them except for Alice and Julius. They formed up behind the Earl and his new Countess, two by two, and they processed down the aisle between the tall urns of bridal-white flowers and the benevolent smiles of their invited guests.

/ It was all done as it should be done, Clio understood. Every detail was in place. Her mother and her aunt, Hugo and even Grace herself had been born with the innate capacity to manage such things. Clio's own fearful conviction that the world was on the edge of some great change, and that these stately rituals of the Church and the county and of the social hierarchy of England itself might not be enacted for very much longer, made this marriage and its significance seem all the more poignant.

It was an odd sentiment to overtake a half-Jewish and wholly skeptical outcast from this very world, Clio reflected. But she was moved, and there were tears in her eyes as she took her place in the procession beside a red-faced Stretton distant cousin she had never even seen before. She held Romy's gloved hand firmly and led her past the flowers and out of the porch into the spring sunshine.

The sudden clash of bells broke out in the square tower above. In the bell room the estate's own ringers had bent to their work at the bellmaster's signal. In their braces and shirtsleeves they hauled on the rope sallies, hand over hand. There would be a full eight-hour peal to celebrate the Earl's marriage.

Outside in the churchyard the music of the seven bells filled the thin air while the eighth, the tenor, wound its intricate way through the triples behind them. The circle of gravel in front of the west door of the church and the grass between the old gravestones was crowded with estate workers and Stretton villagers and pressmen and sightseers. The sound of the bells made them all lift their heads, and for a moment everything else was still.

Then beyond the lych gate, Clio saw Hugo handing his bride up into a high-wheeled carriage. He tucked the swaths of her train tenderly around her. There was a pair of grays waiting in harness with a groom at their heads. The groom handed Hugo the whip, and amidst laughter and cheering and a shower of rice, Hugo gathered the reins and drove his wife across the park and home to Stretton.

Romy had run to Cressida and was tugging longingly at her bouquet. An arm descended on Clio's shoulder.

"Tears?"

She saw that it was Jake.

"Not serious ones. Just for the order of it, the pattern of it all. And for it not lasting after the next thing."

"I know," Jake said simply. "Odd, that, for people like you and me."

He took a large folded white handkerchief out of the pocket of his trousers and handed it to her. From the door of the church Grace was watching them. She hesitated for a moment and then began to move slowly in the opposite direction, toward the lych gate. The churchyard was emptying in the wake of the bridal party. The family would make their way back to the house for the wedding breakfast, and the last preparations for the ball. Jake saw Ruth and his children walking ahead with Nathaniel.

To Clio he said, "Shall we sit here for a little while?"

There was a wooden seat beyond the gravestones, in the shelter of one of the great yew trees that marked the churchyard boundary.

She smiled gratefully. "Yes, please."

The house would be a swarm of last-minute preparations, with men in green baize aprons and hurrying footmen and Blanche sailing through it all as if she were directing and orchestrating some great operatic production. Clio picked her way over the grass behind Jake. She read the inscriptions on the tombstones automatically, as she read everything. The members of the family were all buried in the family vault within the church, but the generations of names out here were still familiar to her. There were Dixeys, and Moores and Bridgers and Walshes, who had provided housemaids and grooms and keepers to the big house for as long as the Strettons had owned it, and who still lived in the village and the lodges and farms beside the estate. There was a stone plaque in the longer grass close to the wall, with a glass jar of fresh daffodils placed beside it. It was a memorial to the sons of the Dixey family who had died in France in 1916.

Clio sat down beside Jake on the wooden seat. It was quiet now, except for the bells, with the last of the congregation and the sightseers filtering away through the old gate. A man in a long green apron appeared and began to sweep up the rice and scattered petals.

Jake closed his eyes and turned his face up to the sun. The light was bright, but there was no warmth in it yet. Clio put her arm through his and lowered her head until it rested against his shoulder.

"Are you all right?" she asked.

"Of course," Jake made his automatic response. He had been thinking about the girl, the miraculous girl called Lottie Brand who had appeared in his surgery and overturned the repetitive business of his life. He had fallen in love with her as soon as he saw her. He thought of Lottie in every private waking moment, but there were not many such moments available to him.

"Ruth looks well."

Ruth had lost some weight, and today she was buttoned into a tight olive-green costume that seemed to keep her snapping energy and her tart disapproval of this ostentatious marriage display of Hugo's only precariously contained.

"Yes, Ruth is well."

Lottie Brand was thirteen years younger than Jake, and she had once been his patient, although he had rapidly made her find another physician.

Jake had had other women, starting from almost immediately after Rachel's birth, but he had never fallen in love with one of them until he met Lottie. She was the daughter of working-class parents from Clerkenwell, a tall girl with a wide smile and a mass of fair hair. Lottie was a dancer and had ambitions to be an actress; in the last year she had even played two bit parts, and now there was talk of some film work. But she was quite ready to earn her keep if necessary as a waitress or a barmaid, or doing whatever else presented itself. Jake loved her for a variety of reasons, but the chief of them was her cheerful acceptance of whatever turned up in her haphazard life. Lottie was always ready to adapt, and she was happy and inquisitive and enthusiastic in ways he had never encountered in anyone else.

She was also the most uninhibited sexual partner he had ever known. Lottie would do anything, and she was capable of suggesting diversions that had never even occurred to him. Occasionally she made him feel like the awestruck boy he had been with Grace, long ago, in the corner beside the hawthorn hedge.

Sometimes, like now, it seemed to Jake extraordinary that such a girl could have any interest in a middle-aged and weary doctor, and also a torture that he could not spend every hour of every day with her, alone with her.

"Jake?"

He opened his eyes on the churchyard, mossy tombstones and the square tower of the church. And the line of yew trees from which he and Julius as boys had illicitly cut branches, imagining that they could make longbows for themselves like the archers at Agincourt in *Henry V.* Hugo had sneered at the idea: rightly as it turned out. The bows had never worked.

"Jake, what are you thinking about?"

"I had a letter from Julius," he said hastily. He searched in the inner pockets of his tailcoat and eventually produced the letter in its envelope. He gave it to Clio.

Clio looked at the black, fluent handwriting. She unfolded the single sheet and read.

Julius had left London, claiming that he found it impossible to work there. He had told everyone that he was composing a piece of music and needed quiet and solitude in order to concentrate on it. He had gone away, to live in a rented cottage at the edge of the sea marshes in a remote corner of North Wales. Clio puzzled for a moment over the multiple consonants of the address, then concentrated on what her twin had written.

Julius explained to Jake that he was sorry that he could not come to Hugo's wedding. It was a long way to travel just at present, and he couldn't leave his cottage because he had adopted a dog. It was a Welsh collie, Julius said. His name was Gelert. He was working, or trying to work. It was difficult, because he could hear the music in his head, but he couldn't take hold of it for long enough to write it down. But the quiet was good, *soothing,* Julius wrote, and he liked to walk on the marshland. He sent his love to Jake, and to everyone in what he had no doubt would turn out to be a fine carnival at Stretton.

That was all.

Clio let the letter fall into her lap.

"Jake, what do you think?" Her voice sounded sharp. "It isn't a long way to travel from North Wales to Shropshire."

"No. He doesn't want to be here. It's the old trouble, isn't it?"

Jake's thoughts looped from Lottie to Julius and to Grace in the long-ago field. Longing and desire seemed to twist and snake through the broken stalks of the years, tracking him, scenting his steps. What Grace had done to them both, to Julius and himself. He wondered if she knew it. He remembered how in the church today she had sat as still as a figure in a portrait.

"The old trouble," Clio said bitterly.

She was distressed that Julius had written to Jake and not to her. The letter itself made her fearful. His voice in it sounded muffled, deliberately so, as if Julius were cloaking some other truth with these distracted excuses about marshlands and elusive music. She wondered if he had not written to her because he knew that with her twin's intuition, she might read beyond the plain words.

Anxiety twitched in her, like a muscle tic.

"When this is over, I'm going to go up there to see him."

"Will he want you to?" Jake asked. There were another twenty-four hours before Ruth and he could leave Stretton, twenty-four more stretching after that before he could hope to be with Lottie again.

Clio said loudly, "Whether he wants it or not. He needs somebody. I'll take Romy and say the two of us need a holiday by the sea, we needn't stay where he is. Just near enough to see him and make sure there's nothing wrong. We can try this town, what is it called? Abergele. How do you think you pronounce it?"

"You could do that," Jake conceded.

The sun had dropped behind the tower. At once it was cold in the graveyard. Clio shivered in her wedding clothes. Jake took the letter from her gloved hands and folded it away in its envelope. He touched her cheek with the back of his hand. "Don't worry," he advised.

They stood up and walked across the shadowed grass. The families and the clergy and the more important of the church guests who had received an invitation would all be back at the house by now. A magnificent tea centered on one of three successive wedding cakes had been laid out in the salon. Jake looked at his watch and sighed.

"Time—just time—for a quick snooze before we have to assemble on parade again. I am exhausted, and I have only been here for a day. How can Hugo and Lucy possibly endure it?"

Clio smiled. "They can do it precisely because it is what one does. There is a kind of magnificence in it, don't you think?"

The dinner held for Hugo and Lucy's wedding was for close members of their families alone, but even so the great mahogany table in the Stretton dining room was extended to its full length to accommodate almost forty people.

The footmen in their places behind each alternate chair wore white gloves and the Stretton livery, and their hair was powdered. There had been complaints from below stairs that the flour made the men's heads itch intolerably in the heat, but Blanche had been implacable. Tonight, for Hugo's wedding ball, no touch of grandeur was too grand.

The glow of dozens of candles shone in the silver and crystal

down the length of the table. There were Malmaison carnations
plaited with ivy in the filigree silver bowls.

Hugo sat at the head of the table, with his bride at the foot. Lucy
was still in her wedding gown, but her veil and the little jacket that
she had worn to the church had been removed to reveal a deep
décolleté. The Stretton diamonds glittered around her throat. It
clearly suited her to be the focus of attention. Her cheeks were
pink, and she talked animatedly in this gathering of her parents and
brothers and sisters and cousins.

Lucy would be a fine Countess, Clio reflected. She would charm
the county and direct her household, but she would never do more
than Hugo required of her.

Blanche was at the center of the table. Her dress was dark purple
velvet, cut to show off her fine shoulders, and worn with a feathered and jeweled turban of the same material. Clio thought she
looked queenly, perfectly and fittingly imperious, as if tonight were
the satisfying climax of a life's diligent preparation. She outshone
her daughters. Phoebe seemed faintly peevish, as if she regretted
her own quieter marriage, and Grace had chosen to wear black lace,
with her ropes of pearls as her only jewelry. She was sitting
between two of the Frobisher men, and her head was inclined as she
listened gravely to what one of them was saying to her.

Clio smoothed her own skirts. Her own dress was an old one of
Eleanor's. She had discovered it, shrouded in tissue paper, in one of
the tall cupboards on an upper landing in the Woodstock Road. It
had smelled powerfully of mothballs when she lifted it out, but the
folds of sea-green satin were fresh and unfaded. She had pains-
takingly unpicked the seams, in the quiet evenings in Paradise
Square, and recut the bodice so that it fitted her narrower frame.

When she put it on this evening, Romy had looked seriously at
her. Then she said, "You look very, very pretty."

"Thank you, darling. But not prettier than the bride, I hope. That
would be very bad form."

"Prettier than anyone. Daddy would be proud of you."

Clio put down her comb, her fingers suddenly stiff. She could
hear her own words, her constant reminder, coming out of Romy's
mouth. Was it right to keep this hope alive in her child, or should
she let Rafael slip away, into the painless recesses of her babyhood? She stooped down and put her arms around Romy, drawing
comfort from her, hiding her face from the clear eyes.

"Thank you. I'm glad I look nice for Hugo's party," Clio said.

Now, in her place at the dinner table, Clio lifted the glass of champagne that had been poured for her and drank half of it. She wanted the bubbles to pass directly into her bloodstream. The white-gloved footman at her shoulder placed a bowl of clear soup in front of her. The finest Stretton china had been brought out of storage. It was white and blue and gold, with the family crest in the center of each piece. Clio looked up from her plate and saw Cressida.

She had been placed at the other end of the table, on the opposite side, almost as far away from Clio as it was possible to be. Her neighbors on either hand were occupied with separate conversations. Cressida did not seem to be looking at anything in particular. Slowly, but quite deliberately, she lifted her champagne glass as Clio had done. But when Cressida replaced hers, it was completely empty.

At five minutes to ten, Hugo led Lucy to the top of the great staircase where they would receive their guests. There was a newly installed electric switch on a small plaque to one side of the stairs. At exactly ten o'clock, Lucy pressed the switch. Outside, the whole of the great south front was suddenly floodlit.

Electricians had worked for a week to install the dozens of lights. Now, as the guests began to converge on the house, Robert Adam's serene golden stone facade beneath its crowning dome was bathed in brilliance. The house was instantly visible for miles around, seeming to float in its dark ocean of parkland.

There had been dinners for the ball in all the notable houses within a radius of fifty miles. Every house had its own house party, and now the guests were arriving at Stretton. Hugo and Lucy stood alone, at the top of the stairs, to welcome them.

There were county people, and hunting and sporting friends of Hugo, and girls who had come out in Lucy's year and who were most of them married now, but there was also London Society. There were political friends and allies of both Hugo and Grace, from the Lords and the Commons, and there were cavalry officers from Thomas's world, and the kind of smart young married couples that Anthony and Grace had once been and who were now the contemporaries of Phoebe and her husband. There were the young girls, the debutantes who would be presented at Court later in the Season, with Cressida amongst them, and their brothers and cousins and friends.

Clio watched them all arriving, the family tiaras and the jewels, and the dresses with the trains looped over the wearer's arm, and the magnificent dress uniforms, and the stiff collars and snowy white waistcoats, and she heard the talk and laughter rising and seeming to gather and concentrate under the cool span of the Adam dome. From the Long Library, where the dancing had already begun, she could hear the music of Ambrose's band. There was even a dance card in her own evening bag. Hugo himself had given it to her. She had kissed him, after the dinner, and wished him happiness.

"D'you know, I am happy?" he said, with the same dazed smile. "It seems more than a fellow has any right to expect. Clio, I can't ask you for a dance. Anyhow, I never was much use at it, even with two legs. But will you dance for me, tonight?"

Clio was touched. "Yes, of course I will."

She wandered through the thickening crowds. There were some people she knew, a surprisingly large number, now she was here amongst them. But there were dozens more faces that were familiar. She saw Lady Londonderry and Winston Churchill, Anthony Eden, Nancy Astor with her son Michael, and Lady Diana Cooper and Lord Halifax and Chips Channon and Diana and Oswald Mosley. These people must be here for Grace as much as for Hugo. For whatever reason, the world seemed to have converged on Stretton tonight. Their own miniature creation of a world, at least.

The ball was already in full swing. There was an atmosphere of determined gaiety. Clio could almost hear the resolution that was never spoken aloud, *We should dance while we can. Who knows how soon we shall have to stop?*

She paused at the open doors that led into the ballroom. She saw Eleanor waltzing in Nathaniel's arms, and Blanche with Thomas, and as she watched them the colors of the ball dresses and the flowers and the women's jewels all seemed to blur together.

For an instant the ballroom became as complete and lovely as an Impressionist painting, firmly fixed in its evanescent moment and resistant to closer scrutiny, because when she stared harder at it, the perfection broke up once again into its component dots of dancers and flowers and candles in their sconces, and the picture in its completeness was lost to her again.

Clio stood still, blinking a little. As she surveyed this celebration of privilege and counted herself a part of it, she felt no rush of anger that it should be allowed to happen while in Europe Jews were being dispossessed and beaten and murdered by the Nazis.

Only ten days earlier, Hitler had invaded Prague. Clio lived with her fears and prayers for Rafael, and with her hatred of the evil that had taken away their life together. But she also knew that tonight was one of the pillars supporting the world she had lived in for most of her life. When the celebration was over, this one and all the others like it, the people would do what was necessary to be done.

The war would come. Those who had been pro-Munich were now no longer in favor, even Grace and her Cliveden friends. Grace was fervently anti-Hitler now.

Clio smiled a thin smile.

It was the faces of the young boys that caught her attention, the eighteen-year-olds who were waltzing with girls in white dresses. The thread of melancholy seemed only to emphasize the glitter, and to make the brightness brighter still.

There was someone standing beside her, Clio realized. She looked, and saw that it was Jake again. He made her open her beaded bag and show him her card.

"No dances at all? Not a single *one* booked?"

Clio laughed and protested, "I'm far too old for this. Go and dance with Cressida."

The tiny pencil attached to the card swung at the end of its tasseled silver cord. Where was Cressida?

"I want to dance with you. May I have the pleasure?"

He wrote his initials on the correct line. JNH. It made Clio think of the old desk and the penknife carvings. Was the desk still here somewhere? How long ago it was.

Jake thought, *I have never even danced with Lottie.* He could imagine the muscled warmth of her turning and humming in his arms. His eyes closed, and her face swam in front of him. He wondered how it was that he could go on sleepwalking through these days and nights.

"Penny for them?" Clio asked, as they had asked each other when they were children.

"Topping band, isn't it?" Jake smiled at her.

Julius put down his sheet of manuscript. He had been sitting with it on his lap for a long time, but he had not written anything. The fire had burned low and then died in a heap of cold ash. He was cold; he felt too chilled even to stand up and go through the mechanical business of rekindling it. There were no logs left in the basket, and the old boy from across the fields who had brought the last load hadn't called for two days. Two days, was it, or much longer than that?

He drew his coat around him instead. The smallest movement required an effort of will that was almost beyond his capability. On the rag rug in front of the dead fire, the dog stirred and then lifted his head to look at him. The creature had given up hope that Julius might take him outside and let him run over the sheep-bitten turf toward the sea wall. He lay still, whining occasionally, the whites of his eyes showing when he yawned and shivered.

Julius shifted again and looked across at the window. He did not know if he had fallen asleep or if in his solitude he had forgotten how to distinguish the passage of time. It seemed that at one moment there was daylight outside, and the next there was the gray-purple threat of darkness. The repetitive cycle of the hours pressed on him like a weight.

The wind was rising. He could hear it whipping inland, unimpeded, toward the dour mountains. The wail drowned out the music in his head, but the sound of the wind with all the implacable and majestic associations of the natural world came too late to be a comfort to him. He had tried to harness the music and to transmit it through the orderly systems of notation. It had defied him, shrieking ever more loudly, until its crescendo made him press his hands to his ears and rock, forward and backward, wishing for nothing more than to be left in silence. And now even as he listened to it, the wind and the music became part of each other.

Julius stumbled to his feet. The dog jumped up at once and stood stiff-legged, with his head cocked. He barked once, then ran to the window. He leaped at it and strained with his forepaws against the glass.

"Gelert, boy," Julius said.

He walked through into the tiny kitchen and saw that the dog's bowl was empty. He ran fresh water into it from the single cold tap and then opened the door of the stone pantry that led off the kitchen. The dog came behind him and lapped noisily at the bowl. The shelf in the pantry was bare except for the heel of a loaf and some cold mutton and a covered bowl of dripping. Julius took a tin plate, and working carefully and methodically, he crumbled the bread and then sliced the meat on top of it. He used the blade of the knife to scoop the dripping out of the bowl and mash it into the heap of meat and bread.

Then he carried the piled-up plate into the kitchen and put it on the floor beside the water bowl. The dog ate some of the food while Julius watched, then sat back on his haunches, looking up at him.

"Good boy," Julius said gently.

He went back into the main room of the cottage. There was an upright piano against one wall, with torn sheets of music manuscript scattered on the floor around it. Julius's violin lay on the piano in its closed case. He lifted it up and held it in one hand, looking around the room as if searching for somewhere else for it to rest. There was nowhere, and so he stooped to put it down on the chair in front of the fire. He unclasped his fingers from the handle very slowly. The violin case sat upright in his place, like an abstract of himself.

The windows and ceilings in the cottage were too low for a man of Julius's height, but as he straightened up he could see directly out of the window across the marsh in the direction of the sea. It was almost dark now. There was only a thin greenish line marking the horizon, and above it the impression of weighty clouds rolling in toward the land.

Julius took an old jacket off a hook. As soon as he clicked up the latch of the outside door, the dog bounded in from the kitchen and raced out into the darkness. Julius followed him, and in the gloom he could just see the white patches of his coat as he sprang away toward the sea.

The air was laden with salt. A recollection stirred, and he groped for it in the disorder within himself. Then with a sudden clarity he remembered summer holidays, a beach in Norfolk and a little canvas pavilion with a red pennant fluttering above it. There was the rowing boat, and then Grace, lying on the sand with her wet clothes molded to her body.

Julius's shivering had become a convulsive shudder. The spasms twisted his shoulders and jarred his bones. The wind seemed to cut into him now, driving him backward toward the little house and whatever waited for him within it. He took one more step, then faltered, and then he swung around so the cottage loomed in front of him. A single square of yellow light showed in the lower window, drawing him on.

As he crept back, he thought briefly about Stretton. He could imagine the music, dance music, not the clamor that filled his head. He wondered if Clio was dancing, and Grace, always Grace, with her hand resting lightly on her partner's shoulder. Her head would be tilted a little to one side, as she listened to whatever it was he was saying.

When he reached the cottage again, Julius went into the kitchen and picked up the half-eaten plate of food. He put it outside on the rough ground, so the dog would find it if he came back. Then he retreated again. He closed the door and turned the heavy old key in the lock.

• • •

Clio danced with Jake, then with Thomas and a handful of Stretton cousins and neighbors whom she had known since she was a child. The ballroom was still a sea of changing colors that wove patterns and figures for her pleasure. It was exhilarating to dance in this warm, shining space with the company of friends around her.

But toward midnight she felt suddenly restless. The heat from the dancers and the candles seemed to fall across her like a smothering weight; her hair was damp over her forehead and at the nape of her neck. But at the same time she shivered, as if a cold draft had penetrated the brilliant room.

She excused herself to her latest partner and slipped away from the dancing. She wandered slowly through the house. The ball was at its height; couples wound up and down the great staircase under the family portraits and sat out in the firelit and scented rooms from which all the dust-sheets and -covers had been stripped off and bundled away. It made Clio happy to see Stretton alive again.

Blanche had been right, she thought. She had made Hugo agree to sell two paintings, a Canaletto and a Lely, to pay for this week of celebrations. Hugo had demurred, but Blanche had insisted. In the end the pictures were sold, and so it was all done as it should be done. There was the new Countess in her wedding dress and her diamonds, and the footmen with their powdered hair, and the hundreds of guests. The great house contained them, serene and magnificent, as it was meant to be.

As it was meant to be tonight. After tonight, how many more evenings like this one would there be?

Clio shivered again. A cold finger touched her spine. The division between her happiness and her fear was so fine that she felt herself vibrate between the twin magnetic poles, an oscillation so fine as to be invisible, but she was still possessed by it. She saw all the brightness of tonight, and even as she looked into its lovely face, she saw another reflection, a mirror image, where the soft flesh had peeled away to show the terrible and savage bone beneath.

She caught her breath and looked behind her, as if the embodiment of her fears might stalk her through the golden glow of the ball. But there were only smiling faces, familiar and unfamiliar, pink with champagne and the exertions of dancing and pleasure. There was no skull-face visible in the crowd.

The doors of the salon stood open onto the terrace. A marquee had been erected on the smooth grass below, and an awning covered the stone steps leading down to it. Clio passed out of the terrace doors and under the awning. There were round tables set out in the marquee and hired staff were busy here, under the eye of the butler, preparing to serve supper. A noisy party of what looked like Phoebe's friends was already in possession of one of the tables. Clio wandered out again, sensing the movement of the evening around her like a tide. She stepped aside, from beneath the shelter of the awning, to look up at the front of the house. The stone shimmered under the floodlights, and the windows gave back their own light.

When she turned to look out into the blackness of the park, she felt that the house was a liner sailing in some dark sea.

Cressida had been sitting at the far end of the terrace, huddled on one of the mossy stone seats in a semicircular niche. When she saw Clio standing alone with her face turned out to the darkness, she jumped up and ran toward her. The hem of her golden-yellow bridesmaid's dress brushed over the paving. The clipping of her satin slippers as she hurried sounded remote, as if even her footsteps belonged to someone else.

"Cressida? Is that you?" Clio was startled. "How long have you been out here?"

"I don't know. I can't remember how long."

Clio looked at her. "Aren't you frozen with cold? With only that thin wrap?"

Cressida repeated, "I don't know. It doesn't matter." Then she laughed, a jagged laugh that was too old for her, without any humor in it. "I don't know anything at all. What can you tell me, Clio?"

Clio looked harder at her. She remembered how Cressida had emptied her champagne glass at the dinner table in one swallow. There must have been several more glasses since then.

"Come inside with me, now," she said gently.

Cressida followed her meekly enough. When they stepped into the salon, she shrank in the blaze of light and then half turned back toward the shelter of the darkness. Clio could see that she had been crying. There were tear marks in the dusting of face powder that Grace had permitted her to apply.

"You need to come and get warm, darling. See, your teeth are chattering."

Cressida felt as if the eyes of every one of the overdressed and raucous people in the room were fixed on her. She muttered, "Can we go somewhere? Away from all this stupid show?"

"Of course we can. Come up to my bedroom, and we'll sit by the fire."

For once there were enough servants in the house for fires to have been lit in all the bedroom grates. Amongst Clio's more vivid recent memories of Stretton were bedtimes so cold that frost flowers bloomed on the insides of the windows.

They passed beneath the portrait of the Misses Holborough. It had been cleaned especially for the ball, and the innocent identical faces looked as fresh as they had done when Sargent painted them. Clio glanced up at it, and by automatic reaction at the opposite and corresponding empty space. Cressida kept her swollen eyes fixed grimly on the floor.

When they reached her bedroom, Clio went straight to the tall-boy and took out a thick woollen cardigan. Tabby had knitted it for her. She put it around Cressida's shoulders, wondering at the same time if Tabby was dancing or if she had managed to extricate herself and achieve the no doubt longed-for sanctuary of her own bedroom.

"Sit down here," Clio commanded. There was a little sofa beside the fire.

Cressida sat, and at once shaded her eyes with her hands.

"I thought I would drink some champagne and be delicious fun and dance and flirt like all the others," she muttered.

The other debutantes, Clio supposed.

"All I feel is *sick*."

"Are you going to be sick?"

Cressida shook her head. "Clio, can I ask you something?"

"Of course you can. Anything you like."

Some question about love, or sex. What had Grace told her, or omitted to tell her?

Cressida's head was bent. Clio saw that there was a tiny dark blot on the glowing folds of her full skirt, and then a second one spread beside it. Cressida was crying again. Her weeping seemed worse for its very silence. Clio left her seat and knelt on the floor in front of her. She tried to take her hands between her own, but Cressida's arms were rigid and the fingers still shielded her eyes.

"What is it you wanted to ask me?"

Cressida took a breath. The question had reverberated within her head for so long, and now she wasn't sure if she could bring it out into the plain world of matter-of-fact inquiry and response.

Clio waited patiently.

At last, roughly and without lifting her head, Cressida said, "Who is my real father? My father, or Pilgrim?"

In the silence that followed they could hear the music of the band like a whisper or an echo.

When Clio couldn't answer her because there was no breath in her lungs, Cressida did look up, and then demanded, "Well?"

Clio knew that her silence was as clear an indication of the truth as any words could be. She began, stumblingly, hoping that shock would pass for surprise, "I don't know. I don't know what you mean. What exactly are you asking me?"

It seemed inconceivable that Grace could have given Cressida any cause for suspicion, even inadvertently. She had spent eighteen years shielding her secret, and she had done it so effectively that it was a long time since Clio or Jake or Julius had so much as thought about the old bloodlines. Cressida was Anthony's daughter.

"You are your father's daughter."

Cressida's face twisted. "Yes. But which father?"

Clio thought of Romy, lying asleep in the next room, with her fist held up to her round cheek. Romy was a child, who could be told stories of her father so that he would stay alive in her memory. But Cressida was not a child any longer; what story could Clio tell her?

She said, "I think you should ask Grace that, not me."

"I don't want to ask *Grace*. I don't talk to Grace about anything except my Season, and which dress I should wear, and what behavior is suitable and what is not."

There was a flatness in her refusal that convinced Clio that it was not Grace who had put the suspicion into her head. And although Cressida's complaint used the same limited words that any privileged girl of her generation might have used about her mother, there was a different pain behind it. Clio had observed Grace and Cressida over the years, and she could guess at some of the distance that lay between them.

Not for Romy and me, she vowed again.

"I want you to tell me," Cressida said.

There was the faint echo of music once more. Clio saw that the fire was burning low. She reached for the little brass scuttle and shook out some coal. She had never learned that she was supposed to ring for the maid.

"Anthony or Pilgrim? Please, Clio. I can see that you know. Once I'm certain, we needn't ever talk about it again. It's not being sure, don't you see that?" Cressida was urgent now. Her tears had dried up.

Clio looked at her. Her hand still rested on the polished handle of the coal scuttle. She would either have to lie, or tell the truth.

"Pilgrim," she said.

Cressida breathed in, a sharp snatch of air, as if she had been holding her breath for a long time. But then she leaned back, folding her hands in her lap to cover the tear marks on her dress. She nodded, quite calmly, as if she were relieved.

"Yes. He told me so."

I would like to kill him, Clio thought.

"What else did he tell you?"

Cressida made a small movement, to indicate that there was nothing else, or nothing that could be as important as the single fact.

"Did he tell you how young your mother was, and how innocent? Did he tell you exactly what he did, and how it happened?"

"No. I didn't ask him. I told him I didn't believe him. But at the same time, you know, I did believe it. It seemed to be an explanation of something I had always felt, and never examined in myself because I didn't know what to look for. It was before, before Alice died, that he told me. When you were all in Berlin. Since then, I've put the truth and the illusion to myself over and over again. Like the pros and cons, in a trial?

"But I always knew it would be you that I would have to ask in the end. Because you and my mother—"

Cressida was not notably articulate. Instead of trying to make the words, she held up her two hands to Clio and then pressed the palms together so that they matched. And then she shrugged.

"I don't know why tonight. Because of the champagne, I suppose."

Clio thought, *Not just because of the champagne. Perhaps because even in your imprecise way you sense that tonight is an ending.*

She was suddenly angry.

"I will tell you what happened. Surely you want to know that too? Pilgrim seduced your mother when she was hardly more than a girl. The age that you are now. You may think that you know everything, Cressida. Probably you don't really know very much, but however much it is, it's far more than Grace and I knew. We were as innocent as Romy, although we believed that we were women of the world.

"When Grace found that she was going to have a baby, she knew there was no use in turning to Pilgrim for help. What she did do was to ask me, and Jake and Julius, and we couldn't do anything either. So she married your father."

"Anthony."

"She married Anthony, who loved her. And then much later, she fell in love with him, as you must know. They were noticeably happy together. I envied them."

"He never knew?"

"No, nor never even suspected. I'm sure of that. Grace kept her secret."

Cressida's mouth pulled downward, showing her distaste.

"Don't judge her," Clio said sharply.

And then she wondered, *Why am I defending Grace? My opposite and my reflection, the left hand matching the right . . .*

"I will tell you something else, Cressida. Pilgrim seduced me, too."

Cressida laughed, at first in disbelief and then with the first signs of amusement. "Yes, I can believe that. He would have liked it, wouldn't he? But you were luckier?"

"It was later. I was older, although not much more sensible. Grace was the one he preferred, the one he really wanted."

Clio's anger had evaporated. She sat down beside Cressida again and put her arm around her. "You will be cleverer, won't you, when your turn comes?" As it soon would. Cressida's contemporaries were downstairs, dancing while they might, the young men with their pink faces.

There was another surprise to come.

Cressida faced her abruptly. "Can I come to Paradise Square, to live with you and Romy? I don't want to stay at Vincent Street any longer."

"Yes, you do." Clio tried to be as gentle as she could. "Grace is your mother, and she loves you."

She had seen Grace looking at Cressida as if she were hungry, and had no idea how to assuage the hunger. And Cressida had turned stiffly away. How slowly the pieces fit into place, Clio reflected, and how long it takes us to understand even the simplest things.

She began to say that Cressida must stay with Grace, and that she must not allow the fact of an accident of birth to alter all her life. But Cressida cut her short.

"Yes. I see that. Thank you for telling me the truth."

Then very quietly, so that Clio had to lean forward to hear the words, she added, "It was Anthony I always loved best."

"I know. He loved you very much, too. I remember his face when he looked at you. Grace told me once that when they came in at night, however late it was, he would run up to the nursery to look at you asleep."

"I didn't know that. Thank you."

Cressida examined her face. Clio waited, but there were no more questions. The fire had kindled again, and flames licked at the iron throat of the grate. Cressida jumped up and pirouetted, with a pretense at vivacity. Her skirt swirled around her ankles. The tear spots had vanished.

"Oh, goodness. Look at the time. Almost two."

At two o'clock, it had been arranged, the Earl and Countess would leave the ball. Their guests would stay on until it was daylight again.

"We had better go and wave them off."

"I might catch the bouquet." Cressida pouted.

There was a crush of people at the foot of the great staircase. Cressida and Clio slipped in amongst them. Clio saw Tabby and waved at her in surprise. If Tabby was up, it must be the best party ever given.

Hugo and Lucy appeared at the top of the stairs. There was a huge cheer as they came slowly down the wide curve, arm in arm. When she reached the bottom step, Lucy lifted one arm and tossed her bouquet. It was her sister Venetia who caught it.

The couple crossed the marble floor between the throngs of their guests, under a shower of dried rosepetals. Clio found that there were tears in her eyes. She blinked, then saw Blanche and Eleanor, with their arms around each other's waists, the same expression of happy satisfaction on their faces.

Two footmen were standing holding open the tall doors. Hugo and Lucy turned back to wave, then went slowly out and down the steps with their families and friends surging after them. Hugo's chauffeur was waiting beside a long black car. Lucy's dress seemed almost to fill the back of the car with white froth, but Hugo climbed in and swung his useless leg after him.

There was a last glimpse of their faces, framed together in the oval window at the rear, as the car rolled away.

Clio didn't know where they were going. To the privacy of one of the estate houses, perhaps. She caught herself wondering if Lucy, Countess of Leominster, was a virgin on her wedding night. She remembered the little inn in the forest of Thuringia, and her sudden longing for Rafael clouded her eyes and made her breath catch in her throat.

She found Cressida was standing beside her.

"Why am I crying?" Cressida demanded.

"I don't know. Why am I?"

They smiled at each other.

"I am going to go inside now, and drink some more champagne, and then I shall dance until my feet fall off," Cressida said.

"That's good, I'm glad," Clio told her.

Clio went in too. The band struck up again, and soon the floor was crowded with couples once more. A portly man whom she had known as a plump boy asked her to dance, and she let him draw her into the music.

To her surprise, there was no shortage of partners.

Just once, she caught a glimpse of Cressida, whirling past in the arms of one of the pink boys. Cressida's head was thrown back, and they were both laughing.

A memory flickered within Clio and she tried to catch at it, following the thread of recollection backward. Then she did capture it. It was Grace, dancing and laughing with Anthony Brock, on the night of the coming-out ball that Grace and she had shared at Belgrave Square.

It occurred to Clio that this was the first time that she had ever seen any likeness of Grace reflected in her daughter.

Later, from one of the long windows overlooking the terrace, Clio was surprised to see that the sky was already lightening. Ambrose and his musicians had finished playing, but their place had been taken by another band. Somewhere, breakfast would be being served.

Then, seemingly only five minutes later, when she looked again it was full daylight. She had been dancing with one of Thomas's Army friends, and now he took her arm, not quite steadily. The dance-floor was almost empty, and the musicians weary.

The major boomed, "I'm just about ready for a rasher of bacon and a grilled kidney. What would you say to joining me?"

Clio smiled at him. He had a damp moustache and the whites of his eyes were bloodshot, but he was a good dancer. In retrospect, the night seemed very long.

"That sounds just about right." Clio's thoughts were turning toward her bed. But not yet, not quite yet.

They crossed the floor together. When they reached the doors, Clio stopped, on some impulse, and glanced behind them. There were only a handful of couples left, slowly turning amidst the discarded dance cards and the crushed flowers. In the very middle of the floor, Clio suddenly saw Grace. She had had no idea that she was there, even that she was still up. But there was the black lace dress and the pearls coiled around her throat.

It looked as if she were dancing with Julius.

They were dreamily waltzing with their heads inclined close together. The circle of their intimacy was tight, and complete. It excluded the ballroom, and the other dancers, and all the rest of the intrusive world.

Clio drew in her breath.

Her partner asked her, "I say, are you all right?"

It took Clio five long seconds to realize that the man was not Julius at all.

He was the same height and coloring, but there was no more of a resemblance than that. Their closeness had been an illusion too. Grace's head was drooping because she was tired, and her partner looked as if he might be drunk.

While Clio was still gazing at them, Grace looked up. Their eyes met, but Grace seemed to stare through Clio into another space. Clio shivered a little. Grace and her partner slid into another wide arc across the littered floor.

"Are you all right?" the cavalry major repeated.

Clio turned away from the ballroom. "Yes, thank you, quite all right. Just dizzy, for a moment, that's all."

"Sure? Need to sit down for a minute?"

"No, really. Let's go and find some breakfast, shall we?"

The marquee was almost empty too. It smelled of bruised grass, and cigar smoke and the faded layers of women's perfumes. From outside in the garden Clio could hear the sound of horseplay. There was whooping and cheering, then a loud splash and more cheers. It was nearly, very nearly time for the peace and solitude of her bedroom.

The day after the Stretton Ball—or, as it was, later in the same day—might have been heavy with anticlimax. Armies of men in green baize aprons with brooms and sacks descended on the house, and the outside was noisy with the whistling of electricians as they climbed on scaffolding to dismantle the floodlighting.

But when Clio woke up again, there was sunshine falling in wide bars across the oak floorboards and the high bed. She lay luxuriously between the old linen sheets, lazily stretching and blinking in the sunlight. The hum of satisfaction that possessed the house seemed almost audible.

When she could not justify lying in bed for a moment longer, Clio dressed in loose trousers and an old shirt and wandered downstairs to see whom she could find. There was no sign of Romy or Nanny. At last, in Blanche's little sitting room, she discovered her aunt and her mother perched together over a tray of leftovers that combined late luncheon and early tea. They were dissecting the night's events with their old, inseparable relish.

Clio leaned down to kiss them both. "Aunt Blanche, that was the most heavenly party."

"*Was* it? Do you really think it was? I so much wanted it to be like parties were in the old days, before everything got so grim. Just to show that we could still do it, if we tried."

"Darling, do you remember Norfolk House? And Melton? And the Midsummer Ball at Windlesham?" Eleanor sighed.

"I remember," Blanche said.

Clio saw that they were both tired, and there was a glimpse of frailty in them as they reminisced that she had never noticed before.

"Last night's was the best party I have ever been to," Clio said truthfully. "Every single thing was perfect."

"Perhaps it was." Blanche allowed herself to be persuaded. "Not quite perfect, you know, but as good as we could make it. If only John could have seen it all."

There was a silent wish, too, for Alice. And for Julius.

Clio sat down in the little chair that Blanche indicated for her and took a bone-china cup from the tray. There was a pretty view from this room over the park.

The twins were content. There was a sense of satisfaction and completion, because they had resurrected the old world, however briefly. There was no necessity to express it to each other, but if they had chosen to interpret for Clio, they might have hoped that, after all, there would not be another war. Perhaps last night was not a postscript, and the world they knew and understood would still endure.

Clio recognized the hope, even though she could not share it. Her own fragile optimism crumbled as silently as wood ash.

"Where is everyone?"

"Pappy is asleep, Tabby is out walking. Jake and Ruth and the children are making themselves ready to leave. Why they can't rest a little longer, I do not understand."

Even as Eleanor spoke, there was a clatter outside the door, and then Romy burst in, with Nanny in pursuit.

"You *knock*, Miss Romy—" Nanny remonstrated. Romy was oblivious.

"Mummy! Did you like the party? I picked flowers in the garden, look."

In the face of Nanny's dismay and the mothers' faint disapproval, Clio held out her arms and Romy scrambled onto her lap.

"I loved the party. But I'm even happier to see you."

Romy took her devotion as a matter of course. "Uncle Jake says he's got to go home to London *now*. He doesn't, does he?" Jake was a great favorite.

"If he says he does, then he does."

"He's coming in a minute, to kiss good-bye."

Hirshes and Strettons all went down together to wave good-bye to Jake and his family. Their car was waiting at the foot of the steps, made to look even smaller and shabbier by the house towering above it.

Jake watched them as they came out. He saw Eleanor and Blanche and Nathaniel, and Thomas with his headache, and Grace and Clio, as clearly as he knew that Ruth and his children were standing patiently beside him. Yet all he could focus on was Lottie's face, and the miles that must unravel before he could be in London again, and the steps that would carry him up to her room.

There was a flurry of hugging and handshaking. The Hirshes were, as always, more demonstrative than the Strettons. Jake smiled and kissed cheeks and murmured his thanks, but with each movement he thought *Lottie*. He felt as if he had a fever or were entering into the critical phase of some insidious disease.

Clio and Grace were standing on the bottom step, where the stone balustrade curved behind them to a mossy pillar crowned with a stone pineapple. Cressida stood in front, and a little below them. For an instant, only the briefest second, she seemed to make a third face in the composition of Pilgrim's portrait.

Jake had no attention to spare, for what was left of the magic circle or for anything else.

"Good-bye, darling. Ruth, look after the old boy, won't you? He looks not quite himself."

"I'm fine, Mama." Jake shook off his mother's hand a little

mpatiently and accepted his father's embrace. A moment later, he
elt Grace's cool lips against his cheek, then Clio on the other side,
varmer and more urgent.

"I'll write to Julius, as soon as we're home again. I'll take Romy
p for a visit and make sure that everything is all right."

Grace was walking up the steps, her hands deep in the pockets of
er cardigan.

"Don't worry," Jake repeated mechanically.

They were in the car at last. There was a last press of relatives
round the door, and then they were away, and rolling down the
rive. Ruth folded her hands over her bag, resting in her lap. The
hildren were quiet in the back seat. They passed the Lodge, and
rove through the huge gates.

Ruth said, "Think what we could have done with all that money
t the Clinic or the practice. It must have cost thousands."

"Yes," was all Jake said, partly because he agreed with her
nd partly because his head was too full to leave room for any-
hing else.

lio and Romy traveled back to Oxford the next day, with Tabby
nd Eleanor and Nathaniel. Grace and Cressida had left for London
arlier in the day.

Clio was pleased to be back in Paradise Square. Life in the little
ouse was neat, and circumscribed, and without ambition. She
hought of it as a waiting place that held her and Romy until Rafael
ame back.

The letter to Julius proposing a visit was written and posted.
here was no answer by return, nor on the day after that. Clio
vished that she could telephone; there was no telephone in the
ented cottage, nor did she know of any neighbor who might have
aken a message for him. Anxiety gnawed at her, but she did
othing to assuage it. She began to think that she would not wait for
ulius to extend an invitation. She would travel up to Wales to see
im whether he wanted to be interrupted or not.

On the afternoon of the third day, she was sitting at the table in
he window of her small sitting room. She was typing an article,
nd Romy was perched opposite her. The child was painting a
icture, with her tongue bitten between her teeth.

Clio looked up to see Nathaniel at the front gate.

"What is it, Mummy?" Romy asked.

"I don't know," Clio whispered.

Nathaniel stood beside the door. His face was gray and shrunken, and he leaned against the jamb to support himself.

Clio put out her hands to Romy. She drew the child against her, covering her eyes and ears with rough hands so that she could not see, nor hear what was coming.

Not Rafael.

The shame of her wish was granted. It was not Rafael, but Julius.

Twenty-Three

JULIUS WAS BROUGHT HOME TO Oxford.

It was Jake who traveled to North Wales to see the police and the coroner, and the neighbor who had found Julius's body. Nathaniel tried to insist that he should go too, but Jake made him stay with Eleanor. Eleanor gave herself up to the intensity of her grief, but Nathaniel was silent. Overnight, he became a wandering old man.

Clio and Tabitha made the arrangements for the simple funeral, and Jake brought his brother home. There was no doubt or any shadow of a mystery with which they could comfort themselves against the truth. Julius had hanged himself from a hook in the solid beam of the cottage bedroom. It was three days before the old sheep-farmer from across the marsh came to look for him. There was a single letter on the dresser in the kitchen. It was sealed and addressed in Julius's distinctive black handwriting to Grace.

Julius was buried on All Fools' Day, next to Alice in the church-yard of St. Cross.

It was a cold day, bright and dull in rapid succession as clouds masked the pale sun. They huddled in their black clothes at the grave-mouth while the wind scoured their faces.

Cressida stood next to her mother. She remembered how, in almost the exact same place, she had looked up from Alice's grave and suddenly seen the raw, adult truth of Julius's longing for Grace. She knew that in some way that she could not under-stand, it was because of the longing that Julius was dead. She did not want to speculate about her mother's loves, and the shades and deceptions that had attended them, but the images came to her anyway.

Cressida was cruelly fastidious. The thoughts made her want to separate herself from Grace, who stood immobile with her white face half-hidden by a wisp of veil. Even the hat she wore, and the narrow-waisted black suit, seemed both too chic and too self-conscious for this desolate day. Cressida wished that she could cross over the lips of the grave-mouth to Clio and Jake.

The Hirsh children stood in a close group around Eleanor and Nathaniel, but each of them knew now that they could never fill the invisible spaces that separated them. The adored baby and the favorite son, the musician and the peacemaker, could never be replaced.

Eleanor's hand rested on her husband's arm, but it was Jake who supported them both. Tabitha found her own comfort in her faith. Her lips moved as she prayed.

Clio was as still as Grace. She held herself carefully, as if she were afraid that if she did not, the grief and rage and bitterness would spill out of her. When Nathaniel had mumbled the news barely intelligibly because his mouth seemed frozen and distorted, she had been ashamed because she had wished so fervently that it might not be Rafael. But then, with frightening speed and strength, anger had descended on her. It burned in her then, and now, like a malevolent fire.

At first, the anger had been directed at Julius.

How could he leave them all? How could he have chosen to vanish, to step beyond some curtain so suddenly and completely and leave them, leave *her,* alone?

Until he was dead, Clio had never fully understood that her twin had been half of her. Now she felt as if she were the living trunk of some tree that had been split by lightning. One flank of it had been burned away, to leave the sad pith exposed. The bare wound ached with an intensity of pain that made her afraid of herself. Perhaps the gash would yellow and harden with time, and at length the moss would grow over it, but the tree would never flourish again.

The anger shook her like a gale. He had gone, and left her without a word or a warning.

Then, just like the wind veering, the focus of her anger had shifted. Julius had lived on the margins of his own life because of Grace. Clio had seen him waiting, they had all seen him waiting like some patient monk, at first with a young man's confidence and then, as the years passed, with the beginnings of resignation.

Then there was Berlin. As soon as Julius had achieved happiness, it had been taken away again, and Grace had done that. It was because of Grace that Julius was dead. First Alice, and now Julius. He had gone away, and Clio was left with only her anti-twin.

Clio's anger shifted and then steadied, with Grace at its center.

Clio watched her across the banked-up earth and the mockery of flowers. Julius lay between them under a mask of polished oak. The wind brought the first spots of rain driving into their faces, and the droplets scattered like blemishes over the coffin lid.

After the burial service the mourners drew together outside the churchyard gate. There was no arrangement, as there had been after Alice's funeral, to meet at the house in the Woodstock Road. Eleanor and Nathaniel had not found the strength for it. The few of Julius's friends, mostly musicians, who had heard about his death in time to attend his funeral, moved awkwardly amongst his family and murmured their condolences. The rain grew heavier, and the cars began to move slowly away.

Cressida came to Clio through the helpless group that was left. She held out her hands, not knowing what to ask for. Clio put her arm around her shoulders and held her, rocking her a little, as she might have done with Romy.

"I feel so sad," Cressida whispered.

"I know."

It was a measure of how very young Cressida was that she should be surprised by grief. Or perhaps, Clio thought, it was an indication of her own weariness that it should seem now to be inevitable. She had learned about grief, but not enough about anger.

Clio looked across Cressida's shoulder. A thick strand of the girl's hair had escaped from beneath the brim of her hat, and Clio coiled it around her finger and then tucked it back into place again, as if she were her own daughter.

Grace was watching them. She saw Cressida with Clio, as she had never been with Grace herself. Or had not been since she had grown old enough to turn away, after Anthony's death.

Clio slowly raised her eyes. Between the dark overcoats and bowed heads, she caught Grace's look of pure, clear enmity.

Jake said that one of the family must travel up to Wales again, to sort and pack Julius's possessions and to close up the cottage.

"I would go," he told Clio. "But there is work. And Ruth and I—"

He shrugged. Jake had been with Lottie Brand when Nathaniel telephoned with the news about Julius. Ruth had tried to find him, but he was not where he had claimed to be going, nor had he ever been expected. At first, in the shock and confusion, her discovery of his lie had seemed hardly to matter. There had been no re- crimination; not even a comment. But in the days afterward Ruth had retreated even more bleakly within herself. Jake realized that they had hardly communicated for almost as long as he could remember, but their existence now was in silent and rigid parallel. Jake could not move to one side or the other, either to Lottie or to his wife and children. The spectacle of his own weakness repelled him.

"I understand," Clio said.

"Perhaps Tabby would come with you?"

There was no question that Nathaniel or Eleanor could under- take the journey. The three of them murmured about their parents now as if they were invalids.

"I don't mind going alone," Clio said.

Julius's death had touched Tabby no less significantly than the rest of them. She had announced, in her calm way, that she was making preparations to enter an Anglican convent. It was an open order, she assured them.

"If Mama and Pappy will have Romy for a day or two."

"It would help them, I think," Jake said with relief.

Clio was afraid of the cottage on the sea marshes, but she made the necessary preparations to travel to Wales. Julius's car was still parked in the rough barn beside the Welsh house. Clio could pack it with his belongings, and drive it home again. She did not imagine that it would be a very big load.

Romy went willingly to her grandparents'. When it was time to leave her, Clio was swept with such a wave of possessive love that she did not think she would be able to relinquish her. She knelt down and hugged her and pressed her face against the thick mat of fair curls.

"I'll be back soon," she promised. "Be a good girl for Grandma."

Nathaniel came with her to the gate. He shuffled now, like an arthritic. Clio looked up at the old house, and the turret with the witch's hat. She left it with a heavy heart.

The rain fell all through the long journey northward. Clio changed at Chester, and a slow train took her onward through small seaside towns she had barely heard of. Between low sand dunes crested with coarse grass, she caught occasional glimpses of a vicious-looking sea.

At length, feeling stiff and dirty, she left the train at Llandudno Junction. There was a single dilapidated taxi waiting in the station yard.

Clio gave the driver Jake's directions to the cottage. The man's Welsh accent was so thick, she could barely understand his response.

It was not a very long drive. They passed through a straggling village and then out, on the seaward side, into a wide, flat landscape of low mud banks and salt creeks. Ahead of them Clio could just discern the sea wall, a heavier gray line under the lowering sky. The only living creatures she could see were slow flocks of sheep, huddled in a mass against the wind, and the gulls circling above them.

There was a low farm building to one side of the road, but the taxi passed by. It must be where the farmer lived, the neighbor who had come to look for Julius. A few hundred yards farther on, the road stopped at a five-barred gate. A rutted track led beyond it, and then Clio saw the cottage. It was tiny, and the same gray as the rest of the landscape. A single chimney stuck up from the crooked slate roof.

The driver obligingly took her beyond the gate, over the pot-holed track to the front of the house. There was no enclosure of any kind. The short marsh-grass ran all the way up to the stone walls.

When Clio stepped out of the car, the force of the wind almost overbalanced her. It was searingly cold, and the rain drove into her eyes as if to blind her. She tasted the rankness of salt on her lips.

"Holiday, is it?" the taxi man asked, showing his teeth with a smile.

"Not a holiday, no."

Clio paid him and watched the ancient car bumping away down the track. She felt that her last link with the warm world was being severed. She made herself turn to the cottage door. It had once been painted brown, but the paint had blistered and flaked away in the wind to reveal the split and swollen wood beneath.

There was no key. Jake had told her that. The old lock had had to be broken.

She lifted the latch, and the door swung open. She closed it behind her and at once the wind's howl dropped to a low whistle. A massive wooden sliding bolt would secure the door from the inside.

There was one room, with a stone hearth and an old bread oven to one side of it. There were wood ashes still in the hearth, and an armchair drawn up close to it. Julius's violin was no longer there. Jake had brought that home with him.

There was very little other furniture: a table and two stick-back chairs, a Welsh dresser, and an old upright piano. Sheets of music were neatly stacked on it, some of them manuscript scribbled with angry thickets of notes.

Clio walked very slowly around the small space. With the tips of her fingers she touched the few plates propped on the dresser, and she lifted the lid of the piano and played a single chord. The notes shivered in the close air. Then she looked into the tiny kitchen with the stone-shelved pantry leading off it. The tap was dripping in the sink, over a sea-green stain, and she twisted it tighter.

The precipitously steep staircase was revealed behind a door to the side of the hearth. It was narrow, and there was a dog-leg bend. How had they brought Julius down here, at the end? The pity for him swelled inside her like a wave.

There was only one bedroom, with a kind of cubbyhole beyond it. A window in the gable end, blurred with the rain, looked directly out over the sea. White-capped waves were whipping toward the sea wall. Clio sat down on the brass-framed bed, feeling the horse-hair mattress barely yield beneath her weight. Blankets were neatly folded at the end of it. There was a pine chest of drawers under one window and a three-legged stool that she thought might once have been used for milking. There was an oil lamp on the chest and a box of safety matches beside it. Clio lifted off the glass mantle and held a match to the trimmed wick. The light flared up, blue and then yellow. She replaced the mantle and held up the lamp. Her shadow reared on the wall beside her.

Deliberately, she looked up at the blackened beam that ran the length of the cottage. There was a hook, sturdy enough. She had expected to be disturbed by the sight of it, but she was not.

Clio was no longer afraid of the marsh cottage.

When she watched the taxi driving away, she had wondered how Julius could have come all the way here, to this bleak and remote landscape of all places, but now she began to understand. He had come here exactly in order to remove himself from the world.

She did not know what he had found here, or what demons he had finally confronted, or run away from. But he had chosen to make this journey to the sea and then the final climb up the steep stairs.

The thought of his solitude and the struggle toward death freshened her grief until she had to double over, her knees drawn up to her face, with the springs of the old bed creaking beneath her. She wept, as she had not been able to do before, turning her face into the crook of her arm and giving herself up to her loss.

After a long time, she lifted her swollen face. The meager light outside had entirely faded, and the windows had shrunk to black squares.

Clio listened.

The cottage was full of Julius's presence. She felt close to him now. In his last letter to Jake he had said that this place soothed him. She hoped that much was true, and that he might have found some solace in contemplating the flat land and wide, empty sky. He had also said that he could hear music. She thought that she too could hear it now. It was slow and profoundly solemn.

Some of her sorrow had shifted. Clio was relieved that she had come here and found that there were no terrors within the thick stone walls. This place had held the last of Julius, and she loved it for him.

She had not taken the trouble to bring any food with her, and she was not hungry now. She climbed down the stairs again and took a cup off a hook on the dresser. She ran the cold tap in the kitchen and drank some of the pure, cold water. Then she went back up to the bedroom. Without undressing she wrapped herself in the blankets and lay down to sleep.

At home in Vincent Street, Cressida wandered downstairs from her bedroom to the drawing room, and from the drawing room to her mother's study. Grace's part-time secretary had been in that morning and she had opened and sorted the post. The letters lay in tidy piles now, waiting for Grace's attention when she came in. Cressida thought of making one large and vicious movement, whirling all the letters into the air so that they rose up and settled like litter on the rug. She did not do it. Instead she ran her finger over the telephone receiver resting in its cradle, over the onyx pen-and-ink stand that had been presented by Grace's constituency party, and touched the silver frame containing Anthony's photograph.

She opened her mother's morocco-bound engagements diary and read what was written there. Grace would be home soon.

Cressida was supposed to have been attending a luncheon party, given by the mother of one of her fellow debutantes to enable a selected handful of the girls coming out that year to meet one another. There was one gathering or another almost every day in the weeks leading up to the start of the Season.

"I don't want to go," Cressida had told Grace.

"Don't be silly. One has to go to these things. It's how you make friends. Everyone does their Season."

"Everyone?"

"Everyone like us."

Cressida waited until Grace went out, then she telephoned the hostess and explained that she would not be able to come to lunch today because she had a headache.

She went back up to the drawing room now. After standing at the window looking down into the street for a moment, she sat down on a sofa and began to read a magazine until she heard Grace's taxi drawing up at the street door.

Grace was tired. The morning's committee had been no more than usually tedious, but the simple effort of putting her key in the lock and pushing open the door seemed almost more than she could manage. She walked stiffly into the house and along the hallway to her study. There were piles of letters and memos waiting for her attention, even though she had already dealt with a sheaf of them at the House.

Grace sat down at her desk and rested her head in her hands.

When Julius died, she felt as if the last safeguard had been removed.

Ever since her childhood, for as long as she could remember, there had always been Julius. She knew that he would understand and he would forgive her. Whatever she did and whatever steel or daring or ruthlessness it required of her, she found it and she was capable of it because at the very end, and at the bottom of whatever she reached, Julius would not condemn her.

She had never even properly known it until he was no longer there, and that was as sad as anything she could imagine.

Now that he was dead she felt stripped; exposed and vulnerable as she had never felt before.

She could not have married him, before Alice died. That closeness of the bone was between them, personified in Clio, and it had separated them as well as uniting them. Nor, after Alice died, could she have gone on living with him and physically loving him. That part of her had withered away. She had tried to be honest, believing that it was better to tell him the truth than to pretend. But she had never ceased to depend on him, an airy dependence that might have seemed remote but was in truth as vital as a miner's pit-props. All unknown to her while he was alive, Julius had been the touchstone by which she lived her life.

Now he was dead, and the loss of him had made her weak.

Grace lifted her head from her hands, and she saw Cressida waiting in the study doorway.

"Cressida? I thought you were having lunch with Sarah Stuart-Key?"

"I didn't go," Cressida said deliberately.

She came farther into the room. Watching her, Grace could clearly see the plump, withdrawn child who had faded into this thin, spiky adult. She was shaken by a clumsy pulse of love for both of them, past and present Cressida, love that seemed all the more thick and weighty because it was inarticulate.

"I want to talk to you," Cressida said.

Grace slowly put aside her sheaf of papers. To Cressida, she seemed to make the gesture with reluctance. It was like an emblem of all the years in which her mother had been too busy to mother her. It made her feel hot behind her eyes, and it knotted up the careful words she had planned and made her deliver them like a blow.

"I know about my father. I found out the truth."

Grace was caught, half turned in her chair. "What do you know?"

Cressida leaned over her shoulder and snatched up the framed photograph of Anthony. She held it against her chest with her arms crossed over it.

"I know he isn't my real father, even though I loved him. Pilgrim is, isn't he?"

"Pilgrim?"

Grace was numb with fear and shock. It was unthinkable that the secret should swim up now, out of the depths she had consigned it to. She could only repeat Pilgrim's name, like a fool, like a criminal.

Grace's reaction would have told Cressida everything, even if she had not known it already. She had never seen any emotion reflected so clearly in her mother's face as she saw this flash of guilty fear.

Cressida felt her world shifting on its axis. Giddily, she confronted the new perspectives that were revealed. Her mother was vulnerable. She wielded new power herself; she was no longer a child, even to Grace, who had always made her feel younger and more inadequate than she truly was.

"Who told you?" Grace whispered.

"It doesn't matter. I know, that's all that's important. Why did you do it?" Cressida jerked her chin at the room, and the abrupt gesture took in the rest of the house, the shell that held their lives. "It makes all this seem like a lie. All the way back, to when I was a baby."

Desperately, Grace tried to reassure her. "No, it doesn't. There's no lie. I loved your father, and he loved me. And you were his great pride, every day of his life."

Cressida was afraid that she would cry. It was important that Grace should not see her cry, not at this moment when the notion of power was so finely balanced between them. She concentrated on her anger instead, rubbing at it as if it were a brass kettle that she could cloud with her breath and then polish to a shine with her sleeve.

"You never even let me say good-bye to him. You made me go away, and then he was dead."

Resentment of that was like a black hole buried in her heart. What would everything have been like ever since, Cressida wondered, if she had been able to take her leave of Anthony?

"Cress, listen. That was a terrible day, can't you understand? He was dying, and you were only a little girl."

"He thought I was his *daughter.*"

Only the young could be so cruel, Grace remembered. She had possessed that cruelty once herself.

"I'm sorry," she whispered.

Cressida knew that the balance was tipping toward her, and it was both fearsome and intoxicating. What she did and said *now,* she sensed, might alter the configuration of everything that was to come. She hesitated, then saw again in her mind's eye how Grace had put her papers to one side, with a tiny show of impatience, to let Cressida know that she was interrupting higher things.

There was the heat behind her eyes again, and the unconsidered words.

"Being sorry won't undo anything that is already done, good or bad. All we can do is remember it."

Suddenly Cressida found that she was shouting. There was no chance of choosing the phrases now.

"*I* remember. I remember all the times you were too busy to talk to me, all the times you made me feel stupid, and too fat, and a chore and a burden and an embarrassment. There was a tiny little surface attempt at being a mother, wasn't there? I used to see you putting it on like a lipstick. 'Cressy, darling, do you think those gloves with that frock?' 'Cressy, don't you want to be friends with any girls of your own age?' But it was all a bore for you, wasn't it, and it came out as a sneer and a criticism, every day, for all of my life."

The accusations spilled out of her.

Once she had begun, it seemed, she did not know how to stop herself.

There was every sin of omission and negligence that Grace had ever committed as a mother, significant and trivial, all of them mixed together, a catalogue that was both rending and ridiculous. Cressida's face turned dull crimson, and she held the photograph of Anthony pressed against her as if it might save her life. The words poured out until she was breathless and she had to stop at last, panting and rubbing her mouth with the back of her hand.

Only when she finally faltered into silence was she able to see Grace clearly again. She looked suddenly as she might do when she was old and ugly, if it were possible to imagine that anything of the kind might descend on her beautiful mother.

They faced each other then. The only sound was Cressida's small gasps for breath.

Grace's mouth moved, trying to form an answer. She did not know even how to begin to make a defense against the flood of bitterness. Cressida's outburst had been uncontrolled and the words had been ill-chosen, but Cressida was immature and there was also the thread of cruelty in her that Grace recognized because it had been hers as much as it was now Cressida's. And for all the rage and the wildness, and the confusion of trivial details with major issues, there was a core of truth in everything that she had said.

"Yes," was all Grace said at last, an acknowledgment. With an insight that had never been granted to her before, she could see all the way into Cressida, to her implacable hurt, and she knew that she was the cause of it.

The truth was, Grace understood, that all the love she had ever felt for Cressida had been caught up with guilt for the circumstances of her conception, and grief for Anthony. There was regret for the family that had never properly existed, and a marriage that was hardly begun. All through her childhood Cressida had been a living reminder of Grace's losses and deceptions, and caught in the net of her own concerns, Grace had never found the language by which to express the love instead of her disappointment.

She reached out and gently folded Cressida's fingers away from the silver rim of Anthony's photograph. She slid it out of her hands and replaced it on the desk. When she looked into his eyes, he seemed diminished, receded into the past behind a tiny smiling mask where she could no longer reach him even in her memory. Anthony was gone, and now Julius had followed him.

From Anthony's face she turned to Cressida's. She read defiance in it. It was too late, she recognized with infinite sadness, to be a mother to her daughter. The losses piled against each other, rearing up like monuments.

"What now?" Grace asked her.

"I don't want to live here any longer. If it could be arranged, I would like to go to live in Oxford, with Clio and Romy."

Of course. It must be Clio who had told her. The betrayal of trust, after eighteen years.

"I think I'd be happy there. Clio loves me."

"But I love you too," Grace cried out. The words came easily, whereas she might have imagined them being torn out of her. They were in any case too late. Cressida seemed hardly to hear them.

"I like Oxford. Perhaps I could work there, do something useful."

Grace saw how it would be. There was Clio in her little house in Paradise Square, earth-mothering with Romy and tending the shrine for Rafael Wolf. And there Cressida would be too, happy in the virtuous domestic simplicity of Clio's household.

Clio had a daughter of her own, and yet she would steal Grace's.

Clio had always had Jake and Julius, bound to her by the indissoluble ties of blood instead of the brittle bonds of sex. Now, by some black art, she was undoing the blood tie that should have worked against her, and taking Cressida away.

Clio and Rafael did not deserve what Grace had tried to do for them, even if it had only been the small and pleasurable exercise of power and influence. They would probably never even know about it.

Grace flinched. She was beaten by a terrible hammer-blow of emotion, stronger than any feeling she had ever known.

I hate you, the blood in her veins whispered. *I hate you now, because Cressida loves you, and I will always hate you.*

"What do you think?" Cressida asked. She was almost conciliatory at last, recognizing her victory.

"I don't know. I don't want you to go."

"I know that."

There was the exercise of the new power, absolute and unsoftened. Grace acknowledged it with a small, submissive shrug.

"I could ask Clio."

Cressida seemed to be waiting. Obediently, Grace lifted the telephone receiver and dialed the operator. A message would have to be relayed from the Woodstock Road. Clio did not have a telephone of her own in Paradise Square. But after a brief conversation, Grace replaced the receiver on its hook.

"Uncle Nathaniel says that Clio has just gone up to North Wales. She has gone to pack up Julius's belongings."

She remembered his rooms in Berlin: the few clothes, neatly folded; books and music; almost nothing else.

Cressida nodded. "When she comes back, then." She touched her mother's shoulder lightly, finding a generosity at the end that was only just tainted with irony. Then she went, closing the door behind her.

Grace lowered her head and folded her arms on the desk to make a cradle for it. She lay with her eyes closed, thinking.

Clio was in Wales, touching the last links that Julius had left.

Grace needed to see the place too. The cottage and its associations drew her, strongly and then irresistibly. They were hers as much as they were Clio's. She began to calculate. It was Wednesday. She had planned to travel to Stretton on Friday evening, for a weekend of constituency business. How much farther to North Wales? The route seemed to unravel in front of her, beckoning her onward. Not much farther. Two or three hours' more driving? She could leave in the morning.

As soon as Grace had thought of it, the decision was made.

• • •

Clio woke up the next morning to the sound of wind and driving rain. With the blankets still wrapped around her, she went to the window and looked out toward the sea. The water and the sky were indistinguishable. They rolled toward the house, a single gray mass shot with random gashes of livid light. The marsh grasses were flattened by the vicious wind.

Shivering a little, Clio opened a drawer in the chest and took out a thick, darned sweater of Julius's. She pulled it on over her slept-in clothes. Then she went down to the primitive kitchen and lit the gas under a saucepan of water. When it was heated, she splashed her face at the stained sink, and made herself a pot of tea. She drank the tea without milk, sitting in the old armchair with her fingers laced around the cup for warmth.

She sat for a long time, thinking of Julius.

It had been right to come here. She could feel him close to her, and some of her suffering began to abate. She wandered around the small room, carefully collecting together the scattered music sheets and laying them on top of the piano. Julius's bust of Mozart stood on the deep sill of one of the windows. Clio lifted it up and took her brother's coat off its hook to wrap it in for the journey to Oxford.

Clio went upstairs and opened the drawers of the chest. She took out Julius's few clothes and folded them into tidy piles on the bed. The rain eased while she was working and the wind dropped a little, but the cottage was still filled with the swell and rattle of the weather. The knock at the front door became a rhythmic banging before Clio heard it and separated it from the complaints of the cottage's fabric.

When she pulled back the huge wooden bolt and swung the door open, she saw an old man waiting on the threshold. He was tiny and bent, dressed in brown clothes worn shiny and belted at the waist with hairy string. He was wearing Wellingtons and a flat tweed cap stained the same color as his coat, and when he peered up at Clio she saw that his face was brown too, and creased with exposure to the wind. He looked like some thorn tree bent over on the marsh.

"Morning to you," the man said.

"Good morning," Clio said wonderingly.

"This here's Mr. Hirsh's dog, see?"

The black-and-white collie sat beside him, held on a makeshift eash of the same hairy string. He whined a little and then yawned, lapping his chops with his tongue.

"My brother's dog?" As she spoke, Clio remembered. Julius had written about a dog. His name was Gelert. She stooped down and patted his rough coat and the dog whined again in response. "Good boy," she said softly.

"You must be the farmer?" She looked up at the little man.

He jerked his head sideways toward the marsh. "Sheep."

"Won't you come in? I know you . . . found my brother. I'd like to say thank you for what you did for him."

"Only what anyone would have done, isn't it? Sad thing. I liked what I seen of him. Which wasn't much, mind."

Clio held the door open wider. "Please, won't you come in?"

The farmer shook his head. "Weather," he said, as if that explained everything. "What about the dog, then?"

The dog had been Julius's. The rough black-and-white bundle was another link with him. Clio held out her hand for the loop of string.

"Here, Gelert. Come on, boy."

The dog needed no second invitation. He bounded over the threshold and made for the space in front of the hearth.

"Thank you." Clio turned back to the farmer, but he had pulled at the greasy peak of his cap and was already trudging away down the track toward the gate. Clio shut the door against the wind and saw that the dog was settled in what must be his accustomed place. He rested his head on his paws and watched her.

The time passed slowly, marked by a just detectable strengthening of the light outside that almost immediately began fading again as soon as she had noticed it. In the early afternoon Clio realized that she was hungry. As soon as she went to the door, the dog sprang up and followed her eagerly. She let him out, and he ran in circles around her as she walked to the barn. The keys of Julius's Morris Eight were still in the ignition. The dog jumped in with her and sat in the passenger seat.

The cottage was less isolated than it seemed. A mile or so inland past the farm there was a struggling village of gray stone houses strung out along the road. The mountains were more clearly visible from here, a strong dark rib of them rising out of the coastal plain with the higher peaks like shadows cast behind the foothills. Clio went into the village shop and bought provisions for herself and food for the dog. As she was driving back, the rain doubled its intensity. The single wiper could not cope with the force of it, and she had to drive with her face almost pressed against the streaming windshield.

When she came out of the barn with her arms full of shopping, wind and salt-laden rain beat into her mouth and eyes. Clio ducked her head and ran for the cottage. The sea seemed much closer; she supposed it must be high water. The thunder of the waves against the sea wall was clearly audible.

Clio was sitting in the armchair again, in front of a fire that she had lit with dry wood from the barn, when a sound made her lift her head. The dog sat upright, his muscles quivering.

There was a car coming down the track. They could hear the engine, and the wheels sending out arcs of spray from the huge miry puddles. The car stopped, close to the house. For all the noise of the weather, a silence seemed to descend.

Clio went to the window, and saw Grace. Her white Aston Martin was slewed off to the side of the track with mud splashed over its long bonnet. She came through the rain toward the house, with the sea swelling behind her like a great gray bruise.

A moment later, she was on the threshold, holding up her gloved hand to shield herself from the weather.

"Aren't you going to let me in?" Grace said to Clio.

Clio wanted to answer, *No, never,* but she stood aside and let the door open just wide enough to admit her.

"Why are you here?" Clio asked her. Her voice sounded as it had done when they were children, quarreling on the beach or in the Stretton schoolroom.

Grace turned. There was rainwater shining in her hair, and when she shook off her coat, dark drops spattered over the stone floor.

"For the same reasons as you," she answered.

"No." Clio had shouted before she even realized that she was going to. Her body shook with the intensity of her denial. "I don't want you here. You don't belong here, this is Julius's place."

Grace's clothes were crumpled from the long drive. She took off her suede gauntlets, very slowly, revealing her scarlet-painted nails. "And so, therefore, I do belong in it. You are not the only claimant to his memory, Clio."

Clio saw a red haze of anger and hatred, netted with the dark patterns of veins like a tree against a sunset. Her fists clenched, and the nails bit deep into her palms.

"It is because of you that he is dead."

Grace paused. It struck her suddenly, as it had not done for a long time, how Clio's features mirrored her own. It was like talking to a reflection of herself, only her face looked back at her full of hate and rage.

"No, I believe that Julius is dead because of Julius. I never lied to him, you know. I never promised that I could give him any more than I actually gave. And I loved him, whatever you may choose to believe."

"Oh, Grace, I know that. And I know the destructive power of your love because I have seen it all my life."

Clio went back and hunched beside Gelert in front of the fire. She threw two more logs onto the flames, and a shower of sparks whirled in the black mouth of the chimney.

"Is there anything to drink?" Grace asked.

"Water. Milk."

"I've got some whiskey in the car."

She went out, letting a whirl of cold air into the room, and came back with a bottle of Vat 69. Clio heard her rattling in the kitchen. When Grace leaned over her shoulder with a cup, she reached up automatically and took it. The spirit burned in her throat and made her cough. She sat on the floor and drew up her knees, resting her head on her folded arms. The rough knit of Julius's sweater scraped her cheek, and she caught the faint smell of him lingering in its folds.

Behind her, she sensed Grace prowling through the room with her own cup of whiskey cradled in her hand. The thought of her touching Julius's belongings, even moving through the place where he had been, made the hair at the nape of Clio's neck prickle with cold. She gazed into the flames and at the faces they revealed while Gelert stirred next to her and stretched his paws voluptuously to the warmth of the fire.

Grace stood at one of the tiny windows and stooped to look out. It was dark, and there was nothing to see of the marsh and the sea wall or the clouds and the incessant rain. The roar of the waves seemed to fill her head out of nowhere. She broke away from the window and dragged an upright chair from its place against the wall so that she could sit down in front of the fire.

Grace and Clio sat in silence, not looking at each other, drinking their whiskey out of Julius's cups. The wind and the rain locked them into the close space together.

Grace tipped back the last of her whiskey and reached for the

bottle again. Clio heard the little snick of her lighter as she lit a
cigarette. Grace asked harshly, "Why did you tell Cressida that
Pilgrim is her father?"

Clio did not lift her head. The pictures in the fire hypnotized her.
"I didn't tell her. Pilgrim did."

"When?"

"When we were in Berlin. The last time. When you were with
Julius, before Alice died."

Grace considered.

"You seem to be a part of it, just the same. The conspiracy with
Cressida, against me."

"There is no conspiracy."

"She asked me if she could come to Oxford and live with you
because you love her." Grace blew a plume of smoke between her
teeth, tasting the bitterness. "As if *I* did not, do not."

"She asked me too. I told her that she must stay with you
because you are her mother. She also asked me about her father
because Pilgrim had told her and she did not know whether she
could believe him or not. She needed the truth, and I confirmed it."

Grace exhaled again, a long breath. "So."

It seemed that there was nothing else to say. The hostility between them yawned, dark and ugly as an open wound.

The fire burned low, and Clio threw more logs onto the red
embers. The wind sank to a single note that blew through the
crumbling slates overhead.

Julius seemed close to each of them, a troubled shadow, fretted
and made restless by their division.

At last, Clio went into the kitchen and put together the elements
of a rudimentary meal. She took Julius's books off the table and
laid two places, facing each other, the parody of a domestic tableau.
She set out the cold food, and went to the dresser for two plates. As
clearly as if it were still propped up where he had left it, she saw
Julius's letter, and Grace's name on it. She took the plates from the
shelf and they rattled in her shaking hands.

Grace watched her.

When they sat down facing each other, Grace said, "You can
read the letter if you want to. It's here in my handbag."

They were like Eleanor and Blanche now, looking into each
other's heads without the need for words, but the visions that
danced and sprang before their eyes were neither benign nor reassuring.

Clio took the letter and unfolded it.

Jake had forwarded it to Grace, unopened and without comment. When Grace slit open the plain envelope and read Julius's words, she was powerfully reminded of the letters that Jake had written to her long ago, from the field hospital in France. There was the same eloquence. The fear came from deep within him, and he was unable to express it in music or in words. The brief sentences were disjointed, barely making sense. Except for the last line.

Julius had written, "I love you, Grace. Remember this."

Clio read in her turn:

I can hear music and it makes me afraid.
This was once my language, and I can no longer understand it.
I see holes and spaces where there were once pleasant structures.
Is this what it means to reach an ending?
I am afraid of solitude and I am alone.
I can see absence and darkness, nothing else. Shall I be forgiven for my quietus?
The bare bodkin.
The music goes on, on and on, unstoppable. Silence is welcome.

At the end of the page she saw, *I love you, Grace. Remember this.*

Clio folded the thin sheet of paper and put it back into the envelope. Jealousy bit her for the last time. She had always wanted Julius's love for herself. He was her twin, the good half, and now he was gone forever.

Grace had taken him away.

It was her final act of malice and destruction to come here, to the place where he had died. While she was alone, Clio had dreamed for herself out of the marshes and the old stone walls an image of Julius calm and at peace. Now, because of Grace, she had to see the truth. He was lonely and tormented, and he had preferred to die.

The cottage was filled with the memories of him, and with loss and grief.

Grace took the letter back, and the jaws of her handbag snapped shut on it.

Clio stood up abruptly, the legs of her chair making a harsh scrape on the stone floor. She carried her untouched plate back to the kitchen and dropped the contents into Gelert's bowl. Grace sat on in her place, smoking her long cigarettes and drinking whiskey.

The evening had drained away. At the foot of the steep stairs
Clio said, "There is only one bedroom here. One bed."

Grace did not look around. "I will sleep in the armchair. Just fo
tonight."

Clio went up the steep twist of the stairs and lay down again witl
the blankets wrapped around her. This time she did not sleep s
easily. She listened to the wind, and imagined Grace in the chai
downstairs, smoking and staring into the dying fire with the dog a
her feet.

Grace sat, with her head thrown back and her hands loosel
dangling over the arms. She was full of memories. She thought o
Berlin, and the heat of Julius's body joined to hers came back t
her.

They woke to a world that swelled with water. Rain leaked an
dripped and bubbled all around them. The sea had darkened from
gray to almost black, and the greasy crests of the waves whippe
sullenly into the sea wall.

The two women were stiff and cold, but still the little cottag
held on to them. They stalked each other through the tiny rooms
held captive by the weather and by their jealous guard over the
shadows that remained.

Clio went carefully about the task of packing Julius's belong
ings. She ran out into the rain with the small bundles in her arm
and stowed them into the back of the Morris Eight. She laid the
bust of Mozart, wrapped in Julius's coat, in the passenger seat

"I'll be going this afternoon," Grace said, watching her. "I'm a
Stretton tonight, and seeing constituents all day tomorrow."

Clio nodded. She longed to have the house to herself again, fo
the few hours before she must leave in her turn.

She left Julius's music to the last. She came back from her fina
trip to the barn and the car and shook the rain out of her hair, just a
the dog had done when she let him out earlier. He sat beside the
door now, sniffing the wet air and swishing his tail over the
flagstones. He had been restless all day.

"Gelert, boy." Clio bent to soothe him. She was reconciled to the
idea of taking him back to Paradise Square; she had already imag
ined how she would lead him up to the front door and surprise
Romy.

The sound of the piano made her head jerk up.

Grace was standing with her back to her. She had lifted the lid t
expose the yellowing keys, and the sheets of Julius's music were

pread out around her. She was following the lines of his notation
with one red fingernail, and idly picking out the chords with her left
and. The notes stretched and faded in the thick air.

To Clio it seemed that Grace was picking for amusement in
ulius's exposed heart.

She ran across the room and tore the music away, then slammed
own the piano lid so that Grace had to snatch her hand back. The
eys rattled their faint protest.

The two of them confronted each other. In that second their white
aces were identical, but there was no one to see them and remark on
. Clio's fist had whirled up, and it seemed for a moment that she
vould strike out. They might have fought then, like children, biting
nd scratching and rolling over and over on the stone floor.

But Grace turned sharply away. The house and its ghost were
uddenly unbearably oppressive. She would go out for an hour and
valk Julius's last territory with his dog for company. And afterward
he would drive away to Stretton. She put on her coat and whistled
o the dog, then opened the door that led onto the marshes. The
vind whirled into the room again and blew the sheets of music off
he piano. Rainspots darkened the flags.

Gelert cringed on the threshold, unwilling to venture out, but
Grace saw the length of string that the farmer had brought. She tied
t to his collar, and pulled him out with her.

Clio followed across the room and slid the wooden bolt behind
hem. She went upstairs, with her feet dragging heavily on the
ngled treads. She looked down from the window that faced the sea
nd saw Grace marching away. The collie balked and tugged on the
tring, shrinking from the weather, but Grace held her head up,
urning her face into the driving rain.

Clio sat down on the bed. Afterward, she could not remember
1ow long it was before she looked out of the window again. When
he did raise her head, it was to stare at the sea wall in the distance.

The waves began to lap over the defense. It was high water
gain. Slowly, almost lazily, the ripples spilled over and were
wallowed by the marsh. The universe seemed full of water. There
vas a long, shivering moment of silence when nothing moved in
he sodden world except the idle ripples.

Then the wall split, like the skin of a rotten fruit, and the sea
came bursting through it.

At once a great cliff of water, a wave topped with a crest of dirty
oam as high as a church, raced over the marshland toward the
ottage. Clio watched it, spellbound with fear. In the same instant

she saw Grace running ahead of the thundering water, running with her hands outstretched and Julius's dog like a wolf in front of her.

Clio was frozen. The downstairs door was bolted from within, she had shot the bolt. She would have to open it to let Grace in ahead of the predatory sea, but she only stood at the window, watching her cousin running. The wave was a black wall now, but it moved so fast. Clio did not move.

At last, after an infinity of time chopped into teeming and hurling splinters of memory and longing, Clio whirled away from the window. She threw herself down the dog-leg of the stairs, jarring her bones into flight across the lower room. Her fingers were stretching to the bolt when she heard the terrible drumming of Grace's fists on the other side.

At once there came an overpowering roar as the flood water surged around the house. The sturdy front door held, but a second later the back door was smashed down and the water swirled in. Clio flung herself at the stairs again, clawing herself upward as the torrent swept beneath her.

She found herself standing at the top of the stairwell, gazing down at the inky swell a few feet below her, her breath sobbing in her throat.

Her hands convulsively mimed the gesture of unbolting the door and throwing it open to let Grace in to safety.

Outside the greedy water swept on, eating the flat land past the farm and up to the road that skirted on the marshes.

When the night came, only the upper half of Julius's cottage was visible, sticking up out of the shifting expanse of the redrawn sea.

The night brought a blackness more hideous than anything Clio had ever known. She crouched in the dark like an animal, feeling it touching her skin and pressing like pennies on her eyelids. She forced her eyes wide open. The noise of the wind and water echoed in her head, and swelled louder, and in front of her staring eyes the same images played over and over. There was the black wall of water, and Grace running with the dog, and then a confusion of smashing waves and pounding fists, and a body swept over and over, and her own blind face, under the skin of the sea.

Ever since the day of the *Mabel*, Grace had been afraid of the sea and of death by drowning.

At last, after what seemed like an infinity of time but was only in the gray dawn, the rescue boats came. They brought men in waders, carrying torches and ropes. The men came up the stairs and found

Clio huddled against the inner wall of the bedroom. They lifted her up, gently and kindly, reassuring her in soft Welsh voices. "There now, *geneth bach,* you are safe now. It's all over, you are safe now."

Her white face and staring eyes frightened them, and they saw the little movements that her hands made, to and fro, opening and shutting something that was invisible to them. But she was cold, chilled to her bones, and suffering from shock. She was not hurt, and so she would recover.

Grace's body was recovered five days later, from the rocks of the Anglesey coast. Gelert was lost to the sea.

Twenty-Four

CLIO WAS ILL FOR A long time.

She was taken first to a hospital in Wales, and when it wa
discovered there that she could not eat, or sleep without the aid o
medication, she was moved to a special hospital in Oxford where i
was thought that the proximity of her parents and daughter migh
help her eventual recovery. Her doctors and Jake agreed that he
collapse was the result of shock, and the stress of another bereave
ment following so soon after the loss of Julius.

Nathaniel and Eleanor came to see her, always bringing Rom
with them. They assured her over and over again that the little gi
was safe, and happy with them in the Woodstock Road, becaus
Clio seemed to need their assurances. She would sit silently hold
ing Romy's hand, watching them all with fear and anxiety in he
eyes. After their visits, sitting in the drawing room overlooking th
garden with Romy in bed asleep, the elder Hirshes would remin
each other that Clio and Grace had been close all their lives. They
were born on the same day, and were as much a part of each othe
as blood twins. It was no wonder that Clio was ill, they said. Afte
everything she had suffered.

The old people tried to concentrate their affection and thei
hopes on Romy. The three deaths in such close succession ha
drawn a darkness and fearfulness around them, but they struggle
to hide it from Clio. In time they discovered that Jake was right
they were able to submerge some of their own sadness as they
watched Romy playing in the now overgrown garden.

No one blamed Clio for her breakdown; all through the weeks o
her illness she felt the love and concern of her family gently
pressing against the boundaries of her confusion. She was too ill to
go to Grace's quiet funeral at Stretton, nor was she able to attend the

grand memorial service at Westminster, at which Grace's friends, and her political opponents as well as her allies, paid tribute to her determined spirit.

Afterward, Clio could not remember very much about this time. She was thankful for that. The memories that she did have were of dreams, she knew with hindsight that they must have been dreams, but while she suffered them they were infinitely more real than the hospital ward. She dreamed of water, and faces, and supplicating hands. These horrors came time after time, the same water engulfing her until she feared it so much that she could not turn on a tap to wash her hands, or drink from the beaker on her night table. The hands reached out at her from every shadow and beyond every corner. She folded her own hands into her armpits rather than watch herself fumbling for a bolt that was never drawn back. The faces watched her wherever she went. They were always familiar faces made unfamiliar by their expressions; the features were her own and yet not her own.

There were also visions of punishment. Jailers converged on her and came so close that she cowered away from them before they dissolved and became regiments of teachers and battalions of marching soldiers. She waited in her dreams, wishing for it, whatever it might prove to be, but the threatened punishment was never visited on her.

Then, quite suddenly, she began to recover.

All the time she was ill, Clio knew in some recess of her mind that her illness was an occupation that saved her from having to do anything else.

Almost overnight it came to her that doing something was preferable to occupying the limbo of dreams.

From that day onward, the potency of the visions began to diminish. She began to sleep without needing to swallow pills, and woke up feeling refreshed. The ward she had lived in for weeks became fixed, and no longer dissolved in and out of focus. Its small area reassured her, and then rapidly became boring and confining. Clio began to take walks in the hospital grounds. She found that spring had turned into a hot summer. Horse chestnut trees spread their shade over mown lawns.

One day Nathaniel brought Romy to see her. Clio sat her daughter on her lap and brushed the mass of fair curls back from the child's round face.

"Do you know, Romy, we must do something about your hair?" She heard herself saying it, and saw Nathaniel looking at her in surprised happiness. Clio twisted a thick rope of hair in her fingers, feeling the springy warmth of it.

"We could plait it, or braid it like this, couldn't we? It would make you look so pretty."

Grete had worn her hair in a braid around her head, the same color hair. The last letter from Waltersroda had arrived more than a year ago, and after that there had been silence, and no reply to any of Clio's own letters. Clio could only guess what had happened to Grete and Leopold. Who would wait for Rafael, she thought, if she herself did not?

Clio turned with sudden urgency to her father. She said, "I want to come home. When can I come home?"

Nathaniel's beard was almost completely white, like his hair. He had taken off his old panama hat, and it rested beside his chair with his walking stick. He reached out and took Clio's hand, and held it in his own.

"When you are ready," he told her. "When you feel that you want to."

In another ten days, her doctors agreed that she could be discharged. Clio went home to the Woodstock Road at the beginning of July 1939.

She stayed with Eleanor and Nathaniel for a week. She reabsorbed the sounds and the scents of the old house, moving quietly through the rooms, looking at the shabby furniture and the worn covers. She sat down in front of the open doors that led out onto the balcony, amidst the scent of roses and jasmine, and gazed up at *The Janus Face*.

The staring faces had been part of her hospital dreams, and the separate bodies that grew from the same bud of flesh had been sucked again and again into the churning water.

Now that those horrors had diminished, in the calm of her parents' house with the summer glow of Eleanor's garden spread beneath her, Clio understood what she must learn to endure.

She would have to live forever with her memory of the flood, and her certainty of what she had done on that day.

She had caused Grace's death.

Through her hesitation, the moment of deliberate inaction that was the one sterile fruit springing from all her years of jealousy and rivalry, she had killed Grace. She could have reached the door in time and unbolted it to give her cousin shelter from the wall of water. But by her fatal hesitation she had caused her to drown. That was all, and everything.

Her guilt was her only twin now, and this black twin would never leave her. It would be her companion forever.

The sun in the west struck through the windows and illuminated the portrait. Clio stared up at the webs of color that Pilgrim had woven into their streaming hair, and at the ramparts of solid flesh that forever strained to break apart from each other. It was a good picture, she thought. It revealed the truth, and the truth was not pretty.

Pilgrim had always said that it was his masterpiece.

Romy came to look for her. She held a pack of Happy Families cards. "Mummy, will you play?"

"Of course I will. But we need another person."

"Cressida likes this game."

"I know she does, but Cressy isn't here."

"Grandpappy, then."

"Let's go and find him, shall we?"

They settled down together to Mr. Bun the Baker and his friends. Nathaniel won, and he took just as much pleasure in his triumph as Romy would have done if it had been hers. Watching them, Clio thought how close together youth and old age were. It was she who was isolated, in her middle years.

At six o'clock Nathaniel turned on the radio for the news. They listened to the description of German arms and soldiers pouring into the Baltic port of Danzig.

"We shall be at war soon," Nathaniel said. "There's no hope now."

Romy spread out the cards on the green baize tabletop, then gathered them together in her small hands.

"I think we should move back to Paradise Square," Clio told him. "Romy and I shouldn't trespass on Mama and you forever."

"You can if you wish."

She smiled at him. "I know that. But I'd like to go back to my own house before—anything else happens." She would not say *before the war comes,* although they both knew that it could not be very many days off.

The little house had been kept well aired. Tabby came in sometimes to look after it, in her novice's dress with the ivory crucifix lying snug against a starched bib. Tabby was calm and sure now. She had found her own place, and her family could only try to accept what they could not hope to understand.

Clio and Romy moved back home again at the beginning of

August. Clio found that someone had placed Julius's Mozart in
niche at the angle of the stairs. She supposed that it was Nathanie

The Morris Eight had been recovered when the floodwater
receded, but all of Julius's books and papers and music had bee
destroyed. The marble bust alone had survived, and Clio wa
pleased to find it in her house. She was satisfied to be home agair
She believed that she could go on living here, because she mus
with her black twin. It would be a quiet and uneventful life, live
for Romy's sake.

. The Gilman painting of the bedsitting room hung in the smal
front room, and the Omega Workshops plate was propped on
shelf beneath it. Her possessions were a small comfort, ever
though they seemed to have survived from another existence tha
she could barely recall.

A few days after they had re-established themselves, Tony Hard
came to visit Clio. He brought an advance copy of *Berlin Diary*
She took it and turned it over, looking at the dust jacket printed wit
her name, and the restrained typography, and the tidy pages witl
their paragraphs and punctuation.

She had no sense that the book was anything to do with her at al

"I'm glad you are better," Tony said.

"Thank you."

"Are you pleased with the look of it?" He nodded eagerly at he
novel.

"It's very handsome."

"We shall do pretty well with it, I think. The timing of it, the
latest news from Europe, everything is in our favor."

Even the war, Clio thought. *Rafael.*

But after Grace drowned, she had stopped hoping and praying
for Rafael. That faint, fading chance of happiness was forfeit now

"That's good," Clio said politely. Perhaps the book would earr
her some royalties. She had very little money, and even a tiny extr.
income would make a difference.

Clio gave her publisher tea, and listened to him talking abou
literary London as if he were giving her the latest news from Brazi
or Borneo. After he had gone, she put the novel on a shelf. It looked
no more and no less significant than the other books ranged besid
it. The part of her life it dealt with was behind her. What she di
now was to exist quietly and colorlessly from day to day, and he
black twin always kept step with her.

It was a hot, dry August. Clio sat out in her tiny back garden
watching Romy playing in her cotton sunhat. She wished that sh

could make plants flourish the way Eleanor did. However carefully she dug them in and watered them, Clio's seedlings wilted and died.

The days passed slowly in the haze of the heat. Oxford was almost deserted. On August 20, Clio read *The Times*'s report of the German-Soviet agreement and knew that the last frail thread of hope for peace had been broken.

A letter came from Cressida.

Hugo Leominster was Cressida's legal guardian. After her mother's death she had gone to live with her grandmother and Hugo and Lucy at Stretton; no one had tried to suggest that she should complete her Season.

Blanche was slowly retreating into old age. She was forgetful, and had begun to confuse Cressida with Grace. A dower house was being prepared for her on the estate, to which she would retire with her faithful lady's maid and a handful of staff to care for her. Lucy Leominster was expecting a baby at Christmas. The newlyweds were utterly absorbed in each other, and Cressida was lonely and at a loss in the huge, solemn house.

Her letter said, "Dearest Clio, may I come to stay with you and Romy? Now that you are better again? Not to live with you if you don't want that, but for a visit? I would like it so much. Hugo and Lucy are very kind, but it is not like being with you. Can you understand?"

Watching her mother's expression, Romy said sharply, "What's that?"

"A letter from Cressy."

"Is Cressy coming?" The child's face relaxed and brightened with anticipation.

"I don't know," Clio whispered.

Grace had thought that Clio was trying to steal her daughter away from her.

Was that true, Clio wondered now? Had that been a part of everything else that Grace and she had done to each other?

Perhaps the intention had been in her heart, and she had never known it.

She remembered the races over the Norfolk sand in pursuit of the boys. Grace and she were always running as fast as they could with their sharp elbows out, both of them ready to dig at the other if they could.

That was how it had been, for all of their lives. Yet she had never properly understood the depth of it, the truth that the flaw ran fatally through the rock of both of them. Grace had loved the rock crystals and mineral specimens in the Pitt-Rivers long ago, Clio remembered.

The stone had split apart along its fault line when she stood in the upstairs window and watched the water coming. She had thought then, *This is one race that Grace cannot win.*

It had only been a brief hesitation, an infinity of power and retaliation hotly flowering in those short seconds, but that was what had been in her head. However much she might repent or wish them away, the words and the hesitation were burned into her heart.

"Mummy, you crumpled it." Romy pointed to the letter.

"How silly."

Clio smoothed it out and read it again. Her choice was to deny Cressida because she could not bear to live with this daily reminder of what she had done to her, or to take her in and learn to accept. Clio bowed her head. Her dark *doppelgänger* was here in the house already. There was nothing to deny.

"Shall we ask Cressy to come and stay with us?"

"Yes," Romy crowed in delight.

That evening, from the Woodstock Road, Clio telephoned Stretton.

Cressida came three days later, and Clio went with Romy to meet her at Oxford station. When she stepped down from the carriage, Clio thought, *How like her mother she looks now.*

Romy had drawn and painted a *Welcome Cressy* sign, and they had pinned it up in the Paradise Square hallway. Cressida stopped when she saw it, only half smiling, then turned to put her arms around both of them.

"I'm so glad to be here," she whispered.

Clio felt the warmth of her cheek against her own, and she made herself look down the vista ahead of them both.

"I'm glad you came," she answered.

Cressida unpacked her things and put them away in the little third bedroom. When Romy had gone to sleep that night, the two women sat at the table in the kitchen. Clio had her mending basket, and her head was bent over the heel of one of Romy's socks. Cressida had picked up the pincushion, and now she arranged the pins into a tight circle.

Musingly, almost as if she were talking to herself, Cressida said "I miss her all the time. I look around, or listen for her. Footsteps coming and going, doors opening or a car arriving. She was always so bloody brisk. Busy and intent. I had never considered that she might die. She seemed too powerful to be threatened by death. I used to have a fear for my father, long before he was ever ill, but never for Grace."

Anthony was "my father" again, Clio noticed. She was glad of that.

"All my life I felt that I was trying to move out of the shadow of Grace's influence, and now that she is gone, there is a great space that can't be filled." Cressida shook her head wonderingly. "She was very strong, wasn't she?"

"Yes, she was strong."

"You must miss her too. As much as I do." Cressida was trying to see Clio's face, but she was intent on her darning. "But you felt about her the same way, didn't you?"

Clio never raised her eyes. She went on setting stitch after stitch, drawing the worn threads together.

"She thought that I was trying to take you away. Trying to alienate you from her. She told me so, at Julius's cottage."

"You couldn't have done that. But I know what she was like. I want you to understand that I do know, Clio."

The darn was almost complete. It was nearly time to lay the table for their supper. The pleasure at having Cressida to share the meal with her lifted, then dipped with its counterweight of memory.

"I miss her," Cressida whispered again.

Grace's shadow fell between them. She had always been so strong, she had seemed invincible.

"Yes," Clio said. This was how it would be.

In the basement kitchen of her Islington house, Ruth stood up and turned off the radio. The news made her feel angry with the politicians who had conciliated, and hesitated, and allowed the Nazis to trample as much of Europe as they had done. But it also made her feel heavy with dread. She had wished for resistance, and now that it was coming, she was afraid of it.

She went to the sink and filled a saucepan with cold water, then lifted it onto the stove and lit the gas. Luke was reading at his friend's house and would be coming home soon. It was time to call Rachel down from her bedroom to help with the evening meal.

The front door opened overhead. The footsteps were too heavy and brisk to be Luke's. It must be Jake, home from his evening surgery. Ruth wiped her wet fingers on her apron, feeling the roll of flesh that girdled her middle as she did so. It surprised her, as it sometimes did. She had been intent on other things, and for a moment she had forgotten her weight, and her uncomfortable age, and even the constant reality that Jake had deceived her for the sake of his own pleasure.

Jake came down the stairs. He saw his wife, caught in her apron beside the sink with her hand raised to pat her hair into place. The intention was for him, he knew that. The realization touched him, but at the same time he thought of Lottie, as he did still, in every hour of the day. The physical pain caused by her absence made him move across the kitchen stiffly, like a much older man.

When Ruth had found him out, he had deliberated, pretending to himself that he had some choice to make about the direction of his life, all through a long and agonizing week.

In the end he had given way to his own certainty that he could not leave his wife and children, even for Lottie.

He sat on the bed in her small room, with his head hanging and his clenched fists pressed between his knees, like a condemned man.

He confessed to her that he had weighed their future against his family's and that the two of them had lost. He had told her that he would not see her again. The taste of the words in his mouth made him afraid that he would vomit.

Lottie had been indignant, and then when she saw that he meant what he said, she was violently angry, and finally she cried. Her tears were terrible because he had never seen her cry before.

He had pulled himself out of her arms, disentangling her fingers from his clothes, and walked out of the room. He had walked without knowing where he was going, and he had been sick in the gutter of the Clerkenwell Road. He made himself sit down and drink a whiskey in a pub, and then he went home to Ruth.

"It's over," he told his wife.

Ruth never said anything. She looked at him, and he saw the patina of familiarity accumulated in all their years together, and a new expression that was made up of weariness and mistrust and aversion.

It came as a shock to Jake to realize that Ruth might dislike him

"I'm sorry I have hurt you," he said. "It is all over now. I won't see her again."

Still Ruth said nothing. She had moved away from him, and he had been struck by the vulnerability of her body for all its seemingly armored bulk.

They had lived with each other since as if an awkward truce had been called.

"You're early," Ruth said now.

Jake smiled at her, rubbing his beard with his fingertips. "Small surgery, thank God. Where are the children?"

"Luke is at Benjamin's, and Rachel is upstairs. Shall I call her?"

"In a minute," Jake said. Without knowing what his intention was he put his arm around Ruth's waist. At once the memory of Lottie's narrow and supple body came back to him, as clearly and as powerfully as if he had only relinquished it an hour ago. He pinched the memory down, grinding it away under the thumb of his determination, and kissed Ruth's cheek. Her skin was still smooth and soft, and he saw the old way the color flushed under it.

"Bless you," Jake said simply.

Her head rested against him for an instant.

"I must get the potatoes on," Ruth said. Rachel came down and kissed her father. She did her chores, humming as she set out the knives and forks, and then Luke appeared with his armful of books. The children talked and argued a little as they all moved around each other in the confined space, and Jake looked past them to where Ruth stood at the stove. She worked energetically, as she always did, giving her full attention to the task in front of her.

Jake sat down at the head of the table, and the rest of them arranged themselves in their usual places. It was a family evening exactly like a thousand others, and he felt the resonance of it, the texture of familiarity woven from years of small compromises and unspectacular achievements.

This was what he had, Jake thought.

He felt a small rekindling of self-respect for having tried to preserve it. He did not think he had done so out of cowardice, although he could not be certain of that.

"Did you hear the news?" Luke was asking.

Jake nodded. Chamberlain had announced the Treaty of Alliance with Poland.

"What will happen?"

Jake was already working with the Air Raid Patrol, and as soon as he had eaten, he would be on his way to the church hall at the end of the street to deliver the first in a series of demonstrations of first aid and bandaging. Bandaging had never been one of his particular strengths, he recalled, even when he was a student. Ruth was much better at it. Perhaps he should encourage her to come with him.

Luke and Rachel were looking at him, waiting.

"We'll have to stand up and fight. There's nothing else, now. And we shall win in the end."

He felt different from the prickly, idealistic boy who had watched the outbreak of war with such despair and revulsion. He remembered the field hospital, and the sights and smells of it still came back to him in his dreams, but he would not be a conscientious objector in this war against Hitler. His illusions and principles had been eroded by age and experience—or perhaps, he thought, he no longer felt able to pride himself on the strength of his conscience. The corners of his mouth curled with a thin, self-critical amusement.

There was a poem he recalled reading long ago, in France. He had forgotten most of it, but one couplet came back to him.

> *He ruined me, and I am re-begot*
> *Of absence, darkness, death; things which are not.*

He might even have quoted it in one of his letters to Grace. Amidst the destruction he had imagined himself ruined, but he had later understood that he was not.

He had survived, and he would survive because he was resilient.

It was not a quality that he was proud of; it seemed unambitious and pedestrian and cautious, yet he knew that he possessed it. The poem should have been Julius's, but Jake did not know if his brother had ever read Donne.

The children were still watching him, waiting.

"We'll each of us do what we have to," Jake said calmly. "That is what will happen."

Luke blinked. His eyesight had always been weak, and now he wore dark-rimmed glasses that made him look older than his age. "I shall join up."

Ruth snapped, "You are not even seventeen years old yet. You will sit your exams and get your University place, that's what you will do."

"I'll join the FANYs," Rachel chipped in. Under her mother's stare she added, "When I am old enough, of course."

"Mr. Arkwright says it will be a long war, and I agree with him. There's plenty of time," Luke said.

"We shall do what we have to," Jake repeated. His eyes met Ruth's, and for once she did not look away.

When they had eaten, Luke and Rachel cleared the table and began the washing up. Jake packed a first-aid kit for his lecture and waited by the front door until Ruth came up the stairs from the basement. She liked to sit in their overgrown garden at the end of the day's work and smoke a single cigarette.

Jake said a little too loudly, "I wondered if you'd come with me? I can't demonstrate spiral bandaging to a church hall full of women volunteers and firemen. You'll do it much better."

She hesitated, and in the light from the side window he saw a heavy-bodied woman with dark hair and a faint trace of the same darkness showing on her upper lip. He saw the white skin of her bare solid arms and the features that had molded his children's. This was what he had, this and their mutual resilience.

"Won't you come and help me?"

"I could do. If you like," Ruth said at last.

They went out into the sun-warmed evening. The street was loud with playing children, and a small group of them scattered away from the railings in front of the Hirshes' house. There were the chalk marks of some game on the pavement, and a gaggle of bigger boys running for a ball in the road. In a few more days, perhaps a week, the street would be quiet and almost deserted; most of these city children would be evacuated to safety in the country.

The hall was only two hundred yards away, and Jake could see a trickle of men and women making their way toward it. They were all preparing themselves, in their undramatic way, for what would have to be done. He was suddenly vividly conscious of Ruth walking beside him.

"I'm sorry," he said.

"I know," she answered him.

Jake put his arm awkwardly around her shoulders. Her hip fitted against his, and Ruth lengthened her stride to match his step.

In the doorway of the hall, they looked in at the small audience waiting on their wooden chairs.

"Here's Dr. Hirsh now," somebody called. Jake was a familiar figure in the neighborhood.

Jake said quickly to Ruth, "I have to go to Oxford tomorrow. I promised my father I'd visit him. Won't you come up with me?"

There was a sense for all of them that the visits had best be made sooner rather than later, because nobody knew what might happen after tomorrow.

Ruth shook her head, but she smiled, without resentment. "You go to see your parents. I'll stay here with Luke and Rachel. Just give them all my love, won't you?"

"I'll do that." He touched her hand, then released it again. "Now, shall we go forth and bandage?"

"How did they seem?" Clio asked Jake.

He lifted his glass of whiskey to her, and then drank. The two of them were alone, in Clio's front room with its view of the dusty square. Romy was asleep upstairs, and Cressida had gone to the cinema with the daughter of a neighbor.

"Well enough."

Eleanor and Nathaniel no longer filled the big old house, and there were fewer students and disciples to visit them now, but it seemed to Jake that the old people had drawn into a corner of their domain and found their peace in each other. The losses that they had suffered had in the end brought them closer together and heightened their love and need for each other. Nathaniel's eyes followed Eleanor to the door whenever she left the room, and his face brightened when she came back again. In her turn Eleanor looked to him for confirmation of whatever she said, even the simplest observation.

Jake was touched by the sight of them.

"They have become very frail, just lately," Clio said.

"They are getting old. And they have suffered enough."

Clio stood up quickly, moving awkwardly so that her chair rocked and almost overbalanced. "More Scotch?"

Jake held out his glass. Clio had grown very thin, and her eyes slid away from his when he tried to look into her face. When she leaned over with the whiskey bottle, he caught her hand and held it. After a second she tried to extricate herself, but he held tighter. He reached up and put one of his arms around her shoulder, and pulled her down against him. He felt her body resist the warmth of his, but then, slowly, it slackened until he all but carried the slight weight of her. He moved sideways in his chair to make room for her to sit with his arm still wrapped around her. She was so close that he could feel the rise and fall of her breathing against his chest.

The weight and shape of her was like Grace, the girl she had once been in a water-meadow on a thundery summer afternoon. Jake had never forgotten.

"Talk to me," Clio begged him. Her voice was muffled.

Jake began to talk. They were strongly in his mind, so he talked about their parents. He retold the old stories about their meeting and courtship, and they both remembered how Nathaniel had been delighted to tell them and how Eleanor would murmur, "Nathaniel, really, don't give away all that old nonsense." He talked about their childhoods and growing up in the shabby old house, the five of them strung between the strong poles of their parents.

"Do you remember the plays? *The Sleeping Beauty?*"

"Oh yes, I remember that."

When she was twelve, Clio had written a play based on the old fairy tale. The script had been full of family jokes and outrageous puns, and there had been a role for each of them, even for Alice who was only a baby in arms. Alice had been dressed up in her best lace robe to play the part of the princess at her ill-fated christening.

"Pappy as the prince, in pantomime tights and a blond wig made from teased-out parcel string? And Julius and me as the fairies in ballet skirts? We must have spent a month making costumes and rehearsing."

"Tabby was the grown-up Beauty, do you remember? Very solemn, with the spinning wheel we borrowed from somebody's mother. Mama was the Queen, and I was the King in a horsehair moustache."

The play had been performed amongst the shrubs and creepers at the wild end of the garden on Midsummer's Eve, to an audience of neighbors and schoolfriends.

"Those were good days. Living in the Woodstock Road was like having a common identity, even though we were all so different. It was comfortable and safe, and at the same time interesting and challenging. We had to match and meet the rest of the family. To measure up to what Pappy and Mama expected."

Clio nodded her head, like Romy listening to a story. "Yes, that was what it was like."

Jake drank some more whiskey. He would have to go back to London this evening, but not just yet. He was close to Clio, hooking the net of the shared memories around them. They were separately disabled by their grief, but they should try to hold on to each other more tightly now that Julius and Grace were gone. Now that the circle was broken.

"They were happy, Eleanor and Nathaniel, weren't they?" Jake asked.

"Yes, always."

"There are happy marriages, then." He was not quite sure whether he had said it, or just formed the words within himself, but Clio startled him by sitting upright.

"*Yours* is happy, if you would only see it. If you would only attend to it."

Her vehemence startled him.

Jake unwillingly considered the broken pattern of his years with Ruth. His unfaithfulness was like an irregularity in the design of their lives. Sometimes the strength of the repeat took over and obliterated it, but at other times it glared out, unmissable and hideous, and destroyed all the neat sequences around it. He swerved away from contemplating the havoc it had caused.

"A good marriage," he mumbled. "Our parents', that is. But look. Look at the outcome. Each one of us children. We are all flawed, aren't we? Did they weaken us with their strength?

"There is me, with my failing. You know about that, of course."

The thought of Lottie came to him, and her tears.

"And Alice, and poor Julius."

Clio silently put her hands up, her fingers bent and spread apart to touch her temples. She wanted to close out his voice, but it went on.

"And Tabby, hiding herself away in her nun's habit. All of us are flawed. Except for you, Clio. You are whole, and you must be the strength and the success for the rest of us."

Clio shut her eyes. Within her head she heard the melancholy voice of the sea. She saw the wall of water, and the heavy bolt that held the door shut.

Oh yes, Jake. I am flawed too. If you knew how deeply the fault runs. Because I am a murderer. And that is what I must live with.

She made herself open her eyes and look again. Jake was turning his empty glass in his fingers, watching her.

"I will do my best," she heard herself say, in a voice that seemed to crack and shiver. "Would you like a last drink?"

Jake hesitated and then shook his head.

Clio suddenly said, "Go home, Jake. Go home to Ruth while you can and make things right with her. Then you can be the strength and the success yourself, and you won't have to look to me."

He held her for a moment longer, then patted her bone-ridged shoulder with the flat of his hand.

"Come and see me off?"

"Of course I will."

Clio waited on her front step, with her hand lifted in a wave, until Jake had climbed into his car and driven away out of the square.

Then she went back into her house. She picked up the two empty glasses and rinsed them in the sink, dried them, and replaced them in the cupboard. When the small job was done, she went softly up the stairs to make sure that Romy was sleeping comfortably.

She came down again, and wandered back into her sitting room. She saw the tidy ranks of her books, the picture over the wooden mantel, and the rest of her possessions, carefully and neutrally arranged.

Clio picked up a book and sat down with it, but she did not read.

The hot weather held, and under the hard skies the business of each day unfolded with leaden slowness. There was a sense of waiting and watching, of the world holding its breath.

Reservists were being called up in England and in France, and in Germany two hundred thousand men were massed along the Polish frontier. In the East End of London the people were filling sandbags. Clio and Cressida had made blackout covers for all the windows of the house in Paradise Square.

Clio could not sleep. She sat up late, reading or working or staring at the meaningless pages, and she woke at dawn to prowl restlessly through the rooms while Cressida and Romy still slept. So it was that she was awake, standing at her window surveying the square, when Nathaniel came very early one morning at the end of August. Clio watched him as he crossed the scuffed grass. He was hurrying, with his head down, moving too fast for a man of his age and infirmity. His stick prodded impatiently at the ground.

Clio's body felt heavy with apprehensions as she moved to open the front door. Her fingers were numb and she fumbled with the catch, and she thought again of the bolt that she had never drawn back.

Nathaniel stood on the step. He was gasping for breath, and leaning on his stick for support. He tried to speak, and could not.

Clio held his arm. Her heart began to thump in her chest, a dull rhythm of dread. At last he looked up. She saw that there were tears in the corners of his eyes.

"Not Jake?" she whispered. Nathaniel's head shook as he fought to catch a breath.

"Not Lucy's baby?" There were still four months to go.

No, again.

Clio's fingers tightened, digging into her father's arm, like claws. "Please tell me. *Please*."

He sucked the air into his lungs. He was crying with the effort to speak and with the burden of his message.

His mouth opened. "Rafael," he sobbed. "Rafael is free. He is in Zurich this morning."

Clio reached out to steady herself. She was blind, and dumb, but the tips of her fingers met the wood of her front door, warm with the heat of so many days, grainy and solid and true. The sun had dispersed the thin morning mist, and the birds were singing.

The train steamed and sighed outside Oxford station. From the height of the carriage window, Rafael looked down at the dusty ragwort and nettles and docks that sprawled over the bank beside the track. When he craned forward to look ahead of the idling train, he could just see towers and rounded gray domes in the hazy distance. He was weak and exhausted, but impatience with this last slow mile of the journey made him want to jump up and swing down from the carriage step so that he could run along the track to find her.

There had been so much ground, from the camp to Oxford, but somehow he had covered it and now he was almost there.

Rafael had got away from the work camp, but he would never know if he had escaped or if they had allowed him to slip away. If it had been luck, or Grace's invisible hand working for them at the very end.

He had been among a work party digging the holes for new fencing posts that would enclose a vast new compound. More space was needed to house the thousands of Jews who were being herded into the camp. He had been laboring with three other men, and in one second he had looked up to see that the guards with their rifles were looking in the opposite direction. There was a line of woodland only thirty yards away.

He ran like a hare, and found himself in the shelter of the trees. There was no outcry, and no crack of gunfire.

After that he had walked by night, and hidden himself by day, and he had been helped by a farmer's wife who fed him and gave him a workman's clothes. The farmer's wife had a neighbor who owned a wagon, and at last Rafael had made his way to the Swiss border. In Switzerland there was a Jewish organization that had been formed to help refugees. When he reached them they took him in and they gave him the passport and papers of a Polish Jew, an engineer who had been shot by the Nazis. They had also given him enough money to reach England.

The last link in the chain was the telephone call from Zurich to Nathaniel in Oxford. Nathaniel had agreed to claim the Polish Jew as a relative, and to offer him a home and a sanctuary in England.

And so almost in the last hours of peace, Rafael reached Dover. He traveled by train to London, and from London to Oxford across the little, domestic, gold and green landscape of England.

He was luckier than Grete and Leopold Wolf, who did not escape. The men had come for them, to the little house against the wall of the forest, and they had been taken away.

Rafael bent forward in his seat, wrapping his thin arms around himself. A soldier in a fore-and-aft cap was sitting opposite, watching him.

"You all right, cock?" the soldier asked.

Rafael took a scrap of paper out of the pocket of his shirt and held it out to the man. "Do you know this place, please?"

The soldier frowned a little at the sound of his accent. Then he shrugged. "Paradise Square? It's an easy walk from the station. Left over the road, and up to a big crossroads."

Rafael listened to the man's instructions, plodding through this last stage of the long journey in his head. He felt as if he had been traveling for half a lifetime.

"You got that, mate?"

"Yes. Thank you so much."

There was a jolt and a hiss of steam, and the train began to edge forward again. Engine sheds and signal boxes slid backward past Rafael's staring eyes, and then he saw the chocolate and yellow wooden fretwork of the platform canopy.

Clio watched the black moon of the engine face slowly approaching in its nimbus of smoke. She had met every possible train since Nathaniel had brought her the news, and with each disappointment when Rafael did not appear, she remembered how she had waited in vain for him on the terrible morning in Paris. Anxiety made her shiver even in the thundery heat.

With a final jolt the train stopped. There was a fusillade of shots as the doors slammed open along the length of the platform and passengers flooded out. The station was crowded with a swarm of men in uniform with kitbags and women in bright dresses, and because his eyes and ears were still attuned to the gray monotony of the work camp, Rafael felt confused and afraid of the noise and color. He lifted the small bag that the Jewish group in Switzerland had given to him and climbed down, the last to leave the compartment.

From where she stood at the end of the platform, shading her eyes against the sun, Clio saw a tall man with hair as gray as ash and a face like a skull papered with translucent skin. He had changed almost beyond recognition, but she did not mistake him for an instant.

Rafael hesitated while the crowd ebbed around him, and then he looked toward her. She was thinner and there were lines at the sides of her mouth, but her face was still soft and it burned with love.

He put down his bag and held open his arms, and she ran to him.

CLIO SAT IN HER HOUSE in Little Venice, beneath *The Janus Face* by Quintus Prynne. The portrait was not much admired nowadays, although its strident modernism had once been acclaimed, and the artist himself was all but forgotten. He had been an official war artist, and he had been killed by a stray bomb in 1944.

Clio remembered him, and many other things besides. The memories marched past her as she sat in her high-backed chair. Sometimes she could see the faces clearly, and at other times they were blurred, receding away from her into the gray distance. Sometimes she couldn't even see Rafael's face. Rafael had been her husband for thirty-five happy years, but he had been dead for fifteen, and she was tired now, and bored by her own infirmity and the solitude of old age.

Was it today that the girl was coming, with her machine and her questions? What was it the nurse had said?

And then, as if she had conjured them out of the sea of memories, the nurse appeared, and the girl with her. The girl had long hair, and she was wearing it loose over her shoulders today. Clio eyed it with disapproval. She did not consider it a suitable coiffure for a girl who was not really a girl at all, but a woman of almost forty.

The woman sat down opposite her, and the nurse brought them tea on a tray. Clio didn't want any tea, but she took the cup anyway.

"You are not too tired, are you?" Elizabeth asked. The nurse had warned her that her patient was confused and anxious today.

"I am not tired at all," Clio lied.

The girl was Cressida Brock's daughter, of course. And so she was also Pilgrim's granddaughter, sitting opposite his masterpiece, which she plainly did not care for at all. The realization made Clio want to laugh.

Clio wondered if they had ever talked about Pilgrim, or if she had only imagined it. Elizabeth's questions confused her. She could remember the exact configuration of the patterned linoleum in the old schoolroom in the Woodstock Road, but she could not remember if Cressida's daughter had been here with her questions yesterday, or if it had been last week, or a month ago.

The days played tricks on her now.

Clio could not remember what she had already told the girl and what was still mute memory. She was afraid that she was repeating herself, the stories that she knew to be innocent, in an attempt to suppress what must not be told.

The secrets grew harder to keep with the passage of time.

The dark twin was always with her, the sin she had committed. A sudden longing to confess it swept up inside her, breaking through the careful silence of the decades that seemed no longer as imperative as the truth.

Clio thought that the girl with her long, loose hair looked like Ophelia in a pre-Raphaelite painting. The thoughts crossed and tangled in her mind.

She said loudly, "Nymph, in thy orisons Be all my sins remembered."

That was exactly right. Her sin must be remembered, and this long-haired nymph with her recording machine had been sent to her for the purpose of hearing her confession.

"What was that?" Elizabeth asked.

The stupid girl probably didn't know her Shakespeare at all. What had the line been? Clio realized that she had forgotten it already, and it was so very important.

"What was I saying?" She shook her head in bewilderment.

"Don't worry. It will come back. There's plenty of time."

Elizabeth felt less calm than she sounded. The truth was that she did not have plenty of time. She must finish the book soon.

She knew objectively that Clio had already told her everything she remembered about her cousin from more than fifty years ago.

And yet, something still drew her back to Little Venice, to sit under the terrible portrait. Clio had been closer to Grace than anyone, and she had been deeply shocked by her death. There was probably nothing there, but Elizabeth was still waiting for some extra insight into Grace's life. Some story, perhaps, that she had not heard before.

She repeated, "There's plenty of time."

Clio said, more to herself than to Cressida's daughter, "I don't think so."

The child was mistaken. There was not much time.

She stirred in her chair. "I want to talk about the flood. Are you listening to me?"

As calmly as she could, Elizabeth told her, "I know all about the flood, Aunt Clio. Grace's drowning is very well documented. There are contemporary news reports, diaries, letters. They all describe what happened, and I have read everything there is. It must have been dreadful."

"*I* didn't write any diary," Clio said.

"No."

"And I am the only person who knows what really happened."

"What did happen, Aunt Clio?"

Clio took a great breath. She tried to look around, over her own shoulder, to see the portrait for the last time. But the back of her chair was too high, and she found that she was too weak to crane sideways.

"I killed Grace."

Elizabeth's eyes flicked to the door, in search of the day nurse. Clio was wandering again. She was also prone to making wild claims, Elizabeth had learned that. It was as if she were afraid that her own story was not quite interesting enough; perhaps she had sensed all along that no one would really want to write or read her biography.

Elizabeth reddened guiltily, and leaned forward to flick the stop button. Gently she said, "But Grace was caught in a flood, when the sea wall gave way. She was swept away, no one could have saved her."

Clio only repeated, "I killed her. I wouldn't open the door to her. I wanted her to die."

Her bright eyes had clouded. She stared straight ahead of her, into vacancy.

Elizabeth insisted, "No, Aunt Clio, she was swept away. She didn't reach the door, did she? You felt guilty because you were saved and she was dead, isn't that it? Grace was your friend, almost your twin. But you couldn't have done anything to save her. You mustn't believe it could have been any different. You never said anything about this before, did you? Your memory is playing tricks on you."

Clio sank back in her chair and closed her eyes.

"I am tired now."

All my sins, she thought.

Hamlet, that was it. "All my sins remembered."

She did remember. She had forgotten so much else, but never that. She had kept the secret of Grace and the flood, and that in itself had been a sin. There had been times when she had longed to tell the truth, to people she had loved and to others, strangers caught with her in the fleeting intimacy of ships and airplanes and hotels, but she had kept her secret. The necessity of keeping it had been a great burden, and the solitary shouldering of it had been part of her punishment.

Now the secret was told. Clio was weary and her body ached, but she felt better. Lighter, and stronger, like a girl again, as if a weight had floated away from her.

Elizabeth nodded and began to pack away her tape recorder and her notebook. There was nothing else to learn; she must tell the story that she already knew. When she was ready to leave, she hesitated, looking down at the shrunken face.

Clio opened her eyes. "What were we just talking about?"

Elizabeth smiled at her. "The old things," she answered.

She left Clio to doze in her chair, and went away to tell the nurse that she would let herself out.

When the front door had closed on the brief rattle of street noise, the nurse came briskly through the quiet house. She bent over Clio in the chair, then put her warm hand over her patient's tiny clawed one.

"Come along, Mrs. Wolf, dear," she said. "It's time for your rest."

Clio nodded, smiling a little, ready to sleep.

About the Author

ROSIE THOMAS is the author of many highly successful novels, including *A Woman of Our Times* (a Literary Guild Main Selection) and *Bad Girls, Good Women* (a Main Selection of the Book-of-the-Month Club). She lives in London.

DON'T MISS
THESE CURRENT
BANTAM BESTSELLERS